RITA MAE BROWN

THREE *MORE* MRS. MURPHY MYSTERIES

Pay Dirt

—

Murder, She Meowed

—

Murder on the Prowl

Pay Dirt

Murder, She Meowed

Murder on the Prowl

RITA MAE BROWN

& SNEAKY PIE BROWN

Illustrations by Wendy Wray

THREE *MORE* MRS. MURPHY MYSTERIES IN ONE VOLUME

WINGS BOOKS • NEW YORK

Originally published in three volumes by Bantam Books under the titles:

Pay Dirt, copyright © 1995 by American Artists, Inc.
Illustrations copyright © 1995 by Wendy Wray

Murder, She Meowed, copyright © 1996 by American Artists, Inc.
Illustrations copyright © 1996 by Wendy Wray

Murder on the Prowl, copyright © 1998 by American Artists, Inc.
Illustrations copyright © 1998 by Wendy Wray

This 2005 edition is published by Wings Books®, an imprint of Random House Value Publishing, by arrangement with the Bantam Doubleday Dell Publishing Group, Inc., divisions of Random House, Inc., New York

Wings Books® and colophon are trademarks of Random House, Inc.

Random House
New York • Toronto • London • Sydney • Auckland
www.randomhouse.com

Printed and bound in the United States of America.

A catalog record for this title is available from the Library of Congress.

ISBN 0-517-22522-0

10 9 8 7 6 5 4 3 2 1

Contents

Pay Dirt

Or, Adventures of Ash Lawn

Dedicated to Joan Hamilton & Larry Hodge
and all my horse pals at Kalarama Farm

Cast of Characters

Mary Minor Haristeen (Harry), the young postmistress of Crozet, whose curiosity almost kills the cat and herself

Mrs. Murphy, Harry's gray tiger cat, who bears an uncanny resemblance to authoress Sneaky Pie and who is wonderfully intelligent!

Tee Tucker, Harry's Welsh corgi, Mrs. Murphy's friend and confidante; a buoyant soul

Pharamond Haristeen (Fair), veterinarian, formerly married to Harry

Mrs. George Hogendobber (Miranda), a widow who thumps her own Bible!

Market Shiflett, owner of Shiflett's Market, next to the post office

Pewter, Market's fat gray cat, who, when need be, can be pulled away from the food bowl

Susan Tucker, Harry's best friend, who doesn't take life too seriously until her neighbors get murdered

Big Marilyn Sanburne (Mim), queen of Crozet

Rick Shaw, Albemarle sheriff

Cynthia Cooper, police officer

Paddy, Mrs. Murphy's ex-husband, a saucy tom

Simon, an opossum with a low opinion of humanity

Herbert C. Jones, Pastor of Crozet Lutheran Church, a kindly, ecumenical soul who has been known to share his sermons with his two cats, Lucy Fur and Elocution

Hogan Freely, President of Crozet National Bank, a good banker but not good enough

Laura Freely, a leading guide at Ash Lawn, she is Hogan's wife

Norman Cramer, a respected executive at Crozet National Bank, whose marriage to Aysha Gill set Crozet's gossip mill churning

Aysha Gill Cramer, a newlywed, who watches over her husband like a hawk

Kerry McCray, Norman Cramer's still-flickering old flame, who is beginning to smolder

Ottoline Gill, Aysha's mother, who keeps an eye out for social improprieties—and an eye on her new son-in-law

Introduction

While researching Virginia's historical shrines for my mysteries, I've learned even more about human history but nil about ours.

One of you nonfiction pussycats reading this ought to write the animal history of America. All life-forms are important, but it's hard to get enthusiastic about fish, isn't it—unless you're eating one.

Do pay attention to the fact that humans had to create government because they can't get along with one another. Cats don't need Congress. There's enough danger in life without listening to a gathering of paid windbags. From time to time you might remind your human that he or she is not the crown of creation s/he thinks s/he is.

Ta-ta,

SNEAKY PIE

1

Cozy was the word used most often to describe the small town of Crozet, not *quaint*, *historic*, or *pretty*. Central Virginia in general, and Albemarle County in particular, abounded in quaint, historic, and pretty places, but Crozet was not one of them. A homey energy blanketed the community. Many families had lived there for generations, others were newcomers attracted to the sensuous appeal of the Blue Ridge Mountains. Old or new, rich or poor, black or white, the citizens of the town nodded and waved to one another while driving their cars, called and waved if on opposite sides of the street, and anyone walking along the side of the road was sure to get the offer of a ride. Backyard hedges provided the ideal setting for enriching gossip as gardeners took respite from their labors. Who did what to whom, who said what to whom, who owed money to whom, and, that glory of chat, who slept with whom. The buzz never stopped. Even in the deepest snows, a Crozetian would pick up the phone to transmit the latest. If it was really juicy, he or she would bundle up and hurry through the snow for a hot cup of coffee, that companion to steamy gossip shared with a friend.

The hub of the town consisted of its post office, the three main churches—Lutheran, Baptist, Episcopal, and one small off-shoot, the Church of the Holy Light—the schools—kindergarten through twelfth—Market Shiflett's small grocery store, and Crozet Pizza. Since a person worshiped at one church at a time, the goings-on in the other three might remain a mystery. The small market provided a handsome opportunity to catch up, but you really had to buy something. Also, one had to be careful that Market's fat gray cat, Pewter, didn't steal your food before you had the chance to eat it. Schools were a good source, too, but if you were childless or if your darlings were finally in college, you were out of that pipeline. This left the post office the dubious honor of being the premier meeting place, or Gossip Central.

The postmistress—a title which she preferred to the official one of postmaster—Mary Minor Haristeen rarely indulged in what she termed gossip, which is to say if she couldn't substanti-ate a story, she didn't repeat it. Otherwise, she was only too happy to pass on the news. Her unofficial assistant, Mrs. Miranda Hogendobber, the widow of the former postmaster, relished the "news," but she drew the line at character assassination. If people started dumping all over someone else, Mrs. Hogendobber usu-ally calmed them down or plain shut them up.

Harry, as Mary Minor was affectionately known, performed her tasks wonderfully well. Quite young for her position, Harry benefited from Miranda's wisdom. But Harry's most valuable as-sistants were Mrs. Murphy, her tiger cat, and Tee Tucker, her Welsh corgi. They wallowed in gossip. Not only did the goings-on of the humans transfix them, but so did the shenanigans of the animal community, reported by any dog accompanying its master into the post office. Whatever the dogs missed, Pewter found out next door. When she had something to tell, the round gray cat would run to the back door of the post office to spill it. Over the last few years, the cats had banged on the door so much, creating such a racket, that Harry installed a pet door so the friends could come and go as they pleased. Harry had designed a cover she could lock down over the animals' entrance, since the post office had to be secured each night.

Not that there was much to steal from the Crozet post office —stamps, a few dollars. But Harry diligently obeyed the rules, as she was a federal employee—a fact that endlessly amused her. She loathed the federal government and barely tolerated the state government, considering it the refuge of the mediocre. Still, she drew a paycheck from that bloated government on the north side of the Potomac, so she tried to temper her opinions.

Miranda Hogendobber, on the other hand, vividly remembered Franklin Delano Roosevelt, so her perception of government remained far more positive than Harry's. Just because Miranda remembered FDR did not mean, however, that she would reveal her age.

On this late July day the mimosas were crowned with the pink and gold halos of their fragile blossoms. The crepe myrtle and hydrangeas rioted throughout the town, splashes of purple and magenta here, white there. Not much else bloomed in the swelter of the Dog Days, which began on July 3 and finished August 15, so the color was appreciated.

So far, less than two inches of rain had fallen that month. The viburnums drooped. Even the hardy dogwoods began to curl up, so Mrs. Hogendobber would sprinkle the plants early in the morning and late in the evening to avoid losing too much moisture to evaporation. Her garden, the envy of the town, bore testimony to her vigilance.

The mail sorted, the two women paused for their morning tea break. Well, tea for Harry, coffee for Miranda. Mrs. Murphy sat on the newspaper. Tucker slept under the table at the back of the office.

"Is this a honey day or a sugar day, Mrs. H.?" Harry asked as the kettle boiled.

"A honey day." Miranda smiled. "I'm feeling naturally sweet."

Harry rolled her eyes and twirled a big glob of honey off the stick in the brown crockery honey pot. She then removed the teabag from her own drink, wrapping the string around it on the spoon to squeeze the last drops of strong tea into her cup. Her mug had a horse's tail for a handle, the rest of the cup representing the horse's body and head. Miranda's mug was white with block letters that read WHAT PART OF NO DON'T YOU UNDERSTAND?

"Mrs. Murphy, I'd like to read the paper." Miranda gently lifted the tiger cat's bottom and slid the paper out from underneath.

This action was met with a furious grumble, ears swept back. "*I don't stick my paws on your rear end, Miranda, besides which there's never anything in the paper worth reading.*" She thumped over to the little back door and walked outside.

"In a mood." Miranda sat down and looked over the front page.

"What's the headline?" Harry asked.

"Two people injured on I-64. What else? Oh, this Threadneedle virus threatens to affect our computers August first. I would be perfectly happy if our new computer were fatally ill."

"Oh, now, it's not that bad." Harry reached for the sports page.

"Bad?" Mrs. Hogendobber pushed her glasses up her nose. "If I do one little thing out of sequence, a rude message appears on that hateful green screen and I have to start all over. There are so many buttons to punch. Modern improvements—time wasters, that's what they are, time wasters masquerading as time savers. I can remember more in my noggin than a computer chip can. And tell me, why do we need one in the post office? All we need is a good scale and a good meter. I can stamp the letters myself!''

Seeing that Miranda was in one of her Luddite moods, Harry decided not to argue. ''Not everyone who works in the postal service is as smart as you are. They can't remember as much. For them the computer is a godsend.'' Harry craned her neck to see the photo of the car wreck.

''What a nice thing to say.'' Mrs. Hogendobber drank her coffee. ''Wonder where Reverend Jones is? He's usually here by now. Everyone else has been on time.''

''A thousand years is as a day in the eyes of the Lord. An hour is as a minute to the rev.''

''Careful now.'' Miranda, a devout believer although those beliefs could occasionally be modified to suit circumstances, wagged her finger. ''You know, at the Church of the Holy Light we don't make jokes about the Scripture.'' Miranda belonged to a small church. Truthfully, they were renegades from the Baptist church. Twenty years ago a new minister had arrived who set many parishioners' teeth on edge. After much fussing and fuming, the discontents, in time-honored tradition, broke away and formed their own church. Mrs. Hogendobber, the stalwart of the choir, had been a guiding force in the secession. When the offending minister packed his bags and left some six years after the rebellion, the members of the Church of the Holy Light were so enjoying themselves that they declined to return to the fold.

A tiny rumble at the back door announced that a pussycat was entering. Mrs. Murphy rejoined the group. A louder rumble indicated that Pewter was in tow.

''*Hello,*'' Pewter called.

''Hello there, kitty.'' Mrs. Hogendobber answered the meow. When Harry first took over Mr. Hogendobber's job and brought the cat and dog along with her, Miranda railed against the animals. The animals slowly won her over, although if you asked Miranda how she felt about people who talk to animals, she would declare that she herself never talked to animals. The fact that Harry was a daily witness to her conversations would not have altered her declaration one whit.

"Tucker, Pewter's here," Mrs. Murphy said.

Tucker opened one eye then shut it again.

"Guess I won't tell her the latest." Pewter languidly licked a paw.

Both eyes opened and the little dog raised her pretty head. "Huh?"

"I'm not talking to you. You can't be bothered to greet me when I come to visit."

"Pewter, you spend half your life in here. I can't act as though it's the first time I've seen you in months," Tucker explained.

Pewter flicked her tail, then leapt on the table. "Anything to eat?"

"Pig." Mrs. Murphy laughed.

"What's the worst they can say if you ask? No, that's what," Pewter said. "Then again, they might say yes. Mrs. Hogendobber must have something. She can't walk into the post office empty-handed."

The cat knew her neighbor well because Mrs. Hogendobber had whipped up a batch of glazed doughnuts. As soon as her paws hit the table, Harry reached over to cover the goodies with a napkin, but too late. Pewter had spied her quarry. She snagged a piece of doughnut, which came apart in marvelous moist freshness. The cat soared off the table and onto the floor with her prize.

"That cat will die of heart failure. Her cholesterol level must be over the moon." Mrs. Hogendobber raised an eyebrow.

"Do cats have cholesterol?" Harry wondered out loud.

"I don't see why not. Fat is fat. . . ."

On that note the Reverend Herbert Jones strode through the door. "Fat? Are you making fun of me?"

"No, we've been talking about Pewter."

"Relatively speaking, she's bigger than I am," he observed.

"But you've kept on your diet and you've been swimming. I think you've lost a lot of weight," Harry complimented him.

"Really? Does it show?"

"It does. Come on back here and have some tea." Mrs. Hogendobber invited him back, carefully covering up the doughnuts again.

The good reverend cleaned out his postbox, then swung through the Dutch counter door that divided the public lobby from the back. "This computer virus has everyone's knickers in a twist. On the morning news out of Richmond they did a whole segment on what to expect and how to combat it."

"Tell us." Harry stood over the little hot plate.

"No. I want our computer to die."

"Miranda, I don't think your computer is in danger. This seems to be some sort of corporate sabotage." Reverend Jones pulled up a ladderback chair. "The way I understand it, some person or persons has introduced this virus into the computer bank of a huge Virginia corporation, but no one knows which one. The diseased machine has to be a computer that interfaces with many other computers."

"And what may I ask is interface? In your face?" Miranda's tone dropped.

"Talk. Computers can talk to each other." Herb leaned forward in his chair. "Thank you, honey." He called Harry "honey" as she handed him his coffee. She never minded when it came from him. "Whoever has introduced this virus—"

Miranda interrupted again. "What do you mean, virus?"

The reverend, a genial man who loved people, paused a moment and sighed. "Because of the way in which a computer understands commands, it is possible, easy, in fact, to give one a command that scrambles or erases its memory."

"I don't need a virus for that," Miranda said. "I do it every day."

"So someone could put a command into a computer that says something like, 'Delete every file beginning with the letter A.'" Harry joined in.

"Precisely, but just what the command is, no one knows. Imagine if this is passing throughout the state in a medical data bank. What if the command is 'Destroy all records on anyone named John Smith.' You can see the potential."

"But, Herbie"—Miranda called him by his first name, as they had been friends since childhood—"why would anyone want to do such a thing?"

"Maybe to wipe out a criminal record or cancel a debt or cover up a sickness that could cost them their job. Some companies will fire employees with AIDS or cancer."

"How can people protect themselves?" Mrs. Hogendobber began to grasp the possibilities for mischief.

"The mastermind has sent faxes to television stations saying that the virus will go into effect August first, and that it's called the Threadneedle virus."

"Threadneedle is such an odd name. I wonder what's the connection?" Harry rubbed her chin.

"Oh, there will be a connection, all right. The newspeople are researching like mad on that," he confidently predicted.

"One big puzzle." Harry liked puzzles.

"The computer expert on the morning show said that one way to protect your information base is to tell your computer to disregard any command it is given on August first."

"Sensible." Miranda nodded her head.

"Except that most business is transacted by computer, so that means for one entire day all commercial, medical, even police transactions are down."

"Oh, dear." Miranda's eyes grew large. "Is there nothing else that can be done?"

Herbie finished his tea, setting the mug on the table with a light tap. "This expert reviewed the defenses and encouraged people to program their computers to hold and review any commands that come in on August first. If anything is peculiar, your review program can instruct the computer to void the suspicious command. Naturally, big companies will use their own computer experts, but it sounds as though whatever they come up with will be some variant of the review process."

"I always wanted to put VOID on my license plate," Harry confessed.

"Now, why would you want to do a thing like that?" Mrs. Hogendobber pursed her lips, seashell pink today.

"Because every time my annual renewal payments would go through to the Department of Motor Vehicles, their computer would spit out the check. At least, that's what I thought."

"Our own little saboteur."

"Miranda, I never did it. I just thought about it."

"From little acorns mighty oaks do grow." Mrs. Hogendobber appeared fierce. "Are you behind this?"

The three laughed.

"You know, when I was a young doctor I had a big Thoroughbred I used to hunt named On Call," Herb reminisced. "When someone phoned my office the nurse would say, 'Oh, I'm sorry, the doctor isn't in right now. He's On Call.' "

Harry and Miranda laughed all the more.

"*So what's the scoop, Pewter?*" Tucker asked, then turned her attention to Mrs. Murphy. "*I suppose you already know or you'd have pulled her fur out.*"

With that faint hint of superiority that makes cats so maddening, the tiger twitched her whiskers forward. "*We had a little chat on the back stoop.*"

"*Come on, tell me.*"

Pewter sidled over to the dog, who was now sitting up. "*Aysha Cramer refused, to Mim Sanburne's face, to work with Kerry McCray for the homeless benefit.*"

Mim Sanburne considered herself queen of Crozet. On her expansive days she extended that dominion to cover the state of Virginia.

"*Big deal.*" Tucker was disappointed.

"*It is. No one crosses Mim. She pitched a hissy and told Aysha that the good of the community was more important than her spat with Kerry,*" the rotund kitty announced.

"*Oh, Aysha.*" Tucker laughed. "*Now Mim will give her the worst job* of the benefit—addressing, sealing, and stamping the envelopes. They all have to be handwritten, you know."

"And all this over Norman Cramer. Mr. Bland." Pewter giggled.

The animals caught their breath for a moment.

"Boy, it's a dull summer if we're laughing about that tired love triangle," Mrs. Murphy said wistfully.

"Nothing happens around here," Tucker carped.

"Fourth of July parade was okay. But nothing unusual. Maybe someone will stir up a fuss over Labor Day . . ." Pewter's voice trailed off. "We can hope for a little action."

Mrs. Murphy stretched forward, then backward. "You know what my mother used to say, 'Be careful what you ask for, you might get it.'"

The three friends later would remember this prophecy.

2

Ash Lawn, the Federal home of James and Elizabeth Monroe, reposes behind a mighty row of English boxwoods. When the fifth president and his lady were alive, these pungent shrubs probably rose no higher than waist level. The immense height of them now casts an eerie aura yet lends an oddly secure sense to the entrance. The formal entrance isn't used anymore; people must pass the small gift shop and arrive at the house by a side route.

The warm yellow clapboard creates an accessibility, a familiarity—one could imagine living in this house. No one could ever imagine living in the beautiful and imposing Monticello just over the small mountain from Ash Lawn.

Harry walked among the boxwoods and around the grounds with Blair Bainbridge, her new neighbor—"new" being a relative term in Crozet; Blair had moved there more than a year ago.

A much-sought-after model, he was out of Crozet as much as he was in it. Recently returned from Africa, he had asked Harry to give him a tour of Monroe's home. This irritated Harry's ex-husband, Fair Haristeen, D.V.M., a blond giant who, having repented of his foolishness in losing Harry, desperately wanted his ex-wife back.

As for Blair, no one could divine his intentions toward Harry. Mrs. Hogendobber, that self-confessed expert on the male animal, declared that Blair was so impossibly rugged and handsome that he had women throwing themselves at him every moment, on every continent. She swore Harry fascinated him because she seemed immune to his masculine beauty. Mrs. Hogendobber got it more than half right despite arguments to the contrary from Harry's best friend and her corgi's breeder, Susan Tucker.

Mrs. Murphy chose the shade of a mighty poplar, where she scratched up some grass, then plopped down. Tucker circled three times, then sat next to her as she eyed the offending peacocks of Ash Lawn. The shimmering birds overran the Monroe estate, their heavenly appearance marred by grotesquely ugly pinkish feet. They also possessed the nastiest voices of birddom.

"Oh, how I'd like to wrestle that big showoff to the ground," Tucker growled as a huge male strutted by, cast the little dog a death-ray eye, and then strutted on.

"Probably tough as an old shoe." Mrs. Murphy occasionally enjoyed a wren as a delicacy, but she shied off the larger birds. She prudently flattened herself whenever she perceived a large shadow overhead. This was based on experience because a red-tailed hawk had carried off one of her tiny brothers.

"I don't know why President Monroe kept these birds. Sheep, cattle, even turkeys—I can understand turkeys—but peacocks are useless." Tucker jumped up and whirled around to bite something in her fur.

"Fleas? It's the season." Mrs. Murphy noticed sympathetically.

"No." Tucker grumbled as she bit some more. "Deer flies."

"How can they get through your thick fur?"

"*I don't know, but they do.*" Tucker sighed, then stood up and shook herself. "*Where's Mom?*"

"*Out and about. She's not far. Sit down, will you. If you go off and chase one of those stupid birds, I'll get blamed for it. I don't see why we can't go into the house. I understand why other people's animals can't visit, like Lucy Fur, but not us.*" The younger of Reverend Jones's two cats, Lucy Fur, was aptly named as she was a hellion.

"*Bet Little Marilyn would let us through the back door.*" Tucker winked. She knew Mim Sanburne's daughter loved animals.

"*Good idea.*" The cat rolled in the grass and then bounded up. "*Let's boogie.*"

"*Where'd you hear that?*" Tucker asked as they trotted to the side door. A bench under a small porch made the area inviting. No humans were around.

"*Susan said it yesterday. She picks up that stuff from her kids. Like 'ABC ya' for when you say good-bye.*"

"Oh." Tucker found the semantics of the young of limited interest, since every few years the jargon changed.

Underneath Ash Lawn's main level, docents dressed in period costumes spun, wove, boiled lard for candles, and cooked in the kitchen. Little Marilyn—Marilyn Sanburne, Junior, recently divorced and taking back her maiden name—was the chief docent at Ash Lawn this day. Although only in her early thirties, the younger Marilyn had contributed a great deal financially to Ash Lawn as well as to the College of William and Mary. The college maintained the house and grounds of James Monroe and provided most docents. Little Marilyn was a proud alumna of William and Mary, where she had switched majors so many times, her advisers despaired of her ever graduating. She finally settled on sociology, which greatly displeased her mother, and therefore greatly pleased Little Marilyn.

As Harry had graduated from Smith College in Massachusetts, she was not one of the inner circle at Ash Lawn, but the staff was good at community relations, so Harry and her animals felt welcome there. Of course, everyone at Ash Lawn knew Mrs. Murphy and Tucker.

The other docents that July 30 were Kerry McCray, a pert strawberry-blonde and Little Marilyn's college roommate; Laura Freely, a tall, austere lady in her sixties; and Aysha Gill Cramer, also a friend of Little Marilyn's from William and Mary. As Aysha had been married only the previous April, in a gruesome social extravaganza, it was taking everyone a bit of time to get used to calling her Cramer. Danny Tucker, Susan's sixteen-year-old son, was working as a gardener and loving it. Susan was filling in at the gift shop because the regular cashier had called in sick.

A scheduling snafu had stuck Aysha and Kerry there at the same time. The two despised each other. Along with Little Marilyn, the three had been best friends from childhood all the way through William and Mary, where they pledged the same sorority.

After graduation they traveled to Europe together, finally going their separate ways after a year's time. They wrote volumes of letters to each other. Kerry returned to Crozet first, getting a job at the Crozet National Bank, which had started locally at the turn of the century but now served all of central Virginia. Little Mim followed soon after, married badly, and then divorced. Aysha had returned to Albemarle County only six months ago. Her impeccable French and Italian were not in demand. Career prospects were so limited in this small corner of the world that marriage was still a true career for young women, providing they could find a suitable victim.

The friends picked up where they had left off. Aysha, a bit chubby when she was younger, had matured into a good-looking woman bubbling with ideas.

Little Marilyn, recovering from her divorce, was still blue. She needed her friends.

Kerry, engaged to Norman Cramer, often invited Aysha and Little Marilyn out with them for dinner, the movies, a late night at the Blue Ridge Brewery.

Weedy and timid, Norman possessed a handsome face framing big blue eyes. He, too, worked at the Crozet National Bank as the head accountant. Excitement was not Norman's middle name, so everyone was knocked for a loop when Aysha snaked him away from Kerry. No one could figure out why she wanted him except that she was in her thirties, disliked working, and marriage was an easy way out.

Her mother, Ottoline Gill, far too involved in her daughter's life, seemed thrilled with her new son-in-law. Part of that may have been shock from ever having a son-in-law. She had despaired of Aysha's future, declaring many times over that a girl as beautiful and brilliant as her darling would never find a husband. "Men like dumb women," she would say, "and my Aysha won't play dumb."

Whatever she played or didn't play, she captivated Norman with the result that Aysha and Kerry were now bitter enemies who could barely speak to each other in a civil tone of voice. Norman, away from Aysha's scrutiny, would be pleasant to Kerry, although she wasn't always pleasant back.

Marilyn sent Aysha to work downstairs, packing Kerry out to the slave quarters. It eased the tension somewhat. She knew each one would seek her out in the next day to complain about the mix-up. Kerry would be easier to console than Aysha, who liked nothing better than to have someone at an emotional disadvantage. However, Aysha enjoyed being a docent for Ash Lawn and Marilyn would mollify her, for her sake as well as the good of the place. Bad enough to have Aysha fuss at her, but coping with that harridan of a mother was real hell. And if Ottoline picked up the cudgel, then Marilyn's own mother, Mim, would become involved, too, if for no other reason than to put the pretentious Ottoline in her place.

Mrs. Murphy, tail to the vertical, felt the cool grass under her paws. Grasshoppers shot off before her like green insect rockets. They'd jump, settle, then jump again. Usually she would chase them, but today she wanted to get inside the historic home just to prove she wouldn't be destructive.

As the day drew to a close, most of the tourists had left. A few lingered in the gift shop. The staff of Ash Lawn began closing up. Harry and Blair had entered the house to see if Marilyn needed any help.

A distant roar grew louder. Then a screech, burp, and cutoff announced that a motorcycle had pulled into the parking lot, not just any motorcycle, but a gleaming, perfect black Harley-Davidson. The biker was as disheveled as his machine was gorgeous. He wore a black German World War II helmet, a black leather vest studded with chrome stars, torn jeans, heavy black biker boots, and an impressive chain across his chest like a medieval Sam Browne belt. Wraparound black sunglasses completed the outfit. He was unshaven but handsome in a grungy fashion.

He sauntered up the brick path leading to the front door. Tucker, now on the side of the house by the slave quarters, stopped and began barking at him. Both animals had left the side door to see what was going on.

"*Shut up, Tucker, you'll spoil my strategy,*" the cat warned. She was lying flat by the public entrance just waiting for it to swing open when the visitor entered so she could dart in. Whoever opened the door would let out a yelp as she zipped between their legs. Then they'd have to chase her or cajole her. Harry would have a fit and fall in it. Someone would think to bribe her with food or perhaps fresh catnip from the herb garden. Mrs. Murphy had it all planned. Then she glanced up and saw the Hell's Angel marching toward the door. She decided to stay put.

He opened the door and Little Marilyn greeted him. "Welcome to the home of James and Elizabeth Monroe. Unfortunately our hours are ten to five during the summer and it's five-thirty now. I'm terribly sorry, but you'll have to come back tomorrow."

"I'm not going anywhere." He brushed right by her.

Laura heard this exchange from the parlor and joined Marilyn. Harry and Blair remained in the living room. Aysha was downstairs in the summer kitchen and Kerry was closing up the slave quarters.

"You'll have to leave." Little Marilyn pursed her lips.

"Where's Malibu?" His guttural voice added to his visual menace.

"In California." Blair strode into the front hall.

The biker sized him up and down. Blair was a tall man, broad-shouldered, and in splendid condition. This was no push-over.

"You the resident comedian?" The biker reached into his vest and pulled out a little switchblade. He expertly flipped it open with one hand and began to pick his teeth.

"I am for today." Blair folded his arms across his chest. Harry, too, stepped into the hall behind Blair. "These ladies have informed you that Ash Lawn will be open tomorrow morning. Come back then."

"I don't give a frig about this pile. I want Malibu. I know she's here."

"Who's Malibu?" Harry wedged forward. It occurred to her that the biker's pupils were most likely dilated or the reverse, and he wore sunglasses to cover that fact. He was on something and it wasn't aspirin.

"A thieving slut!" the biker exploded. "I've tracked her down and I know she's here."

"She couldn't possibly be here," Marilyn replied. "All of us who work here know one another and we've never heard of a Malibu."

"Lady, you just never heard the name. She's cunning. She'll hypnotize you, take what she wants, and then strike like a snake!" He pointed his two front fingers at her like fangs and made a striking motion.

Out of the corner of her eye Harry saw Aysha enter through the back door. She could see Kerry out back also on her way to the main house. The biker didn't see them. Harry backtracked, her hands behind her, holding them up in a stop signal. Blair by now had his hand on the biker's shoulder and was gently turning him around toward the front door.

"Come on. You won't find her today. Half the staff's already gone home." Blair's voice oozed reassurance. "I know what you mean, some women are like cobras."

The two men walked outside. Mrs. Murphy stared up at them. The biker smelled like cocaine sweat and grease. She put great store by smell.

The gruff man's voice quivered a touch. "This one, man, this one, oh, you don't know the things she can do to you. She plays with your body and messes with your mind. The only thing she ever really loved was the dollar."

Blair realized he would have to walk this fellow with the stoned expression all the way to his bike because he wasn't budging off the front porch. "Show me your bike."

Mrs. Murphy darted from bush to bush, keeping the men in sight and hearing every word. Tucker dashed ahead of her.

"Tucker, stay behind them."

"You're always telling me what to do!"

"Because you act first and think later. Stay behind. That way if Blair needs help this guy won't know you're there. The element of surprise."

"Well—" The dog realized the cat had a point.

"She wanted to make enough money to sit home, to be a lady." He laughed derisively. "I thought she was joking. A *lady?*"

Blair arrived at the sleek machine, resting on its kickstand. "Bet she hums."

"Yeah, power to burn."

Blair ran his hand over the gas tank. "Had a Triumph Bonneville once. Leaked oil, but she could sing, you know?"

"Good bike." The fellow's lower lip protruded, a sign of agreement, approval.

"Started out with a Norton. How 'bout you?"

"Liked those English bikes, huh?" He leaned against the motorcycle. "Harleys. Always Harleys with me. Started out with a 1960 Hog, 750cc, in pieces. Put her back together. Then I put together a Ducati for a buddy of mine, and before I knew it, I had more work than I could handle."

"BMWs?"

The biker shook his head. "Not for me. Great machines but no soul. And that piston instead of a chain drive—you shift gears on one of those things and it's a lurch. Kill your crotch." He laughed, revealing strong, straight teeth. " 'Course there's no more chains, you know. They use Kevlar." He pointed to the space-age material that had replaced the chain.

"My dad had an Indian." Blair's eyes glazed. "What I wouldn't give for that bike today."

"An Indian. No shit. Hey, man, let me buy you a beer. We've got some serious talking to do."

"Thanks, but my date is waiting for me back at the house. Take a raincheck though." Blair inclined his head back toward Ash Lawn, where Harry stood at the end of the entrance walk. She wanted to make sure Blair was okay.

"I'm staying at the Best Western."

"Okay, thanks." Blair smiled.

"I'm not going anywhere until I find that bitch."

"You seem determined. I'm sure you will."

The biker tapped his head with his fist. "Box of rocks, man, box of rocks, but I never give up. Until then, buddy." He hopped on his machine, turned the key, a velvet purr filling the air. Then he slowly rolled down the driveway.

Mrs. Murphy watched him recede. *"Motorcycles were invented to thin out the male herd."*

Tucker laughed as they fell in with Blair.

"What were you doing out there?" Harry asked as the other women came out of the house and crowded around Blair.

"Talking about motorcycles."

"With that cretin?" Marilyn was incredulous.

"Oh, he's not so bad. He's searching for his girlfriend and

he's staying at the Best Western until he finds her. I might even have a beer with the guy. He's kind of interesting.''

Both Kerry and Aysha had been informed of the search for Malibu.

Laura said, "You're not afraid of him?''

"No. He's harmless. Just a little loaded, that's all.''

"Long as you're not Malibu, maybe he is harmless.'' Harry laughed.

"Can you imagine anyone named Malibu?'' Aysha's frosty tone was drenched in social superiority.

"Think my life would improve if I rechristened myself Chattanooga?'' Kerry joked for the others' benefit. She wanted to smash in Aysha's face.

"Intercourse. Change your name to Intercourse and you'll see some sizzle.'' Harry giggled.

"Ah, yes.'' Laura Freeley's patrician voice, its perfect cadence, added weight to her every utterance. "If I recall my Pennsylvania geography, Intercourse isn't far from Blue Ball.''

"Ladies''—Blair bowed his head—"how you talk.''

3

The John Deere dealership, a low brick building on Route 250, parked its new tractors by the roadside. These green and yellow enticements made Harry's mouth water. Probably a thousand motorists passed the tractors each day on their way into Charlottesville. The county was filling with new people, service people who bought enormous houses squeezed on five acres—riding mowers were their speed. They probably didn't lust after these machines sitting in a neat row. But country people, they'd drive by at dusk, stop the car, and walk around the latest equipment.

Harry's tractor, a 1958 John Deere 420S row crop tractor, hauled a manure spreader, pulled a small bushhog, and felt like a friend. Her father had bought the tractor new and lovingly cared for it. Harry's service manual, a big book, was filled with his notations now crowded by her own. The smaller operator's manual, ragged and thumbed, was protected in a plastic cover.

Johnny Pop, as Doug Minor dubbed his machine, still popped and chugged. Last year Harry bought a new set of rear tires. The originals had finally succumbed. Given this proven reliability, Harry wanted another John Deere, the Rolls-Royce of tractors. Not that she planned to retire Johnny Pop, but a tractor in the seventy-five-horsepower range with a front end loader and special weights for the rear wheels could accomplish many of the larger, more difficult tasks on her farm that were beyond Johnny Pop's modest horsepower. The base price of what she needed ran about $29,000 sans attachments. Her heart sank each time she remembered the cost, quite impossible on a postmistress's wage.

Mrs. Murphy and Tucker waited in the cab of her truck, another item that needed replacing. The Superman blue had faded, the clutch had been repaired twice, and she'd worn through four sets of tires. However, the Ford rolled along. Most people would buy a new truck before a tractor, but Harry, being a farmer first, knew the tractor was far more important.

She strolled around the machines, not a speck of mud on them. Some had enclosed cabs with AC, which seemed sinful to her, although if you ran over a nest of digger bees, that enclosed cab would be a godsend. She liked to dream, climb up to touch the steering wheel, run her fingers along the engine block. That's why dusk appealed to her. It wasn't so much that she didn't want to talk to the salesmen. She'd known them for years, and they knew she hadn't a penny. She hated to waste their time since she wasn't a serious customer.

She opened the door of her truck; a tiny creak followed. She leaned onto the seat but didn't climb in right away.

"Well, kids, what do you think? Pretty fabulous?"

"*They look the same as last time.*" Tucker was hungry.

"*Beautiful, Mom, just beautiful.*" Mrs. Murphy would occasionally ride in Harry's lap when she drove Johnny Pop. "*I vote for the enclosed cab myself and you can put a woven basket with a towel in it for me. I believe in creature comforts.''*

"Ah, well, let's go home.'' She climbed into the truck, cranked the motor, and pulled onto the highway, heading west.

In fifteen minutes she was at the outskirts of Crozet. She passed the old Del Monte food packaging plant and decided to pull into the supermarket.

"I want to go home.'' Tucker whined.

"If you want to eat, then I've got to get you food.'' Harry hopped out of the car.

Tucker inquisitively looked at the cat. *"Do you think she understood what I said?''*

"Nah.'' Mrs. Murphy shook her head. *"Coincidence.''*

"I bet I could jump out the window.''

"I bet I could, too, but I'm not running around this parking lot, not the way people drive.'' She put her paws on the window frame and surveyed the lot. *"Everyone must need dog food.''*

Tucker joined her. *"Mim.''*

"Bet it's her cook. That's the farm car. Mim wouldn't do anything as lowly as shop for her own food.''

"Probably right. Well, there's the silver Saab, so we know Susan is here. . . .''

"Aysha's green BMW. Oh, hey, there's Mrs. Hogendobber's Falcon.''

"And look who's pulling in—Fair. Um-um.'' Tucker's eyes twinkled.

Hurrying down the aisle with a basket on her arm, Harry first bumped into Susan.

"If you're not buying much, you could have gone to Shiflett's Market and saved yourself the checkout line.''

"He closed early tonight. Dentist.''

"Not another root canal?'' Harry counted items in Susan's cart. "Are you having a party or something? I mean, a party without me?''

"No, nosy.'' Susan pushed Harry on the shoulder. "Danny and Brookie want to have a cookout. I said I'd buy the food if they did the work.''

"Danny Tucker behind the barbecue?"

"Well, you see, he's got this new girlfriend who wants to be a chef, so he thinks if he shows an interest in food beyond eating it, he'll impress her. He's talked his sister into helping him."

"Talked or bribed?"

"Bribed." Susan's big smile was infectious. "He's promised to drive her and a friend to the Virginia Horse Center over in Lexington and then he'll look at Washington and Lee University, without Mom, of course."

Mrs. Hogendobber careened around the aisle, her cart on two wheels. "Gangway, girls, I'll miss choir practice."

The two women parted as Miranda roared through tossing items into her cart with considerable skill.

"Great hand-eye," Susan noted.

Nearly colliding with Mrs. Hogendobber, since she entered the aisle from the opposite end, was Aysha Cramer, with her mother, Ottoline. "Oh, Mrs. Hogendobber, I'm sorry."

"Beep! Beep!" Mrs. Hogendobber expertly maneuvered around her and was off.

Ottoline, wearing an off-the-shoulder peasant blouse that revealed her creamy skin and bosoms, plucked the list out of Aysha's cart. "If you're going to waste time talking, I'll work on this list."

Aysha shrugged as her mother continued on and turned the corner. She rolled her cart over to Harry and Susan. "We know she's not DWI."

Mrs. Hogendobber didn't drink.

"Choir practice," Susan said.

"I hope I have as much energy as she does at her age," Aysha said admiringly. "And just what is her age?"

"Mentally or physically?" Susan rocked her cart back and forth.

"Mother says she's got to be in her sixties, because she was in high school when mother was in eighth grade," Aysha volunteered.

Of course, Ottoline the raving bitch never said anything nice about anyone unless it reflected upon her own perceived glory, so Aysha's recounting was a bogus edition of Mrs. Gill's true thoughts.

As if on cue, Ottoline sashayed down the aisle in the opposite direction from which she had left. She dumped items in the cart, nodded curtly to Harry and Susan, only to continue down the aisle, calling over her shoulder, "Aysha, I'm pressed for time."

"Yes, Mumsy." Then she lowered her voice. "Had a fight with the decorator today. She's in a bad mood."

"I thought she'd just redecorated," Susan said.

"Two years ago. Time flies. She's into a neutral palette this time."

"Better than a cleft palate," Harry joked.

"Not funny," Aysha sniffed.

"Oh, come on, Aysha." Harry couldn't stand it when Aysha or anyone behaved like a humorless Puritan.

Apart from the occasional lapse into correctness, Harry thought Aysha had turned out okay except for her unfortunate belief that she was an aristocrat. It was a piteous illusion, since the Gills had migrated to Albemarle County immediately following World War I. To make matters worse, they had migrated from Connecticut. Despite her Yankee roots, Aysha flounced around like a Southern belle. Her new husband, not the brightest bulb on the Christmas tree when it came to women, bought it. He called her "lovegirl." God only knows what she called him. Newlyweds were pretty disgusting no matter who they were.

Susan asked, "Aysha, you've heard about this Threadneedle virus. Tomorrow's the big day. You worried?"

"Oh, heavens no." She laughed, her voice lilting upward before she lowered it. "But my Norman, he's been to meetings about it. The bank is really taking this seriously."

"No kidding." Harry grabbed a few more cans of dog food.

"You can imagine if accounts were mixed up, although Norman says he believes the real target is Federated Investments in Richmond and this whole thing is a cover to get everyone in an uproar while they, or whoever, strikes FI."

"Why FI?" Susan asked the logical question.

"They've been having such hard times. New chairman, shake-ups, and hundreds of people have been let go. Who better but an FI employee to devise a scheme with computers as the weapon? Norman says that by August 2 FI will be in a bigger tangle than a fishing line."

"Ladies!" Fair, framed by a sale sign for charcoal briquets, waved from the end of the aisle.

Aysha smiled at Fair, then looked at Harry to pick up telltale signs of emotion. Harry smiled, too, and waved back. She liked her ex.

"Well, I'd better push on, forgive the pun." Susan headed out. "Danny will be the youngest coronary victim in Crozet if I don't get back with this food."

"Me too."

"Harry, are you cooking?" Aysha couldn't believe it.

Harry pointed to her cart. "Tucker and Mrs. Murphy."

"Give them my best." Aysha moved in the other direction, her laughter tinkling as she went.

Ottoline, hands on hips, appeared at aisle's end. "Will you hurry up?"

Harry reached the end of the aisle, where Fair waited for her. He was pretending to buy charcoal at a discount.

"How you doin'?"

"Fine, what about you?"

"Seeing more shin splints than I can count. Too many trainers are overworking their young horses on this hard ground." Shin splints, or bucked shins, are a common problem among young racehorses.

Harry owned three horses, one of which, still a bit new to

her, had been given to her by Fair and Mim. Lately, Mim had warmed to Harry. In fact, the haughty Mrs. Sanburne seemed to have softened considerably over the past couple of years.

"We're doing pretty good at home. Come on by and let's ride up Yellow Mountain."

"Okay." Fair eagerly accepted. "Tomorrow's a mess, but the day after? I'll swing by at six. Ought to have cooled off a little by then."

"Great. Who do you want to take out?"

"Gin Fizz."

"Okay." She started off knowing that the cat and dog would be crabby from waiting so long.

"Uh, heard you and Blair Bainbridge were up at Ash Lawn yesterday. I thought he was out of town." Fair prayed he would be going out of town again soon—like tomorrow.

"He finished up that shoot and instead of stopping by to see his folks, he came directly home. He's pretty tired, I think."

"How can you get tired wearing clothes and twirling in front of the camera?"

Harry refused to be drawn into this. "Damned if I know, Fair, no one's ever asked me to model." She wheeled away. "See you day after tomorrow."

4

"Get out the shovels," Harry called to Mrs. Hogendobber as she trooped through the back door just as Rob Collier, the mail delivery man, was leaving by the front door.

He ducked his head back in. "Morning, Mrs. H."

"Morning back at you, Rob." She beheld the mammoth bags of mail on the floor. "What in the world?"

"Heck of a way to start August."

As the big mail truck backed out of the driveway, the two women, transfixed by the amount of mail, just stared.

"Oh, hell, I'll get the mail cart and start on bag one."

"I'll be right back." Mrs. Hogendobber hurried out the door and returned in less than five minutes, enough time for Harry to upend the big canvas bag and enough time for Mrs. Murphy to crash full force into the pile, sending letters and magazines scattering. Then she rolled over and bit some envelopes while scratching others.

"Death to the bills!" the cat hollered. She spread all four paws on the slippery pile, looked to the right, then to the left, before springing forward with a mighty leap, sending mail squirting out from under her.

"Get a grip, Murph." Harry had to laugh at the tiger's merry show.

"Here's what I think of the power company." She seized a bill between her teeth and crunched hard. *"Take that. And this is for every lawyer in Crozet."* She pulled her right paw over a windowpane bill, leaving five parallel gashes.

Tucker joined the fun, but not being as agile as Mrs. Murphy, she could only run through the mail and shout, *"Look at me!"*

"All right, you two. This is the only post office in America where people get mail with teeth marks on it. Now, enough is enough."

Mrs. Hogendobber opened the back door just as Pewter was entering through the animal door. *"Hey, hey, wait a minute."*

Mrs. Murphy sat down in the mail debris and laughed as her fat friend swung toward her. Mrs. Hogendobber laughed too.

"Very funny." Pewter, incensed, wriggled out.

"Everyone's loony tunes this morning." Harry bent over to tidy the mess but thought the cat had the right idea. "What is that incredible smell?"

"Cinnamon buns. We need sustenance. Now, I was going to wait and bring these over for our break, but Harry, we'll be working through that." She checked the big old railroad clock on the wall. "And Mim will be here in an hour."

"Mim will have to come back." Harry threw letters in the mail cart and wheeled it to the back side of the mailboxes. "Unless you've got some scoop, turn on the radio." Harry winked as she snatched a hot cinnamon bun and started the sorting.

"I'm not listening to country and western this morning."

"And I don't want to be spiritually uplifted, Miranda."

"Don't fuss." Mrs. Hogendobber clicked on the dial.

The announcer bleated the news. "—an eight-million-dollar loss for this quarter, the worst in FI's sixty-nine-year history. One thousand five hundred employees, twenty-five percent of the famed company's work force, have been let go—"

"Damn." Harry shot a postcard into Market Shiflett's box.

"I imagine those people being handed their pink slips are saying worse than that."

The news continued after a commercial break for the new Dodge Ram. The deep voice intoned, "Threadneedle, the feared computer virus, was already striking early this morning. Leggett's department store has reported some small problems, as has Albemarle Savings and Loan. The full extent of the scramble won't be known until the business day gets under way. But the early birds are reporting light trouble."

"You know, if some computer genius out there really wanted to perform a service for America, he or she would destroy the IRS."

"We are overtaxed, Harry, but you're becoming an anarchist." Miranda wiped a bit of vanilla icing that dripped off her lips, hot coral today to match her square hot coral earrings. Mrs. H. believed in dressing for success, fifties style.

"Ten percent across the board if you make over one hundred thousand and five percent if you make under. Anyone making less than twenty-five thousand a year shouldn't have to pay tax. If we can't run the country on that, then maybe we'd better restructure the country—like FI, we're becoming a dinosaur. . . . Too big to survive. We trip over our own big feet."

Mrs. Hogendobber flipped up another bag. "I don't know—but I do agree we're making a mess of things. Now, what's she doing here?" She saw Kerry McCray coming through the door.

"Hope you don't need your mail," Mrs. Hogendobber called out.

"I tore it up anyway." Mrs. Murphy licked her lips.

"Did you really?" Pewter was impressed.

"Sure, look at this." Mrs. Murphy pushed over an envelope bearing neat fang marks on the upper and lower corners.

"Bet it's a federal offense," the gray cat sagely noted.

"Hope so," Mrs. Murphy saucily replied.

"I'm not here for the mail," Kerry said. "Just wanted to tell you that the Light Opera series at Ash Lawn is doing Don Giovanni on Saturday and really, you've got to come. The lead has such a clear voice. I don't know music like you do, Mrs. Hogendobber, but he is good."

"Why, thank you for thinking of me, Kerry. I will try to swing by."

Harry stuck her head around the mailboxes. "So, Kerry, you been out with the lead singer yet?"

Kerry blushed. "I did show him the University of Virginia."

"You just keep being yourself, honey. He'll soon fall head over heels."

Kerry blushed again, then left, crossing the street to the bank.

"Where does the time go?" Harry shot envelopes into the boxes a bit faster.

"You're too young to worry about time. That's my job."

Harry snagged another cinnamon bun. Pewter had the same idea. "Hey, piggy. That's mine."

"Oh, give her a bite."

"Miranda, you were the person who didn't like cats. The one who thought they were spoiled and sneaky and, as I recall, speaking of time, this was not but two years ago."

Pewter, golden eyes glowing, trilled at Miranda's feet, open-toed wedgies today à la Joan Crawford. "Oh, Mrs. Hogendobber, I looove you."

"I'm gonna puke," Mrs. Murphy growled.

"Now this little darling wants the tiniest nibble." Mrs. Hogendobber pinched off some sweet, flaky dough liberally covered with vanilla icing. The cinnamon scent flooded the room as the bun was broken open. "Here, Pewter. What about you, Mrs. Murphy?"

"*I'm a carnivore,*" Mrs. Murphy declined. "*But thank you.*"

"*I'll eat anything.*" Tailless Tucker wagged her rear end furiously.

Mrs. Hogendobber held a bit aloft, and Tucker stood on her hind feet, not easy for a corgi. She gobbled her reward.

The rest of the day held the usual round of comings and goings, everyone expressed an opinion on the Threadneedle virus, which like so many things reported on television was a fizzle. People also expressed opinions on whether or not Boom Boom Craycroft, the sultry siren of Crozet, would set her cap again for Blair Bainbridge now that he had returned from Africa and she from Montana.

At five to five Mrs. Sanburne reappeared. She'd stopped by at eight-thirty A.M., her usual. Post offices close at five, but this was Crozet, and if anyone needed something, either Harry or Mrs. Hogendobber would stay late.

"Girls," Mim's imperious voice rang out, "Crozet National Bank was infected with the virus."

"Our little bank?" Harry couldn't believe it.

"I ran into Norman Cramer, and he said the darned thing kept inserting information from other companies, feed store companies. Dumb stuff, but they immediately countered with the void commands and wiped it out quickly."

"He's a smart one, that Norman," Mrs. Hogendobber said.

"Sure fell hook, line, and sinker for Aysha. How smart can he be?" Harry giggled.

"I've never seen a woman work *so hard* to land a man. You'd have thought he was a whale instead of a"—she thought for a minute—"small-mouthed bass."

"Three points, Mrs. Sanburne," Harry whooped.

"My favorite moment was when I played through on the

eleventh at Farmington. Aysha, who never so much as looked at a golf club in her life, was caddying for Norman and his golf partner, that good-looking accountant fellow, David Wheeler. Anyway, there she was at the water fountain. She put the golf balls in the fountain. I said, 'Aysha, what are you doing?' and she replied, 'Oh, washing Norman's balls. They get so grass stained.' "

With that the three women nearly doubled over.

Pewter lifted her head as she lay on the back table. Mrs. Murphy was curled next to her, but her eyes were open.

"What do you think of Norman Cramer?"

Mrs. Murphy shot back, *"A twerp."*

"Then why was Aysha so hot to have him?" Tucker, on the floor, asked.

"Good family. Aysha wants to be the queen of White Hall Road by the time she's forty."

"Better make it fifty, Murphy, she's got to be in her middle thirties now." Pewter touched the tiger with her hind paw. Murphy pushed her back.

"Have you seen *Don Giovanni* yet?" Mrs. Hogendobber inquired of Mim. "I was thinking about going tomorrow, Friday."

"Loved it! Little Marilyn can't stand opera, but she did endure. Jim fell asleep, of course. When I woke him he said his duties as mayor of our fair town had worn him out. The only event Jim Sanburne doesn't sleep through that involves music is the Marine Corps band. The piccolo always jolts him awake. Well, I've got a bridge party tonight—"

"Wait, one question. What's the lead singer look like?" Harry was curious.

"She was wearing a wig—"

"I mean the male lead."

"Oh, good-looking. Now, Harry, don't even think about it. You've got two men crazy over you. Your ex-husband and Blair Bainbridge, who I must say is the best-looking man I've ever seen in my life except for Clark Gable and Gary Cooper."

Harry waved off Mim. "Crazy for me? I see Fair from time to time and Blair's my neighbor. Don't whip up a romance. They're just friends."

"We'll see," came the measured reply. With that she left.

Harry washed her hands. The maroon post office ink was smeared into her fingertips. "We should change our ink color every year. I get bored with this."

"And you complain about taxes . . . think what it would cost."

"That's true, but I look at stamps from other countries and the postmark inks, and some of them are so pretty."

"Long as the mail gets there on time," Miranda said. "And when you consider how much mail the U.S. Postal Service moves in one day, one regular business day, it's amazing."

"Okay. Okay." Harry laughed and held up her hands for inspection. "I wouldn't want to waste any valuable ink on my fingers."

"Let's say you have rosy fingertips of a color not found in nature."

"Okay, I'm out of here."

5

The battery flickered on Harry's truck, so she stopped by the old Amoco service station which, a long time ago, was a Mobil station. The ancient Coke machine beckoned. She slipped the coin in and then "walked" the curvaceous bottle through to the end, where the metal jaws opened as she pulled the bottle to freedom. She liked the old machines because you could lift the top up and put your hand into the cool chest. Also, the new soda dispensers were so bright and full of light, she felt she ought to wear sunglasses to use them. A nickel bought a Coke when she was tiny. Then it jumped to a dime when she was in grade school. Now they cost fifty cents, but if one traveled to a big city, the price tag was easily seventy-five. If this was progress, Harry found it deeply depressing.

Usually she headed straight home after work, but the horses grazed on rich pasture. She didn't need to feed grain in the summer. The twilight lingered with intensity. Why hurry?

She absentmindedly nosed the recharged vehicle north up Route 810.

"Where are we going?" Tucker rested her snout on the windowsill.

"Another one of Mom's adventures." Mrs. Murphy curled up behind the long stick shift. She liked that part of the seat best.

"The last time she did this, we ended up in Sperryville. I'm hungry. I don't want to go for such a long drive."

"Whine, then. Get those sweet doggy tears in your eyes. That arouses her maternal instincts." Mrs. Murphy laughed.

"Yeah, well, I can overdo, you know. I've got to save that for special occasions." Tucker was resigned to her fate.

Harry clicked on the radio, then clicked it off. The Preparation H ad disturbed the soft mood of the fading light which blended from scarlet to hazy pink to a rose-gray laced with fingers of indigo.

She slowed at the turn to Sugar Hollow, a favorite spot in western Albemarle County for hikers and campers. The hollow led into a misty crevice in the mountain. No matter how hot the day, the forested paths remained cool and inviting. One could drive a car a few miles into the hollow to a parking lot, then walk.

A roar made Harry hit the brakes so hard that Tucker and Mrs. Murphy tumbled off the seat.

"Hey!" The cat clawed back onto the seat.

A black blur skidded in front of them, hung the turn, and then violently sped down the darkening road away from Sugar Hollow.

Harry squinted after the cycle. It was the black Harley, the driver encased in black leather and on such a hot day. She'd gotten a good look at the bike when Blair had escorted the man out of Ash Lawn. No other motorcycle like it in the area, plus it had California plates.

"Bet he didn't find Malibu in Sugar Hollow either." Harry grimaced.

6

A cold front rolled huge clouds over the mountains together with a refreshing breeze. Although it was the beginning of August, the tang of fall tantalized. In a day or two the swelter would return, but for now Mother Nature, surprising as always, was giving central Virginia a respite.

Harry and Fair turned their horses back toward her barn. The black-eyed Susans swayed in the field along with white Queen Anne's lace and the tall, vibrant purple joe-pye weed. Tucker ran alongside the pair. Mrs. Murphy elected to visit Simon, the possum who lived in the hayloft. A large black snake lived there, too, and Mrs. Murphy gave her a wide berth. The owl slept up in the cupola. The cat and owl couldn't stand one another, but as they kept different schedules, harsh words were usually avoided.

Tucker, thrilled to have the humans all to herself, kept up no matter what the pace. Corgis, hardy and amazingly fast, herd horses as readily as they do cattle. This was a trait Harry had had to modify when Tucker was a puppy, otherwise a swift kick might have ended the dog's career although the breed is nimble enough to get out of the way. Tucker merrily trotted to the side of the big gray mare, Poptart. She hoped that her mother would flirt with Fair. Tucker loved Fair, but Harry had signed off flirting the day of her divorce. Tucker knew Harry was usually forthright, but a little flirting couldn't hurt. She wanted the two back together.

"—right over the ears. Funniest damn thing you ever saw, and when she hit the ground she yelled 'Shit' so loud"—Fair grinned in the telling—"that the judges couldn't ignore it. No ribbon for Little Marilyn."

"Was her mom there?"

"Mim *and* the old guard. All of them. Clucking and carrying on. You'd think she'd have the sense to get away from her mother and go out on her own."

Harry drawled, "Thirty-three is a long, long adolescence. She could have stayed in the house she had with her ex, but she said the colors of the walls reminded her of him. So she moved back to that dependency on Mim's farm. I know I couldn't do it."

"Sometimes I feel sorry for her. You know, everything and nothing."

"I do, too, until I have to pay my bills, and then I'm too jealous for sympathy." A cloud swept low over her head. Harry felt she could reach up and grab a handful of swirling cotton candy. "The hell with money on a day like this. Nature is perfect."

"That she is." Fair spied the old log jump up ahead that Harry and her father had built fifteen years ago, big, solid locust trunks lashed together with heavy rope that Harry replaced every few years. It was three feet six inches. It looked bigger because of the bulk. He squeezed Gin Fizz into a good canter and headed toward the jump, sailing over.

Harry followed. Tucker prudently dashed around the end.

"Who did win the class at the benefit hunter show?" Harry remembered to ask.

"Aysha, with her mother in full attendance and Norman cheering. You'd have thought it was Ascot."

"Good. Say, did I tell you that Aysha was a docent up at Ash Lawn when I was there the other day?"

"She did go to William and Mary, didn't she?" Fair recalled as he slowed to a walk.

"Kerry was there, too, a scheduling foul-up, and Laura Freely. Little Marilyn was in charge, of course, but what set the day off was that this biker came up and had to be escorted off the premises. . . ." She realized that in bringing up Ash Lawn, she would remind Fair that she'd been up there with Blair, which would provoke a frosty response. Her voice trailed off.

"A biker?"

"Hell's Angel type."

"At Ash Lawn?" Fair laughed. "Maybe he's a descendant of James Monroe. What were you and Blair doing up there anyway?"

"Oh—Blair had never seen it. He wanted to do something relaxing."

Fair's lips clamped together. "Oh."

"Now, Fair, don't get in a huff. He's my neighbor. I like him."

"*Yeah, Fair, lighten up.*" The dog added her two cents.

"Are you serious about this guy, or what?"

Harry and her ex-husband had been a pair since kindergarten, and she knew his moods. She didn't want Fair to sink into one of his manly pouts. Men never admitted to pouting, but that's exactly what he did. Sometimes it took her days to pull him out of one. "Number one, I don't have to answer to you. I don't ask you questions." She decided to attack.

"Because I'm not seeing anyone."

"For now."

"That was then. I'm not seeing anyone and I don't want anyone but you. I admit my mistake."

"Make that plural," Harry wryly suggested.

"Well—I admit my mistakes and I repent them. You know you're going to get over this and we'll—"

"Fair, don't be directive. I hate it when you tell me what I'm going to do, and feel and think. That got us into trouble in the first place, and I'm not saying I don't have my share of faults. As wives go, I was a real bust. Can't cook, don't want to learn. Can't iron but I can wash okay. I keep a clean house but sometimes my mind is untidy, and I forgot your birthday more times than I care to admit. Never remembered our anniversary either, for that matter. And the more you'd withdraw from me, the harder I'd work so I wouldn't have to talk to you—I was afraid I'd blow up. I should have blown up."

He pondered that. "You know—maybe you should have."

"Done is done. I don't know what tomorrow will bring, and it's not going to bring togetherness if you get pushy."

"You're the only woman in the world who talks to me like that."

"I suppose the rest of them swoon, bat their lashes, and tell you how wonderful you are. Bet their voices coo."

He suppressed a grin. "Let's just say they shower me with attention. And I have to be nice about it. I can't cut them to shreds over it." He paused. "You make me so mad, I could—I don't know. But I'm never bored with you like I'm bored with the, uh, conventional model."

"Thank you."

"Will you go with me to Mim's party next Saturday?"

"Oh"—her face registered confusion—"I'd love to, but I already have a date."

"Blair?"

"As a matter of fact, yes."

"Dammit to hell!"

"He asked me first, Fair."

"I have to line up for a date with my wife!"

"Your ex-wife."

"You don't feel ex to me." He fumed. "I can't stand that guy. The other day Mim was carrying on about his curly hair. So what? Curly hair? That's a fine recommendation for a relationship."

"Apparently it is for Marilyn Sanburne." Harry couldn't help herself. She wished she were a better person, but his discomfort was too delicious.

"Then I am asking for Thanksgiving, Christmas, and New Year's Eve."

"What about Labor Day weekend?" she teased him.

"Laminitis conference in Lexington," he replied, referring to the hoof disease.

"I was only kidding."

"I'm not. Will you save me those dates?"

"Fair, let's just take it as it comes. I'll say yes to the next summer party—someone's bound to have one—and we can go from there." She sighed. "Given the way the days are clicking off, I ought to say yes to Thanksgiving."

"Tempus fugit," he agreed. "Do you remember Mrs. Heckler singing her congratulations to us?"

"Yeah." She grew wistful. "Isn't it funny what we do remember? I remember that old sweater Dad would wear every homecoming."

"His Crozet football letter sweater." Fair smiled. "I don't think he ever missed a game. Your dad was a good athlete. He lettered in football, baseball, and didn't he play basketball too?"

"Yeah. In those days I think everybody did everything. It was better. Healthier. Tenth-graders now are dreaming of their endorsement contracts. Doesn't anybody play for fun anymore? Dad sure did."

"What year did he graduate?"

"Forty-five. He was too young for the war. Bothered him all his life. He remembered some of the boys who never came home."

"Thank God my father made it back from Korea—seems like no one remembers that war except the guys who fought in it."

"I'm glad he came back too. Where would you be?" She urged Poptart over next to Gin Fizz, reached over, and punched Fair in the arm.

"*Love tap? Mother, can't you brush his hair with your fingertips or something?*" Tucker advised. Tucker had been watching too much TV. She declared it was to study human habits, but Mrs. Murphy said there was plenty of that to study in front of her face. Tucker loved the television because it put her to sleep.

"Tucker, don't yip so loud," Harry pleaded.

"*You're hopeless!*" The dog ran in front of them. She could see Mrs. Murphy sitting in the hayloft door. "*The soul of romance.*"

"*You or Mom?*" Mrs. Murphy laughed.

"*A fat lot you know about love,*" the dog replied.

"*I know it can get you in all kinds of trouble.*"

7

Harry was the first to notice it because she walked to work that Monday morning. The Harley, like a raven with folded wings, was perched in front of the post office. Although Tucker and Mrs. Murphy accompanied her, she had no desire to be alone in the P.O. with that man even if Blair did think he was nonviolent.

She peeped into Market's store. "Hey."

"Hey, back at you," Market called to her.

Pewter thundered out the front door when it was opened, the flab on her belly swaying from side to side. She and Mrs. Murphy immediately ran around the back of the buildings. Tucker was torn whether to join them or stay. She finally followed the cats.

"Where's the biker?"

"The what?" Market wiped his hands on his apron and walked toward Harry behind the counter.

"The Hell's Angel who owns the Harley. If he'd been in your store, you would have noticed."

"Nobody like that this morning. Of course, it's just seven-thirty, so maybe he's out for his morning constitutional and I'll yet have the pleasure." Market offered her a sticky bun. "Is he really a Hell's Angel?"

"Sure looks like one."

"Well, then, Miss Priss, how do you know him? You been hanging around biker bars?" Market teased her.

"He roared up to Ash Lawn the other day when I was giving Blair the tour."

"A cultural Hell's Angel. Harry, you're pulling my leg."

"No, honestly." Harry's inflection rose with her innocence. "Maybe it's a surprise from Fair."

"Sure, sure."

"Blair?"

"Market, what is this? You're getting as bad as the biddies around here, trying to get me tied down again."

"Better than being tied up." He paused. "Then again . . ."

"Have you been talking to Art Bushey?"

As Art was famed for his sense of humor, dwelling mostly on sexual topics, this was not a long-shot question.

"Oh, I'm pricing a new Ford truck over at Art's. I'd like to move up to a three-quarter ton."

"Better sell a lot of potato chips."

"Ain't that the truth."

"This roll is delicious. Are you using a new bakery?"

"Miranda. She's decided she needs pin money, as she puts it, and she's going to be bringing in whatever she whips up. She's such a good baker, I think this arrangement might work."

"Put in a Weight Watchers clinic down the street, and you'll have all your bases covered. There's no way you can eat her concoctions without carrying extra freight."

Aysha and Norman Cramer pushed open the door. Harry stepped aside.

"Hi." Aysha bubbled over. "Sweet'n Low, please. I'm manning, I mean womanning, the phones over at the Junior League charity roundup today. We'll be drinking lots of coffee."

"Norman, what about you?" Market pointed to a sticky bun.

Norman blinked. He blinked a lot, actually, Harry observed.

"I, uh, yeah, I'll try one," he said.

"Now, honey, I don't want any love handles." Aysha pinched him.

"Lovegirl, just a little eensy bite." He smiled. He had beautiful big white teeth.

Laura Freely and Mim entered.

Laura went over to the headache remedies while Mim asked Harry, "And why aren't you in the post office? You're five minutes late."

"Waylaid by a Miranda Hogendobber sticky bun," Harry replied.

Norman swallowed. "They're delicious."

"Don't tempt me!" Laura instructed. "And don't take any to my husband over there at the bank." She nodded in the direction of National Crozet across the street. "Hogan looks at sweets and he gains weight."

Mim hovered over the buns. The odor enticed even her considerable willpower. The swirls in the buns resembled tantalizing pinwheels. "What the heck?" She plunked down a dollar and grabbed two buns. "Does she bring these to work?"

Harry nodded. "She's been baking a lot these last few weeks. She didn't tell me she was going into business though. Guess I was the guinea pig."

"And you don't have an extra pound on your frame," Aysha complimented her.

"Oh, thanks."

Laura pushed her BC Powders on the counter. "If you did all

the farm chores, you wouldn't have to worry either. Harry can probably eat three thousand calories a day and not gain an ounce."

"Speaking of fat, where's Pewter?" Norman, who liked cats, leaned over the counter to look for her.

"Walked out the front door to have a chat with Mrs. Murphy. Well, gang, time to sort your mail."

"Throw out my bills, will you?" Aysha laughed.

"I'm going to give you mine." Harry grinned and left.

She unlocked the front door. Mrs. Hogendobber hadn't come in the back yet. Rob Collier pulled into the front parking space before Harry closed the door. She let it hang open and joined him.

"Only one big bag today."

"Thank God. You about killed us last week."

He noticed the motorcycle. "Who owns that?"

"I don't know his name."

"California plates. A long way from home." Rob hopped out of the truck, bag over his shoulder, and began reminiscing about motorcycles. Motorcycles engendered male nostalgia. "Did I ever tell you about the little Vespa I had? No bigger than a sigh. I wanted to learn to ride a bike, a real bike. I was fourteen, so I gave Jake Berryhill fifty bucks for his brother's old Vespa. Still ran. I didn't get out of second gear for the first month. Then I got the hang of it, so I traded the Vespa in on a 250cc Honda. I thought I was macho man, and I rode that thing on the back roads 'cause I didn't have a license and I didn't have plates."

"How'd you get away with it?"

"Hell, Harry, there weren't but two deputies for the whole of Albemarle County then. They couldn't be bothered with a kid on a Honda." He continued. "Got my license on my sixteenth birthday. Delivered the paper. Saved up and traded up—500cc Honda." He dumped the bag behind the counter, waved to Miranda, and wistfully gazed at the Harley. "You know, I just might have to get me one. Yeah. Slid on your machine, cranked it, and the crank would always fly up and bark your shin. Roll that right wrist in, let out the clutch with your left hand, just nice and easy, pick up your feet and roll—just roll on to freedom."

"Why, Rob, that's poetic," Miranda said.

He blushed. "Happy times." Then he sighed. "What happens? I mean, when is the moment when we get old? Maybe for me it was when I sold that 500cc."

"Honda dealer's in town. There's Harley dealers in Orange and Waynesboro," Harry said.

"Yeah, yeah. I'm going to think about it—seriously."

"While you're thinking, go next door and buy one of Miranda's sticky buns. She's entered the baking business."

"I'll do that." He backed out the door and walked over to Market's.

Miranda beamed. "Do you think it's a good idea?"

"Uh-huh." Harry's tone was positive.

Out back, Mrs. Murphy, Tucker, and Pewter craned their necks upward at the post office drain spout. Little cheeps reverberated from inside.

"Heard it this morning," Pewter solemnly noted. "Haven't seen anyone fly in or out. Of course, I would have caught anyone if they'd tried."

"Dream on, Pewter." Tucker giggled.

"I can catch a bird. I most certainly can," she huffed.

"We aren't catching this one." Mrs. Murphy's whiskers pointed forward, then relaxed. "Come on, time to sort the mail."

"Is there any food in there?" Pewter inquired.

"You work in a market. Why do you always want to know if we have food at the post office?" Tucker's tongue hung out. The day was already heating up.

"Curious. Don't you know anything, Tucker? Cats are by nature curious."

"Brother." The dog pushed open the animal door and entered the post office.

• • •

By noon the biker still had not appeared. Harry couldn't stand it anymore. She went out front and sat on the Harley. It did feel great, nice and lowdown. She checked around to make sure the Hell's Angel wouldn't charge out of a building and scream at her for touching his precious bike.

By three, still no sign of the owner.

"Harry, I'm calling Rick Shaw." Miranda picked up the phone.

Harry considered this a moment. "Wait a second. Let me go get the license plate number." She ran outside and scribbled the number on a scrap of paper.

Miranda dialed the sheriff's department. Cynthia Cooper picked up the phone. "Why aren't you in the squad car?"

Miranda's voice was distinctive. Cynthia knew the caller at once. "I was. What can I do you for?"

"A black Harley-Davidson motorcycle has been parked in front of the post office all day and the owner doesn't seem to be around."

"Do you know the owner?"

"No, but Harry does. Hold on a minute." Miranda handed the phone to Harry.

"Hi, Cynthia. Actually, I don't know the owner but I saw him at Ash Lawn last week."

"Do you suspect anything?"

"Uh, no, I guess we're just wondering why the bike has been here all day. Maybe he copped a ride in a car or something, but we're not a public parking lot. Want the license number?"

"Yeah, okay."

She read off the number. "California plates. Pretty ones."

"They are. Pretty state taxes too. If I paid that much, I'd want gold-plated tags. Okay, Skeezits, I'll run a check and get back to you," she said, calling Harry by her childhood nickname.

The phone rang in fifteen minutes. It was Cynthia.

"The bike belongs to Michael Huckstep, Los Angeles, California. He's a Caucasian—thirty-four years old."

"That was fast." Harry was impressed.

"Computers. If the bike is still there tomorrow, call me. Actually, I'll swing by tonight and check on it anyway, but call me in the morning. Sometimes people do take advantage of federal facilities. It will probably be gone tomorrow."

8

But it wasn't. The next morning, Tuesday, the Harley was right there.

Cynthia cruised on over and inspected the bike while Harry and Mrs. Hogendobber hurried to finish their morning sorting. Mrs. Hogendobber kept running in and out of the office, she was so afraid she'd miss something.

On her last pass into the post office she breathlessly informed Harry, "She's going to have them dust for prints—you know, in case it's stolen."

"Well, if it were stolen, don't you think he'd know it and report it?"

"Not if he's the thief."

Harry cocked her head. "Do criminals have legitimate driver's licenses?"

"Little Marilyn does. The way she drives is a crime." Miranda laughed at her own joke.

Unable to contain her curiosity any longer, Mrs. Murphy strolled out the front door on yet another pass by Miranda. Tucker, lying on her back, legs straight up in the air, was dead to the world. The cat chose not to wake her.

Cynthia, tall and slender, knelt down on the left side of the machine and wrote down the serial number.

Mrs. Murphy jumped on the seat of the motorcycle. She quickly jumped off since it was boiling hot. *"Ouch! Don't they make sheepskin seat covers for bikes?"*

The humans forgot the task at hand for a moment to gossip about Little Marilyn's latest beau—a man both Mrs. Hogendobber and Cynthia considered unsuitable. They moved on to Boom Boom Craycroft's summer vacation, their hope that Kerry McCray would find a decent guy following her loss of Norman, and the delightful fact that Miranda's baked goods were sold out by eight-thirty that morning.

The tiger, her coat shiny as patent leather in the sunlight, sniffed around the motorcycle. She was careful not to get too close, as the metal would be hot as well. A familiar whiff on the right saddlebag, jet black like the rest of the bike, made her stop. She stood on her hind legs, perfectly balanced, and sniffed deeper. Then she got as close as she dared and inhaled. *"Cynthia, Cynthia, there's blood on the saddlebag."*

"—Blair Bainbridge, but you know if Boom Boom lays siege to him again, he might give in. Men find her sexy." Cynthia couldn't help indulging in a light gossip.

"She won't turn his head." Mrs. Hogendobber crossed her arms over her large bosoms.

"They all look at Boom Boom." Cynthia never could understand why a good makeup job and big tits made idiots out of supposedly intelligent men.

"Hey, hey, will someone listen to me!"

"Aren't you a Chatty Cathy?" Miranda reached down to stroke the cat's pretty head.

"*There's blood on the saddlebag. Want me to spell it for you?*" The cat yowled. She vented her frustrations concerning human stupidity.

"My, she is out of sorts." Cynthia brushed her hands on her pants.

"*You're about as smart as a pig's blister.*" Mrs. Murphy spat in disgust.

"I've never seen Mrs. Murphy spit like that." Miranda involuntarily took a step backward.

The cat whirled around and thumped to the front door. She called over her shoulder, "*It's not chicken blood. It's human blood, and it's a couple of days old. If you all would use those pathetic senses of yours, you might even find it yourselves.*" She banged on the door. "*Let me in, dammit. It's hot out here.*"

Since Harry failed to rush right over, Mrs. Murphy, now in a towering rage, shot around to the back of the post office. She smacked open the kitty door, walked in, and whapped Tucker right on the nose.

"*Wake up!*"

"*Ow.*" The dog raised her head, then dropped it. "*You are hateful mean.*"

"*Come outside with me. Now, Tucker. It's important.*"

"*More important than sleeping in the air-conditioning?*"

Mrs. Murphy whapped her again. Harry noticed. "Murphy, retrieve your patience."

"*You can just shut up too. None of you know bugjuice. You rely on your eyes far too much, and they aren't that good anyway. Humans are weak, vain, and smelly!*"

By now Tucker was on her feet and had shaken herself awake. "*Humans can't help being what they are any more than we can.*"

"*Come on.*" She vanished out the door.

Tucker joined her at the motorcycle. Both Miranda and Cynthia had ducked into the market.

"*Here.*" The cat pointed.

Tucker lifted her nose. "Oh, yes."

"Don't touch the bike, Tucker, it's scorching."

"Okay." The corgi moved closer. Her head was tilted back, her eyes bright and clear, her ears forward. "Human. Definitely human and fading."

"I say four days."

"Hard to tell in this heat, but it sure has been a couple of days. It's only a drop or two. If the saddlebag were soaked, even they'd notice it. The aroma of blood is powerful."

"They don't like the smell, assuming they can smell it."

"If there's enough of it, even they can pick it up. I don't know why they don't like it. They eat meat just like we do."

"Yeah, but they eat broccoli and tomatoes too. Their systems are fussier." Mrs. Murphy brushed by Tucker. "I trust your nose. I'm glad you came out with me."

"Have you tried pointing this out to them?"

"Yes." The cat shrugged. "Same old same old. They'll never get it."

"Well, it's a few drops of blood. No big deal—is it?"

"Tucker, a Hell's Angel shows up at Ash Lawn, makes a scene asking for a woman named after a town. Blair gets him out of there. Right?"

"Right."

"Then he sideswipes us as he flies out of Sugar Hollow. And now his motorcycle has been parked in front of the post office for two days."

Tucker scratched her ear. "Something's rotten in Denmark."

9

Actually, something was rotten in Sugar Hollow. A platoon of grade-school hikers on a Wednesday nature trail excursion stumbled upon the remains of a human being. In the high heat the body shimmied with worms.

The stench made the kids' eyes water and some threw up. Then they ran like the dickens down the hollow to the nearest telephone.

Cynthia Cooper picked up the call. She met Sheriff Rick Shaw at the Sugar Hollow parking lot. The nature camp counselor, a handsome nineteen-year-old named Calvin Lewis, led the sheriff and his deputy to the grisly site.

Cynthia pulled out a handkerchief and put it over her mouth and nose. Rick offered one to Calvin. The young man gratefully took it.

"What will you use?" he asked.

"I'll hold my nose. Besides, I've seen more of this than you'll ever want to know." Rick walked over to the corpse.

Cynthia, careful not to touch the body or disturb the scene around it, scanned the blackened mess from end to end.

Then she and Rick walked away from the stench to join Calvin, who wisely had remained at a distance.

"Did you notice anything else when you found the body?" Rick asked.

"No."

Cynthia scribbled in her notebook. "Mr. Lewis, what about broken branches or a path made by the feet of the body if it was dragged through the underbrush."

"Nothing like that at all. If we hadn't been looking for mushrooms—the class is identifying different kinds of mushrooms—I don't think we would have, uh, found . . . that. I smelled it and, uh, followed my nose. It was so strong everywhere that at first I couldn't pinpoint the smell. If I'd known, I would have made the kids stay back. Unfortunately some of them saw him. I didn't mean them to see it—I would have told them it was a dead deer."

Rick put his arm around the young man's shoulders. "Quite a shock. I'm sorry."

"The kids who saw it—I don't know what to tell them. They'll have nightmares for weeks."

Cynthia spoke, "There are a lot of good therapists in the area, people experienced with helping children through trauma." What she didn't say was that most therapists never got this close to raw life or rather, raw death.

After cordoning off the corpse, Rick and Cynthia waited for their team. Calvin rejoined his campers way down at the parking lot.

Rick leaned against a big fiddle oak and lit a cigarette. "Been a long time since I've seen something like this. A real worm's hamburger."

"Whole back blown away. A .357 Magnum?"

"Bigger." Rick shook his head. "Had to have made a loud report."

"People shooting off guns all the time." Cynthia bummed a cigarette off her boss. "Even if it isn't hunting season."

"Yeah. I know."

"A few more days and I think the animals would have been able to pull the arms off, and the legs too. At least the body is intact."

"Let's hope that's a help." He spewed out a stream of soothing blue smoke. "You know, there used to be stills up here. Clear mountain water. Just perfect. Those guys would blow you away pronto. The marijuana growers are more subtle. Here anyway."

"No still around here—at least, I don't think so."

He shook his head. "Not anymore, now that Sugar Hollow is public. Ever drink that stuff?"

"No."

"I did once. Take your head right off. It's not called white lightning for nothing." He glanced over his shoulder at the distant corpse. "Wonder what he got into."

"Guess we'll find out."

"Might take us a while, but you're right. Whenever there's a murder I hope it's an isolated expression of violence and not the start of some, you know . . ."

She knew he meant a serial killer. To date nothing of the kind had ever happened in their area. "I know. Oh, Christ, here come Diana Robb and the crew. If she sees me smoking, I'm going to get Health Lecture 101." Cynthia quickly smashed out her butt in the soft earth.

"Would it do any good?"

"Oh, sure it would—until I wanted the next cigarette."

10

A damp wind slid down the mountains. Harry jounced and jostled along on Johnny Pop. The manure spreader turned, flinging out wood shavings and manure. The sun seemed pinned to the top of the mountain, the shadows from the line of oaks lengthened. Sunrise and sunset were Harry's two favorite times of the day. And today the sweet smell of her red clover filled the air, making the sunset seem richer. Harry kept her fields in alfalfa, red clover, and timothy. She usually produced a very good hay crop from this.

The cat and dog slept in the barn. A full day at the post office wore them out. Tucker heard the noise of a heavy truck crunching down the driveway. She jumped up and awakened Mrs. Murphy.

"*Who goes there?*" Tucker bounded outside.

Blair Bainbridge's dually pulled into sight. Blair stopped and hopped out, shaded his eyes with his hand, saw Harry and sprinted out into the field.

"*That's odd,*" Tucker said to herself. "*He always says hello.*"

Mrs. Murphy, yawning in the doorspan, replied to Tucker's unspoken thought. "*Maybe he's realized he's in love with Mom.*"

"*Don't be sarcastic.*" Tucker sat down, stood up, sat down, finally stood up, and trotted toward the tractor.

Mrs. Murphy rolled over on her other side. She wasn't going anywhere. "*See you later, Alice Gator.*"

Tucker tore after Blair, caught up with him, then blew past him.

Harry, seeing them both, cut the engine. One couldn't hear very well with Johnny at full throttle. "Blair. Hi."

Out of breath, he gasped, "There's been a murder."

"Who?" Harry's eyes enlarged.

"They don't know."

"How'd you find out?"

He put one hand against the seat of the tractor. "Accident."

"Accident or accidentally?" She smiled at herself because she realized that was exactly the kind of question her mother would have asked.

He caught his breath as Tucker circled the tractor. "Accident on 810 at Wyant's Store. I slowed down and noticed Cynthia Cooper just mad as hell, so I pulled over. It was a kid in an old Trooper, driving it like a car. He went off the side of the road, overcorrected, and then sideswiped Cynthia, who was coming from the opposite direction. I mean, she was steamed. The kid was crying, of course, begging her not to tell his parents."

"Is she okay?"

He nodded yes. "Kid too. Anyway, I stayed to help, not that there was much to do, but she isn't the type to get upset. She told me she'd just come out of Sugar Hollow, where a nature group had discovered a dead man. Said it was the grossest mess and she wouldn't be eating dinner tonight. She described what the man was wearing—Harry, I think it's the biker.''

Harry jumped down. ''What?''

He nodded again. ''Heavy black boots, leather vest with symbols and studs—who else fits that description?''

''*Blood on the saddlebags!*'' Tucker yipped.

''Well, he can't be the only man in the country with a black leather vest.'' She stopped a minute and shrugged. A chill overcame her. ''Damn, he about ran me over coming out of Sugar Hollow. Covered from head to toe in leather.''

''Better talk with Cynthia.''

''Did you tell her what you thought?''

''Yeah.'' He stared at the huge tractor wheel. ''He was a little strange. The wheel of fortune, you know.''

Harry watched the sun vanish. ''Someone's up and someone's down—or dead.''

''*Won't somebody listen to me? There's evidence on the motorcycle's saddlebags!*''

''Tucker, hush, I'll feed you in a minute.''

Dejected, Tucker sat on Blair's foot. Blair reached down to pet her.

Blair's lustrous hazel eyes bored into Harry's. ''Do you ever get a feeling about somebody? A real sense of who they are?''

''Sometimes.''

''Despite his appearance and his manner that day, I just felt he was an okay guy.''

''Blair, he can't have been but so okay, or he wouldn't be dead.''

11

A small crowd gathered at the post office parking lot. Harry, Mrs. Hogendobber, Reverend Jones, Market Shiflett, Aysha, Norman, Ottoline, Kerry, the Marilyn Sanburnes—senior and junior, Blair, Mrs. Murphy, Tucker, and Pewter watched as the sheriff's men loaded the motorcycle onto a flatbed gooseneck. Hogan Freely, president of the Crozet National Bank, with his wife, Laura, walked over and joined the crowd.

Cynthia supervised.

Reverend Jones spoke for all of them. "Do you know anything, Cynthia?"

As Cynthia replied, Susan Tucker pulled in. "Wait, wait for me."

"What is this, a town meeting?" Cynthia half joked.

"Kind of." Susan slammed the door of the new Saab. "Fair's on call. He can't make it, but I'll see that your report gets to Fair and Boom Boom, who has a doctor's appointment."

"There's not much to report. A decayed body, a white male most likely in his early thirties, was found in Sugar Hollow yesterday, late afternoon. We have reason to believe, thanks to Blair's accurate description, that the body is that of the owner of this motorcycle. We're running dental checks and we hope to know something soon. That's it."

"Are we in danger?" Mim asked the sensible question.

Cynthia folded her arms over her chest. "There's no way to accurately answer you, Mrs. Sanburne. We suspect foul play, but we don't know for sure. At this point the department isn't worried that there's a killer on the loose, so to speak."

But there was a killer on the loose. The little gathering felt safe because they didn't know the victim and therefore falsely believed they couldn't know the killer.

As Deputy Cooper drove off behind the truck with the motorcycle, the assembled folks squeezed into Market's for some drinks. The motorcycle had conveniently been removed during lunch hour. The sun beat down on them. An ice-cold drink and air-conditioning were welcome.

The animals scooted between legs.

"*Come back here.*" Pewter led them to the back shelves containing household detergents. "*If we get up here we can see everything.*" She jumped onto boxes from the floor to the top shelf. Mrs. Murphy followed her.

"*Raw deal,*" Tucker grumbled.

"*You can go behind the counter. Market's so busy, he won't notice.*"

"*All right.*" Tucker, happier now that she could participate in gleaning information from the humans, worked her way back through the legs to the counter.

Susan, a born organizer, addressed the gathering. "Any of us that've seen the motorcycle before it was parked at the post office ought to write it down for Sheriff Shaw and Deputy Cooper. Obviously, anyone having contact with the deceased should do likewise."

"*Contact?* He barged into Ash Lawn and made such a scene!" Laura blurted out.

"Well, did you tell Deputy Cooper?" Mim inquired.

"No, but I will. I mean, how could I tell her? We just this instant found out—if it really is that same man. Could be some- one else."

Miranda happily watched as people bought her doughnuts, brownies, and tarts—today's batch of goodies. Each day she baked larger quantities and each day they disappeared. She tore herself away from her own products to say, "Those of you who were up at Ash Lawn can go see Sheriff Shaw tomorrow. It would save him time if you go together."

"What happened at Ash Lawn?" Herbie Jones asked the ob- vious.

"This disheveled man, this dirty biker, pushed open the front door after we were closed—" Laura started to say.

"He wasn't that disheveled," Blair interrupted.

"Well, he certainly wasn't well groomed," Laura protested.

"Jeez." Market brought his hand to his face. "If you can't agree on how he looked, I can't wait to hear the rest of it."

"I was in the back, so I can't add anything." Aysha bought a lemon curd tart. She couldn't resist despite her mother's glower- ing gaze.

Harry added to the picture. "Blair and I were in the living room. We didn't see him come in but we heard him. He wasn't rude, really, but he was, uh, intense."

"Intense? He was cracked." Kerry put her hands on her hips. Kerry was a bit of an overreactor. She'd only come in from the slave quarters to catch the tail end of the incident. "He wouldn't leave, and Marilyn, who was in charge that day—"

"I asked him to leave," Little Marilyn chimed in. "He wouldn't go. He said he wanted Marin—"

"Malibu," Harry interrupted.

"Yes, that was it. He wanted this Malibu and he claimed she was at Ash Lawn. Well, of course she wasn't. But he was so insistent."

"Who's Malibu?"

"An old girlfriend," Blair told them.

"That doesn't tell us who she is." Mim, as commanding as ever, hit the nail on the head.

Ottoline sarcastically said, "With a name like Malibu, I suggest we look for someone in a tube top, high heels, short shorts, and with voluminous hair—bleached, of course."

12

The sheriff's office, drab but functional, suited Rick Shaw. He disliked ostentation. His desk was usually neat since he spent most of his time in his squad car. He disliked desk work as much as he disliked ostentation. Mostly he hated being stuck inside.

Today files cluttered his desk, cigarette butts overflowed in the large, deep ashtray and the phone rang off the hook. He'd been interviewed by the local television station, the local newspaper, and the big one from Richmond. Those duties he performed as a necessity. He wasn't a sheriff who loved seeing his face on the eleven o'clock news. Sometimes he'd make Cynthia juggle the interviews.

The coroner worked late into the night taking tissue samples.

No driver's license or identifying papers were found on the body. Cynthia knew the plates were registered to Michael Huckstep. But was the body that of Michael Huckstep? They could assume it was, but until they had a positive ID, they wouldn't know for certain. After all, someone could have killed Huckstep and posed as him.

Rick asked for a list of missing persons as well as stolen motorcycles to be made available to him. They were. Nothing on either California list matched the abandoned Harley or the dead man.

Cynthia scraped into the office. He held up his hand for her to wait. He dispensed with his phone call as soon as he could.

"Mim," he said.

Cynthia emptied the ashtray into the wastebasket. "She wants to be the first to know." She replaced the ashtray. "We went over the bike. Nothing there. No prints. Whoever drove it to the post office wore gloves."

"Bikers usually wear gloves."

"Wonder what he was doing in Sugar Hollow?"

Rick held up his hands as he twirled around in his swivel chair. "Sight-seeing?" He twirled in the opposite direction, then stopped. "Makes me dizzy."

"If it weren't for drugs, we'd be out of work," she joked. "I bet he went in there to make a deal. Sugar Hollow is pretty but not exactly a tourist attraction. He was in there with someone who knows the county—I betcha."

She silently reached over, slipping a cigarette out of his pack, lit it, and spoke. "We searched his motel room. Blair said the biker told him he was staying at the Best Western. The manager, the night manager, and the maids haven't seen Mike Huckstep, the name under which he registered, in days. They don't pay much attention to people coming and going, I guess. No one agrees when they last saw him, but he seemed to be respectful and quiet when he checked in—and he paid in advance for a week."

"Anything in the room?"

"Three T-shirts and a clean pair of jeans. Not another thing.

Not a notepad, a pencil, not even socks and underwear. No paperbacks or magazines. *Nada*."

"I've been reading over the transcripts of your questioning of the Ash Lawn staff as well as Harry and Blair. You know"—he tipped back in his chair and swung his feet onto the folders on the desktop—"this doesn't compute."

"You mean their testimony?"

"No, no, that's fine. I mean the murder. It leads nowhere. Maybe it was a busted deal and the killer took his revenge and the money. There was no money in the pockets of the dead man's jeans."

"Could be . . ." Her voice trailed off, then strengthened again. "But you don't believe it was a busted drug deal, do you?"

"You've been around me too l ..g. You and my wife see right through me." He put his hands behind his head. "No, Coop, I don't believe it. Murder offends me. I can't stand the thought of anyone getting away with it. The rules for getting along in this world are very simple. Thou shalt not kill, thou shalt not steal—seems reasonable to me. Oh, sure, there are times when I could brain my wife and vice versa—but I don't and she doesn't. I count to ten, sometimes I count to twenty. If I can act with a little restraint I figure others can too."

"Yes, but I think murder has to do with something deeper. Something infantile. Underneath it all a killer is saying 'I want my way.' Simple as that. They don't, they can't, even conceive that other people have legitimate needs that might be different and in conflict with their own. It's all me, me, me. Oh, they might dress it up and look mature, concerned, or whatever, but underneath they're infants in a violent, quivering rage."

Rick ran his hands over his receding hairline. "You been reading psychology books on me, Coop?"

"Nah."

The phone rang. Outside Rick's office an officer picked it up, then called out, "Cynthia, Motor Vehicles in California. Want to take it in Rick's office?"

"Sure." She reached over and punched a button. "Deputy Cooper here." She paused, listening. "I'd appreciate that." She gave the station's fax number. "Thank you very much." She hung up the phone. "Mike Huckstep. They're faxing his registration papers and driver's license to us. At least we'll have a physical description."

He grunted. "Who in the hell *is* Mike Huckstep?"

13

Valet parking set the tone for Mim's party. On the invitations she had written that it was a western theme party, complete with square dancing and barbecue. The valet parkers, Susan Tucker's son, Danny, and his high school friends, were dressed in plaid shirts with pointed yokes, jeans, and cowboy boots.

Mim sported beautiful ostrich cowboy boots the color of peanut brittle. Her white leather jeans had been custom made for her, fitting like a glove. She wore a white shirt with a turquoise yoke. Her scarf was Hermès and her Stetson was a 20X beaver. The hat alone must have cost more than $300, since most cowboy hats are only 2X or 4X at most, X being the grade of beaver. The hat, of course, was pure white.

Her husband had donned an old pair of jeans, well-worn

boots, and a nicely pressed Wrangler brushpopper shirt. His belt buckle hinted at the family pocketbook. It was a large, beautifully worked silver oval with gold initials in the center.

All of Crozet attended the hoedown, as it was billed.

Harry borrowed a deerskin shirt with fringe on the yoke, front and back, as well as long fringe on the sleeves. She wore her one pair of Tony Lama boots that Susan had given her for her birthday three years ago. Blair looked like a younger, more handsome Marlboro man, right down to the chaps. Fair fried when he beheld his competition. Not that Fair was bad-looking, he wasn't, but somehow he could never quite synchronize his clothes. Cowboy attire suited his tall frame though, so he looked better than usual.

Mrs. Hogendobber, dangling loads of costume jewelry, swayed in a big red skirt and a Mexican blouse. Her blue cowboy hat hung on her back, the little silken thread like a necklace setting off her throat.

Reverend Jones dug out an old cavalry uniform. He wouldn't tell anyone where he found it. He could have ridden in from 1880.

The music, the food, the ever-flowing liquor, put the group in a wonderful mood.

Kerry McCray arrived early and alone. She said her date, the singer from the Light Opera series, would join them after his show at Ash Lawn. This didn't prevent her from sashaying over to Norman Cramer while Aysha jumped around the dance floor with another partner.

"Norman."

He turned at the sound of the familiar and once-beloved voice. "Kerry."

"Let me ask you something."

"Sure." His tone was hesitant.

"Are you happy?"

A long, long pause followed. He locked his long-lashed blue

eyes into hers. "There are days when I think I am and there are days when I think I've made the biggest mistake of my life. What about you?"

"No. I'm not happy at all." She half smiled. "If nothing else, Norman, we can still be honest with one another."

An agonized expression crossed his features, and then he glanced over Kerry's shoulder, since the music had stopped. "Christ, here comes Aysha." He whispered, "I'll see you at work. Maybe we can have lunch—somewhere, you know."

She watched as he scurried to take his wife by the elbow and hustle her back out onto the dance floor. Tears sprang into Kerry's eyes. Little Marilyn had observed the exchange, although she'd not heard it. She came over.

"He's not worth it."

Kerry sniffed and fought back more tears. "It's not a question of worth, Marilyn. You either love a man or you don't."

Marilyn put her arm around Kerry's waist, walking her away from the dance floor.

Fair and Susan Tucker swung one another around on the floor while the voluptuous widow Boom Boom Craycroft, fabulously dressed, ensnared Blair. He didn't seem to mind. Harry danced with Reverend Jones. She dearly loved the rev and barely noticed the dramas around her. In fact, Harry often shut out those tempests of emotion. Sometimes that was a great idea. Sometimes it wasn't.

After the song ended, the band took a break. The stampede for the bar left the women at the tables as the men jostled for drinks to carry back to "the girls."

Both Blair and Fair arrived at Harry and Susan's table. Mrs. Hogendobber sat at the next table with Herbie and Bob and Sally Taylor, friends from church. Ned was off politicking with the other lawyers.

"Coca-Cola, darling." Fair placed a glass in front of Harry.

Before she could respond, Blair smacked down a gin and tonic. "Harry, you need a real drink."

"She doesn't drink." Fair smiled, baring his fangs.

"She does now." Blair bared his fangs in return.

"Are you trying to get Harry drunk? Pretty crude, Blair."

"Get over it. You divorced her, buddy. I happen to think she's a fascinating woman. Your loss is my gain."

By now the whole party was pretending to be talking with one another, but every ear was cocked in the direction of this exchange.

"She's not a raffle ticket. I haven't lost her and you haven't gained her." Fair squared his massive shoulders.

Blair turned around to sit down. "Cut the crap."

That fast Fair pulled Blair's chair out from under him. Blair sprawled on the ground with a thud.

Blair sprang up. "You stupid redneck."

Fair swung and missed. Blair was quick on his feet.

Within seconds the two strong men were pounding at one another. Blair sent the vet crashing into the table, which collapsed.

"Will you two grow up!" Harry shouted. She was preparing to haul off and sock whoever came closest to her, when a hand closed around her wrist like a steel vise.

"No, you come with me." Reverend Jones yanked her right out of there.

Susan and Mrs. Hogendobber cleared away as the punching and counterpunching increased. As each fist found its target, a thunk resounded over the party. The band hurried back to the bandstand and picked up a tune. Jim Sanburne moved toward the combatants, as did Reverend Jones once he deposited Harry with her hostess.

Harry, red-faced, mumbled, "Mim, I'm so sorry."

"Why apologize for them? You haven't done a thing. Anyway, ever since those drunken swans ruined my Town & Country party I just take it as it comes."

Mim's famed Town & Country party was one she gave years before, filled with stars and business leaders from all over the country. She imported swans for the pool turned lily pond. She drugged the swans for the occasion, but the drugs wore off and the swans invaded the party, got into the liquor and food, becoming pugnacious. Clips of her party made the nightly news on every station in the country. The presidential candidate for whom this extravaganza was planned was shown running from a swan whose wings were outstretched as well as its neck, beak aiming for that large presidential bottom.

"The swans behaved better than these two."

"Harry, I told you both of them are in love with you. You won't listen to me."

"I'm listening now."

Mim slugged back a refreshing gin rickey. "You can't just be friends with men. It doesn't work that way. And don't be mad at them because they can't be friends the way women can. If a man comes around, he wants more than friendship. You know that."

Harry watched as Jim Sanburne and Herbie finally separated the two men she thought of as her friends. Fair had a bloody nose and Blair's lip was split wide open. Boom Boom Craycroft rushed to minister to Blair, who shrugged her off. "I know it. And I hate it."

"Might as well hate men, then."

"You know I don't."

"Then you have to choose between these two or tell them how you feel about them." She paused. "How do you feel about them?"

Harry faltered. "I don't know. I used to love Fair heart and soul, nothing held back. I still love him, but I don't know if I can love him again in that way."

"Maybe trust is the operative word."

"Yeah." She rubbed her right hand over her eyes. Why was life so complicated?

"Blair?"

"He's a tender man. Very sensitive, and I'm drawn to him—

but I'm afraid. Oh, Mim, I just don't know if I can go through loving anyone again."

"Whoever you love will hurt you. You'll hurt him. If you learn to forgive, to go on—you'll have something real." She fingered her Hermès scarf. "I wish I could explain it better than I am. You know that Jim used to cheat on me like there was no tomorrow."

"Uh—" Harry swallowed.

"No need to be polite. He did. The whole town knew it. But Jim was a big, handsome, wild poor boy when I met him and I used my wealth to control him. Running through women was his revenge. I came so close to divorcing him, but, well, I couldn't. When I discovered I had breast cancer, I guess I rediscovered Jim. We opened up and talked to one another. After decades of marriage we finally just *talked* and we forgave one another and—here we are. Now, if a rich bitch like me can take a chance on life and love, I don't see why you can't."

Harry sat quietly for a long time. "I take your point."

"You decide between those two men."

"Blair hasn't exactly declared himself, you know."

"I'm not worried about his feelings right now. I'm worried about yours. Make up your mind."

14

Jangled by the previous night's events, Harry awoke early to a steady rain. As it was desperately needed, she didn't resent the gray one bit. She threw on her ancient Smith College T-shirt, a pair of cutoffs, and sneakers, and dashed to the barn.

After she fed the horses, she hung a bridle on a tack hook in the center aisle, grabbed a bar of saddle soap, a small bucket of water, a sponge, and a cloth to begin cleaning. Rhythmic tasks helped her sort out whatever was going on in her life.

Mrs. Murphy climbed into the hayloft to visit Simon. Being nocturnal, he was sound asleep, so she jumped on a stall door and then to an old but well-cared-for tack trunk. Sitting on four cinder blocks, the wooden trunk was painted blue and gold with M.C.M., Harry's initials, in the middle. Mary Charlotte Minor.

Once divorced, she had kept Haristeen. It was such a bother

to lose your surname in the first place, and then to take it back was too confusing for everyone. That's what she said, but Susan Tucker declared she retained her married name because she wasn't yet done with Fair. Everyone had an opinion on Harry's emotional state and no one minded cramming it down her throat.

She'd had enough emotion and probing questions the night before. She wanted to be left alone. Fat chance.

Blair pulled up the drive to the barn. She had the lights on in the barn, so he knew where she was. Dodging the raindrops, he carried a wicker basket into the aisle.

"This is by way of an apology." He flipped open the wicker lid. Delicious scones, Fortnum and Mason jams and jellies, bite-size ham biscuits, a fragrant Stilton cheese, a small jar of exquisite French mustard, and a large batch of peanut butter cookies were crowded inside. There were even water crackers and tins of pâté stuck in the corners. Before she could reply or thank him, he hurried into the tack room carrying a bag of expensive coffee.

"Blair, I've got only a hotpot down here. I don't have anything for you to make fancy coffee with." She was going to apologize for ending her sentence with a preposition, but then thought, Oh, the hell with it. Grammar and speech were ever diverging currents in the English language.

He silently walked back to his truck, returning with a black Krups coffeemaker, an electric grinder, and a small device for frothing milk for cappuccino.

"You do now." He pointed to the espresso machine. "This will have to go in the kitchen. Now you've got everything you need."

"Blair"—her jaw dropped—"this is so, so, uh, I don't know what to say—thank you."

"I was an ass. I'm sorry. If you'll accept my apology, I'll brew whatever your heart desires. How about a strong cup of Colombian to start? Then we can dig in the basket and follow with espresso or cappuccino, whatever you wish."

"Sounds great to me." Harry vigorously rubbed a rein. "And I do accept your apology."

Mrs. Murphy, tail curled around her, swayed on the tack trunk. She appeared to be sleeping while sitting upright. Humans fell for this trick every time. It was the perfect eavesdropping posture.

Tucker, rarely as subtle, hovered over the basket.

Blair spread a small tablecloth on the rickety table in the tack room. He spied an old coffee tin on a shelf that Harry used as a grain measure. He filled it with water, then dashed outside through the raindrops to pick black-eyed Susans. The coffee was brewed by the time he returned.

"You're soaked."

"Feels good." His hazel eyes were alight.

She put her hands on her hips and looked at the table. "I admire people who are artistic. I couldn't make anything that pretty out of odds and ends."

"You have other talents."

"Name one." Harry laughed.

"*Fishing for compliments,*" Tucker murmured.

"You make people feel good. You have an infectious laugh, and I believe you know more about farming than anyone I've ever met."

"Blair," she laughed, "you didn't grow up on a farm. Anyone who has would seem smart."

"I see other farmers in the county. Their pastures aren't as rich, their fence lines aren't in as good repair, and their use of space and terrain isn't as logical. You're the best."

"Thanks." She bit into a ham biscuit drenched with the mustard. "I didn't know how hungry I was."

They ate, chatted, and ended their meal with spectacular cappuccino.

Blair inhaled the rich smell of leather, saddle soap, pine shavings, the distinct and warm aroma of the horses.

"This barn exudes peace and happiness."

"Dad and Mom poured a lot of love into this place. Dad's family migrated from the Tidewater immediately before the Revolutionary War, but we didn't find this piece of land until the 1840s. The rich Hepworths, that was Mom's family, stayed in the Tidewater. The Minors, hardscrabble farmers, took what they could. The Depression hurt Papaw and Mamaw, so by the time Dad came along and was old enough to pitch in, there was a lot to do. He realized there wasn't a living in farming anymore, so he worked outside and brought home money. Little by little he put things back in order, apples, hay, a small corn crop. Mom worked in the library. Early in the morning, late at night, they'd do the farm chores. I miss them, you know, but I look around and see the love they left."

"They left a lot of love in you too."

Tucker put her head on Harry's knee. *"Say something nice, Mom."*

"Thanks."

"I came over today to apologize and to, well, to tell you I like you a lot. I'm not on my feet . . . I mean, I am financially but I'm not emotionally. I really like you, Harry, and I haven't, oh—" He paused, as this was harder than he had anticipated. "I haven't been fair to you. I know now that our spending time together has had much greater significance to people here than if we lived in New York. I don't mean to be leading you on."

"I don't feel like you are at all. I'm happy with our friendship."

"That's good of you to say. I'm happy, too, but I vacillate. Sometimes I want more, but when I think about what it would mean here, I pull back. If we lived in New York, I'd know what to do. Here, uh, there's more responsibility involved. I love it when I'm here, but I love being on the road, too, and I guess my ego needs it, the attention. I hate to admit that but—"

"Your ego is what makes you good at what you do."

A sheepish smile and blush followed that remark. "Yeah, but there's something silly about standing around in clothes, being photographed. It's just—if I had any balls, Harry, I'd take acting classes, but I think deep down I know I don't have a scrap of talent. I'm just a pretty face." He laughed at his use of an expression generally used to describe women.

"You're more than that. It's up to you and hey, what does it cost to take acting classes—in money and in time? No one is going to throw tomatoes at you in a classroom. If you're any good at it, you'll know. Nothing ventured, nothing gained." She thought a moment. "The University of Virginia has a good drama department."

"You're okay." He reached across the table for her hand but the phone rang.

"Sorry." She stood up and reached for the wall phone. "Hi. Barn."

The deep timbre on the other line, Fair, said, "Will you still speak to me?"

"I'm speaking to you now."

"Very funny. I'm in the truck, had a call over at Mim's, so I'm on my way."

"Not now."

"What do you mean, not now?"

"I have company and—"

"Blair? Is that son of a bitch there?"

"Yes, he came to apologize."

"Goddammit!" Fair switched off his mobile phone.

Harry sat down again.

"Fair?"

"In an emotional tumult, as my mother would have said."

The phone rang again. "I bet that's him. I'm sorry, Blair." She picked up. It wasn't Fair, it was Susan Tucker. "Susan, I'm glad it's you."

"Of course you're glad it's me. I'm your best friend. Scoop."

"I'm ready." Harry mouthed the name Susan to Blair.

"Ned and Rick Shaw had a meeting today about the fund-raiser for the department, and by the bye Rick said the corpse is Mike Huckstep, same fellow that owned the motorcycle. It will be in the papers tomorrow."

"I guess it's not a surprise. I mean, it's what we all figured anyway—that the cycle's owner was the dead man."

"Yeah, I guess that's the end of that. Got a minute?"

"Actually, I don't. Blair's here."

"Ah, that was what I wanted to talk to you about. He came to apologize, I hope."

"Yes."

"We can catch up later, but here it is in a nutshell: Little Marilyn has the hots for Blair."

"A nutshell is where that best belongs." Harry felt that every female under ninety must be swooning over Blair.

"Ah-ha, getting proprietary, are we?"

"No," Harry lied.

"Sure. Okay, I'll call you later for girl talk."

"Spare me. I can't bear one more emotional revelation. Mine or yours or anyone else's. Talk to you later. Bye."

Blair's face clouded over. "Did I just, uh, say too much?"

"Oh, no, no, I don't mean that, but, Blair, all my friends are so busy psychoanalyzing me, you, Fair. I'm sick of it. I'm beginning to think I'm a free movie for everyone."

"I think a single man offends them and a single woman is an object of pity." He held up his hand before she could protest. "It's sexist, but that's the world we live in."

She ran her forefinger over the smooth surface of the high-tech coffeemaker. "Do you want to get married? Wait, I don't mean to me, it's not that kind of question, but in theory, do you want to get married?"

"No. Right now, at this time in my life, the thought scares the hell out of me." He was as honest as a bone. "What about you?"

"Ditto. I mean, I've been married and I thought I was doing a pretty good job at it. Events proved otherwise."

"That was his stupidity, not yours."

"Maybe, but I'm very self-sufficient and I think Fair, and maybe most men, say they admire that quality but in reality they don't. Fair wanted me to be more, well, more conventional, more dependent, and, Blair, that just ain't me."

"Ever notice how people say they love you and then they try to change you?"

She felt so relieved. He said what she felt. "Yeah, I never thought of it that way, but yeah. I am who I am. I'm not perfect and I'm sure not a movie star, but I get along. I don't want to be any other way than the way I am."

"What about sex?"

She gulped. "I beg your pardon?"

He tipped back his head and roared. "Harry, I'm not that forward. What about people's attitudes about sex? If you have an affair, are you a slut in these parts?"

"No, I think that honor belongs to Boom Boom."

"Oooh." He whistled. "But if you sleep with someone, doesn't it imply a commitment? You can't get away with it. Everyone seems to know everything."

She cocked her head to one side. "True. That's why one has to look before one leaps. You can get away with it much more easily than I can. The double standard."

"That double standard you just applied to Boom Boom?"

"Ahhh—no. Boom Boom will have engraved on her tombstone 'At Last She Sleeps Alone.' She overdoes it. But I'd feel the same way about a man. You never met him, but Boom Boom's deceased husband was a real animal. He was fun and all, but if you were a woman, you knew never to trust him."

"*Animal! I take offense.*" Tucker whined, got mad, and padded out to the aisle. She saw Mrs. Murphy and walked over to her friend. She touched her with her nose. "*Wake up.*"

"*I'm not asleep.*"

"*You always say that. You're missing some good stuff.*"

"*No, I'm not.*"

"*Well, you think they'll go to bed?*"

"*I don't know. Not tonight anyway.*"

Back in the tack room Blair and Harry cleaned up. She packed the uneaten items back in the basket.

"Basket's yours too."

"You're being awfully good to me."

"I like you."

"I like you too."

He pulled her to him and kissed her on the cheek. "I don't know what will happen between us, but one thing you can count on, I'll be your friend."

Harry kissed him back, hugged him, and then let go. "That's a deal."

15

The Crozet National Bank, a squat brick building erected in 1910, sat on the corner of Railroad Avenue in a row of buildings that included the old Rexall's drugstore. The woodwork was white, the effect unadorned and businesslike, which suited its purpose.

Thanks to the frugality of a succession of good presidents over the decades, little money had been squandered on the interior. The same old hanging lights swayed overhead. Green-shaded bankers' lamps sat in the middle of heavy wooden desks. The tellers worked at a marble counter behind bronze bars. The austerity lent substance to the bank. The only intrusions of modernity were the computer terminals at each teller station and on each administrative desk.

The office of the bank president, Hogan Freely, was on the

second floor. Mrs. Murphy, accompanying Harry, wandered up the back stairs. She thought she would generously distribute her personality. However, when she strolled into Norman Cramer's office at the far end of the small second story, she decided to hide behind the curtain. Hogan was pitching a major hissy.

"You're telling me you don't know? What in the god-damned hell am I paying you for, Norman?"

"Mr. Freely, please, the situation is highly abnormal."

"Abnormal, it's probably criminal! I'm calling Rick Shaw."

"Let's take this a step at a time." Norman, not the most masculine of men, sounded more masterful than Mrs. Murphy had ever heard him. "If you call in the authorities before I can run a skintight audit, you risk bad publicity, you risk outside auditors being called in. The abnormality in funds may be a glitch in the system. Then we'd be crying wolf. We'd look fool-ish. Crozet National has built its reputation on conservative in-vestment, protecting our customers' assets and good old common sense. I will work day and night if I have to, but give me some time to comb through our records."

Hogan tapped the floor with his right foot. Mrs. Murphy could see his wing tips as she peered from under the curtain. "How many people do you need and how long?" He paused. "And don't ask Kerry to work on this. The tension between you two is disruptive to everyone."

"Give me the whole accounting department and the tellers as well," Norman replied, his ears red from embarrassment.

"How long?"

"Two days and nights, and we'll have to order in food, lots of food."

A long silence followed, then a forceful reply. "All right. You've got until Wednesday closing time or I'm calling the sher-iff. I've got to know why the screen comes up blank when I ask for our assets. And I'm bringing in computer specialists. You work on the books. They'll work on the terminals."

As he started for the door, Norman called to him, "Mr.

Freely, I'm head of this department. The buck stops here. If I can't locate the funds or if the technical experts can't find the computer malfunction, which I really believe this to be, then I will face the press. This is my responsibility.''

"Norman, I'm sorry I blew up at you. I know you'll do your best—I'm jangled. What if the Threadneedle virus did hit us? I have no way of knowing how much money we have. I can't even keep track of simple daily transactions! How can I cover losses if we've had them? The future of this bank depends on your work. We'll be sitting ducks for a takeover.'' His voice cracked. "And how can I face my board of directors?''

"Mim Sanburne most particularly,'' Norman drawled. "We'll find it. Put it out of your mind if you can.''

"Out of my mind—?'' Hogan left before finishing his sentence.

Mrs. Murphy waited, then slipped out the door, jumping the stairs two at a time. She glided over to Harry, who was withdrawing one hundred and fifty dollars. The truck needed a new battery and she hadn't bought groceries in over two weeks.

"Mom, take it all out,'' the cat advised.

Harry felt a familiar rub on her legs. "Visiting done? Let's go back to work.''

"Mom, this bank is in deep doo-doo. You'd better pay attention to me.''

Of course, Harry didn't. She walked back to the post office, Mrs. Murphy glumly following at her heels.

Pewter waited for them outside the market. "Murphy, is it true that the boys got into a fight over Harry?''

"Yes.'' Mrs. Murphy evidenced no interest in the subject.

"Who won?''

"Nobody.''

"You're a sourpuss.'' Pewter fell in alongside her friend.

"Pewts, I was upstairs at the bank and I heard Hogan Freely say that they can't get the computers to report transactions or the amount of money in the bank.''

"Humans put too much faith in money."

"Maybe so . . . I tried to tell Mom, but you know how that goes. She ought to get her money out of there."

"Money. You can't eat it, it doesn't keep you warm. It's pieces of paper. Weird, when you think about it. I believe in the barter system myself."

Mrs. Murphy, lost in thought, missed her friend's comment. "What'd you say?"

"Money's just paper. Not even good enough to shred for a dirt box. But I want to know about the fight."

"I wasn't there."

"Did she say anything about it?"

"No, but Blair came over to apologize."

"Was he horribly contrite?" Pewter wanted the details.

"He bought her an expensive coffeemaking machine. And he brought a big wicker basket full of fancy food."

"What kind of food?" Pewter's mouth watered.

"Uh—liver pâté, crackers, jellies, scones. Stuff."

"Oh, I wish I'd been there. Liver pâté. My favorite."

"Any food is your favorite."

"Strawberries. I hate strawberries," Pewter contradicted her.

"You know, Mom was on the phone with Susan over the weekend, and then this morning she talked to Mrs. Hogendobber about Fair and Blair, in particular; men, in general. She likes them both, but she's . . ." Mrs. Murphy shrugged.

"Burned her fingers. What's that expression? Fool me once, shame on you. Fool me twice, shame on me. Guess it haunts her."

"Here comes Coop. She already picked up her mail."

Cooper pulled into the lot and saw the cats. "Hot outside, girls. Let's go in."

"Okay." The two cats scooted inside when she opened the door.

Miranda glanced up. "Forget something?"

"No. Just a question for you and Harry."

Harry walked up to the counter. "Shoot."

"Oh, Harry, don't say that." Cynthia grinned. "What I want to know is did you notice anyone paying special attention to the bike when it was parked here?"

"Every man that walked by except for Larry Johnson." Larry was the old doctor in town. He hardly ever used his car. He hated machines, walked everywhere, did his own wood chopping and other chores, and enjoyed robust health.

"Names."

"Gee, Cynthia, everyone. Rob Collier, Ned Tucker, Jim Sanburne. Hogan Freely, Fair, Market, Blair—Danny Tucker about died over it and, uh, did I forget anyone?"

Miranda piped up. "Herbie and, let's see, oh, yes, Norman Cramer."

Cynthia furiously scribbled away. "Women?"

"Barely a glance except for me, of course." Harry added, "Why are you asking?"

"I went over that machine with a fine-toothed comb. Then I decided to go over the saddlebags. I was so busy worrying about what was in them—nothing—that I didn't scrutinize the outsides. Couldn't see much anyway since they're black, but I sent them to our little lab, just in case."

Tucker and Mrs. Murphy pricked their ears. Pewter was playing with a cricket in the corner.

"There was a small quantity of blood on one of the bags."

"I told you!" the cat yowled.

"Mrs. Murphy, get a grip," Harry chided her.

"Considering how the man was shot," Mrs. Hogendobber said, "wouldn't blood have splattered everywhere?"

"We know how he was killed, Miranda, but we don't really know where he was killed. We only know where the body was found. And the blood isn't his. The tests came back on the corpse. He had a rare type, AB negative. The blood on the bag was O positive."

"You mean—" Harry didn't finish her sentence.

"There might be another body." Miranda finished it for her.

"Don't jump to conclusions," Cynthia warned. "We've got a team up in Sugar Hollow. If there's anything there, they'll find it. Especially if it's . . ." She delicately left off.

"*Flesh and blood,*" Tucker barked.

16

Harry, Miranda, and Susan combed the forest in the early evening light, the pale golden shafts illuminating spots here and there, the scent of moss and fallen leaves rising around them.

Although Cynthia had told them to keep out of it, they'd do more harm than good, once the sheriff's team left Sugar Hollow, the three women zipped in.

Mrs. Murphy somersaulted as she tried to catch a grasshopper. "*Spit, spit tobacco juice and then I'll let you go.*"

"*Gotta catch him first.*" Tucker thought grasshoppers beneath her attention.

"*I will, O ye of little faith, and when I do I'll say, 'Spit, spit tobacco juice and then I'll let you go.'*"

"*Grasshoppers don't understand English.*" Tucker put her nose to the ground again. She wanted to assist the humans, but any trace of scent other than the smell of rot still hanging on the ground was gone. The humans could no longer smell the decay. *"There's nothing here. We've been walking in circles for an hour and I don't know why they want to stick their noses in it anyway,"* growled Tucker, who stuck her nose in everything.

"A dull summer. Besides, when has Mother ever been able to sit still?"

"I sure can." And with that Tucker plopped down.

The grasshopper or a close relative flipped by Murphy again, and she shot straight up in the air, came down with the insect between her paws, and rolled on the ground.

"Gotcha!"

However, she opened one paw slightly for a close look at her quarry and the grasshopper pushed off with its hind legs, squirting free. Murphy pounced, but the grasshopper jumped high and opened its wings to freedom. In a rage Murphy clawed at the leaves on the ground.

"Ha-ha," Tucker tormented her.

"Oh, shut up, stumpy." She batted the leaves once more in disgust. *"Tucker—"*

"What now?"

"Look."

The corgi reluctantly rose and walked over to the cat's side. She looked at the small clearing Mrs. Murphy made. *"A ring."*

"More than that. A wedding ring." Murphy touched it with one claw. *"There's an inscription inside. You stay here. I'll get Mom."*

"Good luck."

"I'm going straight for the leg. No meowing and brushing by."

"Like I said, good luck."

The leaves crunched underfoot, a fallen tree trunk emanating a dry and powdery aroma blocked her path. The cat soared right over it. She blasted into the middle of the humans.

"Busy bee." Mrs. Hogendobber noticed Murphy's antics.

" 'You ain't seen nothing yet.' " Mrs. Murphy parodied Al Jolson's line. She fixed her gaze on Harry, then turned, ran straight for her leg, and bit it.

"Ouch! What's the matter with you?" Harry swatted at her. Murphy expertly avoided the clumsy hand and bit the other leg.

"Rabies! That cat has rabies." Mrs. Hogendobber stepped backward into a vine and fell right on her large behind.

"Miranda, are you all right?" Susan hurried over to help up the older lady.

"Fortunately, yes. I have ample padding," she grumbled as she brushed off her bottom.

"*Come on.*" Mrs. Murphy ran around in a tight circle, then sat still in front of Harry. "*Okay, Tucker, how about the National Anthem?*"

"*'O say can you see—'*" Tucker warbled.

"What an awful racket." Miranda held her hands over her ears.

Susan laughed. "She doesn't think so."

"*Come on. Follow me. Come on. You'll get it. Watch the pussycat.*" Mrs. Murphy backed up a few steps.

"She's yakking away as well." Susan watched Murphy.

"Might as well see what it is." Harry got the message. "For all I know, Tucker has her foot caught in a root or something. I never know what these two will get into."

"As long as it's not a skunk." Mrs. Hogendobber wrinkled her nose.

"We'd know by now." Susan crawled over the rotted trunk, which Murphy again cleared in one bound.

Mrs. Hogendobber negotiated the obstacle at a slower pace. By the time she was over, Harry had reached Tucker, who didn't budge.

"*'—at twilight's last gleaming, whose broad stripes and—'*"

"*Tucker,*" Mrs. Murphy interrupted this outburst of patriotism, "*you can stop now.*"

"*I was just warming up.*"

"*I know.*" The cat reached down and touched the ring. "*How long do you give them?*"

"*A minute. There's three of them, and unless one of them steps on it, someone will see it.*"

Harry knelt down to pat Tucker. "You okay, girl?"

"Will you look here!" Mrs. Murphy fussed.

Susan did. "Jeez O Pete. Look."

Miranda bent over. "A wedding ring." She reached for it, then withdrew her hand. "Better not."

Harry snapped off a twig from a low branch, slipped it through the ring, and brought it up to her eyes. "M & M 6/12/86."

17

Coop decided not to gripe at Harry, Susan, and Miranda. After all, they did find the wedding ring, about fifty yards from where the body was found. She'd sent it out for prints, although she figured that was hopeless.

It wasn't even noon, but the day was getting away from her. Two accidents during rush hour and both on Route 29, which snarled up traffic. She'd sent out one officer, but with summer vacations depleting the staff, she covered the other one herself.

As soon as Cynthia had received the information from the Department of Motor Vehicles in California, she called the Los Angeles Police Department. She wondered if Huckstep had a criminal record. Sure enough, the answer came back positive for offenses in San Francisco.

The San Francisco Police Department told her Mike Huckstep

had a record for minor offenses: assault and battery, traffic viola-
tions, and one charge of indecent exposure. The officer on duty
suggested she call Frank Kenton, the owner of the Anvil, a San
Francisco bar where Huckstep had worked. When Cynthia asked
why, the officer said that they always believed Huckstep was involved in more than minor crime, but they could never nail him.

Cynthia picked up the phone. It would be eight in the
morning in San Francisco. She'd gotten the phone number of the
Anvil as well as the owner's name and number.

"Hello, Mr. Kenton, this is Deputy Cynthia Cooper of the
Albemarle County Sheriff's Department."

A sleepy, gruff voice said, "Who?"

"Deputy Cooper, Albemarle County Sheriff's Department—"

"Where in the hell is Albemarle County?"

"In central Virginia. Around Charlottesville."

"Well, what in the hell do you want with me? It's early in
the morning, lady, and I work till late at night."

"I know. I'm sorry. You are the owner of the Anvil, are you
not?"

"If you know that, then you should have known not to call
me until after one my time."

"I regret disturbing you, but we're investigating a murder
and I think you can help us."

"Huh?" A note of interest crept into the heavy voice.

"We found a body which we've finally identified as Michael
Huckstep."

"Good!"

"I beg your pardon."

"Good, I'm glad somebody killed that son of a bitch. I've
wanted to do it myself. How'd he get it?" Frank Kenton, wide
awake now, was eager for details.

"Three shots at close range to the chest with a .357 Magnum."

"Ha, he must have looked like a blown tire."

"Actually, he looked worse than that. He'd been out in the woods in the July heat for at least three days. Anything you can tell me, anything at all, might help us apprehend the killer."

"Shit, lady, I think you should give the killer a medal."

"Mr. Kenton, I've got a job to do. Maybe he deserved this, maybe he didn't. That's not mine to judge."

"He deserved it all right. I'll tell you why. He used to bartend for me. Mike had that look. Big broad shoulders, narrow waist, tight little buns. Good strong face and he'd let his beard go a few days. He was perfect for the Anvil. Think of him as gorgeous rough trade."

Cynthia knew that "rough trade" was a term originated by homosexuals that had passed into heterosexual parlance. It meant someone out of the class system, someone with the whiff of an outlaw, like a Hell's Angel. The term had devolved to mean anyone with whom one slept who was of a lower class than oneself. However, Cynthia assumed that Mike Huckstep was the real deal.

"Is the Anvil a straight or gay bar?"

"Gay."

"Was Mike gay?"

"No. I didn't know that, or I wouldn't have hired him. At first I didn't notice anything. He was good at his job, good with people. He flirted with the customers, made a haul in tips."

"You mean you didn't notice that he wasn't gay?"

"Lady, it was worse than that. He brought in his girlfriend, this flat-chested chick named Malibu. Where in the hell he found her, I'll never know. Anyway, he convinced me to let her help out here. Now, I'll never put a chick behind the bar. That's where we need action. But she fit in, worked hard, so I put her at the door. She could screen customers and handle admission."

"You charge for the bar?"

"On weekends. Always have a live band on weekends."

"Did they steal from you?"

"Not a penny. No, what they did was this. Mike would pick out someone rich. Actually, I think Malibu did the grunt work.

Nobody took her seriously. Just another fruit fly, you know what I mean?"

Cynthia understood the term for a woman who hung around gay men. "I know."

"So she'd ask questions, cruise by people's houses if she could track down an address or if they gave it to Mike. Then Mike would trick with the rich guy and Malibu would take pictures."

"Like a threesome?"

"No," he bellowed, "she hid and took pictures and then they'd shake the poor sucker down."

"I thought San Francisco was a mecca for gay America."

"If you work in the financial district, it's not any more of a mecca than Des Moines. And some of the older men—well, they have a different outlook. They have a lot of fear, even here."

"So what happened?"

"One of my regulars, a good man, old San Francisco family, member of the Bohemian Club, wife, kids, the whole nine yards, Mike and Malibu nailed him. He shot himself in the head. A couple of friends told me they suspected maybe Mike was behind it. I finally put the pieces together. He got wind of it, or she did. He never came back to work. I haven't seen him since the day after George Jarvis killed himself, January 28, 1989."

"What about her?"

"Haven't seen her either."

"Were they married?"

"I don't know. They certainly deserved each other."

"One other question, Mr. Kenton, and I can't thank you enough for your help. Did they deal?"

'Frank paused to light a cigarette. "Deputy Cooper, back in the seventies and eighties everyone dealt. Your own mother dealt drugs." He laughed. "Okay, maybe not your mother."

"I see."

"Now, can I ask you a favor?"

"You can try."

"If you've got a photograph of that rotten scumbag, you send it out here to me. I know a lot of people who will want to see Mike dead."

"It's pretty gruesome, Mr. Kenton."

"So was what he did. Send me the pictures."

"Well. . . . Thank you again, Mr. Kenton."

"Next time call after one." He hung up the phone.

Cynthia drummed her fingers on the tabletop. There was no shortage of people who wanted to kill Mike Huckstep. But would they follow him here after years had elapsed? What did Huckstep do between 1989 and now? Was Malibu with him? Where was she?

She called the San Francisco Police Department and spoke to the officer in charge of community liaison. He promised to cooperate. He knew the Anvil, knew Kenton. He'd put someone on the case to ask questions of anyone who might remember Huckstep. It wouldn't be his first priority, but he wouldn't forget.

Then she called the LAPD again. She had asked them to go over to Huckstep's apartment. Yolanda Delgreco was the officer in charge.

"Find anything?" Coop asked when Yolanda picked up the line.

"Funny you should call. I just got back. It's been crazy here. Anyway, I'm sorry I'm late. Place was cleaned out. Even the refrigerator was cleaned out. He wasn't planning on coming back."

"Did the landlord or neighbors know anything about him?"

"His landlord said he didn't work. Had a girlfriend. She dumped him. Huckstep told him he lived off his investments, so I ran a check through the banks. No bank account. No credit cards. Whatever he did was cash and carry."

"Or he had the money laundered."

"Yeah, I thought of that too. When my money's laundered it's because I forgot to clean out my pockets before putting my stuff in the washing machine." Yolanda laughed.

"Hey, thanks a lot. If you ever come to Virginia, stop by. We've got some good women in the department. It will take a while longer here than there probably, but we're working on it."

"Thanks. If I do find myself in Virginia, I'll visit. You have many murders there?"

Cynthia said, "No, it's pretty quiet that way."

"If anything turns up on Mike Huckstep, I'll buzz."

Cynthia hung up the phone. Most of her job on a case like this was footwork, research, asking a lot of questions. Over time and with a bit of luck a pattern usually emerged. So far, no pattern.

18

At seven-thirty in the morning the mercury hovered at a refreshing 63 degrees. Harry intended to jog to work, which took twenty minutes and gave Mrs. Murphy and Tucker exercise too. But she fell behind in her farm chores and hopped in the truck instead. The animals climbed in with her.

"Ready, steady, go." She cut on the ignition. The Superman-blue truck chugged a moment, coughed, and then turned over. "Better let it run a minute or two."

Mrs. Murphy's golden, intelligent eyes were merry. "*Mother, it's not the battery that's the problem. This truck is tired.*"

"*Yeah, we need reliable transportation,*" Tucker carped.

Harry hummed, then pushed in the clutch, popped it in first, and rolled down the driveway. She reached for the knob on the radio. A country music station blared.

"*I hate that stuff.*" The cat slapped at the knob, making the reception fuzzy.

"*Three points.*" Tucker encouraged her.

The tiger's paw shot out again and she moved the dial even more.

"Bless our nation's leaders in this time of moral peril, give them the courage to root out the evil of Satanism masquerading as liberalism, and lest we—"

"Gross." Murphy blasted the radio. "*Humans are weird beyond belief.*"

The strains of a popular tune greeted her kitty ears.

"*Better.*" Tucker's pink tongue hung out. "*Wrinkle music, you know.*"

"*What do you mean, wrinkle music?*" The cat cocked her head at the soothing music.

"*For old people. Haven't you noticed that no one wants to admit they're old? So radio stations advertise that they play hits from the fifties, sixties, seventies up to today. That's bunk. It's wrinkle music, but the listener can pretend he's hip or whatever word they used when they were young.*"

"*I never thought of that.*" Mrs. Murphy admired her friend's insight. "*So how come we don't hear Benny Goodman?*"

"*The Big Band generation is so old, they're going deaf.*"

"*Savage, Tucker. Wait until you get old and I make fun of you.*" The cat laughed.

"*You'll be old right along with me.*"

"*Cats don't age like dogs do.*"

"*Oh, bull!*"

The news crackled over the radio. Harry leaned forward to turn up the sound. "Pipe down, you two. I want to hear the news and thank you, Mrs. Murphy, for manning the stations. Catting the radio? Doesn't sound right."

"*You're welcome.*" Mrs. Murphy put her paws on the dash so she could see through the windshield.

"The state's largest banks are reporting computer breakdowns. For the last week technicians have been working to re-

store full function to the computer systems of Richmond Norfolk United, Blue Ridge Bank, and Federated Investments, all of which are reporting the same problem. Smaller banks are also experiencing problems. Roland Gibson, president of United Trust in Roanoke, counsels people to have patience. He believes this is fallout from the Threadneedle virus, which hit businesses and banks on August first but caused no serious damage, so it was believed. Don't withdraw your money—"

"What do you think of that?" Harry whistled.

"*I think I'd call my banker.*" Murphy arched a silky eyebrow.

"*Yeah, me too,*" the dog echoed.

Harry pulled up behind the post office. When she opened the door the tantalizing aroma of orange-glazed muffins greeted her. Miranda, in a house-cleaning mood, put a checkered tablecloth on the little table. She was measuring the chairs for seat-cover fabric.

"Morning."

Harry's nostrils flared to better capture the scent. "Been reading *House and Garden* again?"

"Threadbare." She pointed to the chair seats. "Couldn't stand another minute of it. Have an orange muffin. My latest."

Harry shoved the muffin in her mouth and said thank you after she ate it. "I sure hope you took some of these next door. These are the best. The best ever." She gulped. "Threadbare. Threadneedle."

"What?" Miranda's lipstick was pearly pink.

A knock on the door diverted Harry's attention from her musing. Susan pushed through the back door. "Where's Rob?"

"Late. Why, are you offering to sort the mail?"

"No." Susan sniffed. "What is that divine smell?"

Harry pointed to the plate of muffins.

Mrs. Hogendobber nodded and Susan's hand darted into the pile. "Oh, oh—" was all she could manage. Swallowing, Susan licked her lips. "I have never tasted anything so delicious in my entire life."

"Now, now, base flattery. You know what the Good Book says about flatterers."

Susan held up her hand for stop. "I don't know what the Good Book says, but I am not flattering you. These are absolutely out of this world!"

"*Well, I want one!*" Tucker yelped.

Mrs. Hogendobber gave the dog a morsel.

"What's up, Susan? It must be pretty good if you're here this early."

"I get up early." She brushed crumbs off her magenta T-shirt. "However, the buzz is that Mim is fit to be tied—in a total, complete, and obliterating rage."

"Why?"

"She owns a large, as in thirty-seven percent, chunk of Crozet National."

"So?" Harry reached for another orange delight.

"Two million dollars is missing from the bank."

"What!" Miranda shouted.

"Two million smackers." Susan ran her fingers through her blond curls. "Ned's on the board and Hogan called him last night to tell him that he has given Norman Cramer until Wednesday night to finish his audit. He's also called in computer whizzes, since that's where the mess seems to have started, but he believes the money is gone. He wants to prepare everyone before he gives a press statement Friday morning. He's not one hundred percent sure about the sum, but that's what the computer types are telling him as they piece the system back together."

"Good Lord." Mrs. Hogendobber shook her head. "What is—"

"It's the Threadneedle virus. Oops, sorry, Miranda, I interrupted you."

Mrs. Hogendobber waved her hand, no matter.

"*I changed the station. That's how she found out,*" the cat bragged.

"But Crozet National?" Susan continued. "It's small beer

compared to United Trust. Of course, they aren't reporting missing funds—yet."

"The Soviets." Miranda smacked the table and scared Tucker, who barked.

"There aren't any more Soviets," Harry reminded her.

"Wrong." Miranda's chin jutted out. "There is no longer a USSR, but there are still Soviets. They're bad losers and they'd love to throw a clinker into capitalist enterprise."

"At Crozet National?" Harry had to fight not to laugh.

"Banks are symbols of the West."

"That's neither here nor there. I want to make sure my money is safe. So I called Hogan myself. Ned could have killed me. Hogan assured me that our money is safe, and even though two million is a terrible loss for the bank, it can absorb it. And the money may yet be found."

"Is Norman Cramer up to the job? I know he's head accountant over there, but—"

"Harry, what does he have to do but punch numbers into a computer? An audit's an audit. It's time consuming, but it doesn't take a lot of gray matter." Miranda, a good bookkeeper, still thought an adding machine could do the job.

The back door swung open. A depressed Mim came in, then brightened. "What is that marvelous—" She spied the muffins. "May I?"

"Indeed." Miranda held out her hand as if bestowing an orange muffin on her old acquaintance.

"Mmm." Mim brushed off her fingers after making short work of the delicious treat. "Susan tell you?"

"Uh—" Harry stalled.

"Yes."

"We can't do much until tomorrow afternoon, when the audit is complete. Worrying won't help." She poured herself a cup of coffee. "Anyone?"

"Any more caffeine and I'll be—"

"*A bitch.*" Tucker finished her mother's sentence.

"Hello!" Pewter arrived through the animal door. "*What a beautiful day.*"

"Hello, gray kitty." Susan stroked Pewter's round head. "What do you know that's good?"

"*I just saw Kerry McCray tell Aysha Cramer to go to bloody hell.*"

"*What?*" the cat and dog asked.

"Isn't she cute?" Mrs. Hogendobber pinched off some muffin for the cat.

Rob Collier tossed the mail bag in the front door as Market Shiflett hustled in the back. Everyone yelled hi at everyone else.

"What a goddamned morning!" Market cursed. "I'm sorry, ladies. Even my cat had to get out of the store."

"What's going on?"

"Cynthia Cooper drove in the minute I opened. She was joking, her usual self, bought coffee and an orange muffin, ah, you brought some here too, Miranda. I'm sold out and it's not even eight. Anyway, Aysha zipped in, and as luck would have it, Kerry followed. They avoided each other just as you'd expect, but they both came to the counter at the same time. Cynthia was leaning against the counter, facing the door. I don't know what kicked it off, but Kerry told Aysha to move her fat butt. Aysha refused to move and called Kerry a cretin. The insults escalated. I never knew women could talk like that—"

"Like what?" Mim's eyes widened.

"Kerry called Aysha a slut. Aysha told Kerry if she'd kept Norman happy he'd have never left her. Well, Kerry said she wasn't a cocksucker, that she would leave that work to Aysha. Before I knew it, Aysha slapped Kerry and Kerry kicked Aysha in the shins. Doughnuts were flying and Cynthia put her coffee on the cake display and separated the two, who were by that point screaming. I just—" He shook his head.

"What despicable language!" Miranda picked up Pewter and held her hand over the cat's ears, realized what she'd done, and quickly removed her hand.

"*Kerry told Aysha she was a fake. She doesn't come from an old family.*" Pewter relished the gossip.

Mrs. Hogendobber stroked the cat, oblivious of the details.

"*It's true.*" Mrs. Murphy sat down and curled her tail around her. "*The Gills are no more first family of Virginia than Blair Bainbridge. The great thing about Blair is he couldn't care less.*"

Market caught his breath. "Aysha scratched Cynthia, by mistake she said. I rushed over to pull Kerry back, since Cynthia was trapped between them, keeping them apart—I was sure they were gonna wreck my store. As we pulled them away from each other, Kerry noticed a wedding ring on the floor. She scooped down to pick it up, I had only one arm on her, you know, and she threw it in Aysha's face. 'You lost your wedding ring. That's bad luck, and I wish you a ton of it.' Aysha checked her left hand. She still had her ring on. But she picked up the ring and said, 'This isn't mine.' She held up her ring finger and that set Kerry off again. She lunged for Aysha. I thought I would never get Kerry out of the store. She apologized profusely once I did and then she burst into tears." He threw up his hands. "I feel bad for her.

"The ring had fallen out of Cynthia's pocket when she jumped into action, so to speak. Actually, I shouldn't make light of it. They were out of control and someone could have been hurt. Aysha handed the ring back to Cynthia. 'Married?' she asked. Cynthia said no, she had no secret life. The ring was found near the corpse in Sugar Hollow. She was a little sheepish about it, but she said if she carried it around, now that it was back from the lab, she was hoping it would give off a vibration and give her an idea."

He shook his head again. "Crazy morning. Oh, and Laura Freely came in just looking like death. What's the matter with her? Hogan running around or something?"

"Hogan doesn't run around," Mim said frostily.

"Kerry's got to get over Norman," Susan jumped in.

"Either that or kill Aysha," Market said.

19

Dark circles under Norman Cramer's eyes made him look like a raccoon. He stood before Hogan Freely, whose office was adorned with golf mementos.

"—the staff was great, but we couldn't find what does appear to be a two-million-dollar deficit. We keep coming up short, but we can't find the location of the loss, so to speak. We've gone over everything and I feel responsible for this—"

Hogan interrupted him. "Don't blame yourself."

"I was hoping this was an isolated accounting error."

"This must be what the Threadneedle virus was really about."

"I don't know, sir. Other banks aren't reporting losses. They're reporting downed computers."

"Norman, go home and get some sleep. I'll face the music."

"I should be there with you. This isn't your fault."

"I appreciate that, but the duty is mine to break the news to our investors and customers. Why don't you just go home and sleep? You look like you need it. I appreciate how hard you've worked on this."

"Well"—Norman folded his hands behind his back—"there has to be an answer."

"Yeah"—Hogan smiled weakly—"I just hope I live long enough to find it. Some slick investigator will figure this out. I spoke to an old college buddy down in Virginia Beach at Atlantic Savings and he said the bank has already retained the services of Lorton & Rabinowitz."

"The experts on corporate sabotage." Norman's pupils widened.

Hogan stood up. "Go on, get some sleep."

Wednesdays Fair worked the western end of Albemarle County. That was his excuse to show up at Harry's farm. He found her repairing fences on the back line of her property.

"In the neighborhood."

"So I see," Harry replied.

"I was wrong. That guy pisses me off, but I was wrong."

"How about an apology for hanging up on me."

"That too. If you'd waited a minute, I would have gotten to that. I'm sorry I swore at you and hung up." He jammed his hands in his pockets.

"Apology accepted."

"Need a hand?"

"Sure."

They worked side by side as they had done for the years of their marriage. The light faded, the mosquitoes appeared, but they pressed on until it was too dark. They knew one another so well, they could work in silence without worrying about it.

20

The hot, hazy, humid days of August fled before a mass of cool, sparkling air from Canada, the second in the last ten days. The clear skies and rejuvenating seventy-degree temperatures delighted everyone's senses except perhaps those of Hogan Freely, Norman Cramer, and Mim Sanburne. Not that people clapped their hands when they heard over the morning radio and local television that money was missing from the bank, but in the relief from summer's swelter it didn't seem so immediately important. Also, they believed Hogan when he declared their funds were secure.

Mrs. Hogendobber drove over to Waynesboro Nursery. She wanted a pin oak for the northern corner of her property, a half-acre lot right behind the post office on the other side of the alleyway.

Mrs. Murphy slept in the mail cart. Tucker stretched out

under the table in the back. Harry boiled water for tea to counter-
act her midmorning slump.

The door opened. Aysha glanced around before stepping inside. "Morning."

"Morning, Aysha. No one's here."

"As long as Kerry's not around." Aysha slipped the key in
her mailbox, opened the heavy little door, and scooped out her
mail. "I suppose you heard what happened yesterday. I guess
everyone has."

"Market said you and Kerry got into it." Harry shrugged.
"It'll blow over."

Aysha placed her mail on the counter. "She's mental. How
can it blow over when she's obsessed with Norman and likewise
obsessed with me—negatively, of course. If he had been in love
with her, if it had been the right combination, he would have
stayed, right?"

"I guess." Harry was never comfortable when people veered
toward analyzing one another. She figured psychology was another set of rules with which to restrain people. Instead of invok-
ing the wrath of God, one now invoked self-esteem, lack of
fulfillment, being out of touch with one's emotions. The list
could go on and on. She tuned out.

"What am I supposed to do?" Aysha wondered. "Hide? Not
appear at any social function where Kerry might be present lest I
bruise her fragile emotions? Everybody wants to be loved by everybody. That's her real problem, it's not just Norman. She has to
be the center of attention. This sure is one way to get it.
Why . . . I even worry about going into the bank. If she had
any decency, she'd transfer to another branch. Norman says he
avoids her like the plague."

Harry thought Kerry a bit emotional, but the Kerry she
knew didn't fit Aysha's description. "Right now neither one of
you can be expected to feel good about the other. Ignore her if
you can."

"Ignore someone who would have killed me if she could?"

"It wasn't that bad."

"You weren't there. She would have killed me if Cynthia hadn't separated us. Thank God she was there. I'm telling you, Harry, the girl is disturbed."

"Love does strange things to people."

Susan and Mim, one by the front door the other by the back, entered at the same time.

"How's Norman?" Mim asked.

"Stressed out. He can't sleep. He's frantic over the missing money." She knitted her eyebrows. "And this episode with Kerry preys on his mind. He insisted on going to work today, on being there when Hogan made his press statement. I keep telling him, 'Honey, no one blames you,' but he blames himself. He needs a vacation, something."

Mim changed the subject. "Marilyn will take your place at Ash Lawn tomorrow. I know she called and left a message on your machine, but since I'm here, I thought I'd tell you."

"Bless her heart." Aysha's face relaxed. "I can spend tomorrow with Norman. Maybe I can slip a tranquilizer into his coffee or something. Poor baby."

Susan, in her tennis blouse and skirt, checked the old railroad clock. "Harry, I'm late for my game. You gonna be around tonight?"

"Uh-huh. I'm on the back fence line."

"Okay. Ned's going to Richmond, so I'll bring a cold supper."

"Great."

Susan left, Aysha swept out, and Mim stayed. She flipped up the divider and walked behind the counter. As Harry's tea water was boiling, she poured Harry's cup of tea and one for herself too. "New seat covers."

"Miranda couldn't stand the old ones. She's so good at stuff like this."

"Harry, will you do me a favor?"

"If I can."

"When you sort the mail, if you see an unusual number of registered letters or large packages from brokerage houses"—she paused—"I guess you can't tell me, but call Rick Shaw immediately."

Harry gratefully sipped the hot beverage. "I can do that."

"I think the money has to go somewhere. Buying large quantities of stock would be one place, although not the safest. I considered that." Her large gold bangle bracelets clanged together when she reached for her cup. "But a person could say the money was inherited or they could even be in collusion with a broker. But the culprit could be anywhere, and two million dollars doesn't disappear."

Harry, not knowing much about high finance, said, "Is it difficult to get one of those numbered accounts in Switzerland?"

"Not really."

"I would think the temptation to spend the money would be overwhelming. I'd buy a new tractor and truck today."

"Whoever did this is patient and highly skilled at deceit, but then, I suppose we all are to one extent or another."

"Patient or deceitful?" Harry laughed.

"Deceitful. We learn early to mask our feelings, to be polite."

"Who would be smart enough to pull this off?"

"Someone with a more rapacious appetite than the rest of us ever realized."

Just then Reverend Jones stepped into the post office.

Mrs. Murphy looked up at her mother just as Mim did. Mim and Harry looked at the portly reverend and said, "Never."

"What are you girls talking about?"

"Appetites," Harry answered.

•   •   •

Kerry McCray nibbled at carrot sticks and celery. She wasn't hungry and she'd cried so much, she felt nauseated. Reverend Jones, just back from the post office, shepherded her to the slate patio in the back of his house, scrounged in the refrigerator for something to eat, and made some iced tea.

"I don't know what to do." She teared up again, her upturned nose sniffing.

"Everyone loses his or her temper. I wouldn't worry too much about that."

"I know, I know, but I love him and I don't think she does. Oh, she fawns all over him for show, but she doesn't really love him. How could she? All she thinks about is herself. She hasn't changed much since grade school except she's better-looking. The boob job helped."

Herb blushed. "I wouldn't know about that."

"How can you miss it?"

"Now, Kerry, if you dwell on Aysha and Norman, you'll worry yourself to a shadow. You've lost weight. You've lost your sparkle."

"Reverend Jones, I pray. I ask for help. I think God's put me on call-waiting."

He smiled. "That's my Kerry. You haven't lost your sense of humor. We are each tested in this life, although I don't know why. I could quote you Scripture. I could even give you a sermon, but I don't really know why we have to suffer as we do. War. Disease. Betrayal. Death. Some of us suffer greater hardships than others, but still, we all suffer. The richest and the poorest alike know heartache. Maybe it's the only way we can learn not to be selfish."

"Then Aysha needs to suffer."

"I've felt that way about a few people I don't much like, too, but you know, leave them to heaven. Trust me."

"I do, Reverend Jones, but I'd like to see her suffer. I don't feel like waiting until I'm forty. In fact, I'd like to kill her."

Kerry's lower lip trembled. "And that's what scares me. I've never hated anyone like I hate her."

"It'll pass, honey. Try to think about other things. Take up a new hobby or a vacation, something to jolt you out of your routine. You'll feel better, I promise."

As Reverend Jones counseled Kerry with his mixture of warmth and good sense, Susan and Harry finished up the fence repairs.

Mrs. Murphy chased a mouse. "*Gotcha!*" She grabbed at the mouse, but the little devil squirmed from under her paw to scoot under a pile of branches that Harry had made when she pruned the trees in the back.

Tucker, also in on the chase, whined, "*Come on out, coward.*"

"*They never do.*" Murphy checked the back of the woodpile just in case.

"Locust posts are hard to find." Harry admired the posts her father put in twenty years earlier. "The boards last maybe fifteen years, but these posts will probably outlast me."

"You'll live a long time. You'll replace them once before you go." Susan picked up her hammer. "I should do this more often. No wonder you never gain an ounce."

"You say that, but you look the same as when we were in high school."

"Ha."

"Don't accept the compliment, then." Harry grinned, checked the ground for nails, and stood up. "Wish we had a little more light. We could take a trail ride."

"Me too. Let's go over the weekend."

"Did I tell you what Mim said to me at her party? She said that men and women couldn't really be friends. Do you believe that?"

"No, but I think her generation does. I've got scads of male friends and Ned has women friends."

"But you still have to settle the issue of sex."

Susan swung her hammer to and fro. "If a man doesn't mention it, I sure don't. I think it's their worry not ours. Think about it. If they don't make a pass at a lady, have they insulted her? I suppose it's more complicated than that, but it seems to me they're damned if they do and damned if they don't. If they take the cue from us that it's okay to forget about it, then I think most of them do. Anyway, after a certain age a man figures out that the first three months sleeping with a new woman will be as thrilling as always. After that it's the same old same old."

"Are we getting cynical?"

"No. Realistic. Everyone you meet in life has problems. If you dump one person and pick up another, you've picked up a new set of problems. It might be that person number two's problems are easier for you to handle, that's all."

"I'm between person number one and person number two and I'm sick of problems. I'm considering being a hermit."

"Everyone says that. Fair's person number one and—"

"It galls me that he thinks he can waltz back into my life."

"Yeah, that would get me too, sometimes, but hey, give him credit for knowing you're the right person and he screwed up."

"Screwed *around*."

"*Mother, give him a break,*" Tucker said.

"Nonetheless, my point stands. As for Blair—"

"Blair hasn't declared himself, so I'm not taking him as seriously as everyone else is."

"But you like him—I mean, *like* him?" Susan's voice was expectant.

"Yeah—I like him."

"You can be maddeningly diffident. I'm glad I'm not in love with you." Susan punched her.

"Don't be ugly."

They trudged toward the barn in the distance. Mrs. Murphy raced ahead, sat down, and as soon as they drew near her, she'd race off again. Tucker plodded along with the humans.

As they put away the tools, Harry blurted out, "Susan, when did the money disappear from the bank?"

"Last week, why?"

"No one has pinpointed an exact time, have they?"

"Not that I recall."

"There's got to be a way to find out." Harry grabbed the phone in the tack room and dialed Norman Cramer. She peppered the tired man with questions, then hung up. "He said he doesn't know for certain the exact time, but yes, it could have started on August first."

Susan rolled the big red toolbox against the corner of the tack room. "The damn virus did work, but doesn't it seem weird to you that other banks aren't reporting missing funds?"

"Yeah, it does. Come on into the house."

Once inside, Harry sat cross-legged on the floor of the library just as she did when she was a child. Books surrounded her. She paged through an *Oxford English Dictionary*. Susan, in Daddy Minor's chair, propped her feet up on the hassock, leafing through a book on the timetables of history.

Mrs. Murphy prowled the bookshelves as Tucker wedged her body next to Harry's.

"They've got all the books they need."

The cat announced, *"There's a mouse in the walls. I don't care about the books."*

"You won't get her out. You haven't been having much luck with mice lately."

"You don't know."

"Say, where's Paddy?" Tucker wondered where Mrs. Murphy's ex, a handsome black and white tom with the charm and wit of the Irish, was living these days.

"Nantucket. His people decided the island would be dull without him, so I guess he's up there chasing seagulls and eating lots of fish."

Harry flipped to "thread." It covered two pages of the unabridged version of the O.E.D.

She found "threadbare," which was first used in writing in 1362. The gap between when a word is used and when it is written down can be decades, not that it mattered in this case.

Her eyes swept down the thin, fine grade of paper. "Ah-ha."

"Ah-ha what?"

"Listen! 'Threadneedle' first appeared in writing in 1751. It's a children's game where all join hands. The players at one end of this human string pass between the last two at the other end and then all pass through."

"I can't see that that has anything to do with the problem."

"Me neither."

"Are there other meanings?"

"Yeah. As a verb phrase, 'thread the needle.' It was written in 1844. It refers to a dancing movement when a lady passes under her partner's arm, their hands being joined." Harry glanced up from the dictionary. "I never knew that."

"Me neither. Anything else?"

"It can also mean to fire a rifle ball through an augur hole barely large enough to allow the ball to pass without enlarging the hole." Harry closed the big volume, making a thick, slapping sound. "What have you found?"

"On August 1, 1137, King Louis VI of France died. So did Queen Anne of Britain in 1714." She read some more. "And Germany declared war on Russia in 1914. Well, that certainly changed the world."

"Let's try another book. There has to be something we're missing."

"It could be a red herring, you know."

"Yeah, I do know, but there's something about this that smells of superiority. Whoever is fooling around—"

"Stealing."

"Right, whoever is stealing money is going to rub our noses in how dumb we are."

"Here." Mrs. Murphy, with her paw, pulled out another book listing events in history. The book fell to the floor.

"Murphy." Harry shook her finger at the cat. "You can break a book's spine doing that."

"*Don't be such a pill.*"

"Back talk." Susan laughed. "It sounds exactly the same whether it's your animals or your children."

"*I never talk back,*" Tucker stated.

"Liar," came the cat's swift reply. She jumped down from the bookshelf to sit next to Harry. Susan left her chair and sat on the floor on the other side of Harry.

"Okay. August first. Slavery was abolished in the British Empire in 1834."

"That reminds me, Mim was talking to Kate Bittner about the Civil War series on PBS. Mim said, 'If I'd known it was going to cause this much fuss, I would have picked the cotton myself.' "

Harry leaned back, hands on knees. "Jeez, what did Kate do?" As Kate was of African descent, this was not an idle question.

"Roared. Just roared."

"Good for her. Think she'll be voted president of the Democratic Party in the county?"

"Yes, although Ottoline Gill and—"

"Ottoline's a Republican."

"Not anymore. She had a fight with Jake Berryhill. Bolted from the party."

"What a tempest in a teapot. Let's see what else. In the Middle Ages, August first was considered an Egyptian Day which was supposed to be unlucky."

"Give me that." Susan took the book from Harry. "You're too slow." Her eyes scanned the dense print. "Harry, here's something." She pointed to the item halfway down the page.

They read aloud, "In 1732, the foundation stone was laid for the Bank of England's building on Threadneedle Street in the City of London."

Harry leapt up and grabbed the phone in the kitchen. "Hey, Coop. Listen to this."

Susan, on her feet now, held the book for Harry to read.

When she finished reading, Harry said, "Susan and I—huh?"

Coop interrupted her, "Keep it right there. Between you and Susan."

Offended, Harry replied, "We aren't going to take out an ad in the paper with this."

"I know, but in your enthusiasm you might spill the beans." Coop apologized. "I'm sorry if I snapped at you. We're understaffed. People rotating off for summer vacation. I'm stressed out and I'm taking it out on you."

"I understand."

"You've done good work. Threadneedle means something . . . I guess. It's about banks. You know, this whole thing is screwy. The Threadneedle virus seemed to be a prank. Then two million dollars cannot be accounted for at Crozet National. There's a rash of car wrecks on 29 and a very dead Mike Huckstep, about whom we know little, is on a slab in the morgue. Everything happens at once."

"Sure seems to." Harry had held the earpiece for Susan, who heard everything.

"Hang in there, Coop," Susan encouraged.

"I will. I'm just blowing off steam," she said. "Listen, thanks for your help. I'll see you soon."

"Sure. Bye."

"Bye."

Harry hung up the phone. "Poor Coop."

"This too shall pass."

"I know that. She knows that, but I don't want my money to pass with it. My money is in Crozet National. It may not be so much, but it's all I have."

"Me too." Susan cupped her hand under her chin, deep in thought. In a moment she asked, "You're getting pretty good on the computer, aren't you?"

Harry nodded.

Susan continued. "I'm not so bad myself. I had to learn in self-defense because Danny and Brookie use the thing constantly. At first I didn't know what they were talking about. It really is great that they learn this stuff at school. To them it's just business as usual."

"Want to raid Crozet National's computer?"

"You read my mind," Susan said, grinning. "We could never get in there though. Hogan might be willing, but Norman Cramer would die if anyone touched his babies. I guess his staff wouldn't be too thrilled about it either. What if we screwed it up?"

"Somebody's done that for us," Harry said. " 'Course, we could sneak in."

"Harry, you're nuts. The building has an alarm system."

"I *could sneak in*," Mrs. Murphy bragged, her ears pricked forward, her eyes flashing.

"*She could. Let her do it*," Tucker agreed.

"You guys must be hungry again." Harry patted Tucker's head and rubbed her long ears.

"*Every time we say anything, she thinks we want to go out or we want to eat*." Mrs. Murphy sighed. "*Tucker, we can go into the bank ourselves*."

"*When do you want to do it?*"

"*Tomorrow night*."

21

A heavy mist enshrouded the buildings. Downtown Crozet seemed magical in the dim, soft night. Mrs. Murphy and Tucker left the house at one-thirty A.M. with Harry sound asleep. Moving at a steady trot, they arrived at the bank by two.

"You stay outside and bark if you need me."

"What if you need me?" Tucker sensibly asked.

"I'll be all right. I wonder if Pewter is awake? She could help."

"If she's asleep, it will take too long to get her up and going." Tucker knew the gray cat only too well.

"You're right." The tiger sniffed the heavy air. A perfumed scent lingered. "Smell that?"

"Yeah."

"Why here?"

"I don't know."

"*Hmm, well, I'm going inside.*" Her tail straight up, the cat moved to the back door with its old wooden steps. Bricks in the foundation had loosened over the years, and a hole big enough for a cat, a possum, or a bold raccoon, accommodated Mrs. Murphy. She swept her whiskers forward, listened intently, then dropped down into the basement. She quickly ran up the stairs to the first floor. She smelled that perfume again. Much stronger now. She jumped on the cool marble counter in front of the teller windows. She trotted down the counter to the end. The carpeted stairway leading to the second floor was nearby. She followed her nose to the stairs, silently leaping two at a time. The only noise was that of her claws in the carpet as she grabbed for a foothold.

As she neared the top of the stairs, she heard human voices, low, urgent. She flattened herself and slunk along the hallway. She arrived at Hogan's office, where sitting on the floor in the dark were Norman Cramer and Kerry McCray. She froze.

"—to do." Norman's voice was ragged.

"Get a divorce."

"She'll never allow it."

"Norman, what's she going to do—kill you?"

He laughed nervously. "She's violently in love with me, or so she says, but I don't think she really loves me. She loves the idea of a husband. When no one's around, she tells me what to do like I'm an idiot. And if she's not telling me what to do, Ottoline takes up the slack."

"Just tell her it isn't working for you. You're sorry."

He sighed. "Yeah, yeah, I can try. I don't know what happened to me. I don't know why I left you. But it was like I had malaria or something. A fever. I couldn't think straight."

Kerry didn't really want to hear this part. "You need to be real clear. Just 'I'm sorry, I want a divorce' is a good way to start. Okay, so she loses her temper and runs you down all over town. Everyone does that when they break up, or almost everyone."

"Yeah—yeah, I know. It's just that I'm under so much pressure now. This mess here at the bank. I don't know if I can handle two crises at the same time. I need to solve one before attacking the other. I'm not stringing you along. I love you, I know that now. I know I've always loved you and I want to spend the rest of my life with you, but can't you wait—until I get things straightened out here? Please, Kerry. Please, you won't regret it."

"I—" She began crying. "I'll try."

"I do love you." He put his arm around her and kissed her.

Mrs. Murphy, belly low, quietly backed away, then turned and tiptoed down the hall to the stairs. Once on the first floor, she raced across the polished parquet in that sanctuary of money, scooted back down into the cellar, and squeezed out the hole to freedom.

Tucker, relieved to see her friend, bounced up and down on her stubby legs.

"Kerry and Norman are in there crying and kissing. Damn." Mrs. Murphy sat and wrapped her tail around her, for the air was quite cool now.

"Where're their cars?" Tucker was curious. "They had to have hidden them. Everyone knows everyone, right? Imagine if Reverend Jones or anybody, really, drove by and found their cars at the bank. I want to know where they've stashed their cars."

"Me too." Mrs. Murphy inhaled the cool air. "I hate love triangles. Someone always gets hurt."

"Usually all three," the dog sagely noted. "Come on. Let's check in the alleyway behind the post office."

They hurried across the railroad tracks. No car rewarded their speedy efforts.

"If you were a human, where would you park your car?" the cat wondered. "Under something or behind something unused or ignored in some way."

They thought for a time.

"There are always cars behind Berryman's garage. Let's look."

They ran back out to Railroad Avenue and loped west, turning south at the railroad underpass onto Route 240. The little garage, freshly painted, was on the next corner.

Stuck behind the other cars waiting to be repaired was Norman's Audi.

"*Score one!*" Tucker yipped.

"*We'd better head home. If we circle the town trying to find Kerry's car, we won't be home by daylight. Mom will be worried. We found one, that's good enough for now.*"

Footsteps in the distance alerted them. Norman Cramer was heading their way.

"*Ssst, here.*" Mrs. Murphy pointed to a truck that was easy to crawl under.

They peered out but remained motionless. Norman, wiping his eyes, quietly opened the driver's door, got in, started the motor, and drove about half a block without lights before turning them on.

"*He looks like Death eating a cracker,*" Tucker said.

They made it home by sunrise. When Harry fed them she noticed grease on Tucker's back. "Damn, Tucker, have you been playing under the truck again? Now I've got to give you a bath."

"*Oh, no!*" Tucker wailed to Murphy. "*See the trouble you got me into.*"

22

"I'm not stupid." Aysha's lower lip stuck out when she pouted. "You weren't at work late last night."

"I was."

"Don't lie to me, Norman. I drove by the bank and your car wasn't parked there."

"I was there until ten-thirty." He devoutly prayed that she hadn't driven by before that, but as she had attended an Ash Lawn meeting, a special fund-raiser, he figured she wouldn't have gotten out until ten-thirty or eleven. "Then I dropped the papers off at Hogan Freely's and he wanted to talk. I couldn't very well give my boss the finger, could I?"

Red-faced, Aysha picked up the phone and dialed. "Laura, hello, Aysha Cramer. I'm calling for Norman. He thinks he left his Mark Cross pen over there from his meeting last night with Hogan. Have you found it?"

"No. Let me ask Hogan, he's right here." Laura returned to the phone. "No, he hasn't found anything either."

"I'm sorry to disturb you."

"No trouble at all. Tell Norman to rest."

"I will, and thank you. Good-bye." She hung up the phone carefully, then faced her husband. "I apologize. You were there."

"Honey, what's the matter with you? Everything is going to be fine. I'm not going to run off or keel over from a heart attack or whatever you're worried about. We're both under pressure. Let's try to relax."

"It's Kerry, I'm worried about Kerry! I know you can handle the job, but I don't know about—"

He put his arms around her waist and nuzzled her neck. "I married you, didn't I?"

23

"*Never, never am I speaking to you again!*" Mrs. Murphy hissed.

"One more," Dr. Parker cooed as she hit up the cat with her rabies booster. "There we go, all over."

Ears flat against her head, hunched up and livid, Mrs. Murphy shot off the examining table. She raced around the room.

"Murphy, calm down."

"*You lied to get me here,*" Mrs. Murphy howled.

The doctor checked her needles. "She'll stop in a minute. She does this once a year and I expect she'll do it next year."

"*I'll remember when the year rolls around. I won't get in the truck.*" Murphy, ears still flat back, sat with her back to the humans.

"Come on," Harry cajoled her.

The sleek tiger refused to budge or even turn her face to her friend. Humans give the cold shoulder. Cats give the cold body.

Scooping her up with one hand under her bottom and the other around her chest, Harry said, "You were a brave girl. Let's go home."

As they rode back into town, Mrs. Murphy stared out the window, back still turned toward Harry.

"Now, look here, Murphy, I hate it when you get in one of your snits. These shots are for your own good. After what you and Tucker did last year, I can't dream of hauling you in to Dr. Parker together. It cost me $123 to replace the curtains in her waiting room. Do you know how long I have to work to make $123? I—"

"Oh, shut up. I don't want to hear how poor you are. My rear end hurts."

"What a yowl. Murphy—Murphy, look at me."

The cat hopped down and crouched on the floor.

Harry's voice rose. "Don't you dare pee in this truck. I mean it." She quickly pulled to the side of the road, got out, and opened the passenger door. She walked into a field, Murphy in her arms. "If you have to go, go here."

"I'm not doing anything you ask me to do." She hunched down amid the daisies.

By the time Harry rolled into Crozet, both cat and human were frazzled. Harry pulled into the market. When she opened the door, Mrs. Murphy nimbly squeezed past her and rushed to the door.

"Open up, Pewter, open up. She's torturing me!"

Harry pushed open the glass door and the cat ran between her legs. Pewter, having heard the complaint, hurried out to touch her nose and have a consoling sniff.

"What happened?"

"Dr. Parker."

"Oh." Pewter licked Mrs. Murphy's ears in sympathy. "I am sorry. I'm sick for a day after those nasty shots."

"Once, just once, I want to go to the doctor with Harry and watch her get the needle." Murphy fluffed her tail.

"Arm or rear?"

"Both! Let her suffer. She won't be able to sit down, and let's see her pick up a hay bale." Murphy licked her lips. "When she opens the door, let's run over to Miranda's. I want to hear her holler."

"Where's Tucker?"

"Susan's."

"There she goes." Murphy trailed Harry's sneaker, and when the door opened, she shot out, followed by Pewter, less speedy. "Follow me."

Harry thought Mrs. Murphy would go to the truck. When the cat zigzagged to the left, she knew this was going to be one of those days. She placed the lettuce and English muffins in the seat of the truck and walked after them. If she ran, then Murphy would run faster. The culprits ambled behind the post office.

"Murphy!" Harry called when she reached the alleyway. She could see a tiger tail protruding from under a blue hydrangea near the alley. Every time she'd call Murphy's name, the cat's tail would twitch.

From opposite ends of the alley drove Kerry McCray in one car and Aysha and Norman Cramer in another. Kerry pulled in behind Market's store and immediately behind her came Hogan Freely, who pulled in next to her. Norman, driving, paused for a moment. Too late to hurry away. Aysha steamed as Harry came up to the window.

"Hi, Harry." Norman called louder to those behind her, "Hello, Hogan. Hi, Kerry."

They nodded and entered the market.

"If you roll on down the alleyway, go slow. Mrs. Murphy and Pewter are on the rampage."

"I'll pull up behind the post office." He smiled. Aysha did not. "Anyway, we're out of paper towels."

"Norman."

"Just a second, honey. I'll be right back."

Wordlessly, she opened her door and followed him. Damned if she'd let him go in there with Kerry alone.

Harry, torn between conflicting desires, was rooted to the

spot. She wanted to catch Murphy. On the other hand, she was only human. What if Kerry and Aysha went ballistic again? Mrs. Hogendobber, in her apron, came out of her back door. Harry motioned her over, quickly explained, and the two tried not to run into the store.

"*Do you believe those two?*" Pewter giggled.

"*I'm insulted. She's supposed to get down on her hands and knees and beg me to come back to the truck.*" Murphy pouted.

Inside the market everyone grabbed a few items off the shelves so as to not look too obvious. As luck would have it, Susan Tucker and Reverend Jones walked in.

"How's your golf game?" Herb asked Hogan.

"Driving's great. The short game . . ." Hogan turned down his thumb.

"I'm sorry to hear about the losses at the bank. I know how much that must weigh on you." The reverend's voice, deep and resonant, made the listener feel better already.

"I have turned that problem inside and out. Upside down. You name it. And still nothing."

Aysha and Norman joined them. Kerry hung back, but she wasn't leaving. Susan joined the circle and Harry stayed a step back with Kerry. Mrs. H. walked behind the counter with Market.

"It's in the computer," Susan blurted out.

"Susan, the computer techies checked our system." Norman grimaced. "Nothing."

"The Threadneedle virus." Susan beamed. "Harry and I—"

"No, wait a minute," Harry protested.

"All right, it was Harry's idea. She said that the moneys were noticed missing within a day or two of the Threadneedle scare—"

"We nipped that in the bud." Norman crossed his arms over his chest.

"That's just it," Harry offered. "Whatever the commands were, there must have been a rider, something to delay and then trigger a transfer of money."

"Like an override." Hogan rubbed his chin, a habit when his mind raced. "Uh-huh. I wonder. Well, we know the problem's not in the machine, so if we can figure out the sequence, we'll know."

"It could be something as simple as, say, whenever you punch in the word *Threadneedle*, a command is given to take money," Susan hypothesized.

"Now, ladies, with all due respect, it isn't that easy. If it were, we would have found it." Norman smiled weakly.

Aysha, eye on Kerry, chimed in. "Let's go, honey, we'll be late for Mother's dinner."

"Oh, sure."

"I think I'll fiddle around tonight at the bank. I work best at night, when it's quiet. You've given me an idea, you two." Hogan glanced from Susan to Harry.

Norman rolled his eyes. Both Aysha and Kerry noticed. Keeping his voice steady, he said, "Now, boss, don't scramble my files." This was followed by an anemic laugh.

"Don't worry." Hogan grabbed his grocery bag. "Those pastries, Miranda—too much." He left.

Norman and Aysha followed.

Kerry, fighting back her urge to trash Aysha, smacked her carton of eggs on the counter so hard, she broke some of them. "Oh, no, look what I've done."

Susan opened the egg carton. "You sure have. Kerry, it's never as bad as you think it is."

"Thanks," came the wobbly reply.

"Where's Tucker?" Harry asked of Susan.

"Back at the house."

"I'm going out to get Murphy. She won't speak to me. Mrs. H.—"

"Yes."

"Vet day. If I can't convince that furry monster to go home with me, will you keep an eye on her? She'll go to the post office or your back door."

"I'll put her in the store with Pewter. Murphy can't resist a bite of sirloin," Market offered.

He was right. Both cats waltzed through the back door about an hour later.

Late that night with the lights out, Murphy told Pewter what she had heard at the bank. They sat in the big storefront window and watched the fog roll down.

"You've never spent a night in the store," Pewter observed. "It's fun. I can go out if I want since Market put in a kitty door like yours, but mostly I like to sit in the window and watch everything."

"It was nice of Market to let me stay. Nice of him to call Harry too. I suppose she thinks I'm learning a lesson. Fat chance. I'll remember the date."

"She fooled you. She took you to the vet on Sunday. Special trip."

Mrs. Murphy thought about that. "She's smarter than I think. Wonder what she had to pay Dr. Parker to make a special trip to the office?"

When Hogan pulled into the bank, his headlights were diffused in the thickening mist. The cats could just make him out as he unlocked the front door and entered. Within a minute the lights went on upstairs, in a fuzzy golden square.

"Diligent," Pewter said. She licked one paw and wiped it over an ear.

Lights turned off in other buildings as the hours passed. Finally only a few neon lights shone in store windows or over signs; the street lamps glowed. The cats dozed, then Mrs. Murphy opened her eyes.

"Pewter, wake up. I heard a car behind us."

"People use the alleyway."

A door slammed, they heard the crunch of human shoes. Then a figure appeared at the corner. Whoever it was had walked the length of the alleyway. They couldn't make out who it was or even what gender, as the fog was now dense. In a moment, swirling gray swallowed the person.

Inside his office Hogan kept blinking. His eyes, exhausted by the screen of the computer, burned. His brain burned too. He tried all manner of things. He punched in the word *Threadneedle*. He remembered the void commands. He finally decided he would review clients' accounts. Something might turn up that Norman had missed. An odd transfer or an offshore transfer. He could go through the accounts quickly since he knew these people and their small businesses. He was at the end of the H's by midnight. An unfamiliar yet familiar name snagged him.

"Huckstep," he said aloud. "Huckstep." He punched in the code to review the account. It had been opened July 30 in the name of Michael and Malibu Huckstep, a joint account. Of course —the murdered man. He must have intended to stick around, if he opened an account. That meant he had an account card with his signature and his wife's. He was going to go downstairs to check the card files, but first the buttons clicked as he checked the amount in the savings account: $4,218.64. Not a lot of money but enough. He rubbed his eyes and checked his wristwatch. Past twelve. Too late to call Rick Shaw. He'd call him first thing in the morning.

Meanwhile he'd go down and check those signature cards. He stood up, interlocked his fingers, and stretched his hands over his head. His knuckles cracked just as the bullet from a .357 tore into his shoulder. He opened his mouth to call out his assailant's name, but too late. The next one exploded his heart and he crashed down into his chair.

Back in the store, the cats heard the gunfire.

"Hurry!" Mrs. Murphy yelled as they both screeched out the kitty door. As they ran toward the bank, they heard through the dense fog footsteps running in the opposite direction, up at the corner.

"*Damn! Damn!*" The tiger cursed herself.

"*What's the matter?*"

"*Pewter, we should have gone around back to see the car.*"

"*Too late now.*" The smallish but rotund gray cat barreled toward the bank.

Arriving at the front step only a couple of minutes after the gunfire, they stopped so fast at the door that they tumbled over one another and landed on a figure slumped in the doorway, a smoking .357 in her hand.

"Oh, NO!" Murphy cried.

24

Kerry McCray lay slumped across the front doorway of the bank. A small trickle of blood oozed from her head. The acrid odor of gunpowder filled the air. The pistol was securely grasped in her right hand.

"*We've got to get Mrs. Hogendobber.*" Mrs. Murphy sniffed Kerry's wound.

"*Maybe I should stay here with her.*" Pewter kept patting Kerry's face in a vain effort to revive her.

"*If only Tucker were here.*" The tiger paced around the inert form. "*She could guard Kerry. Look, Pewter, we'll have to risk that she'll be safe. It's going to take two of us to get Mrs. Hogendobber here.*"

That said, the two sped through the fog, running so low to the ground and so fast that the pads of their paws barely touched it. They pulled up under Miranda's bedroom window which was wide open to catch the cooling night air. A screen covered the window.

"*Let's sing,*" Murphy commanded.

They hooted, hollered, and screeched. Those two cats could have awakened the dead.

Miranda, in her nightdress, shoe in hand, came to the window. She opened the screen and let fly. Mrs. Murphy and Pewter dodged the missile with ease.

"*Bad shot! Come on, Mrs. H., come on!*"

"Pewter?" Miranda squinted into the fog.

The tubby kitty jumped up on the windowsill followed by Mrs. Murphy before Miranda could close the screen.

"*Oh, please, Mrs. Hogendobber, please listen to us. There's terrible trouble—*" Pewter said.

"*Somebody's hurt!*" Murphy bellowed.

"You two are getting on my nerves. Now, you get on out of here." Miranda slid the screen up again.

"*No!*" they replied in unison.

"*Follow me.*" Murphy ran to the door of the bedroom.

Miranda simply didn't get it even though Pewter kept telling her to hurry, hurry.

"*Watch out. She might swat,*" Murphy warned Pewter as she snuck in low and bit Miranda's ankle.

"Ouch!" Outraged, Mrs. Hogendobber switched on the light and picked up the phone. As she did, she noticed the cats circling her and then going back and forth to the door. Their distress affected her, but she wasn't sure what to do and she was mad at Murphy. She dialed Harry.

A dull hello greeted her.

"Your cat has just bit me on the ankle and is acting crazy. Rabies."

"Mrs. Hogendobber—" Harry was awake now.

"Pewter's here too. Screeching under my window like banshees and I opened the window and they jumped in and—" She

bent down as Pewter rubbed her leg. She noticed a bit of blood on Pewter's foreleg and paw where the cat had patted Kerry's head. "Pewter has blood on her paw. Oh, dear, Harry, I think you'd better come here and get these cats. I don't know what to do."

"Keep them inside, okay? I'll be right over, and I'm sorry Murphy bit you. Don't worry about rabies—she's had her shots, remember?" Harry hung up the phone, jumped into her jeans and an old workshirt. She hurried to the truck and cranked it up. As she blasted down the road, she stuck some gum in her mouth. She'd been in too big a rush to brush her teeth.

In seven minutes she was at Miranda's door. As Harry entered the living room Murphy said, "*Try again, Pewter. Mother's a little smarter than Miranda.*"

They both hollered, "Kerry McCray's hurt."

"Something's wrong." Harry reached for Pewter's paw, but the cat eluded her and ran to the front door.

"Rabies." Miranda folded her arms across her bosom.

"No, it isn't."

"That tiger, that hellcat, bit me." She dangled her ankle out from under her nightdress. Two perfect fang marks, not deep but indenting the skin, were revealed.

"*Come on,*" Murphy yowled at the top of her lungs. She scratched at the front door.

"These two want something. I'm going to see. Why don't you go back to bed. And I do apologize."

"I'm wide awake now." Miranda returned to her bedroom, threw on a robe and slippers, and reappeared. "I can't go back to sleep once I've been awakened. Might as well prove that I'm as crazy as you and these cats are." With that she sailed through the open door. "I can barely see my hand in front of my face. How'd you get here so quickly?"

"Drove too fast."

"*Come on. Come on.*" Murphy trotted up ahead in the gray mists, then back. "*Follow my voice.*"

"Harry, we're out on Main Street and they're headed for the railroad tracks."

"I know." The air felt clammy on her skin.

"Is this some cat trick?"

"*Shut up and hurry!*" Pewter's patience was wearing thin.

"Something definitely is agitating them and Murphy's a reasonable cat—usually."

"Cats are by definition unreasonable." Miranda stepped faster.

The bank loomed in the mist, the upstairs light still burning.

The cats called to them through the fog. Harry saw Kerry first, lying facedown, right hand outstretched with the gun in it. Mrs. Murphy and Pewter sat beside her.

"Miranda!"

Mrs. Hogendobber moved faster, then she, too, saw what at first seemed like an apparition and then like a bad dream. "Good heavens."

Harry skidded up to Kerry. She knelt down and felt for a pulse. Miranda was now next to her.

"*Is she all right?*" Mrs. Murphy asked.

"Her pulse is regular."

Miranda watched Pewter touch Kerry's head. "We've got to get an ambulance. I'll go in the bank and call. The door's open. That's odd."

"I'll do it. I have a funny feeling something is really wrong in there. You stay here with her and don't touch anything, especially the gun."

Miranda realized as Harry disappeared into the bank that she'd been so distraught at the sight of the young woman, she hadn't noticed the gun.

Harry returned shortly. "Got Cynthia. Called Reverend Jones too."

"If this is as bad as I think it is, then I suppose Kerry needs a minister." Miranda's teeth were chattering although the night was mild.

Kerry opened her eyes. "Mrs. Murphy."

The cat purred. *"You'll be fine."*

"After the headache goes away," Pewter advised.

"Kerry—"

"Harry—" Kerry reached to touch her head as she rolled onto her side and realized a gun was in her right hand. She dropped it as if it were on fire and sat straight up. "Oh." She clasped her head with both hands.

"Honey, you'd better lie back down." Miranda sat beside her to ease her down.

"No, no—let me stay still." Kerry forced a weak smile.

A coughing motor announced Herb. He pulled alongside the bank and got out. He couldn't see them yet.

"Herbie, we're at the front door," Miranda called loudly to him.

His footsteps came closer. He appeared out of an envelope of thick gray fog. "What's going on?"

"We don't really know," Miranda answered.

Kerry replied, "I feel dizzy and a little sick to my stomach."

Herb noticed the bank door was wide open.

Harry said, "It was open. I used the phone inside, but I didn't look around. Something's wrong."

"Yes—" He felt it too. "I'm going in."

"Take the gun," Miranda advised.

"No. No need." He disappeared into the bank.

"Should we go with him?" Pewter wondered.

"No, I'm not leaving Mother." Murphy continued purring because she thought the soothing sound might calm the humans.

"What little friends you are." Kerry petted the cats, then stopped because even that made her stomach queasy.

"They found you and then they found us—well, it's a long story." Harry sat on the other side of Kerry.

"Herb, what's the matter?" Miranda was shocked when he

reappeared. His face, drained of all color, gave him a frightful appearance. He looked as sick as Kerry.

"Hogan Freely's been murdered." He sat heavily on the pavement almost the way a tired child drops down. "I've known him all my life. What a good man—what a good man." Tears ran down his cheeks. "I've got to tell Laura."

"I'll go with you," Miranda offered. "We can go after the sheriff arrives."

"Kerry." Harry, shaking, pointed to the gun.

Kerry's voice wavered. "I didn't kill him. I don't even own a gun."

"Can you remember what happened?" Harry asked.

"Up to a point, I can." Kerry sucked in air, trying to drive out the pain. "I was over at Mother and Dad's. Dad's sick again, so I stayed late to help Mom. I didn't leave until a little past midnight, and I was crawling along because of the fog. I passed the corner and thought I saw a light in Hogan's office window. It was fuzzy but I was curious. I turned around and parked in the lot. I figured he was up there trying to find the money like he said he was going to do and I was going to surprise him, just kind of cheer him up. I walked up these steps and opened the door, and that's all I remember."

"What about sounds?" Harry asked.

"Or smells?" Pewter added. "Murphy, let's go in and see if we can pick up a scent. Harry's all right. No one's around to hit her on the head and Kerry won't do anything crazy."

"Okay."

The two cats left.

"I remember opening the door. I don't remember footsteps or anything like that, but somebody must have heard me. I didn't think I was making that much noise."

"Luck of the draw," Herb said. "You were going in as he was going out."

The sirens in the distance meant Cynthia was approaching.

•   •   •

The two cats lifted their noses and sniffed.

"Let's go upstairs." Mrs. Murphy led the way.

As they neared Hogan's office, Pewter said in a small voice, "I don't think I want to see this."

"Close your eyes and use your nose. And don't step in anything."

Murphy padded into the room. Hogan was sitting upright in his chair; his shoulder was torn away. Blood spattered the wall behind him. A small hole bore evidence to the bullet that killed him. Murphy could smell the blood seeping into the upholstery of the chair.

Pewter opened one eye and then shut it. "I can't smell anything but blood and gunpowder."

"Blood and gunpowder." Mrs. Murphy leapt onto his desk with a single bound. She tried not to look into Hogan's glassy stare. She liked him and didn't want to remember him like this.

His computer was turned off. His desk drawers were closed. There was no sign of struggle. She touched her nose to every article on his desk. Then she jumped back to the floor. She stopped by the front of his desk.

"Here."

Pewter placed her nose on the spot. "Rubber. Rubber and wet."

"From the misty night, I would think. Rubber won't leave much of a print and not in this carpet. Dammit! Rubber, blood, and gunsmoke. Whoever did this was no dummy."

"Maybe so, Murphy, but whoever did this was in a hurry. The computer is off but still warm." Pewter noticed Hogan's feet under the desk. "Let's talk about this outside. This place gives me the creeps."

"Okay." It bothered Murphy, too, but she didn't want to admit it.

As they walked back down the stairs, Pewter continued. "If someone wanted to dispatch Hogan Freely, there are better ways to do it."

"I agree. So, he was getting close to the missing money."

As the cats passed through the lobby, Rick Shaw entered. He saw them but didn't say anything.

The blue and red flashing lights of the squad car and the ambulance reflected off the fog.

Kerry, on a stretcher, was being carried to the back of the ambulance.

The cats stood next to Harry and Mrs. Hogendobber. Herb, with a slow tread, turned to enter the bank. Cynthia, pad out, was taking notes.

"Herb, I'll go with you."

"Good."

"We'll wait here." Harry pulled Miranda back as she was about to follow. "You'll have nightmares."

"You're right—but I feel so awful. I hate to think of him up there, alone and—"

"Don't think about it and don't let Laura think about it either when you go over there with Reverend Jones. It's too painful. She doesn't have to know all the details."

"You're right." Miranda lowered her eyes. "This is dreadful."

"Dreadful—" Mrs. Murphy whispered, "*and just beginning.*"

25

The hospital smell bothered Harry, reminding her of her mother's last days on earth. She avoided visiting anyone in a hospital if she could, but invariably duty overcame aversion and she would venture down the impersonal corridors.

Kerry was being kept for twenty-four hours to make sure she suffered no further effects from her assault. The doctors treated any blow to the head as serious. Cynthia Cooper was sitting next to Kerry's bed when Harry entered the room.

"How you doing?"

"Okay—considering."

"Hi, Coop."

"Hi." Coop shifted in her seat. "Hell of a night."

Kerry fiddled with her hospital identification wristband.

"Cynthia went with Rick and Herbie to Laura Freely's. Laura collapsed when they told her."

"Who's with her until Dudley and Thea can fly home?" Dudley and Thea were the Freelys' adult children.

"Miranda spent the night there. Mim's with Laura right now. The ladies will take turns even once the children return. There's so much to do and Laura is sedated. She can't make any of the decisions that need to be made. I think Ellie Wood Baxter, Port, and even Boom Boom will work out a schedule." Cynthia stretched her legs.

"Kerry, I dropped by to see if you needed anything from home, what with your dad being sick. I'm happy to pick up stuff for you."

"Thanks, but I'm okay."

"Cynthia—?" Harry's eyebrows pointed upward quizzically.

"I'm here to see she doesn't make a run for it. The .357 in her hand was the gun that killed Hogan. And it's registered to Kerry McCray."

"I don't own a gun." Kerry teared up.

"According to the records, you bought one at Hassett's in Waynesboro, July tenth."

"Are you arresting my friend here?" Harry tried to keep her voice light.

"No, not yet."

"Cynthia, you can't possibly believe that Kerry would kill anyone."

"I'm a police officer. I can't afford emotions."

"Bullshit," came Harry's swift retort.

"Thanks, Harry. We're not close friends, and here you are—thanks." Kerry flopped back on the pillows, then winced because she felt the throb in her head. "I never bought a gun. I've never been to Hassett's. On July tenth I worked all day as usual, handling new accounts."

Cynthia firmly said, "According to records, you showed your driver's license."

"I never set foot in that gun shop."

"What if Kerry is the one who masterminded the bank theft? Maybe Hogan is starting to figure out her m.o." Cynthia used the police shorthand for modus operandi. "She's getting nervous. She knew he was working late in that bank that night. Millions of dollars are at stake. She kills Hogan."

"And hits herself on the head hard enough to knock herself out—yet still keep the gun in her hand?" Harry was incredulous.

"That presents a problem." Cynthia nodded. "But Kerry could have an accomplice. He or she hits her on the head so she looks innocent."

"And I could fly to the moon." Harry sharply inhaled. "This summer is sure turning to crap."

"How elegantly put." Cynthia half smiled.

"Forget being an officer and be one of the girls just for a minute, Coop. Do you really think Kerry killed Hogan?"

Cynthia waited a long time. "I don't know, but I do know that the .357 is the same gun that killed Mike Huckstep."

"What?" Harry felt her throat constrict.

"Ballistics report came back at six this morning. Rick's lashing everyone on. Same gun. We'd like to keep that tidbit out of the papers, but I doubt the boss can. His job is so damned political."

"Huckstep and Hogan Freely." Harry frowned. "One's a Hell's Angel and the other's a bank president."

"Maybe Hogan had a secret life?" Kerry spoke up.

"Not that secret." Harry shook her head.

"You'd be amazed at what people can hide from one another," Cynthia replied.

"I know that, but at some point you've got to trust your instincts," Harry replied.

"Well then, what do your instincts tell you?" Cynthia challenged her.

"Hogan was getting close and that means the answer is in the bank."

"Think you're right."

Kerry moaned. "My goose is cooked, isn't it?"

Cynthia stared hard at her.

26

Because of federal regulations, the bank could not be closed on Monday. In fact, if Hogan had been shot during banking hours, the way the law reads he would have been left there and business would have continued while the sheriff worked. People would have had to step over the body. These stringent rules against closing a bank were born in the 1930s when banks bolted their doors or folded like houses of cards. As is customary when legislators cook up some ameliorative law, it never covers the human condition. The employees of Crozet National worked with black armbands around their left arms. A huge black wreath hung at the end of the lobby, a smaller one on the front door. Out front, the Virginia state flag flew at half mast. Mary Thigpen, the head teller for twenty-five years, kept bursting into tears. Many eyes were red-rimmed.

All the talk about Kerry so outraged Norman that he shouted, "She's innocent until proven guilty, so shut up!"

Rick Shaw had taken over the second floor, squeezing the accounting department, but they managed. The blood splattered on the wall of Hogan's office made Norman woozy. He wasn't the only one.

Mim Sanburne came by after her turn with Laura Freely to inform everyone that the funeral service would be held that Thursday at the Crozet Lutheran Church. The family would receive Wednesday night at home.

A subdued hush followed her announcement.

Over at the post office Harry asked Blair to help while Mrs. Hogendobber organized the food for Wednesday night. Dudley Freely proved incompetent due to shock. Thea, the older Freely child, was better at making some of the decisions forced upon her by the event. What kind of casket, or would it be cremation? What cemetery? Flowers or contributions to charity? She fielded these questions, but sometimes she would have to sit down, fatigued beyond endurance. She didn't realize a great emotional blow is physically exhausting. Mim and Miranda did. They took over. Ottoline Gill and Aysha handled the phone duties. Laura languished in bed. When she regained consciousness she would sob uncontrollably.

Rick and Cynthia tried to question her, but she couldn't get through even a gentle interrogation.

Rick pulled aside Mim outside the post office, as they had both driven in to get their mail. "Mrs. Sanburne, you knew Hogan all his life. Can you imagine him involved in some kind of scheme to defraud people—"

She cut him off. "Hogan Freely was the most honest and generous man I've ever known."

"Don't get huffy, Mrs. Sanburne, I've got two murders on my hands. I have to ask uncomfortable questions. He could have been involved in the theft and had his partner or partners turn on him. It's not an uncommon occurrence."

"I'm sorry, but you must understand. Hogan loved this town and he loved banking. If you knew the people he took chances on, the people he helped get started in business, well, he was about a lot more than money."

"I know. He helped me get my mortgage." Rick opened the door for Mim as they stepped into the post office.

Mrs. Murphy, crouched on the little ledge dividing the mailboxes, waited for Rick and Mim to open their boxes.

Rick opened his first and the tiger reached into his box, swatting his hand as he withdrew his mail.

"Murphy." He walked to the counter and looked around the corner of the boxes.

She looked back at him. *"I wanted to make you feel better."*

"That cat going to grab me?" Mim called.

Harry lifted her from the small counter, ideally suited for sorting into the rows of postboxes. "No, I've got her right here in my arms."

Tucker, head on her paws, said, *"Murphy, nothing is going to make people feel better right now."*

Rick chucked the tiger under the chin. "If only animals could talk. Who knows what she saw the night Hogan was murdered?"

"I didn't see anything because of the fog and I missed a chance to identify the killer's car. I wasn't so smart, sheriff."

"You did the right thing, Murphy, you found help," Tucker lauded her.

Rick left, Mim gave Harry and Blair the information about the family gathering and the funeral, and then she left too.

Harry moved with a heavy tread. "I feel awful."

Blair put his arm around her shoulders. "Everyone does."

27

"We're going to be late." Norman checked his watch as he paced.

"I'm almost ready. I ran into Kate Bittner at the 19th Hole, and you know how she can talk."

He bit his tongue. She was always late. Running into someone at the supermarket was just another excuse. A car turning into the driveway diverted his attention away from pushing Aysha on.

Ottoline, in full regalia, stepped out of her Volvo station wagon.

"Oh, no," he said under his breath.

Ottoline came in the front door without knocking.

"Norman, you look ashen."

"I'm very tired, Ottoline."

"Where's my angel?"

"In the bathroom, where else?"

She squinted at him, her pointy chin sticking out. "A woman must look her best. You men don't understand that these things take time. I have yet to meet the man who wants an ugly woman on his arm."

"Aysha could never be ugly."

"Quite." She click-clacked down the hallway. The bathroom door was open. "You need different earrings."

"But, Mummy, I like these."

"Too much color. We're going to pay our sympathies. This may be a gathering, but it's not a party."

"Well—"

"Wear the drop pearl earrings. Discreet, yet they make a statement."

"All right." Aysha marched into the bedroom, took off her enameled earrings, and plucked out the pendant pearls. "These?"

Exasperated, Norman joined them. "Aysha—please."

"All right, all right," she crossly replied. "I'm ready."

"I hope you'll be made president of the branch now." Ottoline inspected her son-in-law's attire. He passed muster.

"This isn't the time to think about that."

Her lips pursed. "Believe me, there are others not nearly so scrupulous. You need to go into Charlottesville and talk to Donald Petrus. You're young, but you're the obvious person for the job."

"I don't know if that's true."

"Just do as I say," she snapped.

"There are others with more seniority," he snapped back.

"Old women."

"Kerry McCray."

"Ha!" Aysha finally entered into the conversation. "She murdered Hogan Freely."

"Like hell she did. She'll be found innocent."

Ottoline tapped her foot on the floor. "Innocent or guilty . . . she's irrelevant. You must seize the day, Norman."

He looked from mother-in-law to wife and sighed.

28

Harry hated these dolorous social events, but she would attend. Sad as such events were, not to pay one's last respects meant just that, no respect.

She hurried home from the post office. Miranda had spent the day dashing back and forth between the mailboxes and her kitchen. Luckily, Blair had helped drive food over to the Freelys' and had run errands for Miranda, because the mail load, unusually heavy for a Wednesday, kept her pinned to the post office more than she had wished.

Once home, Harry hopped in the shower, applied some mascara and lipstick. Her short hair, naturally curly, needed only a quick run-through with her fingers while it was wet.

"What's she doing in there?" Tucker languidly rolled on the floor, ending up tummy in the air.

"Tarting herself up."

"Did she remember the blusher? She forgets half the time," Tucker noted.

"I'll go see." Mrs. Murphy quietly padded into the small bathroom. Harry had forgotten. The cat leapt onto the little sink and knocked the blusher into the sink. "You need some rose in your cheeks."

"Murphy." Harry reached down and picked up the square black container. "Guess this wouldn't hurt." She touched her cheek with the brush. "There. A raving beauty. I mean, men quiver at my approach. Women's eyes narrow to slits. Kingdoms are offered me for a kiss."

"Mice! Moles! Catnip, all at your feet." Mrs. Murphy enjoyed the dream.

"Who's there? Who's there?" Tucker barreled toward the back door.

Fair knocked, then stepped over the little dog, who immediately stopped barking.

"Hi, cute cakes." Fair smoothed his hand over Tucker's graceful ears, then he called, "It's me."

"I didn't know you were coming," Harry called from the bathroom.

"Uh, I should have called, but it's been one of those days. Had to put down Tommy Bolender's old mare. Twenty-six. He loved that mare and I told him to just go ahead and cry. He did, too, and then I got teary myself. Then that high-priced foal over at Dolan's crashed a fence. Big laceration on her chest. And Patty has thrush."

Patty, a sweet school horse at Sally and Bob Taylor's Mountain Hollow Farm, had taught two generations of people to ride.

Harry joined him. She wore a long skirt, sandals, and a crisp cotton blouse.

"I don't think I've seen you in a skirt since the day we were married."

"That long, huh?" She paused. "Now, Fair, you should have

called me because I'm supposed to go to the Freelys' with Blair and—"

Fair held up his hand in the stop position. "We'll both take you."

"He may not take kindly to that notion."

He held up his hand again. "Leave him out of the loop for a minute. Do you take kindly to it?"

"If you both behave."

"How about this." Tucker wagged her non-tail. "Mom's being escorted by the two best-looking men in the county. The phone lines will burn tonight."

"Boom Boom's will burn the brightest." Mrs. Murphy was now sitting next to Tucker.

"You'll be pleased to know that I called Blair on my way over, since I anticipated this."

"Why didn't you call me?"

"What if you'd said no? Then I'd lose a chance to see you, and in a skirt too."

Another vehicle came down the driveway. Tucker ran barking to the door. She stopped quickly. "Blair, in the Mercedes."

Harry kissed the cat and dog and walked outside with Fair. They both got into Blair's Mercedes and drove off.

"How do you like that?" Tucker watched the red taillights.

"I like it a lot. It proves that Fair and Blair can both learn to get along and put Harry's interests first. That's what I care about. I want someone in Mom's life who makes her life easier. Love shouldn't feel like a job."

29

Flowers, mostly pastels and whites, filled every room of the Freely house. Laura sat in the big wing chair by the living room fireplace. At moments she recognized people. Other times she lapsed into an anguished trance.

Dudley, subdued, greeted people at the door. He'd pulled himself together. A few people cold-shouldered Ned Tucker since they heard he'd taken Kerry McCray's case.

Thea, with the assistance of Mrs. Hogendobber, Mim, and Little Marilyn, accepted condolences, shared memories, made sure that people had something to eat and drink. Ottoline Gill, relishing her self-appointed position, led people to Laura and then quietly led them away toward the food table. Everything was well organized.

In the dining room, Market Shiflett kept replenishing the food supply at his own expense. Hogan had helped him secure his business loan. In the parlor, Aysha and Norman talked to people. From time to time Norman glanced at the front door. He looked miserable. Aysha looked appropriately sad.

Harry's arrival with the two men riveted people's attention until Kerry, released from the hospital that morning, arrived with Cynthia Cooper. At the door she greeted Dudley, who waved off Ottoline. He listened intently, then took Kerry directly to his mother. Ottoline was scandalized, and it showed. A hush fell over the room.

"Laura, I'm so terribly sorry."

Laura lifted her head in recognition. "Did you shoot my Hogan?"

"No. I know it looks bad, but I didn't. I admired and respected him. I would never have done anything so horrible. I'm here to offer my deepest sympathy."

You could have heard a pin drop.

Jim Sanburne took control of the situation. "Folks, we've got to reach out for the best in each other. We'll get through this, we'll celebrate Hogan's life by being more like him, and that's by helping other people."

"And by catching his killer!" Aysha glared directly at Kerry until Norman squeezed her upper arm—hard.

"Hear. Hear." Many in the room shared this sentiment.

As people gathered around Aysha, more people poured into the house. There was barely room to turn around. Norman slipped out. Kerry observed this and left, too, after saying goodbye to Laura. Cooper followed her at a discreet distance.

Norman was lighting a cigarette. He stood, forlorn, in the green expanse of the manicured lawn.

She slipped her arm through his, surprising him. "I must see you."

"Soon." He offered her a cigarette.

A car was heading toward them. He adroitly extricated them from the approaching light. "Maybe we'd better walk away from the house."

As they walked off to the side yard, Kerry pleaded, "I can't live this way, Norman. Are you going to tell her or not?"

"Tell her what?"

"That you're leaving her."

"Kerry, I told you I can't handle a crisis in my home life and at work at the same time. And right now you're looking down the barrel of a gun." He stopped. "Sorry, it's a figure of speech. Let me get through this thing at work and then I can attend to Aysha."

"Attend to Aysha first," she pleaded.

"It's not that easy. She's not that easy."

"I know that. She used to be my best friend, remember?"

"Kerry"—he flicked the cigarette into the grass—"maybe I should give my marriage a chance. Maybe the stress at work has blunted my, uh—kept me from feeling close to Aysha."

Kerry, shaking lightly, said, "Please don't do that. Don't jerk me around. Aysha cares only for Aysha."

"I don't want to jerk you around, but I'm in no condition to make a major decision, and neither are you. Monday I passed Hogan's office. Blood was splattered on the wall. It made me sick. Every time I went downstairs I passed the mess. If you'd seen the blood, you'd be shook too." He shuddered. "I can't take this."

"Time isn't going to make you love Aysha."

"I loved her once."

"You thought you did."

"But what if I do? I don't know what I feel."

Kerry threw her arms around him and kissed him hard. He kissed her back. "What do you feel now?"

"Confused. I still love you." He shrugged. "Oh, God, I don't know anything. I just want to get away for a while."

He reached out and kissed her again. They didn't hear the soft crunch moving toward them.

"Kerry, you slut." Aysha hauled off and belted her. "A murderer and a slut."

Norman grabbed his wife, pulling her away. "Don't hit her. Hit me. This is my fault."

"Shut up, Norman. I know this bitch inside and out. Whatever I have, she has to have it. She's competed with me since we were tiny. It just never stops, does it, Kerry?"

"I had him first!"

The shouting grew louder. Harry and Miranda walked out of the house because of the shouting just as Cynthia Cooper stepped out from behind a big oak. She moved toward the trio.

"You didn't want him. You were going to bed with Jake Berryhill at the same time."

Kerry's face was distorted in rage. "Liar."

"You told me yourself. You said you knew that Norman loved you and he was sweet but he was boring in bed." Aysha relished the moment.

Kerry screamed, "You bitch!"

Again Norman pulled them apart with the help of Cynthia. He was mortified to see her.

"For God's sake, keep your voices down. The Freelys don't deserve this!" Harry's lips tightened as she ran over.

"Norman, tell her you're leaving her."

"I can't." Norman seemed to shrink before everyone's eyes.

Kerry's sobs transformed into white-hot hate. "Then I hope you drop dead!"

She twisted away from Cynthia, who caught her. "Time for a ride home until you are formally charged." She pushed Kerry into the squad car.

Norman meekly addressed the little group, "I apologize."

"Go home," Harry said flatly.

Aysha turned and preceded Norman to their car as her mother pushed open the front door. Ottoline called out to her daughter and son-in-law, but they avoided her.

Miranda folded her arms across her chest and shook her head. "Norman Cramer?"

30

Re-inking the postage meter meant sticky red ink on her fingers, her shirt, and the counter too. No matter how hard she tried, Harry managed to spill some.

Mrs. Hogendobber brought over a towel and wiped up the droplets. "Looks like blood."

Harry snapped shut the top of the meter. "Gives me the willies—what with everything that's happened."

Little Marilyn came in with a brisk "Hello." She opened her mailbox with such force, the metal and glass door clacked into the adjoining box. She removed her mail, sorted it by the waste-bin, then stopped at the counter. "A letter from Steve O'Grady in Africa. Don't you love looking at foreign stamps?"

"Yes. It's a miniature art form," Miranda replied.

"When Kerry and Aysha and I went to Europe after college,

we stayed in Florence awhile, then split up. I had a Eurailpass, so I must have whisked through every country not behind the Iron Curtain. I made a point of sending them postcards and letters more so they could have the stamps than read my scrawl. We were devoted letter writers."

Miranda offered Little Marilyn a piece of fresh banana cake. "You three were best friends for so long. What happened?"

"Nothing. Nothing in Europe anyway. We wanted to do different things, but no one was angry about it. Kerry came home first. She was in London and got homesick. Aysha lived in Paris and I ended up in Hamburg. Mom said either I was to get a job or marry the head of Porsche. I told her he was in Stuttgart, but she wasn't amused. You know, I still have the letters we sent to one another over that time. Aysha wrote long ones. Kerry was more to the point. It was this business with Norman that broke up the three musketeers. Even when I was married and they were single we stayed close. Then, when Kerry was dating Norman and I was divorcing the monster, we went out together."

"Maybe Norman has hidden talents," Harry mused.

"*Very hidden*," Mrs. Murphy called out from the bottom of the mail cart.

"Kerry thought so. They always had stuff to talk about." Marilyn laughed. "As for Aysha, she got panicky. All your friends are married and you're not—that kind of thing. Plus, Ottoline lashed her on."

"*Panic? It must have been a grand mal seizure.*" Mrs. Murphy stuck her head out of the mail cart.

Pewter pushed through the animal door. "*It's me.*"

"*I know*," Murphy called back. Pewter jumped in the mail cart with her.

"Isn't it a miracle the way those two cats found Kerry?" Marilyn watched the two felines roll around and bat at one another in the mail cart.

"The Lord moves in mysterious ways His wonders to perform," Mrs. H. said.

Mrs. Murphy and Pewter stopped.

"You'd think they'd realize that the Almighty is a cat. Humans are lower down in the chain of beings."

"They'll never get it. Too egocentric." Pewter swatted Murphy's tail and renewed the combat.

"I ought to get out those old letters." Little Marilyn headed for the door. "Be interesting to see who we were then and who we are now."

"Bring them in someday so I can look at the stamps."

"Okay."

Miranda cut another piece of banana bread. "Marilyn, do you believe Kerry could kill someone?"

"Yes. I believe any of us could kill someone if we had to do it."

"But Hogan?"

She breathed deeply. "Mrs. H., I just don't know. It seems impossible, but . . ."

"Where did Kerry work in London—if she did?"

"At a bank. London branch of one of the big American banks. That's when she found her vocation, at least that's what she told me."

"I never heard that." Harry's mind raced.

"She's quiet. Then again, how many people are interested in banking, and you two are acquaintances at best. I mean, there's nothing shifty in her not telling you."

"Yeah," Harry weakly responded.

"Well, this is errand day." Marilyn pushed open the door and a blast of muggy air swept in.

So did Rick and Cynthia.

"May I?" Rick pointed to the low countertop door separating the lobby and mailbox area from the work area.

"How polite to ask." Mrs. Hogendobber flipped up the countertop.

Cynthia followed. She placed a folder on the table and opened it. "The owner of a bar in San Francisco where Huckstep worked sent me these." She handed newspaper articles about George Jarvis's suicide to Harry and Mrs. Hogendobber.

Harry finished hers first, then read over Miranda's shoulder.

"The real story is that this man Jarvis, a member of the Bohemian Club, pillar-of-the-community type, was homosexual. No one knew. He was being blackmailed by Mike Huckstep and his girlfriend or wife—we aren't sure if they were really married —Malibu. She must be a cold customer, because she would hide and photograph Mike cavorting with his victims and that's how the blackmailing would start."

"The wedding ring said M & M." Harry handed the clipping back to Cynthia.

"I'm not jumping to conclusions. We've checked marriage records in San Francisco for June 12, 1986. Nothing on Huckstep. It's like finding a needle in a haystack. Checked the surrounding counties too. Given enough time, we'll get through all the records in California."

"Those two could have stood before the ocean and pledged eternal troth." Rick was sarcastic. "Or gone to Reno."

"We've sent out a bulletin to every police department in the nation and to the court of records for every county. Nothing may come of it, but we're sloggin' away."

Cynthia pulled out an eight-by-ten glossy blow-up of a snapshot. "Mike."

"Looking better than when he roared up to Ash Lawn."

"No one has claimed the body," Rick informed them. "We buried him in the county plot. We've got dental records to prove it was really him. We had to get him in the ground, obviously."

"Here's another. This is all Frank Kenton found. He said he called everyone he could remember from those days when Mike tended bar."

A figure, blurred, her back turned, stood in the background of the photo. "Malibu?" Harry asked.

Mrs. Hogendobber put on her glasses. "All I can see is long hair."

"Frank knows little about her. She worked part-time at the Anvil, the bar he owns—caters to gay men. Malibu might as well have been wallpaper as far as the patrons were concerned, plus she seemed like the retiring type. Frank said he can't recall ever having a personal conversation with her."

"Did he know their scam?" Harry stared at the figure.

"Eventually. Huckstep and Malibu left in the nick of time. I suppose they left with a carload of money. They moved to L.A., where they probably continued their 'trade,' although no one seems to have caught them. Easy, I guess, in such a big city."

Rick jumped in when Cynthia finished. "We believe she was in the Charlottesville area when Mike arrived. We don't know if she's still around. Oh, one other sidelight. We've pieced together bits of Mike's background. His social security number helped us there. Frank Kenton had the number in his records. Mike was raised in Fort Wayne, Indiana. Majored in computer science at Northwestern University, where he made straight A's."

"The Threadneedle virus!" Harry clapped her hands.

"That's a long shot, Harry," Rick admonished, then thought a minute. "Puts Kerry right in the perfect place to call in."

Harry folded a mail sack. "If she was smart enough to create their scam or to link up with the computer genius, she sure was dumb to get caught. Somehow it doesn't fit."

"The murder weapon sure fits." Cynthia took a piece of banana bread offered by Miranda.

"Now, you two"—Miranda's voice was laced with humor —"you're not here to show us a photograph of someone's back. I know you have two murders to solve. You'd put most of your effort into finding Hogan's killer, not the stranger's killer. So you must believe they are connected and you must need us in some fashion."

Rick's jaw froze in mid-chew. Mrs. Hogendobber was smarter than he gave her credit for being. "Well—"

"We're trustworthy." Miranda offered him another piece of banana bread.

He gulped. "No question of that. It's just—"

Cynthia interrupted. "We'd better tell them."

A silence followed.

"All right," Rick reluctantly agreed. "You tell them, I'll eat."

Cynthia grabbed a piece of bread before he could devour the whole loaf.

"We've had our people working on Crozet National's computers. It's frustrating, obviously, because the thief has covered his tracks. But we did find one interesting item. An account opened in the name of Mr. and Mrs. Michael Huckstep."

Harry whistled.

Miranda said, "Mr. and Mrs.?"

Cynthia continued. "We pulled the signature cards. But we can't really verify his signature or hers."

"Can't you match it to the signature on his driver's license?" Harry asked.

"Superficially, yes. They match. But to verify it we need a handwriting expert. We've got a lady coming down from Washington." She paused for breath. "As for Mrs. Huckstep's signature . . . it doesn't match, superficially again, anyone's handwriting in the bank."

"When did he or she open the account?" Harry asked.

"July thirtieth. He deposited $4,218.64 in cash." Rick wiped his mouth with a napkin supplied by Miranda. "The bank officer in charge of opening the account was Kerry McCray."

"Not so good." Harry exhaled.

"What if . . ." Mrs. Hogendobber pressed her fingers together. "Oh, forget it."

"No, go on," Rick encouraged her.

"What if Kerry did open the account? That doesn't mean she knew him."

"Kerry declares she never opened an account for Mr. and Mrs. Huckstep even though she was on the floor all of July thirtieth," Rick said heavily. "There's a number on each new account, an identifying employee number. Kerry's is on Huckstep's."

"Is the missing money in his account?" Harry queried.

"No," both answered.

Cynthia spoke. "We can't find a nickel."

"Well, I hate to even ask this. Was it in Hogan Freely's account?" Harry winced under Miranda's scornful reaction.

"No," Rick replied.

"For all we know, the money that disappeared on August first or second could be sitting in an account whose code we can't crack, to be called out at some later, safer date," Cynthia added.

"Maybe the money is in another bank or even another country," Miranda said.

"If two million or more dollars showed up in a personal account, we'd know it by now."

"Rick, what about a corporate account?"

"Harry, that's a bit more difficult because the big companies routinely shift around substantial sums. Sooner or later I think we'd catch it, but the thief and most likely the murderer, one and the same, would have to have someone on the inside of one or more Fortune 500 firms," Rick explained.

"Or someone inside another bank." Harry couldn't figure this out. She didn't even have a hunch.

"Possible." Cynthia cracked her knuckles. "Sorry."

"What can we do?" Miranda wanted to help.

"Everybody tromps through here. Keep your eyes and ears open," Rick requested.

"We do that anyway." Harry laughed. "You know, Big Marilyn asked us to watch for registered letters. Could be stock certificates. Nothing."

"Thank you for the information about Threadneedle." Rick stood up. "I don't think Kerry could pull this off alone."

Miranda swallowed.

As if reading her thoughts, Harry whispered, "Norman?"

"We're keeping an eye on him." Rick shrugged. "We've got

nothing on him at all. But we're scrutinizing everyone in that bank down to the janitor."

"Keep your eyes open." Rick flipped up the Dutch door countertop and Cooper followed.

"If people will kill for a thousand bucks, think what they'll do for two million." Cynthia patted Harry on the back. "Remember, we said watch. We didn't say get involved."

As they left, both Miranda and Harry started talking at once.

"Telling those two to stay out of it is like telling a dog not to wag her tail," Mrs. Murphy said to Pewter.

" 'Cept for Tucker," Pewter teased.

Tucker replied from her spot under the table, "I resent that."

31

"Where does this stuff come from?" Dismayed, Harry surveyed her junk room.

Calling it the junk room wasn't fair to the room, a board-and-batten, half-screened back porch complete with Shaker pegs upon which to hang coats, a heavy wrought iron boot scraper, and big standing bootjack and a long, massive oak table. Dark green and ochre painted squares of equal size brightened the floor. The last line at catching the mud was a heavy welcome mat at the door into the kitchen.

Twice a year the mood would strike Harry and she'd organize the porch. The tools were easy to hang on the walls or take back out to the barn depending on their original home. The boxes of magazines, letters, and old clothes demanded sorting.

Mrs. Murphy scratched in the magazine box. The sound of

claws over shiny, expensive paper delighted her. Tucker contented herself with nosing through the old clothes. If Harry tossed a sweatshirt or a pair of jeans in a carton, they really were old. She was raised in the use-it-up wear-it-out make-it-do-or-do-without school. The clothes would be cut into square pieces of cloth for barn rags. Whatever remained afterward, Harry would toss out, although she swore one day she would learn to make hooked rugs so she could utilize the scraps.

"Find anything?" Tucker asked Mrs. Murphy.

"Lot of old New Yorker magazines. She sees an article she wants to read, doesn't have time to read it then, and saves the magazine. Now, I'll bet you a Milk-Bone she'll sit on the floor, go through these magazines, and tear out the articles she wants to save so she'll still have a pile of stuff to read but not as huge a one as if she'd saved the magazines intact. If she didn't work in the post office, Gossip Central, she'd work in the library like her mother did."

"My bet is the broken bridle will get her attention first. She needs to replace the headstall. She's going to pick it up, mumble, then put it in the trunk to take to Sam Kimball."

"Maybe so. At least that will go quickly. Once she buries her nose in a book or magazine, she takes forever."

"Think she'll forget supper?"

"Tucker, you're as bad as Pewter."

"She fooled us both," the dog exclaimed.

Harry, armed with a pair of scissors, began cutting up the old clothes. "Mrs. Murphy, don't rip apart the magazines. I need to go through them first."

"Give me some catnip. I can be bought off." Mrs. Murphy scratched and tore with increased vigor.

Harry stopped snipping and picked up the magazine box. It was heavier than she anticipated, so she put it back down. "I was going to shake you up."

"Catnip." Murphy's eyes enlarged, she performed a somersault in the box.

"Aren't you the acrobat?" Harry put the box on the oak table. She looked at the hanging herbs placed inside to dry. A large clutch of catnip, leaves down, emitted a sweet, enticing odor. Murphy shot out of the box, straight up, and swatted the tip of the catnip. A little higher and she could have had a slam dunk.

"*Catnip!*"

"Druggie." Harry smiled and snapped off a sprig.

"*Yahoo.*" Mrs. Murphy snatched the catnip from Harry's hands, threw it on the table, chewed it a little, rolled on it, tossed it up in the air, caught it, rolled some more. Her antics escalated.

"Nuts. You're a loony tunes, out there, Blue Angels."

"*Mother, she's always that way. The catnip brings it out more. Now, me, I'm a sane and sober dog. Reliable. Protective. I can herd and fetch and follow at your heels. Even with a bone, which I would enjoy right now, I would never descend to such raucous behavior.*"

"*Bugger off,*" Mrs. Murphy hissed at Tucker. The weed made her aggressive.

"Fair is fair." Harry walked into the kitchen and brought out a bone for Tucker before returning to her task.

As the animals busied themselves, Harry finished off the box of clothing. She reached into the magazine box and flipped through the table of contents. "Umm, better save this article." She clipped out a long piece on the Amazon rain forests.

"*Someone's coming,*" Tucker barked.

"Shut up." Murphy lolled her head. "*You're hurting my ears.*"

"*Friend or foe?*" the corgi challenged as the car pulled into the driveway.

"*Do you really think a foe would drive up to the back door?*"

"*Shut up, yourself. I'm doing my job, and besides, this is the South. All one's foes act like friends.*"

"*Got that right,*" the cat agreed, rousing herself from her catnip torpor. "*It's Little Marilyn. What the heck is she doing here at seven in the evening?*"

"Come on in," Harry called. "I'm doing my spring cleaning, in August."

Marilyn opened the porch door. "At least you're doing it. I've got a ton of my stuff to sort through. I'll never get to it."

"How about an iced tea or coffee? I can make a good pot of hot coffee too."

"Thank you, no."

"If you don't need the iced tea, I do." Harry put down her scissors.

The two humans repaired to the kitchen. Harry's kitchen, scrupulously clean, smelled like nutmeg and cinnamon. She prided herself on her sense of order. She had to pride herself on something in the kitchen, since she couldn't cook worth a damn.

"Milk or lemon?" Harry wouldn't take no for an answer.

"Oh, thank you. Lemon. I'm going to keep you from your chores." Marilyn fidgeted.

"They'll wait. I've been on my feet all day anyway, so it's good to have a sit-down."

"Harry, we aren't the best of friends, so I hope you don't mind my barging in on you like this."

"It's fine."

She cast her eyes about the kitchen, then settled down. "I don't know what to do. Two weeks ago Kerry asked me for a loan. I refused her. I hated to do it, but, well, she wanted three thousand dollars."

"What for?"

"She said she knew her father's cancer was getting worse. If she could invest the money, she could help defray what his insurance won't cover. She said she'd split the profit with me and return the principal in a year's time."

"Kerry's a lot sharper than I thought."

"Yes." Little Marilyn sat stock-still.

"Have you told Rick Shaw or Cynthia?"

"No. I came to you first. It's been preying on my mind. I mean, she's in so much trouble as it is."

"Yeah, I know, but"—Harry held up her hands—"you've got to tell them."

Mrs. Murphy, sitting on the kitchen counter, said, *"What do you really think, Marilyn?"*

"She's hungry." Harry got up to open two cans of food for Mrs. Murphy and Tucker. Tucker gobbled her food while Mrs. Murphy daintily ate hers.

"Thanks for hearing me out. We were all such good friends once. I feel like a traitor."

"You're not. And horrendous as the process is, that's what the courts are for—if Kerry is innocent, she'll be spared. At least, I hope so."

"Don't you know that old proverb? 'Better to fall into the hands of the Devil than into the hands of the lawyers.' "

"You think she's sunk, don't you?"

"Uh-huh." Little Marilyn nodded in the affirmative, tears in her eyes.

32

Every spare moment she had, Kerry punched into the computer in a back office. Cynthia told her she could go to work. She'd be formally arraigned tomorrow. Rick told the acting president, Norman Cramer, to allow Kerry to work. He had a few words with the staff which amounted to "innocent until proven guilty." What he hoped for was a slip on Kerry's part or the part of her accomplice.

The thick carpeting in the officer branch of the bank muffled the footsteps behind her as she frantically pulled up records on the computer. Norman Cramer tapped her shoulder.

"What are you doing?"

"Fooling around. Kind of like you, Norman." Kerry's face burned.

"Kerry, this is none of your business. You'll interfere with Rick Shaw's investigation."

What neither of them knew was that Rick was monitoring Kerry's computer. An officer down in the basement saw everything she called up.

"Hogan Freely's murder is everybody's business. And I'd rather be chewed out by you than not try and come up with some clue, any clue."

His sallow complexion darkened. "Listen to me. Forget it."

"Why don't you and I go outside and talk?"

"And risk another scene? No."

"I knew you were a coward. I hoped it wasn't true. I really believed you when you told me you'd leave Aysha—"

He sharply reprimanded her. "It's not appropriate to discuss personal matters at work."

"You won't discuss them at any other time."

"I can't. Maybe I know things you don't and maybe you should forget about me for a while. You shouldn't have come in today. It upsets everyone." He spun on his heel and walked away.

Steam wasn't hotter than Kerry McCray. She followed him. "You sorry son of a bitch."

He grabbed her arm so hard he hurt her as he half pushed, half dragged her down the narrow corridor to the back door. He practically threw her down the steps into the parking lot. "Take the day off! I don't care if Rick Shaw thinks it's okay for you to be here. I don't. Now, get out and chill out!" He slammed the door.

Kerry sobbed in the middle of the parking lot. She walked over to her car, opened the door, and got inside. Then she put her head on the steering wheel and sobbed some more.

Mrs. Hogendobber passed on her way from the bank. She hesitated but then walked over.

"Kerry, can I help?" she asked through the rolled-down window.

Kerry looked up. "Mrs. Hogendobber, I wish you could."

Mrs. Hogendobber patted her on the back. " 'Love your ene-

mies, bless them that curse you, do good to them that hate
you . . . For if ye love them which love you, what reward have
ye? Do not even the publicans the same?' "

Kerry recovered enough to remark, "Make that Republi-
cans."

"There, there, I knew you'd perk up. I find the Bible always
helps me in time of need."

"I think it was you as much as your quote. I wish I could be
as wise and as calm as you are, Mrs. Hogendobber." She opened
her glove compartment for a tissue. "Do you believe I killed Hogan Freely?"

Miranda said, "No." She waited for Kerry to finish blowing
her nose. "You just don't seem like the type to me. I can imagine
you killing Norman in a lover's rage, but not Hogan." She
paused. "If you live long enough, honey, you see everything.
You're still seeing many things for the first time, including a two-
timing ex-boyfriend. After a while you know what's worth getting het up over and what just to let go. He married Aysha. Let
him go. Reading the Good Book and praying to the Lord never
hurt anyone. You'll find solace there and sooner or later the right
man will come into your life." She inhaled. "It's so hot. You'll
fry in that car. Come on over to the P.O. and I'll make you some
iced tea. I have some chocolate chip cookies, macadamia nut ones
too."

"Thank you. I'm wrung out. I think I'll go home and maybe
I'll take your advice and read the Bible." She wiped her eyes.
"Thank you."

"Don't give it a second thought." Miranda smiled, then
turned for the post office.

Kerry drove off.

Mrs. Hogendobber waited until there was no one else in the
building to tell Harry about the episode. Crozet, being a town of
only 1,733 people, didn't miss much. A few noticed Kerry's pursuit of Norman down the corridor. Boom Boom Craycroft saw
him push her out of the building and fifteen people coming and

going saw Mrs. Hogendobber consoling Kerry in the parking lot. Variations of the events made the rounds. Each telling exaggerated Kerry's unhappiness and surmised guilt until she was suicidal. Norman's handling of her seemed tinged by heroism to many.

By the time Little Marilyn drove up to Ash Lawn to relieve Aysha, the tale was worthy of a soap opera, but then, maybe daily life is a soap opera.

Everyone at Ash Lawn was working double duty since Laura Freely would not be returning for the remainder of the year. Trying to schedule and work in Ottoline, who substituted for Laura, frazzled Little Marilyn, in charge of the docents.

Marilyn combed her hair and straightened up as Aysha finished a tour for a group of sightseers. More were coming, but Marilyn had about ten minutes before she would gather up a new group to commence the tour.

Aysha related her version of the Norman-Kerry episode. Her gloating offended Marilyn Sanburne, Jr.

"She's the loser. You're the winner. Be gracious enough to ignore her."

Aysha threw her shoulders back and squared her chin, prelude to some pronouncement of emotional significance tinged with her imagined superiority. "Who are you to dictate manners to me?"

"I used to be your best friend. Now I wonder."

"You're on her side. I knew it. Oh, don't women just love a victim and Kerry paints herself as a real martyr to love—she's a murderer, for chrissakes!"

"You don't know that and you don't have to wallow in it."

"I'm not."

"You look like you're gloating to me," Marilyn shot back. "Just drop it."

Aysha's voice lowered, a signal that what she was about to impart was really, truly, terribly important and that she'd been keeping it in only because she was such a lady. "She kissed my husband at Hogan Freely's wake."

Since neither Harry nor Cynthia had ever mentioned it, Marilyn didn't know about the kissing part of the incident. As the two rivals had yelled and screamed at the top of their lungs, she certainly knew about the rest of it. She heard every word, as did most of the other mourners. "Look, I'd have been upset. I understand that. I wouldn't want anyone kissing my husband, especially a former lover. But, Aysha, get over it. Every time you react to her, she gets what she wants. She's the center of your attention, Norman isn't, and she's the center of Norman's attention and you're not. Rise above it."

"Easy for you to say. I remember in school how devious she was—so nice to your face, so vicious when you were out of sight—"

"I don't want to hear that stuff." Marilyn advanced toward Aysha a step, realized what she was doing, and stopped. "Keep this up, Aysha, and you'll be as big a bitch as your mother."

"You think you're better than the rest of us because you'll inherit your mother's fortune. If Big Marilyn were my mother, I'd be worried. Every woman turns into her mother. Mine is small potatoes compared to yours."

"I don't care about the money."

"Those who have it never care about it. That's the point! Someday I hope I have as much as you do so I can rub your nose in it."

"Your time is up. I'll take over now." Marilyn quietly walked into the front room to greet the visitors to Monroe's home.

33

Air-conditioning was a luxury Harry couldn't afford. Her house at the foot of Yellow Mountain stayed cool except on the worst of those sultry summer nights. This was one of those nights. Every window was open to catch the breezes that weren't there. Harry tossed and turned, sweated, and finally cursed.

"I don't know how you can sleep through this," she grumbled as she stepped over Tucker and headed toward the bathroom.

As Harry brushed her teeth Mrs. Murphy alighted nimbly on the sink. *"Hotter than Tophet."*

Harry, mouth full of toothpaste, didn't reply to Murphy's observation. After rinsing, she petted the cat, who purred with appreciation.

Walking through the house provided no relief. She wandered into the library, shadowed by Murphy.

"Mother, this is the hottest room in the house. Why don't you put ice cubes on your head and a baseball cap over them? That will help."

"I'm hot too, sweetheart." Harry glanced at the old books her mother gleaned from the library sales she used to administer. "Here's the plan. Let's go into the barn, move the little table from the tack room out into the aisle, and think. The barn's the coolest place right now."

"Worth a try." Murphy raced to the screened-porch door and pushed it open. The hook dangled uselessly because the screw eye was long gone.

As they walked into the barn, the big owl swooshed overhead. "You two idiots will spoil a good night of hunting."

"Tough." Mrs. Murphy's fur fluffed out.

When Harry switched on the lights, the opossum popped his head out of a plastic feed bucket. "Hey."

"Simon, don't worry. She doesn't care. We're going to do some research."

"Here?"

"Too hot inside."

"Feels like being wrapped in a big wet towel out here. Must be even worse in the house," Simon concurred.

Harry, having no idea of the lively conversation taking place between her cat and the possum, carried the small table to the aisle, set up a fan, grabbed a pencil and yellow tablet, sat down, and started making notes. Every now and then Harry would slap her arm or the back of her neck.

"How come the skeeters bite me and leave you alone?" she asked the tiger, who batted at the moving pencil.

"Can't get through the fur. You humans lack most protective equipment. You keep telling the rest of us it's because you're so highly evolved. Not true. An eagle's eyes are much more developed than yours. So are mine, for that matter. Put on mosquito repellent."

"I wish you could talk."

"I can talk. You just can't understand what I say."

"Murphy, I love it when you trill at me. Wish you could read too."

"What makes you think I can't? Trouble is, you mostly write about yourselves and not other animals, so I find few books that hold my interest. Tucker says she can read, but she's pretty shaky. Simon, can you read?"

"No." Simon had moved to another feed bucket, where he picked through the sweet feed. He especially liked the little bits of corn.

Harry listed each of the events as she remembered them, starting with Mike Huckstep's appearance at Ash Lawn.

She listed times, weather, and any other people who happened to be around.

Starting with the Ash Lawn incident, she noted it was hot. It was five of five. Laura Freely was in charge of the docents: Marilyn Sanburne, Jr., Aysha Cramer, Kerry McCray. Susan Tucker ran the gift shop. Danny Tucker was working in the yard to the left of the house. She and Blair were in the living room.

She tried to remember every detail of every incident up to and including Little Marilyn's visit to her concerning Kerry's request for a loan.

"Murphy, I give up. It's still a jumble."

The cat put her paw on the pencil, stopping its progress. "Listen. Whoever is behind this can't be that much smarter than you are. If they came up with this, then you'll figure it out. The question is, if you do figure it out, will you be safe?"

Harry absentmindedly petted Murphy as the cat tried to talk sense to her.

"You know, I've sat up half the night making lists. The so-called facts are leading me nowhere. Sitting here with you, Murphy, no chores, totally quiet, I can think. Time to trust my instincts. Mike Huckstep knew his killer. He walked deep into the woods with him. Hogan Freely may or may not have known his killer, but the murderer certainly knew Hogan, knew he was working that night, and had the good fortune to walk into an unlocked bank, or he or she had a key. Any one of us in Market Shiflett's store knew Hogan would be in the bank. He told us.

Laura knew, but I think we can let her off the hook. I wonder if he told anyone else?''

''*The thick fog gave the killer a real bonus.*'' Mrs. Murphy remembered the night vividly.

Harry tapped the pencil on the table. ''Was it planned or was it impulse?''

Harry wrote out her thoughts and waited for the sunrise. At six, since Mrs. H. was up and baking by then, she phoned her friend. She asked her to cover for her for half an hour. She needed to drop something off at the sheriff's office.

At seven she was at Rick Shaw's office, where she left her notes with Ed Wright, who was ending his night shift. By eight Rick called. He'd read the notes and he thanked her.

She sorted the mail with Miranda while telling her what she wrote down for Sheriff Shaw. On those rare occasions when she was up all night she usually got very sleepy about three in the afternoon. She figured she'd nod out and she warned Mrs. Hogendobber not to be too angry with her. However, the events of the day would keep her wide awake.

34

At the beginning of the day Harry blamed the bizarre chain of events on the fact that it was cloudy. That, however, couldn't explain how the day ended.

At ten-thirty Blair Bainbridge pulled into the front parking lot of the post office on a brand-new, gorgeous Harley-Davidson. It appeared to be black, especially under the clouds, but in the bright sunlight the color would sparkle a deep plum.

"What do you think?" Blair asked.

Harry walked outside to admire the machine. "What got into you?"

"Grabbing at summer." He grinned. "And you know, when I saw Mike Huckstep's Harley, I was flooded with memories. Who says I have to be mature and responsible twenty-four hours a day? How about twenty hours a day, and for four hours I can be wild again?''

''Sounds good to me.''

Miranda opened the front door. ''You'll get killed on that thing.''

''I hope not. Is there a Bible quote for excessive speed?''

''Off the top of my head, I can't think of one. I'll put my mind to it.'' She closed the door.

''Oh, Blair, she'll worry herself to a nub. She'll call her buddies in Bible study class. She won't rest until she finds an appropriate citation.''

''Should I take her for a ride?''

''I doubt it. If it's not her Ford Falcon, she doesn't want to get in it or on it.''

''Bet you five dollars.'' With that he hopped up the steps into the post office.

Harry closed the door behind her as Mrs. Murphy and Tucker greeted Blair.

''Mrs. Hogendobber, I just happen to have two helmets and I want to take you for a ride. We can float across the countryside.''

''Now, isn't that nice?'' But she shook her head no.

Before he could warm up to his subject, the front door flew open and a glowering Norman Cramer stormed in.

''How can you? This is in such bad taste!''

''What are you talking about?'' Blair replied since the hostility was directed at him.

''That, that's what I'm talking about!'' Norman gesticulated in the direction of the beautiful bike.

''You don't like Harleys? Okay, you're a BMW man.'' Blair shrugged.

''Everything was all right around here until the day that motorcycle appeared. How can you ride around on it? How can you even touch it! What'd you do, slip Rick Shaw money under the table? I thought unclaimed property was to go to public auction held by the Sheriff's Department.''

"Wait a minute." Blair relaxed. "That isn't the murdered guy's Harley. It's not even black. Go out and take another look. I just bought this bike."

"Huh?"

"Go look." Blair opened the door for Norman.

The two men circled the bike as the humans and animals observed from inside.

"Norman's losing it." One side of Harry's mouth turned up.

"If you were caught between Kerry and Aysha, I expect you'd unravel too. Scylla and Charybdis."

"Steam was coming out of his ears. And how could he say something like that about Rick Shaw? Jesus, the crap that goes through people's minds."

"Don't take the name of Our Savior in vain."

"Sorry. Hey, here comes Herbie."

The reverend stopped to chat with the men, then entered the building. "Cheap transportation. Those things must get fifty miles to the gallon. If gas taxes continue to rise, then I might get one myself. How about a motorcycle with a sidecar?"

"You going to paint a cross on it? A little sign to hang on the handlebars, 'Clergy'?"

"Mary Minor Haristeen, do I detect a whiff of sarcasm in your tone? Haven't you read of the journeys of St. Paul? Imagine if he'd had a motorcycle. Why, he could have created congregations throughout the Mediterranean, Gaul even. Sped along the process of Christianization."

"On a Harley. I like that image."

"You two. What will you come up with next?" Miranda sauntered over to the counter.

"Imagine if Jesus had a car. What would he drive?" Herbie loved to torment Miranda, and since he was an ordained minister he knew she would have to pay attention to him.

"The best car in the world," Miranda said, "my Ford Falcon."

"Might as well go back to sandals." Harry joined in the game. "I bet he'd drive a Subaru station wagon because the car goes forever, rarely needs to be serviced, and he could squeeze the twelve disciples inside."

"Now, that's a thought." Herb reached down to pat Tucker, who walked out from under the countertop.

Blair rejoined them. Norman too.

"I'm sorry. I'm a little edgy." Norman cast down his eyes.

"Norman, you've got one woman too many in your life, and that's not including Ottoline." Mrs. Hogendobber was forthright.

He blushed, then nodded.

Blair lightheartedly said, "All those men out there looking for a woman, and you've got them to spare. How do you do it?"

"By being stupid." Norman valiantly tried to smile, then left.

"Well, what do you think of that?" Miranda exclaimed.

"I think he's about to check into Heartbreak Hotel," Harry replied.

"Depressed." Blair opened his mailbox.

"Now, now, if he loves Aysha, he'll work it out." Herb believed in the sacrament of marriage. After all, he'd married half the town.

"But what if he doesn't love her?" Harry questioned.

"Then I don't know." Herb folded his arms across his chest. "All marriage is a compromise. Maybe he can find the middle ground. Maybe Aysha can too. Her social climbing tries even my patience."

As Herb left, Cynthia Cooper arrived. "Thanks for your notes."

"Couldn't sleep. Had to do something."

"I was up all night too," Blair added. "If I'd known that, I would have come over."

"You devil." Cynthia would have died to hear him say that to her. "Well, we checked out the signature card handwriting with the signature on Mike Huckstep's income tax statements and driver's license application with the graphologist from Washington. They are authentic. And Mrs. Huckstep's signature is not his handwriting. He didn't forge a signature. It's not Kerry's signature either. Two people signed the card."

"How'd you find out so fast?"

"Wasn't that fast. Try getting the IRS to listen to a tiny sheriff's department in central Virginia. Rick finally called up our congressman and then things started to move. The DMV part was easy."

"Did Mike actually go into the bank and sign cards?"

"Well, no one at the bank remembers seeing a man of his description. Or won't admit to it."

"Coop, how did he sign?" Blair asked.

"At gunpoint?"

"Have you been able to question Laura yet?" Mrs. H. inquired. "She might remember something."

"She's cooperated to the max. Once the shock wore off, she's helped as much as she can because she wants to catch Hogan's murderer. Dudley and Thea are doing all they can too. Unfortunately, Laura says she's never seen anyone matching Huckstep's description. Hogan would occasionally discuss bank problems with Laura, but usually they were people problems. The tension between Norman Cramer and Kerry McCray disturbed him. Other than that, she said everything seemed normal."

"And there's nothing peculiar in anyone's background at Crozet National?" Mrs. Hogendobber played with her bangle bracelets.

"No. No criminal records."

"We're still at a dead end." Harry sighed.

"You know, Harry, you're the only person who has seen the killer," Cooper replied.

"I've wondered about that."

"What do you mean?" Blair and Miranda talked over each other but basically they said the same thing.

"Whoever was riding that motorcycle when it almost side-swiped Harry at Sugar Hollow was most likely our man. Unless Huckstep rode out and rode back later."

"And all I saw was a black helmet with a black visor and someone all in black leather. A real Hell's Angel."

"Why didn't you say anything?" Miranda wanted to know.

"I did. I told Rick and Cynthia. I've racked my brain for anything, a hint, an attitude, but it happened so fast."

After Blair left to go riding around the countryside, Cynthia stayed on for a little bit. People came in and out as always, and at five the friends closed the post office to go home.

Susan Tucker drove over with Danny and Brooks. They left Harry's house about eight. Then Fair called. The night cooled off a bit, so Harry gratefully drifted off to sleep early.

The jangle of the phone irritated her. The big, old-fashioned alarm clock read four-thirty. She reached over and picked it up.

"Hello."

"Harry. It's Fair. I'm coming over."

"It's four-thirty in the morning."

"Norman Cramer's been strangled."

"What?" Harry sat bolt upright.

"I'll tell you everything when I get there. Stay put."

35

Cinnamon-flavored coffee perfectly perked awakened Harry's senses. She'd brought the Krups machine into the kitchen from the barn. It was so fancy, she thought it was too nice to keep in the stable. Mrs. Murphy and Tucker ate an early breakfast with her. The owl, again furious at the invasion of privacy, swept low over Fair's head as he trudged to the back door.

"What happened?" she asked as she poured him a cup and set out muffins on the table.

His face parchment white, he sat down heavily. "Bad case of torsion colic. Steve Alton's big Hanoverian. He brought her over to the clinic and I operated. I didn't finish up until three, three-thirty. Steve wanted to stay with her, but I sent him home to get some sleep. I came in through town and turned left on Railroad Avenue. Not a soul in sight. Then I passed the old Del Monte plant and I saw Norman Cramer sitting in his car. The lights were on, and the motor too. He was just kind of staring into space and his tongue was hanging out kind of funny. I stopped and got out of the truck, and as I drew closer I saw bad bruises around his neck. I opened the door and he keeled over out onto the macadam. Called Rick. He arrived in less than ten minutes—he must have gone a hundred miles an hour. Cynthia made it in twenty minutes. All I'd done was put my fingerprints on the door handle. I didn't touch the body. Anyway, I told them what I knew, stayed around, and then Rick sent me home."

"Fair, I'm sorry." Harry's hands trembled. "If you'd been earlier, the murderer might have gone after you."

"I'll see those dead eyes staring out at me for a long, long time. Rick said the body was still warm." He reached for her hand.

"If I make up the bed in the guest room, do you think you can sleep?"

"No. Let me take a catnap on the sofa. I've got to get back to the clinic by seven-thirty."

She brought out some pillows and a light blanket for the sofa. Fair kicked off his shoes and stretched out. He wistfully looked at Harry as she reached to turn off the light. "I love being in this house."

"It's good to have you here. I'll wake you at six-thirty."

"Are you going back to sleep?"

"No. I've got some thinking to do." He fell asleep before she finished her sentence.

36

Harry used the tack room as an office. She pulled out her trusty yellow legal pad and wrote down everything Fair had just told her. Then she described what she knew about the killer of Mike Huckstep and Hogan Freely. Whether or not the same person or persons killed Norman was up for grabs, but he was head of the accounting department at Crozet National. Her guess was the three murders were tied together.

She wrote:

1. Knows how to operate a computer.
2. Knows the habits of the victims.
3. Knows the habits of the rest of us, although nearly caught after killing Hogan Freely.

4. Kills under pressure. A quick thinker. Knocked out
    Kerry before Kerry could see him, then set her up
    as the killer . . . unless killer is Kerry's
    accomplice. A real possibility.

5. Works in the bank or knows banking routines
    perhaps from another job. Might have key.

6. Possibly knows Malibu. May use her as bait.
    Perhaps Malibu is the killer or the killer's partner.

7. Feels superior to the rest of us. Fed media
    disinformation about the Threadneedle virus and
    then watched us eat it up.

8. Can ride a motorcycle.

At six Harry picked up the old black wall phone and called Susan
Tucker. Murphy sat on the legal pad. The cat couldn't think of
anything to add unless it was "armed and dangerous."

"Susan, I'm sorry to wake you."

"Harry, are you okay?"

"Yes. Fair's asleep on the couch. He found Norman Cramer
strangled early this morning."

"What? Wait a minute. Ned—Ned, wake up." Susan shook
her husband.

Harry could hear him mumble in the background, a pair of
feet hitting the floor, then the extension picked up.

"Harry."

"Sorry to wake you, Ned, but I think this might help Kerry
since you're her lawyer. Fair found Norman Cramer strangled in
his car in front of the Del Monte plant. About three-thirty this
morning. He didn't know he was dead. He opened the door and
Norman keeled over onto the pavement. Fair said huge bruises
around his throat and the condition of his face pointed to stran-
gulation."

"My God." Ned spoke slowly. "You were right to call us."

"Is everyone crazy? Is the murderer going to pick us off one
by one?" Susan exploded.

"If any of us interfere or get too close, I'd say we're next." Harry wasn't reassuring.

"I'm going to call Mrs. H. and Mim. Then I've got to wake up Fair. How about we all meet for breakfast at the café—seven-thirty? Umm, maybe I'd better phone Blair too. What do you think?"

"Yes, to both," Susan answered.

"Good enough. We'll see you there." Ned paused. "And thank you again."

Harry called Mrs. Hogendobber, who was shocked; Big Marilyn, who was both shocked and angry that this could happen in her town; and Blair, awakened from a heavy sleep, was in a daze.

She fed the horses, Mrs. Murphy, and Tucker. Then she woke Fair. They freshened up.

"Mrs. Murphy and Tucker, this is going to be a difficult day. You two stay home." She left the kitchen door open so the animals could go onto the porch. She left each of them a large bowl of crunchies.

"*Take me with you,*" Tucker whined.

"*Forget it,*" Mrs. Murphy said impassively. "*As soon as she's down the drive, I've got a plan.*"

"*Tell me now.*"

"*No, the humans are standing right here.*"

"*They don't understand what you're saying.*"

"*Better safe than sorry.*"

Harry kissed both pets, then hopped in the old truck while Fair climbed into his big Chevy truck. They headed for the downtown café. He had called the clinic. The horse was doing fine, so he decided to join the group for breakfast.

"*Follow me,*" Murphy commanded once the truck motors could no longer be heard.

"*I don't mind doing what you ask, but I hate taking orders,*" Tucker grumbled.

"*Dogs are obedient. Cats are independent.*"

"*You're full of it.*"

Nonetheless, Tucker followed as Mrs. Murphy scampered through the front meadows and the line of big sycamores along the creek that divided the pastures.

"Where are we going?"

"To Kerry McCray's. The fastest way is to head south. We can avoid the road that way too, but we'll have to cross the creek."

"You get your paws wet?"

"If I have to" was the cat's determined reply.

Moving at a sustained trot, the two animals covered ground rapidly. When they reached the big creek, Murphy stopped.

"It's high. How can it be high with no rain?"

Tucker walked to a bend along the bank. *"Here's your answer. A great big beaver dam."*

Mrs. Murphy joined her low-slung friend. *"I don't want to tangle with a beaver."*

"Me neither. But they're probably asleep. We could run over the dam. By the time they woke up, we'd probably be across. It's either that or find a place to ford downstream, where it's low."

"That will take too long." She inhaled deeply. *"Okay, let's run like blazes. Want me to go first?"*

"Sure. I'll be right behind."

With that, Mrs. Murphy shot off, all fours in the air, but running across a beaver dam proved difficult. She had to stop here and there, since heavy branches and stout twigs provided a snaggy surface. Murphy could hear movement inside the beaver lodge. She picked her way through the timber as fast as she could.

"Whatever happens, Murphy, don't hit the water. They'll pull you under. Better to fight it out on top of the dam."

"I know, I know, but there are more of them than us and they're stronger than we are." She slipped, her right front leg pushing into the lodge. She pulled it out as if it were on fire.

Slipping and sliding, Murphy made it to the other side. Tucker, heavier, was struggling. A beaver head popped up in the water at the other end of the dam.

"Hurry!" the cat shouted.

Tucker, without looking back, moved as rapidly as she could. The beaver swam alongside the dam. He was closing in on Tucker.

"*Leave her alone. She's trying to cross the creek. We mean no harm,*" the pretty tiger pleaded.

"*That's what they all say, and the next thing that happens is that men show up with guns, wreck the dam, and kill us. Dogs are the enemy.*"

"*No, man is the enemy.*" Mrs. Murphy was desperate. "*We don't belong to a person like that.*"

"*You may be right, but if I make a mistake, my whole family could be dead.*" The beaver was now alongside Tucker, who was almost to the creek bank. He reached up to grab Tucker's hind leg.

The dog whirled around and snarled. The beaver drew back for an instant. Tucker scrambled off the dam as the large animal advanced on her again. On terra firma both Tucker and Mrs. Murphy could outrun the beaver. They scorched the earth getting out of there.

At the edge of the woods they stopped to catch their breath.

"*How are we going to get back?*" Mrs. Murphy wondered aloud. "*I don't want to travel along the road. People drive like lunatics.*"

"*We'll have to find a place to ford far enough downstream so the beaver can't hear us. We can't swim it now. The lodge will be on alert.*"

"*It's going to take us over an hour to get home, but we'll worry about it later. We can be at Kerry McCray's in another ten minutes if we run.*"

"*I've got my wind back. Let's boogie.*"

They dashed through the fields of Queen Anne's lace, butterfly weed, and tall goldenrod. A small brick rancher came into view. Two squad cars were parked behind Kerry's Toyota. Its trunk lid was up.

"*I hope we're not too late.*" Murphy put on the turbocharger.

Tucker, a speed demon when she needed to be, raced next to her.

They made it to the cars as Kerry was being led out of her house by Sheriff Shaw. Cynthia Cooper carried a woven silk drapery cord with tasseled ends in a plastic bag.

"*Damn!*" Murphy snarled.

"*Too late?*" Tucker, having lived with Mrs. Murphy all her life, figured that the cat had wanted to explore before the cops arrived.

"*There's still a chance. You jump on Cynthia when she reaches to pet you and grab the plastic bag. I'll shred it as quickly as I can. Stick your nose in there and tell me if Kerry's scent is on the rope.*"

Without answering, Tucker charged Cynthia, who smiled at the sight of the little dog.

"Tucker, how did you get over here?" Tucker clamped her powerful jaws on the clear plastic bag, catching Officer Cooper by surprise. "Hey!"

Yanking it out of Cooper's hand, Tucker raced back to Mrs. Murphy, who was crouched back in the field, where Cynthia couldn't see her.

The minute Tucker dropped the bag under Murphy's nose, she unleashed her claws and tore for all she was worth. Cooper advanced on them, although she didn't know Murphy was there.

Tucker stuck her nose in the bag. "*It's not Kerry's scent.*"

"*Whose scent, then?*"

"*Rubber gloves. No scent other than Norman's cologne.*"

"Mrs. Murphy, you're as big a troublemaker as Tucker." Cooper disgustedly picked up the shredded bag.

"*If you had a brain in your head, you'd realize we're trying to help.*" Murphy backed away from Cynthia. "*Tucker, just to be sure, go sniff Kerry.*"

Tucker eluded Cynthia's grasp and ran over to Kerry, who was standing by the squad car.

"Tucker Haristeen." Kerry's eyes filled with tears. "At least I've got one friend."

Tucker licked her hand. "*I'm sorry.*"

Rick moved toward Tucker, and the dog spurted out of his reach. "Tucker, come on back here. Come on, girl."

"*No way.*" The dog barked as she rejoined Mrs. Murphy, lying flat on her belly in the orchard grass.

"Let's head back before they take us to the pound for punishment."

"They wouldn't do that." Tucker glanced back at the humans.

"Coop might." Murphy giggled.

"Kerry's scent isn't on the cord. After checking, I'm doubly positive."

As they leisurely walked back toward their farm, the two animals commiserated over Kerry's fate. The killer planted the murder weapon in the trunk of her car. Given Kerry's threats to kill Norman, which every human and animal in Crozet knew about by now, she had as much chance of being found innocent as a snowball in hell. Even if there was doubt about her shooting Hogan Freely, there would be no doubt about Norman.

By the time they reached the creek, they both felt down.

"Think we're far enough away from the beaver?"

"Murphy, it's not that deep downstream. If we fool around and try to find a fording place you can clear with one leap, we'll be here all day. Just get your paws wet and be done with it."

"Easy for you to say. You like water."

"Close your eyes and run if it's that bad."

Tucker splashed across the creek. Murphy, after ferocious complaining, followed. Once on the other side, Tucker had to wait for her to elaborately shake each paw, then lick it.

"Do that when we get home."

Mrs. Murphy, sitting on her rear end, had her right hind leg straight up in the air. "I'm not walking around with this creek smell on me."

Tucker sat down since she couldn't budge Mrs. Murphy from her toilette. "Think Norman was in on it?"

"That's obvious."

"Only to us." Tucker stretched her head upward.

"The humans will accept that Kerry killed him. A few might think that he was getting too close to the killer in the bank—or that he was her accomplice and he wimped out."

"Kerry could have killed him and used rubber gloves. It's possible that we're wrong."

"Doesn't everything come down to character?"

"Yes, it does."

"Tucker, if Norman wasn't the person behind the computer virus, do you think he was the type to track the killer? To keep on the case?"

"He wasn't a total coward. He could have unearthed something. Since he works in the bank, he'd tell someone. Word would get around—"

Mrs. Murphy finished her ablutions, stood up, and shook. "True enough. But we've got to trust our instincts. Three men have been killed with no sign of struggle. I could kick myself from here to Sunday for not running into the alleyway to see the car. I heard the killer's car the night Hogan was shot. Both Pewter and I did."

"I've told you before, Murphy, you did the right thing." Tucker started walking again. "I don't think the murderer will strike again unless it's another bank worker."

"Who knows?"

37

Harry, Fair, Mrs. Hogendobber, Susan, Ned, Blair, Big Marilyn, and Little Marilyn watched out the café window as Cynthia Cooper drove by in the squad car. Kerry McCray sat in the back seat behind the cage. No sooner had the dolorous spectacle passed than Aysha Cramer, pedal to the metal, roared past the café in her dark green car. Fair stood up, and as he opened the door, a crash could be heard. Within seconds Rick Shaw screeched by, a cloud of dust fanning out behind him. He hit the brakes hard, fishtailing as he stopped.

By now the remainder of the group hurried outside to join Fair, who was running at top speed toward the site of the wreck. Aysha had deliberately sideswiped Cynthia Cooper's squad car, forcing the deputy off the road. Cynthia, ever alert, stayed inside the car and locked the doors. She was talking on the radio.

"I'll kill her! Unlock this door! Goddammit, Cynthia, how can you protect her? She killed my husband!"

Rick pulled in behind Cooper. He leapt out of the car and hurried over to Aysha.

"Aysha, that's enough."

"You're protecting her. Let me at her! An eye for an eye, a tooth for a tooth."

As Rick and Fair struggled with Aysha, who would not release the door handle, Mrs. Hogendobber quoted under her breath, " 'Vengeance is mine, I will repay, says the Lord'—"

From inside the car Kerry screamed, "I did not kill him. You killed him. You drove him to his death!"

Aysha went berserk. She twisted away from the two men, strengthened by blind rage. She picked up a rock and smashed the back window of the car. Fair grabbed her from behind, slipping his powerful arms inside hers. She kicked backward and hit his shin, but he persevered and, with Rick, Ned, and Blair, pulled her away from the car. She collapsed in a heap by the side of the road. Aysha curled up in a ball, rocking back and forth and sobbing.

Cynthia prudently used the moment to pull away.

Rick motioned for the men to help him put Aysha in his car. Fair picked her up and carried her. He placed her in the back seat. She fell over and continued weeping.

Big Marilyn walked around to the other side of the car. Ned stepped in. "Mim, I'll go. If she loses it again, you may not be able to restrain her."

"I'll get in the front with Sheriff Shaw. We'd better get her to Larry." Larry Johnson, the old town doctor, and his partner, Hayden McIntire, treated most of the residents of Crozet.

"That's fine," the sheriff agreed. "I've had to tell many people terrible news, but I've never been through one like this. She ran right over me and jumped into her car."

"Takes everyone differently, I guess." Harry felt awful. "Better call her mother."

As if on cue, Ottoline sped down the road, slammed on the

brakes, and fishtailed in behind her daughter's car. She got out, leaving her door open.

"This doesn't bring him back." Ottoline slid into the back seat of Rick's car.

"I hate her!" Aysha sobbed. "She's alive and Norman's dead." She scrambled out of the other side of the back seat. Ottoline grabbed for her, but too late. Aysha stood by Deputy Cooper's car, screaming, "Why didn't you put her in jail after she shot Hogan Freely? You left a killer out among us, and now . . ." She collapsed in tears.

Ottoline, by now out of Rick's cruiser, helped her to her feet.

Rick hung his head. "There were extenuating circumstances."

"Like what?" Ottoline snarled.

"Like the fact that Kerry McCray had a goose egg on her head and was knocked out cold," Cynthia answered.

"And she had the gun that killed Hogan in her hand!" Aysha lurched away from her mother. She faced Rick. "You're responsible. Norman is dead because of you."

"Come on, honey, let me take you home." Ottoline tugged at Aysha.

"Aysha," Harry said coolly, "did Norman have a close friend in the bank?"

Aysha turned a bloodshot eye on Harry. "What?"

"Did he have a buddy at Crozet National?"

"Everyone. Everyone loved him," Aysha sobbed.

"Come on now. You're going to make yourself sick. Come on." Ottoline pushed her toward her car, the driver's side door still hanging open. She imparted a shot to Harry. "Your sense of timing is deplorable."

"Sorry, Ottoline. I'm trying to help."

"Harry, stick to postcards." Ottoline's tone was withering. Harry had to bite her lip.

As Ottoline with Aysha, and Cynthia with Kerry, drove away,

the remaining friends stood in the middle of the street, bewil-
dered. Market and Pewter were running toward them along with
Reverend Jones. Harry cast her eyes up and down the street. She
could see faces in every window. It was eerie.

Fair brushed himself off. "Folks, I've got to get back to the
clinic. If you need me, call." He slowly walked to his truck,
parked in front of the café.

"Excuse me." Blair trotted to catch up to Fair.

"Oh, my, we forgot to pay," Little Marilyn remembered.

"Let's all go back and settle up." Harry turned for the café
and wondered what the two men were talking about.

38

A dejected Cynthia Cooper returned to her desk after depositing Kerry, in a state of shock, at the county jail. Fortunately, there were no other women in custody, so she wouldn't be hounded by drug addicts, drunks, or the occasional hooker.

Cynthia was plenty disturbed. The phones rang off the hook. Reporters called from newspapers throughout the state and the local TV crew was setting up right outside the department building.

That would put Rick in a foul mood. And if Rick wasn't happy, nobody was happy.

She sat down, then stood up, then down, up, down, up. Finally she walked through the corridors to the vending machines and bought a pack of unfiltered Lucky Strikes. She stared at the bull's-eye in the middle of the pack. She'd better damn well get lucky. She peeled off the thin cellophane cord, slipped off the top, tore a small square in the end, and turned the pack upside down. The aroma of fresh tobacco wafted to her nostrils. Right now that sweet scent smelled better than her favorite perfume. She tapped the base of the pack and three white cigarettes slid down. She plucked one, turned the pack right side up, and slipped it in her front shirt pocket. Matches came down the chute with the pack. She struck one and lit up. Leaning against the corridor wall, she didn't know when a cigarette had tasted this good.

The back door opened, and she heard the garble of reporters. Rick slammed the door behind him, walked past her, grabbed the cigarette out of her mouth, and stuck it in his own.

"Unfiltered," she called out to him.

"Good. Another nail in my coffin." He spun on his heel and returned to her. She had already lit another cigarette. "I should have arrested Kerry right away. I used her for bait and it didn't work."

"I think it did. Even if she killed Norman. He was her accomplice. Cool. Very cool. He married Aysha to throw us off."

"So you don't buy that Kerry McCray took the wind out of Norman's sails?" Rick gave her a sour look.

Cynthia continued. "It was perfect."

"And Hogan?"

"Got too close or—too greedy."

Rick took a long, long drag as he considered her thoughts. "A real cigarette, not some low-tar, low-nicotine crap. If I'm gonna smoke, then I might as well go back to what made me smoke in the first place."

"What was it for you?"

"Camels."

"My dad smoked those. Then he switched to Pall Mall."

"How about you?"

"Oh, Marlboro. At sixteen I couldn't resist the cowboy in the ads."

"I would have thought you'd have gone for one of those brands like Viceroy or Virginia Slims."

"The murder weapon was on the seat of Kerry's Toyota," Cynthia said. "As for Virginia Slims, too nelly . . . know what I mean?"

"Yeah, I do. As to the cord . . . it'll come back no prints. I'll bet you a carton of these babies."

"I'm not taking that bet, but, boss, no prints doesn't mean Kerry wasn't smart enough to wear gloves. She's been threatening to kill Norman for days."

"That's just it, Coop. Smart. If she was smart enough to team up with Norman, to invent the Threadneedle virus, she wouldn't be dumb enough to get caught with a .357 in her hand or that cord in her possession." Rick nearly shouted. "And there's the unfortunate problem of Mike Huckstep."

"Yeah." She thought a minute. "Think she'll get out on bail?"

"I hope not." A blue, curling line of smoke twirled out of his mouth. "She's safer in there and I can keep the reporters happy with the news she's booked for murder."

"Safer?"

"Hell, what if Aysha goes after her?"

"Or she goes after Aysha?"

"More likely. This way we can keep everyone out of our hair for a little bit."

"You're up to something." Coop had observed Rick's shrewdness too many times not to know he was springing a trap.

"You're going to talk Frank Kenton into flying out here from San Francisco."

"Fat chance!"

"We'll pay his way." He held up his hand. "Just leave the wrangling about money to me. Don't worry about it."

"You think he can identify Malibu?"

"He can take a good look at Kerry. That's a start."

"But Kerry never lived in San Francisco."

"How do we know? We'll question her and cross-examine her and it's possible, just possible, that something will slip. I think if she sees him, it will scare the devil out of her."

"Or someone else." Cynthia stubbed out her cigarette in the standing ashtray filled with sand.

"That too. That too. So, topgirl, get on it."

"What's this topgirl stuff?"

"Dunno, just popped into my head."

39

Boom Boom Craycroft dashed into the post office. The place had been a madhouse all day as people hurried in and hurried out, each one with a theory. Pewter curled up in the mail cart. She missed her friends, but she was glad to catch the human gossip.

"Guess you heard I was pushed off the road by Aysha. How was I to know Norman had been killed and she was chasing Kerry."

"None of us knew, and you look none the worse for wear. The Jag seems okay too." Harry's tone was even.

"My guardian angel was working overtime." Boom Boom opened her mailbox. "These bills. Have you ever noticed they come right on time but the checks never do? Then again, the stock market being what it is, who knows from quarter to quarter how much money they have? I hate that. I hate not knowing how much money I've got coming in. Which reminds me. Did you know the bank found $250,000 in Kerry's account?"

"Oh?" Mrs. Hogendobber came over to the counter.

"I just came from there. The place is a beehive—$250,000! She certainly didn't make that much at Crozet National. And it wasn't in her account yesterday. If she'd been patient, she could have had it all, unless, of course, she's a small fry and this is a payoff."

"Boom Boom, who told you? I'd think the bank or at least the Sheriff's Department would want to control this information."

"Control information? You were born and bred in Crozet. You know better than that," Boom Boom hooted.

"How'd you find out?" Mrs. Hogendobber was pleasant.

"Flirted with Dick Williams." She mentioned a handsome bank officer who was always solicitous of the ladies but most especially of his wife, Bea. Boom Boom added, "Well, actually it was Jim Craig who told me and Dick, politely, mind you, told him to hold his cards close to his chest for a while. So I batted my eyes at both of them and swore I'd never tell. Who cares? It will be on Channel 29 tonight."

And with that she breezed out the door.

"What an airhead."

"You don't like her because she took up with Fair after your divorce."

"You don't like her either."

"That's true," Miranda confessed.

Pewter popped her head up over the mail cart. "She's a fake, but half the people you meet are fakes. What's one more?"

"Do you want to come home with me tonight?"

"Harry, I would love to come home with you." Pewter hopped out and vigorously rubbed Harry's legs.

"Lavish with her affections," Mrs. Hogendobber observed. The older woman sat down. "I feel so tired. I shouldn't be. I got enough sleep, but I can't keep my head up."

"Emotions. They're exhausting. We're all ragged out. I know I am."

Before Harry could sit down with Miranda, Susan opened the back door and stuck in her head. "Me."

"Come in," Mrs. Hogendobber invited her. "You usually do."

Susan dropped into the seat opposite Miranda. "Poor Ned. People are calling up, outraged that he's defending Kerry McCray. The fact that every citizen has the right to a trial before their peers escapes them."

"Trial by gossip." Mrs. Hogendobber shook her head.

"If people want to be ugly, there's not a lot you or Ned can do about it. If I were in trouble, I'd sure want Ned as my attorney."

Susan smiled. "I should count my blessings. After all, my husband wasn't killed, and what are a few hate calls?"

"I bet Kerry doesn't even have a toothbrush," Miranda thought out loud. "Girls, we should go over to her house and pack some clothes for her. This is the United States of America. Innocent until proven guilty. Makes no matter what public opinion is, she's innocent under the law until proven guilty. So we shouldn't shun her."

The other two sat quietly.

Finally, Susan replied, "Miranda, you always bring us back to the moral issue. Of course we'll go over there after work."

40

"This place is pin tidy." Mrs. Hogendobber put her hands on her hips. "I had no idea Kerry was such a good housekeeper."

"Remind me never to invite you to my place." Cynthia Cooper carefully packed some toiletries.

Harry, Mrs. Hogendobber, and Susan called Cynthia before going over to Kerry's. The Sheriff's Department scoured the place, so Rick Shaw said okay to the ladies' visit as long as Cynthia accompanied them.

He didn't know that Mrs. Murphy, Pewter, and Tee Tucker accompanied them also.

While Susan and Harry threw underclothes, T-shirts, and jeans as well as a good dress into a carryall bag, the animals went prowling.

"There've been so many people in here, so many scents." Tucker shook her head.

Mrs. Murphy spied the trapdoor to the attic. Pewter craned her neck at the door.

"Think we could get up there?" Pewter asked.

"I'll yodel. Mom hates that worst of all." Tucker laughed, threw her head back, and produced her canine yodel which could awaken the dead.

"My God, Harry, what's wrong with your dog?" Cynthia called from the bathroom.

Harry walked into the hallway to the bedrooms and beheld Tucker yowling in the key of awful. Mrs. Murphy circled around her legs. Pewter was frozen under the attic trapdoor.

"If I go any faster, I'll make myself dizzy." The cat slowed down.

"You three are pests. I should have left you home."

"Oh, yeah?" Murphy reached up with her claws on Harry's jeans, wiggled her rear end, and climbed up Harry so quickly that the young woman barely had time to complain about the claws.

"Ouch" was all she could say as Mrs. Murphy reached her shoulders, then stood on her hind legs and batted at the attic door.

"If she doesn't get it, she's comatose," Pewter wryly noted.

Susan stuck her head out in the hallway. "A human scratching post. What a good idea. What does she see up there?" Susan noticed Murphy's antics.

"A trapdoor, stupid," Tucker yapped.

"Hey. Hey, Cynthia," Pewter called, as did Susan.

Cynthia and Mrs. H. walked out as Susan called. Susan pointed to the trapdoor. Harry cocked her head to one side to see it and then Mrs. Murphy jumped off.

"Did I tell you that your animals were here when we arrested Kerry? Tucker ran off with the plastic bag in which we had the cord, the suspected murder weapon, all sealed up. She dropped it in the field: Mrs. Murphy used her claws like a chainsaw. What a mess. Fortunately, I retrieved it before she damaged the evidence. This place has to be five miles from your house."

"I'm going to start locking you two up. You hear?"

"*We hear but we aren't listening,*" Murphy sassed.

Pewter was impressed. "*Did you really do that?*"

"*Piece of cake,*" Mrs. Murphy bragged.

"*You couldn't have done it without me.*" Tucker was jealous.

Susan brought a chair in from the kitchen, stood on it, and opened the trapdoor. A little whiff of scorching-hot air blasted her in the face.

After searching around, they found a ladder in the basement. Cynthia went up first, with a flashlight from her squad car. "Good. There's a switch here."

Mrs. Murphy, who loved climbing ladders, hurried up as soon as Cynthia crawled into the attic. Tucker, irritably, waited down below. Harry climbed up. Pewter followed.

"Even the attic is neat," Cynthia noted. "You know, I don't think our boys were up here. Don't repeat that. It makes the department look sloppy, and guess what, they were sloppy."

"It's easy to miss what's over your head."

"Harry, we're paid not to miss evidence," Cynthia firmly told her.

"I'm coming up too," Susan called up.

"Well, don't knock down the ladder when you get up here, Susan, or we'll be swinging from the trapdoor."

"Thanks for the vote of confidence." Susan appeared in the attic. "How can you breathe?"

"With difficulty." Harry grimaced.

"What's up there?" Miranda called from below.

"Not much. Two big trunks. An old pair of skis," Harry informed her.

"*A large wasps' nest in the eave.*" Mrs. Murphy fought the urge to chase wasps. The buzz so attracted her. The consequences did not. "*Let's open the trunk.*"

Cynthia pulled a handkerchief out of her pocket and gingerly opened the old steamer trunk. "A wedding dress. Old."

Harry and Susan, on their knees, looked in as Mrs. Murphy gracefully put a paw onto the satin. Cynthia smacked her paw. "Don't even think about it."

"*Lift up the dress.*" The cat held her temper.

"Bet this was Kerry's grandmother's. It's about that vintage." Susan admired the lace.

"Harry, take that end and I'll lift this one," Cynthia directed.

They lifted up the beautiful old dress. Underneath were old family photo albums and some letters from overseas.

Harry picked up a pile neatly tied in a ribbon. The postmark of the top letter was Roanoke, Virginia, 1952. The pile under that was from overseas from the mid-1980s. They were addressed to Kerry's mother. "I think this is her mother's stuff. She probably brought the trunk over here after Barbara McCray died. Do you need to go through it, you know, read the letters and stuff?"

Cynthia rooted through the rest of the trunk, then carefully replaced everything. "I don't know. If Rick wants me to do it, I can, but I'll ask first. Right now we've got a lot on her."

"It's circumstantial," Susan quietly reminded her.

"That $250,000 is a lot of circumstance." Cynthia sighed and closed the lid of the trunk.

Pewter, squatting on the second trunk, directed them. "*Hurry up and open this one. It's hot up here.*"

"*Go downstairs, then,*" Mrs. Murphy told her.

"*No, I might miss something.*"

Cynthia gently lifted Pewter off the trunk. "Heavy little bugger."

Mrs. Murphy laughed while Pewter fumed.

Cynthia lifted the lid. "Oh, boy."

Harry and Susan looked into the trunk. Mrs. Murphy and Pewter, on their hind legs, front paws resting on the trunk, saw it too.

"Her goose is cooked!" Mrs. Murphy exclaimed.

A black motorcycle jacket, black leather pants, and a black helmet were neatly placed in the trunk.

"You know, I had hoped it wasn't her." Cynthia softly closed the trunk lid.

"Me too." Susan sadly agreed.

"It looks bad, but—" Harry lost her voice in the heat, then regained it. "But she'll get a fair trial. We can't convict her over a motorcycle helmet."

"I can tell you, the Commonwealth's Attorney will sure try," Cynthia said.

Susan patted Harry's shoulder. "It's hard to accept."

They climbed down the ladder, Mrs. Murphy first, and filled in the expectant Mrs. Hogendobber.

"Well?" Tucker inquired.

"Motorcycle gear in the trunk." The cat, dejected, licked Tucker's ear. Grooming Tucker or even Harry made her feel useful if not better.

"Oh, dear" was all Mrs. Hogendobber could say.

Pewter clambered down to join them. *"Kerry's going to be stamping out license plates."*

41

Norman Cramer's funeral was as subdued as Hogan Freely's was grand. Aysha, disconsolate, had to be propped up by her mother, immaculate in black linen. Ottoline couldn't bear Aysha's grief, but as she and her daughter were the center of attention, she appeared as noble as she knew how. Although part of it was an act, part of it wasn't, for Ottoline lived for and through her daughter.

The residents of Crozet, stunned at this last murder, sat motionless in the pews. Laura Freely wasn't there, which was proper, as she was in deep mourning. Reverend Jones spared everyone the fluff about how death releases one to the kingdom of glory. Right now no one wanted to hear that. They wanted Kerry McCray tried and sentenced. If hanging were still in the penal code, they'd have demanded to see her swing. Even those who at first gave her the benefit of the doubt were swayed by the money in her account, and the motorcycle gear in her attic.

Mrs. Hogendobber constantly told people the courts decide, not public opinion. No one listened. Susan, as Ned's wife, was particularly circumspect. Harry said little. She couldn't shake the feeling that the other shoe hadn't yet dropped.

She sat in the fourth pew in the front right side of the church, the pews being assigned on the basis of when your family had arrived in Albemarle County. The Minors settled here over two centuries ago. In fact, one of the Minors founded Crozet's Lutheran church and was buried in the old graveyard behind it. The Hepworths, her mother's family, were Church of England, and they held down their own front-line pew in the Tidewater.

She sat there even when the service ended and the congregation filed out. She scrutinized their faces in an unobtrusive way. Harry scanned for answers. Anyone could be in on this. She imagined each person killing the biker, then Hogan, and finally Norman. What kind of person could do that? Then she imagined Kerry's face. Could she kill?

Probably anyone could kill to defend oneself or one's family or friends, but premeditated murder, cold-blooded murder? No. She could so easily picture Kerry bursting into fury and killing Norman or Aysha, but she couldn't imagine her tracking him down or hiding in the back seat of his car, popping up, asking him to pull over, and then choking the life out of him with a rope. It didn't fit.

She walked outside. The overcast sky promised rain but had yet to deliver. Blair and Fair were waiting for her.

"You two a team or something?"

"We thought we might go to the cemetery together. It will keep us from squabbling, now, won't it?" Fair shrugged his shoulders.

"Are you two up to something?"

"What a distrustful thing to say," Blair mildly replied. "Yes, we're up to being gentlemen. I think we both are ashamed of how we acted at Mim's. We've decided to present a united front in public and spare you further embarrassment."

"Remarkable." Harry dully got in the car.

42

Labor Day marked the end of summer. The usual round of barbecues, parties, tubing down the James River, golf tournaments, and last-minute school shopping crammed the weekend.

Over two weeks had passed since Norman was strangled. Kerry McCray, her defense in the hands of Ned Tucker, was freed on $100,000 bail, raised by her much older brother, Kyle, who lived in Colorado Springs. He was shocked when informed of events, but he stuck by his sister. Kerry, ordered by Ned to keep her mouth shut, did just that. Kyle took a leave of absence from his job to stay with her. He feared Kerry would be badly treated. He swore on a month of Sundays that the motorcycle gear was his. When it came back from the lab, no blood or powder burns had been found on it. Most people said he was lying to save his sister's skin, ignoring the fact that in the early seventies he'd had a motorcycle.

The sun set earlier each day, and Harry, much as she loved the soft light of fall and winter, found the shorter days hectic. So often she woke up in the dark and came home in the dark. She had to do her farm chores no matter what.

Fair and Blair took polite turns asking her out. Sometimes it was too much attention. Mrs. Hogendobber told her to enjoy every minute of it.

Cynthia Cooper and Rick Shaw relaxed a little bit. Cynthia hinted that as soon as schedules could be coordinated, they had a person who could sink Kerry's ship.

Mrs. Murphy, Tucker, and even Pewter racked their brains to think if there was a missing link, but no one could find it. Even if the humans could have understood the truth about scent, which never falters—one's scent is one's scent—and even if they could have understood that Kerry's scent was not on the murder weapon, chances were they would have discounted it. Humans tend to validate only those senses they perceive. They ignore any other species' reality, and, worse, they blot out any conflicting evidence. Humans need to feel safe. The two cats and dog were far wiser on that score. No one is ever safe. So why not live as much as you can?

The avalanche of mail at the post office on Tuesday following the holiday astonished Harry and Mrs. Hogendobber.

"Fall catalogues," Harry moaned. "After a while they get heavy."

Little Marilyn walked through the front door and up to the counter. "You must hate holidays."

"Nah." Harry shook her head. "It's these catalogues."

"You know what I've been doing?" She put her purse on the counter. "I've been rereading the letters Kerry and Aysha and I sent to one another when we were abroad and the letters Aysha sent to me when I returned home. I can't find anything unbalanced in Kerry's letters. It's what you would expect of two young women right out of college. We wrote about where we went, what we read, who we met, and who we were dating. I guess I've been searching for some kind of answer to how someone I've known so long could be a murderer.'' She rested her head on her hand. ''No answers. Of course, I still have a shoebox left. Maybe there will be something in there.''

''Would you mind if I read them too?''

''Harry, that's private correspondence.'' Miranda frowned.

''That's why I'm asking. Marilyn can always say no.''

''I'd be happy for you to read them. Maybe you'll catch something I've missed. You know how the keys you're looking for are always the ones right under your nose. You wanted to see the stamps anyway.''

''In that case, would you mind if I joined you?'' Mrs. Hogendobber invited herself, and, naturally, Little Marilyn said she wouldn't mind at all.

Two cups of coffee and a slice each of Mrs. Hogendobber's cherry pie later, the ladies sat in Little Marilyn's living room surrounded by shoeboxes. Mrs. Murphy squeezed herself into one where she slept. Tucker, head on her paws, dozed on the cool slate hearth.

''See, nothing special.''

''Except that everyone expresses themselves well.''

Harry added, ''My favorite was the letter where Aysha said you should lend her a thousand dollars because you have it to lend.''

Little Marilyn waved her hand. ''She got over it. Well, I've finished the last. Might as well put these back in order.''

Big Marilyn knocked on the door. Her daughter lived on a dependency on her mother's estate. Dependency, although the correct word, hardly described the lovely frame house, a chaste Federal with a tin roof and green-black shutters. ''Hello, girls. Find anything?''

"No, Mother. We were just putting the letters back in place."

"You tried, that's the important thing." She breathed deeply. "What an inviting aroma."

"Cherry pie. You need to sample it. I'm branching into pies now. Market sells out of my doughnuts, muffins, and buns by eight-thirty every morning. He says he needs something for the after-work trade, so I'm experimenting with pies. Don't think of this as calories, think of this as market research."

"Bad pun," Harry teased her.

"Just a tad." Mim held her fingers close together as Miranda blithely ignored her and cut out a full portion. As she did so, a drop of cherry sauce plopped on a letter.

"Clumsy me."

"Don't worry about it," Little Marilyn instructed her.

Mrs. Hogendobber placed the knife on the pie plate, then bent over. She carefully wiped the letter with a napkin. "Hmm."

"Really, Mrs. Hogendobber, don't worry about it."

"I'm not, actually." Miranda handed the letter to Harry. "Queer."

Harry studied the airmail envelope from France, postmarked St. Tropez, 1988. "Always wanted to go there."

"Where?" Mim inquired.

"St. Tropez."

"One of Aysha's. I don't think she missed a city in France."

"Look closer." Mrs. Hogendobber pointed to the postmark.

Harry squinted. "The ink."

"Precisely." Mrs. Hogendobber folded her hands, as happy in Harry's progress as if she'd been a star pupil.

"What are you two talking about?" Mim was nosy.

Harry walked over and placed the letter in the elder Marilyn's lap. Mim pulled out her half-moon glasses and held the letter under her nose.

"Look at the color of the ink." Harry cast her eyes around

the piles of letters for another one from France. "Ah, here's one. Paris. Look at the color here. This one is from Kerry."

"Different, slightly but different." Mim removed her glasses. "Aren't inks like dye lots? This letter is from Paris. That one from St. Tropez."

"Yes, but postal inks are remarkably consistent." Harry was now on her hands and knees. She pulled out letters. "The letters from 1986 are genuine. But here, here's one from Florence, December 1987." Harry handed that letter to Little Marilyn while giving her one from Italy the year before.

"There really is a shade of difference." Little Marilyn was surprised.

Within seconds Harry and Mrs. Hogendobber were on their hands and knees tossing the letters into piles segregated by year.

"You two are fast. Let me help." Little Marilyn joined them.

"Want to work in the P.O.?" Harry joked.

Mim stayed in the chair. Her knees hurt and she didn't want to admit it. Finally they had all the piles sorted out.

"There's no doubt about this. Kerry's postmarks are authentic. Aysha's are authentic until 1987. Then the inks change." Harry rubbed her chin. "This is strange."

"Surely, there's a mistake." Mim was confused by the implication.

"Mim, I've worked in the post office since George took over in 1958. This postmark is forged. Any good stationer can create a round stamp. That's simple. Aysha nearly matched the inks, probably from the postmarks on letters she'd received from Little Marilyn and Kerry in Europe, but different countries have different formulas. Well, now, think of stationery itself. Haven't you noticed how the paper of a personal letter from England is a bit different from our own?"

"Then how did the letters get here?" Big Marilyn asked the key question.

"That's easy if you have a friend in Crozet." Harry crossed

her legs like an Indian. "All she had to do was mail these letters in a manila envelope and have her friend distribute them."

"Much as I hate to admit it, but when George was postmaster, he let a lot of people behind the counter. We do too, to tell the truth, as you well know. It wouldn't take much to slip these letters into the appropriate boxes when one's back was turned. Some of the letters are addressed to Little Marilyn in care of Ottoline Gill."

"Well, I guess we know who her friend was," Harry said.

"Why would her mother participate in such subterfuge?" Mim was astounded. But then, Mim was also secure in her social position.

"Because she didn't want anyone to know what Aysha was really doing. Maybe it didn't fit the program," Harry answered.

"Then where was she and what was she doing?" Little Marilyn, eyes wide, asked.

43

Little Marilyn turned over the letters to Rick Shaw that night. He emphatically swore everyone to secrecy when he arrived. Mim demanded to know what he was going to do about it, where it might lead, and he finally said, "I don't know exactly, but I will do everything I can to find out why. I won't set this aside—just trust me."

"I have no choice." She pursed her lips.

After he left, the group broke up to go home. Quietly pulling aside Harry, Little Marilyn nervously asked, "Would you mind terribly—and believe me I understand if you do—but if not, would you mind if I asked Blair to drive over to Richmond with me for the symphony?"

"No, not at all."

"You see, I'm not sure of your status—that's not how I meant to say it, but—"

"I understand. I'm not sure either."

"Do you care for him?" She didn't realize she was holding her hands tightly. Another minute, and she'd be wringing them.

Harry took a deep breath. "He's one of the best-looking men I've ever laid eyes on, and I like him. I know you like his curly hair." She smiled. "But Blair's diffident, for lack of a better word. He likes me fine, but I don't think he's in love with me."

"What about that fight at the party?"

"Two dogs with a bone. I'm not sure it was as much about me as about property rights."

"Oh, Harry, that's cynical. I think they both care for you very much."

"Tell me, Marilyn, what does it mean for a man to care for a woman?"

"I know what they say when they want something—" Little Marilyn paused. "And they buy presents, they work hard, they'll do anything to get your attention. But I'm not an expert on love."

"Is anybody?" Harry smiled. "Miranda, maybe."

"She certainly had George wrapped around her little finger." Then Little Marilyn brightened. "Because she knew the way to a man's heart is through his stomach."

They both laughed, which caused Mim and Mrs. Hogendob-ber to turn to them.

"How can you laugh at a time like this?" Mim snapped.

"Releasing tension, Mother."

"Find another way to do it."

Little Marilyn whispered to Harry, "I could bash her. That would do it for sure."

Harry whispered back, "You'd have help."

"Mother means well, but she can't stop telling everyone what to do and how to do it."

"Will you two speak up?" Mim demanded.

"We were discussing the high heel as a weapon," Harry lied.

"Oh."

Little Marilyn picked up the thread. "With all this violence —guns, strangling—we were talking about what we would do if someone attacked us. Well, take off your heels and hit him in the eye. Just as hard as you can."

"Gruesome. Or hit him on the back of the head when he runs," Harry added.

"Harry." Mim stared hard at her feet. "You only wear sneakers."

"Do you remember Delphine Falkenroth?" Miranda asked Mim.

"Yes, she got that modeling job in New York City right after the war."

"Once she hailed a cab and a man ran right in front of her hopped in it. Delphine said she held on to the door and hit him so many times over the head with her high heel that he swore like a fishmonger, but he surrendered the cab." She waited a beat. "She married him, of course."

"Is that how she met Roddy? Oh, she never told me that." Mim relished the tale.

Harry whispered again to Little Marilyn, "A trip down Memory Lane. I'm going to collect Mrs. Murphy and Tucker and head home."

Once home, she called Cynthia Cooper, who was already informed of the bogus inks and postmarks.

"Coop, I had a thought."

"Yeah?"

"Did you go by Hassett's to see if anyone there remembered Kerry buying the gun?"

"One of the first things I did after Hogan was killed."

"And?"

"The paperwork matched, the driver's license numbers matched up."

"But the salesman—"

"He'd gone on vacation. A month's camping in Maine. Ought to be back right about now."

"You'll go back, of course."

"I will—but I'm hoping I don't have to."

"What are you up to?"

"Can't tell."

44

Cynthia Cooper never expected Frank Kenton to be attractive. She waited in the airport lobby holding a sign with his name on it. When a tall, distinguished man approached her, an earring in his left ear, she thought he was going to ask for directions.

"Deputy Cooper?"

"Mr. Kenton?"

"The same."

"Uh—do you have any luggage?"

"No. My carry-on is it."

As they walked to the squad car, he apologized for how angry he had been the first time she phoned him. Gruff as he'd been, he wasn't angry at her. She declared that she quite understood.

The first place to which she drove him was Kerry McCray's house. Rick Shaw awaited them, and as they all three approached the front door, Kerry hurried out to greet them, Kyle right behind her.

Frank smiled at her. "I've never seen you before in my life."

"Thank you. Thank you." Tears sprang to her eyes.

"Lady, I haven't done a thing."

As Frank and Cynthia climbed back into the squad car, Cynthia exhaled. "I'm half-glad Kerry isn't Malibu and half-disappointed. One always hopes for an easy case—would you like lunch? Maybe we should take a food break before we push on."

"Fine with me."

Mrs. Hogendobber waved as Cynthia cruised by the post office. The deputy pulled a U-turn and stopped. She ran into the post office.

"Hi, how are you this morning?" Miranda smiled.

"I'm okay. What about yourself?"

"A little tired."

"Where's Harry and the zoo?"

"She's up at Ash Lawn with Little Marilyn, Aysha, and Ottoline."

"What in the world is she doing there, and what is Aysha doing there? Norman's hardly cold."

Mrs. Hogendobber frowned. "I know, but Aysha said she was going stir crazy, so she drove up to gather up her things there as well as Laura Freely's. Marilyn's lost two docents, so she's in a fix. Anyway, she begged to have Harry for a day, since she knows the place so well. Harry asked me and I said fine. Of course, she's not a William and Mary graduate, but in a pinch a Smithie will do. Little Marilyn needs to train a new batch of docents fast."

Cynthia stood in the middle of the post office. She looked out the window at Frank in the air-conditioned car, then back to Mrs. Hogendobber. "Mrs. H., I have a favor to ask of you."

"Of course."

"Call Little Marilyn. Don't speak to anyone but her. She's got to keep Aysha there until I get there."

"Oh, dear. Kerry's out on bail. I never thought of that." Miranda's hand, tipped in mocha mist nail polish today, flew to her face. "I'll get right on it."

Then Cynthia darted into Market Shiflett's, bought two homemade sandwiches, drinks, and Miranda's peach cobbler.

She hopped in the squad car. "Frank, here. There's been a change of plans. Hang on." She hit the siren and flew down 240, shooting through the intersection onto 250, bearing right to pick up I-64 miles down the road.

"You'll love the peach cobbler," she informed a bug-eyed Frank.

"I'm sure—but I think I'll wait." He smiled weakly.

Once she'd maneuvered onto I-64, heading east, she said, "It's a straightaway for about fifteen miles, then we'll hit twisty roads again. I don't know how strong your stomach is. If it's cast iron, eat."

"I'll wait. Where are we going?"

"Ash Lawn, home of James Monroe. We get off onto Route 20 South and then hang a left up the road past Monticello. I'm hitting ninety, but I can't go much more than forty once we get on the mountain road. Another fifteen, twenty minutes and we're there." She picked up her pager and told headquarters where she was going. She asked for backup—just in case.

"She's a real cobra."

"I know."

Cynthia turned off the siren two miles from Ash Lawn. She drove down the curving tree-lined drive, turning left into the parking lot, and drove right up to the gift shop. "Ready?"

"Yes." Frank was delighted to escape from the car.

•   •   •

Harry noticed that Little Marilyn was unusually tense. She hoped it wasn't because she was failing as a docent. Harry shepherded her group through the house, telling them where to step down and where to watch their heads. She pointed out pieces of furniture and added tidbits about Monroe's term of office.

Mrs. Murphy and Tucker had burrowed under the huge boxwoods. The earth was cooler than the air.

Aysha was underneath the house collecting the last of Laura Freely's period clothing as well as her own. Ottoline was helping her.

Cynthia and Frank walked to the front door as nonchalantly as possible. Harry was just opening the side door to let out her group as Cynthia and Frank entered through the front.

As it was lunch hour, the visitors to Ash Lawn who would be in the next tour group, which was Marilyn's, had chosen to sit under the magnificent spreading trees, drinking something ice cold.

Harry was surprised to find Cynthia there.

"This is Frank Kenton from San Francisco."

Harry held out her hand. "Welcome to Ash Lawn."

"It's okay, Harry, you don't have to give him the tour." Cynthia smiled tensely.

Little Marilyn, having been warned by Miranda, contained her nervousness as best she could. "Should I call her now?"

"Yes," Cynthia replied.

The candlesticks shook in their holders as Little Marilyn walked by. After a few minutes she returned with Aysha and Ottoline.

Aysha froze at the sight of Frank.

"That's Malibu," he quietly said.

"No!" Ottoline screamed.

Aysha spun around, grabbed Harry, and dragged her into the living room. Ottoline slammed the doors. When Cynthia tried to pursue her, a bullet smashed through the door, just missing her head.

"Get out of here, all of you!" Cynthia commanded.

Marilyn and Frank hurried outside. Marilyn, mindful of her duty, quickly herded the visitors down to the parking lot. The wail of a siren meant help was coming.

Mrs. Murphy leapt up. "Mom. Mom. *Are you okay?*"

Tucker, without a sound, scooted out from under the box-wood and shot toward the house.

Mrs. Murphy squeezed through the front door which was slightly ajar. Tucker had a harder time of it, but managed.

Cynthia was crouched down, her back to the wall by the door into the living room. Her gun was held at the ready. "Come on out, Aysha. Game's up."

"I've got a gun in my hand."

"Won't do you any good."

Aysha laughed. "If I shoot you first it will."

Ottoline called out, "Cynthia, let her go. Take me in her place. She's lost her husband. She's not in her right mind."

Cynthia noticed the cat and dog. "Get out of here."

Mrs. Murphy tore out the front door. Tucker waited a moment, gave Cynthia a soulful look, then followed her feline friend.

"*Tucker, around the side. Maybe I can get in a window.*"

They heard Harry's voice. "Aysha, give yourself up. Maybe things will go easier for you."

"Shut up!"

The sound of Harry's beloved voice spurred on both animals. Mrs. Murphy raced to the low paned window. Closed. Ash Lawn was air-conditioned. Both cat and dog saw Harry being held at gunpoint in the middle of the room.

Ottoline stood off to the side of the doors.

"*Tucker, these old windows are pretty low. Think you can crash through?*"

"*Yes.*"

They ran back fifty yards, then turned and hurtled toward the old hand-blown window. Tucker left the ground a split second before Murphy, ducking her head, and hit the glass with the

top of her head. Mrs. Murphy, her eyes squeezed tight against the shattering glass, sailed in a hairbreadth behind Tucker. Broken glass went everywhere.

Aysha whirled and fired. She was so set on a human opponent, she never figured on the animals. Tucker, still running, leapt up and hit her full force, and she staggered back.

Ottoline screamed, "Shoot the dog!"

Mrs. Murphy leapt up and sank her fangs into Aysha's right wrist while grabbing on to her forearm with front and hind claws. Then she tore into the flesh for all she was worth.

Aysha howled. Harry threw a block into her and they tumbled onto the floor. Tucker clamped her jaws on a leg. Ottoline ran over to kick the corgi.

Mrs. Murphy released her grip and yelled, "*The hand, Tucker, go for the hand.*" Tucker bounded over the struggling bodies. Ottoline's kick was a fraction of a second too late. Aysha was reaching up to bludgeon Harry on the head. Tucker savaged Aysha's hand, biting deep holes in the fleshy palm. Aysha dropped the gun. Ottoline quickly reached for it. Tucker ran quietly behind her and bit her too, then picked up the gun.

Harry yelled, "Coop! Help!"

Mrs. Murphy kept clawing Aysha as Tucker eluded a determined Ottoline, her focus on the gun.

Coop held her service pistol in both hands and blew out the lock on the doors. "It's over, Aysha." She leveled her gun at the fighting women.

Harry, a bruise already swelling up under her left eye, released Aysha and scrambled to her feet. She was struggling to catch her breath. Ottoline ran up behind Coop and grabbed her around the neck, but Coop ducked and elbowed her in the gut. With an "umph" Ottoline let go.

Aysha started to spring out the door, but Harry tackled her.

Coop shoved Ottoline over to where Aysha was slowly getting up.

"You were so smart, Aysha, but you were done in by a dog and a cat." Harry rejoiced as Tucker brought her the gun.

"It's always the one you don't figure that gets you." Cynthia never took her eyes off her quarry.

Rick Shaw thundered in. He grasped the situation and hand-cuffed Aysha and Ottoline together, back to back, then read them their rights.

"Ow." Aysha winced from where Mrs. Murphy and Tucker had ripped her hand.

Harry squatted down and petted her friends. She checked their paws for cuts from the glass.

"Why?" Harry asked.

"Why not?" Aysha insouciantly replied.

"Well, then how?" Cynthia queried.

"I have a right to remain silent."

"Answer one question, Aysha." Harry brushed herself off. "Was Norman in on it?"

Aysha shrugged, not answering the question.

Ottoline laughed derisively. "That coward. He lived in fear of his own shadow." Ottoline turned to Rick Shaw. "You're making a big mistake."

Aysha, still panting, said, "Mother, my lawyer will do the talking."

Harry picked up a purring Mrs. Murphy. "Aysha, your letters to Marilyn from St. Tropez and Paris and wherever—you faked the postmarks and did a good job. But it's much harder to fake the inks."

Ottoline grumbled. "You can't prove that in a court of law. And just because I delivered fake postcards doesn't make my daughter a criminal."

Aysha's eyes narrowed, then widened. "Mother, anything you say can be used against me!"

Ottoline shook her head. "I want to make a clean breast of it. I needed money. Stealing from a bank is ridiculously easy. Crozet National was very sloppy regarding their security. Norman was putty in my hands. It was quite simple, really. When he weakened, I strangled him. As he slowed by the canning plant I popped up out of the back seat and told him to pull over. He was harder to kill than I thought, but I did have the advantage of surprise. At least I didn't have to hear him whine anymore about what would happen if he got caught.''

Mrs. Murphy reached out with her paw, claws extended. *"Aysha, are you going to stand there and let your mother take the rap?"*

"I hate cats," Aysha spat at the little tiger who had foiled her plans.

"Well, this one was smart enough to stop you," Cynthia sarcastically said.

"That's enough." Rick wanted to get mother and daughter down to the station to book them. He pointed toward the squad car. As they were handcuffed back to back, walking proved difficult.

"Did you kill Hogan Freely too?" Harry asked Ottoline.

"Yes. Remember when we were in Market Shiflett's? Hogan said he was going to work late and bang around on the computer. He was intelligent enough that he might have—"

"Mother, shut up!" Aysha stumbled.

"What if Hogan had figured out my system?" Ottoline said, emphasizing "my."

"There is no system, Mother. Norman was stealing from the bank. Hogan threatened him. He killed Hogan and his accomplice inside the bank killed him. Kerry *was* his partner. He betrayed me."

"He did?" Ottoline's eyebrows jumped up. She thought a second, then her tone changed as she followed Aysha's desperate line of reasoning. "What a worm!"

"Aysha, we know you worked at the Anvil. You can't deny that." Harry, still quietly seething with anger, argued as she followed them to the squad car.

"So?"

Ottoline went on rapidly, babbling as though that would get

the people off the track. "I had to do something. I mean, my daughter, a Gill, working in a place like that. She was just going through a stage, of course, but think how it could have compromised her chances of a good marriage once she returned home, which she would do, in time. So I begged her to write postcards as if she were still in Europe. I took care of the rest. As it was, she had drifted away from Marilyn and Kerry so they didn't know exactly where she was. Sending fake postcards wasn't that hard, you see, and her reputation remained unsullied. I don't know why young people have to go through these rebellious stages. My generation never did."

"You had World War Two. That was rebellion enough."

"I'm not that old," Ottoline frostily corrected Harry.

"Ladies, these are good stories. Let's get to the station house and you can make your statements and call your lawyer," Rick prodded them.

Frank Kenton followed Cynthia. As he opened the door to her squad car he gave Aysha a long, hard look.

Defiantly, she stared back.

"I'll live to see you rot in hell." He smiled.

"I like that, Frank. There's a real irony to that—you as a moral force." Aysha laughed at him.

"Don't lower yourself to talk to him," Ottoline snapped.

"She lowered herself plenty in San Francisco," Frank yelled at Ottoline. "Lady, we'd have all been better off if you hadn't been a mother."

Ottoline hesitated before trying to get in the back seat of the squad car. Rick held open the door. The way the two women were handcuffed, they couldn't maneuver their way into the car.

"This is impossible." Aysha stated the obvious.

"You're right." Rick unlocked her handcuffs.

That fast, Aysha sprinted toward the trees.

"Stop or I'll shoot!" Rick dropped to one knee while pulling his revolver.

Cynthia, too, dropped, gun at the ready. Aysha made an easy target.

Tucker dug into the earth, flying after Aysha. Passing the human was easy for such a fast little dog. She turned in front of Aysha just as Rick fired a warning shot. Harry was going to call the dog back but thought it unwise to interrupt Tucker's trajectory. Aysha glanced over her shoulder just as Tucker crouched in front of her. She tripped over the little dog and hit the ground hard.

Cynthia, younger and faster than Rick, was halfway there, when a wobbly Aysha clambered to her feet.

"Goddamned dog!"

"Put your hands behind your head and slowly, I said slowly, walk back to the squad car."

Ottoline, crying uncontrollably, slumped against the white and blue car. "I did it. Really. I'm guilty."

"Shut up, Mother! You never listen."

A flash of parental authority passed over Ottoline's face. "If you'd listened to me in the first place, none of us would be in this mess! I told you not to marry Mike Huckstep!"

"I don't know anyone by that name!" Aysha's whole body contorted with rage.

Ottoline's face fell like a collapsed building. She realized that in her frantic attempt to save her daughter she had spilled the beans.

45

Reverend Jones was the last to join the little group at Harry's farm for a potluck supper hastily arranged by Susan. He greeted Mrs. Hogendobber, Mim, Little Marilyn, Market, Pewter, Ned, Blair, Cynthia, Kerry McCray, and her brother, Kyle.

"What did I miss?"

"Idle gossip. We waited for you," Mrs. Hogendobber told him. "Fair's the only one missing. He'll come when he can."

"Did you ever find out how Aysha transferred the money?" Susan eagerly asked.

"Yes, but we don't know what she's done with it, except for the sum she transferred into Kerry's account. She fully intends to hire the best lawyer money can buy and serve out her jail term if she doesn't get capital punishment. She'll probably be out on good behavior before she's fifty, and then she'll go to wherever she's stashed the money." Cynthia sounded bitter.

"How'd she do it?" Mim asked again.

"There was a rider attached to the void command in the Crozet National computer. Remember all the instructions for dealing with the Threadneedle virus? Well, it was brilliant, really. When the bank would void the command of the virus to scramble files, a rider would go into effect that instructed the computer to transfer two million dollars into a blind account on August first. The money didn't leave the bank. Later Aysha or Norman squirreled it out. For all we know, it may still be in that blind account, or it may be in an offshore account in a country whose bankers are easily bribed."

"Where was Mike Huckstep in all this?" Blair was curious.

"Ah . . ." Cynthia smiled at him. She always smiled at Blair. "That was the fly in the ointment. She had everything perfectly planned, a plan she undoubtedly stole from Huckstep, and he shows up at Ash Lawn just before her trap was set to spring. She wasn't taking any chances and she was shrewd enough to know the death of a biker wouldn't pull at many heartstrings in Crozet. She coolly calculated how to get away with murder. She told him she was enacting his plan. He signed the bank cards willingly, thinking the ill-gotten gain would be pirated into his account. They'd be rich. Norman inserted the account information into the system, not knowing who Mike really was. Meanwhile, Aysha told Mike she wanted him back. He didn't know she was married to Norman, of course. She told him how awful she'd felt running out on him, but she was afraid of total commitment, and when she realized her mistake she couldn't find him—he'd moved from Glover Street, where they used to live. She suggested he pick her up on the motorcycle and they could cruise around. Bam! That was it for Mike Huckstep, her real husband. Not only is she a killer and a thief, she's a bigamist."

"How did he find her?" Harry wondered.

"He knew her real name. Aysha got a break when he showed up at Ash Lawn strung out like he was. He called her by the name he knew best. Of course, Ottoline is claiming Huckstep must have been killed by a drug dealer or some other lowlife—anyone but her precious daughter."

"So, Coop, how did Huckstep find Aysha?" Susan asked.

"Oh," she said, smiling, "I got off the subject, didn't I? He must have tapped into our Department of Motor Vehicle files or he could have zapped the state income tax records. The man seems to have been, without a doubt, a computer genius."

"Imagine if that mind had been harnessed to the service of the Lord," Mrs. Hogendobber mused.

"Miranda, that's an interesting thought." Herbie crossed his arms over his chest. "Speaking of his mind, I wonder what provoked him to look for her."

"Love. He was still in love with her, despite all," Blair firmly stated. "You could see that the day he came to Ash Lawn. Some men are gluttons for that brand of punishment."

"We'll never really know." Cynthia thought Blair's interpretation was on the romantic side.

"Takes some people that way," Kerry ruefully added to the conversation.

"Guess he got more and more lonesome and—" Susan paused. "It doesn't matter, I guess. But what I can't figure out is how he knew to go to Ash Lawn."

"Yeah, that's weird." Little Marilyn recalled his visit.

"My hunch is that Aysha bragged about her pedigree, that old Virginia vice. She probably said she was or would be a docent at Monticello or Ash Lawn or something like that. I doubt we'll ever truly know because she is keeping her mouth shut like a steel trap." Cynthia shook her head. "In fact, if it weren't for the way Ottoline keeps letting things slip, we wouldn't know enough to put together a case."

"Poor Norman, the perfect cog in her wheel." Kerry's eyes misted over.

"Why couldn't Mike put his plan into effect?" Little Marilyn asked.

"A man like that wouldn't have friends inside a bank. He needed a partner who was or could be socially acceptable. I suppose the original plan entailed Aysha working inside a bank," Mim shrewdly noted.

"Aysha decided she could pull it off without him," Cynthia said. "When he showed up she shrewdly told him she'd found a dupe inside the bank. They could be in business pronto. Although Mike probably did love her as Blair believes, she couldn't control him the way she could control Norman. And she definitely had her eyes on the whole enchilada."

"I keep thinking about poor Hogan. There he was in Market's store, telling us he was going to work late that night, telling Aysha." Susan shivered, remembering.

"He scared her for sure. The fog was pure luck." Cynthia glanced over at Blair. He was so handsome, she couldn't keep her eyes off him.

Little Marilyn noticed. "Thank God for Mrs. Murphy and Tee Tucker, they're the real heroes."

"*Don't let it go to your head,*" Pewter chided.

"*You're out of sorts because you missed the fireworks.*" Mrs. Murphy preened.

"*You're right.*" Pewter tiptoed toward those covered dishes in the kitchen.

"Has she shown any remorse?" Mrs. Hogendobber inquired.

"None."

"Ottoline says Aysha is being framed. She insists that Kerry is the culprit while she killed Norman to spare her daughter a dreadful marriage." Mim rose to signal time to eat. "But then, Ottoline always was a silly fool."

"Whose blood was on the saddlebag?" Harry asked.

"What blood?" Mim motioned for Little Marilyn to join her. "I don't know anything about blood."

"A few drops of blood on Mike Huckstep's saddlebags."

Cynthia checked her hands and decided she needed to wash them before eating. "Aysha's. She must have had a small cut."

By now the humans had invaded the kitchen. Much as they wanted to wait for Fair, their stomachs wouldn't. Besides, with a vet, one never knew what his hours would be.

Little Marilyn had cooked crisp chicken.

"Don't forget us," came the chorus from the floor.

She didn't. Each animal received delectable chicken cut into small cubes. As the people carried their plates back into the living room, the animals happily ate.

Miranda asked, "What about Kerry?"

"Aysha was slick, slick as an eel." Cynthia put down her drumstick. "First she used the term Threadneedle because she knew Kerry worked for a bank in London, near the Bank of England, on Threadneedle Street. She figured by the time we unearthed that odd fact, Kerry's neck would be in the noose. Aysha had a fake driver's license made with her statistics and photograph but with Kerry's name, address, and social security number, which she pulled out of the bank computer in Norman's office. She bought the gun at Hassett's that way."

"Fake driver's licenses?" Miranda was surprised.

"High school kids are a big market—so they can buy liquor," Harry said.

"How would you know that?" Miranda demanded.

"Oh—" Harry's voice rose upward.

"It's a good thing your mother is not here to hear this."

"Yes. It is." Harry agreed with Miranda.

"But why would Aysha kill Norman? He was her cover," Marilyn wanted to know.

"She didn't," Harry blurted out, not from knowledge but from intuition and what she had observed at Ash Lawn.

"Norman chickened out after Hogan's murder. White-collar crime was all right, but murder—well, he was getting very shaky. Aysha was afraid he'd crack and give them away. Ottoline, terrified that her daughter might get caught, really did strangle him.

I'm sure the old girl's telling the truth about that, although we don't have any proof."

"So Ottoline knew all along." Harry was astonished.

"Not at first." Cynthia shrugged. "When Mike Huckstep's body was found, Ottoline got her first seismic wake-up call. When Hogan was killed, she had to have known. Aysha may even have told her. Like I said, Aysha denies everything and Ottoline confesses to everything."

"She killed to protect her daughter." Mim shook her head.

"Too late. And planting the weapon in Kerry's Toyota—that was obvious and clumsy."

"Then it was Aysha driving the motorcycle out from Sugar Hollow?" Harry remembered her close call.

"Yes." Cynthia finished off a chicken wing as the others chatted.

"You know," Mim changed the subject, "Ottoline was forever Aysha's safety net. She never let her grow up in the sense that the woman was never accountable for her actions. The wrong kind of love," Mim observed. "Hope I didn't do that to you."

Her daughter answered, "Well, Mother, you'd be happy to live my life for me and everyone else's in this room. You *are* domineering."

A silence descended upon the group.

Big Marilyn broke it. "So . . . ?"

They all laughed.

"*Did you think it was Aysha?*" Pewter spoke with her mouth full.

"*No. We just knew it wasn't Kerry. At least we were pretty sure it wasn't,*" Tucker replied.

"*I'm happy we're alive.*" Murphy flicked her tail. "*I don't understand why humans kill each other. I guess I never will.*"

"*You have to love them for what they are.*" Tucker snuck over to sniff Pewter's plate.

Pewter boxed Tucker on the nose. "*Watch it. I don't have to love a poacher!*"

"*You take so long to eat.*" Tucker winced.

"If you'd eat more slowly you'd enjoy it more," Pewter advised.

They heard the vet truck pull up outside, a door slamming, then Fair pushed open the screen door. The friends, intent on their dinners, greeted him. Then one by one they noticed.

"What have you done?" Mrs. Hogendobber exclaimed.

"Curled my hair a little," he replied in an unusually strong voice. "Didn't come out quite the way I expected."

"Might I ask why you did it?" Harry was polite.

"Works for Blair." He shrugged. "Thought it might work for me."

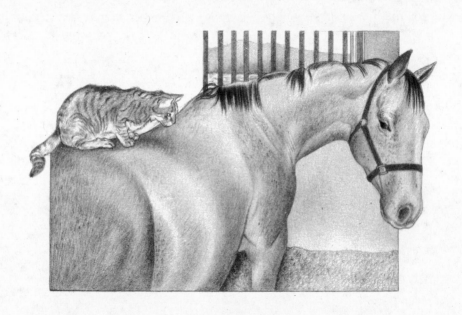

Murder, She Meowed

Dedicated to Pooh Bear and Coye
who love and guard Mrs. William O. Moss

Cast of Characters

Mary Minor Haristeen (Harry), the young postmistress of Crozet, whose curiosity almost kills the cat and herself

Mrs. Murphy, Harry's gray tiger cat, who bears an uncanny resemblance to authoress Sneaky Pie and who is wonderfully intelligent!

Tee Tucker, Harry's Welsh corgi. Mrs. Murphy's friend and confidante; a buoyant soul

Pharamond Haristeen (Fair), veterinarian, formerly married to Harry

Mrs. George Hogendobber (Miranda), a widow who thumps her own Bible!

Market Shiflett, owner of Shiflett's Market, next to the post office

Pewter, Market's fat gray cat, who, when need be, can be pulled away from the food bowl

Susan Tucker, Harry's best friend, who doesn't take life too seriously until her neighbors get murdered

Big Marilyn Sanburne (Mim), queen of Crozet

Rick Shaw, Albemarle sheriff

Cynthia Cooper, police officer

Herbert C. Jones, Pastor of Crozet Lutheran Church, a kindly, ecumenical soul who has been known to share his sermons with his two cats, Lucy Fur and Elocution

Arthur Tetrick, distinguished steeplechase officer and lawyer

Charles Valiant (Chark), young to be a steeplechase trainer but quite talented

Adelia Valiant (Addie), she turns twenty-one in November, catapulting her and Chark into their inheritance. She's a jockey—headstrong and impulsive

Marylou Valiant, Chark and Addie's mother, who disappeared five years ago

Mickey Townsend, a trainer much loved by Addie and much deplored by Chark

Nigel Danforth, recently arrived from England, he rides for Mickey Townsend

Coty Lamont, the best steeplechase jockey of the decade

Linda Forloines, vicious lying white trash whose highest value is the dollar

Will Forloines, on the same ethical level as his wife but perching on a lower intelligence rung

Bazooka, a hot 'chaser owned by Mim Sanburne

Orion, Mim's hunter, who displays an equine sense of humor

Rodger Dodger, Mim's aging ginger barn cat, newly rejuvenated by his girlfriend, Pusskin. Rodger likes to do things by the book

Pusskin, a beautiful tortoiseshell cat, she dotes on Rodger and irritates Mrs. Murphy

Dear Reader:

Thank you for your letters. While I try to answer every one I can answer some of the more frequent questions here.

Do I use a typewriter? No. Mother does. I use a Toshiba laptop that costs as much as a used Toyota. I like the mouse.

Do I write every day? Only when the real mousing is bad.

Do I live with other cats and dogs? Yes, and horses, too, but I'm not giving them any free advertising. After all, I'm the one who writes the books therefore I deserve the lion's share of the attention.

Is Pewter really fat? Well, parts of her have their own zip code. And I just saw her eat a mushroom not ten minutes ago. A mushroom is a fungus. What self-respecting cat eats fungus? She drinks beer, too.

Is Mother fun? Most times. She slides into the slough of despond when she has to pay bills. She had a lot to pay this year because floods washed out part of our road and bridge. The insurance didn't cover it but I could have told her that. She's been working very hard and while I sympathize it does keep her out of my fur.

Am I a Dixiecat? Well, I was born in the great state of Virginia so I believe we're not here for a long time but we're here for a good time. I sure hope you're having as good a time as I am!

Love,

SNEAKY PIE

1

The entrance to Montpelier, once the home of James and Dolley Madison, is marked by two ivy-covered pillars. An eagle, wings outstretched, perches atop each pillar. This first Saturday in November, Mary Minor Haristeen—"Harry"—drove through the elegant, understated entrance as she had done for thirty-four years. Her parents had brought her to Montpelier's 2,700 acres in the first year of her life, and she had not missed a race meet since. Like Thanksgiving, her birthday, Christmas, and Easter, the steeplechase races held at the Madisons' estate four miles west of Orange, Virginia, marked her life. A touchstone.

As she rolled past the pillars, she glanced at the eagles but gave them little thought. The eagle is a raptor, a bird of prey, capturing its victims in sharp talons, swooping out of the air with deadly accuracy. Nature divides into victor and victim. Humankind attempts to soften such clarity. It's not that humans don't recognize that there are victors and victims in life but that they prefer to cast their experiences in such terms as good or evil, not feaster and feast. However she chose to look at it, Harry would remember this crisp, azure day, and what would return to her mind would be the eagles . . . how she had driven past those sentinels so many times yet missed their significance.

One thing was for sure—neither she nor any of the fifteen thousand spectators would ever forget this particular Montpelier meet.

Mrs. Miranda Hogendobber, Harry's older friend and partner at work, rode with her in Harry's battered pickup truck, of slightly younger vintage than Mrs. Hogendobber's ancient Ford Falcon. Since Harry had promised Arthur Tetrick, the race director, that she'd be a fence judge, she needed to arrive early.

They passed through the gates, clambering onto the bridge arching over the Southern Railroad tracks and through the spate of hardwoods, thence emerging onto the emerald expanse of the racecourse circling the 100-acre center field. Brush and timber jumps dotted the track bound by white rails that determined the width of the difficult course. On her right, raised above the road, was the dirt flat track, which the late Mrs. Marion duPont Scott had built in 1929 to exercise her Thoroughbreds. Currently rented, the track remained in use and, along with the estate, had passed to the National Historic Trust upon Mrs. Scott's death in the fall of 1983.

Straight ahead through more pillared gates loomed Montpelier itself, a peach-colored house shining like a chunk of soft sunrise that had fallen from the heavens to lodge in the foothills of the Southwest Range of the Blue Ridge Mountains. Harry thought to herself that Montpelier, built while America labored under the punitive taxes of King George III, was a kind of sunrise, a peep over the horizon of a new political force, a nation made up of people from everywhere united by a vision of democracy. That the vision had darkened or become distorted didn't lessen the glory of its birth, and Harry, not an especially political person, believed passionately that Americans had to hold on to the concepts of their forefathers and foremothers.

One such concept was enjoying a cracking good time. James and Dolley Madison adored a good horse race and agreed that the supreme horseman of their time had been George Washington. Even before James was born in 1752, the colonists wagered on, argued over, and loved fine horses. Virginians, mindful of their history, continued the pastime.

Tee Tucker, Harry's corgi, sat in her lap staring out the window. She, too, loved horses, but she was especially thrilled today because her best friend and fiercest competitor, Mrs. Murphy, a tiger cat of formidable intelligence, was forced to stay home. Mrs. Murphy had screeched "dirty pool" at the top of her kitty lungs, but it had done no good because Harry had told her the crowd would upset her and she'd either run into the truck and pout or, worse, make the rounds of everyone's tailgates. Murphy had no control when it came to fresh roasted chicken, and there'd be plenty of that today. Truth be told, Tucker had no self-control either when it came to savoring meat dishes, but she couldn't jump up into the food the way the cat could.

Oh, the savage pleasure of pressing her wet, cold nose to the window as the truck pulled out of the farm's driveway and watching Mrs. Murphy standing on her hind legs at the kitchen window. Tucker was certain that when they returned early in the evening Murphy would have shredded the fringes on the old couch, torn the curtains, and chewed the phone cord, for starters. Then the cat would be in even more trouble while Tucker, the usual scapegoat, would polish her halo. If she had a tail, she'd wag it, she was so happy. Instead she wiggled.

"Tucker, sit still, we're almost there," Harry chided her.

"There's Mim." Mrs. Hogendobber waved to Marilyn

Sanburne, whose combination of money and bossiness made her the queen of Crozet. "Boiled wool, I see. She's going Bavarian."

"I like the pheasant feather in her cap myself." Harry smiled and waved too.

"How many horses does she have running today?"

"Three. She's having a good year with Bazooka, her big gelding. The other two are green and coming along." Harry used the term that described a young animal gaining experience. "It's wonderful that she's giving the Valiants a chance to train her horses. Having good stock makes all the difference, but then Mim would know."

Harry pulled into her parking space. She fished her gloves out of her pocket. At ten in the morning the temperature was forty-five degrees. By 12:30 and the first race, it might nudge into the high fifties, a perfect temperature for early November.

"Don't forget your badge." Mrs. Hogendobber, a good deal older than Harry, was inclined to mother her.

"I won't." Harry pinned on her badge, a green ribbon with OFFICIAL stamped in gold down the length of it. "I've even got one for Tucker." She tied a ribbon on the dog's leather collar.

The Hepworths, Harry's mother's family, had attended the first running of the Montpelier Hunt Races in 1928 when it was run over a cross-country course. It was always the "Hepworth space" until a few years ago when it became simply number 175.

Harry and Tucker hopped out of the car, ducked under the white rail, sprinted across the soft, perfect turf, and joined the other officials in the paddock area graced by large oak trees, their leaves still splashes of orange and yellow. In the center sat a small green building and a tent where jockeys changed into their silks and picked up their saddle pad numbers. Large striped tents were set up alongside the paddock in a restricted area for patrons of the event. Harry could smell the ham cooking in one tent and hoped she'd have time to scoot in for fresh ham biscuits and a cup of hot tea. Although it was sunny, a light wind chilled her face.

"Harry!" Fair Haristeen, her ex-husband and the race veterinarian, was striding over to her, looking like Thor himself.

"Hi, honey. I'm ready for anything."

Before the blond giant could answer, Chark Valiant and his sister, Adelia, walked over.

Chark, so-called because he was the sixth Charles Valiant, hugged Harry. "It's good to see you, Harry. Great day for 'chasing."

"Sure is."

"Oh, look at Tucker." Addie knelt down to pet her. "I'd trust your judgment anytime."

"A corgi official or an Official Corgi?" Chark asked, his tone arch.

"*The best corgi*," the little dog answered, smiling.

"You ready?" Harry peered at Addie, soon to be twenty-one, who'd followed her older brother into the steeplechasing world. He was the trainer, she was the jockey, a gifted and gutsy one.

"This is our Montpelier." She beamed, her youthful face already creased by sun and wind.

"Mim's the nervous one." Chark laughed because Mim Sanburne, who owned more horses than she could count, paced more than the horses did before the races.

"We passed her on the way in. Looked like she was heading up to the big house." Harry was referring to Montpelier.

"I don't know how she keeps up with her dozens of committees. I thought Monticello was her favorite cause." Fair rubbed his hands through his hair, then put his lad's cap back on.

"It is, but she promised to help give elected officials a tour, and the Montpelier staff is on overload." Harry did not need to explain that in this election year, anyone running for public office, even dogcatcher, would die before they'd miss the races and miss having a photo of themselves at the Madison house run in the local newspaper.

"Well, I'm heading back to the stable." Chark touched Harry on the shoulder. "Find me when the races are over. I hope we'll have something to celebrate."

"Sure."

Fair, called away by Colbert Mason, director of the National Hunt and Steeplechase Association, winked and left Harry and Addie.

"Adelia!" Arthur Tetrick called, then noticed Harry, and a big smile crossed his angular, distinguished face.

Striding over to chat with "the girls," as he called them, Arthur nodded and waved to people. A lawyer of solid reputation, he was not only acting race director for Montpelier but was often an official at other steeplechases. As executor of Marylou Valiant's will, he was also her two children's guardian—their father being dead—until Adelia turned twenty-one later that month and came into her considerable inheritance. Chark, though older than his sister, would not receive his money, either, until Addie's birthday. His mother had felt that men, being slower to mature, should have their inheritance delayed. She couldn't have been more wrong concerning her own offspring, for Chark was prudent if not parsimonious, whereas Addie's philosophy was the financial equivalent of the Biblical "consider the lilies of the field." But Marylou, who had disappeared five years earlier and was presumed dead, had missed crucial years in the development of her children. She couldn't have known that her theory was backward in their case.

"Don't you look the part." Addie kidded her guardian, taking in his fine English tweed vest and jacket.

"Can't be shabby. Mrs. Scott would come back to haunt me. Harry, we're delighted you're helping us out today."

"Glad to help."

Putting his hand over Addie's slender shoulder, he murmured, "Tomorrow—a little sit-down."

"Oh, Arthur, all you want to do is talk about stocks and bonds and—" she mocked his solemn voice as she intoned, "—NEVER TOUCH THE PRINCIPAL. I can't stand it! Bores me."

With an avuncular air, he chuckled. "Nonetheless, we must review your responsibilities before your birthday."

"Why? We review them once a bloody month."

Arthur shrugged, his bright eyes seeking support from Harry. "Wine, women, and song are the male vices. In your case it's horses, jockeys, and song. You won't have a penny left by the time you're forty." His tone was light but his eyes were intense.

Wary, Addie stepped back. "Don't start on Nigel."

"Nigel Danforth has all the appeal of an investment in Sarajevo."

"I like him." She clamped her lips shut.

Arthur snorted. "Being attracted to irresponsible men is a female vice in your family. Nigel Danforth is not worthy of you and—"

Addie slipped her arm through Harry's while finishing Arthur's sentence for him, "—he's a gold digger, mark my words." Irritated, she sighed. "I've got to get ready. We can fight about this after the races."

"Nothing to fight about. Nothing at all." Arthur's tone softened. "Good riding. Safe races. God bless. See you after the day's run."

"Sure." Addie propelled Harry toward the weigh-in stand as Arthur joined Fair and other jovial officials. "You'll adore Nigel—you haven't met him, have you? Arthur's being an old poop, as usual."

"He worries about you."

"Tough." Addie's face cleared. "Nigel's riding for Mickey Townsend. Just started for him. I warned him to get his money at the end of each day, though. Mickey's got good horses but he's always broke. Nigel's new, you know—he came over from England."

Harry smiled. "Americans don't name their sons Nigel."

"He's got the smoothest voice. Like silk." Addie was ignoring the wry observation.

"How long have you been dating him?"

"Two months. Chark can't stand him but Charles the Sixth can be such a moose sometimes. I wish he and Arthur would stop hovering over me. Just because a few of my boyfriends in the past have turned out to be blister bugs."

Harry laughed. "Hey, you know what they say, you gotta kiss a lot of toads before finding the prince."

"Better than getting a blister."

"Addie, anything is better than a blister bug." She paused. "Except drugs. Does Nigel take them? You can't be too careful." Harry believed in grabbing the bull by the horns.

Quickly, Addie said, "I don't do drugs anymore," then changed the subject. "Hey, is Susan coming today?"

"Later. The Reverend Jones will be here, too. The whole Crozet gang. We've got to root for Bazooka."

Chark waved for his sister to join him.

"Oops. Big Brother is watching me." She dropped Harry's arm. "Harry, I'll see you after the races. I want you to meet Nigel."

"After the races then." Harry walked over to get her fence assignment.

Harry, as usual, had been assigned the east gate jump, so-called because it lay closest to the east gate entrance to the main house. She vaulted over the rail to the patrons' tents, put together a ham biscuit and a cup of tea, turned too fast without looking, and bumped into a slender dark man accompanied by a jockey she recognized.

"I'm sorry," she said.

"Another woman falling over you," Coty Lamont said sarcastically.

"Coty, you aren't using the right cologne. Old manure doesn't attract women." The other man spoke in a light English accent.

Harry, who knew Coty slightly—the best jockey riding at this time—smiled at him. "Smells good to me, Coty."

He recognized her since she occasionally worked other steeplechase races. "The post office lady."

"Mary Minor Haristeen." She held out her hand.

He shook her hand. He couldn't extend his hand until she offered hers . . . rough as Coty appeared, he had absorbed the minimum of social graces.

"And this here's Nigel Danforth."

"Pleased to meet you Mr. Danforth." Harry shook his hand. "I'm a friend of Addie's."

Their faces relaxed.

"Ah," Nigel said simply, and smiled.

"Then be ready to part-*tee*," Coty said.

"Uh—sure," Harry, a bit confused by their sudden enthusiasm, said softly.

"See you later." Coty headed for the jockeys' changing tent.

Nigel winked. "Any friend of Addie's . . ." Then he, too, hurried to the tent.

Harry watched the diminutive men walk away from her, struck by how tiny their butts were. She did not know what to make of those two. Their whole demeanor had changed when she mentioned Addie. She felt as if she'd given the password to an exclusive club.

She blinked, sipped some tea, then walked out the east side of the tent area and stepped over the cordon. Tucker ducked under it.

"Come on, Tucker, let's check our fence before the hordes arrive."

"*Good idea,*" Tucker said. "*You know how everyone stops to pass and repass. If you don't get over there now you'll never get over.*"

Harry glanced down at the dog. "You've got a lot to say."

"*Yes, but you don't listen.*"

From the east gate jump Harry couldn't see the cars driving in, but she could hear the steady increase in noise. Glad to be alone, she bit into the succulent ham biscuit and noticed Mim walking back through the gates to the big house, toward the races. She thought to herself that the political tour must be over, another reason she was happy to be in the back—no handshaking.

Working in the Crozet post office allowed Harry weekends and a minimum of hassle. The P.O. was open Saturdays from 8 A.M. to noon. Sally Dohner and Liz Beer alternated Saturdays so Harry enjoyed two full days of freedom. Her friends took their work home with them, fretted, burned the midnight oil. Harry locked the door to the small postal building on Crozet's main drag, drove home, and forgot about work until the next morning. If she was going to fret over something, it would be her farm at the base of Yellow Mountain or some problem with a friend. Often accused of lacking ambition, she readily agreed with her critics. Her Smith College classmates, just beginning to nudge forward in their high-powered careers in New York, Boston, Richmond, and far-flung cities in the Midwest and West, reminded her she had graduated in the top 10 percent of her class. They felt she was wasting her life. She felt her life was lived from within. It was a rich life. She used a different measuring stick than they did.

She had one thing they didn't: time. Of course, they had one thing she didn't: money. She never could figure out how you could have both. Well, Marilyn "Mim" Sanburne did, but she had inherited more money than God. In Mim's defense, she used it wisely, often to help others, but to be a beneficiary of her largesse, one had to tolerate her grandeur. Little Marilyn, Harry's age, who glowered in her mother's shadow, was tiring of good works. A flaming romance would take precedence over good deeds, but Little Mim, now divorced, couldn't find Mr. Right, or rather, her mother couldn't find Mr. Right for her.

Harry's mouth curled upward. She had found Mr. Right who'd turned into Mr. Wrong and now wanted to be Mr. Right again. She loved Fair but she didn't know if she could ever again love him in that way.

A roar told her that the Bledsoe/Butler Cup, the first race of the day, one mile on the dirt, $1,000 winner-take-all—had started. Tempted as she was to run up to the flat track and watch, she knew she'd better stay put.

"Tucker, I've been daydreaming about marriage, men"—she sighed—"ex-husbands. The time ran away with me."

Tucker perked up her big ears. *"Fair still loves you. You could marry him all over again."*

Harry peered into the light brown eyes. "Sometimes you seem almost human—as if you know exactly what I'm saying."

"Sometimes you seem almost canine." Tucker stared back at her. *"But you have no nose, Harry."*

"Are you barking at me?" Harry laughed.

"I'm telling you to stop living so much in your mind, that's what I'm saying. Why you think I'm barking is beyond me. I know what you're saying."

Harry reached over, hugged the sturdy dog, and kissed the soft fur on her head. "You really are the most adorable dog."

She heard the announcer begin to call the jockeys for the second race, the first division of the Marion duPont Scott Montpelier Cup, purse $10,000, two miles and one furlong over brush for "maidens" three years old and upward, a maiden being a horse that had never won a race. She could see people walking over the hill. Many race fans, the knowledgeable ones, wanted to get away from the crowds and watch the horses.

A brand-new Land Rover drove at the edge of the course, its midnight blue shining in the November light. Harry couldn't imagine being able to purchase such an expensive vehicle. She was saving her pennies to replace the '78 Ford truck, which despite its age was still chugging along.

Dr. Larry Johnson stuck his head out the Land Rover's passenger window. "Everything shipshape?"

"Yes, sir." Harry saluted.

"Hello, Tucker." Larry spoke to the sweet-eyed dog.

"Hi, Doc."

"We've got about ten minutes." Larry turned to Jim

Sanburne, Mim's husband and the mayor of Crozet, who was driving. "Don't we, Jim?"

"I reckon." Jim leaned toward the passenger window, his huge frame blotting out the light from the driver's side. "Harry, you know that Charles Valiant and Mickey Townsend are fighting like cats and dogs, so pay close attention to those races where they've both got entries."

"What's the buzz?" Harry had heard nothing of the feud.

"Hell, I don't know. These damn trainers are prima donnas."

"Mickey accused Chark of instructing Addie to bump his jockey at the Maryland Hunt Cup last year. His horse faltered at the sixth fence and then just couldn't quite pick it up."

"Mickey's a sore loser," Jim growled to Larry. "He'll break your fingers if you beat him at checkers—especially if there's money bet on the game."

"Goes back further than that." Harry sighed.

"You're right. Charles hated Mickey from the very first date Mickey had with his mother." Jim ran his finger under his belt. "Takes some boys like that. But you know Charles had sense enough to worry that Townsend only wanted her money."

"Chark couldn't understand how Marylou could prefer Mickey to Arthur." Larry Johnson recalled the romance, which had started seven years ago, ending in shock and dismay for everyone. "I guess any woman who compares Arthur to Mickey is bound to favor Mickey. I don't think it had to do with money."

"Off the top of your head, do you know what races—"

Before Harry could finish her question, Jim Sanburne bellowed, "The third, the fifth, and the sixth."

"Nigel Danforth is riding for Townsend," Larry added.

"Addie told me," Harry said.

"You heard about them too." Jim smiled.

"Kinda. I mean, I know that Addie is crazy for him."

"Her brother isn't." Larry folded his arms across his chest.

"Hey, just another day in Virginia." Harry smacked the door of the Land Rover.

"Ain't that the truth," Jim said. "Put two Virginians in a room and you get five opinions."

"No, Jim, put you in a room and we get five opinions," Larry tweaked him.

Jim laughed. "I'm just the mayor of a small town reflecting the various opinions of my voters."

"We'll come by after the first race. Need anything? Food? Drink?" Larry asked while Jim was still laughing at himself.

"Thanks, no."

"Okay, Harry, catch you in about a half hour then." Jim rolled up the hill as Larry waved.

Harry put her hands on her hips and thought to herself. Jim, in his sixties, and Larry, in his seventies, had known her since she was born. They knew her inside and out, as she knew them. That was another reason she didn't much feel like being the Queen of Madison Avenue. She belonged here with her people. There was a lot that never needed to be said when you knew people so intimately.

This shorthand form of communication did not apply to Boom Boom Craycroft, creaming over the top of the hill like a clipper in full sail. Since Boom Boom had once enjoyed an affair with Harry's ex-husband, the buxom, tall, and fashionable woman was not Harry's favorite person on earth. Boom Boom reveled in the emotional texture of life. Today she reveled in the intense pleasure of swooping down on Harry, who couldn't move away since she was the fence judge.

"Harry!" Boom Boom cruised over, her square white teeth gleaming, her heavy, expensive red cape moving gently in the breeze.

"Hi, Boom." Harry shortened her nickname, one won in high school because her large bosoms seemed to boom-boom with each step. The boys adored her.

"You're dressed for the job." Boom Boom appraised Harry's pressed jeans and L. L. Bean duck boots—the high-topped ones, which reached only nine inches for women, a fact that infuriated Harry since she could have used twelve inches on the farm; only the men's boots had twelve-inch uppers. Harry also wore a silk undershirt, an ironed flannel tartan plaid, MacLeod, and a goosedown vest, in red. If the day warmed up, she would shed her layers.

"Boom Boom, I'm usually dressed this way."

"I know," came the tart reply from the woman standing there in Versace from head to foot. Her crocodile boots alone cost over a thousand dollars.

"I don't have your budget."

"Even if you did you'd look exactly the same."

"All right, Boom, what's the deal? You come over here to give me your fashion lecture 101, to visit uneasiness upon me, or do you want something from Tucker?"

Tucker squeezed next to her mother. *"She's got on too much perfume, Mom. She's stuffing my nose up."*

Boom Boom leaned over to pat the silky head. "Tucker, very impressive with your official's badge."

"Boom, those fake fingernails have got to go," the dog replied.

"I'm here to visit and to watch the first race from the back."

"Have a fight with Carlos?"

Boom Boom had been dating a wealthy South American who lived in New York City and Buenos Aires.

"He's not here this weekend."

"Trolling, then?" Harry wryly used the term for going around picking up men.

"You can be so snide, Harry. It's not your best feature. I'm here to patch up our relationship."

"We don't have a relationship."

"Oh, yes, we do."

"They're lining up, the starter's tape is up,"—the announcer's voice rang out as he waited for the tape to drop—"and they're off."

"I've got to work this race." Harry moved Boom Boom forcibly back, then took up her stance on the rail dead even with the jump. If a rider went down, she could reach the jockey quickly, as soon as all the other horses were over the fence, while the outriders went after the runaway horse.

The first jumps limbered up the horses and settled the jockeys. By the time they reached Harry's jump, the competition would be fierce. The first race over fences covered a distance of two miles and one furlong; competitors would pass her obstacle only once. This race, and in fact all races but the fifth, the Virginia Hunt Cup, were run over brush, meaning the synthetic Grand National brush fences, which had replaced natural brush some years ago. The reasoning behind the change was that the natural brush varied in density. Because steeplechase horses literally "brushed" through the top of these jumps, any inconsistency in texture or depth or solidity could cause a fall or injury. The Grand National fences provided horses with a safer jump. Timber horses, on the other hand, had to jump cleanly over the whole obstacle, although the top timbers were notched on the back so they would give way if rapped hard enough. Even so, the last thing a timber trainer or jockey wanted was for one of their horses to "brush" through a timber fence.

Harry heard the crowd. Then in the distance she heard the thunder. The earth shook. The sensation sent chills up her spine, and in an instant the horses turned the distant corner, a kaleidoscope of finely conditioned bays, chestnuts, and seal browns, hooves reaching out as they lengthened their stride. She recognized the purple silks of Mim Sanburne as well as Addie's determined gaze. The Urquharts, Mim's family, had registered the first year that the Jockey Club was organized, 1894, so their horses ran in solid color silks. Harry also saw the other silks: emerald green with a red hoop around the chest, blue with yellow dots, yellow with a diagonal black sash, the colors intense, rippling with the wind, heightening the sensation of speed, beauty, and power.

The first three horses cleared the brush, their hooves tipping the top of the synthetic cedar, making an odd swishing sound, then she heard the reassuring thump-thump as those front hooves reached the earth followed by the hind. The three leaders pulled away, and the remainder of the pack cleared the jump, a Degas painting come to life.

She breathed a sigh of relief. No one went down at her fence. No fouls. As the hoofbeats died away, moving back up the hill toward the last several jumps and the homestretch, the crowd screamed while the announcer called out the positions of the horses.

"Closing hard, Ransom Mine, but Devil Fox hanging on to the lead, and here they come down the stretch, and Ransom Mine is two strides out, but oh, what a burst of speed, it's Devil Fox under the wire!"

"Hurray for Mim!" Harry whispered. "A strong second."

Boom Boom drew alongside her. "She didn't expect much from Ransom Mine, did she?"

"She's only had him about six months. Picked him up in Maryland, I think."

"Changing trainers helped," Boom Boom said, "Chark is working out really well for her."

"Will and Linda Forloines are still going around telling horror stories about how much they did for Mim, and how vile she was to fire them." Harry shook her head, recalling Mim's former trainer and his wife, a jockey. "Will couldn't find his ass with both hands."

"No, but he sure found the checkbook," Boom Boom said. "And I don't think Will has a clue as to how much Linda makes selling cocaine or how much she takes herself."

"They're lucky Big Mim didn't prosecute them, padding the stable budget the way they did."

"She'd spend thousands of dollars in court and still never see a penny back. They've squandered all of it. Her revenge will

be watching them blow out. Mim's too smart to directly cross druggies. She'll let them kill themselves—or take the cure. Thank God Addie took the cure."

"Yes," Harry said succinctly. She hated people who took advantage of others and justified it by saying the people they were stealing from were rich. If she remembered her Ten Commandments, one said, *Thou Shalt Not Steal.* It didn't say, *Thou Shalt Not Steal Except When the Employer is Wealthy.* Will and Linda Forloines still hung around the edges of the steeplechase world. The previous year Will had been reduced to working in a convenience store outside of Middleburg. Finally they had latched on to a rich doctor who moved down from New Jersey and who wanted to "get into horses." Poor man.

"They're here."

"Here?" Harry said. Boom Boom's deep voice could lull one, it was so lovely, she thought.

"You'd think they'd have the sense not to show their faces."

"Will never was the brightest bulb on the Christmas tree." Harry peeled off her down vest as Boom Boom changed the subject.

"I'm here to tell you that I'm sorry I had a fling with Fair, but it *was* after your divorce. He's a sweet man, but we weren't the right two people. I hadn't dated anyone seriously since Kelly died, and I needed to put my toes in the water."

Harry didn't think it was Boom Boom's toes that had fascinated Fair, but she resisted the urge to make a comment. Also, she didn't believe for one minute that the relationship had magically started right after the divorce. "Can you understand how it would upset me?"

"No. You divorced him."

"That didn't mean I was over him, dammit." Harry decided not to try to pinpoint the exact date of Boom Boom's liaison with Fair. At least they hadn't appeared in public until after the divorce.

"Why take it out on me? Take it out on him."

"I did, sorta."

"Well, Harry, what about the women, uh, while you were married? Those were your enemies, not me."

"Did I ever say I was emotionally mature?" Harry crossed her arms over her chest as Tucker followed the conversation closely.

"No."

"So."

"So what?"

"So, I could see you. I couldn't see those affairettes he was having while we were married. I got mad at you for all of them, I guess. I never said I was right to get mad at you but I did."

"You're still mad at me."

"No, I'm not." Harry half lied.

"You certainly never go out of your way to be nice to me."

"I'm cordial."

"Harry, we're both born and raised in Virginia. You know exactly what I mean." And Boom Boom was right. One could be correct but cool. Virginians practiced cutting one another with precise elegance.

"Yeah, well, since we were both raised in Virginia, we know how to avoid subjects like this, Boom Boom. I have no desire to explore my emotions with you or anybody."

"Exactly!"

Harry squinted at the triumphant face. "Don't start with me."

"We've got to grow beyond our conditioning. We've got to cast aside or break through our repression. You can't hold your emotions in, they'll eat away at you until you become ill or dry up like some people I could mention."

"I'm very healthy."

"You're also not twenty anymore. You've been holding these emotions in for too long."

"Now, look." Harry's voice oozed reasonableness. "What

you call repressed, I call disciplined. I am not teetering on the brink of self-annihilation. I don't drink. I don't take drugs. I don't even smoke. I like my life. I'd like a little more money maybe, but I like my life."

"You're in denial."

"Denial is a river in Egypt."

"Harry," her voice lowered, "that joke's got gray hairs. You don't fool me with your quips. I want you to come with me to Lifeline. It's changed my life, absolutely. Six months ago I would never have been able to approach you, I would have held on to my own anger, but now I want to reach out. I want us to be friends. Lifeline teaches you to take responsibility for yourself. For your own emotions. It's a structured process, and I know you like structure. You *can* learn these things, learn new ways to *be* with people in a group that will encourage you. You'll feel safe. Trust me, Harry, it will make you happy."

Trusting Boom Boom was the last thing Harry would ever do. "I'm not the type."

"I'll even pay for it."

"*What?*"

"I mean it. I'll pay for it. I feel so bad that you're still mad at me. I want us to be friends. Please consider my offer."

"I—" Harry, caught off guard, stuttered, "I, I—Jesus, Boom Boom."

"Think about it. I know you'll find a thousand reasons not to do this, but why don't you take out a pad of paper and list the pros and cons? You might find more reasons to engage in Lifeline than you know."

"Uh—I'll think about it."

"One other little thing."

"Oh, God."

"Think about the fact that you're still in love with Fair."

"I am not! I love him but I'm not in love with him."

"Lifeline." Boom Boom smiled seraphically, moving off.

Harry breathed deeply, conscious of her heart pounding. Jim Sanburne's midnight-blue Land Rover hove into view. She collected herself.

"News?" Larry inquired.

"Clean as a whistle," Harry said.

"Are you all right?" the doctor asked, observing her flushed face and rapid breathing.

"I'm fine. How long till the next race?"

"Half hour. Just about," Jim answered her.

"I need a co—cola."

"You need something," Larry joked. "You're breathing like a freight train. Why don't you come to my office Monday? How long's it been since you had a checkup?"

"Larry, I'm fine. I had a little tête-à-tête with Boom Boom."

"Say no more." He smiled and as the two men drove off, Jim said, "Did she say tit a tat?"

"No." Larry laughed loudly. "Jim, you're just a redneck with money."

Jim grunted. "Sounded like body parts to me, good buddy."

2

"Mom, I'm hungry."

"Tucker, stop yapping, you're getting on my nerves."

"You've had a ham biscuit and I haven't had anything since breakfast." The aroma from the food tents drove Tucker to distraction.

Harry checked her watch. Twenty minutes. She dashed into a tent, grabbed fried chicken, a small container of coleslaw, another one of beans, one cold Coke, and a big cup of hot tea with a plastic cover on it.

As Harry threaded her way through the crowd, she passed the jockeys' tent. A commotion stopped her. The flap of the tent opened to reveal colorful silks on hangers dangling from a rope strung across the tent. Ace bandages, caps, and socks were tossed on low benches.

Nigel, close-cropped black hair gleaming in the sun, charged out. Chark Valiant charged out after him.

"Leave him alone," Addie called after her brother. She opened the tent flap, sticking her head through. She hadn't finished changing and couldn't come all the way out.

"Shut up, Adelia." Chark pushed her head back behind the flaps, then twirled on the young man. "You flaming phony—you don't fool me. If my sister weren't a Valiant, you wouldn't give her the time of day."

Addie popped her head back out of the tent as a florid Mickey Townsend bore down on the scene from one direction.

Arthur Tetrick leaned out of the top of the two-story finish-line tower. "Mickey, don't—" He shut up, realizing he'd cause a bigger scene.

The jockey kept walking away from Chark, who grabbed him by the right shoulder, spinning him around.

"Stop it." Nigel's voice was clipped and furious.

"You stay away from my sister."

"She's old enough to make her own decisions."

Chark shook his finger in Nigel's face. "You want her money, you lying sack of shit."

"Bugger off," Nigel growled.

Chark hauled off to hit him but Mickey Townsend grabbed Chark from behind, pulling him back. "Settle this later."

Chark twisted his head to see Mickey as Nigel returned to Addie, who'd stuck her head out of the tent again. He slipped into the tent with her as three other jockeys slipped out.

"Takes one gold digger to know another." Chark struggled.

Mickey, square-built and powerful, continued dragging him away. "Shove it."

Arthur, who had hurried down from the tower, approached the two men. "Mickey, I'll take over from here."

"Suit yourself." Mickey unleashed his iron grip on the young man.

"Thank you for defusing an embarrassing situation." Arthur grabbed Chark's elbow.

"Yeah, sure." Mickey inclined his handsome, crew-cut head, then ambled back to the paddock.

"Charles, this will not do," Arthur sternly admonished him.

"I'll kill that creep."

Arthur rolled his eyes heavenward. "The more resistance you offer, the more irresistible he becomes. Besides, Adelia's a baby. She's not going to date men you find attractive."

"I don't find men attractive," Chark sassed back.

"A slip of the tongue. You know what I mean." Arthur draped his arm over Chark's shoulder. "Calm down. Ignore this absurd romance. If you do, it will die of its own accord." The horses were now in the paddock. "Tell you what, after the races I have to fax in the paperwork to National from the big house. Take everyone maybe an hour. How about if I meet you at the Keswick Club for a drink? We can talk this over then. Okay? Then we'll look in on Mim's party or she'll banish us to Siberia."

"Okay," Chark replied, trying to settle his churning emotions. "But I just don't get it."

Arthur chuckled. "That's what makes the world go 'round. They don't think like we do—"

Chark interrupted. "They don't think."

"Be that as it may, men and women see the world quite differently. I've got to climb back up to my perch. Keswick Club at eight."

"Yeah." Chark smiled at the man who had become his surrogate father, then headed to the paddock where Addie, already up on a rangy bay called Chattanooga Choo, ignored his approach.

Nigel, in orange silks with three royal blue hoops, rode a striking chestnut beside her as they walked the horses around.

Chark sighed deeply, deciding not to give his sister instructions for the third race. She usually ignored them anyway.

Harry jogged back to her position, nodding to friends as she weaved her way through the dense throng. As they spied the official's badge, they waved her on, a few calling that they'd drop by to see her. She wondered what it was about romantic energy or sexual energy that made everybody crazy, producing a scene like the one she had just witnessed.

She returned to the east gate jump, sat down, and opened her tea. A plume of steam spiraled upward.

"Mother!" Tucker's voice rose.

"Beggar." Harry tore off a piece of hot chicken which Tucker gobbled. "Fat beggar."

"I'm not a beggar, but I can't reach the tables and you can. And I'm not fat. Fat is Pewter." Tucker aptly described the gray cat who worked at Market Shiflett's convenience store next to the post office in Crozet. Pewter couldn't come to the races either, doubling Tucker's supreme satisfaction.

The announcer called out post time. Harry started eating as fast as Tucker. She hadn't realized how famished she was, but she'd been up since five that morning with only a few bites to sustain her.

Each morning Harry fed her three horses, then turned them out into the pasture. She left marshmallows for the possum who lived in the hayloft. Then she'd feed her pets . . . but sometimes she forgot to feed herself. Mrs. Murphy, apart from a good breakfast, had a huge bowl of crunchies in mixed flavors. Usually Harry left open the animal door that she had installed in her back kitchen door. The screen door off the screened-in porch, which ran the length of the kitchen, was easy for Mrs. Murphy and Tucker to push open. But this morning she had closed up the animal door, deciding she'd keep Mrs. Murphy in the house since the cat had been known to follow the car. By the time she left to fetch Mira, she'd put in three hours of hard work on the farm.

The trumpet call to the third race made Harry eat even faster. She rinsed the food down with tea and Coke.

"Got any left?"

"Tucker, get your nose out of that cup."

"Just curious."

Harry brushed herself off, picked up her debris, and stood at her position.

She heard a crack, then a double shot fired. False start. Those wore on the nerves of riders and horses. The announcer called out the renewed lineup. "Horses in position. They're off!" The third race, the Noel Laing Stakes, two and a half miles over brush, was the second biggest race of the day, with a purse of $30,000—60 percent to the winner.

The crowd yelped in anticipation. The horses charged out of sight and Harry heard the rumble of hooves, the ground shaking like Jell-O. The leader, a bright bay, was way ahead of the others. Every one cleared her fence, although one horse faltered. The jockey pulled up, his green silks with a blue cross already pasted with sweat to his body.

Harry knew this race was two and a half miles long. The horses would be around again in a few minutes. She ran out to the jockey, Coty Lamont.

"You okay?"

"He's come up lame. I'll walk up on the inside rail." Coty dismounted, careful to hold on to the reins as Harry held the horse by the bridle. "Vet's up there."

"Blown tendon, I'm afraid, Coty." Harry hoped she was wrong, because tendon injuries took a long time to heal and the risk of reinjury on a bowed tendon was high.

"Yeah." Coty touched his crop to his cap by way of thanks. He slowly walked the gelding across the course and up the inside rail as Harry raced back to her post.

Seconds later the field came around for another lap. All jumped clean.

As Harry waited for the announcer's report on the victor, she saw Will and Linda Forloines walking down the grassy slope toward her. They had in tow a man all but wrapped in Barbour.

Linda called out, "Hello, Harry."

"Hi." Harry waved to both of them. No reason to be impolite, much as she disliked the couple. She knew instantly the fellow in country drag had to be their soon-to-be-fleeced Yankee employer. She also knew that Will and Linda were making a point of showing him they knew everyone in the steeplechase world. Linda, more cunning than Will, wouldn't stop to talk to many people since she knew they would not warmly welcome her. The New Jersey gentleman wouldn't realize she was not on friendly terms since everyone would be polite. They turned and walked in the other direction as the Land Rover drove toward Harry. Linda ducked her head at the sight of Jim Sanburne.

Jim and Larry pulled up again. This time Mim, in the backseat, hopped out. She hadn't seen Will and Linda. The men drove on.

"I want to watch the fourth race from here. I can't bear listening to Boom Boom tell me about spiced cream cheese on endive for another second! It's either endives or Lifeline." She twirled her wool cape behind her.

"This fence is too far away for most people to walk." Harry glanced down the rail. "Uh, but not too far for Greg Satterwaite. I see he's working the outside rail. I guess he'll be going to the outside barns next. God forbid he should miss anyone."

"Don't tell me," Mim exclaimed. "Has the good senator seen me?"

"Not yet. He's busy pumping hands and smiling big." Harry pulled a huge fake smile as demonstration.

Mim scurried behind one of the big trees. A telltale whiff of smoke would give her away should anyone be looking. Harry ignored Mim's cheating; she knew Mim wasn't supposed to smoke. Still, she wasn't going to tell Mim what to do or what not to do.

"Hi, there. How are you?" Satterwaite held out his hand, already swollen.

Harry suppressed an evil urge to squeeze it. "Morning, Senator."

"I surely hope I may count on your vote. This is a tough election for me."

"You can," Harry replied with little enthusiasm. She hated politics.

A jet of smoke shot upward from behind the tree.

"Thank you, thank you for your support." He smiled, capped teeth gleaming, then moved on to his next victim.

A few moments later Mim sneaked out from behind the tree. "Whew! Saved. When a politician knows you have money they'll talk until they're blue in the face. Save us from our government!"

"We're supposed to be a democracy. Save us from ourselves." Harry laughed, then noticed the cigarette still in Mim's fingers; it was burning down to a stub.

Mim stomped it into the ground. "Don't tell Jim."

"I won't." But she was surprised to see Mim gambling with her health after her bout with breast cancer.

Harry checked her program. "You've got Royal Danzig in this race. Congratulations on the first division of the Montpelier Cup, by the way. Ransom Mine took this fence with so much daylight he was flying."

"If he stays sound, he'll be one of the great ones, like Victorian Hill." Mim mentioned a wonderful horse, a star in the early '90s.

"Who was the greatest 'chaser you ever saw?"

Mim replied without hesitation. "Battleship, by Man-O'-War out of Quarantine, bred in 1927. To see that horse in Mrs. Scott's pale blue silks with the pink-and-silver cross was something I'll never forget. I was tiny then, but it made such an impression. This place was hopping because Mrs. Scott was in her prime. To have seen Battleship, that was heaven."

"What about Marylou Valiant's Zinger?" Harry remembered the leggy chestnut colt.

"If he hadn't injured his stifle, yes, I think he could have been very fine indeed." She looked up at the sky. "I hope she's up there watching today. People will say I hired Adelia and Charles out of affection. Granted that may have played some small part, but the truth is they're good . . . and getting better. And the difference in the stable since that dreadful couple is gone!" She crossed her arms over her chest. "You know it was a drip-drip like Chinese water torture after Marylou disappeared. The day I admitted to myself she must be dead was one of the darkest days of my life. And I promised to do what I could for her children."

"You more than kept your promise."

"The hard work was done. Marylou and Charley did that. When Chark went to Cornell and Addie to Foxcroft, I saw them at holidays and special school functions. What was hard was knowing when to be firm." She laughed at herself. "Now with Marilyn I never had trouble with that, but . . . well, their loss had been so profound. I sometimes wonder if I should have been tougher, especially with Addie."

Before Harry could say anything, they both heard the shot. Mim moved back. Harry trained her eyes on the roll of the land where she would first see the field.

Again that eerie rumble, and then the horses, packed tightly together, surged into view. Mim's purple silks were in the middle of the pack, a good place for this point in a race of just over two miles. Goggles over her eyes, Addie concentrated on the jump. Harry listened to the grunts and shouts of the jockeys as they cleared the brush, the whap-whap and whoosh as the hind hooves touched the greenery. And then they were gone, raging on, slipping into the dip of the land, and charging uphill again for the next fence.

Mim strained to hear the announcer call out positions. As they cleared Harry's jump, one horse in the rear of the pack took off too early and crashed through the jump, stumbling on the other side but recovering.

Harry watched the horse, which wasn't injured but was tiring badly. "Dammit, why doesn't he pull up?"

"Because it's Linda Forloines. She'll drive a horse to death."

"But I just saw Linda not twenty minutes ago."

"Zack Merchant's jockey got stepped on in the paddock as he was mounting up. Linda scurried right up to Zack, and of course he was desperate. The results speak for themselves."

The crowd noises followed the horses, an odd muffle of congregated voices, and then the field again appeared on the hill, Royal Danzig still safely in the middle.

Harry shook her head. "Linda's a piece of work."

"Precisely." Mim pursed her lips. She was not one to spread negative gossip, but she despised the Forloines to such a degree it took all her formidable discipline not to share her loathing with anyone who would listen.

"Zack Merchant's not exactly a prince among men either." Harry hated the way he treated horses, although to customers and new clients he put on a show of caring for the animals. Other horsemen knew his brutal methods, but as yet there was no way to address abuse inside the racing game. It was a little like telling a man he couldn't beat his wife. You might hate him for it. You might want to smash his face in, but somehow—you just couldn't until you caught him in the act.

The announcer's voice rose in frenzy. "Four lengths and pulling away, this race is all Royal Danzig, Royal Danzig, Royal Danzig, with Isotone crossing the finish line a distant second followed by Hercule and Vitamin Therapy."

"Congratulations!" Harry shook Mim's hand. Mim wasn't a woman designed for a spontaneous hug.

Mim carefully took the proffered hand. Her face flushed. She was wary against her own happiness. After all, the results weren't official yet. "Thank you." She blinked. "I'll find Chark and Addie. Quite a smart race she rode, staying with the pack until the stretch."

"You're having a sensational day." Harry smiled. "And it's not over yet."

"The official results of the Montpelier Cup, second division, are Royal Danzig, Isotone, and Hercule." The announcer's voice crinkled with metallic sound.

Mim relaxed. "Ah—" She couldn't think of anything to say.

"*Congratulations, Mrs. Sanburne.*" Tucker panted with excitement.

Mim said, "Tucker wants something."

"*No, I'm just happy for you,*" Tucker replied.

"Tucker."

"*Why do you always tell me to be quiet when I'm being polite?*" Tucker's ears swept back and forth.

"I'd better head up to the winner's circle. Oh, here comes my knight in shining armor."

Jim Sanburne rolled down in the Land Rover. "Come on, honeybunch."

"Well done, Mim The Magnificent!" Larry laughed.

"Hi, guys." Harry poked her head in the window. "Tell Fair to check on the horse Linda Forloines rode. He looks wrung out."

"Will do," Larry Johnson said as Jim kissed his wife, who was sliding into the front seat.

Larry Johnson moved to the back, and for an instant as Mim swung her attractive legs under her, close together as befits a proper Southern lady, Harry had an intimation of what Mim must have been like when young: graceful, reserved, lovely. The lovely had turned to impeccably groomed once she reached 39.999 and holding . . . as Miranda Hogendobber had put it when she reached sixty herself. However, the graceful and reserved stayed the course. That Mim was a tyrant and always had been was so much the warp and woof of life in these parts that few bothered to comment on it anymore. At least her tyrannies usually were in the service of issues larger than her own ego.

Harry walked to Mim's tree, leaning against the rough bark. Tucker sat at her feet. The temperature climbed to the high fifties, the sky's startling pure blue punctuated with clouds the color of Devonshire cream. Harry felt oddly tired.

Miranda, her brogues giving her firm purchase on the grass, strode straight over the hill, ducked under the inside rail, crossed the course, and ducked under the outside rail. Her tartan skirt held in place with a large brass pin completed an outfit only Miranda could contemplate. The whole look murmured "country life" except for the hunter-green beret, which Miranda insisted on wearing because she couldn't stand for the wind to muss her hair. "No feathers for me," she had announced when Harry had picked her up. Harry's idea of a chapeau was her Smith College baseball cap or an ancient 10X felt cowboy hat with cattleman's crease that her father had worn.

"Tired blood?" Miranda slowly sat down beside her.

"Hmm, my daily sinking spell."

"Mine comes at four, which you know only too well since I collapse on the chair and force you to brew tea." Miranda folded her hands together. "Mayhem up there. I have never seen so many people, and Mim can't take a step forward or backward. This is her Montpelier."

"Sure seems to be."

"Isn't it wonderful about the Valiant children?" Miranda still referred to them as children. "They're giving Mim what she wants—winners!"

"Uh-huh."

"When I think of what those two young people endured—well, I can't bear it. The loss of both parents when they were not even out of their teens. It makes me think of the Fortieth Psalm." She launched into her spiritual voice. " 'I waited patiently for the Lord; he inclined to me and heard my cry. He drew me up from the desolate pit, out of the miry bog, and set my feet upon a rock, making my steps secure—' " She caught her breath.

Harry broke in, "Miranda, how do you remember so much? You could recite from the Bible two weeks running."

"Love the Good Book. If you would join me at the Church of the Holy Light, you'd see why I lift up my voice—"

Harry interrupted again; not her style, but a religious discussion held no appeal for her. "I come to your recitals."

Miranda, possessed of a beautiful singing voice, responded, "And so you do. Now don't forget our big songfest the third weekend in November. I do wish you'd come to a regular service."

"Can't. Well, I could, but you know I'm a member of the Reverend Jones's flock."

"Oh, Herbie, the silver-tongued! When he climbs up in the pulpit, I think the angels bend down to listen. Still, the Lutheran Church contains many flaws that"—she tried to sound large-minded about it—"are bound to creep in over the centuries."

"Miranda, you know how I am." Harry's tone grew firm. "For some reason I must be today's target. Boom Boom appeared to force a heart-to-heart on me. Large ugh. Then Senator Satterwaite came over, but I didn't give him a chance to turn on the tapedeck under his tongue. And now you."

Miranda squinted. "You get out on the wrong side of bed today?"

"No."

"You shouldn't let Boom Boom control your mood."

"I don't," fired back Harry, who suspected it might be true.

"Uh-huh." This was drenched with meaning. Miranda crossed her arms over her chest.

Harry changed the subject. "You're right, the Valiants have been through a lot. These victories must be sweet."

"What would torment me is not knowing where my mother's body was. We all know she's dead. You can only hope but so long, and it's been five years since Marylou disappeared. But when you don't know how someone died, or where, you can't put it to rest. I can go out and visit my George anytime I want. I like to put flowers on his grave. It helps." George, Miranda's husband, had been dead for nine years. He had been the postmaster at Crozet before Harry took over his job.

"Maybe they don't think about it. They don't talk about it—at least, I've never heard them, but I only know them socially."

"It's there—underneath."

"I don't guess we'll ever know what happened to Marylou. Remember when Mim offered the ten-thousand-dollar reward for any information leading to Marylou's discovery?"

"Everyone played detective. Poor Rick." Miranda thought of the Albemarle County sheriff, Rick Shaw, who had been besieged with crackpot theories.

"After Charley died, Marylou kept company with some unimpressive men. She loved Charles Valiant, and I don't think any man measured up for a long time. Then too, he was only thirty-eight when he died. A massive heart attack. Charley was dead before he hit the ground." Miranda held up her hands, palms outward. "Now I am not sitting in judgment. A woman in her late thirties sliding into her early forties, suddenly alone, is vulnerable, indeed. You may not remember, but she dated that fading movie star, Brandon Miles. He wanted her to bankroll his comeback film. She went through men like popcorn . . . until Mickey Townsend, that is."

"Next race!" Harry got up suddenly. The timber jump was alongside the brush jump.

The fifth race, the $40,000 Virginia Hunt Cup, the final leg of the Virginia Fall Timber Championship Series, provided no problems apart from two riders separating company from their mounts, which served to improve the odds for those still in the saddle. Mickey Townsend and Charles Valiant evidenced no antagonism. Their horses and jockeys were so far apart in the four-mile race that neither could cry foul about the other.

As for Linda Forloines, she had picked up Zack Merchant's other horses and had come in third in the Virginia Hunt Cup.

She'd take home a little change in her pocket, 10 percent of the $4,400 third-prize money.

The sixth race, the first division of the Battleship, named in memory of Mrs. Scott's famous horse, was two miles and one furlong over brush and carried a $6,000 purse. Miranda, weary of the crowd, stayed with Harry. The tension swept over the hill. They could feel the anticipation. Back on the rail, Mim, wound tighter than a piano wire, tried to keep calm. The jockeys circled the paddock. Addie, perched atop Mim's Bazooka, a 16.3-hand gray, would blaze fast and strong if she could keep him focused. She still avoided Chark. Nigel, wearing Mickey Townsend's red silks with the blue sash, joked with her. Both riders looked up when the low gate was opened so they could enter the grassy track. Linda Forloines, in the brown-and-yellow silks of Zack Merchant, spoke to no one. The sixth race would be difficult enough for those jockeys who knew their horses; she didn't. Coty Lamont exuded confidence, smiling to the crowd as he trotted onto the turf.

The gun fired. "They're off!"

It seemed only seconds before the field rounded toward Harry, soared over the east gate fence, and then pounded away.

"Fast pace," Harry remarked to Miranda.

The crowd noise rolled away over the hill, then rose again as the horses appeared where the largest number of spectators waited. Again the noise died away as the field went up the hill and around the far side of the flat track; only the announcer's voice cut through the tension, calling out the positions and the jumps.

Again the rhythm of hoofbeats electrified Harry, and the field flew around the turn, maintaining a scorching pace.

Bazooka, in splendid condition, held steady at fourth. Harry knew from Mim that Addie's strategy, worked out well in advance with Chark, would call for her to make her move at the next to last fence.

As the horses rushed toward her obstacle, she saw Linda Forloines bump Nigel hard. He lurched to the side as his horse stepped off balance.

"Bloody hell!" he shouted.

Linda laughed. Nigel, on a better horse, pulled alongside her, then began to pull away. In front of the fence Harry saw Linda lash out with her left arm and catch Nigel across the face with her whip. Bloody-lipped, Nigel cleared the fence. Linda cleared a split second behind him. She whipped Nigel again, but this time he was ready for her. He'd transferred his whip from his left to his right hand, and he backhanded her across the face, giving her a dose of her own. Linda screamed. Harry and Miranda watched in astonishment as the two jockeys beat at each other away and up the hill.

"Harry, what do you do?"

"Nothing until after the race. Then I'll have to hurry to the tower and file my report. But unless one of them protests, not a thing will happen. If either one does—what a row!"

"Vicious!"

"Linda Forloines?"

"Oh—well, yes, but the other one was almost as bad."

"Yes, but he was in the unenviable position of having to do something or she'd get worse. People like Linda don't understand fair play. They interpret it as weakness. You need to hit them harder than they hit you."

"In a race?" Miranda puffed up the hill behind Harry as the winner was being announced—Adelia Valiant on Bazooka. Tucker, ears back, scampered on ahead.

"In the best of all possible worlds, no, but that's when people like Linda go after you. When they think you can't or won't fight back. I'd have killed her myself."

They reached the tower, Mrs. Hogendobber panting.

"Miranda, climb up here. You're a witness, too."

Miranda stomped up the three flights of stairs to the tower

top where the announcer, Arthur Tetrick, and Colbert Mason, national race director, held sway. Tucker stayed at the foot of the steps.

The horses, cooling down, galloped in front of the stand.

"Harry," Arthur Tetrick said, offering her a drink, "thank you so much for all you've done today. Oh, sorry, Mrs. Hogendobber, I didn't see you."

"Arthur." Harry nodded to Colbert Mason. "Colbert. I'm sorry to report there was a dangerous and unsportsmanlike incident at the east gate jump. Linda Forloines bumped Nigel Danforth. It could have been an accident—"

"These things happen." Colbert, in a genial mood, interrupted, for he wanted to rush down to congratulate Mim Sanburne on the stupendous display of winning two races and placing second in another, all in one day. He was especially pleased that Mim had won the Virginia Hunt Cup.

"But wait, Colbert. Then she struck him across the face with her whip. After the jump they flailed at each other like two boxers. Mrs. Hogendobber witnessed it also."

"Miranda?" Arthur's sandy eyebrows were poised above his tortoise-shell glasses.

"Someone could have been seriously injured out there, or worse," Miranda confirmed.

"I see." Arthur leaned over the desk, shouting down to the second level to the race secretary. "Paul, any protest on this race?"

"No, sir."

Just then Colbert leaned over the stand. "I say . . . ." Now he could see the welts on Nigel's face and his bloody lip as the jockey rode by to the paddock. A look at Linda's face confirmed a battle.

Arthur leaned over to see also. "Good Lord." He shouted, "Nigel Danforth, come here for a moment. Linda Forloines, a word, please."

The two jockeys, neither looking at the other, rode to the

bottom of the tower as their trainers and grooms hurried out to grab the bridles of their horses.

"Have you anything to report on the unusual condition of your faces?" Arthur bellowed.

"No, sir," came the Englishman's reply.

"Linda?" Arthur asked.

She shook her head, saying nothing.

"All right, then." Arthur dismissed them as Mim, floating on a cloud, entered the winner's circle. "Harry, there's nothing I can do under the circumstances, but I have a bad feeling that this isn't over yet. If you'll excuse me, I'm due in the winner's circle. I have the check." He patted his chest pocket. "See you ladies at Mim's party."

As the crowd slowly dispersed, the grooms, jockeys, trainers, and owners went about their tasks, until finally only the race officials remained. Even the political candidates had evaporated. One horse van after another rumbled out of the Madison estate.

Harry, Mrs. Hogendobber, and Tucker hopped into the truck as the sun slipped behind the Blue Ridge Mountains. Darkness folded around them as they slowly cruised down the lane.

"Lights are still on in the big barn," Harry noted. "There's so much to do." The horses required a lot of attention after a race—cold-hosing their legs, checking medications, feeding them, and finally cleaning the tack.

"All done," Miranda sang out.

"Huh?"

"The lights just went out."

"Oh." Harry smiled. "Well, good, someone got to go home early."

An hour later the phone jingled up at Montpelier where Arthur and Colbert had repaired for a bit of warmth, then to collate and fax the day's results to the national office in Elkton, Maryland.

"Hello." Arthur's expression changed so dramatically that Colbert stood to assist him if necessary. "We'll be right over." Arthur carefully replaced the receiver in the cradle.

He ran out to his car with Colbert next to him, headed for the big stable.

3

"Where is he?" Harry grumbled. "You'd think I'd be used to it by now. He's never been on time. Even his own mother admitted he was a week late being born."

"Last time I saw Fair he was checking over that horse with the bowed tendon," Addie said as yet another person came up to congratulate her. "Wherever he is, Nigel's probably with him. He's never on time either."

Mim, champagne glass in hand, raised it. "To the best trainer and jockey in the game, Hip, hip, hooray!"

The assemblage ripped out, "Hip, hip, hooray!"

Chark lifted his glass in response. "To the best owner."

More cheers ricocheted off the tasteful walls of Mim Sanburne's Georgian mansion just northwest of Crozet.

Her husband, Jim, jovially mixed with the guests as servants in livery provided champagne—Louis Roederer Cristal, caviar, sliced chicken, smoked turkey, delicately cured hams, succotash, spoon bread, and desserts that packed a megaton calorie blast.

Many of the serving staff were University of Virginia students. Even with her vast wealth Mim ran a tight ship, and given Social Security, withholding taxes, workers' compensation, and health insurance to pay, she wasn't about to bloat her budget with lots of salaries. She hired for occasions like this, the rest of the time making do with a cook, a butler, and a maid. A farm manager and two full-time laborers rounded out the payroll.

Charles and Adelia Valiant trained her horses, but they trained other people's as well. Once a month Mim received an itemized bill. Since they enjoyed the use of her facilities for half the year, Mim was granted a deep discount. The other half of the year the Valiants wintered and trained in Aiken, South Carolina.

Mim called steeplechasers slow gypsies since they stayed for four to six months and then moved on.

The Reverend Herbert Jones, tinkling ice cubes in his glass, joined Harry as Addie was pulled away by another celebrant.

"Beautiful day. 'Course, you never know with Montpelier. I've stood in the snow, the rain, and I've basked in seventy-four degrees and sunshine. Today was one of the best."

"Pretty good." Harry smiled.

Herb watched Boom Boom Craycroft out of the corner of his eye. She worked the room, moving in a semicircle toward Harry. "Boom Boom's tacking your way." He lowered his gravelly voice.

"Not again."

"Oh?" His eyebrows shot upward.

"She freely shared her innermost feelings with me between the first and second races. Forgiveness and redemption are just around the corner if I'll join Lifeline."

"I thought forgiveness and redemption were mine to dispense." The Reverend Jones laughed at himself. "Well, now, let her ramble. Who knows, maybe this Lifeline really has helped her in some way. I prefer prayer myself."

In the background the phone rang. Rick Shaw, the Sheriff of Albemarle County, was summoned to it.

"He never gets a break. Coop neither," Harry observed. Shaw's deputy was Cynthia Cooper.

"Lots of drunks on the road after Montpelier."

"They don't need the races for an excuse. I figure they IV the stuff."

Rick hung up the phone, whispered something to Mim, and left the party. Mim's face registered shock. Then she quickly regained her social mask.

4

Sheriff Rick Shaw, penlight in hand, pulled back an eyelid. Nothing. He continued carefully examining the body before him, with Dr. Larry Johnson observing. Shaw didn't want the corpse moved yet.

Nigel Danforth sat exactly as Fair Haristeen had found him—upright on a tack trunk, wearing his red silks with the blue sash. A knife was plunged through his heart.

Although the murder appeared to have taken place in Orange County and Rick Shaw was sheriff of the adjoining county, Orange's sheriff, Frank Yancey, had called him in. Rick had handled more murders than he had, and this one was a puzzle, especially since the knife had been plunged through a playing card, the Queen of Clubs, which was placed over Nigel's heart.

Fair, arms crossed, watched, his face still chalky white.

"His body was *exactly* like this when you found him?" Rick asked the lanky vet.

"Yes."

"See anything, anyone?"

"No, I walked in through the north doors and turned on the lights. All the horses should have been removed by then but I thought I'd double-check. He was sitting there. I didn't know anything was wrong, although I thought it was peculiar that he'd sit in the dark. I called to him, and he didn't answer. When I drew closer, I saw the knife sticking out of his chest. I felt his pulse. Goner."

"What about his body temperature when you touched him?"

"Still warm, Larry. Maybe he had been dead an hour. His extremities hadn't started to fill with fluid. He really looked as though he was just sitting there."

"No sign of anybody—anything?" Rick sighed. He'd known Fair for years, respected him as a vet and therefore as a scientific man. Fair's recollections counted heavily in Rick's book.

"None in the barn. A few big vans pulled out across the road. Their noise could have covered someone running away. I checked the stalls, I climbed into the hayloft, tack room. Nothing, Sheriff."

"The card's a neat trick." Frank Yancey shook his head. "Maybe it's a payback for a gambling debt."

"Helluva payback," Larry Johnson said.

"Helluva debt?" Frank gestured, his hands held upward.

"Frank, you've got the photos and prints you need?" Rick continued when Frank nodded in the affirmative, "Well, let's remove the body then. Do you mind if Larry sits in on the autopsy?"

"No, no, I'd be glad to have him there."

"Guess I can't keep this out of the papers." George Miller, Orange's mayor, unconsciously wrung his hands. He had arrived minutes after Yancey's call. "Colbert Mason and Arthur Tetrick were horrified, but they turned cagey pretty fast. They especially didn't want a photo of the body to get into the papers."

"One murder in the steeplechase world doesn't mean it's seething with corruption," Larry remarked sensibly.

"Five years ago there was another murder." Fair's deep baritone sounded sepulchral in the barn.

"What are you talking about?" Frank leaned forward.

"Marylou Valiant."

"Never found her, did they?" Frank Yancey blinked, remembering.

"No," Rick answered. "We know of no connection to steeplechasing other than that she owned a good string of horses. That's not a motive for murder. There are some who think she's not dead. She just walked away from her life."

"They say that about Elvis, too," Fair replied. "Anyone told Adelia Valiant?"

"Why?" Frank and George said simultaneously.

"She was dating Danforth . . . pretty serious, I think."

Frank eyed the big man. "Well—can you tell her?"

Rick and Fair glanced at each other, then at Larry.

"I'll tell her," the old doctor said gently. "But I'd like you fellows with me. And Rick, don't jump right in, okay?"

The sheriff grimaced. He tried to be sensitive, but the drive to catch a murderer could override his efforts. "Yeah, yeah."

Two ambulance attendants rolled the gurney into the barn from the south doors as Fair, Larry, and Rick left through the north.

Rick turned to Fair. "Was he a good jockey?"

"Not bad."

5

Will Forloines's face fell longer and longer. His color deepened. He couldn't hold it in any longer. "That was a damn fool thing you did to Nigel."

"Bullshit."

"Don't cuss at me, Linda. I can still kick your ass into next week."

"I love it when you get mad." She sarcastically parodied old movies.

He shifted his eyes from the road to her. "You're lucky he didn't file a complaint."

"Had him by the short hairs."

"Oh—and what if he'd nailed you? You didn't know he wouldn't file against you."

"Will, let me do the thinking."

The wheel of the brand-new Nissan dropped off the road. Will quickly returned his gaze to the road. "You take too many chances. One of these days it will backfire."

"Wimp." While she insulted him, she took the precaution of dropping her hand into his lap.

"Things are going good right now. I don't want them screwed up."

"Will, relax. Drive. And listen." She exhaled through her nose. "Nigel Danforth has bought a shitload of cocaine over the last two months. He can't squeal."

"The hell he can't. He can finger us as the dealers."

"Better to be mad at me over one race than lose his connection. And if he blew the whistle on us, he'd be blowing it on himself—and his girlfriend. All that money isn't coming from race purses."

Will drove a few minutes. "Yeah, but you're cutting it close."

"Paid for this truck." She moved closer to him.

"Linda, you"—he sputtered—"you take too many risks."

"The risk is the rush."

"Not for me, Babe. The money is the rush."

"And we're sitting in the middle of it. Dr. D'Angelo's loaded, and he's dumb as a post."

"No, he's not," Will contradicted her. "He's dumb about horses. He's not dumb about his job or he wouldn't have made all that money. Sooner or later he'll figure things out if you try to sell him too many horses at once. Take it slow. I'd like to live in one place for a couple of years."

She waited a moment. "Sure."

As this was said with no conviction, Will, irritated, shot back, "I like where we live."

She whispered in his ear, enjoying her disagreement with him just so she could "win" the argument, get him under her control. She might have loved her husband, but she truly needed him. He was so easy to manipulate that it made her feel powerful and smart. "We'll make so much money we can buy our own farm."

"Yeah . . ." His voice trailed off.

She smiled. "Nigel will forget all about it. I guarantee it. He owes me for a kilo. He's coming up tomorrow to pay off the rest of it. I got part of the money today before the race." She laughed, "Bet he couldn't believe it when I whipped him. He'll forget though. He'll be so full of toot, I'll be his best friend."

6

When Fair Haristeen walked through the door of Mim's party, Harry determined to pay no attention to him. However, she couldn't help noticing his jaw muscles tightening, which she recognized as a sign of distress. Dr. Larry Johnson and Sheriff Rick Shaw flanked him, and Larry headed straight for Addie Valiant. Fair turned to follow them.

"Doom and gloom," Susan Tucker observed.

"Hope someone didn't lose a horse," Harry said.

"I know. It was such an unusual Montpelier. The worst was that bowed tendon, pretty fabulous when you consider some of the accidents in the past. But maybe it's because the course is so difficult. People are careful."

"Huh?"

"Harry, are you paying attention?" her best friend said.

"Yes, but I was thinking I'd have to head home before too long. Miranda closes up shop by nine, you know." Harry referred to Miranda's lifelong habit of early retirement and early rising.

"Well, as I was saying before you drifted off, because the course is demanding jockeys stay focused. Sometimes when it's a bit easy they get sloppy."

"Mom, I'm hungry," Tucker pleaded.

Susan dropped a piece of cake for the dog.

"Susan, you spoil Tucker worse than I do." It was Susan who had bred the corgi. Harry noticed Larry taking Addie by the elbow and Rick whispering in Mim's ear. "Something's going on. Damn, I hope it's not some kind of late protest. I wouldn't put anything past Mickey Townsend. He hates to lose."

Five minutes passed before a howl of pain sounded from the library. All conversation stopped. Mim, holding her husband's hand, put her other hand on Chark's shoulder, guiding him to the library. Larry had wanted to inform Addie before bringing her brother into it. The confusion and concern on Chark's face upon hearing his sister's cry alerted even the thickest person in the room to impending sorrow.

Mim shut the library doors behind her. All eyes were now on her. She walked over to the three-sash window and collected herself. Then, her husband at her side, she addressed the gathering.

"I regret to inform you that there appears to have been a"— she cleared her throat—"murder at Montpelier." A gasp went up from the crowd. "Nigel Danforth, the English jockey riding for Mickey Townsend, was found dead this evening in the main stable. Sheriff Shaw says they know very little at this time. He asks for your patience and cooperation over the next few days as he will be calling upon some of us. I'm afraid the party is over, but I want to thank you for celebrating what has been a joyous day— until now." She opened her hands as if in benediction.

Little Marilyn, unable to conceal her agitation, called out. "Mummy, how was he killed?"

"Stabbed through the heart."

"Good God!" Herbie Jones exclaimed, and after that the noise was deafening as everyone talked at once.

"That explains it," Susan said to Harry, who understood she was referring to Fair's miserable countenance. "How about we pay our respects to our hostess and leave?"

Miranda bustled over. "My word, how awful, and how awful for Mim, too. It certainly casts a pall on her triumph. Harry, Herbie's offered to escort me home so I'm leaving with him."

"Fine. I'll see you on Monday."

"Good, then I'll ride with you." Susan piped up then called to her teenaged son, Danny, "One dent in that car and you are toast."

On the way home Harry, Susan, and Tee Tucker wondered why a jockey would be killed after the races. They ran through the usual causes of death in America: money, love, drugs, and gambling. Since they knew little about Nigel, they soon dropped the speculation.

"Another body blow for Addie." Harry cupped her hand under her chin and stared out the window into the sheltering darkness.

"Ever notice how some people are plagued with bad luck and tragedy?"

"*King Lear?*" Harry quipped, not meaning to sound flippant. "Sorry."

"I'm not sure I will ever understand how your mind works," Susan wryly said to her friend.

"There are days when it doesn't work at all."

"Tell me about it. Especially after you have children. What's left of your mind flies out the window." As a mother of two teenagers, Susan both endured and enjoyed her offspring. She pulled down the long driveway to Harry's farm.

"Bet you Boom Boom makes a beeline for Addie once she emerges from the library," Harry grumbled.

"Mim will shoo her out first."

"Ha!" Harry said derisively. "Boom Boom will volunteer to clean up after the party, the sneak. Bet you she pounces on Addie with an invitation to join her at Lifeline. Bloodsucker."

"She does seem to draw sustenance from other people's problems." Susan inhaled. "But then again this program of self-exposure or whatever it is *has* calmed her down."

"I don't believe it."

"You wouldn't." Susan stopped at the screened door at the back of the house. Mrs. Murphy was visible in the window and then disappeared. "A pussycat is anxious to see you."

"Come on in. She wants to see you, too. I'll feed her, then carry you home."

"Good. Then I can look for my black sweater. I know I left it here."

"Susan, I swear I've searched for it. It's not here."

"You won't believe what happened," Tucker called out, eager to tell her friend everything and also eager to watch Mrs. Murphy fume because she'd missed it.

"Tucker, hush." Harry opened the door and ushered Susan inside.

The temperature was in the forties and dropping, and the chill nipped at Harry's heels, so she hurried along behind her friend. The kitchen, deceptively calm, lured her into comfort.

"Here, kitty, kitty."

"*I hate you*," Mrs. Murphy called from the bedroom.

Harry walked into the living room followed by Tucker and Susan.

"Uh-oh." Tucker laid her ears flat.

Susan gasped, "Berlin, 1945!"

The arm of the sofa had been shredded, methodically destroyed. Lamps smashed to the ground bore witness to the tiger

cat's fury. She had also had the presence of mind to scratch, tear, and bite magazines, the newspapers, and a forlorn novel that rested on Harry's wing chair. The pièce de résistance was one curtain, yanked full force, dangling half on and half off the rod.

Harry's mouth dangled almost in imitation of the curtain. She slapped her hands together in outrage.

"Mrs. Murphy, you come out here."

"In a pig's eye." The cat's voice was shrill.

"I know where you're hiding. You aren't that original, you little shit!" Harry tore into her bedroom, clicked on the light, dropped to her knees, and lifted up the dust ruffles. Sure enough, a pair of gleaming green eyes at the furthest recesses of the bed stared back at her.

"I will skin you alive!" Harry exploded.

"You're in deep doo-doo," Tucker whined.

"She'll forget it by morning," came the saucy reply.

"I don't think so. You've wrecked the house."

"I know nothing about it."

7

Since Harry had closed off the animal door, Mrs. Murphy stayed inside. She would have preferred to go out to the barn just in case Harry woke up mad. As it was she prudently waited until she heard the cat food can being opened before she tiptoed into the kitchen.

"You're impossible." Harry, good humor restored by a sound night's sleep, scratched the cat at the base of her tail.

"I hate it when you leave me."

As Harry dished out shrimp and cod into a bowl upon which was prophetically written UPHOLSTERY DESTROYER, Tucker circled her mother's legs.

"Why do you feed her first? Especially after what she's done."

"I'll get to you."

"She feeds me first because I'm so fascinating."

"*Gag me.*" Tucker remembered that the cat knew nothing of yesterday's bizarre event. She forgot her irritation as she settled into the pleasure of tormenting Mrs. Murphy. "*Beautiful day at the races.*"

"*Shut up.*"

"*Boom Boom swept down on Mom, though.*"

Mrs. Murphy, on the counter, turned her head from her food bowl. "*Oh, did Mom cuss her out?*"

"*Nah.*" Tucker jammed her long nose into the canned beef food mixed into crunchies.

Harry brewed tea and rummaged around for odds and ends to toss into an omelet while the animals chatted. Tucker finished her food so quickly it barely impeded her conversational abilities.

The tiger, delicate in her eating habits, paused between mouthfuls, gently brushing her whiskers in case some food was on them. She surveyed the damage in the living room without a twinge of guilt. "*How'd Mim do?*"

"*Second in the second race, won the fourth race, and she won the big one.*"

"*Wow.*" She swatted her food bowl, angry all over again at being left out. "*I grew up with horses. I don't know why Mother thinks I won't behave myself at Montpelier. As if I've never seen a crowd before.*"

"*You haven't. Not that big.*" Tucker licked her lips, relishing her breakfast and the cat's discomfort.

"*I can handle it!*" She glared down at the dog. "*I ride in cars better than you do. I don't bark. I don't ask to be fed every fifteen minutes, and I don't whine to go to the bathroom.*"

"*No, you just do it under the seat.*"

Mrs. Murphy spit, her white fangs quite impressive. "*No fair. I was sick and we were on our way to the vet.*"

"*Yeah, yeah. Tapeworms. I'm tired of that excuse.*"

The pretty feline shuddered. "*I hate those tapeworm shots, but they do work. Haven't had a bit of trouble since. Of course, flea season is over.*"

She had heard the vet explain that some fleas carry the tapeworm larvae. When animals bite the spot where a flea has bitten them, they occasionally ingest an infected flea, starting the cycle wherein the parasite winds up in their intestines. Both cat and dog understood the problem, but when a flea bites, it's hard not to bite back.

Harry sat down to her hot omelet. Mrs. Murphy kept her company on the other side of the plate.

"I am not giving you any, Murphy. In fact, I'm not forking over one more morsel of food for days—not until I clean up the wreckage of this house. I've half a mind to leave you home from work tomorrow, but you'd run another demolition derby."

"*Damn right.*"

Tucker, annoyed at not being able to sit on the table, plopped under Harry's chair, then rose again to sit by her mother's knee. "*Oh, Murph, one little thing . . . a jockey was murdered last night at the Montpelier stable, the big old one.*"

The green eyes grew larger, and the animal leaned over the table. "*What?*"

"Mrs. Murphy, control yourself." Harry reached over to pet the cat, who fluffed her fur.

"*A jockey, Nigel somebody or other—we don't really know him although Adelia Valiant does—he was stabbed. Right through the heart.*" Tucker savored this last detail.

"*You waited all this time to tell me?*" Murphy unleashed her claws, then retracted them.

Tucker smiled. "*Next time you tell me cats are smarter than dogs, just remember I know some things you don't.*"

Murphy jumped down from the table, put her face right up into Tucker's, and growled. "*Don't mess with me, buster. You get to go with Mom to the races. You come home and tell me nothing until now. I would have told you straightaway.*"

The little dog held her ground. "*Maybe you would and maybe you wouldn't.*"

"*When have I withheld important news from you?*"

"*The time you and Pewter stole roast beef from the store.*"

"*That was different. Besides, you know Pewter is obsessed with food. If I hadn't helped her steal that roast beef, I wouldn't have gotten one measly bite of* it. *She would have stolen it herself, but she's too fat to squeeze into the case. That's different."*

"No, it isn't."

Harry observed the Mexican standoff. "What's got into you two this morning?"

"*Nothing.*" Murphy stalked out of the room, taking a swipe at Tucker's rear end when the dog's head was turned.

Harry prudently reached down and grabbed Tucker's collar. "Ignore her."

"*With pleasure.*"

The phone rang. Harry answered it.

"Sorry to call you so early on a Sunday morning," Deputy Cynthia Cooper apologized. "Boss wants me to ask you some questions about the races yesterday."

"Sure. Want to come out here?"

"Wish I could. You ready?"

"Yes."

"What do you know about Nigel Danforth?"

"Not much, Coop. He's a new jockey on the circuit, not attached to a particular stable. What we call a pickup rider or a catch rider. I met him briefly yesterday."

Hearing this, Mrs. Murphy sourly returned to the kitchen. She didn't so much as glance at Tucker when she passed the dog, also eavesdropping.

"*Crab.*"

"*Selfish,*" the cat shot back.

"Did you ever speak to Nigel?"

"Just a 'pleased to meet you.' "

"Do you know anything about his relationship with Addie?"

"She told me yesterday morning that she liked him." Harry thought a minute. "She intimated that she might be falling in love with him, and she wanted us to get together after the races at the party."

"Did you?"

"Well, I was at Mim's party. Addie was there, too." She

added, "First, though, I waited on standby at the tower after the last race to see if Arthur Tetrick or Mr. Mason wanted me to file a report. There was a nasty incident at my fence, the east gate fence, between Nigel Danforth and Linda Forloines."

"I'm all ears."

Harry could hear Cooper scribbling as she described the incident.

"That's quite serious, isn't it? I mean, couldn't they get suspended?"

"Yes. I told Arthur and Colbert Mason, he's the national director, but I guess you know that by now. Neither of the jockeys lodged a protest, though. Without a protest there's nothing the officials can do."

"Who has the authority in a situation like that?"

"The race director. In this case, Arthur."

"Why wouldn't Arthur Tetrick haul both their asses in?"

"That's a good question, Coop." Harry sipped her tea. "But I can give you an opinion—not an answer, just an opinion."

"*We want to hear it,*" the cat and dog said, too.

"Shoot."

"Well, all sports have umpires, referees, judges to see that mayhem is kept to a minimum. But sometimes you have to let the antagonists settle it themselves. Rough justice."

"Expand."

"If an official steps in, it can reach a point where Jockey A is being protected too much. I mean, Coop, if you're going to go out there, then you've got to take your lumps, and part of it is that some riders are down and dirty. If they think no one is looking, they'll foul you."

"But you were looking."

"I don't understand that." Harry recalled the brazenness of the situation.

"Is Linda dumb?"

"Far from it. She's a low-rent, lying, cunning bitch."

"Hey, don't keep your feelings to yourself," Cynthia teased her.

Harry laughed. "There are few people that I despise on this earth, but she's one of them."

"Why?"

"I saw her deliberately lame a horse temporarily, then lie about it to Mim. She took the horse off Mim's hands and sold it at a profit to a trainer out of state. She didn't know that I saw her. I—well, it doesn't matter. You get the point."

"But she's not stupid, so why would she commit a flagrant foul, one that could get her suspended? And right in front of you?"

"It doesn't figure." Harry was stumped.

Coop flipped through her notes. "She can't keep a job, any job, longer than a year. That could mean a lot of things, but one thing it most certainly means is, she can't get along with people over an extended period of time."

"Obviously, she couldn't get along with Nigel Danforth." Harry sipped her tea again.

"Do you have any idea, I don't care how crazy it sounds, why Linda Forloines would hit Nigel in the face?"

Harry played with the long cord of the phone. "I don't have any idea, unless they were enemies—apart from being competitors, I mean. The only other thing I can tell you—just popped into my head—is that people say Linda deals drugs. No one's ever pinned it on her though."

"Heard that, too," Cooper replied. "I'll be back at you later. Sorry to intrude on you so early, but I know you're out before sunup most days. Pretty crisp this morning."

"I'll wear my woollies. Let me ask you a question."

"Okay."

"Can everyone account for their whereabouts at the time of the murder?"

"No," Cooper flatly stated. "We've got a good idea when he

died, within a twenty-minute frame, but really—anybody could have had the time to skip in there and kill him. The commotion of the event wears people out, dulls their senses, to say nothing of the drinking."

"That's the truth. Well, if I think of anything I'll call. I'm glad to help."

Harry hung up the phone after good-byes. She liked Cynthia, and over the years they'd become friends.

"*I couldn't hear what Cynthia was saying. Tell me,*" Murphy demanded.

Harry, cup poised before her lips, put it back down in the saucer. "You know, it *doesn't* make sense. It doesn't make a bit of sense that Linda Forloines would lay into Nigel Danforth right in front of me."

"*What?*" Mrs. Murphy, beside herself with curiosity, rubbed Harry's arm since she had jumped back on the counter.

"*I'll tell you all about that.*" Tucker promised importantly as Harry pulled on an ancient cashmere sweater, slapped the old cowboy hat on her head, and slipped her arms through her down vest.

"Come on, kids, time to rock and roll." Harry opened the door. They stepped out into the frosty November morning to start the chores.

8

Will Forloines stood up when Linda sauntered out of Sheriff Frank Yancey's office. At first the husband and wife had balked at being questioned individually, but finally they gave in. It would look worse if they didn't cooperate.

Will had been surprised at the blandness of Sheriff Yancey's questions—partly because he was scared the cops might be on to their drug dealing. *Where were you at seven on the night of the murder? How well did you know the deceased?* That sort of thing.

Linda turned and smiled at Frank, who smiled back and shut his door.

Will handed Linda her coat and they opened the door. The day, cool but bright, might warm up a bit.

Not until they were in the truck did they speak.

"What did he ask you?" Will didn't start the motor.

"Nothing much." Her upturned nose in profile resembled a tiny ski jump.

"Well, what?" Will demanded.

"Where was I? I told him in the van with Mickey Townsend. The truth."

"What else?" He cranked the truck.

"He wanted to know why I hit Nigel in the face with my whip before the east gate jump."

"And?" Will, agitated, pressed down so hard on the accelerator he had to brake, which threw them forward. "Sorry."

"I said he bumped me, he'd been bumping me and I was damned sick of it. But not sick enough to kill him for it."

"And?"

"That was it."

"You were in there for half an hour, Linda. There had to be more to it than that. Things don't look so good for us. I told you not to take chances. You're a suspect."

She ignored that. "We passed the time of day. He asked how long I'd been riding. Where did I learn? Nothing to the point. I hit the guy in the face. That doesn't mean I killed him."

"I don't like it."

"Hey, who does?"

Will thought for a moment. "Did he ask anything about drugs? I mean, what if Nigel had coke in his system."

"No, he didn't ask anything like that." She folded her hands and gloated. "I did say that since Fair Haristeen was the person who found Nigel, he ought to be investigated. I hinted that Fair's been doping horses. Just enough of a hint to send him on a wild-goose chase."

Will looked at her out of the corner of his eye. He'd grown accustomed to her habitual lying. "Anyone who knows Fair Haristeen won't believe it."

"Hey, it'll waste some of their time."

"You sure he didn't ask anything tricky?" His voice hardened.

"No, goddammit. Why are you on my case?"

"Because he split us up to see if our stories conflicted."

"I don't have any stories except about Fair. I'll get even with him yet, and Mim, too, the rich bitch."

"I wouldn't worry about them now."

Her eyes narrowed. "She fired you, too."

"Someone fires you, you say you quit. People believe what they want to believe. We make good money now. Revenge takes too much time."

She smirked. "Everyone thinks Mim ran us out of business and that we're broke. Bet their eyes fell out of their heads when we drove into Montpelier in a brand-new truck."

She hadn't reckoned on most people being more involved with the races than with her. Few had noticed their new truck, but then Linda related everything to herself.

"You really didn't tell him anything?" A pleading note crept into his voice.

"NO! If you're getting weak-kneed, then stay out of it. I'll do it. Jesus, Will."

"Okay, okay." They headed up Route 15, north. "Our supplier isn't going to be happy if our names get in the paper. Just makes me nervous."

"The sheriff asked me one weird question." She observed his knuckles whiten as he gripped the steering wheel. "Nothing much. But he asked me if I knew anything about Nigel's green card."

"His immigration card? You mean his right-to-work card?"

"Yeah, the green card." She shrugged. "Said I never saw it. Wonder why he'd ask about that?"

9

Mondays Harry and Mrs. Hogendobber shoveled the mail.
Mounds of catalogs, postcards, bills, and letters filled the canvas
mail cart and spilled onto the wooden floor, polished by years of
use.

Mrs. Murphy, disgruntled because she couldn't snuggle in
the mail cart, zipped out via the animal door installed for her
convenience at the back. Tucker snored, asleep on her side in the
middle of the floor where she could create the greatest obstacle.
The cat didn't wake her.

Truth be told, she loved Tucker, but dogs, even Tucker, got
on her nerves. They were so straightforward. Mrs. Murphy enjoyed nuance and quiet. Tucker tended to babble.

The door flapped behind her. She sat on the back stoop of
the post office surveying the alleyway that divided the row of old

business buildings from private backyards. Mrs. Hogendobber's yard sat directly behind the post office. Her garden, mulched and fertilized, usually a source of color, had yielded to winter. She'd clipped off her last blooming of mums.

The cat breathed in that peculiar odor of dying leaves and moist earth. As it was eleven A.M. the frost had melted and the scent of wild animals dissipated with it. Mrs. Murphy loved to hunt in the fall and winter because it was easy to track by scent.

She ruffled out her fur to ward off the chill, then marched over to Market Shiflett's store.

As she approached the back door she hollered, *"Pewter, Pewter, Motor Scooter, come out and play!"*

The animals' door, newly installed at the grocery store, swung open. Pewter rolled out like a gray cannonball.

"Everyone's ass over tit today."

Mrs. Murphy agreed. *"Mondays put humans in a foul mood. Ever notice?"*

"There is that, but the stabbing of that jockey sure has tongues wagging." She lifted her head straight up in the air. *"Let's go root around under Mrs. Hogendobber's porch."*

The two bounded across the alley and ducked under Miranda's porch.

"He was here again last night." Pewter's pupils grew large.

Mrs. Murphy sniffed. *"Like a skunk only, umm, sweeter."* She stepped forward and caught her whiskers in cobwebs. *"I hate spiders!"* She shot out from under the porch.

"Ha, ha." Pewter followed her, highly amused at the cobwebs draped over her friend's whiskers and face. *"You look like a ghost."*

"Least I'm not fat."

Pewter, nonplussed, replied, *"I'm not fat, just round."* She moseyed over to the garden. *"Bet Mrs. H. would have a major hissy if she knew a fox visited her nightly."*

"Pickings must be good."

"I wouldn't want to be undomesticated," Pewter, fond of cooked foods, revealed.

"You sit in that store and dream on. I've never once thought of that."

"Know what else I've thought about?" Pewter didn't wait for a reply. "Sushi. What Crozet needs is a good sushi bar. Imagine fresh tuna every day. Now I enjoy tuna from the can, I prefer it packed lightly, not in heavy oil, mind you. But fresh tuna . . . heaven."

The tiger licked the side of her right paw and swept it up over her ears. "Would we have to use chopsticks?"

"Very funny. I bet I could steal sushi from a pair of chopsticks on their way to some dope's mouth." She imitated her stealing motion, one swift swipe of the paw, claws extended. She shuddered with delight at the thought of it.

"Hey, look." Mrs. Murphy intruded on Pewter's reverie.

Both cats watched Addie Valiant drive up and park behind the post office. She closed the door of her blue Subaru station wagon, the back jammed with tack, wraps, saddle pads, and other equine odds and ends. Turning up the collar of her heavy shirt, she knocked on the back door of the post office, listened, then opened the door.

"Let's go." Murphy ran across the yard.

"What for?" Pewter didn't budge.

"The dead jockey was her boyfriend."

"Oh." Pewter hurried to catch up. Both cats hit the animal door simultaneously, spit at one another, then Murphy slipped in first, a disgruntled Pewter literally on her tail.

Murphy had washed only half her face; the other half was resplendent with cobwebs.

Addie pulled her mail from the back of her mailbox.

Harry checked through the magazine pile to see if anything was there for her.

"Now, honey, you let me know if there's anything we can do. Anything at all." Miranda handed Addie a bun with an orange glaze. An excellent baker, she made a little money on the side by baking for Market Shiflett's store.

"I'm not hungry, thank you."

"I am," Pewter purred.

Tucker, awake now, scrambled to her feet. "Me, too." She noticed Mrs. Murphy's face. "Halloween's over."

Harry noticed at the same time. "Where have you been?"

"Under Miranda's porch."

Harry scooped up the pretty cat, grabbed a paper towel, and wiped off the cobwebs, not as simple as she thought since they were sticky.

Addie dropped into a chair. "Mind if I sit a minute? I'm tired."

"Shocks will do that to you." Miranda patted her on the back.

"Yeah—I know. I guess I didn't think there were any left for me."

"Life has a funny way of being loaded with surprises, good and bad," the kindly woman said.

"Is anyone going to eat that orange bun?" Pewter asked.

"Chatty Cathy." Harry scratched the gray cat behind the ears.

Miranda pulled little pieces of the bun apart and munched on them.

Pewter let out a wail. "Give me some!"

Miranda ignored this so Pewter scrambled onto a chair and thence onto the small table in the back where the buns rested enticingly on a white plate. She licked off the icing while the humans, deep in conversation, never noticed. Mrs. Murphy, not to be outdone, joined her friend.

Tucker complained bitterly. Murphy batted a hardened bit of icing off the table to the dog to shut her up. If she kept up her racket, the humans might notice their uninvited snack.

"They asked me so many questions they made me dizzy." The young woman's hands fluttered to her face. "I couldn't answer half of them. I wasn't much help. They pumped Chark pretty hard, too."

"Rick Shaw said that Frank Yancey's an okay guy, so he was just asking what he had to, I guess." Harry wanted to be helpful, but she didn't know what to do or say.

Addie's big blue eyes misted over. "I was just getting to know him so—"

"Of course, of course." Miranda patted her hand this time. "How long had you known him?"

"Two months, give or take a week. I met him at the Fair Hill races and whammo!" She smacked her hands together.

"Happens that way sometimes." Harry smiled.

"We had so much in common. Horses. Horses and horses," Addie said. "He taught me a lot. You know how some people keep what they know to themselves? Won't share anything. Not Nigel. He was happy to teach me, and he was just as happy to learn from me too."

"Sounds like a lovely young man," Miranda, ever the romantic, replied soothingly.

Harry, far less romantic, nonetheless wanted to be supportive, but her inquiring nature couldn't be suppressed for long. "Do you think he had enemies?"

"Harry, you sound like Frank Yancey." Addie crossed one leg over the other, then winced.

"What'd you do?" Miranda solicitously inquired.

"Knees. They take a beating out there, you know." She turned back to Harry. "As far as I know he didn't have enemies. No one knew him long enough, and besides, he was fun, a real positive person." She paused. "Everyone's got some enemies though."

"His poor parents in England." Miranda shook her head.

"Hadn't thought of that," Harry said. "Do you have any idea why this happened?" Her curiosity had surged.

"No." Addie got up. "Everyone is asking me that."

"I'm sorry. But it's natural."

"I hope whoever killed him rots in hell!" Addie flared, then wiped away the unexpected tears.

" 'Whoever sheds the blood of man, by man shall his blood be shed; for God made man in His own image,' " Mrs. Hogendobber quoted from Genesis.

"I'll happily shed blood." Addie clamped down her lips.

"What do you mean?" Harry asked.

"I mean, if I find the killer first . . ."

"Don't say that," Miranda blurted out.

"Yeah, don't." Harry seconded her older friend's feeling.

"I don't give a damn. If the killer is caught, he'll go to trial. Lots of money will get spent, and the system is so corrupt that he probably won't get convicted, and if he does he'll be out on parole in no time. It's a farce."

Much as Harry tended to agree, she didn't want to encourage Addie to murder. "You know, the scary part is, what if you do find the killer, or get close? What if he turns on you, Addie? Stay out of it. You liked this guy, but you didn't know him well enough to die for him."

"Harry, you can fall in love in an instant. I did."

"Oh, Addie . . ." Harry's voice trailed off.

Miranda draped her arm over Addie's thin shoulder. "Harry's not trying to argue with you or upset you, honey. She doesn't want you to do something impulsive that could ruin your life. And I agree. Neither one of us wants you to expose yourself to danger. After all, no one knows why Nigel was killed. It's not just the who, it's the why, you see. That's where the danger lies."

Addie cried again. "You're right. I know you're right."

Both women comforted her as best they could. When Addie left the post office, she passed the now empty white plate. The cats had fallen asleep next to the scene of their crime.

10

Work continued despite the personal sorrow Adelia Valiant had to absorb. Horses needed to be fed, watered, exercised, groomed, turned out, and talked to over a stall door. The routine, oddly consoling, numbed her mind.

Mim told her to take time off if she needed it, but Addie kept riding. After all, she and her brother had other clients to serve, and when people pay you money, they expect results.

The Valiant fortune, some eighteen million and growing due to good investments directed by Arthur Tetrick, should have ensured that Adelia and Charles Valiant need never labor for their bread and butter.

But Marylou had witnessed the dismal effects of wrapping children in wads of money to soften the hard knocks of life. She didn't want her children to become the weak, petty tyrants she had often observed. She wanted to give them grit.

Enough was drawn annually from the trust fund to pay for lodging, cars, clothes, the necessities. This forced her children to work if they wanted more. If they turned into gilded turnips after Adelia's maturity, so be it.

As it happened, both sister and brother loved their work. There was no doubt in either of their minds that they'd continue working once the inheritance was theirs. They might build a good stable of their own, but they'd continue to train and ride.

Addie's past drug problems had more to do with her personality than with her background. Plenty of poor kids ran aground on drugs too. And plenty of poor kids spent their money as soon as they picked up their paycheck. Addie's impulsiveness and desire for a good time had little to do with class.

Addie wiped down the last horse of the day, a leggy gray, as the white Southern States delivery truck rolled down the drive.

"Feed man."

Chark, at the other end of the barn, called out, "I'll attend to it. You finish up what you're doing."

As Addie rubbed blue mineral ice on the gray's legs, she could hear the metal door clang up on the truck, the dolly clunk when it hit the ground, and the grunts of her brother and the delivery man as they loaded fifty-pound sacks of 14 percent protein sweet feed onto the dolly.

After filling up the zinc-lined feed bins—Mim thought of everything in her stable, but still the mice attacked—the delivery man murmured something to Chark and then drove off.

As her brother, a medium-built, well-proportioned man, ambled toward her, Addie asked, "Are we behind on the bill?"

"Up to date—" He smiled. "—for a change."

"What did he want then?"

"Nothing. Said he was sorry to hear about your friend."

The lines around her mouth relaxed. "That was kind of him. People surprise me."

"Yeah." Chark jammed his hands in his jeans. "Sis, I'm sorry that you're sorry, if you know what I mean, but I didn't like Nigel, and you know it, so I can't be a hypocrite now. Not that I wished him dead."

"You never gave him a chance."

"Oil and water." He ground his heel into the macadam aisle.

She led the gray back to his stall. "You don't much like any man I date."

"You don't much have good taste." Chark sounded harsher than he meant to sound. "Oh, hell, I'm sorry. You have to kiss them, I don't." He stopped making circles off his heel. "Nigel was a fake."

"You hate English accents."

"That I do. They smack of superiority, you know, talking through their noses and telling us how they gallop on the downs of Exmoor. This is America, and I'll train my way."

She put her hands on her hips. "Thought we settled that in 1776. You don't like anyone telling you what to do or making a suggestion that you perceive as a veiled criticism."

"I listen to you." His eyes, almond-shaped like his sister's, darkened.

"Sometimes"—she restlessly jammed her hands in her pockets—"you treated Nigel like dirt. And I—I—" She couldn't go on. Tears filled her eyes.

He stood there wanting to comfort her but not willing to give ground on the detested Nigel. Brotherly love won over and he hugged her. "Like I said, I didn't wish him dead. Maybe Linda Forloines did it."

Addie stiffened. "Linda . . . she made a move like a dope fiend." Addie referred to the whipping incident in stable slang.

"That's just it." Chark released his sister. "I'm willing to bet the barn that those two are selling again. Where else would the Forloines get the money for a new truck?"

"Didn't see it."

"Brand new Nissan. Nice truck." He rubbed his hands together. He had arthritis in his fingers, broken years ago, and the chill of the oncoming night made his joints ache.

She shrugged. "Who knows." But she did know.

"She's probably doping horses as well as people."

"I don't know."

"It wouldn't surprise me if she and Will are—uh, in the mix somehow. A feeling."

"I don't know," she repeated. "But I had my own *Twilight Zone* episode today.

"Huh?"

"I picked up the mail, and Harry and Mrs. H. were really wonderful except Harry's worse than the sheriff—she asks too many questions. Anyway, I lost my temper and said if I found out who killed Nigel before the law, I'd kill him. They both about jumped down my throat and said, 'Don't even say that.' "

"They're right. Crazy things happen."

"What gave me the shivers was their saying that if I got too close to the murderer, maybe he'd turn on me."

"Damn," he whispered.

11

The dagger that killed Nigel Danforth, tagged and numbered, lay on Frank Yancey's desk. Rick Shaw and Cynthia Cooper sat on the other side of the desk.

"That's no cheap piece of hardware." Rick admired the weapon.

Frank touched it with the eraser on his pencil. "The blade is seven and a half inches, and the overall length is twelve and three quarters inches. The blade is double-edged stainless steel, highly polished, as you can see, and the handle is wrapped in wire, kind of like fencing uh—"

"Foils." Cooper found the word for him.

"Right." Frank frowned. "I think this was an impulse killing. Why would someone leave an expensive dagger buried in Nigel's chest?"

"If it was impulse, why the Queen of Clubs?" Rick countered.

Frank stroked the stubble on the side of his jowls. "Well—"

"And another thing, Sheriff Yancey," Cynthia respectfully addressed the older man, "I've been at the computer since this happened. I've talked to Scotland Yard. There is no Nigel Danforth."

"I was afraid of that." Frank grimaced. "Just like I was afraid we'd find no fingerprints. Not a one."

"Well, there are no inland revenue records, no passports, no national health card, no nothing," Cynthia said.

"Who the hell is that on the slab in the morgue?" Frank rhetorically asked.

"About all we can do is get dental impressions and send them over the wires. That will work if the stiff, I mean deceased," Cooper corrected herself, "had a criminal record. Otherwise, your guess is as good as mine."

"I don't like this." Frank smacked his hand on the table. "People want results."

"Don't worry, it's not an election year for you, Frank, and it's not like a serial killer is stalking the streets of Orange. The murder is confined to a small world."

"We hope," Cynthia said.

"I don't like this," Frank repeated. "I'll get Mickey Townsend in here. Why would he hire a man without a green card?"

"Same reason a lot of fruit growers hire Mexicans and don't inquire about their immigration status. They figure they can get the crop in before Immigration busts them. Any American employer whose IQ hovers above his body temperature knows to ask for a green card or go through the bullshit of getting one for the employee." Rick crossed his right leg over his left knee.

"It's the modern version of an indentured servant. You get someone a green card and they owe you for life," Cynthia added.

"Well, we know a few things." Rick folded his hands over

his chest, feeling the Lucky Strikes pack in his pocket and very much wanting a cigarette.

"Sure," Frank said. "We know I'm in deep shit and I have to tell a bunch of reporters we're on a trail colder than a witch's tit."

"No, we also know that the killer likes expensive weapons. Perhaps the dagger has symbolic significance, as does the Queen of Clubs. We also know that Nigel knew his killer."

"No, we don't," Frank said stubbornly.

"I can't prove it, of course, but there are no signs of struggle. He was face-to-face with his killer. He wasn't dragged or we'd have seen the marks on the barn floor."

"The killer could have stabbed him and then carried him to the chair." Cynthia thought out loud.

"That's a possibility, meaning the killer has to be strong enough to lift a—what do you reckon—a hundred-twenty-pound jockey over his shoulder."

"Or her shoulder. A strong woman could lift that." Cynthia scribbled a few notes in her spiral notebook.

"Wish Larry and Hank would call." Frank fidgeted.

"We could go over there, see what they've turned up." Rick stood.

"Bad luck having the county coroner out of town. He's as good as new." Frank, irritated, didn't realize the irony of his remarks.

Just then the phone rang. "Yancey," Frank said.

Hank Cushing's high-pitched voice started spouting out organ weights and stomach contents. "Normal heart and—"

"I don't give a damn about that. Was he stabbed twice or once?" Frank barked into the receiver.

"Twice," Hank responded. "The condition of the liver showed some signs of nascent alcohol damage and—"

"I don't care about that. Send me the report."

"Well, you might want to care about this." Hank, miffed, raised his voice. "He'd put his age down as twenty-six for his jockey application with the National Steeplechase Association, and I estimate his age to be closer to thirty-five. Might be worth sticking that fact in your brain *and* the fact that he had a serious dose of cocaine in his bloodstream. I'll send the file over as soon as I've written up my report." Miffed, Hank hung up on him.

Frank banged down the phone. "Prick."

"Well—?" Both Rick and Cynthia asked in unison.

"Stabbed twice. Full of coke."

"Makes sense. He'd hardly sit there while someone placed a card over his heart."

"Rick, he would if they'd held a gun to his head."

"Good point, pardner." Rick smiled at Cynthia.

"One other thing, Hank said his age was closer to thirty-five than the twenty-six he wrote down for the steeplechase association."

"Hmm," Rick murmured. "Whoever he was, he was a first-rate liar."

"Not so first-rate," Coop rejoined. "He's dead. Someone caught him out."

"Well, I sure appreciate your help." Frank got to his feet. "I figure the good citizens of Orange can sleep safe in their beds at night."

"That's what I'm doing. Going home to bed." Cynthia felt as if sand was in her eyes from staring at the computer screen for the last two and a half days.

On the way back to Charlottesville in an unmarked car, Rick smoked a cigarette, opening the window a crack first. "Frank's in over his head."

"Yep."

"If we're lucky this will be a revenge killing, and that'll be the end of it. If we're not, this will play out at other steeplechase races or other steeplechase stables, which means the good citizens of Orange and Albemarle counties may not sleep so soundly—not if they've got horses in the barn."

Cynthia stretched her long legs. "Horsey people are obsessed."

"I don't much like them," Rick matter-of-factly said.

"I can't say that, but I can say they fall into two categories."

"What's that?"

"They're either very, very intelligent or dumb as a sack of hammers. No in-between."

Rick laughed, exceeding the speed limit.

12

A sleek BMW 750il, the twelve-cylinder model, cruised by the post office at seven-thirty Tuesday morning. Harry noticed Mickey Townsend behind the wheel as she passed by in her truck.

"Some kind of car."

Mrs. Murphy and Tucker dutifully glanced at the metallic silver automobile but, not being car nuts, they returned their attention to more important matters.

"Hey, Ella!" Mrs. Murphy called to Elocution, Herb Jones's youngest cat, as she sat by the minister's front door.

Since the window was rolled up, Elocution couldn't hear, but Harry sure could.

"You'll split my eardrums."

"Mother, I have to listen to you morning, noon and night."

"Yeah, but she's not screeching for her friends."

"*Tucker, shut up.*" The cat boxed that long, inviting nose. Murphy wondered what cats living with pugs, bulldogs, and chows did since those canines' noses were pushed in. Guess they jumped on their backs and bit their necks.

The lights were already on inside as Harry parked the truck.

"Hey," she called as she opened the back door, the aroma of fresh cinnamon curling into her nostrils.

"Morning." Mrs. Hogendobber put whole coffee beans into a cylindrical electric grinder. The noise terrified Tucker, who cowered underneath the empty mail cart.

"Chicken."

"*I hate that noise,*" the dog whimpered.

Harry heated up water on the hot plate. She couldn't drink much coffee so she made tea. Doughnuts, steam still rising off them, were arranged in concentric circles on the white plate.

"Cinnamon?" Harry said.

"And cake doughnuts too. I'm experimenting with two different doughs." A knock at the back door interrupted her. "Who is it?"

"Attila the Hun."

"Come on in," Mrs. Hogendobber answered.

Susan Tucker, pink-faced from the cold, opened the door. "Good frost this morning. Hi, Tucker." She reached down to pet the dog. "Hello, Mrs. Murphy, I know you're in the mail cart because I can see the bulge underneath."

"*Morning,*" came the sleepy reply.

"Saw Mickey Townsend drive by," Susan said.

"Passed him on the way in. Oh, Susan, I've got a registered letter for you."

"Damn." Susan thought registered letters usually meant some unwanted legal notice or, worse, a dire warning from the IRS.

Harry fished out the letter with the heavy pink paper attached, a copy underneath. "Press hard so your signature shows through."

Ballpoint in hand, Susan peered at the return address. "Plaistow, New Hampshire?" She firmly wrote her name.

Harry carefully tore off the pink label, which she kept, the carbon copy remaining with the envelope.

Susan wedged her forefinger under the sealed flap, opening the letter. "Say, this is pretty nice."

"What?" Harry read over her shoulder.

"State Line Tack exhausted their supply of turnout rugs in red and gold. If I'll accept a navy with a red border, they'll give me a further ten percent discount, and they apologize for the inconvenience. They haven't been able to reach me by phone." She snapped the paper. "Because the damn kids never get off it! What a good business."

"I'll say. You know who else is really great: L. L. Bean."

"The best." Mrs. Hogendobber ate a doughnut. "Mmm. Outdid myself."

Susan folded the letter, returning it to its envelope, and then, as is often the case between old friends, she jumped to another subject with no explanation because she knew Harry would understand the connection: signing for letters. "You must know every signature in Crozet."

"We both do." Mrs. Hogendobber wiped crumbs from her mouth. "We could be expert witnesses in forgery cases. I wish you two would try one of these. My best."

Harry grabbed a cinnamon doughnut even though she had sworn she wouldn't.

"Go on." Mrs. Hogendobber noticed Susan salivating over the plate. "I can't eat them all myself."

"Ned told me I can't gain my five winter pounds this year. He even bought me a NordicTrack." Susan stared at the doughnuts.

"Don't eat lunch." Harry saved her the agony of the decision by handing her one.

Once that fresh smell wafted right under her nose, Susan

popped the doughnut straight in. "Oh, hell." She helped herself
to a cup of tea. "Heard some scoop."

"I wait with cinnamon breath—as opposed to bated, that
is." Harry untied the first mailbag.

"Nigel Danforth bet a thousand dollars on the fifth race—
Mim's horse, not Mickey Townsend's."

Miranda wondered out loud. "Is that bad?"

"A jockey wouldn't bet against himself or the stable he's
riding for, plus a jockey isn't supposed to bet at all. That's a fact
for all sports. Remember Pete Rose." Susan, suffering the tortures
of the damned, grabbed another cinnamon doughnut.

"Wouldn't it mean he's fixing the race?"

"It might, but probably not in this circumstance." Susan
continued: "Mickey Townsend's mare didn't have much of a
chance. Of course, Nigel placed the bet through a third party. I
mean, that's what I've heard."

"Yeah but with steeplechasing—one pileup and a goat could
win." Harry leaned over Mrs. Murphy. "Murphy, I need to dump
the mail in."

"No."

"Come on, kitty cat."

"No." To prove her point Murphy rolled over on her back,
exposing her beautiful beige tummy with its crisp black stripes.

"All right then, smartass." Harry poured a little mail on the
cat.

"I'm not moving." Mrs. Murphy rolled over on her side.

"Stubborn." Harry reached in with both hands and plucked
her out, placing her in the fleece teepee she'd bought especially
for the cat.

Grumbling, Mrs. Murphy circled inside three times, then
settled down. She needed her morning nap.

"Doesn't sound cricket to me." Mrs. Hogendobber occasionally used an expression from her youth when, due to World
War II, phrases from the British allies were current.

"It's not the most prudent policy." Harry dumped the remainder of the mail from her sack into the cart, then wheeled it over to the post boxes.

"I'd worry less about that and more about where a jockey got one thousand dollars cash." Susan helped with the third-class mail. "Those guys only get paid fifty dollars a race, you know. If they win, place or show they get a percentage of the purse."

"The wages of sin." Harry laughed.

"You know . . ." Susan's voice trailed off.

"We ought to go over to Mim's stable," Harry said, "at lunch. Larry comes in today." Dr. Larry Johnson, partially retired, filled in at lunch so Harry and Mrs. Hogendobber could run errands or relax over a meal at Crozet Pizza.

"Now, girls, just a minute. You heard a rumor, Susan, not a fact. You shouldn't slander someone even though he is dead."

"I'm not slandering him. I only told you, and I don't think it hurts if we sniff about."

"*I'll do the sniffing,*" Tucker told them.

"*We should talk to the horses. They know what went down. Too bad there weren't any left in the barn when Nigel was stabbed,*" Mrs. Murphy drawled from inside her teepee.

"*Even if there had been, Murphy, chances are that the horse would have been vanned back to its stable and how would we get there? Especially if it was a Maryland horse?*" Tucker lay down in front of the teepee, sticking her nose inside. Mrs. Murphy didn't mind.

The front door opened. The Reverend Herb Jones and Market Shiflett bustled in.

"Got the mail sorted yet?" Market asked.

"Is it eight yet?" Harry tossed mail into boxes.

"No."

"I have yours right here. I did it first because I like you *so* much," Harry teased him.

As Market blew in the front door, Pewter blew into the back.

"What about me?" Herb asked.

"I like you *so* much, too." Harry laughed, handing him a stack of magazines, bills, letters, and catalogs.

Pewter walked around Tucker and stuck her head into the teepee. Then she squeezed in and curled up next to Mrs. Murphy.

"*Boy, you're fat,*" the tiger grumbled.

"*You always say that,*" Pewter purred, for she liked to snuggle. "*But I keep you warm.*"

"Say, I heard that Linda Forloines bet a thousand dollars on the fifth race against the horse she was riding." Herb Jones flipped unwanted solicitations into the trash.

"See," Miranda triumphantly called as she continued her sorting.

"See what?" he asked.

"Susan said that same thing about Nigel Danforth," Miranda called from behind the post boxes.

"Oh." Herb neatly stacked his mail and put a rubber band around it. "Another rumor for the grist mill."

"Well, someone must have bet one thousand dollars on the fifth race." Susan, chin jutting out, wasn't giving up so easily.

Market leaned over the counter. "You know how these things are. The next thing you'll hear is that the body disappeared."

13

Fair stood in the doorway, looking as serious as a heart attack. Normally Harry would have cussed him out because she hated it when he dropped in on her without calling first. Sometimes he forgot they weren't married, an interesting twist since, when they were married, he'd sometimes forgotten that as well.

The paleness of his lips kept her complaint bottled up.

"*Daddy!*" Tucker scurried forward to shower love on Fair.

"*Brown-noser.*" Mrs. Murphy turned her back on him, and the tip of her tail flicked. She liked Fair but not enough to make a fool of herself rushing to greet him. Also, Murphy, having once endured a philandering husband herself, the handsome black-and-white Paddy, keenly felt for Harry.

"Close the door, Fair. It's cold."

"So it is." He gently shut the door behind him, took off

his heavy green buffalo-plaid shirt, and hung it on a peg by the door.

"I'm down to cheese and crackers tonight because I haven't been to the supermarket in weeks. You're welcome to some."

"No appetite. Got a beer?"

"Yep." She reached into the refrigerator, fishing out a cold Sol, popped the cap, grabbed a glass mug, and handed it to him as he headed for the living room. He sank into the overstuffed chair, a remnant from the forties, which Harry's mom had found at a rummage sale. It could have even been from the thirties. It had been recovered so many times that only bits of the original color, a slate gray with golden stars, straggled on the edges where the upholsterer's nails held a few original threads. The last recovering had occurred seven years ago. Mrs. Murphy, claws at the ready, had exposed the wood underneath the fabric and tufting, which was why you could also see the upholsterer's nails. Her steady application of kitty destructiveness forced Harry to throw a quarter sheet over the chair. Now that she'd gotten used to it, she liked the dark green blanket, edged in gold, used to keep horses' hindquarters warm in bitter weather.

"To what do I owe this pleasure?"

Fair pulled long on the beer. "I am under investigation—"

"For the murder of Nigel Danforth?" Harry blurted out.

"No—for doping horses. Mickey Townsend drove over to tell Mim, and Mim told me, and sure enough Colbert Mason from National confirmed it. He was kind enough to say that no one believed it, but he had to go through the motions."

"Has anyone formally accused you?"

"Not yet."

"It's a crock of shit!"

"My sentiments exactly." The deep lines around his light eyes only added to his masculine appeal. He rubbed his forehead. "Who would do such a thing?"

"Whoever tells you they wouldn't," Harry remarked. "Who has something to gain by doing this to you? Another vet?"

"Harry, you know the other equine vets as well as I do. Not one of them would sink that low. Besides, we cooperate with one another."

Murphy brought in her tiny play mouse covered with rabbit's fur, one of her favorite toys. She hoped she could seduce Harry into throwing it so she could chase it. She jumped on the arm of the chair, dropping it into Harry's lap.

"Murphy, go find a real one."

"*I have cleansed this house of mice. I am the master mouser,*" she bragged.

"*Ha!*" Tucker wedged herself on Harry's foot.

"*You couldn't catch a mouse if your life depended on it.*"

"*Well, you couldn't herd cows if your life depended on it, so there.*"

Harry tossed the mouse behind her shoulder, and the cat launched off the chair, tore across the room, skidded past the mouse because she'd put her brakes on too late, bumped her butt on the wall, slid around, got her paws under her, and pounced on the mouse.

"*Death to vermin!*" She tossed the mouse over her head. She batted it with her paws. She lobbed it in the air, catching it on the way down.

"Wouldn't you love to be like that just once?" Harry admired Mrs. Murphy's wild abandon.

"Freedom." Fair laughed as the tiger, play mouse in jaws, leapt over the corgi.

"*I hate it when you do that,*" Tucker grumbled.

Mrs. Murphy said nothing because she didn't want to drop her mouse, so she careened around and vaulted Tucker from the other direction. Tucker flattened on the rug, ears back.

"*Show-off.*"

The cat ignored her, rushing into the bedroom so she could drop the mouse behind the pillows and then crawl under them to destroy the enemy again.

Harry returned to the subject, "Remember those war philosophy books you used to read? *The Art of War* by Shu Tzu was one.

A passage in there goes, 'Uproar in East, strike in West.' Might be what's going on with you."

"You read those books more carefully than I did."

"Liked von Clausewitz best." She crossed her legs under her. "No one who knows you, no one who has watched you work on a horse could ever believe you would drug horses for gain. Since this complaint came out of the steeplechase set, you know it may not relate to the murder, but then again, it gets folks sidetracked, looking east."

"Yeah—they'll waste time on me," he mumbled.

"Like I said, 'Uproar in East, strike in West.' " She paused. "Did you know Nigel?"

"He didn't talk much so it was a nodding acquaintance." He threw his leg over an arm of the chair. "Want to go to a show?"

"Nah. I'm going to paint the bathroom tonight. I can't stand it another minute.

"You work too much."

"Look who's talking."

"*Isn't anyone going to come in here and play with me?*" Murphy called from the bedroom as she threw a pillow on the floor for dramatic effect.

"She's vocal tonight." Fair finished his beer. "Bring me your mousie."

Seeing a six-foot-four-inch man of steel ask for a cat to bring her mousie never struck Harry as strange. Both she and Fair were so attuned to animals that speaking to them was as natural as speaking to a human. Generally, it produced better results.

Murphy ripped out of the bedroom, mouse in jaws again, and dropped the little gray toy on Fair's boots.

"What a *valuable* mouse. Murphy, you're a big hunter. You need to go on a safari." He threw the mouse into the kitchen, and off ran Murphy.

"*You indulge her.*" Tucker sank her head on her paws.

"Miranda and I were going over to Mim's at lunch to poke

around about the rumors of Nigel betting against himself in the sixth race, or was it the fifth?'' She shrugged. '' 'Course, the same rumor floated around about Linda Forloines.''

"The thousand dollars?''

"Guess it's made the rounds.''

"Yeah. Why didn't you go?''

"Larry relieved us late. Miranda got a call from her church group, some crisis to do with the songfest, so I went over to Crozet Pizza. No point in chasing rumors, which is why I can't believe that Colbert Mason is bothering about this one concerning you. Well, I guess he has to go through the motions.''

"You were always better than I was at figuring out people. I'm not a vet just because I love animals. Don't much like people deep down, I suppose—or maybe I just like a few select ones like you.''

"Don't start,'' Harry swiftly replied.

"*Mom, don't be so hard on him.*'' Mrs. Murphy deposited her play mouse next to her food bowl.

"*Yeah, Mom,*'' Tucker chimed in.

"I'm not starting.'' He sighed. "You know I've repented. I've told you. I'm changing. Hell, maybe I'm even growing up.''

"Mother used to say that men don't grow up, they grow old. Actually, I thought Dad was a mature man, but then again a daughter doesn't see a man the same as a wife does.''

"Are you telling me I can't grow up?''

"No.'' She uncrossed her legs, leaning forward, "I'm not good at these topics. The conventional wisdom is that women can talk about emotions and men can't. I don't see that I'm good at it, and I don't see any reason to learn. I mean, I know what I feel. Whether I can or want to express it is my deal, right? Anyway, emotions are like mercury, up, down, and if you break the thermometer, the stuff runs out. Poof.''

"Mary Minor, don't be so tough. A little introspection can't hurt.''

"Not the therapy rap again?'' She threw up her hands.

He ignored the comment. "I hated going, but I'd made such a mess of my life it was that or sucking on a gun barrel." He paused. "Actually look forward to those sessions. I'm taking a college course and the subject is me. Guess it means I'm egotistical." He smiled wryly.

"What matters is that for you it's a—" she rummaged around for the right word, "an enlarging experience. You're open to it and getting a lot from it. I'm not. I'm closed. It ain't my deal."

"What's your deal?"

"Hard work. Why do you ask what you already know?"

"Wanted to hear you say it."

"You heard me."

"Harry, it's okay to share emotions."

"Goddammit, I know that. It's also okay not to share them. What good does it do, Fair? And what's the line between sharing and whining?"

"Do I sound like I'm whining?"

"No."

They sat in silence. Mrs. Murphy padded in, leaving her mouse by her food bowl.

"*Go to a movie with him, Mom,*" Tucker advised.

"*Yeah,*" Murphy agreed.

"You know if there's any way I can help you with this inquiry, I'll do it."

"I know." He sat waiting to be asked to stay, yet knowing she wouldn't ask. At last he rose, tossed his long-neck bottle in the trash, and lifted his heavy shirt off the peg. "Thanks for listening."

She joined him in the kitchen. "Things will turn out right. It's a waste of time, but dance to their tune for a while."

"Like singing for my supper? Remember when I was starting out, Mim would give me odd jobs at the stable and then feed me? Funny about Mim. She's tyrannical and snobbish, but underneath she's a good soul. Most people don't see that."

"What I remember is Little Marilyn's first husband driving you bananas."

"That guy." Fair shook his head. "I was glad when she was shuck of him, although I guess it was hard for her. Always is, really. Are you glad to be rid of me?"

"Some days, yes. Some days, no."

"What about today?" His eyes brightened.

"Neutral."

He opened the kitchen door and left. "Bye. Thanks for the beer," he called.

"Yeah." She waved good-bye, feeling that phantom pain in her heart like the phantom pain in an amputated limb.

14

Bazooka, sleek, fit, and full of himself, pranced sideways back to the stable. Addie breezed him but he wanted to fly. He hated standing in his stall, and he envied Mim's foxhunters, who led a more normal life, lounging in the pastures and only coming into their stalls at night.

Like most competitive horses, Bazooka was fed a high protein diet with supplements and encouraged to explode during the race. Mostly he felt like exploding at home. He knew he could win, barring an accident or being boxed in by a cagey opposing jockey. He wanted to win, to cover himself with glory. Bazooka's ego matched his size: big. Unlike most 'chasers at other barns, he also knew that when his competitive days drew to a close, Mim wouldn't sell him off. She would retire him to foxhunting, most likely riding him herself, for Mim was a good rider.

The fact that Mim could ride better than her daughter only deepened Little Marilyn's lifelong sulk. Occasional bursts of filial devotion gusted through the younger Mim's demeanor.

Both mother and daughter watched as Bazooka proudly passed them.

"He's on today," Addie called to them.

"The look of eagles." Mim grinned.

"I *am* beautiful!" Bazooka crowed.

"Mom, I didn't know Harry was coming by." Little Marilyn had grown up with Mary Minor Haristeen, but although she couldn't say she disliked Harry, she couldn't say she liked her either. Personalities, like colors, either look good together or they don't. These two didn't.

Mim, by contrast, found it easy to talk to Harry even though she deplored the younger woman's lack of ambition.

The Superman-blue Ford truck chugged to the parking lot behind the stable. Tucker and Mrs. Murphy appeared before Harry did. They spoke their greetings, then ran into the stable as Harry reached Big Mim and Little Mim, occasionally called Mini-Mim if Harry was feeling venomous.

"What have you got there?" Mim asked, noticing that Harry carried a small box.

"The labels for the wild game dinner invitations. Little Marilyn was printing up the invitations."

"Did you run these off a government computer?" Mim folded her arms across her chest.

"Uh—I did. Aren't you glad your taxes have gone to something productive?"

Little Mim snatched the box from Harry's hands. "Thanks."

"How do the invitations look?" Harry asked.

Little Marilyn squinted at Harry, distorting her manicured good looks. "Haven't picked them up yet." Which translated into: She forgot to order them, and the labels told her she'd better get cracking. "I think I'll go get them right now. Need anything from C-ville, Mum?"

"No. I gave my list to your father."

"Good to see you, Harry." The impeccably dressed young Marilyn hot-footed it to her Range Rover.

No point in either her mother or Harry criticizing her. They knew she hadn't done her job, but she'd do it under pressure. Nor was there any point in discussing it with each other.

Harry walked with Mim into the lovely paneled tack room. The air was nippy even though the sun was high.

"Where's Chark?"

"Other end of the barn. He's finishing up the last set. Bang 'em out early, as he says."

Harry sat down as Mim pointed to a seat covered in a handsome dark plaid. Harry could have lived happily in Mim's tack room, which was prettier than her living room.

"Mim, I know that Mickey Townsend drove over to tell you about the unfounded charges leveled against Fair. Fair dropped by last night. This is outrageous"—her face reddened—"for somebody to smear one of the best vets in practice. Do you have any idea who would pull a stunt like this?"

"No." Mim sat down opposite Harry. "I called Colbert and Arthur first thing this morning and told them the inquiry had better be fast and be quiet or I am going to make life sheer hell for everyone." She held up her hand as if requesting silence from an audience. "I also told them it's a waste of time when they have far more important things to do."

"Well, that's why I'm here. You're one of the most powerful people in the association." Mim murmured denial even as she was pleased to hear it, and Harry continued. "I dropped by Ned Tucker's this morning. Susan filled him in. He said he would represent Fair, no charge. He drafted a letter, which I have right here."

As Mim read, her eyebrows knitted together and then she smiled. "Good show, Ned."

The letter said in exhaustive legalese that Fair had no intention of submitting to an inquiry without a formal accusation. If this was allowed to continue, then every veterinarian, trainer, and jockey could be paralyzed by poisonous gossip. He demanded his accuser come forward, that a formal complaint be filed. Once that was accomplished, he would defend himself.

"What do you think? Rather, what do you think the National Steeplechase Association will think?" Harry took the letter back from Mim's outstretched hand, sporting only her wedding band and engagement diamond today.

"I expect they'll nail the accuser straightaway. But can you get Fair to sign this? You know how he is about honor. Nineteenth century, but then that's what makes him such a splendid man."

"Of course I can't get him to sign it. He thinks people should resolve their differences any way they can before resorting to lawyers. He doesn't understand that America doesn't work that way anymore. The minute we're born we put some lawyer on retainer."

"So what's the solution here?"

"Uh—Mim, what I had hoped is that you would fax this to Colbert. Maybe write a note that Ned Tucker came to you with this because he doesn't want the association further embarrassed. You know, the murder, public relations problems, et cetera. You want to give Colbert and Arthur, too, plenty of warning so they can frame a response should the press jump on this." Harry breathed deeply. She hadn't realized how nervous she was.

Mim sank back in the chair, painted nails tapping the armrests. "Harry, you are far more subtle than I give you credit for—of course I'll do it."

"Oh, thank you. Fair will never know unless Colbert tells him."

"I'll hint in my cover letter that if this can be rapidly resolved, the signed letter will never arrive. Fair will drop legal proceedings."

Harry beamed. "You're so smart."

"No—you are. And you're still in love with him."

"That's what everyone says, but no, I'm not." Harry quickly replied. "I love him. It's different. He's a friend and a good man, and he doesn't deserve this smear job. He'd do the same for me."

"Yes, he would."

As Mim and Harry discussed Fair, love, Jim, Bazooka, Miranda's choir group's fund-raiser for the Church of the Holy Light, as well as the kitchen sink, Mrs. Murphy and Tucker chatted up the barn cat, a strong, large ginger named Rodger Dodger. His tortoiseshell girlfriend, Pusskin, slept in the hayloft, worn out from chasing a chipmunk that morning.

Bazooka, being wiped down in the wash stall, listened disappointedly because the other animals weren't talking about him.

"How's hunting?" Rodger Dodger asked Mrs. Murphy.

"Good."

"Oh, yeah, she kills her play mouse nightly." Tucker giggled.

"Shut up. I account for my share of mice and moles."

"Don't forget the blue jay. That put Mom right over the edge." Tucker gloated.

"I hated that blue jay."

"I hate them, too," Rodger solemnly agreed. "They zoom down from twelve o'clock directly above you and peck you. Then peel out and zoom away. I'd kill every one if I could."

"What's going on around here?" Tucker changed the subject from rodent and fowl kills. Now, if they wanted to discuss how to turn cattle or sheep, she could offer many stories.

Rodger swept his whiskers forward, stepping close to the tiger cat and corgi. "Last night someone took Orion out of his stall, put him in the cross ties, and dug around in the stall, but was interrupted. Whoever it was covered the hole back up and put Orion in the stall."

"Can you smell anything in the stall?"

"Earth." Rodger Dodger rested on his haunches.

"Let's take a look." Mrs. Murphy scampered down the aisle. Since Orion was a hunter, he was playing outside in a field. The animals could go into his stall.

Tucker put her nose to the ground. The cats pawed the wood shavings away. The ground had indeed been freshly turned over.

Mrs. Murphy cautiously investigated the other corners of the stall. Nothing.

"Doesn't make sense, does it?" Rodger observed Tucker.

"I don't know." She lifted her head, inhaled fresh air, then put her nose back to the smoothed-over spot. "If we could get someone to dig here I might find something. If anything was removed, I would smell that." She sniffed again. "Right now it's blank."

The three animals sat in the stall.

"Do you know who it was?" Tucker asked.

"No, I was out in the machine shed last night. Good pickings. When Orion made mention of it on his way out this morning, I was too groggy to grill him."

"Let's go ask Orion." Mrs. Murphy left the stall just as Bazooka was put into his stall by Chark Valiant.

"You don't have to ask Orion," the steel gray told them. "I saw who it was. Coty Lamont."

"Coty Lamont!" Mrs. Murphy exclaimed. Rodger jumped on the tack trunk in front of Bazooka's stall and got on his hind legs to chat with the horse. "Bazooka, why was he here?"

"He didn't say," Bazooka sarcastically replied. "But Mickey Townsend tiptoed in and shut the stall door with Coty in there. Coty tried to get out but Mickey wouldn't let him. He told him to cover it back up, and to come with him."

"Old Kotex hates Mickey." Mrs. Murphy used Coty's nickname. "For that matter, so does Chark Valiant."

"Bet Coty didn't go," Tucker said.

"Oh, but he did." Bazooka relished the tale. "Mickey pulled a gun on him and told him he had to go with him."

"Did he go?" Tucker's lustrous eyes widened.

"Sure he did. See, I don't know how he got here. Mickey just tiptoed into the barn," Bazooka added. "*Anyway, Mickey told him to put his hands behind his head. He unbolted the stall, and Coty walked in front of him.*"

"*Boy, is that weird.*" Rodger Dodger scratched his side with his hind leg.

It was more than weird, because that night at dusk Coty Lamont, the best steeplechase jockey of his generation, was discovered on a dirt road in eastern Albemarle County right off Route 22. He was laid out in the bed of his Ford 350 dually pickup truck painted in his favorite metallic maroon. The Queen of Spades was over his heart, a stiletto driven through it.

15

Rick Shaw lost cigarette lighters the way small children lose gloves. He used disposable lighters because of this. Pulling a see-through lime-green lighter from his coat pocket, he studied the corpse in the truck.

Cynthia Cooper scribbled in her notebook, weakened, and lit up a cigarette herself.

The ambulance crew waited at a distance. Kenny Wheeler, Jr., who had found the body, stayed with the sheriff and his deputy.

"Kenny, I know you've told me this before but tell me again because I need to have the sequence right," Rick softly asked the tall, deep-voiced young man.

"I was checking a fence line. Kinda in a hurry because I was losing light and running behind, you know." He stared down at his boots. "This old road is really on my neighbor's property, but I have use of it, so I thought I'd swing through to get to the back acres. Save a minute or two. Anyway, I saw this truck. Didn't recognize it. And as I drew closer I saw him"—he pointed to the body—"in the bed. I thought maybe the guy fell asleep or something—I mean, until I got closer. Well, I stopped my truck, got out, kinda peeped over the sides. I mean, I knew the man was dead, deader than the Red Sox, but I don't know why I called out, 'Hey.' I stood there for a minute and then I got on the mobile, called you first off, then called Mom and Dad. I described the truck. They didn't know it. Dad wanted to come right out, but I told him to stay put. It's better that I'm the only one involved.

"Well, Dad didn't like that. He's a hands-on guy, as you know, but I said, 'Dad, if you come on out here, then you'll get caught in the red tape, and you have enough to do. I found him, so I'll take care of it.' So he said okay finally, and here I am."

Cynthia closed her notebook. "Rick, do you need Kenny anymore?"

"Yeah, wait one minute." Rick, gloves on, pulled out the registration. "The truck is registered to Coty Lamont. That name mean anything to you?" Rick leaned against the open door of the truck.

"Coty Lamont." Kenny frowned. "A jockey. I'm pretty sure I've heard that name before. We don't race, but . . . that name is familiar."

"Thanks, Kenny. You've been a tremendous help. Go on home. I'll call you if I need you. Give your Mom and Dad my regards. Wife, too." Rick clapped him on the back.

As Kenny turned his truck around and drove out, Rick looked back into the bed of the truck. "Notice anything?"

"Yeah, he was shot in the back for good measure. Probably struggled." Cynthia answered.

"Uh-huh. Anything else?"

"Same M.O. as the last one, pretty much."

"The card, Cynthia, check out the card."

"The Queen of Spades." She whistled. "Lot of blood on this one."

"Spades, Coop—the other card was clubs."

Cynthia rubbed her hands on her upper arms. The sunset over the Southwest Range and the night air chilled to the bone. "Clubs, spades—are you thinking what I'm thinking?"

"Diamonds and hearts to go."

16

The glow from the tip of his cigarette shone through Rick Shaw's hand in the starless night. He cupped it to keep out the wind as he leaned over the railing at Montpelier's flat track.

Barry McMullen, who rented the flat track stable, hunched his shoulders against the biting wind, pulling up his collar.

"There's nothing to this thousand-dollar rumor." Barry pushed his chin out assertively. "I've known Coty Lamont ever since he started out as Mickey Townsend's groom. Then he got his first ride on one of Arthur Tetrick's horses back when Arthur kept twenty horses in training. I just don't think Coty would be suckered into a gambling ring, and I know he would never throw a race."

"Not even for a couple hundred thousand dollars?"

Barry considered that. "No jockey that threw a race—and

it's damned easy to do in 'chasing—would get that much money. The stakes are considerably lower than flat racing, considerably lower."

"How much?"

"Maybe five thousand. Tops."

"So we're talking about sums, not character."

Barry growled, "Don't put words into my mouth. Coty Lamont possessed an ego three times his size. He was the best, had to be the best, had to stay the best. He wouldn't throw a race. I think this gambling hunch is off the mark—for him. I don't know Jack Shit about the other guy who was killed. That Nigel fella."

"Neither do we." Rick felt hot ashes drop into his hand. He tilted his palm halfway to drop them on the cold ground, stamping them out with his foot.

"Pleasant enough. Asked to ride here. He was a decent hand with a horse, but I didn't have any room for him." He wrapped his scarf tighter around his neck. "Is there a reason we're standing out here in the cold, Rick?"

"Yes. I don't trust anyone in any barn right now."

Barry's light brown eyes widened. "My barn?"

"Any barn. If you repeat my questions there isn't much I can do about it. After all, I'm a public servant and my inquiry must be aboveboard, but it doesn't have to be broadcast. I don't want anyone eavesdropping while mucking a stall or throwing down hay." He shook his head. "I've got a bad feeling about this business."

Barry's jaw hardened. "Jesus, what do you think is going on?"

"What about a ring that sells horses for high prices, then substitutes cheap look-alikes, keeping the high-priced horses for themselves to win races or to be resold again? Possible?"

"In the old days, yes. Today, no. Every Thoroughbred is tattooed on the lip—"

Rick interrupted. "You could duplicate the tattoo."

Slowly Barry replied, "Hard to do but possible. However, why bother? These days we have DNA testing. The Jockey Club demands a small vial of blood before it will register a foal, and it demands one from the mare, too. The system is ninety-nine point ninety-nine percent foolproof."

"Not if someone on the inside substitutes vials of blood."

This floored Barry. "How do you think of things like that?"

"I deal with miscreants, traffic violators, domestic dragons, thieves, and hard-core criminals day in and day out. If I don't think as they do I'll never nail them." The deep creases around Rick's mouth lent authority to his rugged appearance. "It would have to be an inside job. Meaning the seller, the vet, possibly a jockey or a groom, and maybe even someone at the Jockey Club would have to be in on it."

"Not the Jockey Club." Barry vigorously shook his head. "Never. We're talking about *Mecca*. Sheriff, I would bet my life no one at the Jockey Club would ever desecrate the institution even for a large sum of money, and hey, I don't always agree with them. I think they're turned around backward sometimes, but I trust them, I mean, I trust their commitment to Thoroughbreds."

"Well, I hope you're right. If my bait-and-switch hunch isn't right, I'm lost. Two jockeys have been killed within seven days. Unless we're talking about some kind of bizarre sex club here, or irate husbands, then I'm sticking close to gambling or selling horses."

"You'd better put out that weed, Sheriff Rick." Barry smiled, pointing at Rick's hand.

At just that moment the cigarette burned his palm and Rick flapped his hands, dropping the stub. Its fiery nub burned in the dying grass. Rick quickly stepped on it. "Thanks. Got so preoccupied I forgot I was holding the damn thing."

"They'll kill you, you know."

Rick sardonically smiled. "Better this than a stiletto. Anyway, I've got to die of something." What he kept to himself was the fact that he'd tried to quit three times, the pressure of work always pulling him back to that soothing nicotine. "You know what Nigel was doing in this stable?" He nodded in the direction of the imposing flat track stable lying parallel to the track.

"Picking up gear. I think that's what he was doing. Some jockeys stowed their gear here, away from the crowds."

"Where were you immediately after the races?"

"Enjoying Cindy Chandler's tailgate party."

"And after that?"

He put his hands in his pockets. "Ran into Arthur Tetrick and walked with him on his way to the big house. We chatted about Arthur buying a four-year-old I saw in Upperville. Arthur wants back in the game. We walked toward the gate to the house. I left him there and went to check on one last van pulling out from the back stables, not mine." He pointed northeast of his stable in the direction of the smaller stables, well out of sight. "That's when one of Frank Yancey's deputies called me. Pretty dark by then."

"Don't be surprised if Frank asks you all the same questions that I have. I've talked to him, of course."

Barry, although not a native Virginian, had lived in Orange County since the early '70s. He knew Sheriff Yancey well. "Frank's a good man. Not a smart man, but a good man. I'm glad you're on this now."

Rick couldn't cast aspersions on a fellow law enforcement officer. "Frank might be smarter than you know. You see, Barry, it's not what he knows, it's who he knows. I'm going over to roast"—he savored the word—"Mickey Townsend tomorrow. Maybe he'll turn something up for me. You get on with him?"

"Yeah."

Rick started back toward the squad car. "Oh, one other thing. Anyone play cards in this group, the steeplechase people? I don't mean a friendly hand here and there, but impassioned card players?"

"Hell, Mickey Townsend would kill for an inside straight."

17

Dr. Stephen D'Angelo, a pulmonary surgeon, rode toward the stables. He was immaculately dressed in butcher boots, tan breeches, a white shirt, and tweed hacking jacket.

Linda Forloines rode alongside him. "She's a point and shoot."

"Where did you say this horse hunted?"

"Middleburg, Piedmont, and Oak Ridge."

He patted his horse's neck. "How much?"

"Well, they're asking twenty thousand dollars. But let's go over there. If you ride her and like her, I bet I can get that price down."

"Okay. Make an appointment for Thursday afternoon." He stopped outside the stable door, dismounted, and handed the reins to Linda, who had dismounted first.

Time being precious to him, he scheduled his rides at precisely the same time each day. Then he drove to the hospital, changing there.

He had sworn when he moved down from New Jersey that he'd retire, but word of a good doctor gets around. Before he knew it he was again in practice with two mornings' operating time at the hospital.

Like most extremely busy people in high-pressure jobs, he had to trust those around him. Linda kept the stable clean and the horses worked. He couldn't have known that behind his back she made fun of everything about him.

She mocked his riding ability, calling it "death defying." She moaned about his truck and trailer; she wanted a much more expensive one. She lauded her contributions to his farm to all and sundry even as she bit the hand that fed her.

As soon as the horses were untacked and wiped down, she planned to call her friend in Middleburg who was selling the horse Dr. D'Angelo was interested in for someone else. The horse was worth $7,500. If Dr. D'Angelo liked the mare, Linda would "plead" with her friend to plead with her client to drop the price. They'd counter at $15,000. The owner of the horse would indeed get $7,500. Linda and her friend would split and pocket the additional $7,500 without telling anyone. The original owner wouldn't know because they'd cash the check and pay her in cash. It was done every day in the horse business by people less than honest . . . often selling horses less than sound.

The phone rang as Linda tossed a Rambo blanket over one of the horses.

The wall phone hung on the outside wall.

She picked it up. "Hello."

"Linda," the deep male voice said, "Coty Lamont was found dead in the back of his pickup truck. A knife through the heart."

She gasped. "What?"

"You're losing business." He laughed. Then his voice turned cold. "I know Sheriff Yancey questioned you."

Before he could continue she said, "Hey, I'm not stupid. I didn't say a word."

A long pause followed. "Keep it that way. Liabilities don't live long in this business. Midnight. Tomorrow."

"Yeah. Sure." She hung up the phone, surprised to find her hand shaking.

18

The pale November light spilled over her like champagne, making the deep blacks of Mrs. Murphy's stripes glisten. Her tail upright, her whiskers slightly forward, she loped across the fields to Mim's house. Alongside her and not at all happy about it wobbled Pewter—not an outdoor girl. Tee Tucker easily kept up the pace.

Mim's estate nestled not fifteen minutes from the post office if one cut across yards and fields.

"Oh, can't we walk a bit?"

"We're almost there." Murphy pressed on.

"I know we're almost there. I'm tired," complained the gray cat.

"Hold it!" Tucker commanded.

The two cats stopped, Pewter breathing hard. A rustle in the broom sage alerted them to another presence. The cats dropped to their bellies, ears forward. Tucker stood her ground.

"*Who goes there?*" Tucker demanded.

"*As fine a cat as ever walked the globe,*" came the saucy reply.

"Ugh." Pewter squinted. She had never been able to stand Paddy, Mrs. Murphy's ex-husband.

Murphy stuck her head up, "*Whatever you're doing on this side of Crozet, I don't want to know.*"

"*And you shan't, my love.*" He kissed her on the cheek. "*Pewter, you look slimmer.*"

"*Liar.*"

"*What a pretty thing to say to a gentleman paying you a compliment.*"

"*What gentleman?*"

"*Pewter, be civil.*" Murphy hated playing peacemaker. She had better things to do with her time. "*Come on, you two. If we're going to get back by quitting time, we've got to move on.*"

"*Where are you going?*"

"*Mim's stable. Come along and I'll give you the skinny.*" Mrs. Murphy used an expression that she had heard Mrs. Hogendobber occasionally use when the good lady felt racy.

"*Let's trot. I am not running.*" Pewter pouted.

"*All right. All right,*" Tucker agreed to put her in a better mood. "*Remember, it's because of you that we're on this mission.*"

"*It's not because of me, it's because Coty Lamont turned up dead in the back of a pickup truck, shot in the back and with a knife through his heart. All I did was report the news of it this morning.*"

"*How is it that Harry didn't know first—or the sanctified Mrs. Hogendobber?*" Paddy smelled a heavy scent of deer lingering in the frost.

"*Cynthia told Harry second. She stopped for coffee and one of Mrs. Hogendobber's bakery concoctions. French toast today and a kind of folded-over something with powdered sugar. Next she dropped in at the post office—.*"

Tucker interjected, "*Said they'd read about it in the papers later, so she'd give them the real facts.*"

"*And then I let you talk me into coming out here. Why I will never know.*" Pewter loudly decried her sore paw pads.

"*Because Coty Lamont slipped into Mim's barn on the night or early* morning when he was killed, that's why, and no one knows it but Rodger Dodger, Pusskin, the horses, and us."

Tucker patiently explained again to Pewter. This was like teaching a puppy to hide a bone. Repetition.

Tucker knew that Pewter figured things out just fine, but in bitching and moaning she could be the center of attention. Then, too, her paw pads, unused to hard running, really were tender.

"*Another human knows, all right.*" Mrs. Murphy spied the cupolas on the stable up ahead. "*Coty's killer.*"

"*You don't know that,*" Paddy said and was informed as to the events that had transpired before Coty was found, the events at Mim's stable. Stubbornly, he said, "*That means Mickey Townsend, since Rodger said he snuck in and found him.*"

"*Sure looks that way, but I've learned not to jump to conclusions, only at mice,*" Murphy slyly offered.

"*Don't sound superior, Murphy. I hate it when you do.*" Pewter puffed as they entered the big open doors trimmed in dark green on white.

Addie and Chark Valiant were arguing in the tack room situated in middle of the stable.

"You've got to get serious about the money."

"Bullshit," Addie defiantly replied.

Chark's voice rose. "You'll piss it all away, Addie—"

She interrupted. "All you and Arthur think about is the money. If I burn through my inheritance, that's my tough luck."

"We should keep our funds together and invest. It's the way to make more money."

"I don't want to do that. I have never wanted to do that. You take your share and I'll take mine."

"That's crazy!" he yelled. "Don't you realize what's at stake?"

"I realize that you and Arthur Tetrick went to court two years ago to extend the term of Arthur's trusteeship." Her face was red, "It's my money. Thank God, the judge didn't extend the term!"

"You were loaded on drugs, Addie. We did the right thing to try and protect you."

"Bullshit!" She threw her hard hat on the floor.

Chark tried another approach. "What if we get another adviser?"

"Dump dear Uncle Arthur?" The word uncle was drenched in sarcasm.

"If it would convince you to keep our money together, yes."

A silence ensued, which Addie finally broke. "No. You and Arthur can watch over your money. I'll watch over mine."

"Goddammit, you're so stupid!"

She screamed, "I'm not going to be under your thumb for the rest of my life!"

"No, you'll just be under the thumb of whatever son of a bitch you fall in love with next—just like Mother."

The sound of a slap reverberated throughout the barn. "I could kill you. I wouldn't be surprised if you killed Nigel."

"You're nuts!" Chark stormed out of the tack room and out of the barn.

The animals, not moving, watched as Addie charged out of the tack room, running after her brother and bellowing at the top of her lungs, "I hate you. I really friggin' hate you!"

"Hi," Rodger called down from the hayloft. "Don't pay any attention to them, they're always fighting over money."

"Hi," called Pusskin, Rodger's adored girlfriend, sitting by his side.

"Have you heard?" Pewter loved to be first with the news, any news.

"No." Rodger climbed backward down the ladder to the hayloft. Pusskin followed.

"Coty Lamont was found murdered last night," Pewter breathlessly informed them.

"*How awful.*" Pusskin slipped a rung, putting her hind paw on Rodger's head.

"*That's why we're all here, Rodg,*" Mrs. Murphy said. "*Let's go into Orion's stall.*"

Rodger, knowing of Paddy's reputation with the female of the species, walked between Pusskin and the handsome black cat with the white tuxedo front and white spats on his paws.

Orion stood in his stall, for he was to be clipped today, a process he loathed. The stiff whiskers on his nose and chin would be shaved off with hair clippers like the ones humans used for a buzz cut. His ears would be trimmed and a path on his poll behind his ears would be cut, a bridle path. The stall was latched.

"*Orion, how are you today?*" Rodger called to him from the tack trunk.

"*How do you think? That damned Addie will twitch me and Chark will play barber shop.*" A twitch was used to keep horses standing still for such beauty treatments. A looped piece of rope at the end of a half broom handle was wrapped around his lip.

"*I'll make a deal,*" Mrs. Murphy called out to him.

"*I'm listening.*" Orion walked over to behold the gathering on his tack box. Tucker was seated beside it.

"*I'll open this latch. I think if we cats push on the door, we can slide it back. Now, I don't care if you run out, but will you wait until we stop digging?*"

The handsome horse blinked, his large brown eyes filled with curiosity. "*What's in my stall, anyway? Sure I'll promise.*"

Mrs. Murphy, lean and agile, stretched to reach the bolt on the stall door. About the width of a human little finger, although longer, the metal bolt slid into a latch, a rounded piece of metal on the top, enabling a human to pull back the latch with one finger. Helped Mrs. Murphy, too. After much tugging, she pulled the fingerhold on the bolt downward, then she pushed with all her might to push the whole bolt back through its latch.

"*You did it.*" Pewter was full of admiration.

"*Now let's push.*" Rodger put his paws on the stall door, right below the X, which strengthened the lower door panel. Paddy put

his paws at the very base of the door. Pewter added her bulk to it,
and Tucker nudged with her nose. In no time at all they rolled the
door back as quietly as they could.

"Over here." Rodger bounded to the spot.

"Let's pull the shavings away from it." Pusskin sent shavings flying
everywhere.

All the cats, plus Tucker, were sprayed with little shavings
bits.

"I can't smell anything," Orion added, "and you know I have a good
sense of smell."

"I can't either," Tucker confessed. "But, Orion, if you'll use your
front hooves to crack up the hard-packed earth, we can get digging faster. We
might find something. Treasure, I bet!"

"Treasure is sweet feed drenched in molasses." Orion chuckled as he
tore out chunks of earth.

Mrs. Murphy mumbled. "Too noisy—it'll bring the humans."

Noisy as Orion was, he dug out a deep saucer much more
quickly than the combined cat and dog claws could have done.
They heard footsteps outside.

"I'm out of here." Orion wheeled and trotted out of his stall
just as Addie, over her fury, walked back into the barn from the
other end.

Once outside, Orion jumped the fence into the pasture
where his buddies chewed on a spread-out round bale of hay.

Two other people came into the tack room from outside.
Tucker leapt into the small crater.

"Anything?" Mrs. Murphy asked her trusted companion.

"Can you smell gold?" Pusskin innocently asked.

Pewter bit her tongue. The pretty tortoiseshell was a kitty
bimbo, but she made Rodger happy in his old age.

"I do smell something. Faint, very faint. Maybe another two feet below,
maybe less."

"What?" came the chorus.

"Well, I don't know exactly. A mammal that's been dead for a long, long
time. It's so faint and dusty, like mildew after the sun hits it."

Before the animals could react, Addie, Charles, and Arthur Tetrick lurched into the open stall.

"What the—?" Addie opened her mouth.

"That damned Orion. He's too smart." Charles slapped his thigh. "He heard the clippers."

"How'd he get out?" Addie stared at the animals, not comprehending that they had freed the hunter. "What is this, an animal convention? Mrs. Murphy, Tucker, Pewter, Paddy, Rodger, and Pusskin even."

The animals remained silent with Tucker slinking toward the door.

Arthur inspected the hole. "Better fill this in right away. It's not good for a horse to stand in an uneven stall. Not good at all."

"But that's the funny thing." Charles removed his baseball cap and ran his fingers through his hair. "Orion isn't a digger."

Arthur snorted. "Well, he is now."

"*You would do best to dig further,*" Mrs. Murphy told Addie.

"*Yeah, Adelia, something's down there,*" Rodger added, noticing that Addie was pointedly ignoring her brother and Arthur.

"I'll get the shovel and pack this back down." Charles left the stall.

"*Keep digging!*" Tucker barked.

"That dog has a piercing bark." Arthur frowned. "I never liked little dogs."

"*I never liked fastidious men,*" Tucker snapped back, then ran out of the stall followed by the other animals.

Adelia snapped too, as she walked away from the stall, "You two are as thick as thieves. I'm going to lunch."

"Come on, Addie." Charles said, but she kept walking away.

"*Rodger and Pusskin, keep your eyes open,*" Mrs. Murphy told them as her small group left the barn. "*Anything at all. A change in routine—*"

"*We will,*" Pusskin agreed. "*But what the humans do is their own business.*"

"*Curiosity killed the cat,*" jibed the big ginger.

"*Don't say that, Rodger. I hate that expression.*" Pusskin frowned.

"*I'm sorry, my sweet.*" He rubbed the side of his face against hers.

Pewter stifled a laugh.

"*Bye,*" they called to one another.

As Mrs. Murphy melted back into the field Paddy said, "*You are nosy.*"

"*Well . . .*" The tiger cat thought a moment. "*I didn't much care until Coty was killed and I found out he'd been in the barn the night before. I don't know—guess I am nosy.*"

"*I'm hungry.*"

"*Another ten minutes.*" Tucker babied Pewter. "*Unless you want to run.*"

"*No, not another yard!*"

"*Wish I could figure out a way to get Mom or even Mim to dig up that stall.*" Murphy thought out loud.

"*About all she knows is when to open a can of food.*" Tucker loved Harry but suffered no illusions about her mental capabilities.

"*You're right,*" Murphy sadly agreed.

"*Whatever is in that stall is going to cause a shitload of trouble,*" Paddy sagely noted. "*And Orion's got to stand on it.*"

"*If he digs it up again just out of curiosity they'll either put him in another stall to see if it's pique on his part or put a rubber mat in the stall. I doubt he'll dig, though.*" Tucker was getting hungry herself.

"*Why do you say that?*" Pewter walked more briskly since she was close to home.

"*He'll be in enough trouble for bolting his stall and digging that hole in the first place. He'll lie low for a while.*" Tucker saw Mrs. Hogendobber's house. "*Hey, I'll race you to the door.*"

"*No,*" Pewter adamantly said, but the others took off, leaving her to grumble as she walked to the post office. "*Bunch of show-offs.*"

19

A small nicotine stain marred Arthur Tetrick's lower lip. A dedicated pipe smoker, he contentedly packed in an expensive mix as he relaxed in Mim's living room. He'd walked up to the house after Addie stalked off.

"Smartest horse. Too smart." He tapped down the tender tobacco releasing a sweet unsmoked fragrance. "You're going to have to put a combination lock on his stall door."

Mim, out of the corner of her eye, saw Chark and one of her grooms chasing Orion in the field. This was a holiday, a canceled school day for the hunter, and he was making the most of it.

"Some sherry, Arthur?"

"No, no." He waved his hand. "No libations until the sun's over the yardarm."

"Coffee or tea then? I have some wonderful teas that Little Marilyn gave me for my birthday."

"A bracing darjeeling would do me a world of good." He held the match over the bowl of his burl pipe, the bowl shining with the use of many years, the draw perfect. That same pipe today would cost well over $250, so Arthur cherished it. No true pipe smoker would stick the flame right into the bowl just as no true cigar smoker would ever put the flame to the end of the cigar.

Mim shook a tiny bell. Gretchen appeared at the doorway. Gretchen and Mim had been together so long neither could imagine life without the other no matter how unequal the terms. "Yes, Miz Big." Her shorthand for Big Marilyn.

"Some darjeeling for the gentleman and some Constant Comment for me."

"Morning, Gretchen." Arthur nodded.

"Morning, Mr. Arthur. Cream or sugar?"

"Cream, well, half-and-half if you have it."

"Oh, Miz Big, she got everything." Gretchen turned, her wiry frame almost leaving a puff of smoke, she turned so fast.

"Mim, I'm here on a mercy mission." He cleared his throat. "As you know, Adelia comes into her inheritance November fourteenth, the day after the Colonial Cup. It's a considerable fortune, as you are aware. At that time she may elect to separate her share from Charles's share, which, of course, I oppose. Adelia is a lovely, lovely girl with absolutely no head for business. She should never be allowed to get her hands on her money. The interest is sufficient to allow her to live very well indeed."

"Bonds. Are you talking bonds, Arthur?" Mim shrewdly asked.

"Well, yes and no. As it now stands the Valiant resources are so conservatively invested that they reap barely six percent per annum. I have deliberately invested conservatively so as to run no risks until they inherit. Once that happens, I would still advise them to be prudent but to diversify more than I did when they were minors. They can afford a bit of risk, you know, keep the bulk in secure investments while targeting a small portion for high-risk/high-yield investments. My fear is, Adelia will take her money and—'' He held up his hands. ''Shiny cars, the usual foolish pleasures . . . Mim, you and I have both seen impulsive scions run through more money than Adelia will inherit. Large as the amount is, no well is bottomless. She greatly respects you. She finds me an old bore.''

''Impossible,'' Mim said brightly as Gretchen delivered the tea.

Mim's tea service, which had been in the family on her mother's side since George III, caught the light, holding it prisoner to the lustrous silver. No one with an eye for beauty could behold her tea service without a slight gasp of appreciation.

''Need anything else?'' Gretchen smiled.

''New knees.''

''I told you not to hunker down there in that garden this summer, but you didn't listen to me. You don't listen to anyone.''

''I'm listening to you now, Gretchen dear.''

''Yes, Miz Big, dear.'' Gretchen put her hands on her hips. ''Mr. Arthur, you talk to her. She is the most stubborn woman God ever put on this earth. She don't listen to me. She don't listen to her husband—'course, I don't listen to mine either. She is just a whirlwind of opinion. Uh-huh.'' That said, Gretchen wheeled and vacated the room.

''She is one of a kind.'' Arthur chuckled.

''Thank God. I don't think I could stand two.''

Mim used the delicate silver tongs to drop a sugar cube into her Constant Comment, making it even sweeter. ''Now let me understand you fully. You want me to tell Adelia to be a bit more aggressive with her investments but not to get crazy and, of course, never, ever, on pain of death, to touch the principal. Ideally she will keep the money together with Charles's.'' A beat. ''And you'd like to remain as an adviser, or in some capacity.''

"Um . . ." He nodded in the affirmative and placed his pipe in the pipe ashtray that Mim kept in the living room as he delicately brought the thin teacup to his lips. "I say, this is marvelous tea. My compliments to Little Marilyn."

"Before I have this financial meeting with her, I want to know who you are recommending for handling the portfolio. After all, out of duty you must recommend people other than yourself. We must hope the children will be wise enough to stick with you."

"I rather like Ed Bancroft at Strongbow and McKee."

"Yes, he's very good, but he's older. They might work better with someone in his or her thirties."

Arthur paled. "Too young, too young. A young person hasn't ridden the market through a few cycles. They panic during contractions." He refused to call a recession or a depression just what it was.

"Good point." She leaned back in the silk-covered chair. "Well, you seem to be the best person for the job. There's always Arnie Skaar, should they wish a change—you know, an assertion of independence."

"Yes, Arnie's good."

"Will you be saddened if you lose your job?" she forthrightly asked.

"Oh, I never thought of it as a job, and in some ways Charles has been Adelia's guardian more than I have. Really, I'll continue to guide them as best I can no matter what happens. I was shocked, when Marylou disappeared, to discover she'd made me her executor. I thought she was so besotted with Mickey Townsend that she might have foolishly changed her will. Devastated as I was to lose Marylou, I was heartened by her caution on this matter." He drew on his pipe. "Charles and I have been able to draw together. Adelia favored Mickey, and, well—women are so unpredictable." He held up his hands as if in supplication.

"You've done your best. Being anyone's executor is a time-consuming and sad process. I was Mother's executor, and I learned more in that one year than I think I did in all the years before." Mim poured Arthur more tea. "Terrible news this morning. It's giving us all the chills."

"What?" He inhaled the delicate yet strong tea aroma.

"You haven't heard?" Mim put her cup and saucer down.

"No."

"Coty Lamont was stabbed through the heart on a dirt road off Route Twenty-Two. Dumped in the back of his pickup truck."

"Good God!" Arthur's cup slipped from his hand. He captured it with his saucer but slopped tea everywhere. "I'm so sorry, Mim."

"Scotchgard." She tinkled for Gretchen again. "Works wonders."

"Ma'am." Gretchen perceived the situation as soon as the "Ma'am" was out of her wide and generous mouth. "I'll be back."

She returned quickly with dishtowels, mopping up Arthur and dabbing the rug. "No harm done."

"I do apologize. It was such a shock."

"What shock?" Gretchen wouldn't budge.

"Oh, Gretchen, Sheriff Shaw called to tell me there's been another murder. Coty Lamont."

"That handsome good-for-nothing jockey? Why, he used to ride for you, didn't he, Mr. Arthur, back when you was in the game?"

"Yes, yes, I gave him his start. I gave a lot of men a leg up, so to speak. He left me to ride for Mickey Townsend and then moved on from there. That's the way of the world—the young and ambitious, climbing the ladder." He wiped his brow with a neatly folded linen handkerchief. "This is too much. Why didn't Adelia and Charles say something?"

"They don't know yet. Rick just called. I'd like to think I was his first call, but I doubt it. I'm going to buy one of those CBs that lets me listen to police calls."

"No, you aren't," Gretchen scolded. "You'll be running all

over the county. Bad enough that Mr. Jim does it. 'Course, being mayor he has to, I guess.''

"Something's dreadfully wrong," Mim blurted out. "Arthur, you officiate at different races. Surely, you must know something.''

"No." He wiped his brow again. "Coty Lamont. It doesn't seem possible. And stabbed through the heart, you say?''

Mim nodded. "Apparently he wasn't as easy to kill as Nigel Danforth was because Rick says he was shot first. Of course, they'll do an autopsy, but he believes the shot preceded the stabbing. This grotesque symbol—the stiletto through the heart. And another playing card.''

"What do you mean?" Gretchen asked, curiosity getting the better of her.

"Gretchen . . . oh, sit down and have some tea. I'll get a crick in my neck turning around to talk to you.''

Gretchen quickly fetched another cup, eagerly plopped down and helped herself to some of the darjeeling.

"You see," Mim intoned, "the first man murdered had a playing card over his heart. The Queen of Clubs. Fair Haristeen found him. And Arthur, I must talk to you about Fair. Anyway, this second murder—" She paused. "The Queen of Spades.''

"Mojo." Gretchen downed her tea in one big swallow.

Arthur smiled indulgently. "I don't think anyone knows voodoo in central Virginia.''

"Mojo." She clamped her jaw shut.

"Well, if it isn't mojo, it still means something.''

"Means something wild. You stab a man through the heart, you got to get real close. You got to look in his eyes and smell his breath. You got to hate him worse than the angel hate the Evil One. I know 'bout these things.''

Arthur shuddered. "Gretchen, you are very graphic.''

"When was the last time you saw Coty?" Mim asked him.

"Montpelier. I was always proud of him, you know—that I

saw his talent early and encouraged it. I emphatically did not encourage his arrogance."

Mim's tone flattened a bit. "But he was arrogant—arrogant and too clever by half."

"Ain't clever now."

"That's just it, Gretchen. Maybe he was, and like I said, he was too clever by half always playing odds with the bookies through fronts like Linda Forloines. No one could catch him at it." She smoothed over her skirt. "I suppose I'll go down and tell Charles and Adelia. Arthur, I'll wait a day or two to have that financial discussion with Adelia."

"Of course, of course. Well, I'd better be heading home. I was going to run some errands in town, then go to the office, but I think I'll go straight home and, well—ponder."

"Nothing to ponder. Somebody got a backwards passion. It's worse than hate—reverse love." Gretchen picked up the silver tray and ambled out.

20

"I resent that. I resent this whole damned line of questioning!" Mickey Townsend roared in Rick Shaw's face.

Rick, accustomed to such displays, calmly folded his hands as Cynthia Cooper, behind him, took notes. "I don't think there's any way to make this pleasant. Nigel Danforth rode for you and—"

"Rode for me for two months. How the hell did I know he was, uh—a non-person?"

"You could have checked his green card."

"Well, I didn't. He was a decent jock and I let it go, so call down the damned bloodhounds from Immigration on me. They'll harass me for hiring a skilled Brit, yet they let riffraff pour over the border and go on welfare and we pay for it!"

"Mr. Townsend, I wouldn't know about that," Rick Shaw

replied dryly. "But you are a successful trainer. You have knowledge of the steeplechase world, and two jockeys have been killed within a week of one another under similar circumstances. You knew them both. And they both rode for you at various times."

His face reddened. "Balls! Everyone in the game knew Coty Lamont. I don't like your line of questioning, Shaw, and I don't much like you."

"You're accustomed to having your own way, aren't you?"

"Most successful people are, Sheriff." Townsend folded his burly arms across his chest. "So I'm a prick. That doesn't make me a killer."

"Did you owe Nigel Danforth money?"

"Absolutely not. I pay at the end of the day's race."

"Easier when you don't have withholding taxes and Social Security to worry about, isn't it?"

"You're damned right it is, and taxes will destroy this nation. You mark my words."

"Did you owe Coty Lamont money?"

"Why would I owe Coty Lamont money?" The bushy eyebrows knitted together.

"That's what I'm asking you."

"No."

"Did you like Coty Lamont?"

"No."

"Why?"

"That's my business. He was a talented son of a bitch. That's all I'm prepared to say."

"We'll get a lot further along if you cooperate with me." He swiveled to exchange looks with Coop, who frowned. This was part of their routine before recalcitrant subjects. They could play "good cop, bad cop" but Mick was too smart for that game.

"Well, let me try another tack then. Did either Nigel Danforth or Coty Lamont owe you money?"

"No." Mick rolled his forefinger over his neat black mustache. "Yes."

"Who and how much?"

"Nigel owed me three hundred forty-seven dollars, a collection of poker debts, and Coty owed, oh, about one hundred twenty-two dollars."

"You didn't like Coty but you played poker with him?"

"Hey, there's down time in this business. I don't have to love a guy to let him sit in on a poker game."

"You're a good player?"

Mick shrugged.

Cynthia chimed in, "Everyone says you're slick as an eel."

"They say that because they don't remember which cards are out and which ones are still in the deck. If you're playing stud, that's all you gotta do." He shrugged those powerful shoulders again. "I'm not so smart."

Rick rubbed his receding hairline. It was almost as if he were searching for the hair. "Coop, can you think of anything?"

"One little thing—Mr. Townsend, do the card suits have a special significance?"

"What do you mean?"

"Well, what if—crazy, I know, but what if I had a royal flush in hearts and you had one in spades. Who would win?"

"I would. The suits in ascending order are clubs, diamonds, hearts and spades."

"But wouldn't most people declare it a draw?" Rick puzzled. "I mean most people wouldn't know the significance of the suits. At least, I don't think they would. If a situation like that occurred, wouldn't you draw off the deck, high card takes it?"

"In a situation with two royal flushes, you'd both have cardiac arrest and it wouldn't matter. The odds are impossible."

"But you know the significance of the suits," Rick pressed.

"Yes, I do."

"Isn't there another way to look at the suits, a non-poker way?" Cynthia asked.

He leaned back in his chair. "Sure."

"Can you tell me what that is?"

"You've done your homework. You tell me." He stared at her.

"All right." She smiled at him. "Clubs represent humans at their basest. Spades is a step up. Instead of clobbering one another, they work the earth. Diamonds is a higher level than that, obviously, but the highest type of human would fall into the heart category."

"Well put." Mickey smiled back at the young officer. He couldn't help himself. She was nice-looking.

"A club and a spade have been used," Rick drawled.

"So next comes a diamond. Somebody rich." Mickey folded his arms across his chest. "Won't be me. I'm not rich."

21

Totem, a Thoroughbred hotter than Hades, ditched most people who climbed on his back. The only reason he wasn't turned into Alpo was that he could run like blazes. Dr. D'Angelo had bought him on sight from Mickey Townsend at Montpelier. Linda Forloines, furious that she wasn't in on the deal and hence got no commission, plotted how to get rid of the animal.

She promised Dr. D'Angelo that she would faithfully work Totem. She'd then take a bar of soap and lather him up fifteen minutes before D'Angelo walked into the stable. This way the horse looked as though he'd been exercised. Then Linda would make up a story about how he had behaved, full of little details to cement her lies. As soon as D'Angelo left she'd hose the horse off and turn him out in the paddock.

Will, grabbing the halter with a lead chain over the nose, helped his wife walk the horse to the paddock.

"I'll get this horse out of here in two months' time," she bragged.

"How?"

"Ask Bob Drake to ride him when D'Angelo's here."

"Bob Drake can't ride this horse." Will's eyes widened.

"Exactly." She grunted as the large animal bumped into her. She hit his rib cage with her fist, hoping he'd not bump into her again.

They both breathed a sigh of relief when Totem walked into his paddock and the gate closed behind him.

"Linda, Bob could get hurt—bad."

She shrugged, "He's a big boy. He doesn't have to ride the horse."

Will pondered that. "Well, he gets planted. Then what?"

"Then I tell D'Angelo he could get sued with a horse like this. I'd better take it off his hands."

Will smiled, "The commission ought to be pretty good."

"Just remember"—she winked at him—"we're going to own our own stable—real soon. We can make money in this business. Real money."

"What if D'Angelo won't sell?"

"He will." She rubbed her hands together. "I've got him all figured out. Listen, honey, I've got to make a pick up tonight. I'll be back real late."

He frowned. "I wish you'd let me go with you."

"I'm safe. It's better if only one of us knows who the supplier is. Since I knew him first, it doesn't make sense to drag you into it. And he'd never allow it."

Will shielded his head as a gust of wind blew straw and hay bits everywhere. "It's dangerous."

"Nah."

"Two of our best customers are dead."

"Has nothing to do with us."

"God, I hope not." Will's features drained of animation.

Linda didn't want Will to know the supplier for two reasons. In a tight spot he might spill the beans, ruining everything. And he'd know the exact amount of coke being sold to her. That would never do because she didn't want him to know how much she kept back for herself. She cut it lightly once before bringing it back home. Then she and Will cut it together, using a white powdered laxative.

Will could be the brawn of the outfit. She was the brains. What he didn't know wouldn't hurt him.

Later that night, at ten-thirty, when Linda pulled out of the driveway in the truck, Will hurried outside and jumped into Dr. D'Angelo's old farm truck. He followed her, lights off, until she turned south on Route 15. He allowed a few cars to buffer the zone between himself and his wife. Then he clicked on the lights and followed her to her rendezvous.

22

Silver strands of rain poured over the windshield. Harry could barely see as she drove to work. The windshield wipers sloshed back and forth, allowing momentary glimpses of a road she luckily knew well.

Mrs. Murphy, paws on the dash, alert, helped Harry drive. Tucker wasn't quite able to rest her hind paws on the bench seat and reach for the dash.

"*Big puddle up ahead,*" the cat warned.

Harry slowed, wondering why her tiger was so chatty.

"*Mom, a stranded car dead ahead.*" Mrs. Murphy's claws dug into the dash.

Mickey Townsend's beautiful silver BMW rested by the side of the road, the right wheels in a drainage ditch that had swollen from a trickle to a torrent.

Harry stopped, putting on her turn signal because the old truck's flasher fuse had a tendency to blow. Of course, that wasn't as annoying as having the gear shift stick whenever she tried to put it in third gear. The passenger window looked as though Niagara were pouring over it. She couldn't see a thing.

"Damn." She pulled ahead of the beached vehicle, careful not to suffer the same fate. "Guys, stay here."

"Don't go out in that," Mrs. Murphy told her. "You'll catch your death of cold."

"Stop complaining, Murphy. You stay right here. I mean it."

She clapped her dad's old cowboy hat on her head, which channeled the water away from her face and off the back and front of the hat. She'd never found anything better for keeping the rain out of her eyes. She also wore her Barbour coat, a dark green dotted with mud, and her duck boots. They would keep her dry.

She slipped out, quickly closed the door, and prayed no one would skid around the curve as it appeared Mickey Townsend must have done. She put her hand over her eyes and peered into the driver's seat. Nothing. She walked around to the other side, just to be sure he wasn't bending over outside his car, trying to figure out how to extricate himself from this mess. He wasn't there.

She lifted herself back up into the truck, clicked off the turn signal, and rolled on down the road. By the time she walked through the back door, carrying both Mrs. Murphy and Tucker under her Barbour, Mrs. Hogendobber had sorted out one bag of mail.

"Miranda, I'm sorry I'm late. I couldn't go over twenty-five miles an hour, the visibility was so awful."

"Don't worry about it," Mrs. Hogendobber airily replied. "The water is ready for tea and I whipped up oatmeal muffins last night and another batch of glazed doughnuts. I can't bake enough doughnuts for Market. He sells out by ten o'clock."

"Oh, thanks." Harry gratefully pulled off her raincoat as

Mrs. Murphy and Tucker shook off the few drops of water that had fallen on them. Harry hung up her coat on the coat rack by the back door and poured herself a cup of tea. "I'd die without tea."

"I doubt that, but you'd sure be grouchy in the morning." Miranda helped herself to a second cup.

"Oh, I better call Rick." Harry carried the steaming cup with her to the phone.

"Now what's wrong?"

"Mickey Townsend's BMW is stranded at Harper's Curve." She punched the numbers.

"I hope he's all right. Things are so—queer just now."

Harry nodded. "Sheriff Shaw, please, it's Mary Minor Haristeen." She waited a minute. "Hi, Sheriff. Mickey Townsend's BMW has two wheels dropped in a ditch at Harper's Curve. I got out to check it and it's empty."

"Thanks, Harry. I'll send someone over once things quiet down. It's one fender bender after another on a day like this." He paused a moment. "Did you say Mickey Townsend's car?"

"Uh-huh."

His voice sounded strained. "Thanks. I'll get right on it. That curve can be evil."

The phone clicked and Harry put the receiver back in the cradle.

"Well?"

"At first he didn't seem too worried about it but now he's sending someone right over."

"You know at choir practice last night Ysabel Yadkin swore that Mickey is involved in a big gambling scam and that Nigel Danforth owed him oo-scoobs of money. I asked her what was the last steeplechase she attended and she gave me the hairy eyeball, I can tell you. 'Well, Ysabel,' I said, 'if you're going to tell tales, you ought to at least know the people you're talking about.' She fried. But then after practice she came over and declared that I was being snotty because I had horsey friends. Her Albert knows Mickey Townsend because he works on that expensive car of his."

"Since when did Albert start working on BMWs?"

Mrs. Hogendobber drained her mug, returning to the second mailbag. "Since they offered him more money than Mercedes."

"Mrs. H., sit down, you did that first bag all by yourself. I'll do this one."

"Idle hands do the devil's work. I don't mind."

Together they tipped the bag into the mail cart just as Boom Boom Craycroft sashayed through the front door at eight o'clock sharp.

"What a morning, and the temperature is dropping. I hope this doesn't turn to ice."

"We're a little behind, Boom Boom, and it's my fault."

"I can help."

"Oh, no, don't bother," said Harry, who knew that Boom Boom's idea of help would be to sort for five minutes, then have a fit of the vapors. "Why don't you run a few errands and come on back in about half an hour?"

"I guess I could." She plucked her umbrella out of the stand where she had dropped it. "Isn't it awful about Coty Lamont?"

Before she had the complete sentence out of her mouth a soaking-wet Mickey Townsend pushed open the door and sagged against the wall.

"Mickey, are you all right?" Boom Boom reached out to him.

"Yes, by the grace of God." He began shaking; he was chilled to the bone.

"Come back here." Miranda flipped up the dividing barrier. "You need a hot drink. I'll run to the house and get some of George's clothes. They're too big for you but at least they're dry."

"Oh, Mrs. Hogendobber, a cup of coffee will put me right." His teeth chattered, belying his words.

"Now you stay right here," Miranda commanded as Harry made him a cup of instant coffee.

"Sugar and cream?" Harry opened the tiny refrigerator to reach for the cream.

"Two sugars and a dab of cream." He held out his hand for the cup, then put both hands around it, vainly trying to stop shaking.

Boom Boom joined them as Mickey dripped water all over the floor.

"He's white as a sheet," Tucker noted.

"I stopped by your car." Harry threw her coat over his shoulders.

"How long ago?"

"Fifteen, twenty minutes."

"Just missed me." His teeth hit the rim of the cup. "I couldn't find a house. I headed into the cornfield there but realized I had to come back to the road because I couldn't see anything and I'd get lost. I mean, I know that territory but I couldn't see a damned thing and I was—" He gulped down a few warm mouthfuls of coffee. "God, that tastes good."

Miranda pushed open the back door, turned and shook her umbrella out the door, and then closed it because the wind was blowing the rain into the post office. A shopping bag of clothes hung on her arm. "You go right into the bathroom and towel off. There's a big towel here on top. And get into these clothes."

Mickey did as he was told, finally emerging in pants with rolled cuffs and the sleeves of George's old navy sweater rolled up, too, but he was warm.

"Mrs. Hogendobber never throws anything out." Mrs. Murphy laughed. "I guess it's a good thing."

He ate a glazed doughnut and continued his story. "I found the road again and knew if I could get into town you'd be in the post office early. Say, I'd better call a towing service."

"I already called Rick Shaw."

"What for?"

"I didn't know where you were or whether you were okay—things being what they are," Harry said forthrightly. "So I called him."

"Well, he's not worried about me. He treats me like the chief suspect."

"He sounded worried enough on the phone," Harry stated.

"Yeah—well." Mickey slumped a moment, then straightened his back. "I guess I'm a little worried, too."

"Everyone's worried." Boom Boom nibbled an oatmeal muffin.

"I know that road like the back of my hand. Someone swooped down behind me and ran me off the road."

"People don't pay attention to the weather—" Miranda prepared to launch into a diatribe about the bad driving habits of the younger generation, meaning anyone younger then herself.

Mickey cut her off, "No, whoever this was wanted to run me off the road—or worse."

"What?" Boom Boom stopped mid-bite.

"They nudged me from behind and then drew alongside and pushed me right off the road. If we'd been twenty yards further up the road, it would have been a steep drop, I can tell you that."

"Could you see who it was?" Harry asked.

"Hell, no, not in this rain. It was a big-ass truck, I can tell you that. I'm not even sure about the color, although I thought I caught a glimpse of black or dark blue. GMC maybe, but I don't know. It happened so fast."

"*Why don't they ask him what he was doing down that road in the first place?*" Mrs. Murphy rubbed against Tucker.

"*Too polite.*" Tucker loved it when the cat rubbed on her.

"*This is no time to be polite. And furthermore, I don't believe him.*"

"*You don't believe he was run off the road?*"

"*I believe that.*" The cat's whiskers touched and tickled Tucker's nose. "*But he's hiding something.*"

"Maybe he knows what's in Orion's stall?"

"Tucker, I don't know about that. I don't think we'll ever get the humans to dig down deep enough, and Orion can't help. He's switched to another stall, remember?"

"Yeah. So what is it about Mickey Townsend?"

"You can smell fear as well as I can."

23

Harry, Susan, Fair, Big Mim, Little Marilyn, and Boom Boom all had their noses out of joint because the rain had forced them to bag their long-planned foxhunting with Keswick Hunt Club. The only good thing about the rained-out Saturday was that Harry finally went grocery shopping.

As she wheeled her cart around the pet food aisle, always her first stop, she saw Cynthia Cooper piling bags of birdseed into her cart.

"Coop."

"Hey. Great minds run in the same direction."

"Mrs. Murphy will shred the house if I don't get her tuna. She tore the arm off the sofa last week. I still haven't put it back together."

"Because of tuna?"

"No. I left her home from Montpelier and took Tucker. Made her hateful mean."

Five years ago, hearing a story like that, Cynthia Cooper would have thought it a fabrication. However, she had grown to know Harry's cat and dog as well as other Crozet animals. The stories were true. In fact, Mrs. Murphy had pointed out a skull fragment to her on a case at Monticello. It could have been blind luck but then again—

"One of these days I'll get a cat, but I work the most terrible hours. Maybe I need a husband before the cat. That way he can take care of the cat when I'm on duty."

"Hope you have better luck than I did."

"Doesn't it make you crazy that everyone tries to get you and Fair back together—including Fair?" Cynthia laughed.

Harry rested her elbows on the push bar of the cart. "Lack of imagination. They don't believe another eligible man will come through Crozet."

"Blair Bainbridge." She was referring to the model who had bought the farm next to Harry's a few years back.

"His career takes him away for such long stretches of time. And I think Marilyn Sanburne the younger has set her cap for him."

"Quaint expression."

"I'm trying not to be rude." Harry inadvertently kicked the cart and almost fell on her face as it rolled out from under her.

"How much more shopping?" Cynthia pointed to Harry's long list.

"Forty-five minutes. Why?"

"If you buy pasta I'll make it."

"No kidding?" Harry eagerly said. Not being much of a cook, she loved being asked to dinner or having someone cook for her.

"That way we can catch up." Cynthia put her finger to her lips, the hush sign.

Harry understood right away. "Be back at the house in an hour."

As she rounded the next aisle in a hurry, she beheld Boom Boom, ear pressed to cans of baked beans.

"I'm in this aisle now." Harry had to twit her. "I mean, unless the beans are talking to you."

"You need to do something about your hostility level. I really and truly want to take you to Lifeline with me."

"I am doing something about my hostility level." Harry mimicked Boom Boom's mature and understanding voice, the one reserved for moments of social superiority. With that she pushed her cart away.

"What do you mean?" Boom Boom put her hands on her hips. "Harry, come back here."

Harry twirled around the next aisle without looking back. Boom Boom, miffed, hurried after her. "What do you mean?"

"Nothing," Harry called over her shoulder, throwing items into her cart at a fast clip.

Boom Boom, never one to miss an emotional morsel, cut the corner too close and rammed into a toilet paper display that tumbled over the floor, into her cart, and onto her head.

Harry stopped and laughed. She couldn't help it. Then she turned her cart, threw a couple rolls into it and said to the fuming Boom Boom, "Wiped out, Boom."

"Oh, shut up, Harry!"

"Ha!"

Cynthia hooted as Harry recounted the supermarket incident. She dipped a wooden fork into the boiling water to pluck out a few noodles. "Not quite ready."

Harry set the table. Mrs. Murphy reposed as the centerpiece. Tucker mournfully gazed at the checkered tablecloth.

"Here." Harry tossed the corgi a green milkbone.

"*How can you eat that stuff?*" Murphy curled her front paws under her chest.

"*I'll eat anything that doesn't eat me first.*"

"*Very funny. My grandmother told me that joke.*" The cat flicked her right ear.

"Here we go." Cynthia put the pasta on the table. "Is she going to eat with us?"

"Well—if she bothers you I'll put her on the floor, but she loves pasta with butter, so once this cools I'll fix her a plate."

"Harry, you'll spoil that cat."

"Not enough," came the swift reply as Harry diced pasta for the cat and then made a small bowl for Tucker too. She put butter on her own noodles while Cynthia drenched hers in a creamy clam sauce.

"Can't I interest you in this sauce?"

"You can interest me, but I've got to lose five pounds before winter really sets in or I won't get rid of it until April. Susan and I made a vow last week not to put on winter weight."

"You aren't one pound overweight."

"You don't squeeze into my jeans."

"Harry, you're reading too many fashion magazines. The models are anorexic."

"I don't subscribe to one fashion magazine," Harry proudly proclaimed.

"Of course not. You read whatever comes into the post office."

Harry sheepishly curled her noodles onto the fork. "Well, I suppose I do."

"You're the best-read person in Crozet."

"That's not saying much." Harry laughed.

"The Reverend Jones reads a lot."

"Yes, that's true. How'd you know that?"

"Called on him yesterday in the course of my duties."

"Oh."

"I wondered how well he knew Coty Lamont, Mickey Townsend, and the rest of the steeplechase crowd, and if he knows any knife collectors."

"He knows more people than anyone except Mim and Miranda, I swear. Did he know anything about those—"

"More!" Tucker barked.

"No." Harry sternly reprimanded the greedy dog.

"Said he knew Coty Lamont from years back when he was a groom. I also asked him about Rick's bait and switch idea. Put a fake tattoo on a horse's upper lip and sell it for a lot of money. Herb said it just wouldn't work today. Rick's having a hard time giving up his pet theory since we're running into dead ends. The boss can be very stubborn."

"That's a nice way to put it." Harry scooped more pasta on her plate and used just a little of the clam sauce, which was delicious. "Did he have any ideas about what's going on?"

"No. You know Herb, he likes to rummage around in the past. He took off on a tangent, telling me about when Arthur Tetrick and Mickey Townsend were both in love with Marylou Valiant. Coty Lamont used to spy on Mickey for Arthur."

"Spy?"

"Wrong word. He'd pump the grooms at Mickey's for news about when and if he'd dated Marylou that week. She dated both of them for about six months and then finally broke it off with Arthur." She giggled. "It's hard to imagine Arthur Tetrick being romantic."

"Guess it was hard for Marylou too."

They both laughed.

Cynthia recounted what the minister had told her. "After Marylou disappeared, Herb said Arthur suffered a nervous breakdown."

"He did. They had to hospitalize him for a week or two, which made him feel even worse because he wasn't there for the Valiants. Larry Johnson admitted him."

"Mim took care of the Valiants. That's what Herb said."

"Yeah. It was pretty awful. She offered a ten-thousand-dollar reward for any information leading to Marylou's whereabouts. As soon as Arthur was released, he wanted the Valiants with him. Mim told him a woman was better able to look after their needs than a man. Arthur didn't want Mickey to see them at all and Mim disagreed with that, too. Addie was hurt enough. She needed Mickey. This provoked another huge fight between Arthur and Mickey. So Adelia was sent away to school, Charles graduated from Cornell and worked in Maryland for a while. Addie always came home to visit Mickey during her vacations. Arthur and Mickey really hate one another. Mickey didn't get a cent from Marylou. He wasn't mentioned in her will. They hadn't been together long enough, I guess. Mim did her best for the Valiants—well, for Marylou, I would say. She was a true friend."

Coop asked, "Did Mim inherit anything from Marylou?"

"A bracelet as a memento. I don't think Mim ever accepted money from Arthur for the kids' bills, except maybe tuition. Addie didn't stay at school long, of course. Hated it."

"I was brand-new to the force when all that was going on . . . the disappearance. Had nothing to do with the case. Mostly I answered the telephone and punched information into the computer until I had it out with Rick."

"I didn't know that."

"Oh, yeah. I told him he was giving me secretarial work and I was a police officer. He surprised me because he thought about it and then said, 'You're right.' We've gotten along ever since. More than that. I adore the guy. Like a brother," she hastened to add.

They ate in silence for a few moments. Mrs. Murphy reached onto Harry's plate, pulling off a long noodle. Harry pretended not to notice. Cynthia knew better than to say anything.

"Coop, what is going on?"

"Damned if I know. The autopsy report came back on Coty Lamont. Full of toot. So was Nigel. No fingerprints on the body. No sign of struggle. It's really frustrating."

Harry shook her head. "I bet a lot of those guys are on cocaine. Maybe they owed their dealer."

"Drugs are responsible for most of the crime in this country. One other little tidbit you have to promise not to tell."

"Not even Miranda?"

"No."

Harry sighed deeply. It pained her to keep a secret from Miranda or Susan. "Okay."

"There is no Nigel Danforth."

"Huh?"

"Fake name. We can't find out who he is or was. We're hoping that sooner or later someone who doesn't know he's dead will look for him, file a missing persons report." She rested her fork across the white plate. "That's a long shot though."

"Mickey Townsend doesn't know who he is?"

"No, and Rick put it to him. None too kindly either."

"Whoeee, bet Mickey doubled for Mount Vesuvius."

"He kept it in check."

"That's odd."

"We think so, too."

"*Mickey's scared,*" Mrs. Murphy interjected.

"Honey, you've had enough." Harry thought the cat was talking about food.

"*I wish just once you would listen to me,*" Murphy grumbled. "*He's scared and there's something in Mim's barn.*"

"*Something not nice,*" Tucker added.

Harry stroked the cat while Cynthia fed Tucker a bit of buttered bread. "She has the most intelligent face."

"*Oh, puleese,*" the cat drawled.

"Do you think Mickey's in on the murders?"

"I don't think anything. I'm trying to gather facts. He's got an alibi for the first murder because so many people saw him at the time of the murder. He was loading horses from the smaller barns. But then everyone's got an alibi for that murder. As for the second murder—anyone could have done it. And when we review the principals' time frame at Montpelier, most anyone could have done in Nigel Danforth. We've even reconstructed Charles Valiant's moves about the time of the murder because he and Nigel had an argument at the races. Nothing hangs together.''

"Did you go through mug shots to try and find Nigel?''

"We punched into the computer. Nothing. We've sent out his dental records. Nothing. I think the guy is clean.'' She shrugged. "Then again . . .''

"Before the races Jim Sanburne and Larry Johnson told me to watch out because Charles and Mickey had gotten into it at the Maryland Cup last year,'' Harry said. "They thought there'd be trouble between the jockeys, but then they didn't know that Addie had fallen for Nigel. That's not where the trouble came from, though. Odd.''

"Linda Forloines and Nigel. Yes, we've tried to piece that together. Frank Yancey interrogated Will and Linda separately. We're getting around to them. Rick's instincts are razor sharp. I wanted to drive right up Fifteen North and flush them out, but Rick said 'Wait.' He believes some other bird dog will flush their game.''

"You think they're in on this? Actually, I detest Linda Forloines to such a degree that I'm not a good person to judge.''

"Lots of people detest her,'' Cynthia said. "She's a petty crook and not above selling horses to the knackers while telling the owner she's found them a good home.''

"She's so transparent that it's ludicrous—if you know horses.'' Harry piled more pasta on her plate.

"She's selling cocaine again. Rick thinks she'll lead us to the killer—or killers.''

"You do think she's in on it.'' Harry's voice lowered although no one else was there.

"Linda was the one who indirectly accused Fair of doping horses.''

"I'll kill the bitch!''

"No, you won't,'' Cynthia ordered her. "Frank Yancey saw

right through her when she planted her 'suspicion.' When Colbert Mason at National got a little worried, we sat back to see
what he would do. Mim's faxing off the lawyer's letter pushed
Colbert to contact Linda and tell her she had to file a formal
complaint. She backed off in a hurry."

"What a worthless excuse for a human being she is."

"True, but why did she do that, Harry?"

"Because she likes to stir the pot, fish in muddy waters, use
any phrase you like."

"You can do better than that." Cynthia gathered up the
dishes.

"She's throwing you off the scent."

"We've been watching her. She scurried straight to some of
the people she's been supplying. Less to warn them than to shut
their traps. At least that's what we think. We can't keep a tail on
her around the clock, though. We don't have enough people in
the department. We're hoping she'll lead us to the supplier."

"Did she sell coke to Coty Lamont?"

"Yes. She also sold it to Nigel Danforth. His blood was full
of it, too. Jockeys are randomly tested, and we believe they were
tipped off as to when they would be tested."

Harry whistled in amazement. "Poor Addie."

"Why?"

"Jeez, Cynthia, she was about to get mixed up with a user."

"My instincts tell me she's back on it again."

"I hate to think that."

"You can help me." Cynthia leaned forward. "The stiletto
used in these murders is called a silver shadow. They retail for
anywhere from ninety to one hundred ten dollars. I've checked
every dealer from Washington to Richmond to Charlotte, North
Carolina. They don't keep records of who buys knives. It's not
like guns. Apparently a stiletto is not a big seller because it's not
as useful as a Bowie knife. Only six have been sold in the various
shops I called. Anyway I'm still checking on this, but it's slipping
down on my things-to-do list because we're being overwhelmed

after the second murder. The pressure from the press isn't helping. Rick's ready to trade in the squad car for a tank and roll over
those press buzzards." She paused. "If you should see or hear
anything about knives—tell me."

"Sure."

"One other thing." Harry's expression was quizzical as
Cynthia continued. "If this is about drugs, the person committing these crimes might not be rational."

"Do you think murder can be rational?"

"Absolutely. All I'm saying is, keep your cards close to your
chest." She winced. "I wish I hadn't said that."

"Me, too," the cat chimed in.

24

The foxes stayed in their burrows, the field mice curled up in their nests, and the blue jays, those big-mouthed thieves, didn't venture out. The rains abated finally, but temperatures plummeted, leaving the earth encased in solid ice.

Fortunately, since it was Sunday, there wasn't much traffic. While this cut down on the car accidents, it also made most people feel marooned in their own homes.

Mrs. Murphy hunted in the hayloft while Tucker slept in the heated tack room. Simon, the opossum, was fast asleep on his old horse blanket, which Harry had donated for his welfare. The owl also slept overhead in the cupola.

The tiger knew where the blacksnake slept, so she avoided her. By now the snake was five years old and a formidable presence even when hibernating.

Hunched on top of a hay bale, an aromatic mixture of orchard grass and alfalfa, Murphy listened to the mice twittering in the corner. They'd hollowed out a hay bale in the back corner of the loft and into it dragged threads, pieces of paper, even pencil stubs until the abode was properly decorated and toasty. Mrs. Murphy knew that periodically a mouse would emerge and scurry across the hayloft, down the side of a stall, then slide out between the stall bars. The object was usually the feed room or the tack room. They'd eaten a hole in Harry's faded hunter-green barn jacket. Mrs. Hogendobber patched it for her because Harry couldn't imagine barn chores without that jacket.

Harry fed Tomahawk, Gin Fizz, and Poptart half rations, which caused no end of complaining down below. If the horses couldn't be turned out for proper exercise, Harry cut back on the food. She feared colic like the plague. A horse intestine could get blocked or worse, twisted, and the animal would paw at its belly with its hind hooves, roll on the ground in its torment, and sometimes die rapidly. Usually colic could be effectively treated if detected early.

The three horses—two geldings and one mare—sassy in their robust health, couldn't imagine colic, so they bitched and moaned, clanged their feed buckets against the walls, and called to one another about what a horrible person Harry was to cheat on food.

Mrs. Murphy had half a mind to tell them to shut up and count themselves lucky when one of the mice sped from the nest. The cat leapt up and out into the air, a perfect trajectory for pouncing, but the canny mouse, seeing the shadow and now smelling the cat, zigzagged and made it to the side of the stall.

Mrs. Murphy couldn't go down the stall side, but she walked on the beam over it, dropping down into Poptart's stall just as the mouse cruised through the stall bars. Mrs. Murphy rocked back on her haunches, shot up to the stall bars, grabbed the top with her paws, then slipped back into the stall because her claws couldn't hold on to the iron.

"*Dammit!*" she cursed loudly.

"*You'll never get those mice, Murphy.*" Poptart calmly chewed on her hay. "*They wait for you to appear and then run like mad. She's eating grain in the feed room right now, laughing at you.*"

"*Well, how good of you to tell me,*" Murphy spat. "*I don't see you doing anything to keep the barn free of vermin. In fact, Poptart, I don't see you doing much of anything except feeding your face.*"

Placidly rising above the abuse, the huge creature stretched her neck down until she touched Murphy's nose. "*Hey, shortchange, you're trapped in my stall, so you'd better watch your tongue.*"

"*Oh, yeah.*"

With that the cat leapt onto the horse's broad gray back. Poptart, startled, swung her body alongside the stall bars. With one fluid motion Mrs. Murphy launched herself through the stall bars, landing on the tack trunk outside.

Poptart blinked through the stall bars as Mrs. Murphy crowed, "*You might be bigger but I'm smarter!*"

Having a good sense of humor, the horse chuckled, then returned to her orchard grass/alfalfa mix, which tasted delicious.

The cat trotted into the feed room. Sure enough, she could hear the mouse behind the feed bin. Harry lined her feed bins with tin because mice could eat their way through just about anything. However, grains spilled over and the mice had eaten a tiny hole in the wall. They'd grab some grains, then run into the hole to enjoy their booty.

Mrs. Murphy sat by the hole.

A tiny nose peeped out, the black whiskers barely visible. "*I know you're there and I'm not coming out. Go home and eat tuna.*"

Murphy batted at the hole and the little nose withdrew. "*I'm a cat. I kill mice. That's my job.*"

"*Kill moles. They're more dangerous, you know. If one of these horses steps into a mole hole? Crack.*"

"*Clever, aren't you?*"

"*No, just practical,*" came the squeak.

"*We're all part of the food chain.*"

"Bunk." To prove the point the mouse threw out a piece of crimped oat.

"I will get you in good time," Mrs. Murphy warned. "You fellows can eat a quart of grain a week. That costs my mother money, and she's pretty bad off."

"No, she's not. She has you and she has that silly dog."

"Don't try to flatter me. I am your enemy and you know it."

"Enemies are relative."

Mrs. Murphy pondered this. "You're a philosophical little fellow, aren't you?"

"I don't believe in enemies. I believe there are situations when we compete over resources. If there aren't enough to go around, we fight. If there are, fine. Right now there're enough to go around, and I don't eat that much and neither does my family. So don't eat me . . . or mine."

The tiger licked the side of her paw and rubbed it over her ears. "I'll think about what you said, but my job is to keep this barn and this house clean."

"You already cleaned out the glove compartment of the truck. You've done your job." The mouse referred to Murphy's ferocious destruction of a field mouse family who took up residence in the glove compartment. They chewed through the wires leading into the fuse box, rendering the truck deader than a doornail. Once Murphy dispatched the invaders, Harry got her truck repaired, though it cost her $137.82.

"Like I said, I'll think about it."

"Murphy," Harry called. "Let's go, pussycat."

Murphy padded out of the feed room. Tucker, sleepy-eyed, waddled behind Harry. Fit as she was, Tucker still waddled, or at least that's how she appeared to Mrs. Murphy.

"Whatcha been doing?"

"Trying to catch mice. You should have heard the sneak holed up there in the feed room where I finally trapped him with my blinding speed."

"What did he say?"

"One argument after another about how I should leave him and his family alone. He said enemies were relative. Now that's a good one."

As Harry rolled open the barn door, a blast of frigid air caused the animals to fluff out their fur. Tucker, wide-awake now, dashed to the house through the screen door entrance and into the kitchen through the animal door. Mrs. Murphy jogged alongside Harry, who was sliding toward the back porch.

"I can handle snow but I hate this ice!" Harry cursed as her feet splayed in different directions. She hit the hard ice.

"*Come on, Mom.*" Mrs. Murphy brushed alongside her.

Tucker, feeling guilty, emerged from the house. Her claws, not as sharp as Murphy's, offered no purchase on the ice so she stayed put unless called.

"*Crawl on your hands and knees,*" Tucker advised.

Harry scrambled up only to go down again. She did crawl on her hands and knees to the back door. "How did I get to the barn in the first place?"

"*You moved a lot slower, and the sun is making the ice slicker, I think,*" Mrs. Murphy said.

Finally Harry, with Mrs. Murphy's encouragement, struggled onto the screened-in back porch. She removed her duck boots and opened the door to the kitchen, happy to feel the warmth. Mrs. Murphy kept thinking about the mouse saying enemies were relative. Then another thought struck her. She stopped eating and called down to Tucker, "*Ever notice how much bigger we are than mice, moles, and birds? Our game?*"

"*No, I never thought about it. Why?*"

"*We are. Occasionally I'll bring down a rabbit, but my game is smaller than I am.*"

"*And faster.*"

"*Oh, no, they're not!*" Mrs. Murphy yelled back at Tucker. "*No one is faster than I am. They have a head start on me, and half the time I still bring them down. Anyway, they have eyes on the sides of their heads. They can see us coming, Tucker.*"

"*Yeah, yeah.*" Tucker, pleased that she had twitted feline vanity, rested her head on her paws, her liquid brown eyes staring up at angry green ones.

"I'm not going to continue this discussion. I'll keep my revelation to myself." Haughtily she turned her back on the dog and walked the length of the kitchen counter. She stopped before the painted ceramic cookie jar in the shape of a laughing pig.

"Don't be so touchy." Tucker followed along on the floor.

"I don't see why I should continue a discussion with an animal who has no respect for my skills." She was feeling a little testy since she couldn't nail the barn mouse.

"I'm sorry. You are amazingly fast. I'm out of sorts because of the ice."

Eagerly the cat shared her thoughts, "Well, what I've been thinking is how small jockeys are. Like prey."

25

Tricky November. The mercury climbed to 55°F. The ice melted. The earth, soggy from the rain, slowly began to absorb the water. One confused milk butterfly was sighted flying around Miranda's back door.

Harry and Mrs. Hogendobber sorted through the usual Monday morning eruption of mail. Pewter visited but grew weary of Mrs. Murphy and Tucker describing their dramas on the ice. She fell asleep on the ledge dividing the upper from the lower post boxes. Lying on her side, some of her flabby gray belly hung over.

"Now you are coming, aren't you?" Mrs. Hogendobber asked about her church's songfest. "It's November nineteenth. You write down the date."

"I will."

Mrs. Murphy stuck her nose in Mrs. H.'s mailbag. "Mrs. Murphy, get out of there."

"Don't be an old poop face."

Mrs. Hogendobber reached down into the bag, her bangle bracelets jangling, and grabbed a striped kitty tail.

"Hey, I don't grab your tail!" The cat whirled around.

"Now I told you to get out. I don't even like cats, Murphy. For you I make an exception." Mrs. Hogendobber told half the truth. When Harry took over her husband's job, bringing her animals to work, Mrs. Hogendobber had been censorious. During her period of mourning she would find herself at the post office, not sure how she'd arrived at that destination. She'd helped George for the nearly four decades that he was postmaster. An unpaid assistant, for the Crozet post office, small and out of the way, did not merit more workers. Of course, the volume of mail had increased dramatically over the years. When Harry took over as postmistress, as they preferred to call the position, her youth allowed her to work a bit harder than George could at the end of his career, but even she couldn't keep up with the workload. Entreaties for an assistant fell on deaf federal ears. No surprise there. Out of the 459,025 postal employees, less than 10 percent worked in rural areas. They tended to be ignored, a situation that also had its good side, for rural workers enjoyed much more freedom than urban postal employees, trapped in a standard forty-hour week with some power-hungry supervisor nagging them.

Mrs. Hogendobber began coming once or twice a week to pitch in. At first, Harry had welcomed her company but asked her not to work because she couldn't pay her. But Miranda knew the ins and outs of the routine, the people at the central post office in Charlottesville on Seminole Trail, even the people in Washington, not to mention everyone in Crozet. She proved invaluable. Since George, prudent with money, had left her with enough to be comfortable, and she was making more with her baking, she didn't need the money. More than anything, she needed to be useful.

Over time she and Harry grew close. And over time, despite her reservations, Mrs. Hogendobber grew to love the two furry friends at Harry's side. She'd even learned to love the fat gray cat presently knocked out on the ledge. Not that she wanted anyone to know.

Murphy, having pressed her luck, backed out of the bag, danced sideways to the counter, and leapt on it. She collapsed on her side and rolled over, showing lots of tummy.

"Murphy, you're full of yourself this morning." Harry patted her stomach.

"I'm bored. Pewter's sacked out. Tucker's snoring under the table. It's a beautiful day."

Harry kissed her on the cheek. A light knock at the back door put a stop to the kissing. Mrs. Murphy could take but so many human kisses.

Miranda opened the door. "Adelia, come right in."

Addie, still wearing her chaps, stepped inside.

"Breeze all your babies?" Harry asked as Tucker lifted her head, then dropped it back down again.

"Oh, yeah." Addie sniffed as the vanilla odor from hot sticky buns reached her nostrils.

"Your mail's on the table," Miranda said as she carried two handfuls of mail to the big bottom boxes used by the small businesses in town.

"Thanks."

"Ready for the Colonial Cup?" Harry referred to the famous steeplechase in Camden, South Carolina, which had also been started by Marion duPont Scott.

"Well, Ransom Mine is coming along. You remember, he came in second at Montpelier. Royal Danzig, dunno, off these last couple of days, and Bazooka—I think I need a pilot's license to ride him. Mickey Townsend sent over two horses right after Nigel was killed." She paused a moment. "He said he wanted me to work them. They're really going great. Mickey's always backed me, you know. Chark's crabby about it, but he knows it's extra money so he shut up."

"What are you all talking about, 'breezing' a horse?" Miranda paused, oblivious to Pewter who was rolling over in her sleep.

"*Watch out!*" Mrs. Murphy called.

Too late. Pewter tumbled into one of the large business mailboxes.

"Pewter." Mrs. Hogendobber leaned over the befuddled cat. "Are you all right?" She couldn't help it. She burst out laughing.

"*Fine.*" Pewter picked herself up and marched right out of the box, over to the table where she tore out a hunk of pastry with her claws before Harry could stop her.

"Actually, I think you all have more work with these critters than I do with the horses," Addie observed. "Breezing—uh, I limber up the horse a little, jog a little, and then I do an exercise gallop around the track. Chark gives me the distance. You work a horse for conditioning and for wind. I guess that's the easiest way to describe it."

"Aren't you ever afraid up there?" Miranda asked.

"Right now I'm more afraid down here."

"Why? Has someone threatened you?" Mrs. Hogendobber walked back to Addie.

"No." Addie sat down on the chair by the sticky buns. "Everything's a mess. Arthur bombards me with daily lectures about how to handle my inheritance when I turn twenty-one. Mim's giving me the same lecture but with a lot more class. My brother shrugs and says if I blow it it's my own fault and he's not keeping me, but then I never asked him to. That's on a good day. On a bad day he yells at me. Everybody's acting like I'm going to go hog-wild."

"*Pewter's the one who goes hog-wild,*" Murphy snickered.

"*Shut up,*" Pewter replied, sitting on the other chair at the

table. She thought the humans, engrossed in conversation, wouldn't notice her filching another piece of bun.

They did. Addie stretched over and lightly smacked the outreached paw. "You have no manners."

"*I'm hungry,*" Pewter pleaded.

Mrs. Hogendobber reached into her voluminous skirt pockets and pulled out a few tiny, tiny fish, Haute Feline treats. She lured Pewter away from the table. Mrs. Murphy leapt off the counter and hurried over, too.

"I never thought I'd live to see the day." Harry laughed.

"If I don't do this, there won't be anything left for us." Miranda laughed, too. She turned her attention back to Addie. "One of the terrible things about wealth is the way people treat you."

"Well. Uh, well, I'm not wealthy yet." Addie rubbed her finger on the table making designs only she could see. "Actually, I came by, Harry, to see if you'd lend me a hundred dollars. I'll pay you right after Camden—speaking of money." She smiled sheepishly.

Harry, not an ungenerous soul, hesitated. First, that was a chunk of change to her. Second, what was going on? "Why won't Chark lend you the money?"

"He's mad at me. He's being a butthole." Her voice rose.

"So, what did you do with the money you won at Montpelier?" Harry juggled a load of mail on the way to the post boxes.

"Uh—"

"I'm not lending you a cent until I know why you're short. The *real* reason."

"And what's that supposed to mean?" Addie flushed.

"Means your deceased boyfriend had a coke habit. How do I know you don't have one?"

This stunned Miranda, who stopped what she was doing, as did the cats and dog. All eyes focused on Addie, whose face transformed from a flush to beet red.

"He was trying to stop. Until Linda got hold of him. I hope

she gets a stiletto through her heart. Except she doesn't have one."

"What about you?" Harry pressed.

"I'm off all substances. Anyway, I had the example of Mother."

"Now, now, your mother was a wonderful woman. She was a social drinker, I grant you." Miranda defended Marylou.

"She was a drunk, Mrs. Hogendobber," Addie's voice became wistful. "She'd get real happy at parties and real sad at home alone. She leaned on Mim a lot, but a best friend isn't a lover, and Mother needed that. She'd be morose at home . . . and out would come the bottle.

"Well . . ." Miranda was obviously reluctant to give up her image of Marylou Valiant. "At least she always behaved like a lady."

Harry crossed her arms over her chest. "You still haven't answered my question. Why do you need a hundred dollars?"

"Because I owe Mickey Townsend from a poker game the night before the Montpelier Races," she blurted out.

"He won't wait?" Miranda was curious.

"Mickey's a good guy. I adore him. I wish Mother had married him. But when it comes to poker, I mean, this is *serious*." She rubbed her thumb and forefinger together.

"Come on, he won't let you work off a hundred dollars with the horses he brought over?" Harry waited for the other shoe to drop.

"I haven't asked."

"Addie, I don't believe a word of this!" Harry figured they were long past the point of subtlety. Mickey was a bum excuse.

"I really do owe Mickey a hundred dollars. I just want to get it out of the way. And I don't want Arthur to find out."

"Mickey won't tell him." Mrs. Hogendobber stated the obvious, which had no effect on the young woman.

Out of the blue, Harry fired a question. "And how much did Nigel really owe Mickey?"

Without thinking it through, Addie answered, "About two thousand. He'd have made good on it, you see, because he took a kilo from Linda and Will—"

"A kilo!" Harry exclaimed.

"Yes, he thought he could sell it off after cutting it and make a lot of money." Addie realized she'd let the cat out of the bag. "Don't tell Rick Shaw or Deputy Cooper!"

"This could have some bearing on the case," Mrs. Hogendobber replied sensibly.

"Then why hasn't anyone mentioned the kilo? Where the hell is it? Whoever killed him probably carted it away and is further enriching himself." Harry threw her hands in the air, disgusted that Addie would hold back something so vital.

"I have it." Her voice was small.

"*You what?*" The humans and animals said in unison.

"My God, Adelia, you're crazy. People have killed for less than a kilo of cocaine, and you know that Linda and Will will be on your tail *soon.*" Harry was emphatic.

"They already are." She put her head in her hands. "I put it in my big safe deposit box at Crozet National Bank when Nigel asked me to help him out. No one else knows. The sheriff from Orange County and Rick combed through his truck and his quarters. Nothing. Clean. Linda knows the cops haven't found the coke. She wants it back."

"I'll bet she does!" Harry exploded.

"She says she'll blackmail me if I don't return it. She says nobody will believe that I'm not in on the drug sale, and if I accuse her, it's her word against mine. She says that if I give her back the coke, that will be the end of it."

"So why *do* you need the hundred dollars?" Miranda picked up the refrain.

"For gas for the dually and for pocket change. I'll drive the coke up tonight. I haven't any spare money because I've been paying off money I owe Linda"— she paused, thinking—"over a horse deal."

"How much? Really, how much?" Tucker and Harry both asked.

"Uh . . ." A long pause followed. "As of today, one thousand and fifteen dollars."

"Good God, Addie." Harry sank into the chair that Pewter had vacated when she was offered the Haute Feline. She knew instinctively that Addie owed Linda Forloines on her own drug tab. Addie was lying to her.

"Pretty stupid, huh?" She hung her auburn head.

"Box of rocks." Harry made a fist and tapped her skull.

Miranda's imposing figure overshadowed the two seated young women. "This is foolishness and will lead to more pain. 'As a dog returneth to his vomit, so a fool returneth to his folly,' Proverbs twenty-six eleven."

"*I resent that,*" Tucker barked.

"Gross," Addie said.

"I am not giving you one hundred dollars. And we're calling Rick Shaw right this minute."

"No! He'll tell Arthur, and Arthur'll tell Chark. They'll get the damn trusteeship extended. I'll never get my money!"

"Your mother's will is your mother's will. It can't be broken," Miranda told her.

"Maybe not, but they sure can drag it out. It's my money."

"But you've got to give the sheriff this information. You've got to get out before you get in too deep—you've already aided and abetted a felon."

"Coty Lamont was on cocaine too, wasn't he?" Mrs. Hogendobber inquired.

Addie nodded.

"For all we know, Addie, you deliver that kilo and you'll wind up with a knife through your heart." Harry sighed.

"I can't tell Rick," Addie wailed.

Miranda lifted the receiver from the phone as Addie bolted for the door. Tucker tripped her and Harry pounced on her.

"Let me go."

"Dammit, Addie, you're gonna get killed. You give Linda and Will that kilo and you'll be in business with Linda for the rest of your life. She'll bring you horses. She'll want special favors. If you're lucky, she'll take the kilo and blow town. If she stays . . ."

"If you're not lucky, cement shoes," Pewter matter-of-factly stated.

26

Rick Shaw, being an officer of the law for all his adult life, never expected people to tell him the truth right off the bat. The truth, like diamonds, had to be won by hand, by pick, by dynamite.

His anger when he heard the dismal story at the post office was not so much provoked by Addie's withholding information, although he wasn't happy about that, as by the way she had foolishly placed herself in jeopardy. He also made a mental note that Mickey Townsend had drastically downplayed the amounts of money Nigel and Coty owed him. He had never mentioned Addie's debt at all.

As soon as he dismissed Addie, after taking her back to his office for a full disclosure, he and Cynthia Cooper hopped into the squad car. He'd taken the precaution of calling the president of the bank, advising him not to let Addie into her safe deposit box. It could be opened only in Rick's presence.

"Did you call Culpeper?" Cynthia asked in shorthand, meaning the sheriff of Culpeper County.

"Uh-huh."

They drove in silence. When they reached Dr. D'Angelo's place, Romulus Farms, Sheriff Totie Biswanger was waiting for them.

"Gone," was all he said.

"Both of them?" Cynthia asked.

"Ey-ah," came the affirmative. He pointed to their cottage on Dr. D'Angelo's farm.

"Neat as a hairpin. Nothing moved. Clothes in the closet. Food in the refrigerator."

"Kind of funny, ain't it?" Totie folded his arms over his barrel chest and stared at his shoes.

27

"They dropped the whole damn thing!" Fair's radiant face under-scored the happy news.

Harry had encountered him at Mim's, where she'd gone to deliver an express package. Mim and Chark Valiant, also on hand, were nearly as excited as Harry was at Fair's news.

They were all gathered at the barn, where Mrs. Murphy and Tucker nosed around. Rodger Dodger and Pusskin were nowhere to be found.

"Well, let me have a look at Royal Danzig," Fair said. "Didn't mean to talk so much."

"Oh, he can wait another minute. Once we get down to business, we'll forget to ask the details." Mim invited them into the tack room.

"Where's Addie?" Fair asked.

Mim, who knew, said nothing for Chark was in the dark about his sister's unholy mess. Another request of Rick Shaw's.

"She called from Charlottesville," Chark answered. "Said she was tied up and didn't know when she'd be back."

"Oh, okay." Fair grabbed a cup of coffee. He'd been up since four o'clock that morning because of an emergency at a hunter barn. "As near as I can make out, or as much as Colbert Mason wants to tell me, he contacted my accuser, Linda Forloines. She claimed he entirely misunderstood what she had said. She was furious he'd even think that and she had no intention of bringing charges against me. So that's that." He sat in the comfy old leather chair and immediately regretted it because he knew he wouldn't want to get up.

"Typical," was Mim's reply.

"She's not worth talking about," Chark added.

They all knew Linda's modus operandi. She'd act as though she had inside information, she'd hint, intimate, change the inflection of her voice to convey the full weight of her words. This way she could say that people misunderstood her, implying there must be a problem with you if you could even think such a thing.

"Well, let me take a look at Royal Danzig." Fair forced himself out of the chair.

They walked down the beautiful center aisle and Chark pulled the flashy guy out of his stall. As Fair ran his hands over the horse's legs, Rodger Dodger, fresh from patrolling the paddocks, sauntered into the barn, his beloved Pusskin by his side.

"Royal, what's the buzz?" the old ginger cat asked.

"Kinda tender on my left leg. I think I put a foot wrong when I was turned out in the paddock."

"Hope it's nothing serious," Rodger politely replied.

"Me, too, I want to go to Camden."

"Rodger, how you been?" Mrs. Murphy called out when she heard Rodger's voice. She and Tucker had been in the tack room. It smelled so good and was toasty warm.

"Murphy. Hi, Tucker," Rodger said as Pusskin murmured her greetings.

Mrs. Murphy sat down, curling her tail around her. "*I've got a proposition for you, Rodger.*"

"*What proposition?*" Tucker's ears pointed up. "*Why didn't you tell me?*"

" *'Cause I've been cooking it.*" Mrs. Murphy turned back to Rodger. "*There's a chance your barn mice know what's in Orion's stall.*"

"*Why not ask the horses?*" Tucker asked.

"*I did.*" Rodger flicked his tail for a minute. "*They didn't remember anything, not even Orion, and he's the oldest, being twelve. 'Course, it could be that whatever is in there was buried in summertime years back. The foxhunters are always turned out in the far pastures in summer, so only the mice and I would have been here. I don't remember anything, but summers I go up and rest in the big house because of the air conditioning.*"

"*If you made a deal with the mice, maybe they'd talk to us.*" Mrs. Murphy kept to her agenda.

"*What kind of deal?*"

"*Not to catch them.*"

"*I can't do that. Mim will be furious if I don't deliver mice to the tack room. She asks Chark every day if Pusskin and I have done our duty.*"

"*She's real fussy,*" Pusskin added.

"*I thought of that.*" Mrs. Murphy wanted to bat Pusskin. She tried to make her meow sound pleasant. "*What I propose is that you catch field mice and deliver them to the tack room. The humans don't know the difference.*"

Rodger rubbed his whiskers with his forepaw. He wrinkled his brow. A wise old fellow, he wanted to consider the ramifications of such a bargain. "*It will work for a time, Murphy, but as the grain goes down and the barn mice population doesn't decrease, the humans will figure out something's wrong. I don't want Pusskin or me to get the boot.*"

"*Mim would never do that,*" Tucker rightly surmised.

"*I'd like to think that.*" Rodger knew other cats who were out of work or worse because they got lazy. "*But even if she let us stay, she*" might bring in another cat, and I don't want to be bothered with that. This is my barn."

"What if we asked the barn mice not to show themselves?" Mrs. Murphy tried to figure out a solution. "At least so the humans wouldn't see them. You know how they get about mice."

"Seeing is bad enough. It's the grain I'm worried about," Rodger said sensibly.

"Can't they get by on what the horses throw on the ground? You know, horses are the sloppiest eaters," Pusskin chimed in. Not a bad idea for a slow kitty, Mrs. Murphy admitted.

"Less food. More safety," Rodger purred. "It's a trade-off. Worth a try, I suppose, but Murphy, why do you care what's in Orion's stall?"

"Don't say curiosity," Tucker warned.

Mrs. Murphy breathed in the crisp air. Her head felt quite as clear as the air around her. "I think the murders aren't over, and I think whatever's in Orion's stall might be part of the answer."

"If humans kill one another, that's their business," Pusskin, not a major fan of the human race, hissed.

"But what if this puts Mim in danger? Think about that." Mrs. Murphy reached out with a paw to Pusskin as though she were going to cuff her. "Something has happened in her barn. Something that goes back a few years at least. Mickey Townsend pulled a gun on Coty Lamont in the middle of the night. Coty was in Orion's stall, digging. Mickey makes him cover it back up, then takes him away. Coty's truck wasn't here. He'd walked in from somewhere and Mickey snuck up on him. Pretty peculiar. The next day Coty Lamont is dead in the back of the pickup, a knife through the heart and another playing card on it, the Queen of Spades. That's what Cynthia Cooper told my mom when they had supper night before last." She took a breath.

Pusskin blurted out, "That means Mickey's the killer."

"Maybe yes and maybe no. Addie has a kilo of cocaine in her safe deposit box that she says belonged to Nigel Danforth."

"Oh, no!" Rodger and Pusskin exclaimed together.

"She told Rick Shaw. Now she's in deep doo-doo." Tucker felt the same urgency that her best friend did. "And I don't think she would have told him, but Mom and Mrs. Hogendobber forced her to do it. I reckon we haven't heard the end of it because Addie was supposed to deliver the kilo to Linda Forloines, and what's Linda going to do when it doesn't show up?"

"So Addie might be in danger?" Rodger liked Addie.

"Anybody might be in danger, especially if I'm right about there being a secret in Orion's stall. What if, by pure accident, Mim stumbles on the truth? You can't expose your owner to that kind of danger. I know you aren't house cats, but Mim is fair and she takes care of you. And"—Mrs. Murphy lowered her voice—"what would have happened if she hadn't rescued you all from the SPCA? There are too many kittens, and no matter how good a job the SPCA does—well, you know."

The animals remained silent for some time after that grim reminder.

Finally Rodger spoke, firmly. "It's a debt of honor. We'll do our best for Mim. Pusskin?"

"Whatever you say, darling."

He filled his red chest, licked the side of Pusskin's pretty face, then said, "Let's parlay with the mice."

The mice were partying in the walls of the tack room. Mim had insulated the tack room so there was plenty of space between the two walls, filled with warm insulation, easy for mice to get in and out of because they burrowed from the stall next door. By this time they had created many entrances and exits, driving Rodger Dodger to distraction because even if he and Pusskin divided to cover holes, they'd still miss the mice.

The raucous squeaking stopped when the mice heard and smelled the approaching cats.

"Must be an army of them," the head mouse, a saucy female, warned.

Rodger put his pink nose at the entrance to one of the holes. "Loulou, it's Rodger and Pusskin. Mrs. Murphy and Tucker, the corgi from over by Yellow Mountain, are with us."

"The post office animals," Loulou replied, her high-pitched voice clear and piercing.

"*How do they know that?*" Mrs. Murphy wondered.

"*We know everything. Besides, we have cousins at Market Shiflett's store. Pewter's too fat to run anyone down.*"

Murphy giggled. So did Tucker.

"*Loulou, I've come with an offer you should consider.*"

A moment of silence was followed by a wary Loulou. "*We're all ears.*"

"*Do you know what's buried in Orion's stall?*"

"*As the oldest mouse, I do,*" Loulou swiftly replied. "*But I'm not telling you.*"

Rodger kept his temper in check, but Pusskin complained, "*She's a real smartass.*"

Mrs. Murphy whispered for her to shut up.

"*Loulou, I don't expect something for nothing. Pusskin and I agree not to catch any barn mice for a year*"—that last part was Rodger's own flourish—"*if you agree not to let the humans see you. Otherwise they'll think Pusskin and I are lazing about and we'll get in hot water, and Mim might try to bring in another cat. You can understand our position, can you not?*"

"*Yes.*"

"*Well, a year of freedom for the information—and try not to breed too much, will you?*"

"*It's an open shot to the feed room. The humans will see us.*" Loulou was playing for time as the excited chatter in the background proved.

"*There's plenty of grain under the horses' feed buckets. Just don't show your faces in the barn during the day, and if you hear a human coming at night, duck for cover. Otherwise, we'll all be in a real bad situation.*"

"*I'll get back to you,*" Loulou replied.

The three cats and the dog patiently waited. Harry walked by on her way to the john. "What are you all doing?"

"*High-level negotiations,*" Mrs. Murphy informed her.

"Sometimes you're so cute." Harry smiled and continued on her way.

"*Whew.*" Tucker sighed. "*She could have screwed up the whole deal.*"

"*Yeah, the last thing we want any of them to see is this entrance here with all of us sitting around like bumps on a log.*" Rodger shifted his weight from one haunch to the other.

They heard a chorus of tinny voices. "*Aye.*" Then one lone "*Nay.*"

"*Rodger Dodger!*" Loulou said peeking her little head out of the entrance. She was a feisty mouse and a confident one.

"*Yes.*"

"*We are almost unanimous. We agree to your terms, a free year, but I have a personal favor to ask.*"

"*What?*"

"*Can you talk to Lucy Fur and Elocution, the Reverend Jones's two cats? My youngest sister's family lives behind the tapestry of the Ascension. Lucy Fur and Elocution hassle them constantly. I'm not asking for a moratorium, just a little less hassle, you know?*"

"*I don't know those cats,*" Rodger honestly replied.

"*I do,*" Mrs. Murphy quickly said. "*I'll talk to them. You have my word.*"

"*You must have mice at your barn,*" Loulou pushed.

"*I do, but you all are browns and they are grays. I doubt any of your family is out my way.*"

A pause followed. "*You're probably right, but you will talk to these barn cats?*"

After a long pause Murphy agreed, "*Yes. Now, will you tell us what is in Orion's stall, and whether you remember any of the people involved.*"

Loulou coughed, clearing her throat. "*I was very young. Mother was still alive but I remember it as if it were yesterday. Five years ago last July. Hotter than Tophet. Coty Lamont and a fellow called Sargent dug a deep hole in the corner of the stall. Had to be two in the morning, and about four when they finished. The earth was soft there, so they made good work of it. We could smell how nervous they were. You know, that sharp, ugly odor.*" She caught another big breath. "*They left, then came back with a heavy canvas tarp and a man holding either end. I couldn't see what was in it but I could smell blood.*"

"*Damn,*" Mrs. Murphy whispered.

Loulou listened to a squeak then said, "*Mom and I and the older mice, no longer living, of course, watched from the hayloft. When they lifted the tarp to lower it in, I guess they were tired because they dropped it, and one end unraveled a little. Lots of brassy hair spilled out. Mother got a good look at the face because she ran along the top of the stall beam."

All the animals held their breath as Loulou continued. "It was Marylou Valiant."

28

Livid, Addie Valiant opened her safe deposit box at Crozet National in the presence of five onlookers. Rick Shaw and bank president, Dennis Washington, stared at the brown-paper-wrapped package. By opening the box in the evening they had avoided the regular ebb and flow of banking traffic, diminishing the chances of someone getting wind of Addie's escapade.

"I don't know why everyone has to be here." Addie pouted. Arthur stood next to Dennis. Chark, arms folded across his chest, leaned against a wall of small stainless steel safe deposit boxes.

Cynthia Cooper held the small brass key. She wouldn't give it back to Addie. "Arthur is your guardian until midnight November fourteenth. And I would think you'd be glad your brother is here."

"I'm not glad."

Rick had waited until the last minute to pull in Charles and Arthur, fearing that the earlier he informed them, the likelier they were to leak the news. That could be dangerous.

Addie's young face wrinkled in rage. "I'll hear about my poor judgment for the rest of my life." She wheeled on Arthur. "And I bet you find a way to extend your trusteeship with help *again* from my loving brother!"

"You're under duress," Arthur said in a measured voice. "This was an extremely foolish thing to do. As to your money, the wishes of your mother will be followed to the letter."

"I don't believe that. You think I'm stupid about money."

Arthur opened his mouth, then shut it. Addie, fiery like her mother, wouldn't hear anything he said.

"Sis, I ought to wring your neck for this stunt," Chark said through clenched teeth as Cynthia Cooper reached into the deep safe deposit box and lifted out the wrapped kilo.

"It wasn't what you think. Nigel bought this to pay off his debt to Mickey."

"This goes far beyond a debt to Mickey Townsend," Rick replied. "This represents a lot of money on the street."

"He used you!" Chark yelled.

"He didn't use me."

"Let the dead sleep in peace." Arthur held up his hands to stop the argument. "Whatever his intentions were we'll never know."

Rick motioned for Cynthia to lock up the box.

"I have something to tell you all." Rick's eyes narrowed. "And Addie, if you're holding anything back, out with it." She glared at him as he continued. "There is no Nigel Danforth."

"What do you mean?" Alarm flashed on her face while confusion registered on Chark's and Arthur's visages.

"I mean, there is no record of such a person in England. And there is no green card registered to anyone by that name in this country. Our only hope is his dental records, which we have sent out by computer to every police station we can reach, here and in England. A real long shot. His fingerprints are not on file in either the U.S. or England."

Addie sank like a stone. "I don't understand."

Chark caught his sister and gently lowered her in a chair. "He lied even more than I thought," he said.

She put her head in her hands and sobbed. "But I loved him. Why would he lie to me?"

Arthur placed his hand on her shoulder. "Sheriff, might he perhaps be from some British colony—or French colony?"

"Coop thought of that. Can't find a thing. We don't know who this man was, where he came from, or his exact age. All we know is that he gave a kilo of cocaine to Addie to keep for him. Saying he bought it from Linda Forloines—"

"Well, get them!" Addie wailed.

"We tried to arrest them yesterday. They're gone." Rick, embarrassed, saw the dismay on their faces.

"Is my sister"—Chark could hardly get the words out—"under arrest?"

"No. Not yet anyway," Rick said.

"Now see here, Shaw." Arthur stood up straight. "She's been a foolish girl, but many a woman's been led astray by a man. She is no drug dealer. She isn't even a user anymore."

Shaking, tears down her cheeks, Addie choked, "Well—uh, sometimes."

"Then your brother and I will put you in a clinic." Arthur's tone brooked no contradiction.

"What about Camden? Anyway, I only use a little to celebrate. Really. I'm not an addict or anything. Test my blood."

"We'll settle this between us." Arthur took control. "Sheriff, does Adelia have permission to ride in Camden?"

"Yes, but"—he focused on Addie—"don't try anything stupid—like running away."

"Do you think Will and Linda will show up there?" Chark asked.

"I don't know," Rick replied.

"They're out of the country by now." Addie wiped her red eyes. "Linda always said she was going for one last big hit."

"Why didn't she do that a long time ago?" Arthur's voice was hard.

"Because she was using too. She said she'd cleaned up, though. Now it's strictly business. She wanted a haul. And out of here." Addie dropped her head in her hands again.

"There's lots of this around the steeplechase world, isn't there?" Cynthia jotted notes in her book.

Addie shrugged. "Goes in cycles. I don't think there's any more drug abuse on the backstretch than there is in big corporations."

"In that case, America's in trouble," Chark said.

"We'll deal with America tomorrow." Arthur smiled tightly. "Right now my first priority is getting this young lady straightened out. Sheriff, is there any more that you need from us tonight?"

"No," Rick said. "You're free to go."

Later, when Rick and Cynthia were about to get into the squad car, she asked him, "Do you think she's telling the truth? That she really didn't know about Nigel?"

"What's your gut tell you?"

Cynthia leaned against the door of the car. The night, crystalline and cold, was beautiful. "She didn't know."

"What else?" He offered her a cigarette which she took.

Cynthia bent her head for a light and took a drag. She looked up, noticing how perfectly brilliant the stars were. "Rick, this thing is a long way from being over."

He nodded in agreement, and they finished their cigarettes in silence.

29

The big purple van with the glittering gold lettering—DALMALLY
FARM on both sides and HORSES on the rear—was parked next to an
earthen ramp. The loading ramps, heavy and unwieldy, could
injure your back so Mim had had an earthen ramp built. The
horses walked directly onto the van without hearing that thump-
thump of metal underneath them. Of course, once they were at
the races, the loathed ramp did have to be pulled out from the
side of the van, but still, any easing of physical labor helped.

Harry loved to inspect Mim's vans. Mim also had an aluminum gooseneck trailer for hunting. Although purple was the racing color of her mother's family, for hunting Mim used red and
gold on her three-horse slant-load Trailet. Harry coveted this
trailer as well as the Dodge dually with the Cummins turbo-diesel
engine that pulled it. That was red, too.

She'd stopped by the stable after work to see if Little Marilyn was around. She didn't want to seem as though she was checking up on her peer, but she was. Little Mim had finally sent out the invitations for the wild-game dinner, but she hadn't reported who had RSVPed and who hadn't. As it was, Susan Tucker had had to pick up the invitations from the printer in Charlottesville.

Just as Harry climbed back into her truck, Big Mim cruised into the parking lot in her Bentley Turbo R. Mim never stinted on machines of any sort. It was an irrational thing with Mim: she couldn't resist cars, trucks, or tractors. Fortunately, she could afford them. She probably ran the best-equipped farm in Albemarle County. She even had a rolling irrigation system, a series of pipes connected to huge wheels that ran off a generator.

"Harry."

"Hi. I was trying to find Little Marilyn but no one's around."

"She's in Washington today." Mim opened the heavy door and slid out. "Worried about the dinner?"

"A little."

"Me too. Well, don't worry overmuch. I'll check the messages on the service and tell you who's accepted. I'll resort to the telephone tree, too, if necessary." She mentioned the system wherein designated callers were each responsible for calling ten people.

"I can do that."

"No, she's my daughter, and as usual, she's falling down on the job." Mim fingered her Hermes scarf. "Marilyn hasn't been right since her divorce was final last year. I don't know what to do."

Harry, forthright, said, "She isn't going to learn much if you do it for her."

"Do you want the game dinner to fall apart? My God, the hunt club would have our hides. I'd rather do it and get after her later."

Harry knew that was true. Their foxhunting club, the Jefferson—which chased foxes, rather than truly hunting them—was filled with prickly personalities, big egos, and tough riders as well as those of calmer temperament. Foxhunting by its nature attracts passionate people, which is all very well until the time comes for them to cooperate with one another. Little Marilyn would stir a hornets' nest if the game dinner didn't raise the anticipated revenue.

"I wish I could help you, but Marilyn has never much cared for me."

"Now, Harry, she's not demonstrative. She likes you well enough."

Harry decided not to refute Mim. Instead, her attention turned toward Tucker and Mrs. Murphy chattering loudly about who had been in Orion's stall.

"Mrs. Murphy and Tucker appear to be hungry," Mim said.

"Mim, I wish you'd listen." Mrs. Murphy mournfully hung out the driver's window.

"Yeah, well, let me know if there's anything I can do to help," Harry said.

"You're part of the telephone tree." Mim started for the stable, then turned. "Harry, what are you doing next weekend?"

"Nothing special."

"How would you like to come to Camden this weekend to see the Colonial Cup? It would mean a lot to Adelia and Charles, I'm sure."

"Don't go." A bolt of fear shot through Mrs. Murphy and she didn't know why.

"If Miranda will take care of my babies, I'd love to go."

"I thought Miranda might like to attend as well. Her sister lives in Greenville. Perhaps she could drive over."

"Let me see what I can do about the kids here, but I'd love to go."

"It's Adelia's twenty-first birthday. I thought we could celebrate down there and put her troubles behind us."

"Good idea."

30

Gray clouds hung so low Harry felt she could reach up and grab one. Although the temperature stayed in the mid-forties, the light wind, raw, made her shiver.

She dashed out of the bank on her lunch hour just as Boom Boom dashed in.

"Harry."

"Boom Boom."

"I'm sorry I lost my temper in the supermarket."

"Uh, well, an avalanche of toilet paper will do that to you." Harry continued down the steps.

Boom Boom placed a restraining, manicured hand on her shoulder. "Miranda says you can have the next hour off."

"Huh?"

"I was just in the post office and I asked her if I could borrow you for an hour."

"What?"

"To go to Lifeline with me."

"No."

"Harry, even if you hate it, it's an experience you can laugh about later."

Harry wanted to bat Miranda as well as throttle Boom Boom, a vision in magenta cashmere and wool today. "No. I can't do something like that."

"You need to reach out to other people. Release your fears. We're all knotted up with fear."

Harry breathed deeply, removing Boom Boom's hand from her shoulder. "I'm afraid to die. I'm afraid I won't be able to pay my bills. I'm afraid of sickness, and I guess if I'm brutally honest, I'm afraid to grow old."

"Lifeline can not only banish those fears but teach you how to transform them to life-enhancing experiences."

"Good God." Harry shook her head.

Mickey Townsend walked up behind her, a deposit envelope in his gloved hand. "Harry, Boom Boom. Harry, are you all right?"

"No! Boom Boom keeps pressuring me to go to Lifeline with her. I don't want to go."

"You'd be surprised at the number of people who do go." Boom Boom fluttered her eyelashes. Harry assumed this was for Mickey.

"I've never been to Lifeline, but—" He paused. "When Marylou disappeared I went to Larry Johnson. He prescribed anti-depressants, which made me feel like a bulldozer ran over me, except I could function. I hated that feeling so I went into therapy."

"You?"

"See!" Boom Boom triumphantly bragged.

"Shut up, Boom. Lifeline isn't therapy."

"Did it help? I'm sure it did." Boom Boom smiled expansively.

Mickey lowered his already low voice. "I found out I'm a real son of a bitch, and you know what else I found out?" He leaned toward Boom Boom, whispering, "I like it that way."

Harry laughed as Boom Boom, rising above the situation, intoned, "You could benefit from Lifeline."

"I could benefit from single malt scotch, too." He tipped his hat. "Ladies."

Harry, still laughing, bade her improvement-mad tormentor good-bye.

"You know what, Harry?" Boom Boom shouted to her back. "This is about process, not just individual people. Process. The means, not the ends. There are positive processes and negative processes. Like for Mickey Townsend. Ever since the whole town turned on him for courting Marylou—*negative* process."

Harry stopped and turned around. "What did you say?"

"Process!" Boom Boom shouted.

Harry held up her hands for quiet. "I hear you. I think I'm missing something."

"A lot."

"Go back to Marylou."

"Not unless you come with me to Lifeline."

"Look. I've got to pack now, I'm going to Camden for the weekend. I haven't got time to go with you to Lifeline. Talk to me about process right now. I promise I'll go when I return."

"Set a time frame."

"Huh?"

"You could come back and say you'll go with me next year."

"In a week."

Boom Boom, thrilled, stepped closer, looming over Harry from her much greater height. "Nothing happens in isolation. All emotions are connected like links in a chain. Marylou Valiant couldn't cope without her husband. She began to drink too much. Squander money. That set off Arthur, who loved her. He chased off that greedy movie star and what happens? She falls in love with Mickey Townsend."

"So?"

"Process. No one directly confronts and releases their emotions. Arthur becomes embittered. He wins over Chark. Mickey wins over Addie. The men fight over Marylou through her children."

Harry, silent for a long time, said, "This is Act Two."

"Yes—until everyone involved stops hanging on to hardened, dead patterns. But people's egos get hung up in their anger and their pain. So they pass it along."

"What goes around comes around," Harry said, thinking out loud.

"Not exactly. This is about breaking patterns."

"I understand. I think." She rubbed her temples. "Didn't mean to be, uh, reductive."

"You will go with me?"

"I said I would."

"Shake on it."

Harry extended her hand. She ran back to the post office, pushed the door open. "Miranda, how could you?"

Miranda, glasses down on her neck, said to Herb Jones, "Ignore her."

Harry strode up to the counter, Murphy, Pewter, and Tucker watching her every move. "You told Boom Boom you'd relieve me for an hour so I could go to Lifeline. How could you?"

"I did no such thing. I told her if you wanted to go you could. It's a slow day."

"Damn. I should have known." Harry propped her elbow on the smooth, worn counter. "Well, I am going." She held up her hand for stop. "Not today. Next week."

"Harry, I'm proud of you." The reverend beamed.

"Why?"

"You're showing the first signs of forgiveness."

"I am?"

"You are." He slapped her on the back, reaching over the counter. "You girls enjoy the races."

As he left, Harry repeated to Miranda her entire conversation with Boom Boom Craycroft.

"She wasn't talking about the murders—she was just talking." Miranda pushed her glasses up to the bridge of her nose.

"Yeah, but it made me wonder if Nigel and Coty's murders aren't part of a process—something started before drugs . . . or during drugs. Fixing races. Betting. That was everyone's first thought, remember?"

"Yes. It proved unfounded."

"Well, Mrs. H., they weren't just killed because someone didn't like them. They were links in a chain."

"She surprises me." Pewter lay down crossing her paws in front of her. *"Humans can reason."*

31

Since no one claimed Nigel Danforth's body, he was buried in a potter's grave at the expense of the taxpayers of Ablemarle County.

His belongings were in his tack trunk back in the over-crowded locker room at the station.

Cynthia Cooper called Mickey Townsend to pick them up. The department had tagged and photographed each item.

He followed her back to the locker room.

"I was going to turn this over to Adelia since he had no next of kin. But the more I thought about it, the more I decided against it. It could upset her too much, and the big race is this weekend. You were his employer. You'll have to stand in for next of kin."

"May I open it?"

"Sure."

He knelt down, lifting the brass hasp on the small wooden trunk. A riding helmet rested on top of folded lightweight racing breeches. He placed it on the ground with the breeches beside it. Two old heavy wool sweaters and a short winter down jacket were next. Assorted bats and whips rested on the bottom along with a shaving kit.

"Feel that." Mickey handed her a whip, pointed to the leather square at the end.

"It's heavy. What's in there?"

"A quarter. It's illegal but nothing says he can't use it during workouts. A crack with that smarts, I promise."

"Not much to show for a life, is it?" she said.

"He had some beautiful handmade clothes from London. Turnbull & Asser shirts. That kind of thing. He made money somewhere."

"Yeah. I remember when we went through the cottage. Still, not much other than a few good clothes. The only reason we kept the tack trunk so long is he was sitting on it. We dusted it inside and out."

Mickey slid his hands into the pockets of the down jacket. He checked the inside pocket. Empty.

It wasn't until he got home and hung the jacket on a tack hook, wondering to whom he should give the clothing—maybe some poor, lean kid struggling to make it in the steeplechasing world—that he noticed a folded-over zipper where the collar met the yoke of the down jacket. Nigel had worn the jacket so much that the collar squinched down, covering the zipper. The tack hook straightened out the collar. A hood would be inside, another aid against foul weather.

Out of curiosity, Mickey unzipped it, unfurling the hood. A dull clink drew his eyes to the soft loam of the barn aisle.

He bent over, picking up a St. Christopher's medal. He started to shake so hard he steadied himself against the stall.

Beautifully wrought, the gold medal was the size of a half-dollar. Over the detailed relief of St. Christopher carrying the Christ child was layer after layer of exquisite blue enamel. The engraving in perfect small script on the gold non-enameled back read: *He's my stand-in. Love, Charley.*

Mickey burst into tears, clutching the medal to his chest. "St. Christopher, you failed her."

That medal had hung around Marylou Valiant's neck on a twisted thick gold chain.

Once he regained control of himself, Mickey stood up. He started for the phone in the tack room to call Deputy Cooper. His instinct told him it would have been easy to miss the hood in the collar. If he hadn't hung up the coat, he would have missed it himself.

He sat down behind the old school desk and picked up the receiver.

He thought to himself, *What if they did see it and photograph it? Maybe they're trying to bait me. I'm a suspect.* He put the receiver back in the cradle. *No, no they missed it.* He held the beautiful medal in both palms. *Marylou, this medal will lead me to your killer, and I swear by all that's holy I'll take him out. If Nigel killed you, then may he fry in Hell for eternity.*

He stood up abruptly and slipped the St. Christopher's medal in his pocket.

32

"She's got Susan to take care of us and the horses," Tucker moaned. "She's packing her bags. What are we going to do?"

"I can hide under the seat of the Ford and then jump into the racing van." Mrs. Murphy lay on her side. She'd worried about this so much she was tired.

"But I can't fit under the seat," Tucker wailed. "And you need me. Mother needs me, she just doesn't know it."

"I'm thinking."

Tucker dropped her head between her white paws so that her face was in front of Mrs. Murphy's. "There will be more murders! Everyone will die!"

"Don't get carried away. Anyway, be quiet for a minute. I'm still thinking." Five long minutes passed. "I have an idea."

"What?" Tucker jumped up.

Mrs. Murphy also sat up. She didn't like to have Tucker hanging over her. "*Go into her bedroom and beg, plead, cry. Make her take you.*"

"*What about you?*" Tucker's soft brown eyes filled with worry.

"*She won't take me. We both know that. I can travel as well as you, but Mother has it in her head that cats don't like to travel.*"

"*It's because you—*"

"*I only did that once!*" Mrs. Murphy flared. "*I wish you'd forget it.*"

"*Mother doesn't. I'm trying to think like she does,*" Tucker hedged.

"*The day we think like a human we're in trouble. We outthink them, that's the key. She won't take me. If she'll take you, one of us will be there at least. She needs a keeper, you know. If she blunders into something she could make a real mess. I'm a lot more worried about Mim, actually.*"

"Mim?" Tucker's tongue flicked out for a minute, a pink exclamation point.

"*Marylou Valiant is buried in her barn. Coty Lamont and someone called Sargent put the body there five years ago. Right? Well, Mim may be safe and sound but the fact remains that a murdered woman, a dear friend of hers, is buried on her property. What if she finds out?*"

Tucker, knowing her friend well, picked up her train of thought. "*It's a small circle, these 'chaser people. Mim's important in that world.*"

"*One thing is for sure.*"

"*What?*"

"*The murderer carries a deck of cards.*"

"So does half of America." Murphy brushed against Tucker's chest, tickling the dog's sensitive nose with her tail.

"*Here's what really bothers me. Once a murder is committed, the last thing a murderer would want to do is dig up the corpse. It's the corpse that incriminates them.*"

"*Maybe they forgot to take off her jewelry or there was money buried with her.*"

"*Possible, if the murderer or murderers were rattled. Yes, it's possible but Coty had enough time to collect his wits. He would have stripped her of anything* valuable. I'd bet on that. Then, too, we don't know for sure if Coty or the other guy killed her."

"Don't forget Mickey Townsend."

"I haven't." Murphy paced, her tail flicking with each step. "Mickey must know where Marylou is, though. Otherwise, why did he stop Coty from digging that night?" She paced some more. "But it doesn't feel right, Tucker. Mickey was in love with Marylou."

"Maybe at the last minute she thought Arthur was the better choice. Maybe she told him and he lost it and killed her—lover's passion," Tucker said soberly.

"I don't know, but you've got to go to Camden, Tucker. Mickey will be there. They'll all be there—and that's what scares me."

"I'll do my best."

"Go into that bedroom and put on a show."

Tucker trotted into Harry's bedroom. She'd placed her duffle bag on the floor. Her clothes lay on the bed and she was folding them.

Tucker crawled into the duffle bag. "Mom, you've got to take me."

"Tucker—" Harry smiled. "Get out of there."

Mrs. Murphy bounded on the bed. "Take her, Harry."

"Murphy—" Harry shooed her off a blouse. The cat sat on another one. "Now this is too much."

"Tucker needs to go with you."

"Yes, it's very important," the dog whined.

"Throw back your head and howl. That's impressive," the cat ordered.

Tucker threw back her pretty head, emitting a spine-tingling howl. "I wanna go!"

Harry knelt down and hugged the little dog. "Ah, Tucker, it's only for the weekend."

Tucker repeated her dramatic recitation. "I wanna go! Don't leave me here!"

"Oh, now, come on." Harry comforted the dog.

"Oo-oo-oo!"

"That's good." Mrs. Murphy moved to another blouse. If she

couldn't go she could at least deposit as much cat hair as possible on Harry's clothes.

"Well—" Harry weakened.

"*Oh, please, I'm the best little dog in the world. I won't make you walk me to go to the bathroom. I won't even eat. I'll be real cheap—*"

"*That's pushing it, Tucker,*" Mrs. Murphy grumbled.

"*She's eating it up.*"

"Oh, Tucker, I feel so guilty about leaving you here."

"*Oo-oo-oo!*"

Harry picked up the phone by the bed and punched in Mim's number. "Hello, Mim. I have the unhappiest dog in front of me, curled up in my duffle bag. May I bring Tucker?" She listened to the affirmative reply. "Thank you. Thank you, too, for Tucker." Then she called Sally Dohner, who agreed to fill in for her at the post office.

"*Way to go!*" Mrs. Murphy congratulated her friend.

"*Oh, boy!*" Tucker jumped out of the duffle bag and ran around in small circles until she made herself dizzy and fell down.

"Now how did you know you were going?" Harry laughed at the dog. "Sometimes I think you two understand English." She petted Mrs. Murphy, who nestled down in a sweater. "I'm sorry, Murphy, but you know how you are on a long trip. You take care of Susan—she's going to spend the weekend here. She said she'd love a break from being a wife and mother." Harry sat on the bed. "Bet she brings the whole family with her anyway. Well, you know everyone."

"*Yes. I'll be a good kitty. Just tell her I want lots of cooked chicken.*"

"She even promised to fry pork chops for you."

"*Ooh, I love pork chops.*" Mrs. Murphy purred, then called out to Tucker: "*Tucker, you've got to remember everything you see, smell, or hear.*"

"*Got ya.*"

33

Camden, South Carolina, settled in 1758 and called Pine Tree Hill at that time, sits in a thermal belt, making it perfect for horsemen. While the air freezes, the sand does not, so in wintertime Thoroughbred breeders, trainers, chasers, hunters, and show horse people flock to the good footing and warmer temperatures. While not as balmy as Florida, Camden isn't as crowded either, nor as expensive.

Mrs. Marion duPont Scott had wintered in Camden, falling in love with the town. The relaxed people, blessed with that languid humor peculiar to South Carolina, so delighted her that she decided to use her personal wealth to create the Colonial Cup, a Deep South counterpoint to great and grand Montpelier. She developed a steeplechase course that allowed spectators in the grandstand to see most of the jumps, a novelty.

Over the years the races grew. The crowds poured in. The parties created many a wild scandal. The pockets of the citizens of Camden bulged.

The only bad thing that could be said about this most charming of upcountry towns in South Carolina is that it was the site of a Revolutionary War disaster on April 16, 1780, when General Horatio Gates, with 3,600 men, lost to Lord Cornwallis's 2,000 British troops. After that the British decided to enjoy thoroughly the comforts of Camden and the attentions of the female population, famed for their exquisite manners as well as their good looks.

Harry, thrilled to be a guest at the Colonial Cup, walked around Camden with her mouth hanging open. She and Miranda had decided to tour the town before heading over to the track. The races wouldn't commence until the following day, and they were like schoolgirls at recess. Harry dutifully asked Mim, then Charles, then Adelia, and even Fair if they needed her assistance. As soon as everyone said "No," she shot out of the stable, Tucker at her heels.

"I could get used to this." Harry smiled as she regarded a sweeping porch that wrapped around a stately white frame house. Baskets of flowers hung from the ceiling of the porch, for the temperature remained around 65°F.

"How I remember Mamaw sitting on her swing, passing and repassing, discussing at length the reason why she lined her walkway with hydrangeas and why her roses won prizes. Oh, I wish Didee were coming." Miranda used the childhood name for her sister. "That husband of hers is too much work."

"What husband isn't?"

"My George was an angel."

Harry fought back the urge to reply that he was now. Instead she said, "He had no choice."

Mrs. Hogendobber stopped. The crepe on the bottom of her

sensible walking shoes screeched, which made Tucker bark. That made the West Highland white on the wraparound porch bark. "Do I detect sarcasm?"

"Hush, Tucker."

"*I'm on duty here,*" Tucker stoutly barked right back. "*If that white moppet wants to run his mouth and insult us, I am not remaining silent.*"

"Will you shut up!"

"My husband listened better than your dog."

"Let's move on before every dog in the neighborhood feels compelled to reply. Tucker, I don't know why I brought you. You've been a real pain in the patoutee. You sniffed everything where we slept. You rushed up and down the barn aisles. You ran out in the paddocks. You dashed into every parked van. Are you on canine amphetamines?"

"*I'm searching for information. You're too dumb to know that. I'm not rushing around like a chicken with its head cut off. I have a plan.*"

"Apparently, Tucker isn't too pleased with you either," Mrs. Hogendobber noted.

"She'll settle down. Let's go on up the road. The second oldest polo field in the United States is there."

They walked down a sandy path; the railroad track lay to their right. Within moments the expanse of manicured green greeted them, a small white stable to one side. On the other side of the field were lovely houses, discreetly tucked behind large boxwoods and other bushes.

A flotilla of corgis poured across the field, shooting out of the opened gate of one of the houses. Tee Tucker stopped, her ears straight up, her eyes alert, her non-tail steady. She had not seen so many of her own kind since she was a puppy.

"*Who are you?*" they shouted as they reached midfield.

"*Tee Tucker from Crozet, Virginia. I'm here for the Colonial Cup.*"

Before the words were out of Tucker's lips the corgis swarmed around her, sniffing and commenting. Finally the head dog, a large red-colored fellow, declared, "*This is a mighty fine repre-*

sentative of our breed. *Welcome to the great state of South Carolina. Might I invite you to our home for a refreshing drink or to meet my mistress, a lovely lady who would enjoy showing you Camden hospitality?"*

"Thank you, but I've got to stay close to Mom. On duty, you know."

"Why, yes, I understand completely. My name is Galahad, by the way, and these are my numerous offspring. Some were blessed with intelligence and others with looks." He laughed and they all talked at once, disagreeing with him.

"Have you ever seen so many corgis?" Mrs. Hogendobber watched all those tailless behinds wiggling in greeting.

"Can't say that I have," Harry said, laughing.

"Galahad," Tucker asked politely, *"have there been any murders at the Colonial Cup?"*

"Why, no, not in my recollection, although I think there were many who considered it, humans being what they are. Given their tendency to rely on copious libations for sociability—I'd say it was remarkable that they haven't dispatched one another into the afterlife."

"Oh, Daddy." One of the girls faced Tucker. *"He does go on. Why do you ask a thing like that?"*

"Well, there've been two steeplechase jockeys murdered since Montpelier. I was curious. You know, maybe it's not so unusual."

"Plenty unusual. Steeplechasing doesn't attract the riffraff that flat racing does," Galahad grumbled.

"These days, how can you tell riffraff from quality, Daddy?" the petite corgi asked, knowing full well what the answer would be.

"Bon sang ne sait mentir," came the growled reply.

"What's that?" Tucker's eyebrows quivered.

"Good blood doesn't lie."

"Ah, blood tells," Tucker said. She laughed to herself because that old saw drove Mrs. Murphy wild. Being an alley cat, she would spit whenever Tucker went off on a tangent about pure-bred dogs. *"Well, I am charmed to have met you all. As you can see, the humans are moving off. By the way, I'm staying at Hampstead Farm. If anything should pop into your heads, some stray thought about the racing folks, the 'chasers, I'd appreciate your getting word to me."*

"*You some kind of detective?*" the pretty little one asked.

"*Yes. Exactly.*" Tucker dashed to catch up with Harry and Miranda, hearing the oohs and aahs behind her. She neglected to tell them she worked with a partner, a cat. They'd never meet Mrs. Murphy, so what the heck?

34

Dr. Stephen D'Angelo's farm truck had been discovered in an abandoned barn near Meechum's River in western Albemarle County.

Rick Shaw and his department thoroughly searched the area, turning up nothing, not even a scrap of clothing.

"Think they ditched the truck and stole another?"

"We'd know. I put out a call to the local dealers and to other county departments. Nada. For the first day they were in their truck, the Nissan. After they got rid of D'Angelo's truck."

"By now they know we're on their trail. They've swapped off the Nissan," Coop said.

"That's more like it. No telling, though."

"Sooner or later someone was bound to find this truck."

She sighed. "Well, they've got two days' head start." Cynthia put on her gloves.

"They got it. They could have driven to any airport out of state by now or picked up the train. Or just kept driving. I expect those two have more fake IDs than a Libyan terrorist. They've got seventy-one dollars in cash." He squinted as a tiny sunburst of light reflected off the outside mirror. "Linda withdrew the money at one o'clock on the day they disappeared."

"Let's get this thing dusted for prints."

"Coop, you're methodical. I like that in a woman." He smiled. "Got your bags packed?"

"I always keep a bag packed, why?"

"We're going to Camden."

"No kidding."

"As spectators. If I notify the sheriff down there, it's one more department to fool with. They don't know what we do and I'm not inclined to tell them. It's enough that I have to handle Frank Yancey day in and day out."

"He's getting a lot of pressure from the newspaper." Her mind returned to Linda and Will. "The Forloines have a booming business. And there's someone higher up on the food chain."

"Right. You might want to wear your shoulder holster."

"Good idea."

35

Nerves tight before a race were stretched even tighter today. Fair Haristeen noticed the glum silence between the Valiants when he checked over Mim's horses early that morning.

Brother and sister worked side by side without speaking.

Arthur Tetrick stopped by on his way to the racecourse. He, too, noticed the frosty air between the siblings.

Addie, on sight of her guardian, practically spat at him. "Get out of my face, Arthur."

His eyebrows rose in a V; he inclined his head in a nod of greeting or acquiescence and left.

"Jesus, Addie, you're a bitch today." Charles whirled on her as Arthur shut the door to his car and drove out the sandy lane.

She looked into her brother's face, quite similar in bone structure to her own. "You, of course, are a prince among men!"

"What's that supposed to mean?"

"That you and Arthur are ganging up on me again. That I know he called on Judge Parker the day I spilled the beans about Nigel's stash. God, I was stupid. You'll both use it against me in court."

"This isn't the day to worry about stuff like that."

"You *knew* he went to see Parker, didn't you?"

"Uh"—Chark glanced outside, the sun filtered through the tall pines—"he mentioned it."

"Why didn't you tell me?"

"You'd had enough stress for one day."

"Liar."

"I'm not lying."

"You're withholding. It amounts to the same thing."

"Look who's talking. You lied to me about drugs. You withheld the truth about Nigel. A kilo is a lot of coke, Addie!"

"It wasn't for me!" she shouted.

"Then what were you doing with Nigel?"

"Dating him. Just because he was really into it doesn't mean I was, too."

"Come on, I'm not stupid."

She pointed her finger at him. "So what if I took a line or two. I'm okay. I stopped. This isn't about coke. It's about my money. You want my share."

"No, I don't." He pushed her finger away. "But I don't want to see you ruin everything Dad worked for. You have no sense of—" He struggled.

She filled in the word for him. "Responsibility?"

"Right." His eyes blazed. "We have to nurture that money. It seems like a lot but it can go faster than you think. You can't be cautious and we both know it."

"No risk, no gain."

"Addie." He tried to remain patient. "The only thing you know how to do is spend money. You don't know how to make it."

"Horses."

"Never."

"Then what are you doing as a trainer?" She was so frustrated tears welled up in her eyes.

"I get paid for training. I'm not running my own horses. Jesus, Addie, the board and vet bills alone will eat you alive. 'Chasing is for rich people."

"We *are* rich."

"Not if you try to be a major player overnight. We have to keep that money in solid stocks and bonds. If I can double the money in ten years, then we can think about owning a big string of our own."

"What's life for, Charles?" She used his proper name. "To hoard money? To read balance statements and call our stockbroker daily? Do we buy a sensible little farm or do we rent for ten years? Maybe I think life is an adventure—you take chances, you make mistakes. Hey, Chark, maybe you even lose money but you live."

"Live. You'll wind up with some bloodsucker who married you for your fortune. Then there'll be two of you squandering our inheritance."

"Not our inheritance. My inheritance. You take yours and I'll take mine. It's simple."

"I'm not going to let you ruin yourself."

"Well, brother, there's not a damn thing you can do about it." She stopped, blinked hard, then said in a low voice, "You could have killed Nigel. I don't put it past you." She drew close to his face. "I'll do one thing for you though. You're so worried about me? Well, this is my advice to you. Dump dear old Uncle Arthur. He's a dinosaur. And a very well-off dinosaur, thanks to Mom's will. He got his ten percent as executor. And after you dump the old fart, do something crazy, Chark. Something not useful. Buy a Porshe 911 or go to New York and party every night for a month. For once live your life. Just let go." She turned and walked outside.

He yelled after her, "I didn't kill Nigel Danforth!"

She cocked her head and turned back to face him. "Chark, for all I know you'll kill me, then you can have the whole ball of wax."

"I can't believe you said that." His face was white as a sheet.

"Well, I did. I've got races to run." She left him standing there.

36

The making of a good steeplechaser, like the making of a good human being, is an arduous melding of discipline, talent, luck, and heart. The best bloodlines in the world won't produce a winner, although they might fortify your chances.

Thoroughbreds a trifle too slow for the flat track find their way to the steeplechasing barns of the East Coast. Needing far more stamina than their flat-racing brethren, the 'chasers dazzle the equine world. Many a successful steeplechase athlete has retired to foxhunting, the envy of all who have beheld the creature soaring over fences, coops, ditches, and stone walls.

They gathered at the Springdale track for the $100,000 purse of the Colonial Cup, the last race in the season. After this race the points would be tallied, and the best trainer, horse, and jockey would emerge for the season.

Harry and Mrs. Hogendobber figured the most useful thing they could do was to keep Mim occupied despite her nervousness. They knew better than to disturb the Valiants before a race. Keeping Mim clear of them seemed a good policy.

Tucker, on a leash, complained, but Harry refused to release her. "You don't know where you are and you might get lost."

"*Dogs don't get lost. People do.*"

"She's yappy this morning." Miranda, wearing her favorite plaid wraparound skirt and a white blouse with a red cable knit sweater, seemed the essence of fall.

"The crowd excites her."

"*I'm on a recon mission. I need to chat up any animal who will talk to me.*"

Heedless of Tucker's tasks, Harry pulled her along to the paddock. After being dragged a few feet Tucker decided to give in and heel properly. If she couldn't have her way, she might as well make the best of it.

The lovely live oaks sheltered the paddock. The officials busied themselves in the final hour before the first race.

Colbert Mason spied Mrs. Hogendobber and waved to her. Miranda waved back.

Arthur bustled out of the small officials' office, his Worth and Worth trilby set at a rakish angle. Most of the other men wore hats, too: porkpies, cowboy hats, lads' caps in every imaginable fabric, and one distinguished navy blue homburg. The manufacturers of grosgrain ribbon would survive despite the dressing down of America. Horsemen had style.

The one blond uncovered head among the group belonged to Fair, who had ridden over in the van. He walked over to join his ex-wife and Miranda.

"May I get you ladies a drink or a sandwich?"

"No, but I'd like to sit a spell. This commotion is tiring." Miranda dumped herself on a park bench.

"Imagine how the horses feel." Fair sat next to her.

"*Fair, make her let me go,*" Tucker implored.

He reached down and scratched those big ears. "You're so low to the ground, girl, I bet all these shoes and legs are bewildering."

"No, they're not."

"Ignore her. She's whined and whimpered since the moment we arrived." Harry sternly raised her forefinger to the dog.

"You know, when we were married, I always wanted to bring you here, but somehow I never got the time."

"I'm here now."

"Do you like it?"

"It's wonderful. Miranda and I toured the town. I had no idea it was so lovely."

"People here know how to garden." Miranda's passion, apart from the choir and baking, was gardening. "I'm tempted to ask for cuttings."

"Bet they'd give them to you." Fair smiled. He put his arm around Harry's shoulders.

"Where's Mim?" she said. "We started out with her—"

"We drove over with her and Jim. That's not the same as starting out." Miranda chuckled. "That Mim, no sooner had we parked than she rocketed out of her car."

"Don't worry. Arthur headed her off before she could get to Addie and Chark. And Jim stuck right with her. He's the only one of us capable of dissuading Mim from her plans."

"She doesn't mean to lean on those youngsters." Mrs. Hogendobber stretched her legs out in front of her, wiggling her toes. She'd walked more in the last twenty-four hours than in the preceding month. "Oh, that feels good."

"Nerves," Harry succinctly said.

"There are plenty of owners worse than Mim. We practically had to tranquilize Marylou Valiant in the old days." He laughed.

"If I'd been dating Mickey Townsend I'd have to be tranquilized too." Harry giggled.

"I thought you liked Mickey." Miranda finally released her purse from her death grip and set it on the ground next to her.

"I do like Mickey. He's full of energy. He's got plenty of that burly masculine charm that Marylou could never resist. But he loses money at the races and doesn't pay his staff until he wins it back."

Fair crossed his arms over his chest. "If he'd married Marylou, he wouldn't have had those worries. Racing isn't for folks who need a weekly paycheck. Plus you need nerves of steel. He has them. I worry more about his temper than the money. He comes up with it somehow."

"It's the *somehow* I'm worried about," Harry said under her breath.

"Why?"

"Fair, two jockeys are under the ground and—" She looked up then blurted out, "What the hell—?"

Miranda, Fair, and Tucker turned their heads left in the direction of Harry's amazed look. "Gracious!" Miranda exclaimed.

"Bet you didn't recognize me in street clothes," Cynthia Cooper joked.

Fair, a gentleman, stood up and offered Cynthia Cooper his seat as she and Rick Shaw approached.

"Well, do I look the part?" Rick wore a plaid lad's cap, a tweed jacket, and baggy pants.

"Do you think you're incognito?" Harry smiled at him.

"You look splendid." Miranda praised the sheriff, a man with whom she might have disagreements but for whom her affection never dimmed.

Harry lowered her voice. "You know the Virginia gang will recognize you."

Cynthia replied, "Sure, we know that. We've never seen a steeplechase, and the boss here had an impulse, so . . . voilà!"

Harry, not believing a word of it, simply smiled. Rick and Cynthia were aware none of the three believed them; probably Tucker didn't either, but they'd go along with the story.

Loud voices at the paddock grabbed their attention.

"You're behind this—" Chark's voice rose.

He shut up when Mickey's fist jammed into his mouth.

Within seconds the two men were knocking the stuffing out of each other.

Fair, Cynthia, and Rick rushed over. Tucker lunged to help but Harry held on to the leash.

"I'll kill you, you dumb son of a bitch," Mickey cursed, then landed a right to the breadbasket. "You're too stupid to know who's on your side and who isn't."

"With you as a friend I don't need enemies." Chark gasped, then caught Mickey on the side of the head with a glancing blow. He reeled back, going down on one knee. The St. Christopher's medal fell out of his pocket, face down on the grass.

Rick and Cynthia deftly stepped between the two men. Rick grabbed Mickey as Cynthia pulled Chark's left arm up behind his back and put a hammer lock around his throat.

"Easy, Chark. Let's end this before it gets a whole lot worse." Cynthia's regulation size .357 Magnum flashed as her blazer opened up. Chark couldn't see it, but as she pressed against him he could feel it. He immediately stopped struggling.

Mickey, however, didn't. Fair stepped in and he and Rick took Mickey down together.

"Goddammit, man." Fair shook his head. "Things are bad enough."

Mickey tried to shake them off. "Bad ain't the word. Let me go." He saw the medal and reached over to pick it up. Fair held him. Rick picked up the medal and handed it to Mickey.

Chark noticed but the object didn't fully register at that moment.

Two uniformed police officers arrived at the scene and brusquely told Cynthia, Rick, and Fair to step back. Then the skinny one noticed her gun.

"You got a license to carry that, ma'am?"

"Deputy Cynthia Cooper, Albemarle County Sheriff's department. I'd shake your hand but I'm occupied. Until you all can talk sense into Mickey Townsend there, I'll remain occupied. We can be formally introduced later."

"Want some help with the perp?" the cop asked Cynthia using the shorthand for perpetrator.

"I'll take care of him. Thanks."

"Coop, I'm okay. I lost my temper." Chark sighed. "Why go out of my way to piss on a skunk?"

"Can't comment on that. Come on, I'll walk you back to the weigh-in. Okay?"

"Yeah. On the way you can tell me what you're doing here."

"A first-class chickenshit!" Mickey, oblivious to the crowd around him, spat out the words as Chark walked away.

Fair whispered, "Mickey, shut up."

"Huh?" Fair's words filtered through the hammer pounding in Mickey's brain.

"Two jockeys who owed you money are dead. No one believes you were playing Old Maid. Chill out," Fair warned.

Mickey shut up.

Rick turned to the two uniformed cops. "This man lives in my county. Nothing to worry about." The two cops nodded and watched Rick and Fair walk away, Mickey between them, the crowd bubbling about what they'd just witnessed.

"You're bullshitting me," Mickey said under his breath to Rick. "You don't know one end of a horse from the other."

"Mickey, you are your own worst enemy." Fair shook his head.

"It's obvious, isn't it?" Mickey spoke to the vet he used and trusted. "Rick Shaw's here to spy on me. Everyone thinks I killed Nigel and Coty. Dammit! Why the hell would I kill my own jockey?"

"You tell me," Rick said.

"I didn't! That's the long and short of it." Mickey's handsome face sagged, and he suddenly appeared old.

"Lying takes so much energy. Just tell the truth," Rick said nonchalantly. "You knew Nigel didn't have a green card. Let's start there."

"Ah, man, give me a break." Mickey squared his shoulders, looking his forty-five years again. "I don't give a shit if the guy had a polka-dot card. He knew how to ride a horse. And don't give me this crap about protecting American workers or protecting abused immigrants. I didn't abuse anyone, and if an American worker can do the job as well as the limey, hey, he's hired. Screw the government."

He was so incorrigible, Rick and Fair had to laugh.

"Mickey, if you'd just give it to me straight I wouldn't have to see you as a prime suspect."

Mickey looked up at Fair imploringly. "Suspect for what?"

"Just talk to the man," Fair said in an even tone.

Mickey gazed over the tops of their heads, over the tops of the trees, all the way up to a robin's-egg-blue sky. "All right."

37

With a half hour to the first race, Mickey Townsend asked if he might give directions to his jockey, obviously new to the job.

Fair had returned to the paddocks.

Cynthia and Rick walked along with Mickey, Cynthia flipping open her notebook as they headed back to his horses.

"I will tell you everything, but I've got to see the races."

"That's fine," Rick said. "You're not under arrest—yet. You've got enough time to start talking before the first race."

Mickey exhaled deeply, shut his eyes, and then opened them. "Nigel Danforth owed me two thousand dollars, give or take, on a gambling debt—not horses, poker. Coty Lamont owed me over seven thousand from last season. I owe Harvey Throgmorton five and a half grand. His wife had her first child, he's had a bad-luck year with the horses, and he needs the money. I want to pay him off. I didn't kill Nigel and I didn't kill Coty Lamont." He took another deep breath, involuntarily clasping and unclasping his hands. "I got a little crazy. I thought about beating them up, and Coty really pissed me off. He promised to pay me, and—that was on the night he was killed or early that morning. I'd heard one lie too many. I don't know . . . when he didn't show up at my barn at ten that night as agreed, I roared on over to his house. To make a long story short, I threatened him, pulled a gun, told him he'd better pay me by morning or he would be history." He walked over to the cooler and plucked a soft drink out for himself. "Want some?"

"No, thanks."

"All this talking makes me thirsty." Mickey popped the top and drank. "I left. What he didn't figure on was that I'd wait for him. I waited at the end of the driveway behind a big bush, had my lights off. When he drove out of there about half an hour later, I tailed him. Guess I've seen too many cop shows. Anyway, I followed him to Mim Sanburne's stable. He didn't drive in, though, which was the weird thing. He left his truck behind the old Amoco station about half a mile from her main gate. But here's what really made me wonder—he covered his license plate with a rag or something. Josh at the Amoco is always fixing cars, I mean the lot is always full of stuff, but Coty covered up that license plate.

"He didn't hear me because I stayed way far behind, far enough to muffle my motor, and then I cut it. About twenty minutes later I ran out of patience, so I walked into Mim's myself. Had my gun. I found him in the stable. He had her hunter in the crossties. I walked over to the stall, scared the shit out of him. He'd been digging in the corner of the stall. I asked him what the hell was he doing and he said getting my money. I asked him what was down there and he said pirate's treasure, real smartass, you know. I was so mad, I said, 'Cover the hole back up, you're jerking me around—if there was anything of value down there you'd have claimed it by now.' Coty always thought people were stupid, that he could stay one step ahead. He was about to tell me something but then he shut up and we both got scared for a minute because we heard a noise. Turned out it was nothing but mice in the hayloft. You know, when it's real quiet at night you hear things like their feet, those little claws. Damnedest thing.

"Well, he filled the hole back in. He hadn't gotten very deep anyway. Put the horse back in the stall. I walked him out to my car by the road, then drove him back to his truck and told him he had until five o'clock before I took his truck as collateral.

"That was the last I saw of Coty Lamont." Pale, he finished his soda, then said as an afterthought, "Doesn't look too good for me, does it?"

"No," Rick said.

"If you're telling the truth, you'll be all right," Cynthia added.

"Do you know about the coke?" Rick listened as the call to the first race was announced.

"Uh—" Mickey stalled.

"Were they users?" Rick asked.

"Yes."

"Are you?"

"I wouldn't have lasted this long in the business if I were hooked on that stuff."

"Do you know who sells it?"

"Sheriff, it's not hard to get."

"That's not what I'm asking."

"Linda Forloines."

"Thank you, Mickey. After the races you'd best go back to Albemarle County and not leave without checking in with me. Go on, the first race is about to start."

Mickey rose, his knees cracking. He walked to the course, his hands deep in his pockets, his fingers wrapped around Marylou's medallion. He was tempted to tell Cynthia and Rick, sorely tempted, but he'd keep the St. Christopher's medal a secret for a little bit longer.

Cynthia flipped her notebook shut. "You believe him?"

"You know better than to ask me something like that."

"Yeah, but I always do, don't I?"

38

The light breeze made Arthur Tetrick's sky-blue official's ribbon flap. His brisk walk assisted the flapping.

Chark and Addie sat behind the weigh-in station. As they had no horse in the first race they watched everyone else.

"Are you all right?" Arthur asked, noticing Chark's swollen lip.

"I'm embarrassed." Chark ignored the dribble from his bleeding lip.

"What happened?"

"Mickey Townsend acted like Mickey Townsend." Chark spoke ruefully. "I walked out of the official's tent and bumped into him. By mistake. I wasn't looking where I was going. I've got Ransom Mine on my mind, you know. He made some crack about how I excel at the bump and run. He's still pissed off about the Maryland Hunt Cup last year. 'Course, I'm a little tense . . ."

"That's the understatement of the year." Addie spoke out of the side of her mouth.

He held up his hands in supplication. "I saw red. No excuses. I was wrong. I made a spectacle of myself."

"No harm done. I'll head off Mim if I can." Arthur checked his watch. "Hmm. I take that back. I'll try to find Harry and Miranda. Maybe they can keep Mim occupied so you don't have to go over the whole story again. Or get chewed out."

Chark winced as Addie dabbed at his lip with a handkerchief. She couldn't stand the dripping blood anymore. "I'm so ashamed."

"If I had half a chance I'd like to thrash him myself."

Addie peered up at Arthur. "I still like Mickey. You two will never cut him a break."

Arthur snapped, "Mickey Townsend cares for nobody but Mickey Townsend. For reasons I will never fathom he casts a spell over the female of the species."

"Yeah, sure." Addie threw down the hankie. "Arthur, I know you went to see Judge Parker."

Arthur's face clouded. "Just a formality."

"No, it wasn't. You were filing papers to extend your trusteeship."

"I did no such thing." He glared at her. "You inherit your fortune at midnight on your birthday . . . tomorrow night. The paperwork will be done on Monday. That's why I went to see Judge Parker."

"You think I'm not competent. Because of the drugs."

Arthur lowered his voice. "This is neither the time nor the place! But Adelia, I have come to the mournful conclusion that I can do nothing to help you. You may not believe me, but I will be relieved to no longer be your trustee or the executor of your mother's will. I wash my hands of you." He drew in a gulp of sweet air. "I only hope your mother will forgive me if she's looking down upon us."

"What rot." Addie left them. She needed to push everything and everybody out of her mind to concentrate on the horses and the course. Each time she saw Arthur or talked to her brother, she felt she was being pulled back into a white-hot rage. This was the first race without Nigel, and that hit her harder than she thought it would.

Arthur followed her with his eyes, then sadly said, "Well, I've upset her. I didn't mean to but . . ."

"She started it."

"So she did, Charles, but I'm old enough to know better."

"You're right about Mickey though. He twisted Mom around his little finger and Addie thought he could do no wrong. Know what else I don't get?" Chark stood up, found he was a trifle shaky, and started to sit back down.

"Here, Chark, you're hurt." Arthur put his hand under Chark's arm to steady him.

"I'm shook up, not hurt. I can't believe I lost control like that."

"You're too hard on yourself." Arthur discreetly glanced at his wristwatch, then sat next to Chark for a moment. "Now, what is it that you don't understand? You lost your train of thought."

"If Mom was so in love with Mickey, why did she refuse to marry him?"

"Ah—" Arthur tipped back his head. "I'd like to think because she knew it wouldn't work in the long run."

"Addie says it was because I didn't like Mickey. Makes me feel guilty as hell."

"Oh, now—"

"You know how she was. She'd do anything for Addie. I used to beg her to marry you. Funny, isn't it?"

"Not to me," Arthur said sadly.

"I used to scream at her that Mickey was a gold digger.

When I think of the stuff I said to my mother," he hung his head, covering his eyes, "I feel so terrible."

Arthur put his arm around Chark. "There, there. You're overwrought. You were young. She forgave you. Mothers always do, you know."

Chark shook his head. "I know, but—"

"Let's talk about something pleasant. I picked up Adelia's birthday cake. It's three tiers high since I figured everyone will wind up back at Mim's place anyway. It's got a jockey's cap on it, Mim's colors, with two crossed whips. Chocolate inside, vanilla icing on the outside. Her favorite."

"That's great, Arthur—just great."

"Big birthday, twenty-one." His own twenty-first had receded into memory, a kind of warm blur. "I've got to go. I'll do my best to find Harry or Mim before I take up my post."

"Thanks."

"Don't mention it." Arthur walked away, the sandy soil crunching underfoot.

39

Addie found Mickey under a huge sweet gum tree on the back side of the course. His stopwatch in his hand, he furtively checked between it and the announcer's stand.

"You mad at me, too?" he said.

"Nah." She drew alongside him.

" 'Bout five more minutes," he said.

"You might win this race."

"Oh, I might win every race." He smiled weakly. "Just depends who the gods smile on that day, right?"

"I think it depends upon the brilliance of the jockey and the heart of the horse."

"That helps." He shifted his weight from one foot to the other. "Do you know why Nigel and Linda beat each other up at the Montpelier Races? He never would tell me, and I think it might be why he's dead."

"Nigel bought a kilo of cocaine from Linda. Or at least I thought he bought it. He was going to sell it to pay off debts, yours being one, and then buy a little place and start training horses himself. He said he knew he couldn't be a jockey forever."

"Yeah, well, you don't just go from being a jockey to being a trainer." Mickey folded his arms across his chest. "Think he was hooked?"

"No."

"Did you tell the sheriff?"

"Finally I did. I mean, I'm in a lot of trouble because I stashed the kilo in my safe deposit box."

"Addie—"

"Yeah, well, I told them that, too. They've impounded it."

Mickey chewed the inside of his lip. "What else did you tell them?"

"Not any more than I had to. Look, just because you're a riverboat gambler doesn't mean you killed anybody. It wasn't enough money to kill someone over."

"What do you think?"

"No way." She grinned.

"Tell you one thing, pretty girl." He felt protective toward Addie, who reminded him a lot of Marylou. "We need a soothsayer to help us."

"Soothsayer won the Eclipse Award. Hell, if we had a soothsayer life would be perfect."

He laughed. "You're too young to remember that horse."

Her face darkened a moment. "There's one thing I did lie about, though."

"Huh?" His senses sharpened.

"Nigel never paid for the cocaine. He said he'd pay as soon as he sold it. He only paid for about a fourth of it. I told Sheriff

Shaw that Nigel paid for it." She helplessly held up her hands. "I don't know why I lied."

"Addie!" He blanched.

"I don't want Linda coming after me." Her face flushed. "If Linda thinks I set her up, hey . . ." She didn't need to finish the thought.

Mickey rolled his shoulders forward and back, something he did to relax his muscles. "She's in so much shit. Hell, they know she sells it. She's a suspect with or without your help."

"Selling ain't killing. You coming to my birthday party?" She fell in with his step.

"No."

"I'll talk to Chark."

"Don't. Let well enough alone, Adelia. I'd be a wet blanket."

"Oh, please come. You'd make me happy." She sighed. "Be a lot happier if Nigel were still here."

He patted her on the back. "Believe it or not, honey, I know how you feel. There isn't a day that goes by that I don't miss your mother." He waited, cleared his throat. "Addie, you aren't the only person withholding information from the sheriff." He reached into his pocket, placing the beautiful St. Christopher's medal into Adelia's hand.

She stared, blinked, then the tears gushed over her cheeks. She brought the medal to her lips, kissing it. "Oh, no. Oh, no." Although she knew her mother must be dead, the medal brought home the full force of the loss; not a vestige of hope remained.

"Where did you get this?" she whispered.

Mickey, crying too, said, "From Nigel Danforth's down jacket." He explained the whole sequence of events to her. "This will lead us to her murderer. My gut tells me it wasn't Nigel. But how did he get this medal?"

"Mickey, let me have it."

"After we flush out the rat."

"No. Let me have it now. I want to wear it just like Mom did."

"Addie, it's too dangerous."

"Please. You can stick close to me. I want Mom's medal, and I want everyone to see it."

40

Despite being on a leash, Tucker wiggled with excitement. The smells alone thrilled her: aromas of baked ham, smoked turkey, roast beef, and fried chicken mingled with the tang of hot dogs, hamburgers, and mustard. Three-bean salad, seven-layer salad, simple cole slaw, and rich German potato salad emitted a fragrance not as tantalizing as the meats, but food was food and Tucker wasn't picky. The brownies, angel food cakes, pound cakes with honey drizzled on top, and pumpkin pies smelled enticing, too. The sour mash whiskey, bracing single malt scotches, sherries, port, gin, and vodkas turned her head away because these odors stung her nostrils and her eyes.

For Tucker, the Colonial Cup was a kaleidoscope of smells and of more people than she could possibly greet. Tucker knew her social obligations. She was to rush out and sniff each human nearing her mother. If she knew them, she would wag her nonexistent tail. If she didn't, she'd bark her head off, the cheapest and most effective alarm system yet devised. But with thousands of people swarming about, she couldn't bark at everyone. Instead she practiced her steely gaze technique. If someone approached Harry, she braced herself, never removing her eyes from the person's face. Once she felt sure the person was not going to lunge for Harry or Mrs. Hogendobber, she relaxed.

Although bred for herding, corgis are also mindful of their special human and will defend that person to the best of their ability. In Tee Tucker's opinion the best dog for human defense was and ever would be a chow chow. Fanatically devoted to their masters, chows first growled a warning and then, if the warning was ignored, the dog would nail the potential attacker, whether it was another canine, a human, or whatever. Tucker wasn't that ferocious but she was devoted to Harry. Sometimes she wished Harry had another dog. Mrs. Murphy could be so superior sometimes, and she hated it when the cat looked down at her from a table or a countertop. She loved Murphy, but she couldn't play rough with her or the cat would shred her sensitive nose.

"*Mother, these tailgates tempt me. If I have to walk by you, you should beg food for me.*"

The day had warmed up, and the time between races was more exhausting than the races themselves. Miranda, parched from the dust and the sun, pulled Harry toward a drink stand.

Harry longingly viewed the bar set out on the back of a station wagon, but since she didn't know the jolly people celebrating the sunshine, the horses, the day, and one another, she moved on, to the stand.

"I thought Fair wasn't going to work this race," Miranda said.

"You know how that goes." Harry bought a Coke, glanced down at her panting pooch, and asked for an empty paper cup.

She walked over to the water fountain, filled it up, and Tucker happily slurped.

"Guess being married to a vet is like being married to a doctor."

"I'm not married to him."

"Oh, will you stop."

"Yes, it's like being married to a doctor, and Fair is so conscientious. He works on animals whether the people pay or not. I mean, they always tell him they're going to pay, but they don't. If an animal is in trouble, he's there."

"Isn't that why you loved him?"

"Yes." Harry finished her Coke.

"Mmm." Miranda watched the three jockeys, their silks brilliant, standing in the paddock.

Harry followed her gaze, particularly noticing one wiry fellow, hand on hip, crop in hand. "Funny, isn't it? Those behemoth football players get paid a fortune and we worship them for their strength, but these guys have more courage. Women, too. Pure guts, gristle, and brains out there."

"Well, I've never understood how—" Miranda stopped. "Harry, is it rude to talk to jockeys before they ride? I would guess it is."

"They aren't up next. I recognize the silks."

Miranda charged over to the three men. One looked much younger than the others—about sixteen. "Excuse me," she said.

Tucker bounded forward, surprising Harry, who was pulled off balance.

"Ma'am." The eldest of the three, a man in his middle forties, removed his cap.

"Did you know Nigel Danforth?" Miranda demanded.

"I did." The teenager spoke up.

"This may sound like an odd question, but, did you like him?"

"Didn't really know him." The older man spoke up quickly. The youngest one, in flame-orange silks with two black hoop bands on each sleeve, said, "He acted like he was better than the rest of us."

Harry smiled. That English accent set off people every time.

As if reading her thoughts, the middle jockey, twenty-five or so, added, "It wasn't his accent, which sounded phony to me. He used to strut about, cock of the walk. And brag."

"That he was a better rider?" Harry joined in.

"No," the younger one said. "That he was going to marry Addie Valiant. Addie deserves better than that."

"Yes, she does," Harry agreed.

Now the oldest jockey, in deep green silks with pale blue circles on them, decided to talk. "Don't get me wrong. None of us hated him enough to kill him, and he wasn't a dirty rider, so you have to give the man credit for that, but there was something about him, something shifty. You'd ask him a question, any question, and he'd dance around it like he needed time to think of an answer."

"What did Addie see in him?" the youngest one asked, eyebrows quizzical. His longing tone betrayed a crush on Addie.

Miranda, in her "Dear Abby" voice, replied, "She wasn't thinking clearly. She would have come to her senses."

"Why do you want to know about Nigel Danforth?" the older man asked.

Harry jumped in. "Guess we were as curious as you all were—we couldn't figure out what she saw in him either."

They exchanged a few more words, then Harry, Miranda, and Tucker hastened to the small paddock where jockeys mounted their horses before they were led out onto the track.

Addie, riding for a client other than Mim in this race, walked around led by Chark. Her mother's medal gleamed on her neck. She had the top button of her silks undone. Chark, taut before the race and upset over Mickey Townsend as well as his argument with his sister, didn't notice.

Colbert Mason, the Sanburnes, Fair Haristeen, Arthur Tet-

rick, Mickey Townsend, Rick Shaw, and Cynthia Cooper, plus
hundreds of others, observed the horses. Within a few minutes
they'd be called toward the starting cord.

Miranda's mouth fell open. "It can't be," she half-
whispered.

"What?" Harry leaned toward her.

"Look at Adelia's neck."

Harry peered, the light bouncing off the royal blue enamel.
"Some kind of medal. I don't remember it. Must be an early
birthday present."

"No early present. I'd know that medal anywhere. It was
Marylou's. She never took it off her neck after Charley died. Not
even for fancy balls. She'd drape her rubies and diamonds over
it."

Harry focused on the medal. "Uh—yes, now that you mention it. I recall Marylou wearing that."

Mim, across the paddock, also stared at the medal. She
grabbed Jim's arm.

Mim, Miranda, and Jim converged on Rick Shaw, pulling
him away from the rail and possible eavesdroppers.

Once he persuaded them to talk in sequence, he listened
intently as did Deputy Cooper.

"You don't know if it's the exact medal. Someone could
have given her a replica," Rick said.

"Flip it over." Mim's lips were white from emotion.

"Even if it carries the same message, it could be a replica."
Rick pursued his line of thought.

"It was made by Cartier expressly for Marylou." Mim
wrung her hands.

"I appreciate this. I really do. After the races we can ask
Adelia to remove the medal so you all can have a closer look, and
she can tell us where she got it." Rick hoped the medal was
meaningful, but he needed to keep Marylou's old friends calm.
He wanted to approach this evidence quietly and sensibly.

"The minute the Colonial Cup is run." Mim was pleading, unusual for her.

"I promise," Rick said firmly.

The trumpet called contestants from the paddocks to the track.

Harry, Mrs. Hogendobber, the Sanburnes, and Tucker raced to the stands. The horses lined up, the cord sprang loose, and they shot off. Addie hung in the pack, easily clearing the fences, but on the second lap the horse was bumped over a fence and lost a stride or two. She couldn't make it up by the finish line, and they were out of the money.

As the humans hollered and exchanged money among themselves, Tucker, happy to see another dog come up into the stands, a jaunty Jack Russell, called out, "Hello."

"Hi," the Jack Russell answered. "I hope we sit near one another. I've had about all the humans I can stand. My name is The Terminator."

"Mine is Tucker."

Fortunately, the owner, a nervous-looking, thin, middle-aged woman, took a seat in front of Tucker. "This is good luck. Are you with anyone in the races?"

"Mim Sanburne," Tucker replied.

"She might win the cup this year," the Russell said sagely. "My human, ZeeZee Thompson—she's a trainer, you know—thinks Mim has a good chance. In fact, my human has been in the top five trainers in winnings for the last ten years."

"Oh." Tucker sounded impressed.

"ZeeZee used to ride in England, but she took a bad fall, ruptured her spleen and damaged her liver plus she broke some ribs. So as soon as she recovered, she learned how to train."

"She must have known Nigel Danforth in England."

The Terminator paused, lowering her voice. "Nigel Danforth is no more a Brit than you or I, my friend. My mother's afraid to talk about him 'cause of the murders, you see. She doesn't want to be next."

"Is she in danger?" Tucker surged forward on her leash. Harry

paid no attention, so Tucker moved next to the smooth-coated Jack Russell.

"I hope not, but you see, she is the only person who knows where Nigel came from, and if the killer figures that out, she might be in trouble."

"The killer's only taking out jockeys." Tucker comforted the other dog.

"I don't know, but whoever is doing this knows 'chasing inside and out."

"How did your mother know Nigel Danforth?"

"Montana. One summer—I guess it must have been six years ago, when I was a puppy—we went out to Bozeman. He was a ranch hand, but he was good with a horse. Mom told him the money back East was better than punching cows. He had a full mustache and beard then. Men look real different to humans when they shave them off. They smell the same, of course."

"What was his real name? Do you remember that?"

"Sargent Wilcox." Tucker's eyes widened as the little dog continued. "I sure hope my mother is safe. Wilcox only worked for Mom for a little bit. He was too wild for her."

Tucker hoped so, too, because she was beginning to get the picture, not the whole picture but the very beginning, and it was terrifying.

41

The Colonial Cup, for which they had waited, was about to be run.

Mim joined her husband, Harry, Mrs. Hogendobber, and Fair in the box in the grandstand. She'd run up from the paddock where she'd smiled at Addie and wished her well, all the while keeping her eyes on the St. Christopher's medal. When Chark gave his sister a leg up, Mim returned to the grandstand for fear her own nerves would make the Valiants agitated. Her beige suede outfit topped with her ubiquitous Hermes scarf showed not a wrinkle, crease, or stain despite her dashing about. She sat down, jaw tight. Little Marilyn would have gladly tightened the scarf around her mother's neck. She hated it when Mim tensed up like this, so she sat with ZeeZee Thompson down the aisle.

No one spoke. Not even Tucker, who sat motionless in Harry's lap.

Addie, shimmering in purple silks, circled on Bazooka, then came into the starting area. The yellow rope stretched across the track. The horses lined up, prancing sideways and snorting. Then twang—the rope snapped back—and off they shot.

Bazooka gunned out front. Chark, down near the starting area, ran back toward the grandstand for a better view and in the process ran into Mickey Townsend again. He said he was sorry and kept going, leaving Mickey to dust himself off. The horse Mickey trained, a client's from West Virginia, was in the middle of the pack.

"She's on too fast a pace," Mim murmured through the tension-narrowed slit that was her mouth.

"Don't fret, honey. Addie knows what she's doing."

Arthur Tetrick, up in the race director's box for this one, stood, mouth hanging open. He peeked over Colbert Mason's shoulder at the big digital timer. "She'll never make it."

"A scorcher," Colbert laconically replied.

Bazooka's stride lengthened with every reach of his black hooves. Addie appeared motionless on top of him, moving only as they landed after each successful jump.

Try as it might, no horse could get near her. The race, so perfect, seemed like a dream to Addie's cheering section. The crowd screamed as much in disbelief as in excitement.

At the next to last fence, Bazooka vaulted over, another perfect landing, and four strides after the fence Addie and the saddle slipped off and under Bazooka. She hit the ground with a thud.

If she'd fallen off at a jump she would have been thrown clear. But the saddle dropped to the left side and slightly underneath Bazooka. His left hind hoof grazed her head. She rolled into a ball.

One fractious horse, seeing Addie on the ground, exploded. The rider fought hard but the animal plunged right over the fallen jockey.

Bazooka crossed the finish line first just as the ambulance reached an unconscious Addie on the track.

42

Chark, with Mickey Townsend not far behind, tore down the grass track. Arthur Tetrick blasted out of the booth and ran down the concrete grandstand steps faster then anyone thought possible.

Huge Jim Sanburne was immediately behind them. Fair was already on the track on the other side of the finish line. An outrider led Bazooka over to him.

Rick Shaw grabbed Cynthia Cooper's arm as they ran out from the tailgate section.

"I should have seen it coming. Damn me!" He cursed. "You stay here. You know what to do. I'll ride in the ambulance."

"I'll finish up at Hampstead Farm."

"Right." He flashed his badge at a shocked track official and sprinted out to the ambulance, where Addie's unconscious form was being carefully slid into the back. Chark, tears in his eyes, hopped in with her.

Arthur reached the ambulance the same time Rick did. "Sheriff." Rick opened his badge for the ambulance attendants. "Arthur, go back to the booth and get me a video of this race. Now!"

"Yes, of course." Arthur turned and ran back to the grandstand, passing the two slow-moving Camden police.

"Jim, get her saddle. See that no one touches it but you. Hurry before some do-gooder gets there first," Rick commanded.

Jim, without comment, lurched toward the next to last jump.

"Mickey, go find Deputy Cooper. She'll be in the paddock . . . help her. You know these people. They'll talk to you."

"You got it." Mickey peeled off toward the paddock, jumping the track rail in his hurry.

"Chark, I'm coming with you." He hoisted himself into the back of the ambulance.

The driver's assistant closed the heavy door behind them. With its flashers turned on, the vehicle rolled along the side of the track. The driver, savvy about horses, would save his siren until they reached the highway.

"Who saddled the horse?" Rick waved to the gesticulating policemen.

"I did." Chark held his sister's hand.

"Where do you keep your tack?"

"At the stalls."

"Hampstead Farm?"

"No, no—the stalls at the track. We pick up the saddle pad number, we draw for position first, then we saddle up."

"Wouldn't be hard for someone to mess with the saddle or the—" Rick stopped to think of the term.

"Girth," Chark said.

"Girth, yes."

"Yes, but I saddled Bazooka. I'd have seen it." He squeezed

his sister's hand, the tears coming down his face. He reached over and touched the St. Christopher's medal, turning it over. "What in God's name . . ." he whispered.

"What is it?"

"This is Mother's. We haven't seen it since the day she disappeared." He stared, uncomprehending, at Rick.

The emergency rescue worker held Adelia's head firmly between her hands. If Addie's neck were broken, one bump could make a bad situation very much worse.

Rick, on his knees, bent over. He read aloud the inscription: He's my stand-in. Love, Charley

"Dad gave that to Mom the year they were married."

"And you haven't seen this since your Mother disappeared?"

"No."

Rick sat back on his haunches as the ambulance sped to the hospital.

"Sheriff."

"Huh?" Rick's mind was miles away.

"Whoever had this killed my mother."

Rick reached over and put his hand on Chark's shoulder. He said nothing, but he was praying hard, praying that Adelia would live, praying she wouldn't be paralyzed, and praying he could persuade Camden's police to provide twenty-four-hour protection until she could be moved to Albemarle County.

"Charles, you understand that my job forces me to ask unseemly questions."

"I do, sir."

"Could your sister have killed your mother?"

"Never." Chark's voice was level even as the tears kept flowing.

"Adelia comes into her majority tomorrow. Did you want her dead?"

"No," Chark whispered, shaking his head.

"What about Arthur Tetrick? Would he gain by your sister's death?"

Chark regained his voice, "No. His term as executor expires tomorrow at midnight. Even if"—he choked—"she doesn't make it, he has nothing to gain."

"Do you have any idea who would do this?"

"I can only think of one person. Linda Forloines. Because of the cocaine."

"We thought she might show up. Disguised. It's a bit far-fetched, but"—he squeezed Chark's shoulder—"we were worried."

"She could have paid someone to do this."

"Yes. Deputy Cooper is working over the officials and jockeys pretty hard right about now."

"Sheriff, I had a stupid fight with Addie. If anything should happen—" he covered his eyes, "I couldn't live. I couldn't."

"She's going to be okay." Rick lied, for he couldn't know. "You'll have plenty of time to mend your fences."

Rick looked imploringly at the rescue-squad woman, who looked down at Addie.

43

A small incident occurred during the questioning of track personnel, owners, trainers, and jockeys.

When Jim Sanburne brought Addie's light, small racing saddle to Deputy Cooper, Mickey Townsend reached for it and Arthur Tetrick slammed him across the chest with a forearm.

They slapped each other around until the men in the paddock quickly separated them.

"He's trying to smear the prints," Arthur protested.

"No, I wasn't!" Mickey shouted from the other side of the paddock.

After they quieted down, Cynthia resumed her questioning. Harry and Miranda helped by organizing people in a line and by quickly drawing up a checklist of who was in the paddock area.

Fair turned Bazooka over to a groom after checking the animal thoroughly for injury. As a precaution he drew blood to see if Bazooka could have been doped. An amphetamine used on a horse as high octane as Bazooka was a prescription for murder. He conferred with a reputable local equine vet, an acquaintance, Dr. Mary Holloway. She took the vial, jumped into her truck, and headed for the lab.

Fair reached the paddock and joined Coop. "What can I do?"

"Got a pair of rubber gloves?"

"Right here." He pulled the see-through gloves from his chest pocket.

"Inspect the saddle, will you? But be careful—remember, it has to be fingerprinted. Jim Sanburne, Chark and Addie will have prints on the saddle. We're looking for—well, you know."

"I'll be careful." Fair picked up the saddle, lifted the small suede flap. The leathers, beltlike with buckles, were solid on both sides. Then he inspected the girth, torn in two. "That's how they did it." He flipped over the girth and could see on the underside the razor cut, which ran its width. As the outside of the girth was not cut, someone could tighten the girth and not realize it was cut underneath.

"Would someone need to know a lot about horses or racing to do that?" Cooper asked.

"It would help. But with a little direction anyone could do it."

Troubled, Coop pressed her lips together. "Next."

A slight young man stepped forward. "Randy Groah. I ride for Michael Stirling here in Camden."

"Where were you before the last race?"

As Cynthia questioned, Harry wrote down everyone's statistics, name, address, phone number, etc. . . .

Tucker, having easily slipped her collar, followed The Terminator. They checked the changing room, hospitality tents, and the on-site stables. They turned up nothing except for doughnut crumbs, which they ate, certain the food had nothing to do with the case.

A long, low whistle stopped the Jack Russell. "*That's my mom.*"

"*I'll follow you over.*" Tucker trotted alongside her feisty new friend.

"Terminator, let's go." ZeeZee clapped her hands.

"*I'll walk along for a bit.*" Tucker fell in beside The Terminator. They reached the stables, where ZeeZee's Explorer was parked in front.

"Come on, Term." She scooped up the little guy and put him on the passenger seat.

"*Good luck,*" the Jack Russell called out.

"*You, too.*" Tucker scampered back to the paddock while ZeeZee peeled out of there.

Three and a half hours later Harry, Miranda, Fair, and Cynthia Cooper finished questioning jockeys and track officials. The Sanburnes left for the hospital as soon as Cynthia dismissed them. Mim had told Coop about the St. Christopher's medal, and Miranda confirmed it.

Coop stopped by the jockeys' changing tent to check over Addie's gear bag. She unzipped it. "I will slice and dice this son of a bitch!"

On top of Addie's clothes rested a Queen of Diamonds.

44

When Harry finally walked into her kitchen at 2:30 A.M. and saw Susan, all the horrors of the day, which now seemed years ago, began to spill out. Susan had heard about Addie's accident on the radio and had waited at the farm to talk to her friend.

The two dear friends sat down at the kitchen table. Harry told her that Chark was under suspicion but hadn't been arrested.

"*So you see, Sargent Wilcox is Nigel and it was Sargent who, along with Coty Lamont, buried Marylou Valiant.*" Tucker lay down nose to nose with Mrs. Murphy, flat out on her stomach.

"*And you say this Jack Russell met Nigel in Bozeman, Montana?*" Mrs. Murphy gently swished her tail back and forth like a slender reed in slowly moving water. "*Not that I would put much faith in anything a Jack Russell says, but still—*"

"*This was a reputable Russell, not one of those yappers.*"

"Oh, you'll stick up for any dog."

"No, I won't. You've never heard me say anything good about a Chihuahua, have you?"

The cat allowed as to how that was a fact. She flicked her pink tongue over her black lips. "Apart from ZeeZee Thompson, no one there knows that Nigel Danforth is Sargent Wilcox."

"No," Tucker said, "but that's not all. Mrs. Hogendobber and Mim— Jim, too—were upset about a St. Christopher's medal Addie wore after the first race."

"Why?"

"It was her mother's. No one has seen it since Marylou disappeared."

"Maybe that's why Coty Lamont was digging"—she paused—"except he didn't reach the body. Oh, this is giving me a headache!"

"Whoever had the St. Christopher's medal has had it for the last five years. And you know what else?" Tucker panted. "Someone put the Queen of Diamonds in Addie's gear bag."

Mrs. Murphy put her paws over her eyes, "Tucker, this is terrible."

45

"Son of a bitch!" Rick Shaw exploded.

"You couldn't have known." Cynthia offered him a cigarette. He snatched one out of the pack.

"He's playing with us." He lit his cigarette and clenched so hard on the weed that he bit it in half, sending the burning tip falling into his crotch. He batted out the fire.

Cynthia, too, smacked at the glowing tip. "Sorry."

He paused a minute, then glanced down at her hand in his crotch. "Ah—I'm sure there's something I could say to cover this situation, but I can't think of it right now." He dropped the stub in the ashtray.

Cynthia lit him another cigarette. "Don't bite, just inhale."

It was five in the morning and they circled the growing city of Charlotte with ease—too early for traffic. Rick and Cynthia had stayed to assist the Camden police since the crimes in their respective jurisdictions were most likely linked. The Camden police had insisted on booking Charles Valiant on suspicion of attempted murder. Rick finally let them, figuring twenty-four hours in Camden's jail would be twenty-four hours in which they would know Chark's whereabouts. Arthur would free him on bail early Monday morning.

"The Queen of Diamonds! Son of a bitch!"

"Boss, you've been saying that for the last hour and a half. There's one bloody queen left and—"

"Bloody queen is right. I know this guy will strike again, I know it. If only I could figure out the significance of the cards." He slammed the dash.

"Your blood pressure's going to go through the roof."

"Shut up and drive!" He glowered out the window and then turned to her. "I'm sorry."

"It's a bitch. I never saw it coming, either," she said sympathetically.

"If we only knew what they had in common."

"Jockeys."

"Not enough." He shook his head.

"They all knew one another."

"Yes." He began to breathe a bit more regularly.

"They're all young people."

"Yes."

"They owed money to Mickey Townsend. They all used cocaine."

"Yes." He rubbed his eyes with the back of his hands. "Oh, Coop, it's staring me right in the face and I can't see it."

46

It was a subdued group that gathered at Miranda's on Sunday night: Harry, Rick Shaw, and Cynthia Cooper, plus Pewter, Mrs. Murphy, and Tucker.

The big news from Camden was that Addie had suffered a severe concussion. The doctors, afraid that her brain would swell, insisted on keeping her in the hospital for two more days. She'd also broken her collarbone. Given what could have happened, the consensus was that she was a lucky woman. And a rich one. She had attained her majority.

The Camden police, in a burst of efficiency, arrested Mickey Townsend on suspicion of the murders of Nigel Danforth and Coty Lamont. A pack of cards found tucked in his car's side pocket was missing the queens of clubs, spades, and diamonds. A stiletto rested under the seat of his silver BMW.

He protested his innocence. He'd be sent up to Ablemarle County as soon as the paperwork was completed between Rick's department and Camden's. Rick didn't protest the Camden police holding Mickey. Secretly, he felt Mickey'd be safer in custody.

Harry told Rick she didn't think Mickey was the killer. The gambling debts, though sizable, weren't large enough to kill over, and Mickey wasn't that stupid.

Rick, hands interlocking over his stomach, listened. "You don't buy Charles Valiant as the murderer?"

All said, "No."

Cynthia added, "Bazooka wasn't doped. The blood tests came back negative. Fair was on the ball to pull blood."

"Rick, what haven't you told us?" Miranda addressed him in familiar fashion as she offered him one of her famous scones.

Delicately he bit off a piece and chewed before answering. "I know that Mickey Townsend followed Coty Lamont to Mim's stable on the night of Coty's death. He admits to pulling a gun on Coty and marching him out of there. He swears he didn't kill him."

"Why was he in Mim's stable?" Miranda picked up her knitting needles then dropped them in the basket.

"That I don't know. Coty was digging in a stall in the back. Said he would pay Mickey when he unearthed the treasure, well, I don't think those were his exact words. He told me that at Camden yesterday. Lord, it seems like a week ago." He wiped his forehead. "Guess we'd better visit the stable."

At the mention of Mim's stable, Mrs. Murphy sprang to her feet. *"Go crazy! Run around! Bark! Steal a scone! We've got to let them know they need to go over there right now!"*

Mrs. Murphy ran toward the wall, banked off it then jumped clean over Mrs. Hogendobber's laden tea trolley, narrowly missing the steaming tea pot.

"I say—" Miranda's mouth fell agape.

"Go to the stable! Go to the stable now!" Tucker barked.

Pewter, lacking in the speed department, hurried to the center of the living room, rolled over, displayed her gargantuan tummy, and said, "*Pay attention to us! Right now, you stupid mammals!*"

Tucker ran in faster circles and Mrs. Murphy ran with her. Pewter jumped up, considered jumping over the tea trolley, realized she couldn't and instead leapt on the armchair and patted Harry's cheek.

"Harry, these animals are tetched," Miranda finally sputtered.

"*No, we're not. We know what's in Orion's stall. We've known for days, but we haven't been able to tell you. You're on track now. GO TO THE STABLE!*" Mrs. Murphy lifted her exquisite head to heaven and yowled.

Harry stood up and walked over to the cat who eluded her grasp. "Calm down, Murph."

"Maybe she's got rabies." Miranda drew back.

"You say that any time an animal gets excited. She's cutting a shine. Aren't you, Murphy?"

"*No, I am not.*"

"*Me neither. Listen to us,*" Pewter pleaded.

"*Murphy, I'm exhausted. Can I stop now?*" Tucker continued circling the humans.

"*Sure.*"

The dog conveniently dropped by the tea trolley where some crumbs had fallen on the rug.

Rick clapped his hands on his knees. "Well, I'm going over to Mim's to see if she'll let us dig up that stall. Which stall was it?"

Cynthia checked her notes. "Orion's."

"*Hallelujah!*" Mrs. Murphy declared.

47

The cold crept into the stable. At first nobody noticed, but as
Harry, Miranda, and the two animals stood watching Rick Shaw's
team dig into Orion's stall, the chill crept into their bones.

When the sheriff's crew arrived, they surveyed the fourteen-
foot-square stall and didn't know where to start, so Tucker began
digging at the spot. The humans followed suit because Cynthia
Cooper remarked that dogs, thanks to their keen noses, could
smell things humans could not.

Mrs. Murphy grew tired of sitting on the center aisle floor,
so she climbed into the hayloft where, with Rodger Dodger,
Pusskin, and the mice, she gazed down as the humans labored.
Spadeful after spadeful of crush-or-run and then clay was carefully piled to the side.

Mim, her shearling jacket pulled tightly around her, joined the humans. "Anything?"

"No," Harry answered.

"You don't think this is some kind of nutty tale on Mickey's part—a wild-goose chase?" she asked.

Rick, arms folded across his chest, replied, "I've got to try everything, Mrs. Sanburne. Don't worry, we'll put everything back just as we found it."

A car pulled up outside, the door slammed, and a haggard Arthur Tetrick strode into the stable. "Mim?" he called out. "Are you out here?"

"Here."

Arthur shouted as he walked up. "I've gotten Chark released! He'll fly home tomorrow. An ambulance will bring up Adelia on Thursday if the doctors agree." He noticed the digging. "What's going on?"

"We don't know exactly," Mim answered.

Harry shivered.

"Why don't you go back to the tack room," Miranda suggested. "You don't have enough meat on your bones to ward off the cold. Not like I do."

"No. I'll walk around a bit." Harry jiggled her legs and walked up and down the aisle. Tucker walked with her.

"*You racking up brownie points, Tucker?*" the tiger hollered.

"*Oh, shut up. You can be so green-eyed sometimes.*"

That made Rodger Dodger and Pusskin laugh because Mrs. Murphy had beautiful green eyes.

One of the officers hit something hard. "Huh?"

Rick and Cynthia drew closer. "Be careful."

The other two officers carefully pushed their spades into the earth. "Yeah." Another light click was heard.

They worked faster now, each shovelful getting closer until a rib cage appeared.

"Oh, my God!" Mim exclaimed.

"What is it?" Arthur pushed his way to the edge, saw the rib cage and a now partially exposed arm as the men feverishly dug.

Arthur hit the ground with a thud.

"*Wuss.*" Mrs. Murphy turned her nose up.

48

Charles Valiant appeared far older than his twenty-five years. Dark circles under his eyes marred his handsome appearance. He'd eaten nothing since Addie's fall. Neither Fair nor any of his friends could get him to eat. Boom Boom took a turn with him as did everyone. She spoke passionately of Lifeline, leaving him some literature, but he was far too depressed to respond.

Fair sat with him in the living room of the little cottage on Mim's estate. Harry boiled water for a cup of instant soup. Mrs. Murphy and Tucker quietly lay on the rug.

"Chark, you've got to eat something," Harry pleaded.

"I can't," he whispered.

A knock on the door propelled Fair out of a comfortable old chair. He opened the door. "Arthur."

A subdued Arthur came inside, quickly shutting the door behind him. He forced a smile. "Well, we know one thing."

"What?" Fair's blond stubble made him look like a Viking.

"It can't get any worse."

Harry said nothing for she thought it could indeed get worse, and if the killer weren't apprehended soon, it would.

"Charles, Adelia will be fully recovered before you know it. She'll be home before the week is out. Please eat something so she doesn't worry about *you*," Arthur reasoned.

"He's right," Fair said.

"Well, I stopped by to see how you're doing." Arthur held out his hand. "I nearly forgot. Congratulations on coming into your inheritance. I know you'll use it wisely."

"Oh," Chark's voice sounded weak, "I'd forgotten all about it."

"This troublesome time will pass. All will be well, Charles. And as for Adelia"—he folded his hands together—"perhaps she is right. She needs to go her own way and be her own person. I truly believe things will work out for the best."

"Thanks, Arthur." Chark shook his hand.

"Well, I'd better be on my way."

"I'll walk you to your car." Harry opened the front door, asking as they walked, "Do they know yet who it was in Orion's stall? I mean conclusively?"

Arthur shook his head. "No, but I think we all know." A strangled cry gurgled in his throat. "To see her like that when I thought never to see her again . . ." He collected himself. "I will advise Mim on an excellent criminal lawyer, of course."

"Why?" Harry innocently asked.

"The body was found on her property. I should think she'll be a suspect and possibly even arrested."

Harry's voice rose. "Has everyone lost their minds? Marylou Valiant was one of her *best* friends."

"Most murders are committed among people who are family or friends." He held up his hands. "Not that I, for one min-

ute, think that Mim Sanburne murdered her. But right now, Mim
is in a vulnerable position. Go inside before you catch your
death.''

Harry walked back into Chark's cottage, closing the door
tightly behind her, and thought about the phrase ''catch your
death''—as though death were a baseball hurtling through the
azure sky.

49

Mrs. Murphy left the stable at six-thirty in the morning, cutting across the hay fields . . . she needed time to herself to think. She brushed by some rattleweed, causing the odd metallic sound that always startled city people upon first hearing it. The light frost, cool on her pads, would melt by ten in the morning, lingering only in areas of heavy shade or along the creek bottom.

A deep, swift creek divided Harry's farm from Blair Bainbridge's land, property that had once belonged to the family of the Reverend Herbert Jones. Murphy hoped Blair would return soon, because she liked him. As a model he was one of that growing number of Americans who made a lot of money at his job but preferred to live somewhere lovely instead of in a big city. He was often on the road, though.

She stopped at the creek, watching the water bubble and

spray over the slick rocks. Mrs. Murphy, never overfond of water, liked it even less when the mercury was below 60°F. She bent over the deep bank, for there were quiet pools, and if she stayed still she could see the small fish that congregated there. She'd watched Paddy, her ex, catch a small-mouth bass once, a performance that must have heated up her ardor for him although now she couldn't understand what she had ever seen in that faithless tom. Still, he was handsome and likable.

A flip of a tail alerted her to the school of fish below. She sighed, then trotted to where Jones's Creek, as it was known, flowed into Swift Run and thence into Meechum's River.

The scent of fallen and still dropping leaves presaged winter. They crunched underfoot, which made hunting field mice a task. She followed the twists and turns of Jones's Creek, admiring the sycamores, their bark distinctive by the contrasts of gray peeling away to beige. She startled ravens picking grain out of a cornfield. They hollered at her, lifted up over her head, circled, and returned after she passed.

Another ten minutes and she reached the connection where the creek poured into Swift Run. A big willow, upturned in last week's rains and wind, had crashed off the far bank into the river. A lone blue heron, a silent sentinel, was poised about fifty yards downstream from the willow.

As Mrs. Murphy was on the opposite shore, the heron, enormous, worried not at all about the small predator. Then again, the bird was so big that if Mrs. Murphy had swum Swift Run and catapulted onto her back, the heron could have soared into the air, taking the cat with her.

She looked up from her fishing, giving Mrs. Murphy a fierce stare. The heron's methods depended on stillness followed with lightning-fast reflexes as she grabbed a fish—or anything else that caught her fancy—with her long beak.

The tiger cat sat and watched the great bird. An odd ripple of current under the willow's trunk drew her gaze away from the heron. The water would strike the obstacle and whirl around it,

the obstacle would roll a bit, then the water would break free on its way downstream.

She walked along the bank to get a better look, reveling in her good eyes, so much better than human or dog eyes. She focused and another little gusher of water lifted up the obstacle. An arm broke through the surface and then sank again. Another hard rain and the corpse would be free from the branches of the willow.

Mrs. Murphy, fur fluffed out, watched. The next surge of water pushed the body up a bit farther, and she saw what was left of Linda Forloines's face. The eyes and nose were gone, courtesy of hungry fish and crawdads. The face was bleached even whiter and bloated, but it was Linda Forloines without a doubt. Mrs. Murphy remembered her from when she had worked at Mim's stable.

She trotted back to her original spot and called out to the heron, "I'm sorry to disturb your hunting. Is this your territory?"

"Of course it's my territory," came the curt reply.

"Do you know there's a dead human back at the willow?"

"Yes."

"Do you know how long it's been there?"

The heron cocked her head, her light violet-crested plume swept back over her head. "Not quite a week. There's another body one mile from here as I fly, more miles on the ground. That one is stuck in a truck." She snapped her long powerful beak. "I wish they'd have the decency to bury their dead."

"The murderer was in a hurry," the cat called over the creek.

"Ah." She stretched her graceful neck to the sky then re-coiled it. "They exhibit a strange penchant for killing one another, don't they?"

"A genetic flaw, I suppose." Mrs. Murphy also thought human violence most unanimal-like. After all, she and her kind only killed other species, and then for food, although she had a diffi-cult time resisting dispatching the occasional mouse for sport.

The heron spread her wings, exposing each feather to the

warming sun. "Oh, that feels good. You know, if I felt like it, I could fly right over there and pick you up by your tail."

"You'd have to catch me first," Mrs. Murphy countered.

"You'd be surprised at how fast I can fly."

"You'd be surprised at how fast I can zig and zag." Mrs. Murphy's toes tingled. She unsheathed her claws. "Tell you what. I'll get a head start and you see if you can catch me. Don't pick me up, though, because I haven't hurt you—why hurt me? Just a game, okay?"

"All right." The heron flapped her wings while still standing.

Mrs. Murphy took off like a shot. She raced along the edge of Jones's Creek back toward the cornfields as the heron lifted off to her cruising altitude. She ducked into the cornfields, which infuriated the crows, who soared up like pepper dashed into the sky. They saw the heron approaching and complained at the top of their considerable lungs.

The heron swooped low over the corn calling, "No fair."

"You never said I couldn't seek cover."

The crows dive-bombed back into the corn, forgetting for a moment about Mrs. Murphy, who leapt forward, nearly swatting one iridescent black tail.

"HEY!" The crow clamped its yellow beak together, then zoomed out of there, the others following.

The heron circled, landing at the edge of the cornfield, eyes glittering. Mrs. Murphy walked to the end of the corn row. She was maybe ten feet from the huge creature.

"You could run out and attack me before I could get airborne," the heron taunted the cat.

"Maybe I could, but why would I want to pull feathers from a bird as elegant as yourself?" Mrs. Murphy flattered her. She knew that gleam in the eye, and she didn't trust the heron even though she wasn't on the bird's customary menu.

The compliment pleased the heron. She preened. "Why, thank you." She stepped toward Mrs. Murphy, who didn't back into the corn row. "You know that dead woman back there at the willow?"

"I know who it was. No one I care about, but there's been a rash of murders among the humans."

"Um. My mother used to tell me that she could give me a fish or she could teach me how to fish. Naturally, I was lazy and wanted her to give me the fish. She didn't. She swallowed it right in front of me. It made me so mad." The big beak opened, revealing a bright pink tongue. "But I got the message, and she taught me how to fish. If you don't know how to fish you look at everyone as a free meal or you become bait yourself. I expect that dead thing back there couldn't fish."

"Partly true. She liked fishing in troubled waters." The cat intently watched the heron. Those huge pronged feet looked out of place in the cornfield.

"Ah. Well, I enjoyed talking to you, pussycat. I'm going back to my nest."

"I enjoyed you too."

With that the heron rose in the sky, circling once. Mrs. Murphy walked out of the cornfield, then made a beeline back to the old barn as the heron made a wider circle and cawed out to her below. Even though she felt the heron wouldn't attack, the sound of that caw pushed her into a run. She flew, belly flat to the land, the whole way home.

"Why, Mrs. Murphy, you look as though you've seen a ghost," Harry said as Murphy careened into the barn, her eyes as big as billiard balls.

"No, just Linda Forloines."

Tucker tilted her head. "Not in the best of health, I presume." Then she laughed at her own joke.

"She was useless in life. At least she's useful in death."

"How?"

"Fish food."

50

"Do you know what you're doing?" Miranda paced, her leather-soled shoes sliding along the worn shiny floorboards of the post office.

The old railroad clock on the wall read 7:20. Darkness had enveloped the small building. The shades were drawn and only a glimmer of light from the back room spilled out under the back window. The front door, kept unlocked, every now and then opened and closed as Crozet residents, on the way home from work or to a party, dashed in and picked up their mail if they had been unable to get there during the day.

As a federal facility, a post office, no less, the front part of the building where the boxes were had to be kept open to the public. The back was locked, and the crenelated door was pulled down to the counter much like a garage door, and locked from behind.

"I'll be at your choir show a tad late," Harry said.

"You shouldn't be here alone. Not with a killer on the loose."

"She's right," Mrs. Murphy, Tucker and Pewter echoed.

Pewter, seeing the light, had sauntered in from next door. "Market's open until eleven, but still someone could sneak in here and he'd never know. He's too busy watching television."

"Harry, come on. You can do this tomorrow."

"I can't. I've got this one little hunch."

"If you're not at our choirfest by intermission, I am calling Rick Shaw. Do you hear me?"

"Yes."

With reluctance, Mrs. Hogendobber closed the door, and Harry locked it behind her.

Working with the mail meant she saw every catalog under the sun. She knew of three hunting catalogs, five gun catalogs, which also featured knives, and one commando catalog for those who envisioned themselves soldiers of fortune. If the police hadn't traced the knives that the killer used, it might very well be because they had confined themselves to local stores.

She started calling. Since all the catalog companies had twenty-four-hour 800 numbers, she knew she'd get someone on the end of the line.

An hour later she had found Case XX Bowie knives for over $200, replicas of sabers, double-edged swords, saracens, and even stilettos, but not the kind she wanted. She'd spoken to college kids moonlighting, crusty old men who wanted to discuss the relative merits of government-issue bayonets, and even one aggressive man who asked her for a long-distance date.

The two cats nestled into the mail cart, since there wasn't anything they could do to help. Tucker fell asleep.

Having exhausted her supply of catalogs, Harry had hit a dead end. She couldn't think what to do next. She'd even called a uniform supply company on the outside chance someone there might be a cutlery enthusiast, as she put it.

"*Call L.L. Bean. They know everything,*" Mrs. Murphy called out from the bottom of the mail cart.

Harry made herself a cup of tea. She checked the clock. "If I don't get over to the Church of the Holy Light in about twenty minutes Mrs. H. will fry me for breakfast."

"*I told you, call L.L. Bean.*"

Harry sat down, sipped her tea. She felt more awake now. She kept an L.L. Bean catalog, her own, stacked next to the sugar bowl.

"*Tucker, has she got it yet?*"

"*No.*" The dog lifted her head. "*Forget it.*"

"*Sometimes people drive me around the bend!*" the sleek cat complained, leaping out of the mail bin.

"*Why bother?*" Pewter stretched out in the bottom. "*She won't listen about Linda's body. She won't listen now either.*"

Mrs. Murphy jumped onto the table, rubbed Harry's shoulder then stuck out her claws and pulled the L.L. Bean catalog toward Harry.

"Murph—" Harry reached out and put her hand on the catalogue, fearful the cat would shred it. "Hmm." She flipped open the pages, filled with merchandise photographed as accurately as possible.

She gulped down a hot swallow, jumped up, and dialed the 800 number.

"Could I talk to your supervisor, please?"

"Certainly." The woman's voice on the other end was friendly.

Harry waited a few moments and then heard, "Hello, L.L. Bean, how may I help you?"

"Ma'am, pardon me for disturbing you. This has nothing to do with L.L. Bean, but do you know of any mail-order company that specializes in knives?"

"Let me think a minute," the voice said, that of a middle-

aged woman. "Joe, what's the name of that company in Tennessee specializing in hunting knives?" A faint voice could be heard
in the background. "Smoky Mountain Knife Works in Sieverville,
Tennessee."

"Thank you." Harry scribbled down the information,
"You've been great. May I make one suggestion about your duck
boots? I mean, I always call them duck boots."

"Sure. We want to hear from our customers."

"You know the Bean Boot you all started making in 1912?
Well, I love the boot. I've had mine resoled twice."

"I'm glad to hear that."

"But women's sizes don't carry a twelve-inch upper. Ours
only go to nine inches, and I work on a farm. I would sure like to
have a twelve-inch upper."

"What's your shoe size?"

"Seven B."

"You wear a seven and a half in this—you know, a little
bigger for heavy socks."

"Yes, thank you for reminding me."

"Tell you what, can you call me back tomorrow and I'll see
what we can do? The sales force is twenty-four hours, but I'll
have to wait until regular hours tomorrow to see if I can accom-
modate your request. What's your name?"

"Mary Minor Haristeen."

"Okay then, Miss Haristeen, you call me tomorrow afternoon and ask for Glenda Carpenter."

"Thank you, I will."

Harry pressed the disconnect button and got the phone
number for the Sieverville company. Hurriedly she punched in
the phone number.

A man answered, "Smoky Mountain."

"Sir, hello, this is Mary Minor Haristeen from the Crozet
post office in central Virginia. I am trying to trace back orders for
folks here. A resident says he had the knives sent to my post

office, and I swear they must have gone to the main post office in Charlottesville instead. It's no mistake on your part, by the way— just one of those things."

"Gee—that could be a lot of orders."

"Maybe I can help you. It would either be repeat orders or a bulk order for that beautiful stiletto, uh, I forget the name, but the handle is wrapped in wire and it's about a foot long."

The voice filled with pride. "You mean the Gil Hibben Silver Shadow. That's some piece of hardware, sister."

"Yes, yes, it is." Harry tried not to shudder since she knew the use to which it had been put.

"Let me pull it up on the computer here." He hummed. "Yeah, I got one order to Charlottesville. Three knives. Ordered for Albemarle Cutlery. Nice store, huh?"

"Yes. By the way, is there a person's name on that?" Harry didn't tell him there was no Albemarle Cutlery. The name had to be a front.

"No. Just the store and a credit card. I can't read off the number, of course."

"No, no, I understand, but at least I know where the shipment has gone."

"Went out two months ago. Hasn't been returned. I hope everything is okay."

"It will be. You're a lifesaver."

She bid her good-byes and then called down to the central post office on Seminole Road.

"Carl?" She recognized the voice that answered.

"Harry, what's doing, girl?"

"It only gets worse. Between now and December twenty-fifth we might as well forget sleep. Will you do me a favor?"

"Sure."

"Do you have a large post office box registered to Albemarle Cutlery?"

"Hold on." He put the phone down.

Harry heard his footsteps as he walked away, then silence. Finally the footsteps returned. "Albemarle Cutlery. C. de Bergerac."

"Damn!"

"What?"

"Sorry, Carl, it's not you. That's a phony name. Cyrano de Bergerac was a famous swordsman in the seventeenth century. The subject of a famous romance."

"Steve Martin. I know," Carl confidently replied.

"Yes, well, that's one way to remember." Harry laughed and wondered what Rostand, the playwright, would make of Steve Martin as his hero. "Listen, would you fax me his signature from the receipt?"

"Yeah, sure. You up to something?"

"Well—yes."

"Okay, I'll keep my mouth shut. I'll pull the record and fax it right over. Good enough?"

"More than good enough. Thanks."

"*Mother, calm down,*" Mrs. Murphy told her. "*The fax will come through in a minute.*"

Harry froze when she heard the whirr and wheeze of the fax. Her hands trembled as she pulled the paper out. Mrs. Murphy hopped on her shoulder.

"It can't be!" Harry's hands shook harder when she saw the left-leaning, bold script.

"*Well, who is it?*" Pewter called from the mail bin.

"*I don't know,*" Murphy called back. "*I don't see the handwriting of people like Mother does. I mean, I know Mom's, Fair's, Mim's, and Mrs. Hogendobber's, but I don't know this one.*"

Tucker scrambled to her feet. "*Mother, call Rick Shaw. Please!*"

But Harry, dazed by what she now knew, wasn't thinking straight. Shaken, she folded the paper, slipping it into the back pocket of her jeans.

"Come on, gang, we've got to get to church before Mrs. Hogendobber pitches a hissy."

"Don't worry about Mrs. Hogendobber," Pewter sagely advised. "Call the sheriff."

"Everyone will be at the choirfest, so she can see him there," Tucker added.

"That's what I'm afraid of." Mrs. Murphy fluffed out her fur and jumped off Harry's shoulder.

"What do you mean?" Pewter asked as she crawled out of the mail bin. She was too lazy to jump.

"Everybody will be there—including the killer."

51

The heater, slow in working, sent off a faint aroma in Harry's blue truck. She gripped the steering wheel so tightly her knuckles were white. Puffs of breath lazed out into the air as she sped along, a big puff from her, a medium puff from Tucker, and two small puffs from Mrs. Murphy and Pewter.

"I'm proud of Mom," Tucker said. "She figured this one out all by herself. I couldn't tell her about Nigel being Sargent, although we still don't know all that we need to know about him."

"Humans occasionally use their deductive powers." Mrs. Murphy wedged close to Harry's leg, Pewter next to her, as they huddled down to get warm.

"But if she figured out about the knife place, don't you think Rick Shaw and Cynthia have figured that out as well?" Pewter asked.

"Maybe, but only Mom knows the signatures."

"*Maybe he's afraid of exposing her to risk. Whoever this is is ruthless. Let's not forget that this started years ago,*" Mrs. Murphy prudently noted.

The parking lot of the Church of the Holy Light, jammed from stem to stern, testified to the popularity of the evening's entertainment. The choirfest, one of the church's biggest fund-raisers, drew music lovers from all over the county. They might not be willing to accept the Church's strict message, but they loved the singing.

Harry scanned the lot for a place to park but had to settle for a spot along the side of the road. She noticed that the squad car was near the front door. Mim's Bentley Turbo R, Susan and Ned's Conestoga—as they called their station wagon—were there, Herbie's big Buick Roadmaster; in fact, it looked as though everyone was at the choirfest but her.

She forgot to tell the animals to stay in the truck. They hopped out when she opened the door, following her into the church just as the choir made its measured entrance to enthusiastic applause. Intermission was over and the folks could expect a rousing second half.

Harry noticed her little family as did some of the other people who turned to greet her. Tucker quietly sat down next to Fair. Mrs. Murphy and Pewter, not exactly sacrilegious but not overwhelmed either, decided to check out the gathering before picking their spot.

"You kitties come back here," Harry hissed, staying at the back of the church.

"*Don't look at her,*" Mrs. Murphy directed her fat gray sidekick.

"Mrs. Murphy! Pewter!" Harry hissed, then stopped because the choirmaster had lifted his baton, and all eyes were on him. The organist pressed the pedals and the first lovely notes of "Swing Low, Sweet Chariot" swelled over the group.

Tucker, realizing Harry wouldn't chase after her, decided to follow the cats, who generally led her into temptation.

Chark Valiant sat in the front row with the Sanburnes and Arthur Tetrick. Rick and Cynthia stood off to the side. Harry, not finding a seat, leaned against the wall, hoping to catch Rick's or Cynthia's eye unobtrusively.

Mrs. Hogendobber stepped forward for her solo. Her rich contralto voice coated the room like dark honey.

"Mrs. H.?" Mrs. Murphy was so astonished to hear the good woman that she walked right in front of everyone and sat in front of Miranda, her pretty little head tilted upward to watch her friend, the lady who formerly didn't like cats.

Miranda saw Mrs. Murphy, now joined by Pewter and Tucker. The two kitties and the dog, enraptured, were immobile. A few titters rippled throughout the audience, but then the humans were oddly affected by the animals listening to Miranda singing one of the most beautiful spirituals, a harmonic record of a harsher time made endurable by the healing power of music.

Herb, also in the front row, a courtesy seat from the church, marveled at the scene.

When Miranda finished, a moment's hush of deep appreciation was followed by thunderous applause.

"*You were wonderful,*" Mrs. Murphy called out, then trotted down the center aisle to check over each face in her passing.

"*What are we looking for?*" Pewter asked.

"*Someone guilty as sin.*"

"*Ooh-la,*" she trilled.

"*And in church, too,*" Tucker giggled.

"Will you get back here!" Harry whispered.

"*Ignore her. No matter how red in the face she gets, just ignore her.*"

"*You're going to get it,*" Pewter warned.

"*She has to catch me first, and remember, she left me to go to Montpelier and then Camden. I just pray*"—she remembered she was in a church—"*we can get her out of here before the fur flies.*"

The next song, a Bach chorale, held everyone's attention. Mrs. Murphy jumped onto a low table along the back wall near Harry but far enough away so she could jump off if Harry came after her. Pewter followed. Tucker lagged behind.

"Count the exits."

"Double front doors, two on either side of the nave. There's a back stair off the balcony but that probably connects with the doors off the nave."

"And I'm willing to bet there's another back door." She swept her whiskers forward. "Tucker, get up here."

"Tucker, there are four exits. The one behind, two on the side, and one behind the proscenium, I think. If something goes wrong, if he gets scared or anything, we can run faster than he can. You go back to the nave exit, we'll stay by this one. If anything happens, stay with Mom and we'll go out our door and catch up with you. We'll be out the door before the humans know what hit them."

"Well, let's hope nothing happens." Pewter, not the most athletic girl, wanted to stay put.

Rick edged his way toward Harry, careful not to make noise. Cynthia moved to the front door.

Harry reached in her back pocket and pulled out the fax. "Come outside with me for a minute."

The sheriff and his deputy tiptoed out with Harry. Keenly, Miranda observed them as she sang. A few other people noticed out of the corners of their eyes.

"Harry, you've been meddling again," Rick said in a low voice as they closed the doors behind them.

"I couldn't help it. I figured if we could trace the knives we'd have a first down, goal to go."

Cynthia studied the fax sheet with a little pocket flashlight.

Rick held it steady in his hands, as Harry told him whose handwriting it was. "I'm not surprised," he said.

"Was the body Marylou Valiant's?" Harry asked.

"Yes." Cynthia answered. "Dr. Yarbrough brought the dental records right over a half hour ago. It is Marylou."

"Did you have any idea?" Harry asked Rick.

"Yes, but I thought this was about money. It's not." He rubbed his nose, the tip of which was cold. "The cards and knife in Mickey Townsend's car—right over the top. That brought me back to the real motive: jealousy." He shook his head. "When you get down to it, motives are simple. Crimes may be complicated, but motives are always simple."

"What do we do now?" Harry shuffled her feet.

"*We* don't do anything," Rick said as more applause broke out inside. "We wait."

"He's got good alibis," Coop commented.

"But if you broke down each murder, minute by minute, wouldn't you find the loophole?"

"Harry, it's not that easy. We've pinpointed the time of the murders as close as we can, but that still gives him a healthy thirty-minute comfort zone. A good lawyer can chip away at that very easily, you know, try to get the jury to believe the coroner's report is fuzzy. Things like the temperature inside the barn versus the temperature outside would affect the corpse, as would the victim's health while alive. They'll erode the time frame of each murder as well as planting doubt in the jury's mind as to how he could have escaped notice at Montpelier. Then they'll indulge in character assassination for each prosecution witness. Right now it's a cinch he'll get off with a good lawyer. Case is totally circumstantial." Rick hated the way the system worked, especially if a defendant had money.

"Yes, but what about Marylou's murder?" Harry's lips trembled she was so angry. "Can't we pin him down there?"

"Maybe if Coty were alive," Coop said. "He obviously knew where Marylou was buried."

"Rick, you *can't* let that son of a bitch go free."

"If I arrest him before I've built my case, he will go free, scot free, Harry." Rick's jaw clenched. He folded the fax. "This is a big help and I thank you for it. I promise you, I will do everything I can to close in."

More applause from inside roused Harry. "I guess I'd better go back in and make sure Murphy hasn't caused another commotion."

"A musical cat." Cynthia smiled, patting Harry on the back. "I know this is upsetting, but we just can't go out and arrest people. We'll keep working until we can make it stick. It's the price we pay for being a democracy."

"Yeah." Harry exhaled from her nose, then opened the door a crack and squeezed through.

The two cats remained on the table.

The last song, a great big burst from Handel's *Messiah*, raised the rafters. The audience cheered and clapped for an encore. The choir sang another lovely spiritual and then took a final bow, separating in the middle and filing out both sides of the stage.

The audience stirred. Harry walked over to the table, ready to scoop up Mrs. Murphy and Pewter when Mim, Jim, Charles, and Arthur came over, Fair immediately behind them.

Harry, overcome with emotion at the sight of the murderer, blurted out, "How could you? How could you kill all those people? How could you kill someone you loved?"

Arthur's face froze. He started to laugh but a horrible flash of recognition gleamed in Mim's eyes and in Chark's. Lightning fast he grabbed Harry, pulled a .38 from under his coat, and put it to her head. "Get out of the way."

Fair ducked low to tackle him. Arthur fired, grazing his leg. Fair's leg collapsed under him as people screamed and ran.

Mrs. Hogendobber, not yet off the stage, ran out the side door and hopped into her Ford Falcon. She started the motor.

Rick and Cynthia, hearing the shot, rushed back in through the double doors just as Arthur dragged Harry out.

"You come one step closer and she's dead."

"What's another one, Arthur? You're going to kill me anyway." Harry thought how curious it was to die with everyone looking on. She felt the cold circle of the barrel against her head, saw the contorted anguish on the faces of her friends, the snarling rage of her dog.

No one noticed the two cats streaking by. Tucker stayed with Harry.

"Don't rile him, Mother. The minute he shifts his eyes I'll nail him," the sturdy little dog growled.

"Arthur Tetrick!" Mim shrieked. "You'll rot in hell for this. You killed Marylou Valiant, didn't you?"

Arthur fired over her head just for the joy of seeing Mim frightened. Except she wasn't. People around her hit the ground but she shook her fist at him. "You'll never get away with it."

Chark, the time for talk past, lunged for Arthur. A crack rang out and the young man slumped to the ground, grabbing his shoulder.

Arthur ran outside now, propelling Harry, the cold air clarifying his senses, but then Arthur was always coolly assessing the odds in his life. His car was parked near the front. He pushed Harry into the driver's side, keeping the gun on her at all times, making her slide over to the passenger seat.

"Can you get a shot off?" Rick, on one knee, asked Cynthia, also on one knee, pistol out.

"No. Not without jeopardizing Harry."

Fair limped out, trailing blood. Herbie Jones ran after him, struggling to hold him back. "He'll kill her, Fair!"

"He'll kill her for sure if we don't stop him."

"Fair. Stay where you are!" Rick commanded.

Tucker had reached the car where Harry was and grabbed Arthur's ankle as he started to get in. Arthur shook the dog off, not noticing that Mrs. Murphy and Pewter had leapt into the backseat. He quickly turned the gun back on Harry, who had her hand on the passenger door handle.

"*Keep down in the backseat,*" Mrs. Murphy told Pewter. "*Once he gets in the driver's seat and reaches for the ignition, we've got him.*"

Pewter, too excited to reply, crouched, her fur standing on end, her fangs exposed.

To Arthur's shock, Mrs. Hogendobber roared through the parking lot, stopping the Falcon directly in front of him.

"I'll kill that meddling biddy!" he screamed, losing his temper for the first time.

He opened the driver's window and took aim, firing through her passenger window. Mrs. Hogendobber opened her door and rolled out, lying flat on the ground. Arthur could no longer see her.

"Run for it, Miranda, he's going to ram the car!" Herb shouted as he rushed forward, crouching to help Miranda. She scrambled to her feet, her choir robes dragging in the stone parking lot.

Just as Arthur cut on his ignition he heard two hideous yowls behind him.

"*Die, human!*" Mrs. Murphy and Pewter leapt from the backseat into the front, attacking his hands.

Murphy tore deeply into his gun hand before he registered what had happened.

Seizing the opportunity, Harry grabbed his right hand, smashing his wrist on the steering wheel. He tried to reach over the steering wheel for her with his left hand but Pewter sank her fangs to their full depth into the fleshy part of his palm. He screamed.

Harry smashed his wrist again as hard as she could against the steering wheel. He dropped the gun. She reached down to grab it. He kicked at her but she retrieved it.

Now Arthur Tetrick felt the cold barrel of a gun against his right temple.

Rick Shaw, his .357 Magnum pressed against Arthur's left temple, said, "You are under arrest for the murders of Nigel Danforth, Coty Lamont and Marylou Valiant. You have the right to remain silent—" Rick rattled off Arthur's rights.

Cynthia opened the passenger door as Arthur howled, "Call off your cats!"

Harry slid out the opened door. "Come on, girls!"

Mrs. Murphy took one last lethal whack for good measure, then leapt out followed by Pewter, who appeared twice her already impressive size.

Tucker and Fair, both limping, reached Harry at the same time. Fair grabbed Harry and held her close. He couldn't speak.

Harry began to shake. Curious how she had felt so little fear when she was in danger. Now it flooded over her. She hugged her ex-husband, then broke to rush to Miranda, being attended to by Herbie and Mim.

"Miranda, you could have been killed!" Tears rolled down Harry's cheeks. She stopped to scoop up the two cats, clutching them to her, repeatedly kissing their furry heads, then knelt down to kiss her sturdy corgi.

"Well, if he'd gotten out of this parking lot, you would have been killed," Miranda stated flatly, oblivious to her own heroism.

"I'd say two hellcats and Miranda saved your life." The Reverend Jones reached out to pet the cats.

"And Tucker. Brave dog." Harry again kissed a happy Tucker.

Arthur Tetrick sat bolt upright in his car. He'd never felt so much pain in his life, and being the self-centered man that he was, it did not occur to him that what he had inflicted upon his victims was much, much worse.

52

The whole crowd—Miranda, Fair, Cynthia, Rick, Big Mim, Little Marilyn, Jim, Susan, Herbie, Market Shiflett, Mrs. Murphy, Pewter, and Tucker—sat in the back of the post office the next day. Addie had come home from the hospital, but now Chark was in. She had the ambulance take her to Martha Jefferson Hospital to be with her brother; he would recover, but the bullet had shattered some bone.

Arthur had confessed to the murders of Marylou Valiant, Sargent Wilcox, a.k.a. Nigel Danforth, and Coty Lamont. As a lawyer he knew that after his behavior at the church he was dog meat, so he planned to throw himself on the mercy of the court with a guilty plea and thereby escape the death penalty.

Rick, who had interrogated Arthur, continued his story.

"—probably the only time Arthur ever acted out of passion, but once he killed Marylou Valiant, he had to get rid of the body. Coty and Sargent, through pure dumb luck, walked in on him as he was dragging her to his car. Sargent had been at Arthur's barn for only ten days, but he proved willing and flexible. He and Coty helped him bury Marylou in the last place anyone would ever look—Mim's barn. Sargent must have pocketed the St. Christopher's medal when no one was looking. Shortly after that Arthur gave up steeplechasing."

Mim chimed in, "I remember that. He said he couldn't go on without Marylou. It was her sport. He'd officiate but he'd run no more horses. What an actor he was."

"When Marylou disappeared, the two prime suspects were Arthur and Mickey Townsend for obvious reasons. We had no way of knowing whether Marylou was even dead, though. Technically we had no crime, we had no victim, we had a missing person," Rick said.

"And Arthur was a most conscientious executor of Marylou's will." Jim Sanburne hooked his fingers in his belt.

"Well, then, what happened to start this killing spree?" Fair stretched his bandaged leg out slowly. It felt better if he moved it around every now and then.

"Sargent came back," Cynthia said. "Wooed Addie. And stirred up Coty, who had been content up until then, to make more demands."

"Oh, that must have scared the bejesus out of Arthur," Herbie blurted out.

"Not as much as seeing Marylou's St. Christopher's medal around Addie's neck before the Colonial Cup," Cynthia said.

"He thought she knew?" Miranda questioned.

"He realized Sargent or Coty must have taken the medal. He feared Nigel—Sargent—had told Addie and that she would tell Rick after the race. Imagine his shock when he saw that royal blue medal just before she went out on the course," Rick said.

"I know how shocked I was to see it." Mim shook her head.

"Sargent and Coty were bleeding him heavily. He had no designs other than killing them. Addie upset the applecart," Cynthia added.

"What about Linda and Will? They're still missing."

Rick held up his palms, "Don't know. We have no idea if they're alive. Their absence is certainly not lamented and I doubt Arthur would need to kill them. I don't think they knew anything. We only know that sooner or later drug dealers sometimes get what they deserve."

As the group talked, Harry fed the cats and dog tidbits from the ham sandwiches Market had brought over.

"What was the significance of the queens?" Mim asked.

"Arthur said that was just meant to drive us all nuts. The bloody queen, he said and laughed in my face. Marylou was a bloody queen when she dumped him for Mickey. Arthur exploded . . . and strangled her."

"Addie is lucky to be alive," Miranda said softly. "Poor children. What they've been through."

"Yes." Mim reached in her purse for a handkerchief to dab her eyes.

Mrs. Murphy chimed in, "*Men like Arthur aren't accustomed to rejection.*"

"Here, have some more ham." Miranda offered a piece to the cat since she interpreted the meows as requests for food.

"I bet he ran Mickey Townsend off the road that terrible rainy day—he was quietly going out of control." Miranda remembered that cold day.

Harry watched Pewter as she reached up and snagged half of a ham sandwich. "Market, we should share Pewter. What if I take her home with me every night, but she can work in the store during the day and work here, too?"

"*Yes!*" Pewter meowed.

Market laughed, "Think of the money I'll save."

"*Yeah, Pewter's a lion under the lard,*" Mrs. Murphy teased her friend.

The phone rang. Harry answered it. "Oh, hello, Mrs. Carpenter. You can? That's great. Let me give you my credit card number." Harry reached into her purse, pulled out a credit card, and read off her number.

"What are you buying?" Miranda demanded.

"L.L. Bean is making me a special pair of duck boots in my size, with twelve-inch uppers."

53

Poised on a hay bale, Mrs. Murphy waited. Pewter stayed inside with Harry. Mrs. Murphy rather liked having another cat around. Tucker didn't mind either.

There'd been so much commotion this weekend, she needed to be alone to collect her thoughts. She heard the squeaks from inside the hay bale. When an unsuspecting mouse darted out, with a jet-fast pounce Mrs. Murphy had her.

"*Gotcha!*"

The mouse stayed still under the cat's paws. "*Make it fast. I don't want to suffer.*"

Mrs. Murphy carefully lifted the corner of her paw to behold those tiny obsidian eyes. She remembered the help of Mim's barn mice. "Oh, *go on. I just wanted to prove to you that I'm faster than you.*"

"*You aren't going to kill me?*"

"No, but don't run around where Harry can see you."

"I won't." The tiny creature streaked back into the hay bale, and Mrs. Murphy heard excited squeals. Then she walked outside the barn and watched through the kitchen window. Harry was filling up her teapot, a task she performed at least twice a day. Mrs. Murphy was struck by how divine, how lovely, how unique such a mundane task could be. She purred, realizing how lucky she was, how lucky they all were to be alive on this crisp fall day.

Harry, glancing out of the kitchen window, observed Mrs. Murphy, tail to the vertical, come out of the barn.

The phone rang.

"Hello."

"Harry, it's Boom Boom. You were supposed to go with me to Lifeline last week, but considering all the excitement I didn't call. How about Monday at one o'clock?"

"Sure."

"I'll pick you up at the P.O."

"Fine."

"See you then. Bye-bye." Boom Boom signed off.

"Damn!" Harry hung up the phone. She looked out at Mrs. Murphy in the sunlight and thought how wonderful, how glorious, how relaxing it must be to be a cat.

Murder on the Prowl

To Mr. Wonderful—sometimes
David Wheeler

Cast of Characters

Mary Minor Haristeen (Harry), the young postmistress of Crozet

Mrs. Murphy, Harry's gray tiger cat

Tee Tucker, Harry's Welsh corgi, Mrs. Murphy's friend and confidante

Pharamond Haristeen (Fair), veterinarian, formerly married to Harry

Mrs. George Hogendobber (Miranda), a widow who works with Harry in the post office

Market Shiflett, owner of Shiflett's Market, next to the post office

Pewter, Market's shamelessly fat gray cat, who now lives with Harry and family

Susan Tucker, Harry's best friend

Big Marilyn Sanburne (Mim), Queen of Crozet society

Rick Shaw, sheriff

Cynthia Cooper, police officer

Herbert C. Jones, pastor of Crozet Lutheran Church

Roscoe Fletcher, headmaster of the exclusive St. Elizabeth's private school

Naomi Fletcher, principal of the lower school at St. Elizabeth's. She supports her husband's vision 100%

Alexander Brashiers (Sandy), an English teacher at St. Elizabeth's who believes he should be headmaster

April Shively, secretary to the headmaster, whom she loves

Maury McKinchie, a film director who's lost his way, lost his fire, and seems to be losing his wife

Brooks Tucker, Susan Tucker's daughter. She has transferred to St. Elizabeth's

Karen Jensen, irreverent, a star of the field hockey team, and lusted after by most of the boys

Jody Miller, another good field hockey player, she seems to be suffering the ill effects of an evaporating romance with Sean Hallahan

Sean Hallahan, the star of the football team

Roger Davis, calm, quiet, and watchful, he is overshadowed by Sean

Kendrick Miller, driven, insular, and hot-tempered, he's built a thriving nursery business as he's lost his family . . . he barely notices them

Irene Miller, a fading beauty who deals with her husband's absorption in his work and her daughter's mood swings by ignoring them

Father Michael, priest at the Catholic church, a friend of the Reverend Herbert Jones

Jimbo Anson, owner of the technologically advanced car wash on Route 29

Coach Renee Hallvard, a favorite with the St. Elizabeth's students, she coaches the girls' field hockey team

1

Towns, like people, have souls. The little town of Crozet, Virginia, latitude 38°, longitude 78° 60′, had the soul of an Irish tenor.

On this beautiful equinox day, September 21, every soul was lifted, if not every voice—for it was perfect: creamy clouds lazed across a turquoise sky. The Blue Ridge Mountains, startling in their color, hovered protectively at the edge of emerald meadows. The temperature held at 72° F with low humidity.

This Thursday, Mary Minor Haristeen worked unenthusiastically in the post office. As she was the postmistress, she could hardly skip out, however tempted she was. Her tiger cat, Mrs. Murphy, and her corgi, Tee Tucker, blasted in and out of the animal door, the little flap echoing with each arrival or departure. It was the animals' version of teenagers slamming the door, and each whap reminded Harry that while they could escape, she was stuck.

Harry, as she was known, was industrious if a bit undirected.

Her cohort at the P.O., Mrs. Miranda Hogendobber, felt that if Harry remarried, this questioning of her life's purpose would evaporate. Being quite a bit older than Harry, Miranda viewed marriage as purpose enough for a woman.

"What are you humming?"

" 'A Mighty Fortress Is Our God.' Martin Luther wrote it in 1529," Mrs. H. informed her.

"I should know that."

"If you'd come to choir practice you would."

"There is the small matter that I am not a member of your church." Harry folded an empty canvas mail sack.

"I can fix that in a jiffy."

"And what would the Reverend Jones do? He baptized me in Crozet Lutheran Church."

"Piffle."

Mrs. Murphy barreled through the door, a large cricket in her mouth.

Close in pursuit was Pewter, the fat gray cat who worked days next door at the grocery store: nights she traveled home with Harry. Market Shiflett, the grocer, declared Pewter had never caught a mouse and never would, so she might as well go play with her friends.

In Pewter's defense, she was built round; her skull was round, her ears, small and delicate, were round. Her tail was a bit short. She thought of herself as stout. Her gray paunch swung when she walked. She swore this was the result of her having "the operation," not because she was fat. In truth it was both. The cat lived to eat.

Mrs. Murphy, a handsome tiger, stayed fit being a ferocious mouser.

The two cats were followed by the dog, Tee Tucker.

Mrs. Murphy bounded onto the counter, the cricket wriggling in her mouth.

"That cat has brought in a winged irritant. She lives to kill," Miranda harrumphed.

"A cricket doesn't have wings."

Miranda moved closer to the brown shiny prey clamped in the cat's jaws. "It certainly is a major cricket—it ought to have wings.

Why, I believe this cricket is as big as a praying mantis." She cupped her chin in her hand, giving her a wise appearance.

Harry strolled over to inspect just as Mrs. Murphy dispatched the insect with a swift bite through the innards, then laid the remains on the counter.

The dog asked, *"You're not going to eat that cricket, are you?"*

"No, they taste awful."

"I'll eat it," Pewter volunteered. *"Well, someone has to keep up appearances! After all, we are predators."*

"Pewter, that's disgusting." Harry grimaced as the rotund animal gobbled down the cricket.

"Maybe they're like nachos." Miranda Hogendobber heard the loud crunch.

"I'll never eat a nacho again." Harry glared at her coworker and friend.

"It's the crunchiness. I bet you any money," Miranda teased.

"It is." Pewter licked her lips in answer to the older woman. She was glad cats didn't wear lipstick like Mrs. Hogendobber. Imagine getting lipstick on a cricket or mouse. Spoil the taste.

"Hey, girls." The Reverend Herbert Jones strolled through the front door. He called all women girls, and they had long since given up hope of sensitizing him. Ninety-two-year-old Catherine I. Earnhart was called a girl. She rather liked it.

"Hey, Rev." Harry smiled at him. "You're late today."

He fished in his pocket for his key and inserted it in his brass mailbox, pulling out a fistful of mail, most of it useless advertisements.

"If I'm late, it's because I lent my car to Roscoe Fletcher. He was supposed to bring it back to me by one o'clock, and here it is three. I finally decided to walk."

"His car break down?" Miranda opened the backdoor for a little breeze and sunshine.

"That new car of his is the biggest lemon."

Harry glanced up from counting out second-day air packets to see Roscoe pulling into the post office parking lot out front. "Speak of the devil."

Herb turned around. "Is that my car?"

"Looks different with the mud washed off, doesn't it?" Harry laughed.

"Oh, I know I should clean it up, and I ought to fix my truck, too, but I don't have the time. Not enough hours in the day."

"Amen," Miranda said.

"Why, Miranda, how nice of you to join the service." His eyes twinkled.

"Herb, I'm sorry," Roscoe said before he closed the door behind him. "Mim Sanburne stopped me in the hall, and I thought I'd never get away. You know how the Queen of Crozet talks."

"Indeed," they said.

"*Why do they call Mim the Queen of Crozet?*" Mrs. Murphy licked her front paw. "*Queen of the Universe is more like it.*"

"*No, just the Solar System,*" Tucker barked.

"*Doesn't have the same ring to it,*" Mrs. Murphy replied.

"*Humans think they are the center of everything. Bunch of dumb Doras.*" Pewter burped.

The unpleasant prospect of cricket parts being regurgitated on the counter made Mrs. Murphy take a step back.

"How do you like your car?" Roscoe pointed to the Subaru station wagon, newly washed and waxed.

"Looks brand-new. Thank you."

"You were good to lend me wheels. Gary at the dealership will bring my car to the house. If you'll drop me home, I'll be fine."

"Where's Naomi today?" Miranda inquired about his wife.

"In Staunton. She took the third grade to see the Pioneer Museum." He chuckled. "Better her than me. Those lower-school kids drive me bananas."

"That's why she's principal of the lower school, and you're headmaster. We call you 'the Big Cheese.' " Harry smiled.

"No, it's because I'm a good fund-raiser. Anyone want to cough up some cash?" He laughed, showing broad, straight teeth, darkened by smoking. He reached into his pocket and pulled out a pack of Tootsie Rolls, then offered them around.

"You're not getting blood from this stone. Besides, I graduated from Crozet High." Harry waved off the candy.

"Me, too, a bit earlier than she did," Miranda said coyly.

"I graduated in 1945," Herb said boldly.

"I can't get arrested with you guys, can I? You don't even want my Tootsie Rolls." Roscoe smiled. He had a jovial face as well as manner. "Tell you what, if you win the lottery, give St. Elizabeth's a little bit. Education is important."

"For what?" Pewter stared at him. "You-all don't do a damn thing except fuss at each other."

"Some humans farm," Tucker responded.

Pewter glared down at the pretty corgi. "So?"

"It's productive," Mrs. Murphy added.

"It's only productive so they can feed each other. Doesn't have anything to do with us."

"They can fish," Tucker said.

"Big deal."

"It's a big deal when you want your tuna." Murphy laughed.

"They're a worthless species."

"Pewter, that cricket made you out of sorts. Gives you gas. You don't see me eating those things," Mrs. Murphy said.

"You know, my car does look new, really." Herb again cast his blue eyes over the station wagon.

"Went to the car wash on Twenty-ninth and Greenbrier Drive," Roscoe told him. "I love that car wash."

"You love a car wash?" Miranda was incredulous.

"You've got to go there. I'll take you." He held out his meaty arms in an expansive gesture. "You drive up—Karen Jensen and some of our other kids work there, and they guide your left tire onto the track. The kids work late afternoons and weekends—good kids. Anyway, you have a smorgasbord of choices. I chose what they call 'the works.' So they beep you in, car in neutral, radio off, and you lurch into the fray. First, a yellow neon light flashes, a wall of water hits you, and then a blue neon light tells you your undercarriage is being cleaned, then there's a white light and a pink light and a green light—why it's almost like a Broadway show. And"—he pointed outside—"there's the result. A hit."

"Roscoe, if the car wash excites you that much, your life needs a pickup." Herb laughed good-naturedly.

"You go to the car wash and see for yourself."

The two men left, Herb slipping into the driver's seat as Harry and Miranda gazed out the window.

"You been to that car wash?"

"No, I feel like I should wear my Sunday pearls and rush right out." Miranda folded her arms across her ample chest.

"*I'm not going through any car wash. I hate it,*" Tucker grumbled.

"*You hear thunder and you hide under the bed.*"

The dog snapped at Murphy, "*I do not, that's a fib.*"

"*Slobber, too.*" Since Murphy was on the counter, she could be as hateful as she pleased; the dog couldn't reach her.

"*You peed in the truck,*" Tucker fired back.

Mrs. Murphy's pupils widened. "*I was sick.*"

"*Were not.*"

"*Was, too.*"

"*You were on your way to the vet and you were scared!*"

"*I was on my way to the vet because I was sick.*" The tiger vehemently defended herself.

"*Going for your annual shots,*" Tucker sang in three-quarter time.

"*Liar.*"

"*Chicken.*"

"*That was two years ago.*"

"*Truck smelled for months.*" Tucker rubbed it in.

Mrs. Murphy, using her hind foot, with one savage kick pushed a stack of mail on the dog's head. "*Creep.*"

"Hey!" Harry hollered. "Settle down."

"*Vamoose!*" Mrs. Murphy shot off the counter, soaring over the corgi, who was mired in a mudslide of mail, as she zoomed out the opened backdoor.

Tucker hurried after her, shedding envelopes as she ran.

Pewter relaxed on the counter, declining to run.

Harry walked to the backdoor to watch her pets chase one another through Miranda's yard, narrowly missing her mums, a riot of color. "I wish I could play like that just once."

"They are beguiling." Miranda watched, too, then noticed the sparkling light. "The equinox, it's such a special time, you know. Light and darkness are in perfect balance."

What she didn't say was that after today, darkness would slowly win out.

2

On her back, legs in the air, Mrs. Murphy displayed her slender beige tummy, the stripes muted, unlike the tiger stripes on her back, which were shiny jet-black. She heard the Audi Quattro a quarter of a mile down the driveway, long before Harry realized anyone had turned onto the farm drive.

Tucker, usually on guard, had trotted over to the creek that divided Harry's farm from Blair Bainbridge's farm on the southern boundary. A groundhog lived near the huge hickory there. Tucker, being a herding animal, possessed no burning desire to kill. Still, she enjoyed watching quarry, occasionally engaging a wild animal in conversation. She was too far away to sound a warning about the car.

Not that she needed to, for the visitor was Susan Tucker, Harry's best friend since toddler days. As Susan had traded in her old Volvo for an Audi Quattro, the tire sound was different and Tucker wasn't used to it yet. Mrs. Murphy possessed a better memory for such sounds than Tucker.

Pewter, flopped under the kitchen table, could not have cared less about the visitor. She was dreaming of a giant marlin garnished with mackerel. What made the dream especially sweet was that she didn't have to share the fish with anyone else.

Harry, on an organizing jag, was dumping the contents of her bureau drawers onto her bed.

Mrs. Murphy opened one eye. She heard the slam of the car door. A second slam lifted her head. Usually Susan cruised out to Harry's alone. Escaping her offspring saved her mental health. The back screen door opened. Susan walked in, her beautiful fifteen-year-old daughter, Brooks, following behind. No escape today.

"Toodle-oo," Susan called out.

Pewter, irritated at being awakened, snarled, *"I have never heard anything so insipid in my life."*

Mrs. Murphy rested her head back down on her paw. *"Crab."*

"Well, that's just it, Murphy, I was having the best dream of my life and now—vanished." Pewter mourned the loss.

"Hi, Murphy." Susan scratched behind the cat's delicate ears.

"Oh, look, Pewts is underneath the kitchen table." Brooks, who loved cats, bent down to pet Pewter. Her auburn hair fell in a curtain across her face.

"What I endure," the gray cat complained; however, she made no effort to leave, so the complaint was pro forma.

"I'm organizing," Harry called from the bedroom.

"God help us all." Susan laughed as she walked into the chaos. "Harry, you'll be up all night."

"I couldn't stand it anymore. It takes me five minutes to find a pair of socks that match and"—she pointed to a few pathetic silken remnants—"my underwear is shot."

"You haven't bought new lingerie since your mother died."

Harry plopped on the bed. "As long as Mom bought the stuff, I didn't have to—anyway, I can't stand traipsing into Victoria's Secret. There's something faintly pornographic about it."

"Oh, bull, you just can't stand seeing bra sizes bigger than your own."

"I'm not so bad."

Susan smiled. "I didn't say you were, I only hinted that you are a touch competitive."

"I am not. I most certainly am not. If I were competitive, I'd be applying my art history degree somewhere instead of being the post-mistress of Crozet."

"I seem to remember one vicious field hockey game our senior year."

"That doesn't count."

"You didn't like BoomBoom Craycroft even then," Susan re-called.

"Speaking of jugs . . . I hear she seduced my ex-husband wearing a large selection of lingerie."

"Who told you that?"

"She did, the idiot."

Susan sat down on the opposite side of the bed because she was laughing too hard to stand up.

"She did! Can you believe it? Told me all about the black lace teddy she wore when he came out to the farm on a call," Harry added.

Pharamond Haristeen, "Fair," happened to be one of the best equine vets in the state.

"Mom, Pewter's hungry," Brooks called from the kitchen.

Tucker, having raced back, pushed open the screen door and hurried over to Susan only to sit on her foot. As it was Susan who bred her and gave her to Harry, she felt quite close to the auburn-haired woman.

"Pewter's always hungry, Brooks; don't fall for her starving kitty routine."

"Shut up," Pewter called back, then purred and rubbed against Brooks's leg.

"Mom, she's really hungry."

"Con artist." Walking back to the kitchen, Harry sternly addressed the cat, who was frantically purring. "If they gave Academy Awards to cats, you would surely win 'best actress.' "

"I am so-o-o-o hungry," the cat warbled.

"If I could use the electric can opener, I'd feed you just to shut you up." Mrs. Murphy sat up and swept her whiskers forward, then back.

Harry, arriving at the same conclusion, grabbed a can of Mariner's Delight. "What's up?"

"We're having a family crisis." Brooks giggled.

"No, we're not."

"Mom." Brooks contradicted her mother by the tone of her voice.

"I'm all ears." Harry ladled out the fishy-smelling food. Pewter, blissfully happy, stuck her face in it. Mrs. Murphy approached her food with more finesse. She liked to pat the edge of her dish with her paw, sniff, then take a morsel in her teeth, carefully chewing it. She believed this was an aid to digestion, also keeping her weight down. Pewter gobbled everything. Calorie Kitty.

"I hate my teachers this year, especially Home Room." Brooks dropped on a brightly painted kitchen chair.

"Miss Tucker, you were not invited to sit down." Susan put her hands on her hips.

"Mom, it's Harry. I mean, it's not like I'm at Big Mim's or anything." She referred to Mim Sanburne, a fierce enforcer of etiquette.

"Practice makes perfect."

"Please have a seat." Harry invited her to the seat she already occupied.

"Thank you," Brooks replied.

"Just see that you don't forget your manners."

"Fat chance." Brooks laughed at her mother.

They strongly resembled each other, and despite their spats, a deep love existed between mother and daughter.

Danny, Susan's older child, was also the recipient of oceans of maternal affection.

Brooks abruptly got up and dashed outside.

"Where are you going?"

"Back in a flash."

Susan sat down. "I ask myself daily, sometimes hourly, whatever made me think I could be a mother."

"Oh, Susan." Harry waved her hand. "Stop trolling for compliments."

"I'm not."

"You know you're a good mother."

Brooks reappeared, Saturday newspaper in hand, and placed it on the table. "Sorry."

"Oh, thanks. I didn't get out to the mailbox this morning." She took the rubber band off the folded newspaper. The small white envelope underneath the rubber band contained the monthly bill. "I don't know why I pay for this damned paper. Half the time it isn't delivered."

"Well, they delivered it today."

"Hallelujah. Well—?" Harry shrugged. "What's the family crisis?"

"We're not having a family crisis," Susan replied calmly. "Brooks doesn't like her teachers, so we're discussing—"

"I hate my teachers, and Mom is getting bent out of shape. Because she graduated from Crozet High, she wants me to graduate from Crozet High. Danny graduates this year. That ought to be enough. Batting five hundred, Mom," Brooks interrupted.

Harry's eyes widened. "You can't drop out, Brooks."

"I don't want to drop out. I want to go back to St. Elizabeth's."

"That damned snob school costs an arm and a leg." Susan looked up at Pewter, who was eating very loudly. "That cat sounds like an old man smacking his gums."

Pewter, insulted, whirled around to face Susan, but she only proved the statement as little food bits dangled from her whiskers.

Susan smiled. "Like an old man who can't clean his mustache."

"*Ha!*" Mrs. Murphy laughed loudly.

"*She really does look like that,*" Tucker agreed as she sat on the floor under the counter where Pewter chowed down. In case the cat dropped any food, Tucker would vacuum it up.

"Hey, I've got some cookies," Harry said.

"Thank you, no. We ate a big breakfast."

"What about coffee, tea?"

"No." Susan smiled.

"You don't think you can get along with your teachers or over-look them?" Harry switched back to the subject at hand.

"I hate Mrs. Berryhill."

"She's not so bad." Harry defended a middle-aged lady wid-owed a few years back.

"Gives me heaves." Brooks pretended to gag.

"If it's that bad, you aren't going to learn anything."

"See, Mom, see—I told you."

"I think it's important not to bail out before you've given it a month or two."

"By that time I'll have *failed French!*" She knew her mother espe-cially wanted her to learn French.

"Don't be so dramatic."

"Go on, be dramatic." Harry poked at Susan's arm while en-couraging Brooks.

"We need a little drama around here." Tucker agreed with Harry.

"I won't learn a thing. I'll be learning-deprived. I'll shrink into oblivion—"

Harry interrupted, "Say, that's good, Brooks. You must be read-ing good novels or studying vocabulary boosters."

Brooks smiled shyly, then continued. "I will be disadvantaged for life, and then I'll never get into Smith."

"That's a low blow," said Susan, who had graduated from Smith with Harry.

"Then you'll marry a gas station attendant and—"

"Harry, don't egg her on. She doesn't have to pay the bills."

"What does Ned say?" Harry inquired of Susan's husband, a lawyer and a likable man.

"He's worried about the money, too, but he's determined that she get a good foundation."

"St. Elizabeth's is a fine school even if I do think they're a bunch of snobs," Harry said forthrightly. "Roscoe Fletcher is doing a good job. At least everyone says he is. I can't say that I know a lot about education, but remember last year's graduating class put two kids in Yale, one in Princeton, one in Harvard." She paused. "I think everyone got into great schools. Can't argue with that."

"If I'm going to spend that much money, then I should send her to St. Catherine's in Richmond," Susan replied to Harry.

"Mom, I don't want to go away from home. I just want to get out of Crozet High. I'll be away soon enough when I go to college. Smith, Mom, Smith," she reminded her mother.

"Well—" Susan considered this.

"Call Roscoe Fletcher," Harry suggested. "Brooks has only been in school for two weeks. See if he'll let her transfer now or if she'll have to wait for the second semester."

Susan stood up to make herself a cup of tea.

"I asked you if you wanted tea," Harry said.

"I changed my mind. You want some?"

"Yeah, sure." Harry sat back down.

"I already called Roscoe. That officious bombshell of a secretary of his, April Shively, took forever to put me through. It's a contradiction in terms, bombshell and secretary." She thought a moment, then continued. "Of course, he said wondrous things about St. Elizabeth's, which one would expect. What headmaster won't take your money?"

"He has raised a lot of money, at least, that's what Mim says." Harry paused, "Mim graduated from Madeira, you know. You'd think she would have gone to St. Elizabeth's. Little Mim didn't graduate from St. Elizabeth's either."

"Mim is a law unto herself," Susan replied.

"Miranda will know why Big Mim didn't go there."

"If she chooses to tell. What a secret keeper that one is." Susan loved Miranda Hogendobber, being fully acquainted with her quirks. Miranda's secrets usually involved age or the petty politics of her various civic and church organizations.

"The big question: Can Brooks get in?"

"Of course she can get in," Susan replied in a loud voice. "She's carrying a three point eight average. And her record was great when she was there before, in the lower school."

"What about Danny? Will he be jealous?"

"No," Brooks answered. "I asked him."

Harry took her cup of tea as Susan sat back down.

"I just bought that Audi Quattro," Susan moaned. "How can I pay for all of this?"

"I can work after school," Brooks volunteered.

"I want those grades to stay up, up, up. By the time you get into college, you might have to win a scholarship. Two kids in college at the same time—when I got pregnant, why didn't I space them four years apart instead of two?" She wailed in mock horror.

"Because this way they're friends, and this way Danny can drive Brooks everywhere."

"And that's another thing." Susan smacked her hand on the table. "They'll be going to different after-school activities. He won't be driving her anywhere."

"Mom, half my friends go to St. Elizabeth's. I'll cop rides."

"Brooks, I am not enamored of the St. Elizabeth's crowd. They're too—superficial, and I hear there's a lot of drugs at the school."

"Get real. There's a lot of drugs at Crozet High. If I wanted to take drugs, I could get them no matter where I went to school." She frowned.

"That's a hell of a note," Harry exclaimed.

"It's true, I'm afraid." Susan sighed. "Harry, the world looks very different when you have children."

"I can see that," Harry agreed. "Brooks, just who are your friends at St. Elizabeth's?"

"Karen Jensen. There's other kids I know, but Karen's my best friend there."

"She seems like a nice kid," Harry said.

"She is. Though she's also older than Brooks." Susan was frustrated. "But the rest of them are balls-to-the-wall consumers. I'm telling you, Harry, the values there are so superficial and—"

Harry interrupted her. "But Brooks is not superficial, and St. E isn't going to make her that way. It didn't before and it won't this time. She's her own person, Susan."

Susan dipped a teaspoon in her tea, slowly stirring in clover honey. She hated refined sugar. "Darling, go visit Harry's horses. I need a private word with my best bud."

"Sure, Mom." Brooks reluctantly left the kitchen, Tucker at her heels.

Putting the teaspoon on the saucer, Susan leaned forward. "It's so competitive at that school, some kids can't make it. Remember last year when Courtney Frere broke down?"

Trying to recall the incident, Harry dredged up vague details. "Bad college-board scores—was that it?"

"She was so afraid she'd disappoint her parents and not get into a good school that she took an overdose of sleeping pills."

"Now I remember." Harry pressed her lips together. "That can happen anywhere. She's a high-strung girl. She got into, uh, Tulane, wasn't it?"

"Yes." Susan nodded her head. "But it isn't just competitive between the students, it's competitive between the faculty and the administration. Sandy Brashiers is still fuming that he wasn't made upper-school principal."

"Politics exists in every profession. Even mine," Harry calmly stated. "You worry too much, Susan."

"You don't know what it's like being a mother!" Susan flared up.

"Then why ask my opinion?" Harry shot back.

"Because—" Susan snapped her teaspoon on the table.

"*Hey!*" Tucker barked.

"Hush, Tucker," Harry told her.

"What's the worst that can happen?" Harry grabbed the spoon out of Susan's hand. "If she hates it, you take her out of there. If she falls in with the wrong crowd, yank her out."

"This little detour could destroy her grade-point average."

"Well, she'll either go to a lesser college than our alma mater or she can go to a junior college for a year or two to pull her grades back up. Susan, it isn't the end of the world if Brooks doesn't do as well as you wish—but it's a hard lesson."

"I don't think Mrs. Berryhill is that bad."

"We aren't fifteen. Berryhill's not exactly a barrel of laughs even for us."

Susan breathed deeply. "The contacts she makes at St. Elizabeth's could prove valuable later, I suppose."

"She's a good girl. She'll bloom where planted."

"You're right." Susan exhaled, then reached over for the folded paper. "Speaking of the paper, let's see what fresh hell the world is in today."

She unfolded the first section of the paper, the sound of which inflamed Mrs. Murphy, who jumped over from the counter to sit on the sports section, the living section, and the classifieds.

"Murphy, move a minute." Harry tried to pull the living section out from under the cat.

"*I enjoy sitting on the newspaper. Best of all, I love the tissue paper in present boxes, but this will do.*"

Harry gently lifted up Mrs. Murphy's rear end and pulled out a section of paper as the tail swished displeasure. "Thank you."

"*I beg your pardon,*" Mrs. Murphy grumbled as Harry let her rear end down.

"Another fight in Congress over the federal budget," Susan read out loud.

"What a rook." Harry shrugged. "Nobody's going to do anything anyway."

"Isn't that the truth? What's in your section?"

"Car wreck on Twenty-ninth and Hydralic. Officer Crystal Limerick was on the scene."

"Anything in there about Coop?" She mentioned their mutual friend who was now a deputy for the Albemarle County Sheriff's Department.

"No." Harry flipped pages, disappointed that she didn't find what she was looking for.

"You've got the obit section, let's see who went to their reward."

"You're getting as bad as Mom."

"Your mother was a wonderful woman, and it's one's civic duty to read the obituary column. After all, we must be ready to assist in case—"

She didn't finish her sentence because Harry flipped open the section of the paper to the obituary page suddenly shouting, "Holy shit!"

3

"I just spoke to him yesterday." Susan gasped in shock as she read over Harry's shoulder the name Roscoe Harvey Fletcher, forty-five, who died unexpectedly September 22. She'd jumped up to see for herself.

"The paper certainly got it in the obit section quickly." Harry couldn't believe it either.

"Obit section has the latest closing." Susan again read the information to be sure she wasn't hallucinating. "Doesn't say how he died. Oh, that's not good. When they don't say it means suicide or—"

"AIDS."

"They never tell you in this paper how people die. I think it's important." Susan snapped the back of the paper.

" 'The family requests donations be made to the Roscoe Harvey

Fletcher Memorial Fund for scholarships to St. Elizabeth's. . . .'
What the hell happened?" Harry shot up and grabbed the phone.

She dialed Miranda's number. Busy. She then dialed Dr. Larry
Johnson. He knew everything about everybody. Busy. She dialed the
Reverend Herbert Jones.

"Rev," she said as he picked up the phone, "it's Mary Minor."

"I know your voice."

"How did Roscoe die?"

"I don't know." His voice lowered. "I was on my way over
there to see what I could do. Nobody knows anything. I've spoken to
Mim and Miranda. I even called Sheriff Shaw to see if there had been
a late-night accident. Everyone is in the dark, and there's no funeral
information. Naomi hasn't had time to select a funeral home. She's
probably in shock."

"She'll use Hill and Wood."

"Yes, I would think so, but, well—" His voice trailed off a
moment, then he turned up the volume. "He wasn't sick. I reached
Larry. Clean bill of health, so this has to be an accident of some kind.
Let me get over there to help. I'll talk to you later."

"Sorry," Harry apologized for slowing him down.

"No, no, I'm glad you called."

"Nobody called me."

"Miranda did. If you had an answering machine you'd have
known early on. She called at seven A.M., the minute she saw the
paper."

"I was in the barn."

"Called there, too."

"Maybe I was out on the manure spreader. Well, it doesn't
matter. There's work to be done. I'll meet you over at the Fletchers'.
I've got Susan and Brooks with me. We can help do whatever needs to
be done."

"That would be greatly appreciated. See you there." He breathed
in sharply. "I don't know what we're going to find."

As Harry hung up the phone, Susan stood up expectantly.
"Well?"

"Let's shoot over to the Fletchers'. Herbie's on his way."

"Know anything?" They'd been friends for so long they could speak in shorthand to each other, and many times they didn't need to speak at all.

"No."

"Let's move 'em out." Susan made the roundup sign.

Tucker, assisted by Brooks, sneaked into the roundup. She lay on the floor of the Audi until halfway to Crozet. Mrs. Murphy and Pewter, both livid at being left behind, stared crossly as the car pulled out of the driveway.

Once at the Fletchers' the friends endured another shock. Fifty to sixty cars lined the street in the Ednam subdivision. Deputy Cynthia Cooper directed traffic. This wasn't her job, but the department was shorthanded over the weekend.

"Coop?" Harry waved at her.

"Craziest thing I've ever heard of," the nice-looking officer said.

"What do you mean?" Susan asked.

"He's not dead."

"WHAT?" all three humans said in unison.

Tucker, meanwhile, wasted no time. She walked in the front door, left open because of the incredible number of friends, acquaintances, and St. Elizabeth's students who were paying condolence calls. Tucker, low to the ground, threaded her way through the humans to the kitchen.

Brooks quickly found her friends, Karen Jensen and Jody Miller. They didn't know anything either.

As Harry and Susan entered the living room, Roscoe held up a glass of champagne, calling to the assembled, "The reports of my death are greatly exaggerated!" He sipped. "Bierce."

"Twain," Sandy Brashiers corrected. He was head of the English department and a rival for Roscoe's power.

"Ambrose Bierce." Roscoe smiled but his teeth were clenched.

"It doesn't matter, Roscoe, you're alive." Naomi, a handsome woman in her late thirties, toasted her husband.

April Shively, adoringly staring at her florid boss, clinked her glass with that of Ed Sugarman, the chemistry teacher.

"Hear, hear," said the group, which contained most of Harry's best friends, as well as a few enemies.

Blair Bainbridge, not an enemy but a potential suitor, stood next to Marilyn, or Little Mim, the well-groomed daughter of Big Mim Sanburne.

"When did you get home?" Harry managed to ask Blair after expressing to Roscoe her thanks for his deliverance.

"Last night."

"Hi, Marilyn." She greeted Little Mim by her real name.

"Good to see you." It wasn't. Marilyn was afraid Blair liked Harry more than herself.

Fair Haristeen, towering above the other men, strode over to his ex-wife, with whom he was still in love. "Isn't this the damnedest thing you've ever seen?" He reached into the big bowl of hard candies sitting on an end table. Roscoe always had candy around.

"Pretty weird." She kissed him on the cheek and made note that Morris "Maury" McKinchie, Roscoe Fletcher's best friend, was absent.

Meanwhile Tucker sat in the kitchen with Winston, the family English bulldog, a wise and kind animal. They had been exchanging pleasantries before Tucker got to the point.

"What's going on, Winston?"

"I don't know," came the grave reply.

"Has he gone to doctors in Richmond or New York? Because Harry heard from Herb Jones that he was healthy."

"Nothing wrong with Roscoe except too many women in his life."

The corgi cocked her head. *"Ah, well,"* she said, *"a prank, I guess, this obit thing."*

"Roscoe now knows how many people care about him. If people could attend their funerals, they'd be gratified, I should think," Winston said.

"Never thought of that."

"Umm." Winston waddled over to the backdoor, overlooking the sunken garden upon which Naomi lavished much attention.

"Winston, what's worrying you?"

The massive head turned to reveal those fearsome teeth. *"What if this is a warning?"*

"*Who'd do a thing like that?*"

"Tucker, Roscoe can't keep it in his pants. I've lost count of his affairs, and Naomi has reached the boiling point. She always catches him. After many lies, he does finally confess. He promises never to do it again. Three months, six months later—he's off and running."

"*Who?*"

"*The woman?*" The wrinkled brow furrowed more deeply. "*April, maybe, except she's so obvious even the humans get it. Let's see, a young woman from New York, I forget her name. Oh, he's made a pass at BoomBoom, but I think she's otherwise engaged. You know, I lose count.*"

"Bet Naomi doesn't," the little corgi sagely replied.

4

That evening a heavy fog crept down Yellow Mountain. Harry, in the stable, walked outside to watch a lone wisp float over the creek. The wisp was followed by fingers spreading over the meadow until the farm was enveloped in gray.

She shivered; the temperature was dropping.

"Put on your down vest, you'll catch your death," Mrs. Murphy advised.

"What are you talking about, Miss Puss?" Harry smiled at her chatty cat.

"You, I'm talking about you. You need a keeper." The tiger sighed, knowing that the last person Harry would take care of would be herself.

Tucker lifted her head. Moisture carried good scent. *"That bobcat's near."*

"Let's get into the barn then." The cat feared her larger cousin.

As the little family plodded into the barn, the horses nickered. Darkness came as swiftly as the fog. Harry pulled her red down vest off a tack hook. She flipped on the light switch. Having stayed overlong at Roscoe Fletcher's to celebrate, she was now behind on her farm chores.

Tomahawk, the oldest horse in the barn, loved the advent of fall. A true foxhunting fellow, he couldn't wait for the season to begin. Gin Fizz and Poptart, the younger equines, perked their ears.

"*That old bobcat is prowling around.*" Mrs. Murphy leapt onto the Dutch door, the top held open by a nickel-plated hook.

Tomahawk gazed at her with his huge brown eyes. "*Mean, that one.*"

Two bright beady black eyes appeared at the edge of the hayloft. "*What's this I hear about a bobcat?*"

"*Simon, I thought you'd still be asleep,*" Tucker barked.

The opossum moved closer to the edge, revealing his entire light gray face. "*You-all make enough noise to wake the dead. Any minute now and Flatface up there will swoop down and bitterly chastise us.*"

Simon referred to the large owl who nested in the cupola. The owl disliked the domesticated animals, especially Mrs. Murphy. There was also a black snake who hibernated in the hayloft, but she was antisocial, even in summertime. A cornucopia of mice kept the predators fat and happy.

The hayloft covered one-third of the barn, which gave the space a lighter, airier feeling than if it had run the full length of the structure. Harry, using salvaged lumber, had built a hay shed thirty yards from the barn. She had painted it dark green with white trim; that was her summer project. Each summer she tried to improve the farm. She loved building, but after nailing on shingles in the scorching sun, she had decided she'd think long and hard before doing that again.

Mrs. Murphy climbed the ladder to the hayloft. "*Fog is thick as pea soup.*"

"*Doesn't matter. I can smell her well enough.*" Simon referred to the dreaded bobcat.

"*Maybe so, but she can run faster than anyone here except for the horses.*"

"*I'm hungry.*"

"*I'll get Mom to put crunchies in my bowl. You can have that.*"

Simon brightened. *"Goody."*

Mrs. Murphy walked the top beam of the stalls, greeting each horse as she passed over its head. Then she jumped down on the tall wooden medicine chest standing next to the tack-room door. From there it was an easy drop to the floor.

Harry, having fed the horses, knelt on her hands and knees in the feed room. Little holes in the wooden walls testified to the industry of the mice. She lined her feed bins in tin, which baffled them, but they gobbled every crumb left on the floor. They also ate holes in her barn jacket, which enraged her.

"Mother, you aren't going to catch one."

"Murphy, do something!"

The cat sat next to Harry and patted the hole in the wall. *"They've got a system like the New York subway."*

"You're certainly talkative," Harry commented.

"And you don't understand a word I'm saying." The cat smiled. *"I'm hungry."*

"Jeez, Murphy, lower the volume."

"Food, glorious food—" She sang the song from *Oliver.*

Tucker, reposing in the tack room, hollered, *"You sing about as well as I do."*

"Thanks. I could have lived my whole life without knowing that."

Her entreaties worked. Harry shook triangular crunchies out of the bag, putting the bowl on top of the medicine cabinet so Tucker wouldn't steal the food.

"Thanks," Simon called down, showing his appreciation.

"Anytime." Murphy nibbled a few mouthfuls to satisfy Harry.

"I suppose Pewter will be hungry." Harry checked her watch. "She's not an outdoor girl." She laughed.

"If she gets any fatter, you'll need to buy a red wagon so you can haul her gut around," Mrs. Murphy commented.

Harry sat on her old tack trunk. She glanced around. While there were always chores to be done, the regular maintenance ones were finished: feed, water, muck stalls, clean tack, sweep out the barn.

As soon as the horses finished eating, she would turn them out. With the first frost, usually around mid-October, she would flip their schedule. They'd be outside during the day and in their stalls at night. In the heat of summer they stayed inside the barn during the day; it was well ventilated from the breeze always blowing down the mountain. Kept the flies down, too.

She got up, her knees cracking, and walked to the open barn door. "You know, we could have an early frost." She returned to Fizz's stall. "I wonder if we should get on the new schedule now."

"*Go ahead. If there are a couple of hot days, we'll come inside during the day. We're flexible.*"

"*Let's stay inside.*" Poptart ground his sweet feed.

"*Who wants to argue with the bobcat? I don't,*" Tomahawk said sensibly.

Harry cupped her chin with her hand. "You know, let's go to our fall schedule."

"*Hooray!*" the horses called out.

"Nighty night," she called back, turning off the lights.

Although the distance between the stable and the house couldn't have been more than one hundred yards, the heavy fog and mist soaked the three friends by the time they reached the backdoor.

The cat and dog shook themselves in the porch area. Harry would pitch a fit if they did it in the kitchen. Even Harry shook herself. Once inside she raced to put on the kettle for tea. She was chilled.

Pewter, lounging on the sofa, head on a colorful pillow, purred, "*I'm glad I stayed inside.*"

"*You're always glad you stayed inside,*" Tucker answered.

Harry puttered around. She drank some tea, then walked back into her bedroom. "Oh, no." In the turmoil of the day, she'd rushed out with Susan and Brooks, forgetting the mess she had left behind. The contents of her bureau drawers lay all over her bed. "I will not be conquered by underpants."

She gulped her tea, ruthlessly tossing out anything with holes in it or where the fabric was worn thin. That meant she had only enough socks left for half a drawer, one satin bra, and three pairs of underpants.

"*Mom, you need to shop,*" said Mrs. Murphy, who adored shopping although she rarely got the opportunity for it.

Harry beheld the pile of old clothes. "Use it up, wear it out, make it do, or do without."

"You can't wear these things. They're tired," Pewter, now in the middle of the pile, told her. "I'm tired, too."

"You didn't do anything." Murphy laughed.

Harry stomped out to the pantry, returning armed with a big scissors.

"What's she going to do?" Pewter wondered aloud.

"Make rags. Mother can't stand to throw anything out if it can be used for something. She'll cut everything into squares or rectangles and then divide the pile between the house and the barn."

"The bras, too?"

"No, I think those are truly dead," Mrs. Murphy replied.

"Harry is a frugal soul," Pewter commented. She herself was profligate.

"She has to be." Tucker cleaned her hind paws, not easy for a corgi. "That post office job pays for food and gas and that's all. Luckily, she inherited the farm when her parents died. It's paid for, but she doesn't have much else. A little savings and a few stocks her father left her, but he wasn't a financial wizard either. Her one extravagance, if you can call it that, is the horses. 'Course, they help in 'mowing' the fields."

"Humans are funny, aren't they?" Pewter said thoughtfully. "Big Mim wallows in possessions, and Harry has so little. Why doesn't Mim give things to Harry?"

"You forget, she gave her Poptart. She and Fair went halfsies on it."

"I did forget. Still, you know what I mean."

Tucker shrugged. "They're funny about things. Things mean a lot to them. Like bones to us, I guess."

"I couldn't care less about bones. Catnip is another matter," the tiger said gleefully, wishing for a catnip treat.

"Ever see that T-shirt? You know, the one that says 'He who dies with the most toys wins'?" Pewter, snuggling in the new rag pile, asked.

"Yeah. Samson Coles used to wear it—before he was disgraced by dipping into escrow funds." Tucker giggled.

"Stupid T-shirt," Mrs. Murphy said briskly. "When you're dead, you're dead. You can't win anything."

"*That reminds me. The bobcat's out there tonight,*" Tucker told Pewter.

"*I'm not going outside.*"

"*We know that.*" Mrs. Murphy swished her tail. "*Wonder if the Fletchers will find out who put that phony obituary in the paper? If they don't, Mother will. You know how nosy she gets.*"

The phone rang. Harry put down her scissors to pick it up. "Hi."

Blair Bainbridge's deep voice had a soothing quality. "Sorry I didn't call on you the minute I got home, but I was dog tired. I happened to be down at the café when Marilyn ran in to tell me about Roscoe dying. We drove over to his house, and I—"

"Blair, it's okay. She's crazy about you, as I'm sure you know."

"Oh, well, she's lonesome." Since he was one of the highest paid male models in the country, he knew perfectly well that women needed smelling salts in his presence. All but Harry. Therefore she fascinated him.

"Susan and I are riding tomorrow after church if you want to come along."

"Thanks. What time?"

"Eleven."

He cheerfully said, "I'll see you at eleven, and, Harry, I can tack my own horse. Who do you want me to ride?"

"Tomahawk."

"Great. See you then. 'Bye."

" 'Bye."

The animals said nothing. They knew she was talking to Blair, and they were divided in their opinions. Tucker wanted Harry to get back with Fair. She knew it wasn't unusual for humans to remarry after divorcing. Pewter thought Blair was the better deal because he was rich and Harry needed help in that department. Mrs. Murphy, while having affection for both men, always said that Mr. Right hadn't appeared. Be patient.

The phone rang again.

"Coop. How are you?"

"Tired. Hey, don't want to bug you, but did you have any idea who might have put that false obit in the papers?"

"No."

"Roscoe says he hasn't a clue. Naomi doesn't think it's quite as funny as he does. Herb doesn't have any ideas. April Shively thinks it was Karen Jensen since she's such a cutup. BoomBoom says Maury McKinchie did it, and he'll use our reactions as the basis for a movie. I even called the school chaplain, Father Michael. He was noncommittal."

"What do you mean?"

Father Michael, the priest of the Church of the Good Shepherd between Crozet and Charlottesville, had close ties to the private school. Although nondenominational for a number of years, St. Elizabeth's each year invited a local clergyman to be the chaplain of the school. This exposed the students to different religious approaches. This year it was the Catholics' turn. Apart from a few gripes from extremists, the rotating system worked well.

"He shut up fast," Coop replied.

"That's weird."

"I think so, too."

"What does Rick think?" Harry referred to Sheriff Shaw by his first name.

"He sees the humor in this, but he wants to find out who did it. If kids were behind this, they need to learn that you can't jerk people around like that."

"If I hear of anything, I'll buzz."

"Thanks."

"Don't work too hard, Coop."

"Look who's talking. See you soon. 'Bye."

Harry hung up the phone and picked up the small throw-out pile. Then she carefully divided the newly cut rags, placing half by the kitchen door. That way she would remember to take them to the barn in the morning. She noticed it was ten at night.

"Where does the time go?"

She hopped in the shower and then crawled into bed.

Mrs. Murphy, Pewter, and Tucker were already on the bed.

"What do you guys think about Roscoe's fake obituary?" she asked her animal friends.

Like many people who love animals, she talked to them, doing her best to understand. They understood her, of course.

"*Joke.*" Pewter stuck out one claw, which she hooked into the quilt.

"*Ditto.*" Tucker agreed. "*Although Winston said Naomi is furious with him. Mad enough to kill.*"

"*Humans are boring—*" Pewter rested her head on an outstretched arm.

"See, you think like I do." Harry wiggled under the blankets. "Just some dumb thing. For all I know, Roscoe did it himself. He's not above it."

"*Winston said Roscoe's running the women. Can't leave them alone.*" Tucker was back on her conversation with the bulldog.

"*Maybe this isn't a joke.*" Mrs. Murphy, who had strong opinions about monogamy, curled on Harry's pillow next to her head.

"*Oh, Murphy, it will all blow over.*" Tucker wanted to go to sleep.

5

The woody aroma of expensive tobacco curled up from Sandy Brashiers's pipe. The leather patches on his tweed jacket were worn to a perfect degree. His silk rep tie, stripes running in the English direction, left to right, was from Oxford University Motor Car Club. He had studied at Oxford after graduating from Harvard. A cashmere V neck, the navy underscoring the navy stripe in the tie, completed his English-professor look.

However, the Fates or Sandy himself had not been kind. Not only was he not attached to a university, he was teaching high-school English, even if it *was* at a good prep school. This was not the future his own professors or he himself had envisioned when he was a star student.

He never fell from grace because he never reached high enough to tumble. Cowardice and alcohol already marred his good looks at forty-two. As for the cowardice, no one but Sandy seemed to know why he hung back when he was capable of much more. Then again, perhaps even he didn't know.

He did know he was being publicly humiliated by headmaster Roscoe Fletcher. When the ancient Peter Abbott retired as principal of the upper school at the end of last year's term, Sandy should have automatically been selected to succeed Abbott. Roscoe dithered, then dallied, finally naming Sandy principal pro tem. He declared a genuine search should take place, much as he wished to promote from within.

This split the board of directors and enraged the faculty, most of whom believed the post should go to Sandy. If Roscoe was going to form a search committee each time a position opened, could any faculty member march assuredly into administration?

Fortunately for Brooks Tucker, she knew nothing of the prep school's politics. She was entranced as Mr. Brashiers discussed the moral turpitude of Lady Macbeth in the highly popular Shakespeare elective class.

"What would have happened if Lady Macbeth could have acted directly, if she didn't have to channel her ambition through her husband?"

Roger Davis raised his hand. "She would have challenged the king right in his face."

"No way," pretty Jody Miller blurted before she raised her hand.

"Would you like to expand on that theme after I call on you?" Sandy wryly nodded to the model-tall girl.

"Sorry, Mr. Brashiers." She twirled her pencil, a nervous habit. "Lady Macbeth was devious. It would be out of character to challenge the king openly. I don't think her position in society would change that part of her character. She'd be sneaky even if she were a man."

Brooks, eyebrows knit together, wondered if that was true. She wanted to participate, but she was shy in her new surroundings even though she knew many of her classmates from social activities outside of school.

Sean Hallahan, the star halfback on the football team, was called on and said in his deep voice, "She's devious, Jody, because she has to hide her ambition."

This pleased Sandy Brashiers, although it did not please Jody Miller, who was angry at Sean. Ten years ago the boys rarely understood the pressures on women's lives, but enough progress had been made that his male students could read a text bearing those pressures in mind.

Karen Jensen, blond and green-eyed, the most popular girl in the junior class, chirped, "Maybe she was having a bad hair day."

Everyone laughed.

After class Brooks, Karen, and Jody walked to the cafeteria—or the Ptomaine Pit, as it was known. Roger Davis, tall and not yet filled out, trailed behind. He wanted to talk to Brooks. Still awkward, he racked his brain about how to open a conversation.

He who hesitates is lost. Sean scooted by him, skidding next to the girls, secure in his welcome.

"Think the president's wife is Lady Macbeth?"

The three girls kept walking while Jody sarcastically said, "Sean, how long did it take you to think of that?"

"You inspire me, Jody." He cocked his head, full of himself.

Roger watched this from behind them. He swallowed hard, took two big strides and caught up.

"Hey, bean," Sean offhandedly greeted him, not at all happy that he might have to share the attention of three pretty girls.

If Roger had been a smart-ass kid, he would have called Sean a bonehead or something. Sean was bright enough, but his attitude infuriated the other boys. Roger was too nice a guy to put someone else down, though. Instead he smiled and forgot what he was going to say to Brooks.

Luckily, she initiated the conversation. "Are you still working at the car wash?"

"Yes."

"Do they need help? I mean, I'd like to get a job and—" Her voice faded away.

"Jimbo always needs help. I'll ask him," Roger said firmly, now filled with a mission: to help Brooks.

Jimbo C. Anson, as wide as he was tall, owned the car wash, the local heating-fuel company, and a small asphalt plant that he had bought when the owner, Kelly Craycroft, died unexpectedly. Living proof of the capitalist vision of life, Jimbo was also a soft touch. Brooks would be certain to get that after-school job.

Brooks was surprised when she walked through the backdoor of her house that afternoon to find her mother on the phone with Roger. He'd already gotten her the job. She needed to decide whether to work after school, weekends, or both.

After Brooks profusely thanked Roger, she said she'd call him back since she needed to talk to her mother.

"I guess you do." Susan stared at her after Brooks hung up the phone.

"Mom, St. Elizabeth's is expensive. I want to make money."

"Honey, we aren't on food stamps. At least, not yet." Susan sighed, loath to admit that the few fights she ever had with Ned were over money.

"If I can pay for my clothes and stuff, that will help some."

Susan stared into those soft hazel eyes, just like Ned's. Happy as she was to hear of Brooks's willingness to be responsible, she was oddly saddened or perhaps nostalgic: her babies were growing up fast. Somehow life went by in a blur. Wasn't it just yesterday she was holding this beautiful young woman in her arms, wondering at her tiny fingers and toes?

Susan cleared her throat. "I'm proud of you." She paused. "Let's go take a look at the car wash before you make a decision."

"Great." Brooks smiled, revealing the wonders of orthodontic work.

"Yeehaw!" came a holler from outside the backdoor.

"I'm here, too," Tucker barked.

Neither Mrs. Murphy nor Pewter was going to brazenly advertise her presence.

The Tuckers' own corgi, Tee Tucker's brother, Owen Tudor, raced to the backdoor as it swung open. Their mother had died of old age that spring. It was now a one-corgi household.

"Tucker." Owen kissed his sister. He would have kissed the two cats except they deftly sidestepped his advances.

"I didn't hear your truck," Susan said.

"Dead. This time it's the carburetor." Harry sighed. "One of these years I will buy a new truck."

"*And the cows will fly,*" Pewter added sardonically.

"*Mom might win the lottery.*" Tucker, ever the optimist, pricked up her ears.

"Need a ride home?" Susan offered.

"I'll walk. Good for me and good for the critters."

"*It's not good for me,*" Pewter objected instantly. "*My paws are too delicate.*"

"*You're too fat,*" Mrs. Murphy said bluntly.

"*I have big bones.*"

"*Pewter—*" Tucker started to say something but was interrupted by Susan, who reached down to pet her.

"Why don't you all hop in the car, and we'll go to the car wash? Brooks took a job there, but I want to check it out. If you go with me, I'll feel better."

"Sure."

Everyone piled into the Audi. Mrs. Murphy enjoyed riding in cars. Pewter endured it. The two dogs loved every minute of it, but they were so low to the ground the only way they could see out the window was to sit on human laps, which were never in short supply.

They waved to Big Mim in her Bentley Turbo R, heading back toward Crozet.

Mrs. Murphy, lying down in the back window, watched the opulent and powerful machine glide by. "*She's still in her Bavarian phase.*"

"*Huh?*" Tucker asked.

"*Caps with pheasant feathers, boiled wool jackets. For all I know she's wearing lederhosen, or one of those long skirts that weigh a sweet ton.*"

"*You know, if I were German, I'd be embarrassed when Americans dress like that,*" Pewter noted sagely.

"*If I were German, I'd be embarrassed if Germans dressed like that,*" Owen Tudor piped up, which made the animals laugh.

"You-all are being awfully noisy," Harry chided them.

"They're just talking," Brooks protested.

"If animals could talk, do you know what they'd say?" Susan

then told them: "What's to eat? Where's the food? Can I sleep with it? Okay, can I sleep on it?"

"I resent that," Mrs. Murphy growled.

"Who cares?" Pewter airily dismissed the human's gibe.

"What else can they do but joke about their betters? Low self-esteem." Owen chuckled.

"Yeah, and whoever invented that term ought to be hung at sundown." Mrs. Murphy, not one given to psychologizing, put one paw on Harry's shoulder. "In fact, the idea that a person is fully formed in childhood is absurd. Only a human could come up with that one."

"They can't help it," Tucker said.

"Well, they could certainly shut up about it," Mrs. Murphy suggested strongly.

"BoomBoom Craycroft can sure sling that crap around." Tucker didn't really dislike the woman, but then again, she didn't really like her either.

"You haven't heard the latest!" Pewter eagerly sat up by Brooks in the backseat.

"What?" The other animals leaned toward the cat.

"Heard it at Market's."

"Well!" Mrs. Murphy imperiously prodded.

"As I was saying before I was so rudely interrupted—"

"I did not interrupt you." Tucker was testy.

Owen stepped in. "Shut up, Tucker, let her tell her story."

"Well, BoomBoom was buying little glass bottles and a mess of Q-Tips, I mean enough Q-Tips to clean all the ears in Albemarle County. So Market asks, naturally enough, what is she going to do with all this stuff. Poor guy, next thing you know she launches into an explanation about fragrance therapy. No kidding. How certain essences will create emotional states or certain smells will soothe human ailments. She must have blabbed on for forty-five minutes. I thought I would fall off the counter laughing at her."

"She's off her nut," Owen said.

"Market asked for an example." Pewter relished her tale. "She allowed as how she didn't have any essence with her but, for instance, if he felt a headache coming on, he should turn off the lights, sit in a silent room, and put a pot of water on the stove with a few drops of sage essence. It would be even better if he had a wood-burning stove. Then he could put the essence of sage in the little humidifier on top."

"Essence of bullshit," Mrs. Murphy replied sardonically.

"Will you-all be quiet? This is embarrassing. Susan will never let you in her car again," Harry complained.

"All right by me," Pewter replied saucily, which made the animals laugh again.

Brooks petted Pewter's round head. "They have their own language."

"You know, that's a frightening thought." Susan glanced at her daughter in the rearview mirror, surrounded as she was by animals. "My Owen and poor dear departed Champion Beatitude of Grace—"

"Just call her Shortstop. I hate it when Susan uses Mom's full title." Owen's eyes saddened.

"She was a champion. She won more corgi firsts than Pewter and Murphy have fleas," Tucker said.

Murphy swatted at Tucker's stump. "If you had a tail, I would chew it to bits."

"I saw you scratching."

"Tucker, that was not fleas."

"What was it then, your highness? Eczema? Psoriasis? Hives?"

"Shut up." Mrs. Murphy bopped her hard.

"That is enough!" Harry twisted around in the front passenger seat and missed them because the car reached the entrance to the brand-new car wash, and the stop threw her forward.

Roger dashed out of the small glass booth by the entrance to the car-wash corridor.

"Hi, Mrs. Tucker." He smiled broadly. "Hi, Brooks. Hi, Mrs. Haristeen . . . and everybody."

"Is Jimbo here?"

"Yes, ma'am."

A car pulled up behind them, and one behind that. Roscoe Fletcher squirmed impatiently in the second car.

"Roger, I want to zip through this extravaganza." Susan reached in her purse for the $5.25 for exterior wash only.

"Mom, let's shoot the works."

"That's eleven ninety-five."

"I'll contribute!" Harry fished a five out of her hip pocket and handed it to Roger.

"Harry, don't do that."

"Shut up, Suz, we're holding up traffic."

"Here's the one." Brooks forked over a one-dollar bill.

"Okay then, a little to the right, Mrs. Tucker. There, you've got it. Now put your car in neutral and turn off the radio, if you have it on. Oh, and roll up the windows."

She rolled up the driver's side window as Roger picked up a long scrub brush to scrub her headlights and front grille while Karen Jensen worked the rear bumper. She waved.

"Hey, I didn't know Karen worked here. Jody, too." She saw Jody putting on mascara as she sat behind the cash register.

"Brooks, don't you dare open that window," Susan commanded as she felt the belt hook under the left car wheel. They lurched forward.

"Hey, hey, I can't see!" Pewter screeched.

"Early blindness," Mrs. Murphy said maliciously as the yellow neon light flashed on, a bell rang, and a wall of water hit them with force.

Each cleansing function—waxing, underbody scrub and coat, rinsing—was preceded by a neon light accompanied by a bell and buzzer noise. By the time they hit the blowers, Pewter frothed at the mouth.

"Poor kitty." Brooks petted her.

"Pewter, it really is okay. We're not in any danger." Mrs. Murphy felt bad that she had tormented her.

The gray kitty shook.

"Last time I take her through a car wash." Harry, too, felt sorry for the cat's plight.

They finally emerged with a bump from the tunnel of cleanliness. Susan popped the car in gear and parked it in a lot on the other side of the car wash.

As she and Brooks got out to meet with Jimbo Anson, Harry

consoled Pewter, who crawled into her lap. The other animals kept quiet.

A light rap on the window startled Harry, she was so intent on soothing the cat.

"Hi, Roscoe. You're right, it is like a Broadway show with all those lights."

"Funny, huh?" He offered her a tiny sweet, a miniature strawberry in a LaVossienne tin, French in origin. "Just discovered these. Les Fraises Bonbon Fruits pack a punch. Go on and try one."

"Okay." She reached in and plucked out a miniature strawberry. "Whooo."

"That'll pucker those lips. Naomi is trying to get me to stop eating so much sugar but I love sweetness." He noticed Brooks and Susan in the small office with Jimbo Anson. "Has she said anything about school?"

"She likes it."

"Good, good. You been to the vet?"

"No, we're out for a family drive."

"I can't remember the times I've seen you without Mrs. Murphy and Tucker. Now you've got Pewter, too. Market said she was eating him out of house and home."

"No-o-o," the cat wailed, shaken but insulted.

"*Hey, Pewter, we'll get even. We can pee on his mail before Mom stuffs it in his box,*" Murphy sang out gaily. "*Or we could shred it to bits, except the bills. Keep them intact.*"

St. Elizabeth's mail was delivered directly to the school. Personal mail was delivered to the Crozet post office.

"*Yeah.*" Pewter perked up.

"Good to see you, the animals, too." He waved and Harry hit the button to close the window.

Then she called after him, "Where'd you get the strawberry drops?"

"Foods of All Nations," he replied.

She noticed Karen Jensen making a face after he passed by. Roger laughed. "Kids," Harry thought to herself. Then she remembered the time she stuck Elmer's Glue in the locks of her most unfavorite teacher's desk drawer.

After ten minutes Susan and Brooks returned to the car.

Brooks was excited. "I'll work after school on Monday 'cause there's no field hockey practice, and I'll work Saturdays. Cool!"

"Sounds good to me." Harry held up her hand for a high five as Brooks bounced into the backseat.

Susan turned on the ignition. "This way she won't miss practice. After all, part of school is sports."

"*Can we go home now?*" Pewter cried.

"Roscoe must live at this place," Susan said lightly as they pulled out of the parking lot.

6

Little squeaks behind the tack-room walls distracted Harry from dialing. She pressed the disconnect button to redial.

Mrs. Murphy sauntered into the tack room, then paused, her ears swept forward. *"What balls!"*

"Beg pardon?" Pewter opened one chartreuse eye.

"Mouse balls. Can you hear them?"

Pewter closed her eye. *"Yes, but it's not worth fretting over."*

Harry, finger still on the disconnect button, rested the telephone receiver on her shoulder. "What in the hell are they doing, Murphy?"

"Having a party," the tiger replied, frustrated that she couldn't get at her quarry.

Harry lifted the receiver off her shoulder, pointing at the cat with it. "I can't put down poison. If you catch a sick mouse, then you'll die. I can't put the hose into their holes because I'll flood the tack room. I really thought you could solve this problem."

"*If one would pop out of there, I would.*" The cat, angry, stomped out.

"Temper, temper," Harry called out after her, which only made things worse.

She redialed the number as Murphy sat in the barn aisle, her back to Harry and her ears swept back.

"Hi, Janice. Harry Haristeen."

"How are you?" the bright voice on the other end of the line responded.

"Pretty good. And you?"

"Great."

"I hope you'll indulge me. I have a question. You're still editing the obituary page, aren't you?"

"Yep. Ninety-five cents a line. Five dollars for a photo." Her voice softened. "Has, uh—"

"No. I'm curious about how Roscoe Fletcher's obituary appeared in the paper."

"Oh, that." Janice's voice dropped. "Boy, did I get in trouble."

"Sorry."

"All I can tell you is, two days ago I received a call from Hallahan Funeral Home saying they had Roscoe's body as well as the particulars."

"So I couldn't call in and report a death?"

"No. If you're a family member or best friend you might call or fax the life details, but we verify death with the funeral home or the hospital. Usually they call us. The hospital won't give me cause of death either. Sometimes family members will put it in, but we can't demand any information other than verification that the person is dead." She took a deep breath. "And I had that!"

"Do you generally deal with the same people at each of the funeral homes?"

"Yes, I do, and I recognize their voices, too. Skip Hallahan called in Roscoe's death."

"I guess you told that to the sheriff."

"Told it to Roscoe, too. I'm sick of this."

"I'm sorry, Janice. I made you go over it one more time."

"That's different—you're a friend. Skip is being a bunghole, I can tell you that. He swears he never made the call."

"I think I know who did."

"Tell me."

"I will as soon as I make sure I'm right."

7

The high shine on Roscoe Fletcher's car surrendered to dust, red from the clay, as he drove down Mim Sanburne's two-mile driveway to the mansion Mim had inherited from her mother's family, the Urquharts.

He passed the mansion, coasting to a stop before a lovely cottage a quarter mile behind the imposing pile. Cars parked neatly along the farm road bore testimony to the gathering within.

Raising money for St. Elizabeth's was one of Little Mim's key jobs. She wanted to show she could be as powerful as her mother.

Breezing through Little Mim's front door, Roscoe heard Maury McKinchie shout, "The phoenix rises from the ashes!"

The members of the fund-raising committee, many of them alumnae, laughed at the film director's quip.

"You missed the resurrection party, my man." Roscoe clapped McKinchie on the back. "Lasted until dawn."

"Every day is a party for Roscoe," April Shively, stenographer's notebook flipped open at the ready, said admiringly.

April, not a member of the committee, attended all meetings as the headmaster's secretary, which saved the committee from appointing one of its own. It also meant that only information deemed important by Roscoe made it to the typed minutes. Lastly, it gave the two a legitimate excuse to be together.

"Where were you this time?" Irene Miller, Jody's mother, asked, an edge of disapproval in her voice since Maury McKinchie missed too many meetings, in her estimation.

"New York." He waited until Roscoe took a seat then continued. "I have good news." The group leaned toward him. "I met with Walter Harnett at Columbia. He loves our idea of a film department. He has promised us two video cameras. These are old models, but they work fine. New, this camera sells for fifty-four thousand dollars. We're on our way." He beamed.

After the applause, Little Mim, chair of the fund-raising committee, spoke. "That is the most exciting news! With preparation on our part, I think we can get approval from the board of directors to develop a curriculum."

"Only if we can finance the department." Roscoe folded his hands together. "You know how conservative the board is. Reading, writing, and arithmetic. That's it. But if we can finance one year— and I have the base figures here—then I hope and believe the positive response of students and parents will see us through the ensuing year. The board will be forced into the twentieth century"—he paused for effect—"just as we cross into the twenty-first."

They laughed.

"Is the faculty for us?" Irene Miller asked, eager to hitch on to whatever new bandwagon promised to deliver the social cachet she so desired.

"With a few notable exceptions, yes," Roscoe replied.

"Sandy Brashiers," April blurted out, then quickly clamped her mouth shut. Her porcelain cheeks flushed. "You know what a purist he is," she mumbled.

"Give him an enema," Maury said, and noted the group's

shocked expression. "Sorry. We say that a lot on a film shoot. If someone is really a pain in the ass, he's called the D.B. for douche bag."

"Maury." Irene cast her eyes down in fake embarrassment.

"Sorry. The fact remains, he is an impediment."

"I'll take care of Sandy," Roscoe Fletcher smoothly asserted.

"I wish someone would." Doak Mincer, a local bank president, sighed. "Sandy has been actively lobbying against this. Even when told the film department would be a one-year experimental program, totally self-sufficient, funded separately, the whole nine yards, he's opposed—adamantly."

"Has no place in academia, he says." Irene, too, had been lobbied.

"What about that cinematographer you had here mid-September? I thought that engendered enthusiasm." Marilyn pointed her pencil at Roscoe.

"She was a big hit. Shot film of some of the more popular kids, Jody being one, Irene."

"She loved it." Irene smiled. "You aren't going to encounter resistance from parents. What parent would be opposed to their child learning new skills? Or working with a pro like Maury? Why, it's a thrill."

"Thank you." Maury smiled his big smile, the one usually reserved for paid photographers.

He had enjoyed a wonderful directing career in the 1980s, which faded in the '90s as his wife's acting career catapulted into the stratosphere. She was on location so much that Maury often forgot he had a wife. Then again, he might have done so regardless of circumstances.

He had also promised Darla would lecture once a year at St. Elizabeth's. He had neglected to inform Darla, stage name Darla Keene. Real name Michelle Gumbacher. He'd cajole her into it on one of her respites home.

"Irene, did you bring your list of potential donors?" Little Mim asked. Irene nodded, launching into an intensely boring recitation of each potential candidate.

After the meeting Maury and Irene walked out to his country car, a Range Rover. His Porsche 911 was saved for warm days.

"How's Kendrick?" he inquired about her husband.

"Same old, same old."

This meant that all Kendrick did was work at the gardening center he had built from scratch and which at long last was generating profit.

She spied a carton full of tiny bottles in the passenger seat of the Rover. "What's all that?"

"Uh"—long pause—"essences."

"What?"

"Essences. Some cure headaches. Others are for success. Not that I believe it, but they can be soothing, I suppose."

"Did you bring this stuff back from New York?" Irene lifted an eyebrow.

"Uh—no. I bought them from BoomBoom Craycroft."

"Good God." Irene turned on her heel, leaving him next to his wildly expensive vehicle much favored by the British royals.

Later that evening when Little Mim reluctantly briefed her mother on the meeting—reluctant because her mother had to know everything—she said, "I think I can make the film department happen."

"That would be a victory, dear."

"Don't be so enthusiastic, Mother."

"I am enthusiastic. Quietly so, that's all. And I do think Roscoe enjoys chumming with the stars, such as they are, entirely too much. Greta Garbo. *That* was a star."

"Yes, Mother."

"And Maury—well, West Coast ways, my dear. Not Virginia."

"Not Virginia," a description, usually whispered by whites and blacks alike to set apart those who didn't measure up. This included multitudes.

Little Mim bristled. "The West Coast, well, they're more open-minded."

"Open-minded? They're porous."

8

"What have you got to say for yourself?" A florid Skip Hallahan glared at his handsome son.

"I'm sorry, Dad," Sean muttered.

"Don't talk to me. Talk to him!"

"I'm sorry, Mr. Fletcher."

Roscoe, hands folded across his chest, unfolded them. "I accept your apology, but did you really think phoning in my obituary was funny?"

"Uh—at the time. Guess not," he replied weakly.

"Your voice does sound a lot like your father's." Roscoe leaned forward. "No detentions. But—I think you can volunteer at the hospital for four hours each week. That would satisfy me."

"Dad, I already have a paper route. How can I work at the hospital?"

"I'll see that he does his job," Skip snapped, still mortified.

"If he falters, no more football."

"What?" Sean, horrified, nearly leapt out of his chair.

"You heard me," Roscoe calmly stated.

"Without me St. Elizabeth's doesn't have a prayer," Sean arrogantly predicted.

"Sean, the football season isn't as important as you learning: actions have consequences. I'd be a sorry headmaster if I let you off the hook because you're our best halfback . . . because someday you'd run smack into trouble. Actions have consequences. You're going to learn that right now. Four hours a week until New Year's Day. Am I clearly understood?" Roscoe stood up.

"Yes, sir."

"I asked you this before. I'll ask it one last time. Were you alone in this prank?"

"Yes, sir," Sean lied.

9

A ruddy sun climbed over the horizon. Father Michael, an early riser, enjoyed his sunrises as much as most people enjoyed sunsets. Armed with hot Jamaican coffee, his little luxury, he sat reading the paper at the small pine breakfast table overlooking the church's beautifully tended graveyard.

The Church of the Good Shepherd, blessed with a reasonably affluent congregation, afforded him a pleasant albeit small home on the church grounds. A competent secretary, Lucinda Payne Coles, provided much-needed assistance Mondays through Fridays. He liked Lucinda, who, despite moments of bitterness, bore her hardships well.

After her husband, Samson, lost all his money and got caught with his pants down in the bargain in an extramarital affair, Lucinda sank into a slough of despond. She applied when the job at the church became available and was happily hired even though she'd never worked a day in her life. She typed adequately, but, more important, she knew everyone and everyone knew her.

As for Samson, Father Michael remembered him daily in his prayers. Samson had been reduced to physical labor at Kendrick Miller's gardening business. At least he was in the best shape of his life and was learning to speak fluent Spanish, as some of his coworkers were Mexican immigrants.

Father Michael, starting on a second cup of coffee—two lumps of brown sugar and a dollop of Devonshire cream—blinked in surprise. He thought he saw a figure sliding through the early-morning mist.

That needed jolt of caffeine blasted him out of his seat. He grabbed a Barbour jacket to hurry outside. Quietly he moved closer to a figure lurking in the graveyard.

Samson Coles placed a bouquet of flowers on Ansley Randolph's grave.

Father Michael, a slightly built man, turned to tiptoe back to the cottage, but Samson heard him.

"Father?"

"Sorry to disturb you, Samson. I couldn't see clearly in the mist. Sometimes the kids drink in here, you know. I thought I could catch one in the act. I am sorry."

Samson cleared his throat. "No one visits her."

"She ruined herself, poor woman." Father Michael sighed.

"I know. I loved her anyway. I still loved Lucinda but . . . I couldn't stay away from Ansley." He sighed. "I don't know why Lucinda doesn't leave me."

"She loves you, and she's working on forgiveness. God sends us the lessons we need."

"Well, if mine is humility, I'm learning." He paused. "You won't tell her you saw me here, will you?"

"No."

"It's just that . . . sometimes I feel so bad. Warren doesn't visit her grave, and neither do the boys. You'd think at least once they'd visit their mother's grave."

"They're young. They think if they ignore pain and loss, it will fade away. Doesn't."

"I know." He turned, and both men left the graveyard, carefully shutting the wrought iron gate behind them.

At the northwest corner of the graveyard a massive statue of the Avenging Angel seemed to follow them with his eyes.

"I just so happen to have some of the best Jamaican coffee you would ever want to drink. How about joining me for a cup?"

"I hate to trouble you, Father."

"No trouble at all."

They imbibed the marvelous coffee and talked of love, responsibility, the chances for the Virginia football team this fall, and the curiousness of human nature as evidenced by the false obituary.

A light knock on the backdoor got Father Michael out of his chair. He opened the door. Jody Miller, one of his parishioners, wearing her sweats as she was on her way to early-morning field hockey practice, stood in the doorway, a bruise prominent on her cheek and a red mark near her eye that would soon blacken.

"Father Michael, I have to talk to you." She saw Samson at the table. "Uh—"

"Come on in."

"I'll be late for practice." She ran down the back brick walkway as Father Michael watched her with his deep brown eyes. He finally closed the door.

"Speaking of curious." Samson half smiled. "Everything is so important at that age."

It was.

Five minutes after Samson left, Skip Hallahan pulled into Father Michael's driveway with Sean in the passenger seat. Reluctantly, Sean got out.

"Father!" Skip bellowed.

Father Michael stuck his head out the backdoor. "Come in, Skip and Sean, I'm not deaf, you know."

"Sorry," Skip mumbled, then launched into Sean's misdeed before he'd taken a seat.

After Skip ranted for a half hour, Father Michael asked him to leave the room for a few minutes.

"Sean, I can see the humor in calling in the obituary. I really can. But can you see how you've upset people? Think of Mrs. Fletcher."

"I'm getting the idea," Sean replied ruefully.

"I suggest you call on Mrs. Fletcher and apologize. I also suggest you call Janice Walker, editor of the obituary page at the paper, and apologize, and lastly, write a letter of apology and send it to 'Letters to the Editor.' After that, I expect the paper will take your route away from you." The good priest tried to prepare him for retaliation.

Sean sat immobile for a long time. "All right, Father, I will."

"What possessed you to do this? Especially to your headmaster."

"Well, that was kind of the point." Sean suppressed a smile. "It wouldn't have been nearly as funny if I'd called in, uh, your obituary."

Father Michael rapped the table with his fingertips. "I see. Well, make your apologies. I'll calm down your father." He stood up to summon Skip Hallahan.

Sean stood also. "Thanks, Father."

"Go on. Get out of here." The priest clapped the young man on the back.

10

Every hamlet and town has its nerve centers, those places where people congregate to enjoy the delights of gossip. Not that men admit to gossiping: for them it's "exchanging information."

A small group of men stood outside the post office on the first Monday in October in buttery Indian-summer sunshine. The Reverend Herbert Jones, Fair Haristeen, Ned Tucker, Jim Sanburne—the mayor of Crozet—and Sandy Brashiers spoke forcefully about the football teams of Virginia, Tech, William and Mary, and, with a shudder, Maryland.

"Maryland's the one to beat, and it hurts me to say that," the Reverend Jones intoned. "And I never will say it in front of John Klossner."

John, a friend of Herb's, graduated from Maryland and never let his buddies forget it.

Another one of the "in" group, Art Bushey—absent this morning—had graduated from Virginia Military Institute, so there was no reason for argument there. Poor VMI's team couldn't do squat, a wretched reality for those who loved the institution and a sheer joy for those who did not.

"This is the year for Virginia, Herb. I don't care how hot Maryland has been up to now." Sandy Brashiers crossed his arms over his chest.

"Say, why aren't you in school today?" Herb asked.

"I've worked out a schedule with King Fletcher, so I don't go in until noon on Mondays." Sandy breathed in. "You know, I love young people, but they'll suck you dry."

"Too young to know what they're asking of us." Fair toed the gravel. "Now before we get totally off the subject, I want to put in a good word for William and Mary."

"Ha!" Jim Sanburne, a huge man in his middle sixties, almost as tall as Fair but twice as broad, guffawed.

"Give it up, Fair." Ned laughed.

"One of these days the Tribe will prevail." Fair, an undergraduate alumnus, held up the Victory V.

"How come you don't root for Auburn? That's where you went to veterinary school," Sandy said.

"Oh, I like Auburn well enough."

Harry, from the inside, opened the door to the post office and stood, framed in the light. "What are you guys jawing about? This is government property. No riffraff."

"Guess you'll have to go, Fair," Ned said slyly.

The other men laughed.

"We're picking our teams for this year." Jim explained the reasoning behind each man's choice.

"I pick Smith!"

"Since when does Smith have a football team?" Sandy Brashiers asked innocently.

"They don't, but if they did they'd beat VMI," Harry replied. "Think I'll call Art Bushey and torment him about it."

This provoked more laughter. Mrs. Murphy, roused from a midmorning catnap, walked to the open doorway and sat down. She exhaled, picked up a paw, and licked the side of it, which she rubbed on her face. She liked football, occasionally trying to catch the tiny ball as it streaked across the television screen. In her mind she'd caught many a bomb. Today football interested her not a jot. She ruffled her fur, smoothed it down, then strolled alongside the path between the post office and the market. She could hear Harry and the men teasing one another with outbursts of laughter. Then Miranda joined them to even more laughter.

Mrs. Murphy had lived all her life on this plot of Virginia soil. She watched the news at six and sometimes at eleven, although usually she was asleep by then. She read the newspapers by sitting right in front of Harry when she read. As near as she could tell, humans lived miserable lives in big cities. It was either that or newspapers worked on the Puritan principle of underlining misery so the reader would feel better about his or her own life. Whatever the reason, the cat found human news dull. It was one murder, car wreck, and natural disaster after another.

People liked one another here. They knew one another all their lives, with the occasional newcomer adding spice and speculation to the mix. And it wasn't as though Crozet never had bad things happen. People being what they are, jealousy, greed, and lust existed. Those caught paid the price. But in the main, the people were good. If nothing else they took care of their pets.

She heard a small, muffled sob behind Market Shiflett's store. She trotted to the back. Jody Miller, head in hands, was crying her heart out. Pewter sat at her sneakers, putting her paw on the girl's leg from time to time, offering comfort.

"I wondered where you were." Murphy touched noses with Pewter, then stared at the girl.

Jody's blackening eye caught her attention when the girl removed her hands from her face. She wiped her nose with the back of her hand, blinking through her tears. "Hello, Mrs. Murphy."

"Hello, Jody. What's the matter?" Murphy rubbed against her leg.

Jody stared out at the alleyway, absentmindedly stroking both cats.

"*Did she say anything to you?*"

"No," Pewter replied.

"*Poor kid. She took a pounding.*" Mrs. Murphy stood on her hind legs, putting her paws on Jody's left knee for a closer look at the young woman's injury. "*This just happened.*"

"*Maybe she got in a fight on the way to school.*"

"*She has field hockey practice early in the morning—Brooks does, too.*"

"*Oh, yeah.*" Pewter cocked her head, trying to capture Jody's attention. "*Maybe her father hit her.*"

Kendrick Miller possessed a vicious temper. Not that anyone outside of the family ever saw him hit his wife or only child, but people looked at him sideways sometimes.

The light crunch of a footfall alerted the cats. Jody, still crying, heard nothing. Sandy Brashiers, whose car was parked behind the market, stopped in his tracks.

"Jody!" he exclaimed, quickly bending down to help her.

She swung her body away from him. The cats moved out of the way. "I'm all right."

He peered at her shiner. "You've been better. Come on, I'll run you over to Larry Johnson. Can't hurt to have the doctor take a look. You can't take a chance with your eyes, honey."

"Don't call me honey." Her vehemence astonished even her.

"I'm sorry." He blushed. "Come on."

"No."

"Jody, if you won't let me take you to Dr. Johnson, then I'll have to take you home. I can't just leave you here."

The backdoor of the post office swung open, and Harry stepped out; she had heard Jody's voice. Miranda was right behind her.

"Oh, dear," Miranda whispered.

Harry came over. "Jody, that's got to hurt."

"I'm all right!" She stood up.

"That's debatable." Sandy was losing patience.

Miranda put a motherly arm around the girl's shoulders. "What happened?"

"Nothing."

"*She got pasted away,*" Pewter offered.

"I suggested that I take her to Larry Johnson—to be on the safe side." Sandy shoved his hands into his corduroy pockets.

Jody balefully implored Miranda with her one good eye. "I don't want anyone to see me."

"You can't hide for two weeks. That's about how long it will take for your raccoon eye to disappear." Harry didn't like the look of that eye.

"Now, Jody, you just listen to me," Miranda persisted. "I am taking you to Larry Johnson's. You can't play Russian roulette with your health. Mr. Brashiers will tell Mr. Fletcher that you're at the doctor's office so you won't get in trouble at school."

"Nobody cares about me. And don't call Mr. Fletcher. Just leave him out of it."

"People care." Miranda patted her and hugged her. "But for right now you come with me."

Encouraged and soothed by Miranda, Jody climbed into the older woman's ancient Ford Falcon.

Harry knitted her eyebrows in concern. Sandy, too. Without knowing it they were mirror images of one another.

Sandy finally spoke. "Coach Hallvard can be rough, but not that rough."

"Maybe she got into a fight with another kid at school," Harry said, thinking out loud.

"*Over what?*" Pewter asked.

"*Boys. Drugs. PMS.*" Mrs. Murphy flicked her tail in irritation.

"*You can be cynical.*" Pewter noticed a praying mantis in the crepe myrtle.

"*Not cynical. Realistic.*"

Tucker waddled out of the post office. Fast asleep, she had awakened to find no one in the P.O. "*What's going on?*"

"*High-school drama.*" The cats rubbed it in. "*And you missed it.*"

Larry Johnson phoned Irene Miller, who immediately drove to his office. But Jody kept her mouth shut . . . especially in front of her mother.

Later that afternoon, Janice Walker dropped by the post office.

"Harry, you ought to be a detective! How did you know it was Sean Hallahan? When you called me back yesterday to tell me, I wasn't sure, but he came by this morning to apologize. He even took time off from school to do it."

"Two and two." Harry flipped up the divider between the mail room and the public area. "He sounds like his dad. He can be a smart-ass, and hey, wouldn't it be wild to do something like that? He'll be a hero to all the kids at St. Elizabeth's."

"Never thought of it that way," Janice replied.

"You know, I was thinking of calling in BoomBoom Craycroft's demise." Harry's eyes twinkled.

Janice burst out laughing. "You're awful!"

11

Roscoe glanced out his window across the pretty quad that was the heart of St. Elizabeth's. Redbrick buildings, simple Federal style, surrounded the green. Two enormous oaks anchored either end, their foliage an electrifying orange-yellow.

Behind the "home" buildings, as they were known, stood later additions, and beyond those the gym and playing fields beckoned, a huge parking lot between them.

The warm oak paneling gave Roscoe's office an inviting air. A burl partner's desk rested in the middle of the room. A leather sofa, two leather chairs, and a coffee table blanketed with books filled up one side of the big office.

Not an academic, Roscoe made a surprisingly good headmaster. His lack of credentials bothered the teaching staff, who had originally wanted one of their own, namely Sandy Brashiers or even Ed Sugarman. But Roscoe over the last seven years had won over most of them. For one thing, he knew how to raise money as he had a "selling" personality and a wealth of good business contacts. For another, he was a good administrator. His MBA from the Wharton School at University of Pennsylvania stood him in good stead.

"Come in." He responded to the firm knock at the door, then heard a loud "Don't you dare!"

He quickly opened the door to find his secretary, April, and Sandy Brashiers yelling at each other.

April apologized. "He didn't ask for an appointment. He walked right by me."

"April, stop being so officious." Sandy brushed her off.

"You have no right to barge in here." She planted her hands on her slim hips.

Roscoe, voice soothing, patted her on her padded shoulder. "That's all right. I'm accustomed to Mr. Brashiers's impetuosity."

He motioned for Sandy to come in while winking at April, who blushed with pleasure.

"What can I do for you, Sandy?"

"Drop dead" was what Sandy wanted to say. Instead he cleared his throat. "I'm worried about Jody Miller. She's become withdrawn, and this morning I found her behind the post office. She had a bruised cheek and a black eye and refused to talk about it."

"There is instability in the home. It was bound to surface in Jody eventually." Roscoe did not motion for Sandy to sit down. He leaned against his desk, folding his arms across his chest.

"A black eye counts for more than instability. That girl needs help."

"Sandy," Roscoe enunciated carefully, "I can't accuse her parents of abuse without her collaboration. And who's to say Kendrick hit her? It could have been anybody."

"How can you turn away?" Sandy impulsively accused the florid, larger man.

"I am not turning away. I will investigate the situation, but I advise you to be prudent. Until we know what's amiss or until Jody herself comes forward, any accusation would be extremely irresponsible."

"Don't lecture me."

"Don't lecture me."

"You don't give a damn about that girl's well-being. You sure as hell give a damn about her father's contributions to your film project—money we could use elsewhere."

"I've got work to do. I told you I'll look into it." Roscoe dropped his folded arms to his sides, then pointed a finger in Sandy's reddening face. "Butt out. If you stir up a hornet's nest, you'll get stung worse than the rest of us."

"What's that shopworn metaphor supposed to mean?" Sandy clenched his teeth.

"That I know your secret."

Sandy blanched. "I don't have any secrets."

Roscoe pointed again. "Try me. Just try me. You'll never teach anywhere again."

Livid, Sandy slammed the door on his way out. April stuck her blond-streaked head back in the office.

Roscoe smiled. "Ignore him. The man thrives on emotional scenes. The first week of school he decried the fostering of competition instead of cooperation. Last week he thought Sean Hallahan should be censured for a sexist remark that I think was addressed to Karen Jensen—'Hey, baby!'" Roscoe imitated Sean. "Today he's frothing at the mouth because Jody Miller has a black eye. My God."

"I don't know how you put up with him," April replied sympathetically.

"It's my job." Roscoe smiled expansively.

"Maury McKinchie's on line two."

"Who's on line one?"

"Your wife."

"Okay." He punched line one. "Honey, let me call you back. Are you in the office?"

Naomi said she was, her office being in the building opposite his on the other side of the quad. He then punched line two. "Hello."

"Roscoe, I'd like to shoot some football and maybe field hockey practice . . . just a few minutes. I'm trying to pull together dynamic images for the alumni dinner in December."

"Got a date in mind?"

"Why don't I just shoot the next few games?" The director paused. "I've got footage for you to check. You'll like it."

"Fine." Roscoe smiled.

"How about a foursome this Saturday? Keswick at nine?"

"Great."

Roscoe hung up. He buzzed April. "You handled Sandy Brashiers very well," he told her.

"He gives me a pain. He just pushed right by me!"

"You did a good job. Your job description doesn't include tackling temporary principals and full-time busybodies."

"Thank you."

"Remind me to tell the coaches that Maury will be filming some football and hockey games."

"Will do."

He took his finger off the intercom button and sat in his swivel chair, feeling satisfied with himself.

12

Harry sorted her own mail, tossing most of it into the wastebasket. She spent each morning stuffing mailboxes. By the time she got to her own mail, she hadn't the patience to wade through appeals for money, catalogs, and flyers. Each evening she threw a canvas totebag jammed with her mail onto the bench seat of the old Ford truck. On those beautiful days when she walked home from work, she slung it over her shoulder.

She'd be walking for the next week regardless of weather because not only was the carburetor fritzed out on the truck, but a mouse had nibbled through the starter wires. Mrs. Murphy needed to step up her rodent control.

Harry dreaded the bill. No matter how hard she tried, she couldn't keep up with expenses. She lived frugally, keeping within a budget, but no matter how careful her plans, telephone companies changed rates, the electric company edged up its prices, and the county commissioners lived to raise Albemarle taxes.

She often wondered how people with children made it. They'd make it better if they didn't work for the postal service, she thought to herself.

Gray clouds, sodden, dropped lower and lower. The first big raindrop splattered as she was about two miles from home. Tee Tucker and Mrs. Murphy moved faster. Pewter, with a horror of getting wet, ran ahead.

"I've never seen that cat move that fast," Harry said out loud.

A dark green Chevy half-ton slowly headed toward her. She waved as Fair braked.

"Come on, kids," she called as the three animals raced toward Fair.

As if on cue the clouds opened the minute Harry closed the passenger door of the truck.

"Hope you put your fertilizer down."

"Back forty," she replied laconically.

He slowed for another curve as they drove in silence.

"You're Mary Sunshine."

"Preoccupied. Sorry."

They drove straight into the barn. Harry hopped out and threw on her raincoat. Fair put on his yellow slicker, then backed the truck out, parking at the house so Pewter could run inside. He returned to help Harry bring in the horses, who were only too happy to get fed.

Mrs. Murphy and Tucker stayed in the barn.

"These guys look good." Fair smiled at Gin Fizz, Tomahawk, and Poptart.

"Thanks. Sometimes I forget how old Tomahawk's getting to be, but then I forget how old I'm getting to be."

"We're only in our thirties. It's a good time."

She scooped out the sweet feed. "Some days I think it is. Some days I think it isn't." She tossed the scoop back into the feed bin. "Fair, you don't have to help. Lucky for me you came along the road when you did."

"Many hands make light work. You won't be riding tonight."

The rain, like gray sheets of iron, obscured the house from view.

"The weatherman didn't call for this, nor did Miranda."

"Her knee failed." He laughed. Miranda predicted rain according to whether her knee throbbed or not.

She clapped on an ancient cowboy hat, her rain hat. "Better make a run for it."

"*Why don't you put me under your raincoat?*" Mrs. Murphy asked politely.

Hearing the plaintive meow, Harry paused, then picked up the kitty, cradling her under her coat.

"Ready, steady, GO!" Fair sang out as he cut the lights in the barn.

He reached the backdoor first, opening it for Harry and a wet Tucker.

Once inside the porch they shook off the rain, hung up their coats, stamped their feet, and hurried into the kitchen. A chill had descended with the rain. The temperature plunged ten degrees and was dropping still.

She made fresh coffee while he fed the dog and cats.

Harry had doughnuts left over from the morning.

They sat down and enjoyed this zero-star meal. It was better than going hungry.

"Well—?"

"Well, what?" She swallowed, not wishing to speak with her mouth full.

"What's the matter?"

She put the rest of her glazed doughnut on the plate. "Jody Miller had a black eye and wouldn't tell anyone how she got it. The kid was crying so hard it hurt to see her."

"How'd you find out?"

"She cut classes and was sitting on the stoop behind Market's store."

"*I found her first.*" Pewter lifted her head out of the food bowl.

"*Pewter, you're such an egotist.*"

"*Look who's talking,*" the gray cat answered Mrs. Murphy sarcastically. "*You think the sun rises and sets on your fur.*"

"Miranda carried her over to Larry Johnson's. She stayed until Irene arrived. Irene wasn't too helpful, according to Miranda, a reliable source if ever there was one."

"Jody's a mercurial kid."

"Aren't they all?"

"I suppose." He got up to pour himself another coffee. "I'm finally warming up. Of course, it could be your presence."

"*I'm going to throw up.*" Pewter gagged.

"*You don't have a romantic bone in your body,*" Tucker complained.

"*In fact, Pewter, no one can see the bones in your body.*"

"*Ha, ha,*" the gray cat said dryly.

"Do you think it would be nosy if I called Irene? I'm worried."

"Harry, everyone in Crozet is nosy, so that's not an issue." He smiled. "Besides which, you and Miranda found her."

"*I found her,*" Pewter interjected furiously.

"You are not getting another morsel to eat." Harry shook her finger at the gray cat, who turned her back on her, refusing to have anything to do with this irritating human.

Harry picked up the old wall phone and dialed. "Hi, Irene, it's Mary Minor." She paused. "No trouble at all. I know Miranda was glad to help. I was just calling to see if Jody's all right."

On the other end of the line Irene explained, "She got into a fight with one of the girls at practice—she won't say which one—and then she walked into chemistry class and pulled a D on a pop quiz. Jody has never gotten a D in her life. She'll be fine, and thank you so much for calling. 'Bye."

" 'Bye." Harry hung up the receiver slowly. "She doesn't know any more than I do. She said the girls got into a fight at field hockey practice, and Jody got a D on a pop quiz in chemistry."

"Now you can relax. You've got your answer."

"Fair"—Harry gestured, both hands open—"there's no way that vain kid is going to walk into chemistry class with a fresh shiner. Jody Miller fusses with her makeup more than most movie stars. Besides, Ed Sugarman would have sent her to the infirmary. Irene Miller is either dumb as a stick or not telling the truth."

"I vote for dumb as a stick." He smiled. "You're making a

mountain out of a molehill. If Jody Miller lied to her mother, it's not a federal case. I recall you fibbing to your mother on the odd occasion."

"Not very often."

"Your nose is growing." He laughed.

Harry dialed Ed Sugarman, the chemistry teacher. "Hi, Ed, it's Mary Minor Haristeen." She paused a moment. "Do I need chemistry lessons? Well, I guess it depends on the kind of chemistry you're talking about." She paused. "First off, excuse me for butting in, but I want to know if Jody Miller came to your class today."

"Jody never came to class today," Ed replied.

"Well—that answers my question."

"In fact, I was about to call her parents. I know she was at field hockey practice because I drove by the field on my way in this morning. Is something wrong?"

"Uh—I don't know. She was behind Market's store this morning sporting a black eye and tears."

"I'm sorry to hear that. She's a bright girl, but her grades are sliding . . ." He hesitated. "One sees this often if there's tension in the home."

"Thanks, Ed. I hope I haven't disturbed you."

"You haven't disturbed me." He paused for a moment and then said as an aside, "Okay, honey." He then returned to Harry. "Doris says hello."

"Tell Doris I said hello also," Harry said.

Harry bid Ed good-bye, pressed the disconnect button, and thought for a minute.

"Want to go to a movie?"

"I'm not going out in that."

The rain pounded even harder on the tin roof. "Like bullets."

"I rented *The Madness of King George*. We could watch that."

"Popcorn?"

"Yep."

"If you'd buy a microwave, you could pop the corn a lot faster." He read the directions on the back of the popcorn packet.

"I'm not buying a microwave. The truck needs new starter

wires—the mice chewed them—needs new tires, too, and I'm even putting that off until I'm driving on threads." She slapped a pot on the stove. "And it needs a new carburetor."

After the movie, Fair hoped she'd ask him to stay. He made comment after comment about how slick the roads were.

Finally Harry said, "Sleep in the guest room."

"I was hoping I could sleep with you."

"Not tonight." She smiled, evading hurting his feelings. Since she was also evading her own feelings, it worked out nicely for her, temporarily, anyway.

The next morning, Fair cruised out to get the paper. The rain continued steady. He dashed back into the kitchen. As he removed the plastic wrapping and opened the paper, an eight-by-ten-inch black-bordered sheet of paper, an insert, fell on the floor. Fair picked it up. "What in the hell is this?"

13

"Maury McKinchie, forty-seven, died suddenly in his home October third," Fair mumbled as he read aloud Maury's cinematic accomplishments and the fact that he lettered in football at USC. He peered over Mrs. Murphy, who jumped on the paper to read it herself.

Both humans and the cat stood reading the insert. Pewter reposed on the counter. She was interested, but Murphy jumped up first. Why start the day with a fight? Tucker raced around the table, finally sitting on her mother's foot.

"What's going on?" Tucker asked.

"Tucker, Maury McKinchie is dead," Mrs. Murphy answered her.

"Miranda," Harry said when she picked up the phone, "I've just seen it."

"Well, I just saw Maury McKinchie jog down the lane between my house and the post office not ten minutes ago!"

"This is too weird." Harry's voice was even. "As weird as that rattail hair of his." She referred to the short little ponytail Maury wore at the nape of his neck. Definitely not Virginia.

"He wore a color-coordinated jogging suit. Really, the clothes that man wears." Miranda exhaled through her nostrils. "Roscoe was jogging with him."

"Guess he hasn't read the paper." Harry laughed.

"No." She paused. "Isn't this the most peculiar thing. If Sean's behind this again, he realized he can't phone in an obituary anymore. It can't be Sean, though—his father would kill him." She thought out loud.

"And he lost his paper route. Fired. At least, that's what I heard," Harry added.

"*Bombs away!*" Pewter launched herself from the counter onto the table and hit the paper, tearing it. Both cats and paper skidded off the table.

"Pewter!" Fair exclaimed.

"Aha!" Mrs. Hogendobber exclaimed when she heard Fair's voice in the background. "I knew you two would get back together," she gloated to Harry.

"Don't jump the gun, Miranda." Harry gritted her teeth, knowing a grilling would occur at the post office.

"See you at work," Miranda trilled.

14

"Not another prank!" the Reverend Herbert Jones said when he picked up his mail, commenting on the obituary insert in his paper that morning.

"A vicious person with unresolved authority-figure conflicts," BoomBoom Craycroft intoned. "A potent mixture of chamomile and parsley would help purify this tortured soul."

"Disgusting and not at all funny," Big Mim Sanburne declaimed.

"A sick joke," Lucinda Payne Coles said, picking up her mail and that of the Church of the Good Shepherd.

"Hasn't Maury been working with you on the big alumni fund-raising dinner?" Harry inquired.

"Yes," Little Mim replied.

"What's going on at St. Elizabeth's?" Harry walked out front.

"Nothing. Just because Roscoe and Maury are associated with

the school doesn't make the school responsible for these—what should I call them—?" Little Mim flared.

Her mother, awash in navy blue cashmere, tapped Little Mim's hand with a rolled-up magazine.

"Premature death notices." Mim laughed. "Sooner or later they will be accurate. Sean Hallahan has apologized to everyone involved. At least, that's what his father told me. Who has the paper route? That's the logical question."

Marilyn sniffed. Her mother could get her goat faster than anyone on earth. "Roger Davis has the paper route."

"Call his mother," Mim snapped. "And . . . are you listening to me?"

"Yes, Mother."

"Whoever is writing these upsetting things knows a lot about both men."

"Or is a good researcher," Herb's grave voice chimed in.

"Don't look at me," Harry joked. "I never learned how to correctly write in footnotes. You have to do that to be a good researcher."

"Don't be silly. You couldn't have graduated from Smith with honors without learning how to do footnotes." Big Mim unrolled the magazine, grimaced at the photo of an exploded bus, and rolled it back up again. "I'll tell you what's worse than incorrect footnotes . . . lack of manners. Our social skills are so eroded that people don't write thank-you notes anymore . . . and if they did, they couldn't spell."

"Mother, what does that have to do with Roscoe's and Maury's fake obits?"

"Rude. Bad manners." She tapped the magazine sharply on the edge of the counter.

"Hey!" Little Mim blurted, her head swiveling in the direction of the door.

Maury McKinchie pushed through, beheld the silence and joked, "Who died?"

"You," Harry replied sardonically.

"Ah, come on, my last movie wasn't that bad."

"Haven't you opened your paper?" Little Mim edged toward him.

"No."

Herb handed the insert to Maury. "Take a look."

"Well, I'll be damned." Maury whistled.

"Who do you think did this?" Miranda zoomed to the point.

He laughed heartily. "I can think of two ex-wives who would do it, only they'd shoot me first. The obit would be for real."

"You really don't have any idea?" Herb narrowed his eyes.

"Not a one." Maury raised his bushy eyebrows as well as his voice.

Big Mim checked her expensive Schaffhausen watch. "I'm due up at the Garden Club. We vote on which areas to beautify today. A big tussle, as usual. Good-bye, all. Hope you get to the bottom of this."

" 'Bye," they called after her.

Maury, though handsome, had developed a paunch. Running would remove it, he hoped. Being a director, he had a habit of taking charge, giving orders. He'd discovered that didn't work in Crozet. An even bigger shock had befallen him when Darla became the bread-winner. He was searching for the right picture to get his career back on track. He flew to L.A. once a month and burned up the phone and fax lines the rest of the time.

"Mother wants to create a garden around the old railroad sta-tion. What do you bet she gets her way?" Little Mim jumped to a new topic. There wasn't anything she could do about the fake obituary anyway.

"The odds are on her side." Harry picked up the tall metal wastebasket overflowing with paper.

"I can do that for you." Maury seized the wastebasket. "Where does it go?"

"Market's new dumpster," Miranda said.

"Take me one minute."

As he left, Little Mim said, "He's a terrible flirt, isn't he?"

"Don't pay any attention to him," Harry advised.

"I didn't say he bothered me."

Maury returned, placing the wastebasket next to the table where people sorted their mail.

"Thank you," Harry said.

He winked at her. "My pleasure. You can say you've encountered an angel today."

"Beg pardon?" Harry said.

"If I'm dead, I'm living uptown, Harry, not downtown." He laughed and walked out with a wave.

Susan Tucker arrived just as Miranda had begun her third degree on the subject of Fair staying over.

"Miranda, why do you do this to me?" Harry despaired.

"Because I want to see you happy."

"Telling everyone that my ex-husband spent the night isn't going to make me happy, and I told you, Miranda, nothing happened. I am so tired of this."

"Methinks the lady doth protest too much." Mrs. Hogendobber coyly quoted Shakespeare.

"Oh, pul-lease." Harry threw up her hands.

Susan, one eyebrow arched, said, "Something did happen. Okay, maybe it wasn't sex, but he got his foot in the door."

"And his ass in the guest room. It was raining cats and dogs."

"*I beg your pardon*," Mrs. Murphy, lounging in the mail cart, called out.

"All right." Harry thought the cat wanted a push so she gave her a ride in the mail cart.

"*I love this.* . . ." Murphy put her paws on the side of the cart.

"Harry, I'm waiting."

"For what?"

"For what's going on with you and Fair."

"NOTHING!"

Her shout made Tucker bark.

Pewter, hearing the noise, hurried in through the back animal door. "*What's the matter?*"

"*Mrs. H. and Susan think Mom's in love with Fair because he stayed at the house last night.*"

"Oh." Pewter checked the wastebasket for crumbs. "*They need to stop for tea.*"

Susan held up her hands. "You are so sensitive."

"Wouldn't you be?" Harry fired back.

"I guess I would."

"Harry, I didn't mean to upset you." Miranda, genuinely contrite, walked over to the small refrigerator, removing the pie she'd baked the night before.

Pewter was ecstatic.

Harry sighed audibly. "I want his attention, but I don't think I want him. I'm being perverse."

"Maybe vengeful is closer to the mark." Miranda pulled no punches.

"Well—I'd like to think I was a better person than that, but maybe I'm not." She glanced out the big front window. "Going to be a nice day."

"Well, my cherub is playing in the field hockey game, rain or shine," Susan said. "Danny's got football practice, so I'll watch the first half of Brooks's game and the last half of Danny's practice. I wish I could figure out how to be in two places at the same time."

"If I get my chores done, I'll drop by," Harry said. "I'd love to see Brooks on the attack. Which reminds me, got to call and see if my truck is ready."

"I thought you didn't have the money to fix it," Susan said.

"He'll let me pay over time." As she was making the call, Miranda and Susan buzzed about events.

"Miranda, do you think these false obituaries have anything to do with Halloween?" Harry asked as she hung up the phone.

"I don't know."

"*It's only the first week of October.*" Tucker thought out loud. "*Halloween is a long way away.*"

"*What about all those Christmas catalogs clogging the mail?*" Pewter hovered over the pie.

"*Humans like to feel anxious,*" Tucker declared.

"*Imagine worrying about Christmas now. They might not live to Christmas,*" Mrs. Murphy cracked.

The other two animals laughed.

"*You know what I would do if I were one of them?*" Pewter flicked off the dishcloth covering the pie. "*I'd go to an Arab country. That would take care of Christmas.*"

"*Take care of a lot else, too,*" Mrs. Murphy commented wryly.

Miranda noticed in the nick of time. "Shoo!"

Harry grabbed the phone. "Hello, may I have the obituary department?"

Miranda, Susan, the two cats, and the dog froze to listen.

"Obituary."

"Janice, have you heard about the insert?"

"Yes, but it's only in the papers of one route, Roger Davis's route. I can't be blamed for this one."

"I wouldn't want to be in Roger Davis's shoes right now," Harry said.

15

"I didn't do it." Roger, hands in his pants pockets, stared stubbornly at the headmaster and the temporary principal.

"You picked up the newspapers from the building at Rio Road?" Sandy questioned.

"Yes."

"Did you go through the papers?" Roscoe asked.

"No, I just deliver them. I had no idea that death notice on Mr. McKinchie was in there."

"Did anyone else go with you this morning? Like Sean Hallahan?"

"No, sir," Roger answered Roscoe Fletcher. "I don't like Sean."

Sandy took another tack. "Would you say that you and Sean Hallahan are rivals?"

Roger stared at the ceiling, then leveled his gaze at Sandy. "No. I don't like him, that's all."

"He's a bit of a star, isn't he?" Sandy continued his line of reasoning.

"Good football players usually are."

"No, I mean he's really a star now for putting the false obituary in the paper, Mr. Fletcher's obituary."

Roger looked from Sandy to Roscoe, then back to Sandy. "Some kids think it was very cool."

"Did you?" Roscoe inquired.

"No, sir," Roger replied.

"Could anyone have tampered with your papers without you knowing about it?" Roscoe swiveled in his chair to glance out the window. Children were walking briskly between classes.

"I suppose they could. Each of us who has a route goes to pick up our papers . . . they're on the landing. We've each got a spot because each route has a different number of customers. We're supposed to have the same number, but we don't. People cancel. Some areas grow faster than others. So you go to your place on the loading dock and pick up your papers. All I do is fold them to stick them in the tube. And on rainy days, put them in plastic bags."

"So someone could have tampered with your pile?" Roscoe persisted.

"Yes, but I don't know how they could do it without being seen. There are always people at the paper. Not many at that hour." He thought. "I guess it could be done."

"Could someone have followed after you on your route, pulled the paper out of the tube and put in the insert?" Sandy liked Roger but he didn't believe him. "One of your friends, perhaps?"

"Yes. It would be a lot of work."

"Who knows your paper route?" Roscoe glanced at the Queen Anne clock.

"Everyone. I mean, all my friends."

"Okay, Roger. You can go." Roscoe waved him away.

Sandy opened the door for the tall young man. "I really hope you didn't do this, Roger."

"Mr. Brashiers, I didn't."

Sandy closed the door, turning to Roscoe. "Well?"

"I don't know." Roscoe held up his hands. "He's an unlikely candidate, although circumstances certainly point to him."

"Damn kids," Sandy muttered, then spoke louder. "Have you investigated the Jody Miller incident further?"

"I spoke to Coach Hallvard. She said no fight occurred at practice. I'm going to see Kendrick Miller later today. I wish I knew what I was going to say."

16

Rumbling along toward St. Elizabeth's, Harry felt her heart sink lower and lower. The truck repairs cost $289.16, which demolished her budget. Paying over time helped, but $289 was $289. She wanted to cry but felt that it wasn't right to cry over money. She sniffled instead.

"*There's got to be a way to make more money,*" Mrs. Murphy whispered.

"*Catnip,*" Pewter replied authoritatively. "*She could grow acres of catnip, dry it, and sell it.*"

"*Not such a bad idea—could you keep out of the crop?*"

"*Could you?*" Pewter challenged.

They pulled into the school parking lot peppered with Mercedes Benzes, BMWs, Volvos, a few Porsches, and one Ford Falcon.

The game was just starting with the captains in the center of the field, Karen Jensen for St. Elizabeth's and Darcy Kelly for St. Anne's Belfield from Charlottesville.

Roscoe had pride of place on the sidelines. Naomi squeezed next to him. April Shively sat on Roscoe's left side. She took notes as he spoke, which drove Naomi wild. She struggled to contain her irritation. Susan and Miranda waved to Harry as she climbed up to them. Little Mim sat directly behind Roscoe. Maury, flirtatious, amused her with Hollywood stories about star antics. He told her she was naturally prettier than those women who had the help of plastic surgery, two-hundred-dollar haircuts, and fabulous lighting. Little Mim began to brighten.

Pretty Coach Renee Hallvard, her shiny blond pageboy swinging with each stride, paced the sidelines. St. Anne's won the toss. While Karen Jensen trotted to midfield, the other midfielder, Jody Miller, twirled her stick in anticipation.

Irene and Kendrick Miller sat high in the stands for a better view. Kendrick had requested that he and Roscoe get together after the game. His attendance was noted since he rarely turned up at school functions, claiming work kept him pinned down.

People commented on the fact that Sean Hallahan and Roger Davis weren't at the game. Everyone had an opinion on that.

St. Anne's, a powerhouse in field hockey and lacrosse, worked the ball downfield, but Karen Jensen, strong and fast, stole the ball from the attacker in a display of finesse that brought the Redhawk supporters to their feet.

Brooks, an attacker, sped along the side, then cut in, a basic pattern, but Brooks, slight and swift, dusted her defender to pick up Karen's pinpoint pass. She fired a shot at the goalie, one of the best in the state, who gave St. Anne's enormous confidence.

The first quarter, speedy, resulted in no score.

"Brooks has a lot of poise under pressure." Harry was proud of the young woman.

"She's going to need it," Susan predicted.

"Quite a game." Miranda, face flushed, was remembering her days of field hockey for Crozet High in 1950.

The second quarter the girls played even faster and harder. Darcy Kelly drew first blood for St. Anne's. Karen Jensen, jogging back to the center, breathed a few words to her team. They struck back immediately with three razor-sharp passes resulting in a goal off the stick of Elizabeth Davis, Roger's older sister.

At halftime both coaches huddled with their girls. The trainers exhausted themselves putting the teams back together. The body checks, brutal, were taking their toll.

Sandy Brashiers, arriving late, sat on the corner of the bleachers.

"Jody's playing a good game." Roscoe leaned down to talk low to Sandy. "Maybe this will be easier than I thought."

"Hope so," Sandy said.

"Roscoe," Maury McKinchie teased him, "what kind of headmaster are you when a kid puts your obituary in the paper?"

"Looks who's talking. Maury, the walking dead," Roscoe bellowed.

"Only in Hollywood," Maury said, making fun of himself. "Oh, well, I've made a lot of mistakes on all fronts."

Father Michael, sitting next to Maury, said, "To err is human, to forgive divine."

"To err is human, to forgive is extraordinary." Roscoe chuckled.

They both shut up when Mrs. Florence Rubicon, the aptly, or perhaps prophetically, named Latin teacher, waved a red-and-gold Redhawks pennant and shouted, "*Carpe diem—*"

Sandy shouted back, finishing the sentence, "*Quam minimum credula postero.*" Meaning "Don't trust in tomorrow."

Those who remembered their Latin laughed.

A chill made Harry shiver.

"Cold?" Miranda asked.

"No—just"—she shrugged—"a notion."

The game was turning into a great one. Both sides cheered themselves hoarse, and at the very end Teresa Pietro scored a blazing goal for St. Anne's. The Redhawks, crestfallen, dragged off the field, hurt so badly by the defeat that they couldn't rejoice in how spectacularly they had played. It would take time for them to realize they'd participated in one of the legendary field hockey games.

Jody Miller, utterly wretched because Teresa Pietro had streaked by her, was stomping off the field, her head down. Her mother ran out to console her; her father stayed in the stands to talk to people and to wait for Roscoe, besieged, as always.

When Maury McKinchie walked over to soothe her, she hit him in the gut with her stick. He keeled over.

Irene, horrified, grabbed the stick from her daughter's hand. She looked toward Kendrick, who had missed the incident.

Coach Hallvard quickly ran over. Brooks, Karen, Elizabeth, and Jody's other teammates stared in disbelief.

"Jody, go to the lockers—NOW," the coach ordered.

"I think she'd better come home with me," Irene said tightly.

"Mrs. Miller, I'll send her straight home. In fact, I'll drive her home, but I need to talk to her first. Her behavior affects the entire team."

Jody, white-lipped, glared at everyone, then suddenly laughed. "I'm sorry, Mr. McKinchie. If only I'd done that to Teresa Pietro."

Maury, gasping for breath, smiled gamely. "I don't look anything like Teresa Pietro."

"Are you all right?" Coach Hallvard asked him.

"Yes, it's the only time I've been grateful for my spare tire."

Coach Hallvard put her hand under Jody's elbow, propelling her toward the lockers.

Roscoe turned around to look up to Kendrick, who was being filled in on the incident. He whispered to his wife, "Go see what you can do for Maury." Then he said to April, hovering nearby, "I think you'd better go to the locker room with Coach Hallvard and the team, right?"

"Right." April trotted across the field, catching up with Naomi, who pretended she was happy for the company.

Father Michael felt a pang for not pursuing Jody the morning she came to see him. He was realizing how much she had needed him then.

Brooks, confused like the rest of her teammates, obediently walked back to the locker room while the St. Anne's team piled on the bus.

Mrs. Murphy, prowling the bleachers now that everyone was down on the sidelines, jerked her head up when she caught a whiff, a remnant of strong perfume.

"Ugh." Pewter seconded her opinion.

They watched Harry chat with her friends about the incident as Roscoe glided over to Kendrick Miller. Sandy Brashiers also watched him, his eyes narrow as slits.

The two men strolled back to the bleachers, not thinking twice about the cats sitting there.

Kendrick glanced across the field at a now upright Maury attended by Irene and Naomi. "He's got both our wives buzzing around him. I guess he'll live."

Roscoe, surprised at Kendrick's cool response, said, "Doesn't sound as if you want him to—"

Kendrick, standing, propped one foot on the bleacher higher than the one he was standing on. "Don't like him. One of those dudes who comes here with money and thinks he's superior to us. That posture of detached amusement wears thin."

"Perhaps, but he's been very good to St. Elizabeth's."

Quickly Kendrick said, "I understand your position, Roscoe, you'd take money from the devil if you had to. You're a good businessman."

"I'd rather be a good headmaster," Roscoe replied coolly. "I was hoping you could illuminate me concerning Jody."

"Because she hit Maury?" His voice rose. "Wish I'd seen it."

"No, although that's an issue now. She skipped school the other day with a black eye. She said she got it in practice, but Coach Hallvard said, no, she didn't and as far as she knew there were no fights after practice. Does she roughhouse with neighborhood kids or—?"

"Do I beat her?" Kendrick's face darkened. "I know what people say behind my back, Roscoe. I don't beat my daughter. I don't beat my wife. Hell, I'm not home enough to get mad at them. And yes—I have a bad temper."

Roscoe demurred. "Please, don't misunderstand me. My concern is the well-being of every student at St. Elizabeth's. Jody, a charming young girl, is, well, more up and down lately. And her grades aren't what they were last year."

"I'll worry about it when the first report card comes out." Kendrick leaned on his knee.

"That will be in another month. Let's try to pull together and get those grades up before then." Roscoe's smile was all mouth, no eyes.

"You're telling me I'm not a good father." Kendrick glowered. "You've been talking to my bride, I suppose." The word "bride" dripped with venom.

"No, no, I haven't." Roscoe's patience began to erode.

"You're a rotten liar." Kendrick laughed harshly.

"Kendrick, I'm sorry I'm wasting your time." He stepped down out of the bleachers and left a furious Kendrick to pound down and leave in the opposite direction.

Sandy Brashiers awaited Roscoe at the other end. "He doesn't look too happy."

"He's an ass." Roscoe, sensitive and tired, thought he heard implicit criticism in Sandy's voice.

"I waited for you because I think we need to have an assembly or small workshop about how to handle losing. Jody's behavior was outrageous."

Roscoe hunched his massive shoulders. "I don't think we have to make that big a deal out of it."

"You and I will never see eye to eye, will we?" Sandy said.

"I'll handle it," Roscoe said sternly.

A pause followed, broken by Sandy. "I don't want to make you angry. I'm not trying to obstruct you, but this gives us a chance to address the subject of winning and losing. Sports are blown out of proportion anyway."

"They may be blown out of proportion, but they bring in alumni funds." Roscoe shifted his weight.

"We're an institution of learning, not an academy for sports."

"Sandy, not now. I'm fresh out of patience," Roscoe warned.

"If not now, when?"

"This isn't the time or place for a philosophical discussion of the

direction of secondary education in general or St. Elizabeth's in particular.'' Roscoe popped a hard strawberry candy in his mouth and
moved off in the direction of the girls' locker room. Perhaps April
had some information for him. He noticed that Naomi had shepherded Maury toward the quad, so he assumed she would be serving
him coffee, tea, or spirits in her office. She had a sure touch with
people.

The cats scampered out from under the bleachers, catching up
with Harry, who was in the parking lot calling for them.

17

Late that night the waxing moon flitted between inky boiling clouds. Mrs. Murphy, unable to sleep, was hunting in the paddock closest to the barn. A sudden gust of wind brought her nose up from the ground. She sniffed the air. A storm, a big one, was streaking in.

Simon, moving fast for him, ran in from the creek. Overhead Flatface swooped low, banked, then headed out to the far fields for one more pass before the storm broke.

"That's it for me." Simon headed to the open barn door. "Besides, bobcat tracks in the creekbed."

"Good enough reason."

"Are you coming in?"

"In a minute." She watched the gray animal with the long rat tail shuffle into the barn.

A light wind rustled the leaves. She saw the cornstalks sway, then wiggle in Harry's small garden by the corner of the barn. This proved a handy repository for her "cooked" manure. A red fox, half grown, sashayed out the end, glanced over her shoulder, beheld Mrs. Murphy, put her nose up, and walked away.

Mrs. Murphy loved no fox, for they competed for the same game.

"You stay out of my corn rows," she growled.

"You don't own the world," came the belligerent reply.

A lone screech froze both of them.

"She's a killer." The fox flattened for a minute, then got up.

"You're between a storm and a bobcat. Where's your den?"

"I'm not telling you."

"Don't tell me, but you'd better hike to it fast." A big splat landed on the cat. She thought about the fox's predicament. "Go into the shavings shed until the storm blows over and the bobcat's gone. Just don't make a habit of it."

Without a word the fox scooted into the shavings shed, burrowing down in the sweet-smelling chips as the storm broke overhead.

The tiger cat, eyes widened, listened for the bobcat. Another more distant cry, like a woman screaming, told her that the beast headed back to the forest, her natural home. Since the pickings were so good in the fall—lots of fat mice and rats gorged on fallen grain plus fruits left drying on the vine—the bobcat ventured closer to the human habitation.

The wind stiffened, the trees gracefully bent lower. The field mouse Mrs. Murphy patiently tracked wanted to stay dry. She refused to poke her nose out of her nest.

More raindrops sent the cat into the barn. She climbed the ladder. Simon was arranging his sleeping quarters. His treasures, spread around him, included a worn towel, one leather riding glove, a few scraps of newspaper, and a candy bar that he was saving for a rainy day, which it was.

"Simon, don't you ever throw anything out?"

He smiled. "My mother said I was a pack rat, not a possum."

The force of the rain, unleashed, hit like a baseball bat against the north side of the barn. Flatface, claws down, landed in her cupola. She glanced down at the two friends, ruffled her feathers, then shut her eyes. She disdained earthbound creatures.

"*Flatface,*" Simon called up to her, "*before you go to sleep, how big is the* bobcat?"

"*Big enough to eat you.*" She laughed with a whooing sound.

"*Really, how big?*" he pressed.

She turned her big head nearly upside down. "*Thirty to forty pounds and still growing. She's quick, lightning-quick, and smart. Now, if you two peons don't mind, I'm going to sleep. It's turning into a filthy night.*"

Mrs. Murphy and Simon caught up on the location of the latest beaver dam, fox dens, and one bald eagle nest. Then the cat told him about the false obituaries.

"*Bizarre, isn't it?*"

Simon pulled his towel into his hollowed-out nest in the straw. "*People put out marshmallows to catch raccoons. Us, too. We love marshmallows. Sure enough, one of us will grab the marshmallow. If we're lucky, the human wants to watch us. If we're unlucky, we're trapped or the marshmallow is poisoned. I think a human is putting out a marshmallow for another human.*"

Mrs. Murphy sat a long time, the tip of her tail slowly wafting to and fro. "*It's damned queer bait, Simon, telling someone he's dead.*"

"*Not just him—everyone.*"

18

The storm lashed central Virginia for two days, finally moving north to discomfort the Yankees.

Harry's father said storms did Nature's pruning. The farm, apart from some downed limbs, suffered little damage, but a tree was down on the way to Blair Bainbridge's house.

On Saturday, Harry borrowed his thousand-dollar power washer. Merrily she blasted the old green-and-yellow John Deere tractor, her truck, the manure spreader, and, in a fit of squeaky-clean mania, the entire interior of the barn. Not a cobweb remained.

The three horses observed this from the far paddock. By now they were accustomed to Harry's spring and fall fits.

Other humans feeling those same urges worked on Saturday. Miranda aired her linens as she planted her spring bulbs. She'd need the rest of Sunday to finish the bulbs.

The Reverend Jones stocked his woodpile and greeted the chimney sweep by touching his top hat. A little superstition never hurt a pastor.

Fair Haristeen decided to run an inventory on equine drugs at the clinic only to repent as the task devoured the day.

BoomBoom Craycroft, adding orange zest to her list of essences, peeled a dozen of them.

Susan Tucker attacked the attic while Ned edged every tree and flower bed until he thought his fillings would fall out of his teeth from the vibrations of the machine.

Big Mim supervised the overhaul of her once-sunk pontoon boat.

Little Marilyn transferred the old records of St. Elizabeth's bene-factors to a computer. Like Fair, she was sorry she had started the job.

Sandy Brashiers made up the questions for a quiz on *Macbeth*.

Jody Miller worked at the car wash with Brooks, Karen, and Roger.

Because of the storm, the car wash was jam-packed. The kids hadn't had time for lunch, so Jody took everyone's order. It was her turn to cross Route 29 and get sandwiches at the gas station—deli on the southwest corner. The Texaco sat between the car wash and the intersection. If only that station had a deli, she wouldn't have to cross the busy highway.

Jimbo Anson slipped her twenty-five dollars for everyone's lunch, his included, as they were famished.

As the day wore on, the temperature climbed into the mid-sixties. The line of cars extended out to Route 29.

Roscoe Fletcher, his Mercedes station wagon caked in mud, pa-tiently waited in line. He had turned off Route 29 and moved forward enough to be right in front of the Texaco station. The car wash was behind the gas station itself, so the kids did not yet know their headmaster was in line and he didn't know how many cars were in front of him. The car stereo played *The Marriage of Figaro*. He sang aloud with gusto.

The line crept forward.

Jody headed down to the intersection. Five minutes later she dashed back into the office.

"Where's the food?" Roger, hungry, inquired as he reached in for another dry towel.

She announced, "Mr. Fletcher is in line! He hasn't seen me yet. I'll go as soon as he gets through the line."

"I'll starve by then," Roger said.

"He'll be cool." Karen stuck her head in the door as Roger threw her a bottle of mag washer for aluminum hubcaps.

"Maybe—but I don't want a lecture. I know I was wrong to hit Mr. McKinchie." Her voice rose. "I've had about all the help I can stand. I was wrong. Okay. I apologized. Guess you don't want to see him either." She pointed at Roger, who ignored her.

"Well, he's past the Texaco station. You'd better hide under the desk," Karen yelled. "Jeez, I think everyone in the world is here today." She heard horns beeping out on Route 29. Irene Miller had pulled in behind Roscoe, then Naomi Fletcher in her blue Miata. BoomBoom Craycroft, car wafting fragrances, was just ahead of him.

Roger waved up another car. He bent his tall frame in two as the driver rolled down the window. "What will it be?"

"How about a wash only?"

"Great. Put it in neutral and turn off your car radio."

The driver obeyed instructions while Karen and Brooks slopped the big brushes into the soapy water, working off the worst of the mud.

"Hey, there's Father Michael." Karen noticed the priest's black old-model Mercury. "You'd think the church would get him a better car." She yelled so Jody, scrunched under the desk, could hear her.

"It runs," Brooks commented on the car.

"How many are in the line now?" Roger wiped the sweat from his forehead with the back of his arm as Jimbo walked down to the intersection to direct drivers to form a double line. He needed to unclog the main north-south artery of Charlottesville.

"Number twenty-two just pulled in," Brooks replied.

"Unreal." Karen whistled.

Roscoe rolled down his window, flooding the car wash with Mozart. He was three cars away from his turn.

"You-all should learn your Mozart," he called to them. "Greatest composer who ever lived."

His wife shouted from her car, "It's the weekend, Roscoe. You can't tell them what to do."

"Right!" Karen laughed, waving at Naomi.

"I bet you listen to Melissa Etheridge and Sophie B. Hawkins," Roscoe said as he offered her strawberry hard candy, which she refused.

"Yeah." Karen turned her attention to the car in front of her. "They're great. I like Billy Ray Cyrus and Reba McEntire, too."

Irene rolled her window down. "Where's Jody?"

"She went to the deli to get our lunches, and I hope she hurries up!" Roger told a half-truth.

"What about Bach?" Roscoe sang out, still on his music topic.

"The Beatles," Karen answered. "I mean, that's like rock Bach."

"No, Bill Haley and the Comets are like rock Bach," Roscoe said as he sucked on the candy in his mouth. "Jerry Lee Lewis."

The kids took a deep breath and yelled and swung their hips in unison, "Elvis!"

By the time Roscoe put his left tire into the groove, everyone was singing "Hound Dog," which made him laugh. He noticed Jody peeking out of the office. The laughter, too much for her, had lured her from under the desk.

He pointed his finger at her. "You ain't nothin' but a hound dog."

She laughed, but her smile disappeared when her mother yelled at her. "I thought you were at the deli?"

"I'm on my way. We're backed up," she said since she'd heard what Roger told her mother.

"Mr. Fletcher, shut your window," Karen advised as the station wagon lurched into the car wash.

"Oh, right." He hit the electric button, and the window slid shut with a hum.

As the tail end of the Mercedes disappeared in a sheet of water, the yellow neon light flashed on and Karen waved Irene on. "He's so full of shit," she said under her breath.

BoomBoom hollered out her window, "Stress. Irene, this is too much stress. Come meet me at Ruby Tuesday's after the car wash."

"Okay," Irene agreed. Her left tire was in the groove now. "I want the works." Irene handed over fifteen dollars. Karen made change.

Roger, at the button to engage the track, waited for Roscoe to finish. The light telling him to put through the next vehicle didn't come on. Minutes passed.

"I'm in a hurry." Irene tried to sound pleasant.

"It's been like this all day, Mrs. Miller." Karen smiled tightly.

Brooks looked down the line. "Maybe Mr. Fletcher's out but the light didn't come on. I'll go see."

Brooks loped alongside the car wash, arriving at the end where the brown station wagon, nose out, squatted. The tail of the vehicle remained on the track. The little metal cleats in the track kept pushing the car.

Brooks knocked on the window. Roscoe, sitting upright, eyes straight ahead, didn't reply.

"Mr. Fletcher, you need to move out."

No reply. She knocked harder. Still no reply.

"Mr. Fletcher, please drive out." She waited, then opened the door. The first thing she noticed was that Mr. Fletcher had wet his pants, which shocked her. Then she realized he was dead.

19

It wasn't funny, but Rick Shaw wanted to laugh. Mozart blared through the speakers, and the car's rear end shone like diamonds after endless washings.

Naomi Fletcher, in shock, had been taken home by an officer.

Diana Robb, a paramedic with the rescue squad, patiently waited while Sheriff Shaw and Deputy Cooper painstakingly examined the car.

Jimbo Anson turned off the water when Rick told him it was okay.

Roger Davis directed traffic around the waiting line. He was relieved when a young officer pulled up in a squad car.

"Don't go yet," Tom Kline told Roger. "I'll need your help."

Obediently, Roger continued to direct traffic onto the Greenbrier side street. He wanted to comfort Brooks for the shock she had suffered, but that would have to wait.

Rick said under his breath to Coop, "Ever tell you about the guy who died on the escalator over in Richmond? I was fresh out of school. This was my first call as a rookie. No one could get on or off until cleared, and the store didn't turn off the motor. People were running in place. Super aerobics. 'Course the stiff rolled right up to the step-off, where his hair caught in the steps. By the time I reached him, he was half scalped."

"Gross." She knew that Rick wasn't unfeeling, but a law enforcement officer sees so much that a protective shell develops over emotions.

"Let's have the boys take photos, bag the contents of the station wagon." He reached in and, with his gloves on, snapped off the stereo. "Okay, we're done," he called over his shoulder to Diana Robb and Cooper behind him.

"Sheriff, what do you think?" the paramedic asked him.

"Looks like a heart attack. He's the right age for it. I've learned over the years, though, to defer to the experts. Unless Mrs. Fletcher objects, we'll send the body to Bill Moscowitz—he's a good coroner."

"If you don't stop smoking those Chesterfields, I'll be picking you up one of these days."

"Ah, I've stopped smoking so many times." He should have taken his pack out of his pocket and left it in the unmarked car; then she wouldn't have noticed. "Drop him at the morgue. I'll stop by Naomi's, so tell Bill to hold off until he hears from me." He turned to Coop. "Anything else?"

"Yeah, Roscoe's obituary was in the paper, remember?"

He rubbed his chin, the light chestnut stubble already appearing even though he'd shaved at six this morning. "We thought it was a joke."

"Boss, let's question a few people, starting with Sean Hallahan."

He folded his arms and leaned against the green unmarked car. "Let's wait—well, let me think about it. I don't want to jump the gun."

"Maury McKinchie's obituary was stuffed in the paper as well."

"I know. I know." He swept his eyes over the distressed Irene Miller and BoomBoom. Father Michael had administered the last rites. In the corner of his eye the lumpish figure of Jimbo Anson loomed. "I'd better talk to him before he runs to Dunkin' Donuts and eats another dozen jelly rolls." Jimbo ate when distressed. He was distressed a lot.

He half whispered, "Coop, take the basics from these folks, then let them go. I think BoomBoom is going to code on us." He used the medic slang word for "die."

Rick straightened his shoulders and walked the thirty yards to Jimbo.

"Sheriff, I don't know what to do. Nothing like this has ever happened to me. I just feel awful. Poor Naomi."

"Jimbo, death always upsets the applecart. Breathe deeply." He clapped the man on the back. "That's better. Now you tell me what happened."

"He went through the car wash, well I mean, I didn't see him, the kids were up front, and when the car didn't roll off she, I mean Brooks, ran around to see if the pedal hadn't released on the belt and, well, Roscoe was gone."

"Did you see him at all?"

"No, I mean, not until I came back with Brookie. Kid had some sense, I can tell you. She didn't scream or cry. She ran to my office, told me Roscoe was dead, and I followed her to there." He pointed.

"That's fine. I may be talking to you again, but it looks like a heart attack or stroke. These things happen."

"Business was great today." A mournful note crept into his voice.

"You'll be able to reopen before long. I'm going to impound the car, just routine, Jimbo. You won't have to worry about the vehicle being parked here."

"Thanks, Sheriff."

Rick clapped him on the back again and walked into the air-conditioned office—the day had turned unusually hot—where Brooks, Jody, and Karen sat. Cooper was already there.

"Sheriff, we were establishing a time line." Coop smiled at the three young women.

"One thirty, about," Brooks said.

"Mr. Anson said you showed presence of mind," Rick complimented Brooks.

"I don't know. I feel so bad for Mr. Fletcher. He helped me get into St. Elizabeth's after the semester started."

"Well, I'm not the Reverend Jones but I do believe that Roscoe Fletcher is in a better place. Much as you'll miss him, try to think of that."

"Jody, did you notice anything?" Coop asked.

"No. He said 'hi' and that was it. Karen and Brooks scrubbed down his bumpers. I think Roger pressed the button to send him in."

"Where is Roger?" Rick said.

"Directing traffic," Karen replied.

"Good man to have around."

This startled the two girls, who had never thought of Roger as anything other than a tall boy who was quiet even in kindergarten. Brooks was beginning to appreciate Roger's special qualities.

"Was there anything unusual about Mr. Fletcher or anyone else today?"

"No." Karen twirled a golden hair around her forefinger.

"Girls, if anything comes to mind, call me." He handed around his card.

"Is something wrong, something other than the fact that Mr. Fletcher is dead?" Brooks inquired shrewdly.

"No. This is routine."

"It's weird to be questioned." Brooks was forthright.

"I'm sorry you all lost Mr. Fletcher. I know it was a shock. I have to ask questions, though. I don't mean to further upset you. My job is to collect details, facts, like little pieces of a mosaic."

"We understand," Karen said.

"We're okay," Brooks fibbed.

"Okay then." He rose and Coop also handed her card to the three girls.

As she trudged across the blacktop to motion Roger from Green-brier Drive, she marveled at the self-possession of the three high school girls. Usually, something like this sent teenage girls into a crying jag. As far as she could tell, not one tear had fallen, but then BoomBoom, never one to pass up the opportunity to emote, was crying enough for all of them.

20

Johnny Pop, the 1958 John Deere tractor, rolled through the meadow thick with goldenrod. Tucker pouted by a fallen walnut at the creek. Mrs. Murphy sat in Harry's lap. Tucker, a trifle too big and heavy, envied the tiger her lap status.

As the tractor popped by, she turned and gazed into the creek. A pair of fishy eyes gazed right back. Startled, Tucker took a step back and barked, then sheepishly sat down again.

The baking sun and two days of light winds had dried out the wet earth. Harry, determined to get one more hay cutting before winter, fired up Johnny Pop the minute she thought she wouldn't get stuck. She couldn't hear anything, so Mrs. Hogendobber startled her when she walked out into the meadow.

Tucker, intent on her bad mood, missed observing the black Falcon rumbling down the drive.

Miranda waved her arms over her head. "Harry, stop!"

Harry immediately flipped the lever to the left, cutting off the motor. "Miranda, what's the matter? What are you doing out here on gardening day?"

"Roscoe Fletcher's dead—for real, this time."

"What happened?" Harry gasped.

Mrs. Murphy listened. Tucker, upon hearing the subject, hurried over from the creek.

Pewter was asleep in the house.

"Died at the car wash. Heart attack or stroke. That's what Mim says."

"Was she there?"

"No. I forgot to ask her how she found out. Rick Shaw told Jim Sanburne, most likely, and Jim told Mim."

"It's ironic." Harry shuddered.

"The obit?"

Harry nodded. Mrs. Murphy disagreed. "*It's not ironic. It's murder. Wait and see. Cat intuition.*"

21

Sean Hallahan pushed a laundry cart along a hallway so polished it reflected his image.

The double doors at the other end of the corridor swung open. Karen and Jody hurried toward him.

"How'd you get in here?" he asked.

Ignoring the question, Jody solemnly said, "Mr. Fletcher's dead. He died at the car wash."

"What?" Sean stopped the cart from rolling into them.

Karen tossed her ponytail. "He went in and never came out."

"Went in what?" Sean appeared stricken, his face white.

"The car wash," Jody said impatiently. "He went in the car wash, but at the other end, he just sat. Looks like he died of a heart attack."

"Are you making this up?" He smiled feebly.

"No. We were there. It was awful. Brooks Tucker found him."

"For real," he whispered.

"For real." Jody put her arm around his waist. "No one's going to think anything. Really."

"If only I hadn't put that phony obituary in the paper." He gulped.

"Yeah," the girls chimed in unison.

"Wait until my dad hears about this. He's going to kill me." He paused. "Who knows?"

"Depends on who gets to the phone first, I guess." Karen hadn't expected Sean to be this upset. She felt sorry for him.

"We came here first before going home. We thought you should know before your dad picks you up."

"Thanks," he replied, tears welling in his eyes.

22

Father Michael led the assembled upper and lower schools of St. Elizabeth's in a memorial service. Naomi Fletcher, wearing a veil, was supported by Sandy Brashiers with Florence Rubicon, the Latin teacher, on her left side. Ed Sugarman, the chemistry teacher, escorted a devastated April Shively.

Many of the younger children cried because they were supposed to or because they saw older kids crying. In the upper school some of the girls carried on, whipping through boxes of tissues. A few of the boys were red-eyed as well, including, to everyone's surprise, Sean Hallahan, captain of the football team.

Brooks reported all this to Susan, who told Harry and Miranda when they joined her at home for lunch.

"Well, he ate too much, he drank too much, and who knows what else he did—too much." Susan summed up Roscoe's life.

"How's Brooks handling it?" Harry inquired.

"Okay. She knows people die; after all, she watched her grandma die by inches with cancer. In fact, she said, 'When it's my time I want to go fast like Mr. Fletcher.' "

"I don't remember thinking about dying at all at her age," Harry wondered out loud.

"You didn't think of anything much at her age," Susan replied.

"Thanks."

"Children think of death often; they are haunted by it because they can't understand it." Miranda rested her elbows on the table to lean forward. "That's why they go to horror movies—it's a safe way to approach death, scary but safe."

Harry stared at Miranda's elbows on the table. "I never thought of that."

"I know I'm not supposed to have my elbows on the table, Harry, but I can't always be perfect."

Harry blinked. "It's not that at all—it's just that you usually are—perfect."

"Aren't you sweet."

"Harry puts her feet on the table, she's so imperfect."

"Susan, I do not."

"You know what was rather odd, though?" Susan reached for the sugar bowl. "Brooks told me Jody said she was glad Roscoe was dead. That she didn't like him anyway. Now that's a bit extreme even for a teenager."

"Yeah, but Jody's been extreme lately." Harry got up when the phone rang. Force of habit.

"Sit down. I'll answer it." Susan walked over to the counter and lifted the receiver.

"Yes. Of course, I understand. Marilyn, it could have an impact on your fund-raising campaign. I do suggest that you appoint an interim headmaster immediately." Susan paused and held the phone away from her ear so the others could hear Little Mim's voice. Then she spoke again. "Sandy Brashiers. Who else? No, no, and no," she said after listening to three questions. "Do you want me to call anyone? Don't fret, doesn't solve a thing."

"She'll turn into her mother," Miranda predicted as Susan hung up the receiver.

"Little Mim doesn't have her mother's drive."

"Harry, not only do I think she has her mother's drive, I think she'll run for her father's seat once he steps down as mayor."

"No way." Harry couldn't believe the timid woman she had known since childhood could become that confident.

"Bet you five dollars," Miranda smugly said.

"According to Little Mim, the Millers are divorcing."

"Oh, dear." Miranda hated such events.

"About time." Harry didn't like hearing of divorce either, but there were exceptions. "Still, there is no such thing as a good divorce."

"You managed," Susan replied.

"How quickly you forget. During the enforced six months' separation every married couple and single woman in this town invited my ex-husband to dinner. Who had me to dinner, I ask you?"

"I did." Miranda and Susan spoke in chorus.

"And that was it. The fact that I filed for the divorce made me an ogre. He was the one having the damned affair."

"Sexism is alive and well." Susan apportioned out seven-layer salad, one of her specialties. She stopped, utensils in midair. "Did either of you like Roscoe Fletcher?"

"*De mortuis nil nisi bonum*," Miranda advised.

"Speak nothing but good about the dead," Harry translated although it was unnecessary. "Maybe people said that because they feared the departed spirit was nearby. If they gave you trouble while alive, think what they could do to you as a ghost."

"Did you like Roscoe Fletcher?" Susan repeated her question.

Harry paused. "Yes, he had a lot of energy and good humor."

"A little too hearty for my taste." Miranda found the salad delicious. "Did you like him?"

Susan shrugged. "I felt neutral. He seemed a bit phony sometimes. But maybe that was the fund-raiser in him. He had to be a backslapper and glad-hander, I suppose."

"Aren't we awful, sitting here picking the poor man apart?" Miranda dabbed her lipstick-coated lips with a napkin.

The phone rang again. Susan jumped up. "Speaking of letting someone rest in peace, I'd like to eat in peace."

"You don't have to answer it," Harry suggested.

"Mothers always answer telephones." She picked up the jangling device. "Hello." She paused a long time. "Thanks for telling me. You've done the right thing."

Little Mim had rung back to say St. Elizabeth's had held an emergency meeting by conference call.

Sandy Brashiers had been selected interim headmaster.

23

Late that afternoon, a tired Father Michael bent his lean frame, folding himself into the confessional.

He usually read until someone entered the other side of the booth. The residents of Crozet had been particularly virtuous this week because traffic was light.

The swish of the fabric woke him as he half dozed over the volume of Thomas Merton, a writer he usually found provocative.

"Father, forgive me for I have sinned," came the formalistic opening.

"Go on, my child."

"I have killed and I will kill again." The voice was muffled, disguised.

He snapped to attention, but before he could open his mouth, the penitent slipped out of the booth. Confused, Father Michael pondered what to do. He felt he must stay in the booth for the confessional hours were well-known—he had a responsibility to his flock—but he wanted to call Rick Shaw immediately. Paralyzed, he grasped the book so hard his knuckles were white. The curtain swished again.

A man's voice spoke, deep and low. "Father forgive me for I have sinned."

"Go on, my child," Father Michael said as his mind raced.

"I've cheated on my wife. I can't help myself. I have strong desires." He stopped.

Father Michael advised him by rote, gave him a slew of Hail Marys and novenas. He kept rubbing his wristwatch until eventually his wrist began to hurt. As the last second of his time in the booth expired, he bolted out, grabbed the phone, and dialed Rick Shaw.

When Coop picked up the phone, he insisted he speak to the sheriff himself.

"Sheriff Shaw."

"Yes."

"This is Father Michael. I don't know"—sweat beaded on his forehead; he couldn't violate what was said in the confessional booth—"I believe a murder may have taken place."

"One has, Father Michael."

The priest's hands were shaking. "Oh, no. Who?"

"Roscoe Fletcher." Rick breathed deeply. "The lab report came back. He was poisoned by malathion. Not hard to get around here, so many farmers use it. It works with the speed of light so he had to have eaten it at the car wash. We've tested the strawberry hard candy in his car. Nothing."

"There couldn't be any mistake?"

"No. We have to talk, Father."

After Father Michael hung up the phone, he needed to collect his thoughts. He paced outside, winding up in the graveyard. Ansley Randolph's mums bloomed beautifully.

A soul was in peril. But if the confession he had heard was true, then another immortal soul was in danger as well. He was a priest. He should do something, but he didn't know what. It then occurred to him that he himself might be in danger—his body, not his soul.

Like a rabbit who hears the beagle pack, he twitched and cast his eyes around the graveyard to the Avenging Angel. It looked so peaceful.

24

His shirtsleeves rolled up, Kendrick Miller sat in his favorite chair to
read the paper.

Irene swept by. "Looking for your obituary?" She arched a delicate eyebrow.

"Ha ha." He rustled the paper.

Jody, reluctantly doing her math homework at the dining-room
table so both parents could supervise, reacted. "Mom, that's not
funny."

"I didn't say it was."

"Who knows, maybe your obituary will show up." She dropped
her pencil inside her book, closing it.

"If it does, Jody, you'll have placed it there." Irene sank gracefully onto the sofa.

Jody grimaced. "Sick."

"I can read it now: 'Beloved mother driven to death by child—and husband.' "

"Irene . . ." Kendrick reproved, putting down the paper.

"Yeah, Mom."

"Well"—she propped her left leg over an embroidered pillow—"I thought Roscoe Fletcher could have sold ice to Eskimos and probably did. He was good for St. Elizabeth's, and I'm sorry he died. I was even sorrier that we were all there. I would have preferred to hear about it rather than see it."

"He didn't look bad." Jody opened her book again. "I hope he didn't suffer."

"Too quick to suffer." Irene stared absently at her nails, a discreet pale pink. "What's going to happen at St. Elizabeth's?"

Kendrick lifted his eyebrows. "The board will appoint Sandy Brashiers headmaster. Sandy will try to kill Roscoe's film-course idea, which will bring him into a firefight with Maury McKinchie, Marilyn Sanburne, and April Shively. Ought to be worth the price of admission."

"How do you know that?" Jody asked.

"I don't know it for certain, but the board is under duress. And the faculty likes Brashiers."

"Oh, I almost forgot. Father Michael can see us tomorrow at two thirty."

"Irene, I have landscaping plans to show the Doubletree people tomorrow." He was bidding for the hotel's business. "It's important."

"I'd like to think I'm important. That this marriage is important," Irene said sarcastically.

"Then you pay the bills."

"You turn my stomach." Irene swung her legs to the floor and left.

"Way to go, Dad."

"You keep out of this."

"I love when you spend the evening at home. Just gives me warm fuzzies." She hugged herself in a mock embrace.

"I ought to—" He shut up.

"Hit me. Go ahead. Everyone thinks you gave me the shiner."
He threw the newspaper on the floor. "I've never once hit you."
"I'll never tell," she goaded him.
"Who did hit you?"
"Field hockey practice. I told you."
"I don't believe you."
"Fine, Dad. I'm a liar."
"I don't know what you are, but you aren't happy."
"Neither are you," she taunted.
"No, I'm not." He stood up, put his hands in his pockets. "I'm going out."
"Take me with you."
"Why?"
"I don't want to stay home with her."
"You haven't finished your homework."
"How come you get to run away and I have to stay home?"
"I—" He stopped because a determined Irene reentered the living room.
"Father Michael says he can see us at nine in the morning," she announced.
His face reddening, Kendrick sat back down, defeated. "Fine."
"Why do you go for marriage counseling, Mom? You go to mass every day. You see Father Michael every day."
"Jody, this is none of your business."
"If you discuss it in front of me, it is," she replied flippantly.
"She's got a point there." Kendrick appreciated how intelligent his daughter was, and how frustrated. However, he didn't know how to talk to her or his manipulative—in his opinion—wife. Irene suffocated him and Jody irritated him. The only place he felt good was at work.
"Dad, are you going to give St. E's a lot of money?"
"I wouldn't tell you if I were."
"Why not?"
"You'd use it as an excuse to skip classes." He half laughed.
"Kendrick"—Irene sat back on the sofa—"where do you get these ideas?"

"Contrary to popular opinion, I was young once, and Jody likes to—" He put his hand out level to the floor and wobbled it.

"Learned it from you." Jody flared up.

"Can't we have one night of peace?" Irene wailed, unwilling to really examine why they couldn't.

"Hey, Mom, we're dysfunctional."

"That's a bullshit word." Kendrick picked his paper up. "All those words are ridiculous. Codependent. Enabler. Jesus Christ. People can't accept reality anymore. They've invented a vocabulary for their illusions."

Both his wife and daughter stared at him.

"Dad, are you going to give us the lecture on professional victims?"

"No." He buried his nose in the paper.

"Jody, finish your homework," Irene directed.

Jody stood up. She had no intention of doing homework. "I hated seeing Mr. Fletcher dead. You two don't care. It was a shock, you know." She swept her books onto the floor; they hit with thuds equal to their differing weights. She stomped out the front door, slamming it hard.

"Kendrick, you deal with it. I was at the car wash, remember?"

He glared at her, rolled his paper up, threw it on the chair, and stalked out.

Irene heard him call for Jody. No response.

25

"You cheated!" Jody, angry, squared off at Karen Jensen.

"I did not."

"You didn't even understand *Macbeth*. There's no way you could have gotten ninety-five on Mr. Brashiers's quiz."

"I read it and I understand it."

"Liar."

"I went over to Brooks Tucker's and she helped me."

Jody's face twisted in sarcasm. "She read aloud to you?"

"No. Brooks gets all that stuff. It's hard for me."

"She's your new best friend."

"So what if she is?" Karen tossed her blond hair.

"You'd better keep your mouth shut."

"You're the one talking, not me."

"No, I'm not."

"You're weirding out."

Jody's eyes narrowed. "I lost my temper. That doesn't mean I'm weirding out."

"Then why call me a cheater?"

"Because"—Jody sucked in the cool air—"you're on a scholarship. You have to make good grades. And English is not your subject. I don't know why you even took Shakespeare."

"Because Mr. Brashiers is a great teacher." Karen Jensen glanced down the alleyway. She saw only Mrs. Murphy and Pewter, strolling through Mrs. Hogendobber's fall garden, a riot of reds, rusts, oranges, and yellows.

Taking a step closer, Jody leaned toward her. "You and I vowed to—"

Karen held up her hands, palms outward. "Jody, chill out. I'd be crazy to open my mouth. I don't want anyone to know I went to bed with a guy this summer, and neither do you. Just chill out."

Jody relaxed. "Everything's getting on my nerves . . . especially Mom and Dad. I just want to move out."

Karen noticed the tiger cat coming closer. "Guess everyone feels that way sometimes."

"Yeah," Jody replied, "but your parents are better than mine."

Karen didn't know how to answer that, so she said, "Let's go in and get the mail."

"Yeah." Jody started walking.

Pewter and Murphy, now at the backdoor of the post office, sat on the steps. Pewter washed her face. Mrs. Murphy dropped her head so Pewter could wash her, too.

"Didn't you think the newspaper's write-up of Roscoe's death was strange?" Murphy's eyes were half closed.

"You mean the bit about an autopsy and routine investigation?"

"If he died of a heart attack, why a routine investigation? Mom better pump Coop when she sees her—and hey, she hasn't been in to pick up her mail for the last two days."

"Nothing in there but catalogs." Pewter took it upon herself to check out everyone's mailbox. She said she wasn't being nosy, only checking for mice.

Shouting in the post office sent them zipping through the animal door.

They crossed the back section of the post office and bounded onto the counter. Both Harry and Mrs. Hogendobber were in the front section as were Jody, an astonished Samson Coles, and Karen Jensen. Tucker was at Harry's feet, squared off against Jody. The animals had arrived in the middle of an angry scene.

"You're the one!"

"Jody, that's enough," Mrs. Hogendobber, aghast, admonished the girl.

Samson, his gravelly voice sad, said quietly, "It's all right, Miranda."

"You're the one sleeping with Mom!" Jody shrieked.

"I am not having an affair with your mother." He was gentle.

"Jody, come on. I'll ride you home." Karen tugged at the tall girl's sleeve, at a loss for what to do. Her friend exploded when Samson put his arm around her shoulders, telling her how sorry he was that the headmaster had died.

"You cheated on Lucinda—everyone knows you did—and then Ansley killed herself. She drove her Porsche into that pond because of you . . . and now you're fucking my mother."

"JODY!" Mrs. Hogendobber raised her voice, which scared everyone.

Jody burst into tears and Karen pushed her out the front door. "I'm sorry, Mrs. Hogendobber and Mr. Coles. I'm sorry, Mrs. Haristeen. She's, uh . . ." Karen couldn't finish her thought. She closed the door behind her.

Samson curled his lips inward until they disappeared. "Well, I know I'm the town pariah, but this is the first time I've heard that I caused Ansley's death."

A shocked Miranda grasped the counter for support. "Samson, no one in this town blames you for that unstable woman's unfortunate end. She caused unhappiness to herself and others." She gulped in air. "That child needs help."

"*Help? She needs a good slap in the face.*" Pewter paced the counter.

Tucker grumbled. *"Stinks of fear."*

"They can't smell it. They only trust their eyes. Why, I don't know—their eyes are terrible." Mrs. Murphy, concerned, sat at the counter's edge watching Karen force Jody into her car, an old dark green Volvo.

"We'd better call Irene," Harry, upset, suggested.

"No." Samson shook his head. "Then the kid will think we're ganging up on her. Obviously, she doesn't trust her mother if she thinks she's having an affair with me."

"Then I'll call her father."

"Harry, Kendrick's no help," Mrs. Hogendobber, rarely a criticizer, replied. "His love affair with himself is the problem in that family. It's a love that brooks no rivals."

This made Harry laugh; Miranda hadn't intended to be funny, but she had hit the nail on the head.

Samson folded his arms across his chest. "Some people shouldn't have children. Kendrick is one of them."

"We can't let the child behave this way. She's going to make a terrific mess." Miranda added sensibly, "Not everyone will be as tolerant as we are." She tapped her chin with her forefinger, shifting her weight to her right foot. "I'll call Father Michael."

Samson hesitated, then spoke. "Miranda, what does a middle-aged priest know of teenage girls . . . of women?"

"About the same as any other man," Harry fired off.

"Touché," Samson replied.

"Samson, I didn't mean to sound nasty. You're probably more upset than you're letting on. Jody may be a kid, but a low blow is a low blow," Harry said.

"I could leave this town where people occasionally forgive but never forget. I think about it, you know, but"—he jammed his hands in his pockets—"I'm not the only person living in Crozet who's made a mistake. I'm too stubborn to turn tail. I belong here as much as the next guy."

"I hope you don't think I'm sitting in judgment." Miranda's hand fluttered to her throat.

"Me neither." Harry smiled. "It's hard for me to be open-minded about that subject, thanks to my own history . . . I mean,

BoomBoom Craycroft of all people. Fair could have picked some-one—well, you know."

"That was the excitement for Fair. That BoomBoom was so obvious." Samson realized he'd left his mail on the counter. "I'm going back to work." He scooped his mail up before Pewter, recovering from the drama, could squat on it. "What I really feel bad about is tampering with the escrow accounts. That was rotten. Falling in love with Ansley may have been imprudent, but it wasn't criminal. Betraying a responsibility to clients, that was wrong." He sighed. "I've paid for it. I've lost my license. Lost respect. Lost my house. Nearly lost Lucinda." He paused again, then said, "Well, girls, we've had enough soap opera for one day." He pushed the door open and breathed in the crisp fall air.

Miranda ambled over to the phone, dialed, and got Lucinda Coles. "Lucinda, is Father Michael there?"

He was, and she buzzed the good woman through.

"Father Michael, have you a moment?" Miranda accurately repeated the events of the afternoon.

When she hung up, Harry asked, "Is he going to talk to her?"

"Yes. He seemed distracted, though."

"Maybe the news upset him."

"Of course." She nodded. "I'm going to clean out that refrigerator. It needs a good scrub."

"Before you do that, there's a pile of mail for Roscoe Fletcher. Why don't we sort it out and run it over to Naomi after work?"

The two women dumped the mail out on the work table in the back. A flutter of bills made them both feel guilty. The woman had lost her husband. Handing over bills seemed heartless. Catalogs, magazines, and handwritten personal letters filled up one of the plastic boxes they used in the back to carry mail after sorting it out of the big canvas duffel bags.

A Jiffy bag, the end torn, the gray stuffing spilling out, sent Harry to the counter for Scotch tape.

Tucker observed this. She wanted to play, but the cats were hashing over the scene they'd just witnessed. She barked.

"Tucker, if you need to go to the bathroom, there's the door."

"Can't we walk, just a little walk? You deserve a break."

"Butterfingers." Harry dropped the bag. The tiny tear in the cover opened wider.

Mrs. Murphy and Pewter stopped their gabbing and jumped down.

"Yahoo!" Mrs. Murphy pounced on the tear and the gray stuffing burst out.

"Aachoo." Pewter sneezed as the featherlight stuffing floated into the air.

"I've got it!" Mrs. Murphy crowed.

Pewter pounced, both paws on one end of the bag, claws out as the tiger cat ripped away at the other corner, enlarging the tear until she could reach into the bag with her paw.

If Mrs. Murphy had been a boxer, she would have been hailed for her lightning hands.

Lying flat on her side, she fished in the Jiffy bag with her right paw.

"Anything to eat?"

"No, it's paper, but it's crisp and crinkly."

The large gray cat blinked, somewhat disappointed. Food, the ultimate pleasure, was denied her. She'd have to make do with fresh paper, a lesser pleasure but a pleasure nonetheless.

"You girls are loony tunes." Tucker, bored, turned her back. Paper held no interest for her.

"Hooked it. I can get it out of the bag. I know I can." Murphy yanked hard at the contents of the package, pulling the paper partways through the tear.

"Look!" Pewter shouted.

Mrs. Murphy stopped for a second to focus on her booty. "Wow!" She yanked harder.

Tucker turned back around thanks to the feline excitement. "Give it to Mom. She needs it."

Mrs. Murphy ripped into the bag so fast the humans hadn't time to react, and the cat turned a somersault to land on her side, then put her paw into the bag. Her antics had them doubled over.

However funny she was, Mrs. Murphy was destroying government property.

"Mom, we're rich!" Mrs. Murphy let out a jubilant meow.

Harry and Miranda, dumbfounded, bent over the demolished bag.

"My word." Miranda's eyes about popped from her head. She reached out with her left hand, fingers to the floor, to steady herself.

The humans and animals stared at a stack of one-hundred-dollar bills, freshly minted.

"We'd better call Rick Shaw. No one sends that much money in the mail." Harry stood up, feeling a little dizzy.

"Harry, I don't know the law on this, but we can't open this packet."

"I know that," Harry, a trifle irritated, snapped.

"It's not our business." Miranda slowly thought out loud.

"I'll call Ned."

"No. That's still interfering in the proper delivery of the mail."

"Miranda, there's something fishy about this."

"Fishy or not, we are employees of the United States Postal Service, and we can't blow the whistle just because there's money in a package."

"We sure could if it were a bomb."

"But it's not."

"You mean we deliver it?"

"Exactly."

"Oh." Mrs. Murphy's whiskers drooped. *"We need that money."*

26

Naomi Fletcher called Rick Shaw herself. She asked Miranda and Harry to stay until the sheriff arrived.

Mrs. Murphy, Pewter, and Tucker languished in the cab of the truck. When the sheriff pulled in with Cooper at his side, the animals set up such a racket that Cynthia opened the truck door.

"Bet you guys need to go to the bathroom."

"Sure," they yelled over their shoulders as they made a beeline for the front door.

"*You'd better stop for a minute,*" Tucker advised the cats.

"*I'm not peeing in public. You do it,*" the tiger, insulted, replied.

"Fine." The corgi found a spot under a tree, did enough to convince Cynthia that she had saved the interior of Harry's truck, then hurried to the front door.

Once inside they huddled under the coffee table while Cynthia dusted the bag and the bills for prints.

After an exhaustive discussion Rick told Roscoe Fletcher's

widow to deposit the money in her account. He could not impound the cash. There was no evidence of wrongdoing.

"There are no assumptions in my job, only facts." He ran his right hand through his thinning hair.

Naomi, both worried and thrilled, for the sum had turned out to be seventy-five thousand dollars, thanked the sheriff and his deputy for responding to her call.

Rick, hat in hand, said, "Mrs. Fletcher, brace yourself. The story will be out in the papers tomorrow. A coroner's report is public knowledge. Bill Moscowitz has delayed writing up the autopsy report for as long as he can."

"I know you're doing your best." Naomi choked up.

Harry and Miranda, confused, looked at each other and then back at Rick.

Naomi nodded at him, so he spoke. "Roscoe was poisoned."

"*What!*" Tucker exclaimed.

"*I told you,*" Mrs. Murphy said.

"*Don't be so superior,*" Pewter complained.

"Naomi, I'm sorry, so very sorry." Mrs. Hogendobber reached over and grasped Naomi's hand.

"*Who'd want to kill him?*" Pewter's long white eyebrows rose.

"*Someone who failed algebra?*" Mrs. Murphy couldn't resist.

"*Hey, where's Tucker?*" Pewter asked.

Tucker had sneaked off alone to find Winston, the bulldog.

Harry said, "I'm sorry, Naomi."

Naomi wiped her thin nose with a pink tissue. "Poisoned! One of those strawberry drops was poison."

Cooper filled in the details. "He ingested malathion, which usually takes just minutes to kill someone."

Harry blurted out, "I ate one of those!"

"When?" Rick asked.

"Oh, two days before his death. Maybe three. You know Roscoe . . . always offering everyone candy." She felt queasy.

"Unfortunately, we don't know how he came to be poisoned. The candy in his car was safe."

They squeezed back into Harry's truck, the cats on Miranda's lap. Tucker, between the two humans, told everyone what Winston had said. "*Naomi cries all the time. She didn't kill him. Winston's positive.*"

"*There goes the obvious suspect in every murder case.*" Pewter curled up on Miranda's lap, which left little room for Mrs. Murphy.

"*You could move over.*"

"*Go sit on Harry's lap.*"

"*Thanks, I will, you selfish toad.*"

Tucker nudged Murphy. "*Winston said Sandy Brashiers is over all the time.*"

"*Why?*" Pewter inquired.

"*Trying to figure out Roscoe's plans for this school year. He left few documents or guidelines, and April Shively is being a real bitch—according to Winston.*"

"*Secretaries always fall in love with their bosses,*" Pewter added nonchalantly.

"*Oh, Pewter.*" Murphy wrinkled her nose.

"*They do!*"

"*Even if she was in love with him, it doesn't mean she'd be an obstructionist—good word, huh?*" Tucker smiled, her big fangs gleaming.

"*I'm impressed, Tucker.*" The tiger laughed. "*Of course she's an obstructionist. April doesn't like Sandy. Roscoe didn't either.*"

"*Guess Sandy's in for a rough ride.*" Pewter noticed one of Herb Jones's two cats sitting on the steps to his house. "*Look at Lucy Fur. She always shows off after her visit to the beauty parlor.*"

"*That long hair is pretty, but can you imagine taking care of it?*" Mrs. Murphy, a practical puss, replied.

"I don't know what this world is coming to." Miranda shook her head.

"Poison is the coward's way to kill someone." Harry, still shaken from realizing she had eaten Roscoe's candies, growled, "Whoever it was was chickenshit."

"That's one way to put it." Miranda frowned.

"The question is, where did he get the poison and is there a tin

of lethal candies out there waiting for another innocent victim?''
Harry stroked Murphy, keeping her left hand on the wheel.

"We know one thing," Miranda pronounced firmly. "Whoever
killed him was close to him . . . if malathion kills as fast as Coop
says it does."

"Close and weak. I mean it. Poison is the coward's weapon."

In that Harry was half right and half wrong.

27

A light wind from the southeast raised the temperature into the low seventies. The day sparkled, leaves the color of butter vibrated in the breeze, and the shadows disappeared since it was noon.

Harry, home after cub hunting early in the morning, had rubbed down Poptart, turned her out with the other two horses, and was now scouring her stock trailer. Each year she repacked the bearings, inspected the boards, sanded off any rust, and repainted those areas. Right now her trailer resembled a dalmatian, spots everywhere. She'd put on the primer but didn't finish her task before cub hunting started, which was usually in September. Cubbing meant young hounds joined older ones, and young foxes learned along with the young hounds what was expected of them. With today's good weather she'd hoped to finish the job.

Blair lent her his spray painter. As Blair bought the best of everything, she figured she could get the job done in two hours, tops.

She'd bought metallic Superman-blue paint from Art Bushey, who gave her a good deal.

"*That stuff smells awful.*" Tucker wrinkled her nose at the paint cans.

"*She's going to shoot the whole afternoon on this.*" Pewter stretched. "*I'll mosey on up to the house.*"

"*Wimp. You could sleep under the maple tree and soak up the sunshine,*" Mrs. Murphy suggested.

"*Don't start one of your outdoor exercise lectures about how we felines are meant to run, jump, and kill. This feline was meant to rest on silk cushions and eat steak tartare.*"

"*Tucker, let's boogie.*" Mrs. Murphy shook herself, then scampered across the stable yard.

"*I'm not going, and don't you come back here and make up stories about what I've missed,*" Pewter called after them. "*And I don't want to hear about the bobcat either. That's a tall tale if I ever heard one.*" Then she giggled. " *'Cept they don't have tails.*" By now she was heading toward the house, carrying on a conversation with herself. "*Oh, and if it isn't the bobcat, then it's the bear and her two cubs. And if I hear one more time about how Tucker was almost drug under by an irate beaver while crossing the creek . . . next they'll tell me there's an elephant out there. Fine, they can get their pads cut up. I'm not.*" She sashayed into the screened-in porch and through the open door to the kitchen. "Mmm." Pewter jumped onto the counter to gobble up crumbs of Danish. "*What a pity that Harry isn't a cook.*"

She curled up on the counter, the sun flooding through the window over the sink, and fell fast asleep.

The cat and dog trotted toward the northwest. Usually they'd head to the creek that divided Harry's land from Blair Bainbridge's land, but as they'd seen him this morning when he brought over the paint sprayer on his way to cubbing, they decided to sprint in the other direction.

"*Pewter cracks me up.*" Mrs. Murphy laughed.

"Me, too." Tucker stopped and lifted her nose. "*Deer.*"

"*Close?*"

"*Over there.*" The corgi indicated a copse of trees surrounded by high grass.

"Let's not disturb them. It's black-powder season, and there's bound to be some idiot around with a rifle."

"I don't mind a good hunter. They're doing us a favor. But the other ones . . ." The dog shuddered, then trotted on. "Mom and Blair didn't have much to say to each other, did they?"

"She was in a hurry. So was he." Mrs. Murphy continued, "Sometimes I worry about her. She's getting set in her ways. Makes it hard to mesh with a partner, know what I mean?"

"She likes living alone. All that time I wanted Fair to come back, which he's tried to do—I really think she likes being her own boss."

"Tucker, she was hardly your typical wife."

"No, but she made concessions."

"So did he." Mrs. Murphy stopped a moment to examine a large fox den. "Hey, you guys run this morning?"

"No," came the distant reply.

"Next week they'll leave from Old Greenwood Farm."

"Thanks."

"Since when did you get matey with foxes?" Tucker asked. "I thought you hated them."

"Nah, only some of them."

"Hypocrite."

"Stick-in-the-mud. Remember what Emerson said, 'A foolish consistency is the hobgoblin of little minds.' "

"Where are we going?" Tucker ignored Murphy's reference.

"Here, there, and everywhere." Mrs. Murphy swished her tail.

"Goody." The dog loved wandering with no special plan.

They ran through a newly mown hayfield. Grasshoppers flew up in the air, the faint rattle of their wings sounding like thousands of tiny castanets. The last of the summer's butterflies swooped around. Wolf spiders, some lugging egg sacs, hurried out of their way.

At the end of the field a line of large old hickories stood sentinel over a farm road rarely used since the Bowdens put down a better road fifty yards distant.

"Race you!" the cat called over her shoulder as she turned left on the road heading down to a deep ravine and a pond.

"Ha!" The dog bounced for joy, screeching after the cat.

Corgis, low to the ground, can run amazingly fast when stretched out to full body length. Since Mrs. Murphy zigged and zagged when she ran, Tucker soon overtook her.

"I win!" the dog shouted.

"*Only because I let you.*"

They tumbled onto each other, rolling in the sunshine. Springing to their feet, they ran some more, this time with the tiger soaring over the corgi, dipping in front of her and then jumping her from the opposite direction.

The sheer joy of it wore them out. They sat under a gnarled walnut at the base of a small spring.

Mrs. Murphy climbed the tree, gracefully walking out on a limb. "*Hey, there's a car over that rise.*"

"*No way.*"

"*Wanna bet?*"

They hurried up and over the small rise, the ruts in the road deeper than their own height. Stranded in the middle of the road was a 1992 red Toyota Camry with the license plates removed. As they drew closer they could see a figure in the driver's seat.

Tucker stopped and sniffed. "*Uh-oh.*"

Mrs. Murphy bounded onto the hood and stared, hair rising all over her body. Quickly she jumped off. "*There's a dead human in there.*"

"*How dead?*"

"*Extremely dead.*"

"*That's what I thought. Who is it?*"

"*Given the condition of the body, your guess is as good as mine. But it was once a woman. There's a blue barrette in her hair with roses on it, little yellow plastic roses.*"

"*We'd better go get Mom.*"

Mrs. Murphy walked away from the Camry and sat on the rise. She needed to collect her thoughts.

"*Tucker, it won't do any good. Mother won't know what we're telling her. The humans don't use this road anymore. It might be days, weeks, or even months before anyone finds this, uh, mess.*"

"*Maybe by that time she'll be bones.*"

"*Tucker!*"

"Just joking." The dog leaned next to her dear friend. "Trying to lighten the moment. After all, you don't know who it is. I can't see that high up. Humans commit suicide, you know. Could be one of those things. They like to shoot themselves in cars or hotel rooms. Drugs are for the wimps, I guess. I mean, how many ways can they kill themselves?"

"Lots of ways."

"I never met a dog that committed suicide."

"How could you? The dog would be dead."

"Smart-ass." Tucker exhaled. "Guess we'd better go back home."

On the way across the mown hayfield Murphy said out loud what they both were thinking. "Let's hope it's a suicide."

They reached the farm in twenty minutes, rushing inside to tell Pewter, who refused to believe it.

"Then come with us."

"Murphy, I am not traipsing all over creation. It's soon time for supper. Anyway, what's a dead human to me?"

"You'd think someone would report a missing person, wouldn't you?" Tucker scratched her shoulder.

"So many humans live alone, they aren't missed for a long time. And she's been dead a couple of weeks," Murphy replied.

28

Puce-faced Little Marilyn, hands on hips, stood in the middle of Roscoe Fletcher's office, as angry as April Shively.

"You hand those files over!"

Coolly, relishing her moment of power, April replied, "Roscoe told me not to release any of this information until our Homecoming banquet."

Little Mim, a petite woman, advanced on April, not quite petite but small enough to be described as perky. "I am chair of the fund-raising committee. If I am to properly present St. Elizabeth's to potential donors, I need information. Roscoe and I were to have our meeting today and the files were to be released to me."

"I don't know that. It's not written in his schedule book." April shoved the book across his desk toward Marilyn, who ignored it.

Marilyn baited her. "I thought you knew everything there was to know about Roscoe."

"What's that supposed to mean?"

"Take it any way you like."

"Don't you dare accuse me of improper conduct with Roscoe! People always say that. They say it behind my back and think I don't know it." Her words were clipped, her speech precise.

"You *were* in love with him."

"I don't have to answer that. And I don't have to give you this file either."

"Then you're hiding something. I will convene the board and request an immediate audit."

"What I'm hiding is something good!" She sputtered. "It's a large donation by Maury McKinchie for the film department."

"Then show it to me. We'll celebrate together." Little Mim reached out her left hand, with the pinkie ring bearing the crest of the Urquharts.

"No! I take his last words to me as a sacred duty."

Exasperated, tired, and ready to bat April silly, Little Mim left, calling over her shoulder, "You will hear from a lawyer selected by the board and from an accounting firm. Good or bad, we must know the financial health of this institution."

"If Roscoe were alive, you wouldn't talk to me this way."

"April, if Roscoe were alive, I wouldn't talk to you at all."

29

Little Mim was as good as her word. She convened an emergency board meeting chaired by Sandy Brashiers. Sandy had the dolorous duty of telling the group that he believed April had removed files from Roscoe's office: she refused to cooperate even with Sheriff Shaw. The suspicion lurked in many minds that she might have taken other items, perhaps valuable ones like Roscoe's Cartier desk clock.

Alum bigwigs blew like bomb fragments. Kendrick Miller called Ned Tucker at home, asking him to represent the board. Ned agreed. Kendrick then handed State Senator Guyot his mobile phone to call the senior partner of a high-powered accounting firm in Richmond, rousing him from a tense game of snooker. He, too, agreed to help the board, waiving his not inconsiderable fee.

Maury McKinchie, the newest member of the board, suggested

this unsettling news not be discussed until the Homecoming banquet. He made no mention of his large bequest.

Sandy Brashiers then made a motion to dismiss April from her post.

Fair Haristeen, serving his last year on the board, stood up. "We need time to think this over before voting. April is out of line, but she's overcome by grief."

"That doesn't give her the right to steal school records and God knows what else." Sandy leaned back in his chair. Underneath the table he tapped his foot, thrilled that revenge was so quickly his.

"Perhaps one of us could talk to her," Fair urged.

"I tried."

"Marilyn," Maury folded his hands on the table, "she may resent you because you're a strong supporter of Sandy."

"I am," Little Mim said forthrightly, as Sandy tried not to grin from ear to ear. "We have put our differences behind us."

"I don't want to open a can of worms—after all that has happened—but there had been tension inside the administration, two camps, you might say, and we all know where April's sympathies rest," Fair said.

"As well as her body," Kendrick said, a bit too quickly.

"Come on, Kendrick!" Fair was disgusted. "We don't know that."

"I'm sorry," Kendrick said, "but she's grieving more than Naomi."

"That's inappropriate!" Maury banged the table, which surprised them all.

"She spent more time with him than his wife did." Kendrick held up his hands before him, palms outward, a calm-down signal.

"Who then will bell the cat?" Sandy returned to business, secretly loving this uproar.

No one raised a hand. An uncomfortable silence hung over the conference room.

Finally Maury sighed. "I can try. I have little history with her, which under the circumstances seems an advantage. And Roscoe and I were close friends."

Little Mim smiled wanly. "Thank you, Maury, no matter what the consequences."

"Hear, hear!"

Sandy noticed the lights were on in the gymnasium after the meeting adjourned. He threw on his scarf and his tweed jacket, crossing the quad to see what activity was in progress. He couldn't remember, but then he had a great deal on his mind.

Ahead of him, striding through the darkness, was Maury Mc-Kinchie, hands jammed into the pockets of an expensive lambskin jacket.

"Maury, where are you going?"

"Fencing exhibition." Maury's voice was level but he had little enthusiasm for Sandy Brashiers.

"Oh, Lord, I forgot all about it." Sandy recalled the university fencing club was visiting St. Elizabeth's hoping to find recruits for the future. One of Coach Hallvard's pet projects was to introduce fencing at the secondary-school level. It was her sport. She coached field hockey and lacrosse, and had even played on the World Cup lacrosse team in 1990, but fencing was her true love.

Sandy jogged up to Maury. "I'm starting to feel like the absent-minded professor."

"Goes with the territory," came the flat reply.

"I know how you must feel, Maury, and I'm sorry. Losing a friend is never easy. And I know Roscoe did not favor me. We were just—too different to really get along. But we both wanted the best for St. Elizabeth's."

"I believe that."

"I'm glad you're on the board. We can use someone whose vision and experience is larger than Albemarle County. I hope we can work together."

"Well, we can try. I'm going to keep my eye on things, going to try to physically be here, too—until some equilibrium is achieved."

Both men sidestepped the volatile question of a film department.

And neither man yet knew that Roscoe had been poisoned, which would have cast a pall over their conversation.

Sandy smiled. "This must seem like small beer to you—after Hollywood."

Maury replied, "At least you're doing something important: teaching the next generation. That was one of the things I most respected about Roscoe."

"Ah, but the question is, what do we teach them?"

"To ask questions." Maury opened the gym door for Sandy.

"Thank you." Sandy waited as Maury closed the door.

The two men found places in the bleachers.

Sean Hallahan was practicing thrusts with Roger Davis, not quite so nimble as the football player.

Karen Jensen, face mask down, parried with a University of Virginia sophomore.

Brooks and Jody attacked each other with épées.

Jody flipped up her mask. "I want to try the saber."

"Okay." Coach Hallvard switched Roger and Sean from saber to épée, giving the girls a chance at the heavier sword.

"Feels good," Jody said.

Brooks picked up the saber, resuming her position. Jody slashed at her, pressing as Brooks retreated.

Hallvard observed this burst of aggression out of the corner of her eye. "Jody, give me the saber."

Jody hesitated, then handed over the weapon. She walked off the gym floor, taking the bleacher steps two at a time to sit next to Maury.

"How did you like it?" he asked her.

"Okay."

"I never tried fencing. You need quick reflexes."

"Mr. McKinchie." She lowered her voice so Sandy Brashiers wouldn't hear. His attention was focused on the UVA fencers. "Have you seen the BMW Z3, the retro sports car? It's just beautiful."

"It is a great-looking machine." He kept his eyes on the other students.

"I want a bright red one." She smiled girlishly, which accentuated her smashing good looks.

He held his breath for an instant, then exhaled sharply. She squeezed his knee, then jumped up gracefully and rejoined her teammates.

Karen Jensen flipped up her face mask, glaring at Jody, who glared right back. "Did you give out already?"

"No, Coach took away my saber."

Roger, in position, lunged at Brooks. "Power thighs."

"Sounds—uh—" Brooks giggled, not finishing her sentence.

"You never know what's going to happen at St. E's." With Sean in tow, Karen joined them. "At least this is better than shooting those one-minute stories. I hated that."

"If it's not sports, you don't like it," Jody blandly commented on Karen's attitude.

"Took too long." Karen wiped her brow with a towel. "All that worrying about light. I thought our week of film studies was one of the most boring things we ever did."

"When did this happen?" Brooks asked.

"First week of school," Karen said. "Lucky you missed it."

"That's why Mr. Fletcher and Mr. McKinchie are, I mean, were, so tight," Sean said. " 'Cause Mr. Fletcher said if we are to be a modern school, then we have to teach modern art forms."

"Stick with me, I'll make you a star." Jody mimicked the dead headmaster.

"Mr. McKinchie said he'd try to get old equipment donated to the school."

"I didn't think it was boring," Sean told Brooks.

"Mr. Fletcher said we'd be the only prep school in the nation with a hands-on film department," Karen added. "Hey, see you guys in a minute." She left to talk to one of the young men on the fencing team. Sean seethed.

"She likes older men," Jody tormented him.

"At least she likes men," Sean, mean-spirited, snarled at her.

"Drop dead, Hallahan," Roger said.

Jody, surprisingly calm considering her behavior the last two weeks, replied, "He can call me anything he wants, Roger. I couldn't care less. This dipshit school is not the world, you know. It's just his world."

"What's that supposed to mean?" Sean, angry, took it out on Jody.

"You're a big frog in a small pond. Like—who cares?" She smiled, a hint of malice in her eyes. "Karen's after bigger game than a St. Elizabeth halfback."

Sean's eyes followed Karen.

"She's not the only woman in the world." He feigned indifference.

"No, but she's the one you want," Jody said, needling him more.

Roger gently put his hand under Brooks's elbow, wheeling her away from the squabbling Jody and Sean. "Would you go with me to the Halloween dance?"

"Uh—" She brightened. "Yes."

30

Harry dropped the feed scoop in the sweet feed when the phone rang in the tack room.

She hurried in and picked up the phone. It was 6:30 A.M.

"Miranda, it had to be you."

"Just as Rick Shaw said, the story of Roscoe's poisoning is finally in the paper. But no one is using the word 'murder.' "

"Huh—well, what does it say?"

"There's the possibility of accidental ingestion, but deliberate poisoning can't be ruled out. Rick's soft-pedaling it."

"What has me baffled is the motive. Roscoe was a good headmaster. He liked the students. They liked him, and the parents did, too. There's just something missing—or who knows, maybe it was random, like when a disgruntled employee put poison in Tylenol."

"That was heinous."

"Except—I don't know—I'm just lost. I can't think of any reason for him to be killed."

"He wasn't rich. He appeared to have no real enemies. He had disagreements with people like Sandy Brashiers, but"—Miranda stopped to cough—"well, I guess that's why we have a sheriff's department. If there is something, they'll find it."

"You're right," Harry responded with no conviction whatsoever.

31

The repeated honking of a car horn brought Harry to the front window of the post office. Tucker, annoyed, started barking. Mrs. Murphy opened one eye. Then she opened both eyes.

"Would you look at that?" Harry exclaimed.

Miranda, swathed in an old cashmere cardigan—she was fighting off the sniffles—craned her neck. "Isn't that the cutest thing you ever saw?"

Pewter bustled out of Market's store. She had put in an appearance today, primarily because she knew sides of pork would be carried in to hang in the huge back freezer.

Jody Miller, her black eye fading, emerged from a red BMW sports car. The fenders were rounded, the windshield swept back at an appealing angle. She hopped up the steps to the post office.

Harry opened the door for her. "What a beautiful car!"

"I know." The youngster shivered with delight.

"Did your father buy you that?" Miranda thought of her little Ford Falcon. As far as she was concerned, the styling was as good as this far more expensive vehicle's.

"No, I bought it myself. When Grandpa died, he left money for me, and it's been drawing interest. It finally made enough to buy a new car!"

"Has everyone at school seen it?" Harry asked.

"Yeah, and are they jealous."

Since she was the first student to come in to pick up mail that day, neither woman knew what the kids' responses were to the newspaper story.

"How are people taking the news about Mr. Fletcher?" Miranda inquired.

Jody shrugged. "Most people think it was some kind of accident. People are really mad at Sean, though. A lot of kids won't talk to him now. I'm not talking to him either."

"Rather a strange accident," Miranda mumbled.

"Mr. Fletcher was kind of absentminded." Jody bounced the mail on the counter, evening it. "I liked him. I'll miss him, too, but Dad says people have a shelf life and Mr. Fletcher's ran out. He said there really aren't accidents. People decide when to go."

"Only the Lord decides that." Miranda firmly set her jaw.

"Mrs. Hogendobber, you'll have to take that up with Dad. It's"—she glanced at the ceiling, then back at the two women—"too deep for me. 'Bye." She breezed out the door.

"Kendrick sounds like a misguided man—and a cold-blooded one." Miranda shook her head as Pewter popped through the animal door, sending the flap whapping.

"Hey, I'd look good in that car."

"Pewter, you need a station wagon." Mrs. Murphy jabbed at her when she jumped on the counter.

"I am growing weary, very weary, of these jokes about my weight. I am a healthy cat. My bones are different from yours. I don't say anything about your hair thinning on your belly."

"Is not!"

"Mmm." The gray cat was noncommittal, which infuriated the tiger.

"*Do cats get bald?*" Tucker asked.

"*She is.*"

"*Pewter, I am not.*" Mrs. Murphy flopped on her back, showing the world her furry tummy.

Harry noticed this brazen display. "Aren't you the pretty puss?"

"*Bald.*"

"*Am not.*" Mrs. Murphy twisted her head to glare at Pewter.

"Wouldn't you love to know what this is about?" Harry laughed.

"Yes, I would." Miranda looked at the animals pensively. "How do I know they aren't talking about us?"

"And this coming from a woman who didn't like cats."

"Well—"

"You used to rail at me for bringing Mrs. Murphy and Tucker to work, and you said it was unclean for Market to have Pewter in the store."

Mrs. Hogendobber tickled Mrs. Murphy's stomach. "I have repented of my ways. 'O Lord, how manifold are thy works! In wisdom hast thou made them all: the earth is full of thy riches.' Psalm one hundred four." She smiled. "Cats and dogs are part of His riches."

As if on cue, the Reverend Herbert Jones strolled in. "Girls."

"Herb, how are you?"

"Worried." He opened his mailbox, the metal rim clicking when it hit the next box because he opened it hard. "Roscoe Fletcher murdered . . ." He shook his head.

"The paper didn't say he was murdered—just poisoned," Harry said.

"Harry, I've known you all your life. You think he was murdered, just as I do."

"I do. I wanted to see if you knew something I didn't," she replied sheepishly.

"You think his wife killed him?" Herb closed the mailbox, ignoring her subterfuge.

"I don't know," Harry said slowly.

"Fooling around, I'll bet you," Miranda commented.

"A lot of men fool around. That doesn't mean they're killed for it." Herb lightly slapped the envelopes against his palm.

Miranda shook her head. "Perhaps retribution is at work, but there's something eerie about Roscoe's obituary appearing in the paper. The murderer was advertising!"

"Some kind of power trip." He paused, staring at Mrs. Murphy. "And Sean Hallahan is the cat's-paw."

"Yes, Herb, just so." Miranda removed her half glasses to clean them. "I know I've harped to Harry about the obituary, but it upsets me so much. I can't get it out of my mind."

"So the killer, who I still say is a coward, is taunting us?"

"No, Harry, the killer was taunting Roscoe, although I doubt he recognized that. He thought it was a joke, I really believe that. The killer was someone or is someone he discounted." Herb waved his envelopes with an emphatic flourish. "And Sean Hallahan was the fall guy."

"In that case I wouldn't want to be in Maury McKinchie's shoes or Sean's."

"Me neither." Harry echoed Miranda.

"Then perhaps the killer is someone we've discounted." The Reverend Jones pointed his envelopes at Harry.

"You've got to be pushed to the edge to kill. Being ignored or belittled isn't a powerful enough motive to kill," Harry said sensibly.

"I agree with you there." Herb's deep voice filled the room. "There's more to it. You think Rick is guarding McKinchie?"

"I'll ask him." Miranda picked up the phone. She explained their thinking to Rick, who responded that he, too, had considered that Maury and Sean might be in jeopardy. He didn't have enough people in the department for a guard, but he sent officers to cruise by the farm. Maury himself had hired a bodyguard. Rick requested that Miranda, Harry, and Herb stop playing amateur detective.

Miranda then replayed this information minus the crack about being amateurs.

"Cool customer," Herb said.

"Huh?"

"Harry, Maury never said anything about a bodyguard."

"I'd sure tell—if for no other reason than hoping it got back to the killer. It'd put him on notice."

"Miranda, the killer could be in Paris by now," Herb said.

"No." Miranda pushed aside the mail cart. "We'd know who it is then. The killer can't go, and furthermore, he or she doesn't want to go."

"*The old girl is cooking today, isn't she?*" Pewter meowed admiringly.

"*That body in the Toyota has something to do with this,*" Mrs. Murphy stated firmly.

"*Nah.*"

"*Pewter, when we get home tonight, I'll take you there,*" Mrs. Murphy promised.

"*I'm not walking across all those fields in the cold.*"

"Fine." Mrs. Murphy stomped away from her.

Susan walked in the backdoor. "Harry, you've got to help me."

"Why?"

"Danny's in charge of the Halloween maze at Crozet High this year. I forgot and like an idiot promised to be a chaperon at the St. Elizabeth's Halloween dance."

"You still haven't figured out how to be in two places at the same time?" Harry laughed at her. As they had exhaustively discussed Roscoe's demise over the phone, there was no reason to repeat their thoughts.

"All the St. Elizabeth's kids will go through the maze and then go on to their own dance." Susan paused. "I can't keep everyone's schedules straight. I wouldn't even remember my own name if it wasn't sewn inside my coat."

"I'll do it"—Harry folded her arms across her chest—"and extract my price later."

"I do not have enough money to buy you a new truck." Susan caught her mail as Harry tossed it to her, a blue nylon belt wrapped around it. "Actually, your truck looks new now that you've painted it."

"*Everything on our farm is Superman blue,*" Murphy cracked, "*even the manure spreader.*"

That evening Mrs. Murphy and Tucker discussed how to lure a human to the ditched car. They couldn't think of a way to get Harry to follow them for that great a distance. A human might go one hundred yards or possibly even two hundred yards, but after that their attention span wavered.

"*I think we'll have to trust to luck.*" Tucker paced the barn center aisle.

"*You know, they say that killers return to the scene of the crime.*" Mrs. Murphy thought out loud.

"*That's stupid,*" Pewter interjected. "*If they had a brain in their head, they'd get out of there as fast as they could.*"

"*The emotion. Murder must be a powerful emotion for them. Maybe they go back to tap into that power.*" The tiger, on the rafters, passed over the top of Gin Fizz's stall.

Pewter, curled on a toasty horse blanket atop the tack trunk, disagreed. "*Powerful or not, it would be blind stupid to go down Bowden's Lane. Think about it.*"

"*I am thinking about it! I can't figure out how to get somebody out there.*"

"*You really don't want Mother to see it, do you?*" Tucker saw a shadowy little figure zip into a stall. "*Mouse.*"

"*I know.*" Mrs. Murphy focused on the disappearing tail. "*Does it to torment. Anyway, you're right. It's a grisly sight, and it would give Mother nightmares. Didn't like it much myself, and we're tougher about those things than humans.*"

"*In the old days humans left their criminals hanging from gibbets or rotting in cages. They put heads on the gates in London.*" Tucker imagined a city filled with the aroma of decay, quite pleasing to a dog.

"*Those days are long gone. Death is sanitized now.*" Pewter watched the mouse emerge and dash in the opposite direction. "*What is this, the Mouse Olympics?*"

A squeaky laugh followed this remark.

"*Those mice have no respect,*" Tucker grumbled.

32

Hands patiently folded in his lap, Rick sat in the Hallahan living room. Sean, his mother, father, and younger brother sat listening.

Cynthia had perched on the raised fireplace hearth and was taking notes.

"Sean, I don't want to be an alarmist, but if you did not act alone in placing that obituary, you've got to tell me. The other person may have pertinent information about Mr. Fletcher's death."

"So he was murdered?" Mr. Hallahan exclaimed.

Rick soothingly replied, opening his hands for effect, "I'm a sheriff. I have to investigate all possibilities. It could have been an accident."

Sean, voice clear, replied, "I did it. Alone. I wish I hadn't done it. Kids won't talk to me at school. I mean, some will, but others are acting like I killed him. It's like I've got the plague."

Sympathetically Cooper said, "It will pass, but we need your help."

Rick looked at each family member. "If any of you know anything, please, don't hold back."

"I wish we did," Mrs. Hallahan, a very pretty brunette, replied.

"Did anyone ever accompany your son on his paper route?"

"Sheriff, not to my knowledge." Mr. Hallahan crossed and uncrossed his legs, a nervous habit. "He lost the route, as I'm sure you know."

"Sean?" Rick said.

"No. No one else wanted to get up that early."

Rick stood up. "Folks, if anything comes to mind—anything—call me or Deputy Cooper."

"Are we in danger?" Mrs. Hallahan asked sensibly.

"If Sean is telling the truth—no."

33

Later that evening Sean walked into the garage to use the telephone. His father had phones in the bathrooms, bedrooms, kitchen, and in his car. Sean felt the garage was the most private place; no one would walk in on him.

He dialed and waited. "Hello."

"What do you want?"

"I don't appreciate you not talking to me at school. That's a crock of shit."

Jody seethed on the other end of her private line. "That's not why I'm ignoring you."

"Oh?" His voice dripped sarcasm.

"I'm ignoring you because you've got a crush on Karen Jensen. I was just convenient this summer, wasn't I?"

A pause followed this astute accusation. "You said we were friends, Jody. You said—"

"I know what I said, but I hardly expected us to go back to school and you try to jump Karen's bones. Jeez."

"I am not trying to jump her bones."

"You certainly jumped mine. I can't believe I was that stupid."

"Stupid. You wanted to do it as much as I did."

"Because I liked you."

"Well, I liked you, too, but we were friends. It wasn't a"—he thought for a neutral word—"like a hot romance. Friends."

"Friends don't sleep with each other's best friends . . . and besides, you wouldn't be the first."

"First what?"

"First guy to sleep with Karen. She tells me *everything*."

"Who did she sleep with?" Tension and a note of misery edged his voice.

"That's for me to know and for you to find out," she taunted. "I'm never letting you touch me again." As an afterthought she added, "And you can't drive my BMW either!"

"Do your parents know about the car?" he asked wearily, his brain racing for ways to get the information about Karen from Jody.

"No."

"Jody, if you had wanted . . . more, I wish you'd told me then, not now. And if you don't speak to me at school, people will think it's because of the obit."

"All you think about is yourself. What about me?"

"I like you." He wasn't convincing.

"I'm convenient."

"Jody, we have fun together. This summer was—great."

"But you've got the hots for Karen."

"I wouldn't put it like that."

"You'd better forget all about Karen. First of all, she knows you've slept with me. She's not going to believe a word you say. And furthermore, I can make life really miserable for you if I feel like it. I'll tell everyone you gave me my black eye."

"Jody, I never told anyone I slept with you. Why would you tell?" He ignored the black eye threat. Jody had told him her father gave her the black eye.

"Because I felt like it." Exasperated, she hung up the phone, leaving a dejected Sean shivering in the garage.

34

Larry Johnson removed his spectacles, rubbing the bridge of his nose where they pinched it. He replaced them, glanced over Jody Miller's file, and then left his office, joining her in an examining room.

"How are you?"

"I'm okay, I think." She sat on the examining table when he motioned for her to do so.

"You were just here in August for your school physical."

"I know. I think it's stupid that I have to have a physical before every season. Coach Hallvard insists on it."

"Every coach insists on it." He smiled. "Now what seems to be the problem?"

"Well"—Jody swallowed hard—"I, uh, I've missed my period for two months in a row."

"I see." He touched his stethoscope. "Have you been eating properly?"

"Uh—I guess."

"The reason I ask that is often female athletes, especially the ones in endurance sports, put the body under such stress that they go without their period for a time. It's the body's way of protecting itself because they couldn't bring a baby to term. Nature is wise."

"Oh." She smiled reflexively. "I don't think field hockey is one of those sports."

"Next question." He paused. "Have you had sexual relations?"

"Yes—but I'm not telling."

"I'm not asking." He held up his hand like a traffic cop. "But there are a few things I need to know. You're seventeen. Have you discussed this with your parents?"

"No," she said quickly.

"I see."

"I don't talk to them. I don't want to talk to them."

"I understand."

"No, you don't."

"Let's start over, Jody. Did you use any form of birth control?"

"No."

"Well, then"—he exhaled—"let's get going."

He took blood for a pregnancy test, at the same time pulling a vial of blood to be tested for infectious diseases. He declined to inform Jody of this. If something turned up, he'd tell her then.

"I hate that." She turned away as the needle was pulled from her arm.

"I do, too." He held the small cotton ball on her arm. "Did your mother ever talk to you about birth control?"

"Yes."

"I see."

She shrugged. "Dr. Johnson, it's not as easy as she made it sound."

"Perhaps not. The truth is, Jody, we don't really understand human sexuality, but we do know that when those hormones start flowing through your body, a fair amount of irrationality seems to flow with them. And sometimes we turn to people for comfort during difficult times, and sex becomes part of the comfort." He smiled.

"Come back on Friday." He glanced at his calendar. "Umm, make it Monday."

"All right." She paled. "You won't tell anyone, will you?"

"No. Will you?"

She shook her head no.

"Jody, if you can't talk to your mother, you ought to talk to another older woman. Whether you're pregnant or not, you might be surprised to learn that you aren't alone. Other people have felt what you're feeling."

"I'm not feeling much."

He patted her on the back. "Okay, then. Call me Monday."

She mischievously winked as she left the examining room.

35

Not wishing to appear pushy, Sandy Brashiers transferred his office to the one next to Roscoe Fletcher's but made no move to occupy the late headmaster's sacred space.

April Shively stayed just this side of rude. If Naomi asked her to perform a chore, retrieve information, or screen calls, April complied. She and Naomi had a cordial, if not warm, relationship. If Sandy asked, she found a variety of ways to drag her heels.

Although the jolt of Roscoe's death affected her every minute of the day, Naomi Fletcher resumed her duties as head of the lower school. She needed the work to keep her mind from constantly returning to the shock, and the lower school needed her guidance during this difficult time.

During lunch hour, Sandy walked to Naomi's office, then both of them walked across the quad to the upper school administration building—Old Main.

"Becoming the leader is easier than being the teacher, isn't it?" Naomi asked him.

"I guess for these last seven years I've been the loyal opposition." He tightened the school scarf around his neck. "I'm finding out that no matter what decision I make there's someone to 'yes' me, someone to 'no' me, and everyone to second-guess me. It's curious to realize how people want to have their own way without doing the work."

She smiled. "Monday morning quarterbacks. Roscoe used to say that they never had to take the hits." She wiggled her fingers in her fur-lined gloves. "He wasn't your favorite person, Sandy, but he was an effective headmaster."

"Yes. My major disagreement with Roscoe was not over daily operations. You know I respected his administrative skills. My view of St. Elizabeth's curriculum was one hundred eighty degrees from his, though. We must emphasize the basics. Take, for instance, his computer drive. Great. We've got every kid in this school computer literate. So?" He threw up his hands. "They stare into a lighted screen. Knowing how to use the technology is useless if you have nothing to say, and the only way you can have something to say is by studying the great texts of our culture. The computer can't read and comprehend *The Federalist Papers* for them."

"Teaching people to think is an ancient struggle," she said. "That's why I love working in the lower school . . . they're so young . . . their minds are open. They soak up everything."

He opened the door for her. They stepped into the administration building, which also had some classrooms on the first floor. A blast of warm radiator heat welcomed them.

They climbed the wide stairs to the second floor, entering Roscoe's office from the direction that did not require them to pass April's office.

She was on her hands and knees putting videotapes into a cardboard box. The tapes had lined a bottom shelf of the bookcase.

"April, I can do that," Naomi said.

Not rising, April replied, "These are McKinchie's. I thought I'd return them to him this afternoon." She held up a tape of *Red River*. "He lent us his library for film history week."

"Yes, he did, and I forgot all about it." Naomi noticed the girls of the field hockey team leaving the cafeteria together. Karen Jensen, in the lead, was tossing an apple to Brooks Tucker.

"April, I'll be moving into this office next week. I can't conduct meetings in that small temporary office. Will you call Design Interiors for me? I'd like them to come out here." Sandy's voice was clear.

"What's wrong with keeping things just as they are? It will save money." She dropped more tapes into the box, avoiding eye contact.

"I need this office to be comfortable—"

"This is comfortable," she interrupted.

"—for me," he continued.

"Well, you might not be appointed permanent headmaster. The board will conduct a search. Why spend money?"

"April, that won't happen before this school year is finished." Naomi stepped in, kind but firm. "Sandy needs our support in order to do the best job he can for St. Elizabeth's. Working in Roscoe's shadow"—she indicated the room, the paintings—"isn't the way to do that."

April scrambled to her feet. "Why are you helping him? He dogged Roscoe every step of the way!"

Naomi held up her hands, still gloved, in a gesture of peace. "April, Sandy raised issues inside our circle that allowed us to prepare for hard questions from the board. He wasn't my husband's best friend, but he has always had the good of St. Elizabeth's at heart."

April clamped her lips shut. "I don't want to do it, but I'll do it for you." She picked up the carton and walked by Sandy, closing the door behind her.

He exhaled, jamming his hands in his pockets. "Naomi, I don't ask that April be fired. She's given long years of service, but there's absolutely no way I can work with her or her with me. I need to find my own secretary—and that will bump up the budget."

She finally took off her gloves to sit on the edge of Roscoe's massive desk. "We'll have to fire her, Sandy. She'll foment rebellion from wherever she sits."

"Maybe McKinchie could use her. He has enough money, and she'd be happy in his little home office."

"She won't be happy anywhere." Naomi hated this whole subject. "She was so in love with Roscoe—I used to tease him about it. No one will ever measure up to him in her eyes. You know, I believe if he had asked her to walk to hell and back, she would have." She smiled ruefully. "Of course, she didn't have to live with him."

"Well, I won't ask her to walk that far, but I guess you're right. She'll have to go."

"Let's talk to Marilyn Sanburne first. Perhaps she'll have an idea—or Mim."

"Good God, Mim will run St. Elizabeth's if you let her."

"The world." Naomi swung her legs to and fro. "St. Elizabeth's is too small a stage for Mim the Magnificent."

April opened the door. "I know you two are talking about me."

"At this precise moment we were talking about Mim."

Sourly, April shut the door. Sandy and Naomi looked at each other and shrugged.

36

"How did I get roped into this?" Harry complained.

Her furry family said nothing as she fumbled with her hastily improvised costume. Preferring a small group of friends to big parties, Harry had to be dragged to larger affairs. Even though this was a high school dance and she was a chaperon, she still had to unearth something to wear, snag a date, stand on her feet, and chat up crashing bores. She thought of the other chaperons. One such would be Maury McKinchie, fascinating to most people but not to Harry. Since he was a chaperon, she'd have to gab with him. His standard fare, those delicious stories of what star did what and to whom on his various films, filled her with ennui. Had he been a hunting man she might have endured him, but he was not. He also appeared much too interested in her breasts. Maury was one of those men who didn't look you in the eye when he spoke to you—he spoke to your breasts.

Sandy Brashiers she liked until he grew waspish about the other faculty at St. Elizabeth's. With Roscoe dead he would need to find a new whipping boy. Still, he looked her in the eye when he spoke to her, and that was refreshing.

Ed Sugarman collected old cigarette advertisements. He might expound on the chemical properties of nicotine, but if she could steer him toward soccer, he proved knowledgeable and entertaining.

Coach Hallvard could be lively. Harry then remembered that the dreaded Florence Rubicon would be prowling the dance floor. Harry's Latin ebbed away with each year but she remembered enough Catullus to keep the old girl happy.

Harry laughed to herself. Every Latin teacher and subsequent professor she had ever studied under had been an odd duck, but there was something so endearing about them all. She kept reading Latin partly to bask in the full bloom of eccentricity.

"I can't wear this!" Harry winced, throwing off a tight pump. The patent leather shoe scuttled across the floor. She checked the clock, groaning anew.

"There's time," Mrs. Murphy said. "Can the tuxedo. It isn't you."

"I fed you."

"Don't be obtuse. Get out of the tuxedo." Murphy spoke louder, a habit of hers when humans proved dense. "You need something with imagination."

"Harry doesn't have imagination," Tucker declared honestly.

"She has good legs," Pewter replied.

"What does that have to do with imagination?" Tucker wanted to know.

"Nothing, but she should wear something that shows off her legs."

Mrs. Murphy padded into the closet. "There's one sorry skirt hanging in here."

"I didn't even know Mom owned a skirt."

"This has to be a leftover from college." The tiger inspected the brown skirt.

Pewter joined her. "I thought she was going to clean out her closet?"

"She organized her chest of drawers; that's a start."

The two cats peered upward at the skirt, then at each other.

"Shall we?"

"Let's." Pewter's eyes widened.

They reached up, claws unsheathed, and shredded the skirt.

"*Wheee!*" They dug in.

Harry, hearing the sound of cloth shredding, poked her head in the closet, the single light bulb swaying overhead. "Hey!"

With one last mighty yank, Mrs. Murphy scooted out of the closet. Pewter, a trifle slower, followed.

Harry, aghast, took out the skirt. "I could brain you two. I've had this skirt since my sophomore year at Crozet High."

"*We know,*" came the titters from under the bed.

"*Cats can be so destructive.*" Tucker's soulful eyes brimmed with sympathy.

"*Brownnoser!*" Murphy accused.

"*I am a mighty cat. What wondrous claws have I. I can rip and tear and even shred the sky,*" Pewter sang.

"Great. Ruin my skirt and now caterwaul underneath the bed." Harry knelt down to behold four luminous chartreuse eyes peeking at her. "Bad kitties."

"*Hee hee.*"

"I mean it. No treats for you."

Pewter leaned into Murphy. "*This is your fault.*"

"*Sell me out for a treatie.*" Mrs. Murphy bumped her.

Harry dropped the dust ruffle back down. She stared at the ruined skirt.

Murphy called out from her place of safety, "*Go as a vagabond. You know, go as one of those poor characters from a Victor Hugo novel.*"

"Wonder if I could make a costume out of this?"

"*She got it!*" Pewter was amazed.

"*Don't count your chickens.*" Mrs. Murphy slithered out from under the bed. "*I'll make sure she puts two and two together.*"

With that she launched herself onto the bed and from the bed she hurtled toward the closet, catching the clothes. She hung there, swaying, then found the tattiest shirt she could find. She sank her claws in and slid down to the floor, the intoxicating sound of rent fabric heralding her descent.

"You're crazy!" Harry dashed after her, but Murphy blasted into the living room, jumped on a chair arm, then wiggled her rear end as though she was going to leap into the bookshelves filled not only with books but with Harry's ribbons and trophies. "Don't you dare."

"*Then leave me alone,*" Murphy sassed, "*and put together your vagabond costume. Time's a-wasting.*"

The human and the cat squared off, eye to eye. "You're in a mood, pussycat."

Tucker tiptoed out. Pewter remained under the bed, straining to hear.

"What's got into you?"

"*It's Halloween,*" Murphy screeched.

Harry reached over to grab the insouciant feline, but Mrs. Murphy easily avoided her. She hopped to the other side of the chair, then ran back into the bedroom where she leapt into the clothes and tore them up some more.

"*Yahoo! Banzai! Death to the Emperor!*"

"*Have you been watching those World War Two movies again?*" Tucker laughed.

"*Don't shoot until you see the whites of their eyes.*" Murphy leapt in the air, turning full circle and landing in the middle of the clothes.

"*She's on a military kick.*" Pewter snuck out from under the bed. "*If you get us both punished, Murphy, I will be really upset.*"

Murphy catapulted off the bed right onto Pewter. The two rolled across the bedroom floor, entertaining Harry with their catfight.

Finally Pewter, put out, extricated herself from the grasp of Murphy. She stalked off to the kitchen.

"*Fraidycat.*"

"*Mental case,*" Pewter shot back.

"Anything that happens tonight will be dull after this," Harry said with a sigh.

Boy, did she have a wrong number.

37

Little Mim, taut under her powdered face, wig bobbling, wandered across the highly polished gym floor to Harry. At least she thought it was Harry because the vagabond's escort, a pirate, was too tall to be anyone but Fair.

The dance was turning into a huge success, thanks to the band, Yada Yada Yada.

The curved sword, stuck through his sash, gave Fair a dangerous air. Other partyers wore swords. There was Stonewall Jackson and Julius Caesar. A few wore pistols that upon close examination turned out to be squirt guns.

Karen Jensen, behind a golden mask, drove the boys wild because she came as a golden-haired Artemis. Quite a bit of Karen was showing, and it was prime grade.

But then, quite a bit of Harry was showing, and that wasn't bad either.

Little Mim put her hand on Harry's forearm. "Could I have a minute?"

"Sure. Fair, I'll be right back."

"Okay," he replied from under his twirling mustache.

Marilyn pulled Harry into a corner of the auditorium. Madonna and King Kong were making out behind them. King Kong was having a hard time of it.

"I hope you aren't cross with me. I should have called you."

"About what?"

"I asked Blair to the dance. Well, it wasn't just that I needed an escort, but I thought I might interest him in the school and—"

"I have no claim on him. Anyway, we're just friends," Harry said soothingly.

"Thanks. I'd hoped you'd understand." Her wig wobbled. "How did they manage with these things?" She glanced around. "Can you guess who Stonewall Jackson is?"

"Mmm, the paunch means he's a chaperon," Harry stated.

"Kendrick Miller."

"Where's Irene? It isn't World War Three yet with those two, is it?"

"Irene's over there. It'd be a perfect costume if she were twenty years younger. Some women can't accept getting old, I guess." She indicated the woodland fairy, the wings diaphanous over the thin wire. Then, lowering her voice, "Did you see April Shively? Dressed as a witch. How appropriate."

"I thought you liked April?"

Realizing she might have said too much, Little Mim backtracked. "She's not herself since Roscoe's death, and she's making life difficult for everyone from the board on down to the faculty. It will pass."

"Or she will," Harry joked.

"Two bewitching masked beauties." Maury McKinchie complimented them from behind his Rhett Butler mask.

"What a line!" Harry laughed, her voice giving her away.

"May I have this dance?" Maury bowed to Harry, who took a turn on the floor.

Little Mim, happy she wasn't asked, hastened to Blair as fast as her wig would allow.

Sean Hallahan, dressed as a Hell's Angel, danced with Karen Jensen. After the dance ended, he escorted her off the floor. "Karen, is everyone mad at me?"

Jody, dragged along by her mother, glared at Sean. She was in a skeleton outfit that concealed her face, but Sean knew it was Jody.

"Jody is."

"Are you mad at me?"

"No."

"I feel like you've been avoiding me."

"Field hockey practice takes up as much time as football practice." She paused, clearing her throat. "And you've been a little weird lately—distant."

"Yeah, I know."

"Sean, you couldn't help the way things turned out—Mr. Fletcher's dying—and until then it was pretty funny. Even the phony obituary for Mr. McKinchie was funny."

"I didn't do that."

"I know, it was on Roger's paper route, and he says he didn't do it either."

"But I *really* didn't." He sensed her disbelief.

"Okay, okay."

"That's an incredible costume," he said admiringly.

"Thanks."

"Karen—do you like me a little?"

"A little," she said teasingly, "but what about Jody?"

"It's not—well, you know. We're close but not that way. We practiced a lot this summer and—"

"Practiced what?"

"Tennis. It's our spring sport." He swallowed hard.

"Oh." She remembered Jody's version of the summer.

"Will you go out with me next Friday after the game?"

"Yes," she said without hesitation.

He smiled, pushing her back out on the dance floor.

Coach Renee Hallvard, dressed as Garfield the cat, sidled up next to Harry.

"Harry, is that you?"

"Coach?"

"Yes, or should I say 'Meow'?"

"Wonder what Mrs. Murphy would say about this?"

Coach reached back, draping her tail over her arm. "Get a life."

They both laughed.

"She probably would say that."

"If you don't mind, I'll drop off this year's field hockey rule book on Monday."

"Why?" Harry murmured expectantly.

"I need a backup referee—just in case. You know the game."

"Oh, Coach. Make Susan do it."

"She can't." Coach Hallvard laughed at Harry. "Brooks is on the team."

"Well—okay."

Coach Hallvard clapped her on the back. "You're a good sport."

"Sucker is more like it."

Rhett Butler asked Harry to dance a second time. "You've got beautiful legs."

"Thank you," she murmured.

"I ought to give you a screen test."

"Get out of here." Harry thumped his back with her left hand.

"You're very attractive. The camera likes some people. It might like you." He paused. "What's so curious is that even professionals don't know who will be good on-screen and who won't."

"Rhett," she joked because she knew it was Maury, "I bet you say that to all the girls."

"Ha." He threw his head back and laughed. "Just the pretty ones."

"In fact, I heard you have a car full of vital essences, so you must have said something to BoomBoom."

"Oh!" His voice lowered. "What was I thinking?"

Part of Maury's charm was that he never pretended to be better than he was.

"Hey, I'll never tell."

"You won't have to. She will." He sighed, "You see, Harry, I'm a man who needs a lot of attention, female attention. I admit it."

Stonewall and Garfield, dancing near them, turned their heads. "You don't give a damn who you seduce and who you hurt. You don't need attention, you need your block knocked off," Kendrick Miller, as Stonewall, mumbled.

Rhett danced on. "Kendrick Miller, you're a barrel of laughs. I say what I think. You think being a repressed Virginian is a triumph. I think you're pathetic."

Kendrick stopped. Coach Hallvard stepped back.

"Guys. Chill out," Harry told them.

"I'll meet you after the dance, McKinchie. You say where and when."

"Are we going to fight a duel, Kendrick? Do I get the choice of weapons?"

"Sure."

"Pies. You need a pie in the face."

Harry dragged Maury backward. She had heard about Kendrick's flash temper.

"Since we can't use guns, we can start with fists," Kendrick called after him as Renee Hallvard pulled him in the direction opposite Maury.

As the dancers closed the spaces left by the vacating couples, a few noticed the minor hostilities. Fortunately, most of the students were wrapped up in the music and one another.

Jody put her hands on her hips, turned her back on her father, and walked to the water fountain. She had to take off the mask to drink.

"What a putz!" Maury shook his head.

"No one has ever accused Kendrick of having a good time or a sense of humor." Harry half laughed.

"Totally humorless." Maury emphasized the word. "Thank God his kid doesn't take after him. Funny thing, though, the camera liked Jody, and yet Karen Jensen is the more beautiful girl. I noticed that when we had our one-day film clinic."

"Hmm."

"Ah, the camera . . . it reveals things the naked eye can't see." He bowed. "Thank you, madam. Don't forget your screen test."

She curtseyed. "Sir." Then she whispered, "Where's your bodyguard?"

He winked. "I made that up."

Fair ambled over when he'd gone. "Slinging the bull, as usual?"

"Actually, we were talking about the camera . . . after he had a few words with Kendrick Miller. Testosterone poisoning."

"If you keep saying that, I'll counter with 'raging hormones.' "

"You do, anyway, behind our backs."

"I do not."

"Most men do."

"I'm not most men."

"No, you aren't." She slipped her arm through his.

The evening progressed without further incident, except that Sean Hallahan had a flask of booze in his motorcycle jacket. No one saw him drinking from it, but he swayed on his feet after each return from outside.

He got polluted, and when someone dressed as a Musketeer showed up at the party, sword in hand, and knocked him down, he couldn't get up.

As Yada Yada Yada played the last song of the evening, some of the kids began sneaking off. Roger and Brooks danced the last dance. They were a hit as Lucy and Desi.

A piercing scream didn't stop the dancers. After all, ghosts and goblins were about.

The piercing scream was followed by moans that seemed frightening enough. Finally, Harry and Fair left the dance to investigate. They found Rhett Butler lying bleeding on the hall floor, gasping for breath as the blood spurted from his throat and his chest. Bending over him, sword in hand, was a paunchy Stonewall Jackson.

38

Maury McKinchie died before the rescue squad arrived at St. Elizabeth's. Rick Shaw, sirens blaring, arrived seconds after his final gurgle.

Rick lifted Kendrick's bloodied sword from his hand.

"It wasn't me, it was the Musketeer. I fought him off, but it was too late," Kendrick babbled.

"Kendrick Miller, I am booking you under suspicion of murder. You have the right to remain silent . . ." Rick began.

Harry, Fair, Little Mim, and the other chaperons quickly cordoned off the hallway leading to the big outside doors, making sure that Irene was hurried out of the gym. Florence Rubicon ushered the dancers out by another exit at the end of the gym floor. Still, a few kids managed to creep in to view the corpse.

Karen and Sean, both mute, simply stared.

Jody walked up behind them, her mask off, her hair tousled, the horror of the scene sinking in. "Dad? Dad, what's going on?"

Cynthia flipped open her notebook and started asking questions.

Sandy Brashiers, in a low voice, said to Little Mim, "People are going to yank their kids out of here. By Monday this school will be a ghost town."

39

A light brown stubble covered Rick Shaw's square chin. As his thinning hair was light brown, the contrast amused Cynthia Cooper, although little was amusing at the moment.

The ashtray in the office overflowed. The coffee machine pumped out cup after cup of the stimulant.

Cynthia regretted Maury McKinchie's murder, not just because a man was cut down, literally, but because Sunday, which would dawn in a couple of hours, was her day off. She had planned to drive over to the beautiful town of Monterey, almost on the West Virginia border. She'd be driving alone. Her job prevented her from having much of a social life. It wasn't that she didn't meet men. She did. Usually they were speeding seventy-five miles per hour in a fifty-five zone. They rarely smiled when they saw her, even though she was easy on the eyes. The roundup of drunks at the mall furnished her with scores of men, and they fell all over her—literally. The occasional white-collar criminal enlivened her harvest of captive males.

Over the last years of working together she and Rick had grown close. As he was a happily married man, not a hint of impropriety tainted their relationship. She relied on his friendship, hard won because when she joined the force as the first woman Rick was less than thrilled.

The one man she truly liked, Blair Bainbridge, set many hearts on fire. She felt she didn't have a chance.

Rick liked to work from flow charts. He'd started three, ultimately throwing out each of them.

"What time is it?"

"Five thirty."

"It's always darkest before the dawn." Rick quoted the old saw. He swung his feet onto his desktop. "I hate to admit that I'm stumped, but I am."

"We've got Kendrick Miller in custody."

"Not for long. He'll get a big-money lawyer, and that will be that. And it had occurred to me that Kendrick isn't the kind of man to get caught committing a murder. Standing over a writhing victim doesn't compute."

"Could have lost his head." She emptied her cup. She couldn't face another swig of coffee. "But you're not buying, are you?"

"No." He paused. "We deal in the facts. The facts are, he had a bloody sword in his hand."

"And there were two other partyers wearing swords. One of whom vanished into thin air."

"Or knew where to hide."

"Not one kid there knew who the Musketeer was or had heard him speak." Cooper leaned against the small sink in the corner of the old room. She held her fingers to her temples, which throbbed. "Boss, let's back up. Let's start with Roscoe Fletcher."

"I'm listening."

"Sandy Brashiers coveted Roscoe's job. They never saw eye to eye."

He held up his hand. "Granted, but killing to become headmaster of St. Elizabeth's—is the game worth the candle?"

"People have killed for less."

"You're right. You're right." He folded his hands over his chest and made a mental note to dig into Sandy's past.

"Anyone could have poisoned Roscoe. He left his car unlocked, his office unlocked. It wouldn't take a rocket scientist to put a hard candy drenched in poison in his car or in his pocket or to hand it to him. Anyone could do it."

"Who would want to do it, though?" She put her hands behind her head, "Not one trace of poison was found in the tin of strawberry hard candies in his car. And the way he handed out candy, half the county would be dead. So we know the killer had a conscience, sort of."

"That's a quaint way of looking at it."

"I have a hunch Roscoe was sleeping with Irene Miller." Cynthia shook her feet, which were falling asleep in her regulation shoes. "That would be a motive for the first murder."

"We have no proof that he was carrying on an extramarital affair."

Cynthia smirked. "This is Albemarle County."

Rick half laughed, then stood up to stretch. "Everyone's got secrets, Coop. The longer I work this show, the more I realize that every single person harbors secrets."

"What about that money in the Jiffy bag?" Cynthia said.

"Too many prints on the bag and not a single one on the money." Rick sighed. "I am flat running into walls. The obvious conclusion is drug money, but we haven't got one scrap of evidence."

Cynthia shot a rubber band in the air. It landed with a flop on Rick's desk. "These murders are tied together, I'll bet my badge on that, but what I can't figure out is what an expensive school like St. Elizabeth's has to do with it. All roads lead back to that school."

"Roscoe's murder was premeditated. Maury's was not—or so it

appears. Kendrick Miller has a tie to St. Elizabeth's, but—" He shrugged.

"But"—Cooper shot another rubber band straight in the air— "while we're just postulating—"

"Postulating? I'm pissing in the wind."

"You do that." She caught the rubber band as it fell back. "Listen to me. St. Elizabeth's is the tie. What if Fletcher and McKinchie were filching alumni contributions?"

"Kendrick Miller isn't going to kill over alumni misappropriations." He batted down her line of thought.

The phone rang. The on-duty operator, Joyce Thomson, picked it up.

Cynthia said, "I've always wanted to pick up the phone and say, 'Cops and Robbers.' "

Rick's line buzzed. He punched in the button so Cynthia could listen. "Yo."

"Sheriff," Joyce Thomson said, "it's John Aurieano. Mrs. Berryhill's cows are on his land, and he's going to shoot them if you don't remove them."

Rick punched the line and listened to the torrent of outrage. "Mrs. Berryhill's a small woman, Mr. Aurieano. She can't round up her cattle without help, and it will take me hours to send someone over to help. We're shorthanded."

More explosions.

"Tell you what, I'll send someone to move them, but let me give you some friendly advice. . . . This is the country. Cows are part of the country, and I'll let you in on something quite shocking—they can't read 'No Trespassing' signs. You shoot the cows, Mr. Aurieano, and you're going to be in a lot more trouble than you can imagine. If you don't like the way things are, then move back to the city!" He put the phone down. "You know, there are days when this job is a real pain in the ass."

40

A subdued congregation received early-morning mass. Jody Miller and her mother, Irene, sat in a middle pew. The entire Hallahan family occupied a pew on the left. Samson Coles made a point of sitting beside Jody. Lucinda squeezed next to Irene. Whatever Kendrick Miller may or may not have done, the opprobrium shouldn't attach to his wife and child.

Still, parishioners couldn't help staring.

Rick and Cooper knelt in the back row. Rick's head bobbed as he started to drift off, and his forehead touched his hand. He jerked his head up. "Sorry," he whispered.

He and Cynthia waited in the vestibule while people shuffled out after the service. Curious looks passed among the churchgoers as everyone watched to see if the police would stop Irene. She and Jody passed Rick without looking right or left. The Hallahans nodded a greeting but kept moving.

Finally, disappointed, the rest of the congregation walked into the brisk air, started their cars, and drove away.

Rick checked his watch, then knocked on the door at the left of the vestibule.

"Who's there?" Father Michael called out, hearing the knock.

"Rick Shaw and Deputy Cooper."

Father Michael, wearing his robe and surplice, opened the door. "Come in, Sheriff, Deputy."

"I don't mean to disturb you on Sunday. I have a few quick questions, Father."

He motioned. "Come in. Sit down for a minute."

"Thanks." They stepped inside, collapsing on the old leather sofa. "We're beat. No sleep."

"I didn't sleep much myself. . . ."

"Have you been threatened, Father?" Rick's voice cracked from fatigue.

"No."

"In your capacity as chaplain to St. Elizabeth's, have you noticed anything unusual, say, within the faculty? Arguments with Roscoe? Problems with the alumni committee?"

Father Michael paused a long time, his narrow but attractive face solemn. "Roscoe and Sandy Brashiers were inclined to go at it. Nothing that intense, though. They never learned to agree to disagree, if you know what I mean."

"I think I do." Rick nodded. "Apart from the inviolate nature of the confessional, do you know or have you heard of any sexual improprieties involving Roscoe?"

"Uh—" The middle-aged man paused a long time again. "There was talk. But that's part and parcel of a small community."

"Any names mentioned?" Cynthia said. "Like Irene Miller, maybe?"

"No."

"What about Sandy Brashiers and Naomi Fletcher?"

"I'd heard that one. The version goes something like, Naomi tires of Roscoe's infidelities and enlists his enemy, or shall we say rival, to dispose of him."

Rick stood up. "Father, thank you for your time. If anything occurs to you or you want to talk, call me or Coop."

"Sheriff"—Father Michael weighed his words—"am I in danger?"

"I hope not," Rick answered honestly.

41

April Shively was arrested Monday morning at the school. She was charged with obstructing justice since she had consistently refused to hand over the school records, first to Sandy, then to the police. As she and Roscoe had worked hand in glove, not even Naomi knew how much April had removed and hidden.

Sandy Brashiers wasted no time in terminating her employment. On her way out of the school, April turned and slapped his face. Cynthia Cooper hustled her to the squad car.

St. Elizabeth's, deserted save for faculty, stood forlorn in the strong early November winds. Sandy and Naomi convened an emergency meeting of faculty and interested parties. Neither could answer the most important question: What was happening at St. Elizabeth's?

The Reverend Herbert C. Jones received an infuriating phone call from Darla McKinchie. No, she would not be returning to Albemarle County for a funeral service. She would be shipping her late husband's body to Los Angeles immediately. Would the Reverend please handle the arrangements with Dale and Delaney Funeral Home? She would make a handsome contribution to the church. Naturally, he agreed, but was upset by her high-handed manner and the fact that she cared so little for Maury's local friends, but then again, she seemed to care little for Maury himself.

Blue Monday yielded surprises every hour on the hour, it seemed. Jody Miller learned that yes, she was pregnant. She begged Dr. Larry Johnson not to call her mother. He wouldn't agree since she was under twenty-one, so she pitched a hissy fit right there in the examining room. Hayden McIntire, the doctor's much younger partner, and two nurses rushed in to restrain Jody.

The odd thing was that when Irene Miller arrived it was she who cried, not Jody. The shame of an out-of-wedlock pregnancy cut Irene to the core. She was fragile enough, thanks to the tensions inside her house and now outside it as well. As for Jody, she had no shame about her condition, she simply didn't want to be pregnant. Larry advised mother and daughter to have a heart-to-heart but not in his examining room.

At twelve noon Kendrick Miller was released on $250,000 bail into the custody of his lawyer, Ned Tucker. At one in the afternoon, he told his divorce lawyer not to serve papers on Irene. She didn't need that crisis on top of this one, he said. What he really wanted was for Irene to stand beside him, but Kendrick being Kendrick, he had to make it sound as though he were doing his wife a big favor.

At two thirty he blasted Sandy Brashiers on the phone and said he was taking his daughter out of that sorry excuse for a school until things got straightened out over there. By three thirty the situation was so volatile that Kendrick picked up the phone and asked Father Michael for help. For him to admit he needed help was a step in the right direction.

By four forty-five the last surprise of the day occurred when BoomBoom Craycroft lost control of her shiny brand-new 7 series BMW. She had roared up the alleyway behind the post office where she spun in a 360-degree turn, smashing into Harry's blue Ford.

Hearing the crash, the animals rushed out of the post office.

BoomBoom, without a scratch herself, opened the door to her metallic green machine, put one foot on the ground, and started to wail.

"Is she hurt?" Tucker ran over.

Mrs. Murphy, moving at a possum trot, declared, "Her essences are shaken."

In the collision the plastic case in which BoomBoom kept her potions slammed up against the dash, cracking and spilling out a concoction of rose, sage, and comfrey.

Harry opened the backdoor. "Oh, no!"

"I couldn't help it! My heel got stuck in the mat." BoomBoom wept.

Mrs. Hogendobber stuck her head out the door. Her body immediately followed. "Are you all right?"

"My neck hurts."

"Do you want me to call the rescue squad?" Harry asked, dubious but giving BoomBoom the benefit of the doubt.

"No. I'll go over to Larry's. It's probably whiplash." She viewed the caved-in side of the truck. "I'm insured, Harry, don't worry."

Harry sighed. Her poor truck. Tucker ran underneath to inspect the frame, which was undamaged. The BMW had suffered one little dent in the right fender.

Pewter, moving at a slower pace, walked around the truck. "We can still drive home in it. It's only the side that's bashed in."

"I'll call the sheriff's department." Miranda, satisfied that BoomBoom was fine, walked back into the post office.

Market Shiflett opened his backdoor. "I thought I heard something." He surveyed the situation.

Before he could speak, BoomBoom said, "No bones broken."

"Good." He heard the front door ring and ducked back into his store.

"Come inside." Harry helped her former rival out of the car. "It's cold out here."

"My heel stuck in that brand-new mat I bought." She pointed to a fuzzy mat with the BMW logo on it.

"BoomBoom, why wear high heels to run your errands?"

"Oh—well—" Her hand fluttered.

"Where have you been? You always come down to pick up your mail."

"I've been under the weather. These murders upset me."

Once inside, Mrs. Hogendobber brewed a strong cup of tea while they waited for someone to appear from the sheriff's department.

"I think it's dreadful that Darla McKinchie, that self-centered nothing of an actress, isn't having the service here." BoomBoom, revived by the tea, told them about Herb's phone call. She'd seen Herbie Jones at the florist.

"That is pretty cold-blooded." Harry bent down to tie her shoelaces. Mrs. Murphy helped.

"Someone should sponsor a service here."

"That would be lovely, BoomBoom, why don't you do it?" Miranda smiled, knowing she'd told BoomBoom to do what she wanted to do anyway.

After the officer left, having asked questions about the accident and taken pictures, the insurance agent showed up and did the same. Then he was gone, and finally BoomBoom herself left, which greatly relieved Harry, who strained to be civil to a woman she disliked. BoomBoom said she was too rattled to drive her car, so Lucinda Coles picked her up. BoomBoom left her car at the post office, keys in the ignition.

42

"April, cooperate, for Christ's sake." Cooper, exasperated, rapped her knuckles on the table.

"No, I'll stay here and live off the county for a while. My taxes paid for this jail." She pushed back a stray forelock.

"Removing documents pertinent to the murder of Roscoe Fletcher—"

April interrupted. "But they're not! They're pertinent to the operations of St. Elizabeth's, and that's none of your business."

Cooper slapped her hand hard on the table. "Embezzlement is my business!"

April, not one to be shaken by an accusation, pursed her lips. "Prove it."

Cynthia stretched her long legs, took a deep breath, counted to ten, and started anew. "You have an important place in this community. Don't throw it away to protect a dead man."

Folding her arms across her chest, April withdrew into hostile silence.

Cooper did likewise.

Twenty minutes later April piped up, "You can't prove I had an affair with him either. That's what everyone thinks. Don't give me this baloney about having an important place in the community."

"But you do. You're important to St. Elizabeth's."

April leaned forward, both elbows on the table. "I'm a secretary. That's nothing"—she made a gesture of dismissal with her hand—"to people around here. But I'm a damned good secretary."

"I'm sure you are."

"And"—she lurched forward a bit more—"Sandy Brashiers will ruin everything we worked for, I guarantee it. That man lives in a dream world, and he's sneaky. Well, he may be temporary headmaster, but headmaster of what! No one was at school today."

"You were."

"That's my job. Besides, no one is going to kill me—I'm too low on the totem pole."

"If you know why Roscoe was killed, they might."

"I don't know."

"If you did, would you tell me?"

A brief silence followed this question as a clap of thunder follows lightning.

Looking Cynthia square in the eye, April answered resolutely. "Yes. And I'll tell you something else. Roscoe had something on Sandy Brashiers. He never told me what it was, but it helped him keep Sandy in line."

"Any ideas—any ideas at all?"

"No." She gulped air. "I wish I knew. I really do."

43

Kendrick stared at Jody's red BMW as she exploded. "No! I paid for it with Grandpa K's money. He left the money to me, not you."

"He left it to pay for college, and you promised to keep it in savings." His face reddened.

Irene, attempting to defuse a full-scale blowup, stepped in. "We're all tired. Let's discuss this tomorrow." She knew perfectly well this was not the time to bring up the much larger issue of Jody's pregnancy.

"Stop protecting her," Kendrick ordered.

"You know, Dad, we're not employees. You can't order us around."

He slammed the side door of the kitchen, returning inside with the BMW keys in his hand. He dangled them under his daughter's nose. "You're not going anywhere."

She shrugged since she'd stashed away the second set of keys.

Kendrick calmed down for a moment. "Did you pick the car up today?"

"Uh—"

"No, she's had it for a few days."

"Three days."

Irene didn't know how long Jody had had the car, but that was hardly a major worry. She'd become accustomed to her daughter's lying to her. Other parents said their children did the same, especially in the adolescent years, but Irene still felt uneasy about it. Getting used to something didn't mean one liked it.

"If you've had this car three days, where was it?"

"I lent it to a friend."

"Don't lie to me!" The veins stood out in Kendrick's neck.

"Isn't it a little late to try and be a dad now?" she mumbled.

He backhanded her across the face hard. Tears sprang into her eyes. "The car goes back!"

"No way."

He hit her again.

"Kendrick, please!"

"Stay out of this."

"She's my daughter, too. She's made a foolish purchase, but that's how we learn, by making foolish mistakes," Irene pleaded.

"Where did you hide the car?" Kendrick bellowed.

"You can beat me to a pulp. I'll never tell you."

He raised his hand again. Irene hung on to it as Jody ducked. He threw his wife onto the floor.

"Go to your room."

Jody instantly scurried to her room.

Kendrick checked his watch. "It's too late to take the car back now. You can follow me over tomorrow."

Irene scrambled to her feet. "She'll lose a lot of money, won't she?"

"Twenty-one percent." He turned from Irene's slightly bedraggled form to walk into the kitchen, where he turned on the television to watch CNN.

He forgot or didn't care that Jody had a telephone in her room, which she used the second she shut her door.

"Hello, is Sean there?"

Moments later Sean picked up the phone.

"It's Jody."

"Oh, hi." He was wary.

"I just found out today that I'm pregnant."

A gasp followed. "What are you going to do?"

"Tell everyone it was you."

"You can't do that!"

"Why not? You didn't find me that repulsive this summer."

A flash of anger hit him. "How do you know it was me?"

"You asshole!" She slammed down the receiver.

A shaken, lonely Sean Hallahan put the receiver back on the cradle.

44

The front-office staff at Crozet High, frazzled by parental requests to accept transfers from St. Elizabeth's, stopped answering the phone. The line in the hall took precedence.

The middle school and grammar school suffered the same influx.

Sandy Brashiers took out an ad in the newspaper. He had had the presence of mind to place the full-page ad the moment Maury was killed. Given lag time, it ran today.

The ad stated that the board of directors and temporary headmaster regretted the recent incidents at St. Elizabeth's, but these involved adults, not students.

He invited parents to come to his office at Old Main Building or to visit him at home . . . and he begged parents not to pull their children out of the school.

A few parents read the ad as they stood in line.

Meanwhile, the St. Elizabeth's students were thoroughly enjoying their unscheduled vacation.

Karen Jensen had called Coach Hallvard asking that the hockey team be allowed to practice with Crozet High in the afternoon until things straightened out.

Roger Davis used the time to work at the car wash. Jody said she needed money, so she was there, too.

Karen borrowed her daddy's car, more reliable than her own old Volvo, and took Brooks with her to see Mary Baldwin College in Staunton. She was considering applying there but wanted to see it without her mom and dad.

The college was only thirty-five miles from Crozet.

"I'd rather finish out at St. Elizabeth's than go to Crozet High." Karen cruised along, the old station wagon swaying on the highway. "Transferring now could mess up my grade-point average, and besides, we're not the ones in danger. So I'd just as soon go back."

"My parents are having a fit." Brooks sighed and looked out the window as they rolled west down Waynesboro's Main Street.

"Everybody's are. Major weird. BoomBoom Craycroft said it's karma."

"Karma is celestial recycling," Brooks cracked.

"Three points."

"I thought so, too." She smiled. "It is bizarre. Do you think the killer is someone at St. Elizabeth's?"

"Sean." Karen giggled.

"Hey, some people really think he did kill Mr. Fletcher. And everyone thinks Mr. Miller skewered Mr. McKinchie. He just got out of jail because he's rich. He was standing over him, sword in hand."

Brooks stared at the sumac, reddening, by the side of the road as they passed the outskirts of Waynesboro. "Did you hear April Shively's in jail? Maybe she did it."

"Women don't kill," Karen said.

"Of course they do."

"Not like men. Ninety-five percent of all murders are committed by men, so the odds are it's a man."

"Karen, women are smarter. They don't get caught."

They both laughed as they rolled into Staunton on Route 250.

45

November can be a tricky month. Delightful warm interludes cast a soft golden glow on tree limbs, a few still sporting colorful leaves. The temperature hovers in the high fifties or low sixties for a few glorious days, then cold air knifes in, a potent reminder that winter truly is around the corner.

This was one of those coppery, warm days, and Harry sat out back of the post office eating a ham sandwich. Sitting in a semicircle at her feet, rapturous in their attentions, were Mrs. Murphy, Pewter, and Tucker.

Mrs. Hogendobber stuck her head out the backdoor. "Take your time with lunch. Nothing much is going on."

Harry swallowed so she wouldn't be talking with her mouth full. "It's a perfect, perfect day. Push the door open and sit out here with me."

"*Bring a sandwich,*" Pewter requested.

"Later. I am determined to reorganize the back shelves. Looks like a storm hit them."

"Save it for a rainy day. Come on," Harry cajoled.

"Well, it is awfully pretty, isn't it?" She disappeared quickly, returning with a sandwich and two orange-glazed buns, her specialty.

Although Mrs. Hogendobber's house was right across the alley from the post office, she liked to bring her lunch and pastries to work with her. A small refrigerator and a hot plate in the back allowed the two women to operate Chez Post, as they sometimes called it.

"The last of my mums." Miranda pointed out the deep russet-colored flowers bordering her fall gardens. "What is there about fall that makes one melancholy?"

"Loss of the light." Harry enjoyed the sharp mustard she'd put on her sandwich.

"And color, although I battle that with pyracantha, the December-blooming camellias, and lots of holly in strategic places. Still, I miss the fragrance of summer."

"Hummingbirds."

"*Baby snakes.*" Mrs. Murphy offered her delectables.

"*Baby mice,*" Pewter chimed in.

"*You have yet to kill a mouse.*" Mrs. Murphy leaned close to Harry just in case her mother felt like sharing.

Pewter, preferring the direct approach, sat in front of Harry, chartreuse eyes lifted upward in appeal. "*Look who's talking. The barn is turning into Mouse Manhattan.*"

Tucker drooled. Mrs. Hogendobber handed her a tidbit of ham, to the fury of the two cats. She tore off two small pieces for them, too.

"*Mine has mustard on it,*" Mrs. Murphy complained.

"*I'll eat it,*" Tucker gallantly volunteered.

"*In a pig's eye.*"

"*Aren't we lucky that Miranda makes all these goodies?*" Pewter nibbled. "*She's the best cook in Crozet.*"

Cynthia Cooper slowly rolled down the alleyway, pulling in next to BoomBoom's BMW. "Great day."

"Join us."

She checked her watch. "Fifteen minutes."

"Make it thirty, and leave your radio on." Harry smiled.

"Good idea." Cynthia cut off the ignition, then turned the volume up on the two-way radio. "Mrs. H., did you make sandwiches for Market today?"

"Indeed, I did."

Cynthia sprinted down the narrow alley between the post office and the market. Within minutes she returned with a smoked turkey sandwich slathered in tarragon mayonnaise, Boston lettuce peeping out from the sides of the whole wheat bread.

The three sat on the back stoop. Every now and then the radio squawked, but no calls for Coop.

"Why did you paint your fingernails?" Harry noticed the raspberry polish.

"Got bored."

"Isn't it funny how Little Mim changes her hairdo? Each time it's a new style or color, you know something is up," Miranda noted.

Sean Hallahan ambled down the alleyway.

"You look like the dogs got at you under the porch." Harry laughed at his disheveled appearance.

"Oh"—he glanced down at his wrinkled clothes—"guess I do."

"Is the football team going to practice at Crozet High? Field hockey is," Harry said.

"Nobody's called me. I don't know what we're going to do. I don't even know if I'm going back to St. Elizabeth's."

"Do you want to?" Cynthia asked.

"Yeah, we've got a good team this year. And it's my senior year. I don't want to go anywhere else."

"That makes sense," Mrs. Hogendobber said.

He ran his finger over the hood of the BMW. "Cool."

"Ultra," Harry replied.

"*Just a car.*" Pewter remained unimpressed by machines.

He bent over, shading his eyes, and peered inside. "Leather. Sure stinks, though."

"She spilled her essences," Harry said.

"*Don't be squirrelly,*" Mrs. Murphy advised.

Sean opened the door, and the competing scents rolled out like a wave. "I hope I get rich."

"Hope you do, too." Harry gave the last of her sandwich to the animals.

He turned on the ignition, rolled down the windows, and clicked on the radio. "Too cool. This is just too cool."

"Where is BoomBoom, anyway?" Cynthia drank iced tea out of a can.

"Who knows? She needs someone to follow her to the BMW dealer. She slightly dented her bumper, not even a dent actually—she rubbed off some of the finish." Harry indicated the spot.

Sean, paying no attention to the conversation, leaned his head back and turned up the radio a bit. He was surrounded by speakers. Then he let off the emergency brake, popped her in reverse, and backed out into the alleyway. He waved at the three women and three animals and carefully rolled forward.

"Should I yank his chain?" Cynthia craned her neck.

"Nah."

They waited a few moments, expecting him to go around the block and reappear. Then they heard the squeal of rubber.

Cooper put down what was left of her sandwich. She stood up. The car was pulling away.

Mrs. Hogendobber listened. "He's not coming back."

"I don't believe this!" Cooper hurried to the squad car as Tucker scarfed down the sandwich remains. She pulled out the speaker, telling the dispatcher where she was and what she was doing. She didn't ask for assistance yet because she thought he was taking a joyride. She hoped to catch him and turn him back before he got into more trouble—he was in enough as it was.

"Can I come?" Harry asked.

"Hop in."

Harry opened the door. Mrs. Murphy and Tucker jumped in with her. "Miranda, do you care?"

"Go on." She waved her off, then glanced down. "Pewter, are you staying with me?"

"*Yes, I am.*" The gray cat followed her back into the post office.

Cynthia turned left, heading toward Route 250. "Sounded like he was heading this way."

"Don't you think he'll make a big circle and come back?"

"Yeah, I do. Right under my nose. . . . Jeez, what a dumb thing to do." She shook her head.

"He hasn't shown the best judgment lately."

Mrs. Murphy settled in Harry's lap while Tucker sat between the humans.

As they reached Route 250, they noticed a lumber truck pulling off to the right side of the road. Cynthia slowed, putting on her flashers. "Stay here." She stepped out. Harry watched as the driver spoke to her and pointed toward the west. A few choice words escaped his tobacco-stained lips. Coop dashed back to the car.

She hit the accelerator and the sirens.

"Trouble?"

"Yep."

Other cars pulled off to the right as Cynthia's car screeched down Route 250 to the base of Afton Mountain. Then they started the climb to the summit, some 1850 feet.

"You think he got on Sixty-four?"

"Yeah. A great big four-lane highway. He's gonna bury the speedometer."

"Shit, Cooper, he's going to bury himself."

"That thought has occurred to me."

Mrs. Murphy leaned over Harry and said to Tucker, "*Fasten your seat belt.*"

"*Yeah,*" the dog replied, wishing there were seat belts made for animals.

Cynthia hurtled past the Howard Johnson's at the top of the mountain, turning left, then turning right to get onto Interstate 64. Vehicles jerked to the right as best they could but in some places on the entrance ramp the shoulder was inadequate. She swerved to avoid the cars.

The Rockfish Valley left behind was supplanted by the Shenandoah Valley. There was a glimpse of Waynesboro off to the right as they got onto I 64.

Remnants of fall foliage blurred. Cynthia negotiated the large sweeping curves on top of the Blue Ridge Mountains.

"What if he took the Skyline Drive?" Harry asked.

"I'm going to have to call in the state police and Augusta County's police, too. Damn!"

"He asked for it," Harry replied sensibly.

"Yes, he did." Cooper called the dispatcher, gave her location, and requested assistance as well as help on the Skyline Drive.

"*Doesn't compute.*" Mrs. Murphy snuggled as Harry held her in the curves.

"*That he stole the car?*"

"*That he did it right in front of them. He wants to get caught.*" Her eyes widened as they hung another curve. "*He's in on it, or he knows something.*"

"*Then why steal a car in front of Coop?*" Tucker asked the obvious question.

"*That's what I mean—something doesn't compute,*" Murphy replied.

Up ahead they caught sight of Sean. Cynthia checked her speedometer. She was hitting ninety, and this was not the safest stretch of road in the state of Virginia.

She slowed a bit. "He's not only going to hurt himself, he's going to hurt someone else." She clicked on the black two-way radio button. "Subject in sight. Just past Ninety-nine on the guardrail." She repeated a number posted on a small metal sign. "Damn, he's going one hundred." She shook her head.

As good as the BMW was, Sean was not accustomed to driving a high-performance machine in challenging circumstances. The blue flashing lights behind him didn't scare him as much as the blue flashing lights he saw in the near distance, coming from the opposite direction. He took his eyes off the road for a split second, but a split second at 100 miles an hour is a fraction too long. He spun out, steered hard in the other direction, and did a 360, blasting through the guardrail and taking the metal with him as he soared over the ravine.

"Oh, my God!" Harry exclaimed.

Cynthia screeched to a stop. The BMW seemed airborne for an eternity, then finally crashed deep into the mountain laurels below.

Both Cynthia and Harry were out of the squad car when it stopped. Mrs. Murphy and Tucker could run down the mountainside much better than the two humans could as they stumbled, rolled, and got up again.

"We've got to get him before the car blows up!" Mrs. Murphy shouted to the corgi, who realized the situation also.

The BMW had landed upside down. The animals reached it, and Tucker tried to open the door by standing on her hind legs.

"Impossible."

The tiger raced around the car, hoping windows would have been smashed to bits on the other side.

Harry and Cooper, both covered in mud, scratched, and torn, reached the car. Cooper opened the door. Sean was held in place upside down by the safety belt. She reached in and clicked the belt. Both she and Harry dragged him out.

"Haul," Cynthia commanded.

Harry grabbed his left arm, Cynthia his right, and Tucker grabbed the back of his collar. They struggled and strained but managed to get the unconscious, bloodied boy fifty yards up the mountainside. Mrs. Murphy scampered ahead.

The BMW made a definite clicking sound and then *boom*, the beautiful machine was engulfed in flames.

The two women sat for a moment, holding Sean so he wouldn't slide back down. Mrs. Murphy walked ahead, searching for the easiest path up. Tucker, panting, sat for a moment, too.

They heard more sirens and a voice at the lip of the ravine.

Tucker barked. "We're down here!"

Harry, still holding Sean, turned around to see rescue workers scrambling down to help. She felt for the vein in his neck; a faint pulse rippled underneath her fingertips. "He's alive."

Mrs. Murphy said under her breath, "For how long?"

46

The cherry wood in the fireplace crackled, releasing the heavy aroma of the wood. Tucker, asleep in front of the fire, occasionally chattered, dreaming of squirrels.

Mrs. Murphy curled up in Harry's lap as she sat on the sofa while Pewter sprawled over Fair's bigger lap in the other wing chair. Exhausted from the trauma as well as the climb back up the deep ravine, Harry pulled the worn afghan around her legs, her feet resting on a hassock.

Fair broke the stillness. "I know Rick told you not to reveal Sean's condition, but you can tell me."

"Fair, the sheriff has put a guard in his hospital room. And to tell the truth, I don't know his condition."

"He was mixed up in whatever is going on over at St. Elizabeth's?"

"I guess he is." She leaned her head against a needlepoint pillow. "In your teens you think you know everything. Your parents are out of it. You're invincible. Especially Sean, the football star. I wonder how he got mixed up in this mess, and I wonder what's really behind it."

"I heard April was released from jail today, and she didn't want to leave," Fair remarked. "She must know what's going on, too."

"That's so strange. She doesn't look like a criminal, does she?"

"I always thought she was in love with Roscoe and that he used her," Fair said.

"Slept with her?"

"I don't know. Maybe"—he thought a moment—"but more than that, he used her. She jumped through all his hoops. April was one of the reasons that St. E's ran so smoothly. Sure as hell wasn't Roscoe. His talents rested in directions other than details." He rose and tossed another log on the fire. "He ever offer you candy?"

"Every time he saw me."

"*Never offered me catnip,*" Pewter grumbled.

"*Mom's got that look on her face. She's having a brainstorm.*" Tucker closely observed Harry.

"*Humans are fundamentally irrational. They use what precious rationality they have justifying their irrational behavior. A brainstorm is an excuse not to be logical,*" Pewter said.

"*Amen.*" Murphy laughed.

Harry tickled Murphy's ears. "Aren't we verbal?"

"*I can recite entire passages from Macbeth, if you'd care to hear it. 'Tomorrow and tomorrow and tomorrow creeps—' *"

"*Show-off.*" Pewter swished her tail once. "*Quoting Shakespeare is no harder than quoting 'Katie went to Haiti looking for a thrill.' *"

"*Cole Porter.*" Mrs. Murphy sang the rest of the song with Pewter.

"What's going on with these two?" Harry laughed.

"*Mrs. Murphy's telling her about her narrow escape from death.*"

"*That's the first thing I did when we got home.*" Mrs. Murphy sat up now and belted out the chorus from "Katie Went to Haiti."

"*Jesus,*" Tucker moaned, flattening her ears, "*you could wake the dead.*"

Pewter, on a Cole Porter kick, warbled, *"When They Begin the Beguine."*

The humans shook their heads, then returned to their conversation.

"Maybe the link is Sean's connection to Roscoe and Maury." Harry's eyes brightened. "He could easily have stuffed Roger's newspapers with the second obituary. Those kids all know one another's schedules. They must have been using Sean for something—" Her brow wrinkled; for the life of her she couldn't figure out what a teenage boy might have that both men wanted.

"Not necessarily." Fair played devil's advocate. "It really could be coincidence. Just dumb luck."

Harry shook her head, "No, I really don't think so. Sean is up to his neck in this mess."

Fair cracked his knuckles, a habit Harry had tried to forget. "Kendrick Miller stabbed Maury. Maury's murder has nothing to do with Roscoe's. And the kid liberated the BMW, so to speak, and just got carried away. Started something he didn't know how to finish."

"But Rick Shaw's guarding him in the hospital." Harry came back to that very important fact.

"You're right—but connecting him to Roscoe's murder and Maury's seems so far-fetched."

Harry leapt off the sofa. "Sorry, Murphy."

"I was so-o-o comfortable," Murphy moaned angrily. *"Pewter, let's give it to them. Let's sing 'Dixie.' "*

The two cats blended their voices in a rousing version of the song beloved of some folks south of the Mason-Dixon Line.

"You're a veterinarian. You shut them up," Tucker begged.

Fair shrugged, laughing at the two performers.

"Here." Harry tossed Fair a bag of treats. "I know this works." It did, and she dialed Susan. "Hey, Suz."

"Miranda's here. Why didn't you tell me!"

"I am."

"How long have you been home? Oh, Harry, you could have been barbecued."

"I've been home an hour. Fair's here."

"Tell me what happened."

"I will, Susan, tomorrow. I promise. Right now I need to talk to Brooks. Are you sending her to St. Elizabeth's tomorrow?"

"No. Although she wants to go back." Susan called her daughter to the phone.

Harry got right to the point. "Brooks, do you remember who Roscoe Fletcher offered candy to when he waited in line at the car wash?"

"Everybody."

"Try very hard to remember, Brooks."

"Uh, okay . . . when I first saw him he was almost out on Route Twenty-nine. I don't think he talked to anyone unless it was the guys at the Texaco station. I didn't notice him again until he was halfway to the entrance. Uh—" She strained to picture the event. "Mrs. Fletcher beeped her horn at him. He got out to talk to her, I think. The line was that slow. Then he got back in. Mrs. Miller talked to him. Karen walked over for a second. He called her over. Jody, when she saw him, hid back in the office. She'd been reamed out, remember, 'cause of losing her temper after the field hockey game. Uh—this is hard."

"I know, but it's extremely important."

"Roger, once Mr. Fletcher reached the port—we call it the port."

"Can you think of anyone else?"

"No. But, I was scrubbing down bumpers. Someone else could have walked over for a second and I might not have seen them."

"I realize that. You've done a good job remembering."

"Want Mom back?"

"Sure."

"What are you up to?" Susan asked.

"Narrowing down who was offered candy by Roscoe at the car wash."

Susan, recognizing Harry was obsessed, told her she would see her in the morning.

Harry then dialed Karen Jensen's number. She asked Karen the same questions and received close to the same answers, although Karen thought Jody had been off the premises of the car wash, had walked back, seen Roscoe and ducked inside Jimbo's office. She remembered both Naomi and Irene waiting in line, but she couldn't recall if they got out of their cars. She wanted to know if Sean was all right.

"I don't know."

Karen's voice thickened. "I really like Sean—even if he can be a jerk."

"Can you think of any reason why he'd take Mrs. Craycroft's car?"

"No—well, I mean, he's sort of a cutup. He would never steal it, though. He just wouldn't."

"Thanks, Karen." Harry hung up the phone. She didn't think Sean would steal a car either. Joyride, yes. Steal, no.

She called Jimbo next. He remembered talking to Roscoe himself, then going back into his office to take a phone call. Harry asked if Jody was in the office with him. He said yes, she came in shortly after he spoke to Roscoe, although he couldn't be precise as to the time.

She next tried Roger, who thought Roscoe offered candy to one of the gas jockeys at the Texaco. He had glanced up to count the cars in the line. He remembered both Naomi and Irene getting out of their cars and talking to Roscoe as opposed to Roscoe getting out to talk to his wife. He was pretty sure that was what he saw, and he affirmed that Jody emphatically did not want to talk to Roscoe. He didn't know when Jody first caught sight of Roscoe. She was supposed to be picking up their lunch, but she never made it.

The last call was to Jody. Irene reluctantly called her daughter to the phone.

"Jody, I'm sorry to disturb you."

"That's okay." Jody whispered, "How's Sean? It's all over town that he wrecked BoomBoom Craycroft's new car."

"I don't know how he is."

"Did he say anything?"

"I can't answer that."

"But you pulled him out of the vehicle. He must have said something . . . like why he did it."

"Sheriff Shaw instructed me not to say anything, Jody."

"I called the hospital. They won't tell me anything either." A note of rising panic crept into her voice.

"They always do that, Jody. It's standard procedure. If you were in there with a hangnail, they wouldn't give out information."

"But he's all right, isn't he?"

"I can't answer that. I honestly don't know." Harry paused. "You're good friends, aren't you?"

"We got close this summer, playing tennis at the club."

"Did you date?"

"Sort of. We both went out with other people." She sniffed. "He's got to be okay."

"He's young and he's strong." Harry waited a beat, then switched the subject. "I'm trying to reconstruct how many people Mr. Fletcher offered strawberry drops to since, of course, anyone might have been poisoned." Harry wasn't telling the truth of what she was thinking, although she *was* telling the truth, a neat trick.

"Everyone."

Harry laughed. "That's the general consensus."

"Who else have you talked to?"

"Roger, Brooks, Karen, and Jimbo. Everybody says about the same thing although the sequence is scrambled."

"Oh."

"Did Mr. Fletcher offer you candy?"

"No. I chickened out and ran into Mr. Anson's office. I was in the doghouse."

"Yeah. Well, it was still a great game, and you played superbly."

"Really?" She brightened.

"You could make All-State. That is, if St. Elizabeth's has a season. Who knows what will happen with so many people taking their kids out of there."

"School's school." Jody confidently predicted, "I'm going back,

others will, too. I'd rather be there than''—she whispered again—
"here."

"Uh, Jody, are your mother and father near?"

"No, but I don't trust them. Dad's truly weird now that he's out
on bail. Mom could be on the extension for all I know."

"Only because she's worried about you."

"Because she's a snoop. Hear that, Mom? If you're on the line,
get off!"

Harry ignored the flash of bad manners. "Jody, can you tell me
specifically who Mr. Fletcher offered candy to, that is, if you were
watching from Jimbo's office?"

"Mr. Anson went out to talk to him. I sat behind the desk. I
didn't really notice."

"Did you see Mrs. Fletcher or your mom get out of their cars
and talk to Mr. Fletcher?"

"I don't remember Mom doing anything—but I wasn't really
watching them."

"Oh, hey, before I forget it, 'cause I don't go over there much,
the kids said you were on lunch duty that day. Where do you get
good food around there?"

"You don't."

"You were on lunch duty?" Harry double-checked.

"Yeah, and Roger got pissed at me because he was starving and I
saw Mr. Fletcher before I crossed the road so I ran back. If I'd crossed
the road he would have seen me. The line was so long he was almost
out at the stoplight."

"Did he see you?"

"I don't think so. He saw me in the office later. He wasn't even
mad. He waved."

"Did you give Jim his money back?" Harry laughed.

"Uh—no." Jody's voice tightened. "I forgot. It was—uh—well,
I guess he forgot, too."

"Didn't mean to upset you."

"I'll pay him back tomorrow."

"I know you will." Harry's voice was warm. "Thanks for giving me your time. Oh, one more thing. I forgot to ask the others this. What do you, or did you, think of Mr. Fletcher's film department idea?"

" 'Today St. Elizabeth's, tomorrow Hollywood,' that's what he used to say. It was a great idea, but it'll never happen now."

"Thanks, Jody." Harry hung up the phone, returning to the sofa where she nestled in.

Mrs. Murphy crawled back in her lap. *"Now stay put."*

"Satisfied?" Fair asked.

"No, but I'm on the right track." She rested her hand on Mrs. Murphy's back. "I'm convinced. The real question is not who Roscoe offered candy to but who gave him candy. Rick Shaw must have come to the same conclusion." She tickled Murphy's ear. "He's not saying anything, though."

"Not to you."

"Mmm." Harry's mind drifted off. "Jody's upset over Sean. I guess they had a romance and I missed it."

"At that age you blink and they're off to a new thrill." He put his hands behind his head, stretching his upper body. Pewter didn't budge. "Everyone's upset. BoomBoom will be doubly upset." He exhaled, wishing he hadn't mentioned that name. "I'm surprised that you aren't more upset."

"I am upset. Two people are dead. Sean may well join them in the hereafter, and I can't figure it out. I hate secrets."

"That's what we pay the sheriff to do, to untie our filthy knots of passion, duplicity, and greed."

"Fair"—Harry smiled—"that's poetic."

He smiled back. "Go on."

"BoomBoom Craycroft." Harry simply repeated the name of Fair's former lover, then started laughing.

He smiled ruefully. "A brand-new BMW."

"She's such a flake. Pretty, I grant you that. I think I could have handled just about anyone else but BoomBoom." Harry took a side-swipe at Fair.

"That's not true, Harry, a betrayal is a betrayal, and it wouldn't have mattered who the woman was. You'd still feel like shit, and you'd say the same thing you're saying now but about her. I am rebuilding my whole life, my inner life. My outer life is okay." He paused. "I want to spend my life with you. Always did."

"Do you know why you ran around?"

"Fear."

"Of what?"

"Of being trapped. Of not living. When we married, I'd slept with three other women. I was a dutiful son. I studied hard. Kept my nose clean. Went to college. Went to vet school. Graduated and married you, the girl next door. I hit thirty and thought I was missing something. Had I married you at thirty, I would have gotten that out of my system." He softened his voice. "Haven't you ever worried that you're missing out?"

"Yeah, but then I watch the sunrise flooding the mountains with light and I think, 'Life is perfect.'"

"You aren't curious about other men?"

"What men?"

"Blair Bainbridge."

"Oh." She took her sweet time answering, thoroughly enjoying his discomfort. "Sometimes."

"How curious?"

"You just want to know if I'm sleeping with anyone, and that's my business. It's all about sex and possession, isn't it?"

"It's about love and responsibility. Sex is part of that."

"This is what I know: I like living alone. I like answering to no one but myself. I like not having to attend social functions as though we are joined at the hip. I like not having a knot in my stomach when you don't come home until two in the morning."

"I'm a vet."

She held up her hand. "With so many chances to jump ladies' bones, I can't even count them."

"I'm not doing that." He took her hand. "Our divorce was so painful, I didn't think I could live through it. I knew I was wrong. I didn't know how to make it right. Enough time has passed that I can be trusted, and I can be more sensitive to you."

"Don't push me."

"If I don't push you, you do nothing. If I ask anyone else to a party or the movies because I'd like to enjoy someone's companionship, you freeze me out for a week or more. I'm damned if I do and damned if I don't."

"*He's right, Mom,*" Mrs. Murphy agreed with Fair.

"*Yeah,*" Tucker echoed.

"*They talk too much.*" Pewter, weary from her singing and all the spoon bread she'd stolen, wanted to sleep.

"Cheap revenge, I guess." Harry honestly assessed herself.

"Does it make you happy?"

"Actually, it does. Anyone who underestimates the joy of revenge has no emotions." She laughed. "But it doesn't get you what you want."

"Which is?"

"That's just it. I don't really know anymore."

"I love you. I've always loved you, and I always will love you." A burst of passion illuminated his handsome face.

She squeezed his hand. "I love you, too, but—"

"Can't we get back together? If you aren't ready for a commitment, we can date."

"We date now."

"No, we don't. It's hit or miss."

"You're not talking about dating. You're talking about sleeping together."

"Yes."

"I'll consider it."

"Harry, that's a gray reply."

"I didn't say no, nor did I say maybe. I have to think about it."

"But you know how I feel. You know what I've wanted."

"Not the same as a direct request—you just made a direct request, and I have to think about it."

"Do you love me at all?"

"The funny part of all this is that I do love you. I love you more now than when we married, but it's different. I just don't know if I can trust you. I'd like to, truly I would, because apart from Susan,

Miranda, and my girlfriends, I know you better than anyone on the face of the earth, and I think you know me. I don't always like you. I'm sure I'm not likable at times, but it's odd how you can love someone and not like them." She hastened to add, "Most times I like you. Really, it's just when you start giving orders. I hate that."

"I'm working on that. Most women want to be told what to do."

"Some do, I know. Most don't. It's a big fake act they put on to make men feel intelligent and powerful. Then they laugh at you behind your back."

"You don't do that."

"No way."

"That's why I love you. One of the many reasons. You always stand up to me. I need that. I need you. You bring out the best in me, Harry."

"I'm glad to hear it," she replied dryly, "but I'm not on earth to bring out the best in you. I'm on earth to bring out the best in me."

"Wouldn't it be right if we could do that for each other? Isn't that what marriage is supposed to be?"

She waited a long time. "Yes. Marriage is probably more complicated than that, but I'm too tired to figure it out . . . if I ever could. And every marriage isn't the same. Our marriage was different from Miranda and George's, but theirs worked for them. I think you do bring out good things in me—after all, I wouldn't be having this conversation with anyone else, and that's a tribute to you. You know I loathe this emotional stuff."

He laughed. "Harry, I do love you."

She got up and kissed his cheek, disturbing a disgruntled Murphy one more time. "Let me think."

He mused. "I never knew love could be this complicated, or even that I could be this complicated!" He laughed. "I always knew you were complicated."

"See—and I think I'm simple."

Mrs. Murphy settled down in front of the fireplace to stare into the flames. "*You know what worries me?*"

"*What?*" Pewter yawned.

"*If Sean is part of Roscoe's murder, if he's in on this somehow, Mother was one of the last people to be with him. Only Cooper knows he didn't speak to her and Rick.*"

"*So?*" The gray cat fluttered her fur.

"*So, Pewter, the killer might think he told Mother what's what.*"

Pewter's eyes opened wide as did Tucker's. They said in unison, "I never thought of that."

47

The antiseptic odor of hospitals turned Deputy Cooper's stomach. It stung her nostrils even though it wasn't as overpowering as, say, garbage. She wondered if the real offender was the associations she had concerning hospitals, or if truly she just hated the antiseptic.

Shorthanded though the department was, Rick was ferocious about maintaining vigilance over Sean. He'd broken half the bones in his body, his legs being the worst. His left arm was smashed in two places. His spleen was ruptured, and his left lung was punctured by his rib, which caved inward.

His right arm was fine. His skull was not crushed, but the force of the impact had created a severe concussion with some swelling in the brain. He had not regained consciousness, but his vital signs, though weak, had stabilized.

There was a good chance he'd live, although he'd never play

football again. Sean's mother and father took turns watching over him. His grandparents flew in from Olathe, Kansas, to help.

Cynthia half dozed on the hard-backed chair. On the other side of the bed his mother slept in another chair, equally uncomfortable.

A low moan alerted Cynthia. Her eyes opened, as did Sean's.

He blinked strongly to make sense of where he was.

"Sean," Cynthia said in a clear low voice.

His mother awakened with a start and leaned over her son. "Honey, honey, it's Mom."

He blinked again, then whispered, "I'm a father." His lips moved but no more sound escaped. Then, as if he had never spoken, he shut his eyes again and lost consciousness.

48

A howitzer ripped through Harry's meticulously planned schedule. Each night before retiring she would take a sheet of tablet paper, eight by eleven inches, fold it in half, and number her chores in order of priority. She used to watch her mother do it, absorbing the habit.

Harry was an organized person. Her disorganization involved major life questions such as "Whither thou goest?" She told herself Americans put too much emphasis on direction, management, and material success instead of just jumping into life.

Awaking each morning between five thirty and six, she first drank a piping hot cup of tea, fed the horses, picked out the stalls, stripping them on Saturdays, turned the horses out, fed Mrs. Murphy, Tucker, and now Pewter. Then she usually walked the mile out to the road to get her paper. That woke her up. If she was running behind or the weather proved filthy, she'd drive out in the blue truck.

Thanks to BoomBoom, the blue truck reposed again at the service station. Fortunately, BoomBoom's insurance really did cover the damages. And she'd get a new BMW since Sean had destroyed hers. Harry's worry involved the ever-decreasing life span of the 1978 Ford. She had to get a new truck. Paying for it, even a decent used one, seemed impossible.

The morning, crisp and clear at 36° F, promised a glorious fall day ahead. She jogged back, never opening the newspaper. Reading it with her second cup of tea and breakfast rewarded her for finishing the farm chores before heading off to the post office. She adored these small rituals of pleasure. Another concept she'd learned from her mother.

She bit into a light biscuit . . . then stopped, the biscuit hanging from her mouth. As she opened her mouth, the biscuit dropped onto the plate.

She knocked the chair over calling Susan. "You up?"

"Barely."

"Open the paper."

"Mmm. Holy shit! What's going on around here?" Susan exploded.

On the front page of the newspaper ran the story of the high-speed car chase. Harry was quoted as saying, "Another ten seconds and he'd have been blown to bits."

But what caused Susan's eruption was a story in the next column concerning April Shively's release on twenty thousand dollars' bail. That was followed by April's declaring she would not release the papers she had taken from St. Elizabeth's until the board of governors audited the current accounting books in the possession of the temporary headmaster, Sandy Brashiers. She all but accused him of financial misdeeds just this side of embezzlement.

As Harry and Susan excitedly talked in the background, Mrs. Murphy sat on the newspaper to read. Pewter joined her.

"Sean's not in the obit column, so we know he's still fighting." Murphy touched her nose to the paper.

"Going to be a hell of a day at the post office," Tucker predicted.

How right she was. A gathering place in the best and worst of times, it was packed with people.

Big Mim, hoisted up on the counter by the Reverend Jones, clapped her hands. "Order. Could I have some order, please?"

Accustomed to obeying the Queen of Crozet, they fell silent.

"Honeybun, we could move to city hall," her husband, the mayor, offered.

"We're here now, let's get on with it." Mim sat down and crossed her legs. Mrs. Murphy and Pewter flanked her. Tucker wandered among the crowd. The animals decided they would pay attention to faces and smells. Someone might give himself or herself away in a fashion a human couldn't comprehend.

Mim stared sternly at Karen, Jody, Brooks, and Roger. "Why aren't you in school?"

Karen answered for all of them. "Which school? We want to go back to St. Elizabeth's. Our parents won't let us."

"Then what are you doing here?" She pounded them like a schoolmarm.

"The post office is where everything happens, sort of," Brooks replied.

"Smart kid," Mrs. Murphy said.

Irene called out, "Marilyn, can you guarantee my child's safety?"

"Irene, no school can do that anymore, but within reason, yes." Marilyn Sanburne felt she spoke for the board.

Harry leaned across the counter. "Guys, I don't mind that you all meet here, but if someone comes in to get their mail, you have to clear a path for them. This is a federal building."

"The hell with Washington," Market Shiflett brazenly called out. "We had the right idea in 1861."

Cheers rose from many throats. Miranda laughed as did Harry. Those transplanted Yankees in the crowd would find this charming, anachronistic proof that Southerners are not only backward but incapable of forgetting the war.

What Southerners knew in their souls was that given half the chance, they'd leave the oppressive Union in a skinny minute. Let the Yankees tax themselves to death. Southerners had better things to do with their time and money, although it is doubtful those "better things" would be productive.

"Now we must remain calm, provoking as these hideous events have been." Mim turned to Harry. "Why don't you call Rick Shaw? He ought to be here."

"No." Herbie gently contradicted her. "If you'll forgive me, madam"—he often called Mim "madam"—"I think we'll all be more forthcoming without the law here."

"Yes." Other voices agreed.

Mim cast her flashing blue gaze over the crowd. "I don't know what's going on, I don't know why it's going on, but I think we must assume we know the person or persons responsible for Roscoe's demise as well as Maury's bizarre death. This community must organize to protect itself."

"How do we know the killer isn't in this room?" Dr. Larry Johnson asked.

Father Michael replied, "We don't."

"Well, Kendrick was found bending over Maury. Sorry, Irene, but it's true," Market said.

"Then we're telling the killer or killers our plans. How can we protect ourselves?" Lucinda Payne Coles, her brow furrowed, echoed what many others felt as well.

Harry raised her hand, a gesture left over from school.

"Harry." Mim nodded toward her.

"The question is not if the killer or killers could be in this room. The question is, why are people being killed? We'll worry ourselves into a fit if we think each of us is vulnerable."

"But we are!" Market exclaimed. "Two people are dead—and one seventeen-year-old boy who admitted planting the first obituary is in the hospital. Who or what next?"

Harry replied evenly, "Marilyn, I know you don't want to hear this, but everything points to St. Elizabeth's."

"Does that mean we're suspects?" Jody Miller joked.

Irene put her hand on her daughter's shoulder. "No one is

suspecting students, dear." She cast a knowing look at Larry Johnson. She needed to talk to him. Jody was in the first trimester of her pregnancy. A major decision had to be made. On the other hand, she watched Father Michael and thought maybe she should talk to him. It didn't occur to her that Jody was the one who needed to do the talking.

Neither Sandy Brashiers nor any faculty members from the school were there to defend themselves or the institution. They were holding back a tidal wave of questions, recriminations, and fear at their own faculty meeting. The reporters, like jackals, camped at the door.

"You must put aside April's absurd accusations," Marilyn said nervously, "and we will audit the books this week to lay her accusations to rest. She's only trying to divert our attention."

"It's true," Roger said in his quiet voice. "The problem is at St. E's."

Mim asked, "Do you have any idea, any idea at all, what is going on at your school? Is there a drug problem?"

"Mrs. Sanburne, drugs are everywhere. Not just at St. E's," Karen said solemnly.

"But you're rich kids. If you get in trouble, Daddy can bail you out." Samson Coles bluntly added his two cents even though many people shunned him.

"That's neither here nor there," Market said impatiently. "What are we going to do?"

"Can we afford more protection? A private police force?" Fair was pretty sure they couldn't.

"No." Jim, towering over everyone but Fair, answered that query. "We're on a shoestring."

"The rescue squad and other groups like the Firehouse gang could pitch in." Larry, getting warm, removed his glen plaid porkpie hat.

"Good idea, Larry." Mim turned to her husband. "Can we do that? Of course we can. You're the mayor."

"I'll put them on patrol. We can set up a cruise pattern. It's a start."

Mim went on. "While they're doing that, the rest of us can go over our contacts with Roscoe, April, Maury, and Sean. There may be a telling clue, something you know that seems unimportant but is really significant, the missing link, so to speak."

"Like, who gave Roscoe Fletcher candy at the car wash?" Miranda said innocently. "Harry thinks the killer was right there and gave him the poisoned candy right under everyone's nose."

"*She just let the cat out of the bag.*" Murphy's eyes widened.

"*What can we do?*" Tucker cried.

"*Pray the killer's not in this room,*" Mrs. Murphy said, knowing in her bones that the killer was looking her right in the face.

"*But Rick Shaw and Cynthia must have figured out the same thing.*" Pewter tried to allay their fears.

"*Of course they have, but until this moment the person who wiped out Roscoe didn't realize Mom had figured out most people were approaching Roscoe's murder backward. Now they'll wonder what else she's figured out.*"

"*It's Kendrick Miller.*" Pewter licked her paw, rubbing her ear with it.

"*If he is the one, he can get at Mom easily,*" Tucker responded. "*At least he's not here.*"

"*Don't worry, Irene will repeat every syllable of this meeting.*" Murphy's tail tip swayed back and forth, a sign of light agitation.

"*We need to ask Fair to stay with Mom.*" Tucker rightly assumed that would help protect her.

"*Fat chance.*" Murphy stood up, stretched, and called to her friends, "*Come on out back with me. Humans need to huff and puff. We've got work to do.*"

Tucker resisted. "*We ought to stay here and observe.*"

"*The damage is done. We need to hotfoot it. Come on.*"

Tucker threaded her way through the many feet and dashed through the animal door. Once outside she said, "*Where are we going?*"

"*St. Elizabeth's.*"

"*Murphy, that's too far.*" Pewter envisioned the trek.

"*Do you want to help, or do you want to be a wuss?*"

"*I'm not a wuss.*" Pewter defiantly swatted at the tiger cat.

"*Then let's go.*"

Within forty-five minutes they reached the football and soccer fields. Tired, they sat down for a minute.

"Stick together. We're going to work room to room."

"What are we looking for?"

"I'm not sure yet. If April took other books, they're truly cooked now. But none of these people thought they were going to be killed. They must have left unfinished business somewhere, and if the offices are clean as a whistle, then it means April knows the story—the whole story, doesn't it?"

49

Eerie quiet greeted the animals as they padded down the hallway of the Old Main Building, the administration building. The faculty meeting was heating up in the auditorium across the quad. Not one soul was in Old Main, not even a receptionist.

"*Think the cafeteria is in Old Main?*" Pewter inquired plaintively.

"*No. Besides, I bet no one is working in the cafeteria.*" Tucker was anxious to get in and get out of the place before the post office closed. If Harry couldn't find them, she'd pitch a fit.

"*Perfect.*" Mrs. Murphy read HEADMASTER in gold letters on the heavy oak door, slightly ajar. The cat checked the door width using her whiskers, knew she could make it, and squeezed through. Fatty behind her squeezed a little harder.

Tucker wedged her long nose in the door. Mrs. Murphy turned around and couldn't resist batting Tucker.

"*No fair.*"

"*Where's your sense of humor? Pewter, help me with the door.*"

The two cats pulled with their front paws as Tucker pushed with her nose. Finally the heavy door opened wide enough for the corgi to slip through. Everything had been moved out except for the majestic partner's desk and the rich red Persian carpet resting in front of the desk.

"*Tucker, sniff the walls, the bottom of the desk, the bookcases, everything. Pewter, you check along the edge of the bookcases. Maybe there's a hidden door or something.*"

"*What are you going to do?*" Pewter dived into the emptied bookshelves.

"*Open these drawers.*"

"*That's hard work.*"

"*Not for me. I learned to do this at home because Harry used to hide the fresh catnip in the right-hand drawer of her desk . . . until she found out I could open it.*"

"*Where does she hide it now?*" Pewter eagerly asked.

"*Top of the kitchen cabinet, inside.*"

"*Damn.*" Pewter rarely swore.

"*Let's get to work.*" Mrs. Murphy flopped on her side, putting her paw through the burnished brass handle. Using her hind feet she pushed forward. The long center drawer creaked a bit, then rolled right out. Pens, pencils, and an avalanche of paper clips and engraved St. Elizabeth's stationery filled the drawer. She stuck her paws to the very back of the drawer. Mrs. Murphy shivered. She wanted so badly to throw the paper on the floor, then plunge into it headfirst. A paper bag was fun enough but expensive, lush, engraved laid bond—that was heaven. She disciplined herself, hopping on the floor to pull out the right-hand bottom drawer. The contents proved even more disappointing than the center drawer's: a hand squeezer to strengthen the hand muscles, a few floppy discs even though no computer was in the room, and one old jump rope.

"*Anything?*" She pulled on the left-hand drawer.

Tucker lifted her head, "*Too many people in here. I smell mice. But then that's not surprising. They like buildings where people go home at night—less interference.*"

"Nothing on the bookshelves. No hidden buttons."

Murphy, frustrated at not finding anything, jumped into the drawer, wiggling toward the back. Murphy's pupils, big from the darkness at the back of the drawer, quickly retracted to smaller circles as she jumped out. She noticed a small adhesive mailing label, ends curled, which must have fallen off a package. "Here's an old mailing label. Neptune Film Laboratory, Brooklyn, New York—and three chewed pencils, the erasers chewed off. This room has been picked cleaner than a chicken bone."

"We could go over to where Maury McKinchie was killed, in the hall outside the gymnasium," Tucker suggested.

"Good idea." Mrs. Murphy hurried out the door.

"She could at least wait for us. She can be so rude." Pewter followed.

The cavernous gymnasium echoed with silence. The click of Tucker's unretractable claws reverberated like tin drums.

"Know what hall?"

"No," Mrs. Murphy answered Tucker, "but there's only one possibility. The two side halls go to the locker rooms. I don't think Maury was heading that way. He probably went through the double doors, which lead to the trophy hall and the big front door."

"Then why did we come in the backdoor?" Pewter grumbled.

"Because our senses are sharper. We could pick up something in the lockers that a human couldn't. Not just dirty socks but cocaine lets off a sharp rancid odor, and marijuana is so easy a puppy could pick it up."

"I resent that. A hound puppy is born with a golden nose."

"Tucker, I hate to tell you this but you're a corgi."

"I know that perfectly well, smart-ass." Ready to fight, she stopped in front of a battered light green locker. "Wait a minute." She sniffed around the base of the locker, putting her nose next to the vent. "Sugary, sticky."

"Hey, look at that." Pewter involuntarily lifted her paw, taking a step back.

"Dead." Mrs. Murphy noted the line of dead ants going into the locker. She glanced up. "Number one fourteen."

"How do we get in there? I mean, if we want to?" Pewter gingerly leapt over the ants.

"*We don't.*" Tucker indicated the big combination lock hanging on the locker door.

"*Why go to school if you have to lock away your possessions? Kids stealing from kids. It's not right.*"

"It's not right, but it's real," Mrs. Murphy answered pragmatically. "*We aren't going to get anyone into this locker. Even the janitor has burnt rubber.*"

"He rides a bicycle," Tucker said laconically, picturing Powder Hadly, thirties and simpleminded. He was so simpleminded he couldn't pass the written part of the driving test although he could drive just fine.

"You get my drift." The tiger bumped into the corgi. Tucker bumped back, which made the cat stumble.

"*Twit.*"

"*It's all right if you do it. If I do anything you bitch and moan and scratch.*"

"*What are you doing then?*"

"*Describing your behavior. Flat facts.*"

"The flat facts are, we can't do diddly." She halted. "*Well, there is one trick if we could get everyone to open their lockers. Not that the dead-ant locker has poison in it. That would be pretty stupid, wouldn't it? But who knows what's stashed in these things.*"

"Do the faculty have lockers?" Pewter asked.

"*Sure.*"

"*How do you know the faculty lockers from the kids'?*"

"I don't know. *We're on the girls' side. Maybe there's a small room we've missed that's set aside for the teachers.*"

They scampered down the hall and found a locker room for the female faculty. But there was nothing of interest except a bottle of Ambush perfume that had been left on the makeup counter. The men's locker room was equally barren of clues.

"*This was a wasted trip, and I'm famished.*"

"Not so wasted." Murphy trotted back toward the post office.

"*I'd like to know why. Roscoe's office was bare. We passed through April's office, nothing there. The sheriff has crawled over everything, fouling the scent. The gym is a tomb. And my pads are cold.*"

"*We found out that the killer had to have left the gym before Maury McKinchie to wait outside the front doors. They're glass so he could see Maury come out, or he waited behind one of the doors leading to the boys' locker room or the girls'. He dashed out and stabbed Maury and then either ran outside or he ran back into the gym. In costume, remember. He knew this setup.*"

"Ah." Tucker appreciated Mrs. Murphy's reasoning. "*I see that, but if the killer had been outside, more people would have seen him because he was in costume—unless he changed it. No time for that, I think.*" Tucker canceled her own idea.

"*He was a Musketeer, if Kendrick is telling the truth. My hunch is he came from the side. From out of the locker rooms. No one had reason to go back there unless they wanted to smoke or drink, and they could easily do that outside without some chaperon or bush patrol. No, I'm sure he ran out the locker-room side.*"

"*You don't believe Kendrick did it?*" Pewter asked, knowing the answer but wanting to hear her friend's reasons.

"*No.*"

"But what if Maury was sleeping with Irene?" Tucker logically thought that was reason enough for some men to murder.

"*Kendrick wouldn't give a damn. A business deal gone bust; or some kind of financial betrayal might provoke him to kill, but he'd be cold-blooded about it. He'd plan. This was slapdash. Not Kendrick's style.*"

"*No wonder Irene mopes around,*" Pewter thought out loud. "*If my husband thought money was more important than me, I'd want a divorce, too.*"

"*Could Maury have been killed by a jilted lover?*"

"*Sure. So could Roscoe. But it doesn't fit. Not two of them back-to-back. And April Shively wouldn't have vacuumed out the school documents if it was that.*"

They reached the post office, glad to rush inside for warmth and crunchies.

"Where have you characters been?" Harry counted out change.

"*Deeper into this riddle, that's where we've been.*" Mrs. Murphy watched Pewter stick her face into the crunchies shaped like little fish. She didn't feel hungry herself. "*What's driving me crazy is that I'm missing something obvious.*"

"Murphy, I don't *see* how we've overlooked anything." Tucker was tired of thinking.

"No, it's obvious, but whatever it is, our minds don't want to see it." The tiger dropped her ears for a moment, then pricked them back up.

"Doesn't *make sense*," Pewter, thrilled to be eating, said between garbled mouthfuls.

"What is going on is too repulsive for our minds to accept. We're blanking out. It's right under our noses."

50

The uneasiness of Crozet's residents found expression in the memorial service for Maury McKinchie.

There was a full choir and a swelling organ but precious few people in Reverend Jones's church. Darla had indeed flown the body back to Los Angeles, so no exorbitantly expensive casket rested in front of the altar. Miranda, asked to sing a solo, chose "A Mighty Fortress Is Our God" because she was in a Lutheran church and because no one knew enough about Maury's spiritual life to select a more personal hymn. BoomBoom Craycroft wept in the front left row. Ed Sugarman comforted her, a full-time job. Naomi Fletcher, in mourning for Roscoe, sat next to Sandy Brashiers in the front right row. Harry, Susan, and Ned also attended. Other than that tiny crew, the church was bare. Had Darla shown her famous and famously kept face, the church would have been overflowing.

Back at the post office Harry thought about what constituted a life well lived.

At five o'clock, she gathered up April Shively's mail.

"Do you think she'll let you in?"

Harry raised her eyebrows. "Miranda, I don't much care. If not, I'll put it by her backdoor. Need anything while I'm out there? I'll pass Critzer's Nurseries."

"No, thanks. I've put in all my spring bulbs," came the slightly smug reply.

"Okay then—see you tomorrow."

Ten minutes later Harry pulled into a long country lane winding up at a neat two-story frame colonial. Blair Bainbridge had lent Harry his truck until hers was fixed. When she knocked on the door, there was no answer. She waited a few minutes, then placed the mail by the backdoor. As she turned to leave, the upstairs window opened.

"I'm not afraid to come in and get my mail."

"Your box was overflowing. Thought I'd save you a trip."

"Anybody know if Sean's going to make it?"

"No. The hospital won't give out information, and they won't allow anyone to visit. That's all I know."

"Boy doesn't have a brain in his head. Have you seen Sandy Brashiers or Naomi?" April half laughed. Her tone was snide.

Harry sighed impatiently. "I doubt they want to see you any more than you want to see them. Marilyn's not your biggest fan now either."

"Who cares about her?" April waved her hand flippantly. "She's a bad imitation of a bad mother."

"Big Mim's okay. You have to take her on her own terms."

"*Think we can get inside?*" Tucker asked.

"No," Murphy replied. "*She's not budging from that window.*"

"What are they saying about me?" April demanded.

"Oh—that you hate Sandy, loved Roscoe, and you're accusing Sandy to cover your own tracks. If there's missing money, you've got it or know where it is."

"Ha!"

"But you do know something, April. I know you do," Murphy meowed loudly.

"That cat's got a big mouth."

"So's your old lady," Murphy sassed her.

"Yeah!" Pewter chimed in.

"April, I wish you'd get things right." Harry zipped up her jacket. "The school's like a tomb. Whatever you feel about Sandy—is it worth destroying St. Elizabeth's and everything Roscoe worked so hard to build?"

"Good one, Mom." Tucker knew Harry had struck a raw nerve.

"Me destroy St. Elizabeth's! If you want to talk destruction, let's talk about Sandy Brashiers, who wants us to commit our energies and resources to a nineteenth-century program. He's indifferent to computer education, hostile to the film-course idea, and he only tolerates athletics because he has to—if he takes over, you watch, those athletic budgets will get trimmed and trimmed each year. He'll take it slow at first, but I know him! The two-bit sneak."

"Then come back."

"They fired me!"

"If you give back the papers—"

"Never. Not to Brashiers."

Harry held up her hands. "Give them to Sheriff Shaw."

"Fat lot of good that will do. He'll turn them over to St. Elizabeth's."

"He can impound them as evidence."

"Are you that dumb, or do you think I am?" April yelled. "Little Mim will whine, and Mommy will light the fires of hell under Rick Shaw's butt. Those papers will go to the Sanburne house if not St. Elizabeth's."

"How else can you clear your name?"

"When the time comes, I will. You just wait and see."

"I guess I'll have to." Harry gave up, walking back to the truck. She heard the window slam shut.

"Time has a funny way of running out," Mrs. Murphy noted dryly.

51

Driving back into Crozet, Harry stopped and cajoled Mrs. Hogendobber to drive her through the car wash in her Falcon. Pewter, hysterical
at the thought, hid under the seat. Harry filled Miranda in on the
conversation with April, a belligerent April.

As they pulled right off Route 29, coasting past the Texaco station, Harry observed the distance between the gas pumps and the
port of the car wash. It was a quick sprint away, perhaps fifty yards at
the most. The Texaco station building blocked the view of the car
wash.

"Go slow."

"I am." Miranda scanned the setup, then coasted to a stop before the port.

Jimbo Anson rolled out, the collar of his jacket turned up against
the wind. "Welcome, Mrs. Hogendobber. I don't believe you've ever
been here."

"No, I haven't. I wash the car by hand. It's small enough that I can do it, but Harry wants me to become modern." She smiled as Harry reached across her and paid the rate for "the works."

"Come forward . . . there you go." He watched as Miranda's left wheel rolled onto the track. "Put her in neutral, and no radio." Jimbo punched the big button hanging on a thick electrical cord, and the car rolled into the mists.

A buzzer sounded, the yellow neon light flashed, and Miranda exclaimed, "My word."

Harry carefully noted the time it took to complete the cycle as well as how the machinery swung out from the side or dropped from above. The last bump of the track alerted them to put the car in drive. Harry mumbled, "No way."

"No way what?"

"I was thinking maybe the killer came into the car wash, gave Roscoe the poisoned candy, and ran out. I know it's loony, but the sight of someone soaking wet in the car wash, someone he knew, would make him roll down the window or open a door if he could. It was a thought. If you run up here from the Texaco station, which takes less than a minute, no one could see you if you ducked in the car wash exit. But it's impossible. And besides, nobody noticed anyone being all wet."

" 'Cain said to Abel, his brother, "Let us go out to the field." And when they were in the field, Cain rose up against his brother Abel, and killed him. Then the Lord said to Cain, "Where is Abel your brother?" He said, "I do not know; am I my brother's keeper?" And the Lord said, "What have you done? The voice of your brother's blood is crying to me from the ground." ' " Mrs. Hogendobber quoted Genesis. "The first murder of all time. Cain didn't get away with it. Neither will this murderer."

"Rick Shaw is working overtime to tie Kendrick to both murders. Cynthia called me last night. She said it's like trying to stick a square peg in a round hole. It's not working, and Rick is tearing his hair out."

"He can ill afford that." Mrs. Hogendobber turned south on Route 29.

"I keep coming back to cowardice. Poison is the coward's tool."

"Whoever killed McKinchie wasn't a coward. A bold run-through with a sword shows imagination."

"McKinchie was unarmed, though," Harry said. "The killer jumped out and skewered him. Imagination, yes, but cowardice, yes. It's one thing to plan a murder and carry it out, a kind of cold brilliance, if you will. It's another thing to sneak up on people."

"It is possible that these deaths are unrelated," Miranda said tentatively. "But I don't think so; that's what worries me." She braked for a red light.

She couldn't have been more worried than Father Michael, who, dozing in the confession booth, was awakened by the murmur of that familiar muffled voice, taking pains to disguise itself.

"Father, I have sinned."

"Go on, my child."

"I have killed more than once. I like killing, Father. It makes me feel powerful."

A hard lump lodged in Father Michael's thin throat. "All power belongs to God, my child." His voice grew stronger. "And who did you kill?"

"Rats." The disguised voice burst into laughter.

He heard the swish of the heavy black fabric, the light, quick footfall. He bolted out of the other side of the confession booth in time to see a swirl of black, a cloak, at the side door, which quickly closed. He ran to the door and flung it open. No one was there, only a blue jay squawking on the head of the Avenging Angel.

52

"Nobody?"

Lucinda Payne Coles, her heavy skirt draped around her legs to ward off the persistent draft in the old office room, said again, "Nobody. I'm at the back of the church, Sheriff. The only way I'll see who comes in and out of the front is if I walk out there or they park back here."

Cynthia, also feeling the chill, moved closer to the silver-painted radiator. "Have you noticed anyone visiting Father Michael lately, anyone unusual?"

"No. If anything it's quieter than normal for this time of year."

"Thanks, Mrs. Coles. Call me any time of the day or night if anything occurs to you."

Rick and Cynthia walked outside. A clammy mist enshrouded them in the graveyard. They bent down at the side door. Depressions on leaves could be seen, a slight smear on the moisture that they tracked into the cemetery.

"Smart enough to cover his tracks," Cynthia said.

"Or hers. That applies to every country person in the county," Rick replied. "Or anyone who's watched a lot of crime shows." He sat on a tombstone for a moment. "Any ideas?"

"Nope."

"Me neither."

"We know one thing. The killer likes to confess."

"No, Coop, the killer likes to brag. We've got exactly one hope in hell."

"Which is?" She told herself she wasn't really a smoker as she reached into her pocket for a pack.

"I'll take one of those." Rick reached out.

They lit up, inhaling.

"Wonder how many people buried here died of emphysema?"

"Don't know." He laughed. "I might be one of them some-day."

"What's your one hope, boss?"

"Pride goeth before a fall."

53

Rick Shaw set up a temporary command post in April Shively's office. Little Mim and Sandy Brashiers requested over the radio and in the newspaper that students return to St. Elizabeth's for questioning.

Every hand Rick could spare was placed at the school. Little Mim organized and Sandy assisted.

"—the year started out great. Practice started out great—" Karen Jensen smiled at the sheriff. "Our class had a special film week. We wrote a story, broke it down into shots, and then Friday, we filmed it. Mr. McKinchie and Miss Thalman from New York directed us. That was great. I can't think of anything weird."

"Sean?"

"Oh, you know Sean, he likes playing the bad boy, but he seemed okay." She was relaxed, wanting to be helpful.

"If you think of anything, come on back or give me a call." Rick smiled reflexively. When Karen had left, he said to Cooper, "No running nose, no red eyes or dilated pupils or pupils the size of a pin. No signs of drug abuse. We're halfway through the class—if only Sean would regain consciousness."

"If he is going to be a father, that explains a lot."

"Not enough," Rick grumbled.

Cynthia flipped through her notes. "He used to run errands for April Shively. Jody Miller said Sean had a permanent pink pass." She flipped the notebook shut.

A bark outside the door confused them for a moment, then Cynthia opened the door.

Fur ruffled, Tucker bounded in. *"We can help!"*

With less obvious enthusiasm Mrs. Murphy and Pewter followed.

"Where's Harry?"

As if to answer Coop's question, Harry walked through the door carrying a white square plastic container overflowing with mail. "Roscoe's and Maury's mail." She plopped the box on the table. "I put Naomi's mail in her mailbox."

"Anything unusual?" Rick inquired.

"No. Personal letters and bills, no Jiffy bags or anything suspicious."

"Has she been coming to pick up her mail?"

"Naomi comes in each day. But not today. At least not before I left."

Cynthia asked, "Does she ever say anything at all?"

"She's downcast. We exchange pleasantries and that's it."

"Good of Blair to lend you his Dually." Coop hoped her severe crush on the handsome man wouldn't show. It did.

"He's a good neighbor." Harry smiled. "Little Mim's pegged him for every social occasion between now and Christmas, I swear."

"He doesn't seem to mind."

"What choice does he have? Piss off a Sanburne?" Her eyebrows rose.

"Point taken." Cynthia nodded, feeling better already.

"When you girls stop chewing the fat, I'd be tickled pink to get back to business."

"Yes, boss."

"Spoilsport," Harry teased him. "If we take our minds off the problem, we usually find the answer."

"That's the biggest bunch of bull I've heard since 'Read my lips: No new taxes,' " Rick snorted.

"*Read my lips: Come to the locker room.*" The tiger cat let out a hoot.

"Was that a hiccup?" Cynthia bent down to pat Mrs. Murphy.

"*Let's try the old run away—run back routine.*" Tucker ripped out of the room and ran halfway down the hall, her claws clicking on the wooden floor, then raced back.

"*Let's all do it.*" Mrs. Murphy followed the dog. Pewter spun out so fast her hind legs slipped away from her.

"Nuts." Rick watched, shaking his head.

"Playful." Coop checked the mail. There wasn't anything that caught her eye as odd.

Halfway down the hall the animals screeched to a halt, bumping into one another.

"*Idiots.*" Mrs. Murphy puffed her tail. The fur on the back of her neck stood up.

"*We could try again.*" Tucker felt that repetition was the key with humans.

"*No. I'll crawl up Mother's leg. That gets her attention.*"

"*Doesn't mean she'll follow us,*" Pewter replied pragmatically.

"*Have you got a better idea?*" The tiger whirled on the gray cat.

"*No, Your Highness.*"

The silent animals reentered the room. Mrs. Murphy walked over to Harry, rubbed against her leg, and purred.

"Sweetie, we'll go in a minute."

That fast Murphy climbed up Harry's legs. The jeans blunted the claws, yet enough of those sharp daggers pierced the material to make Harry yelp.

"*Follow me!*" She dropped off Harry's leg and ran to the door, stopping to turn a somersault.

"*Show-off,*" Pewter muttered under her breath.

"*You can't do a somersault,*" Murphy taunted her.

"Oh, yes, I can." Pewter ran to the door and leapt into the air. Her somersault was a little wobbly and lopsided, but it was a somersault.

"You know, every now and then they get like this," Harry explained sheepishly. "Maybe I'll see what's up."

"I'll go with you."

"You're both loose as ashes." Rick grabbed the mail.

As Harry and Cynthia followed the animals, they noticed a few classrooms back in use.

"That's good, I guess," Cynthia remarked.

"Well, once you-all decided to work out of the school to question students, some of the parents figured it would be safe to send the kids back." Harry giggled. "Easier than having them at home, no matter what."

"Are we on a hike?" Cynthia noticed the three animals had stopped at the backdoor to the main building and were staring at the humans with upturned faces.

When Harry opened the door, they shot out, galloping across the quad. "All right, you guys, this is a con!"

"No, it isn't." The tiger trotted back to reassure the two wavering humans. "Come on. We've got an idea. It's more than any of you have."

"I could use some fresh air." Cynthia felt the first snowflake of winter alight on her nose.

"Me, too. Miranda will have to wait."

They crossed the quad, the snowflakes making a light tapping sound as they hit tree branches. The walkway was slick but not white yet. In the distance between the main building and the gymnasium, the snow thickened.

"Hurry up. It's cold," Pewter exhorted them.

The humans reached the front door of the gym and opened it. The animals dashed inside.

Mrs. Murphy glanced over her shoulder to see if they were behind her. She ran to the girls' gym door at one corner of the trophy hall. The other two animals marched behind her.

"This is a wild-goose chase." Cynthia laughed.

"Who knows, but it gives you a break from Rick. He's just seething up there."

"He gets like that until he cracks a case. He blames himself for everything."

They walked into the locker room. All three animals sat in front of 114. The line of dead ants was still there.

Since each locker wore a combination lock like a ring hanging from a bull's nose, they couldn't get into the locker.

But it gave Cynthia an idea. She found Coach Hallvard, who checked her list. Number 114 belonged to Jody Miller. Cynthia requested that the coach call her girls in to open their lockers.

An hour later, Coach Hallvard, an engine of energy, had each field hockey player, lacrosse, basketball, track and field, anyone on junior varsity or varsity standing in front of her locker.

Harry, back at work, missed the fireworks. When 114 was opened, an open can of Coca-Cola was the source of the ant patrol. However, 117 contained a Musketeer costume. The locker belonged to Karen Jensen.

54

Rick paced, his hands behind his back. Karen sobbed that she knew nothing about the costume, which was an expensive one.

"Ask anybody. I was Artemis, and I never left the dance," she protested. She was also feeling low because a small amount of marijuana had been found in her gym bag.

Rick got a court order to open lockers, cutting locks off if necessary. He had found a virtual pharmacy at St. Elizabeth's. These kids raided Mom and Dad's medicine chest with regularity or they had a good supplier. Valium, Percodan, Quaaludes, speed, amyl nitrate, a touch of cocaine, and a good amount of marijuana competed with handfuls of anabolic steroids in the boys' varsity lockers.

Hardened though he was, he was unprepared for the extent of drug use at the school. When he pressured one of the football players, he heard the standard argument: if you're playing football against guys who use steroids and you don't, you get creamed. If a boy wants to excel at certain sports, he's got to get into drugs sooner or later. The drug of choice was human growth hormone, but none of the kids could find it, and it was outrageously expensive. Steroids were a lot easier to cop.

The next shocker came when Cynthia checked the rental of the Musketeer costume using a label sewn into the neck of the tunic. She reached an outfitter in Washington, D.C. They reported they were missing a Musketeer costume, high quality.

It had been rented by Maury McKinchie using his MasterCard.

55

The snow swirled, obscuring Yellow Mountain. Harry trudged to the barn, knowing that no matter how deep the snow fell, it wouldn't last. The hard snows arrived punctually after Christmas. Occasionally a whopper would hit before the holidays, but most residents of central Virginia could count on real winter socking them January through March.

The winds, stiff, blew the fall foliage clean off the trees. Overnight the riotous color of fall gave way to the spare monochrome of winter.

A rumble sent Tucker out into the white. Fair pulled up. He clapped his cowboy hat on his head as he dashed for the barn.

"Harry, I need your help."

"What happened?"

"BoomBoom is pitching a royal hissy. She says she has to talk to someone she can trust. She has a heavy heart. You should hear it."

"No, I shouldn't."

"What should I do?" He fidgeted. "She sounded really distressed."

Harry leaned against a stall door. Gin Fizz poked his white nose over the top of the Dutch doors, feed falling from his mouth as he chewed. Usually he'd stick his head out and chat. Today he was too hungry and the feed was too delicious.

"*Mom, go along. That will give BoomBoom cardiac arrest.*" Murphy laughed.

"I'll tell you exactly what I think. She was sleeping with Maury McKinchie."

"You don't know that for a fact." He removed his hat and shook his head.

"Woman's instinct. Anyway, if you don't want to hear what I have to say, I'll go back to work and you can do whatever."

"I want to know."

"The more I think about the horrible events around here, the more it points to the battle between Roscoe and Sandy Brashiers over the future direction of St. Elizabeth's." She held up her hand. "I know. Doesn't take a genius to figure that out."

"Well, I hadn't thought about it that way."

"Comfort BoomBoom—within reason. She might have a piece of the puzzle and not know it. Or she may be in danger. On the other hand, BoomBoom won't miss a chance to emote extravagantly." She smiled. "And, of course, you'll tell me everything."

56

What was working on BoomBoom was her mouth. She confessed to Fair that she had been having an affair with Maury McKinchie. She had broken it off when she discovered he was having affairs with other women or at least with one important woman. He wouldn't tell her who it was.

She thought that the Other Woman, not his wife, of course, might have killed him.

"What a fool I was to believe him." Her expressive gray-blue eyes spilled over with salty tears.

Fair wanted to hug her, console her, but his mistrust of her ran deep enough for him to throttle his best impulses. One hug from him and she'd be telling everyone they had engaged in deep, meaningful discussions. Gossip would take it from there.

"Did he promise to divorce Darla?"

"No. She was his meal ticket."

"Ah, then what was there to believe? I'm missing a beat here. I don't mean to be dense."

"You're not dense, Fair, darling, you're just a man." She forgot her misery long enough to puff up his ego. "Men don't look below the surface. Believe? I believed him when he said he loved me." She renewed her sobs and no amount of light sea kelp essence could dispel her gloom.

"Maybe he did love you."

"Then how could he carry on with another woman? It was bad enough he had a wife!"

"You don't know for certain—do you?"

"Oh, yes, I do." She wiped her eyes with her handkerchief. "I ransacked his car when he was 'taking a meeting,' as he used to say, with Roscoe. He kept everything important in that car. Here." She reached into her silk robe, a luscious lavender, and pulled out a handful of envelopes, which she thrust into his hands. "See for yourself."

Fair held the light gray envelopes, Tiffany paper, wrapped in a white ribbon. He untied the ribbon. "Shouldn't you give these to Rick Shaw?"

"I should do a lot of things; that's why I need to talk to you. How do I know Rick will keep this out of the papers?"

"He will." Fair read the first letter rapidly. Love stuff only interested him if it was his love stuff. His mood changed considerably when he reached the signature at the bottom of the next page. In lovely cursive handwriting the name of "Your Naomi" appeared. "Oh, shit."

"Killed him."

"You think Naomi killed him?"

"She could parade around in a Musketeer costume as easily as the rest of us."

"Finding that costume in Karen Jensen's locker sure was lucky for Kendrick." Fair raised an eyebrow. "I wouldn't let him off the hook yet myself. That guy's got serious problems."

"Heartless. Not cruel, mind you, just devoid of feeling unless there's a dollar sign somewhere in the exchange." BoomBoom tapped a long fingernail in the palm of her other hand. "Think how easy it would have been for Naomi to dump that costume in a kid's locker. Piece of cake."

"Maybe." Fair handed the envelopes back to BoomBoom.

"You aren't going to read the rest of them? They sizzle."

"It's none of my business. You should hand them over to Rick. Especially if you think Naomi killed McKinchie."

"That's just it. She must have found out about me and let him have it after offing Roscoe. Ha. She thought she was free and clear, and then she finds out there's another woman. I give him credit for energy. A wife and two lovers." She smirked, her deep dimple, so alluring, drawing deeper.

"I guess it's possible. Anything's possible. But then again, who's to say you didn't kill Maury McKinchie?" Fair, usually indirect in such circumstances, bluntly stated the obvious.

"Me? Me? I couldn't kill anyone. I want to heal people, bind their inner wounds. I wouldn't hurt anyone."

"I'm telling you how it looks to a—"

"A scumbag! Anyone who knows me knows I wouldn't kill, and most emphatically not over love."

"Sex? Or love?"

"I thought you'd be on my side!"

"I am on your side." He leveled his gaze at the distressed woman, beautiful even in her foolishness. "That's why I'm asking you questions."

"I thought I loved Maury. Now I'm not so sure. He used me. He even gave me a screen test."

"From a sheriff's point of view, I'd say you had a motive."

"Well, I didn't have a motive to kill Roscoe Fletcher!"

"No, it would appear not. Did anyone have it in for Roscoe? Anyone you know?"

"Naomi. That's what I'm telling you."

"We don't know that he was cheating on her."

"He gathered his rosebuds while he may. Don't all you men do that—I mean, given the opportunity, you're all whores."

"I was." His jaw locked on him.

"Oh, Fair, I didn't mean you. You and Harry weren't suited for each other. The marriage would have come apart sooner or later. You know I cherish every moment we shared, and that's why, in my hour of need, I called you."

How could he have ever slept with this woman? Was he that blinded by beauty? A wave of disgust rose up from his stomach. He fought it down. Why be angry at her? She was what she was. She hadn't changed. He had.

"Fair?" She questioned the silence between them.

"If you truly believe that Naomi Fletcher killed her husband because she wanted to be with Maury McKinchie and then killed him in a fit of passion because she found out about you, you must go to the sheriff. Turn over those letters."

"I can't. It's too awful."

He changed his tack. "BoomBoom, what if she comes after you—assuming your hypothesis is correct."

"No!" Genuine alarm spread over her face.

"What about April Shively?" he pressed on.

"A good foundation base would have changed her life. That and rose petals in her bathwater." BoomBoom's facial muscles were taut; the veins in her neck stood out. "O-o-o, I'm cramping up. A charley horse. Rub it out for me."

"Your calf is fine. Don't start that stuff with me."

"What stuff?" She flared her nostrils.

"You know. Now I'm calling the sheriff. You can't withhold evidence like this."

"Don't!"

"BoomBoom, for once put your vanity aside for the public good. A murderer is out there. It may be Naomi, as you've said, but"—he shrugged—"if news leaks out that you had a fling with Maury, it's not the end of the world."

"Easy for you to say."

"I thought the man was a perfect ass."

"He made me laugh. And I can act as well as half of those people you see on television."

"I would never argue that point." He paused a moment, a

flicker, a jolt to the brain. "BoomBoom, have you ever watched any of Maury's movies?"

"Sure. Every one."

"Did you like them? I mean, can you tell me something about them?"

"He used hot, hot leading ladies. He gave Darla her big break, you know."

"Hot? As in sex?"

"Oh"—she flipped her fingers downward, a lightning-fast gesture, half dismissal—"everything Maury did was about sex: the liberating power of sex and how we are transformed by it. The true self is revealed in the act. I mean, the stories could be about the Manhattan district attorney's office or about a Vietnamese immigrant in Los Angeles—that's my favorite, *Rice Sky*—but sex takes over sooner or later."

"Huh." He walked over to the phone.

"Don't leave me."

"I'm not." He called Harry first. "Honey, I'm waiting for Rick Shaw. I'll explain when I get to your place. Is your video machine working? Good. I'm bringing some movies. We're going to eat a lot of popcorn." Then he dialed Rick.

In fifteen minutes Rick and Cynthia arrived, picked up the envelopes, and left after commanding BoomBoom not to leave town.

When she begged Fair not to leave, he replied, not unkindly, "You need to learn to be alone."

"Not tonight! I'm scared."

"Call someone else."

"You're going back to Harry."

"I'm going to watch movies with her."

"Don't do it. It's a big mistake."

"Do what?"

"Fall in love with her."

"I never fell out of love with her. I lost me first, then I lost my wife. Sorry, BoomBoom."

57

"Girl, you'd better have a good explanation." Kendrick's eyes, blood-shot with rage, bored into his daughter.

"I told you. I paid with Grandpa's legacy."

"I checked the bank. You're a minor, so they gave me the information. Your account is not missing forty-one thousand dollars, which is what that damned BMW cost!".

"The check hasn't cleared yet," she replied coolly.

"Pegasus Motor Cars says you paid with a certified check. Who gave you the money!"

"Grandpa!" She sat on the edge of the sofa, knees together like a proper young lady.

"Don't lie to me." He stepped toward her, fists clenched.

"Dad, don't you dare hit me, I'm pregnant."

He stopped in his tracks. "WHAT?"

"I . . . am . . . pregnant."

"Does your mother know?"

"Yes."

If Irene had appeared at that moment, Kendrick might have killed her. Luckily she was grocery shopping. He transferred his rage to the man responsible.

"Who did this to you?"

"None of your business."

"It is my business. Whoever he is, he's going to make good on this deal. He'll marry you."

"I don't want to get married."

"Oh, you don't?" Venom dripped from his voice. "Well, what you want is irrelevant. You got into this mess by following your wants. My God, Jody, what's happened to you?" He sat down with a thud, the anger draining into fear and confusion.

"Don't be mad at Mom. She did what a mother is supposed to do. She went to the doctor with me—once I knew. We were going to tell you, Dad, but with everything that's happened to you—we put it off."

"Who is the father?"

"I'm not sure."

"How many boys have you slept with?" His voice cracked.

"A couple."

"Well, who do you think it is?"

"Sean Hallahan—maybe."

"Oh, shit."

58

"Don't lie to me." Susan hovered over Brooks.

"I'm not. I don't do drugs, Mom."

"You hang out with someone who does."

"Jensen's not a druggie. She had one joint in her bag. Chill out."

Ned stepped in. "I think it's time we all went to bed."

"Danny's already in bed." Brooks envied her brother, off the hook on this one.

"Now look, daughter, if you are hiding something, you'd better come clean. Whatever you're doing, we'll deal with it."

"I'm not doing anything."

"Susan." Ned rubbed his forehead. A headache nibbled at his temples.

"I want to get to the bottom of this. Sheriff Shaw asked each of you questions after the marijuana was found and after that costume showed up. I can't believe it. It's too preposterous. Karen Jensen."

"Mom, Karen didn't kill Mr. McKinchie. Really. It's nuts."

"How do you suppose the costume got in her locker?"

"Easy. Everyone on the team knows everyone else's combination. We're always borrowing stuff."

Susan hovered over Brooks. "What do you know about Karen Jensen that we don't?"

"Karen's okay. She's not a druggie. The only thing I know about Karen is that she was dating an older guy from UVA this summer and got a little too close. Really. She's okay."

Susan put her arm around her daughter's shoulders. "I hope you are, too."

Later Susan called Harry, relaying the conversation with Brooks. Harry treated her to a synopsis of *Rice Sky*.

"Sounds boring."

"Made a lot of money. I think the real reason Roscoe was pushing the film-department idea was to punch up Maury. He was so overshadowed by Darla. Roscoe was smart. Cater to Maury and good things would follow."

"Money. Tons of money."

"Sure. They'd name the department after Maury. He'd donate all his scripts, round up old equipment; the whole thing would be an ego trip."

"How much do you think an ego trip like that would cost?"

"It would take at least a million-dollar endowment, I'd think. Probably more." Harry scribbled on a brown paper bag. "I'm not too good at knowing what it would be worth, really, but it would have to be a lot."

"What's Fair think?"

"Millions," he called out.

"Sandy Brashiers can't be that stupid," Harry said. "For a couple of million dollars even he would cave in on the film-department idea."

"I doubt Roscoe put it in dollars and cents."

"Yeah. Maybe it's in April's books."

"Susan, if that's all that's in there, what's to hide?"

"Damned if I know. We called about Sean, by the way. No change."

"I called, too."

"That kid has to know something. Larry Johnson said he'd heard the main swelling was diminishing. Maybe he'll snap out of the coma once the swelling is down."

"He's lucky to be alive."

59

"Why don't you just tell me the truth?" Rick rapped his fingers on the highly polished table.

"You have no right to push me like this." Naomi Fletcher had her back up.

"You know more than you're telling me." He remained cool and professional.

"No, I don't. And I resent you badgering me when I'm in mourning."

Wordlessly, Cynthia Cooper slid the packet of envelopes, retied with a neat bow, across the table to Naomi. Her face bled bone white.

"How—?"

"The 'how' doesn't matter, Naomi. If you are in on these murders, come clean." Cynthia sounded sympathetic. "Maybe we can work a deal."

"I didn't kill anyone."

"You didn't kill Roscoe to clear the way for McKinchie to marry you?" Rick pressured her.

"Marry Maury McKinchie? I'd sooner have a root canal." Her even features contorted in scorn.

"You liked him enough to sleep with him." Cynthia felt the intimate information should best come from her, not Rick.

"That doesn't mean I wanted to spend my life with him. Maury was a good-time Charlie, and that's all he was. He wasn't marriage material."

"Apparently, neither was Roscoe."

She shrugged. "He was in the beginning, but men change."

"So do women." Cynthia pointed to the envelopes.

"What's good for the gander was good for the goose, in this instance. The marriage vows are quite lovely, and one would hope to live up to them, but they are exceedingly unrealistic. I didn't do anything wrong. I didn't kill anyone. I played with Maury McKinchie. You can't arrest me for that."

"Played with him and then killed him when you learned he wasn't serious about you and he was sleeping with another woman."

"BoomBoom." She waved her hand in the air as though at an irritating gnat. "I'd hardly worry about her."

"Plenty of other women have." Cynthia bluntly stated the truth.

"BoomBoom was too self-centered for Maury. One was never really in danger of a rival because he loved himself too much, if you know what I mean." She smiled coldly.

"You were at the car wash the day your husband died. You spoke to him. You could have easily given him poisoned candy."

"I could have, but I didn't."

"You're tough," Rick said, half admiringly.

"I'm not tough, I'm innocent."

"If I had a dollar for every killer who said that, I'd be a rich man." Rick felt in his coat pocket for his cigarettes. "Mind if I smoke?"

"I most certainly do. The whole house will stink when you leave, which I hope is soon."

Cynthia and Rick shared a secret acknowledgment. No Southern lady would have said that.

"How well did you know Darla?"

"A nodding acquaintance. She was rarely here."

"If you didn't kill Roscoe, do you know who did?"

"No."

"How does withholding evidence sound to you, Mrs. Fletcher?" Rick hunched forward.

"Like a bluff."

"For chrissake, Naomi, two men are dead!" Cynthia couldn't contain her disgust. Then she quickly fired a question. "Was your husband sleeping with April Shively?"

"God, no," Naomi hooted. "Roscoe thought April was pretty but deadly dull." Naomi had to admit to herself that dullness didn't keep men from sleeping with women. However, she wasn't going to admit that to Shaw and Cooper.

"Do you think Kendrick killed Maury?" Rick switched his bait.

"Unlikely." She closed her eyes, as if worn-out.

Cooper interjected. "Why?"

Naomi perked up. "Kendrick doesn't have the balls."

"Did you love your husband?" Rick asked.

She grew sober, sad even. "You live with a man for eighteen years, you tend to know him. Roscoe might wander off the reservation from time to time. He could indulge in little cruelties—his treatment of Sandy Brashiers being a case in point. He kept Sandy in the dark about everything." She paused, "Did I love him? I was accustomed to him, but I did love him. Yes, I did."

Cynthia mustered a smile. "Why?"

Naomi shrugged. "Habit."

"What did Roscoe have against Sandy Brashiers?"

"Roscoe always had it in for Harvard men. He said the arrogance of their red robes infuriated him. You know, during academic ceremonies only Harvard wears the crimson robe."

"Do you have any feeling about the false obituaries?" Cynthia prodded.

"Those?" Naomi wrinkled her brow. "Kids' prank. Sean apologized."

"Do you think he was also responsible for the second one?"

"No. I think it was a copycat. Sean got the luxury of being a bad dude. Very seductive at that age. Another boy wanted the glory. Is it that important?"

"It might be." Rick reached for his hat.

"Have you searched April Shively's house?" Naomi asked.

"House, car, office, even her storage unit. Nothing."

Naomi stood up to usher them out. "She doesn't live high on the hog. I don't think she embezzled funds."

"She could be covering up for someone else." Cynthia reached the door first.

"You mean Roscoe, of course." Naomi didn't miss a beat. "Why not? He's dead. He can be accused of anything. You have to find criminals in order to keep your jobs, don't you?"

Rick halted at the door as Naomi's hand reached the knob. "You work well with Sandy, don't you? Under the circumstances?"

"Yes."

"Did you know that Sandy got a student pregnant at White Academy, the school he worked at before St. Elizabeth's?"

Cooper struck next. "Roscoe knew."

"You two have been very busy." Her lips tightened.

"Like you said, Mrs. Fletcher, we have to find criminals in order to keep our jobs." Rick half smiled.

She grimaced and closed the door.

60

Mrs. Murphy leaned against the pillow on the sofa. She stretched her right hind leg out straight and held it there. Then she unsheathed her claws and stared at her toes. What stupendously perfect toes. She repeated the process with the left hind leg. Then she reached with her front paws together, a kitty aerobic exercise. Satisfied, she lay back on the pillow, happily staring into the fire. She reviewed in her mind recent events.

Harry dusted her library shelves, a slow process since she'd take a book off the shelf, read passages, and then replace it. A light snow fell outside, which made her all the happier to be inside.

Tucker snored in front of the fire. Pewter, curled in a ball at the other end of the sofa, dreamed of tiny mice singing her praise. "O Mighty Pewter, Queen of Cats."

"Lord of the Flies." Harry pulled the old paperback off the shelf. "Had to read it in college, but I hated it." She dropped to the next shelf. "Fielding, love him. Austen." She turned to Mrs. Murphy. "Literature is about sensibility. Really, Murphy, John Milton is one of the greatest poets who ever lived, but he bores me silly. I have trouble liking any art form trying to beat a program into my head. I suppose it's the difference between the hedgehog and the fox."

"*Isaiah Berlin.*" Mrs. Murphy recalled the important work of criticism dividing writers into hedgehogs or foxes, hedgehogs being fixed on one grand idea or worldview whereas foxes ran through the territory; life was life with no special agenda. That was how she thought of it anyway.

"What I mean is, Murphy, readers are hedgehogs or foxes. Some people read to remember. Some read to forget. Some read to be challenged. Others want their prejudices confirmed."

"*Why do you read, Mother?*" the cat asked.

"I read," Harry said, knowing exactly what her cat had asked her, "for the sheer exultant pleasure of the English language."

"*Ah, me, too.*" The tiger purred. Harry couldn't open a book without Mrs. Murphy sitting on her shoulder or in her lap.

Sometimes Pewter would read, but she favored mysteries or thrillers. Pewter couldn't raise her sights above genre fiction.

Mrs. Murphy thought the gray cat might read some diet books as well. She stretched and walked over to Harry. She jumped on a shelf to be closer to Harry's face. She scanned the book spines, picking out her favorites. She enjoyed biographies more than Harry did. She stopped at Michael Powell's *My Life In The Movies.*

She blinked and leapt off the shelf, cuffing Tucker awake. "*Come on, Tucker, come on.*"

"*I'm so comfortable.*"

"*Just follow me.*" She skidded out the animal door, Tucker on her heels.

"What in God's name gets into her?" Harry held *The Iliad.*

Forty-five minutes later both animals, winded, pulled up at Bowden's pond where the Camry and the grisly remains still sat, undiscovered by humans.

"*Tucker, you cover the east side of the pond. I'll cover the west. Look for a video or a can of film.*"

Both animals searched through the snow, which was beginning to cover the ground; still the shapes would have been obvious.

An hour later they gave up.

"Nothing," Tucker reported.

"Me either."

A growl made their hair stand on end.

"The bobcat!" Mrs. Murphy charged up the slippery farm road, leaping the ruts. Tucker, fast as grease, ran beside her.

They reached the cutover hayfields, wide open with no place to hide.

"She's gaining on us." Tucker's tongue hung out.

And she was, a compact, powerful creature, tufts on the ends of her ears.

"This is my fault." The cat ached from running so hard.

"Save your breath." Tucker whirled to confront the foe, her long fangs bared.

The bobcat stopped for a moment. She wanted dinner, but she didn't want to get hurt. She loped around Tucker, deciding Murphy was the better chance. Tucker followed the bobcat.

"Run, Murphy, run. I'll keep her busy."

"You domesticated worm," the bobcat spat.

Seeing her friend in danger, Murphy stopped panting. She puffed up, turning to face the enemy. Together she and Tucker flanked the bobcat about twenty yards from her.

The bobcat crouched, moving low toward Mrs. Murphy, who jumped sideways. The bobcat ran and flung herself in the air. Murphy sidestepped her. The big cat whirled and charged just as Tucker hurtled toward her. The dog hit the bobcat in the legs as she was ready to pounce on Murphy. The bobcat rolled, then sprang to her feet. Both friends were side to side now, fangs bared.

"In here!" a voice called from the copse of trees a spring away.

"Let's back toward it," Murphy gasped.

"Where are we going?" Tucker whispered.

"To the trees."

"She's more dangerous there than in the open."

"It's our only hope."

"*You two are worthless.*" The bobcat stalked them, savoring the moment.

"*That's your opinion.*" Mrs. Murphy growled deep in her throat.

"*You're the hors d'oeuvre, your canine sidekick is the main meal.*"

"*Don't count your chickens.*" Murphy spun around and flew over the snow.

Tucker did likewise, the bobcat closing in on her. She heard breathing behind her and then saw Mrs. Murphy dive into a fox hole. Tucker spun around and snapped at the bobcat's forelegs, which caught her completely by surprise. It gave Tucker the split second she needed to dive into the fox hole after her friend.

"*I can wait all night,*" the bobcat muttered.

"*Don't waste time over spilt milk,*" Mrs. Murphy taunted.

"*I'm glad some of you are big foxes.*" Tucker panted on the floor of the den. "*I'd have never gotten into your earth otherwise.*"

The slight red vixen said to Murphy, "*You told me once to stay in the shed during a bad storm. I owe you one.*"

"*You've more than repaid me.*" Murphy listened as the bobcat prowled around, unwilling to give up.

"*What were you two doing out here tonight?*"

"*Looking for a film or a video back where the dead human in the car is,*" Tucker said.

"*Nobody will find that human until deer-hunting season starts, and that's two weeks away,*" the vixen noted wisely.

"*Did you-all see anything?*"

"*No, although when we first found her at the end of September she'd only been dead a few weeks.*"

"*September! I think the killer threw the evidence in the pond.*" Murphy was a figuring cat.

"*How do you know?*" Tucker knew that the feline was usually a few steps ahead of her.

"*Because the murders are about film and Roscoe's film department. It was right in front of my face, but I didn't see it. Whoever is in that car is the missing link.*"

"Murphy," Tucker softly said, "have you figured out what's going on?"

"*Yes, I think I have, but not in time—not in time.*"

61

Kendrick and Jody sat on a bench outside the intensive care unit. An officer guarded Sean inside. His grandfather was there, too.

Kendrick stopped Dr. Hayden McIntire when he came out of the room. "How is he?"

"We're guardedly optimistic." He looked at Jody. "Quite a few of his friends have stopped by. He's a popular boy."

"Has Karen Jensen been here?" Jody asked.

"Yes. So were Brooks Tucker, Roger Davis, and the whole football team, of course. They can't go in, but it was good that they came."

"Well, that's nice." Kendrick smiled unconvincingly.

After Hayden left, Kendrick took his daughter by the elbow. "Come on, he isn't going to rise up and walk just because you're here."

She stared at the closed doors. "I wish he would."

"I'll attend to Sean in good time."

"Dad, you can't make anybody do anything. One mistake isn't cured by making a bigger one."

They walked down the hall. "That's a mature statement."

"Maybe I'm learning something."

"Well, learn this. I'm not having bastards in my house, so you're going to marry somebody."

"It's my body."

He grabbed her arm hard. "There is no other option."

"Let me go or I'll scream bloody murder right here at University of Virginia Hospital. And you're in enough trouble." She said this without rancor.

"Yes." He unhanded her.

"Did you kill Maury McKinchie?"

"What?" He was shocked that she asked.

"Did you kill Maury McKinchie?"

"No."

62

Neither Mrs. Murphy nor Tucker returned home all night. Harry had called and called. Finally she fed the horses and, last of all, Pewter.

Walking down to get the paper, she heard Tucker bark. *"We're safe!"*

"Yahoo!" Mrs. Murphy sped beside the dog, stopping from time to time to jump for joy, straight in the air, the snow flying up and catching the sunlight, making thousands of tiny rainbows.

"Where have you two been?" Harry hunched down to gather them both in her arms. "I was worried sick about you." She sniffed. "You smell like a fox."

"We spent the night with our hosts," Murphy said.

Tucker, turning in excited circles, interrupted. *"We think there's evidence in Bowden's pond, and then we stayed too late and the bobcat tracked us. Oh, it was a close call."*

"Tucker was brave!"

"You, too."

"Such talk." Harry laughed at their unintelligible chatter. "You must be starving. Come on. We've got to hurry or I'll be late for work."

Driving Blair's Dually into Crozet, Harry noticed the snow lying blue in the deep hollows.

The three rushed into the post office, nearly getting stuck in the animal door. Mrs. Hogendobber, who usually greeted them, was so excited, she barely noticed their entry.

"Hi, Miranda—"

"Where have you been?" Miranda clapped her hands in anticipation of telling her the news.

"What is the matter?"

"Kendrick Miller confessed to Rick Shaw that he had killed Maury McKinchie and Roscoe Fletcher. He had made up the story about the Musketeer because he remembered the Musketeer was wearing a sword. The costume hanging in Jensen's locker was irrelevant to the case. He confessed last night at midnight."

"I don't believe it," Mrs. Murphy exclaimed.

63

A crowd had gathered at Mim's . . . a good thing, since she put them to work stuffing and hand-addressing envelopes for the Multiple Sclerosis Foundation in which she was typically active.

Brooks, Roger, and Karen were relieved now that St. Elizabeth's could return to normal. Sandy Brashiers, at the head of the envelope line, told them to pipe down.

Gretchen, Mim's cook, served drinks.

When Cynthia walked through the door, everyone cheered. Accorded center stage, she endured question after question.

"One at a time." Cynthia laughed.

"Why did he do it?" Sandy Brashiers asked.

Cynthia waited a moment, then said, "These were crimes of passion, in a sense. I don't want to offend anyone but—"

"Murder is the offense," Sandy said. "We can handle his reasons."

"Well—Roscoe was carrying on an affair with Irene Miller and Kendrick blew up."

"*Roscoe?* What about Maury?" Fair Haristeen, tired from a day in the operating room, sat in a chair. Enough people were folding and stuffing. He needed a break.

"Kendrick has identified the poison used. He said Maury was on to him, knew he'd killed Roscoe, and was going to prove it. He killed him to shut him up."

Harry listened with interest. She felt such relief even as she felt sorrow for Irene and Jody. Irene had had an affair. No cheers for that, but to have a husband snap and go on a killing spree had to be dreadful. No wonder Jody had beaned Maury McKinchie at the hockey game. The tension in the Miller household must have been unbearable. "*Nouveau riche,*" Mim cried.

"I'd rather be *nouveau riche* than not *riche* at all," Fair rejoined, and since Mim adored her vet, he could get away with it.

Everyone truly laughed this time.

"How did Kendrick get such powerful poison?" Reverend Herb Jones wondered.

"The nursery and gardening business needs pesticides."

Harry noticed BoomBoom's unusual reticence. "Aren't you relieved?"

"Uh—yes," said the baffled beauty. She'd had no idea about Roscoe and Irene. Why didn't Maury tell her? He'd relished sexual tidbits.

Sandy Brashiers put his hands on his hips. "This still doesn't get April Shively off the hook. After all, she is withholding papers relevant to school operation."

"Maybe she will come forward now," Little Mim hoped out loud.

"How do you know for sure it was Mr. Miller?" Karen said to everyone's amazement.

Cynthia answered, "A detailed confession is about as close to a lock as you can get."

"Why'd he tell?" Harry wondered aloud.

Cynthia winked at her. "Couldn't live with the guilt. Said he confessed to Father Michael first, and over time realized he had to give himself up."

"Well, it's over. Let's praise the Lord for our deliverance," Miranda instructed them.

"Amen," Herb agreed and the others joined in.

"You know, I keep thinking about Irene and Jody sitting home alone. They must be wretched. We should extend our sympathy." Miranda folded her hands as if in prayer.

Everyone looked at Mrs. Hogendobber, thought for a moment, and then agreed that she had a point. It might not be fun to go over to the Millers', but it was the right thing to do.

After the work party, Harry, Fair, Big Mim, Little Mim, Herb Jones, Miranda, and Susan Tucker drove over. The kids piled into Roger's old car. Father Michael had been with the family since Kendrick gave himself up late that afternoon. It was the priest who answered the door. Surprised to see so many people, he asked Irene if she would be willing to see her neighbors. She burst into tears and nodded "yes."

The first person Irene greeted was Big Mim, who after the formalities offered them a sojourn in one of her farm dependencies if they should need privacy from the press.

Irene thanked her and began crying again.

Miranda put her arm around her. "There, there, Irene. This is too strange to contemplate. You must be feeling confused and terrible."

"Bizarre," Jody said forthrightly. "I can't believe he lost it like that."

Irene, not ready to give up on her husband, sputtered, "He's no murderer!"

"He confessed," Jody said flatly.

"We're your friends, no matter what." Softhearted Roger couldn't bear to see Jody's mother cry.

"Mom, I want to go back to school. I know this won't go away, but something in our lives has to be normal."

"Jody, that only puts more pressure on you." Irene worried about the reaction of the other students.

"Hey, I'm not responsible for Dad. I need my friends."

"We'll see."

"Mom, I'm going."

"We'll watch over her," Karen volunteered.

As this issue was hashed out, Father Michael and Herb Jones huddled in a corner. Father Michael, secure in the company of another cleric, whispered to him that he was tremendously relieved that Kendrick was behind bars. After all, he himself was likely to be the next victim.

"Bragging?"

"Not exactly. The first confession was straightforward. The second one, he said he liked killing. He liked the power. I can't say I ever recognized his voice."

"Was there a sense of vindication?" Herb inclined his head close to Father Michael's.

"I couldn't say."

"A touch dramatic."

"The entire episode was certainly that."

Later that evening Harry told Mrs. Murphy, Tucker, and Pewter all that had transpired at Big Mim's and then over at Irene Miller's. Angry though they were at not being included, they listened as she babbled while doing her chores.

"They're so far away from the truth it hurts," Tucker said and Pewter agreed, since Mrs. Murphy had briefed them on what she felt was truly going on.

"It's going to hurt a whole lot more." Mrs. Murphy stared out the window into the black night. Try as she might, she couldn't think of what to do.

64

Typical of central Virginia in late November, a rush of warm wind rolled up from the Gulf of Mexico. Temperatures soared into the low sixties.

Students were now back at St. Elizabeth's, thanks to Kendrick's midnight confession.

Harry and Miranda shoveled through the landslide of mail.

Jody Miller and Karen Jensen pulled in front of Market Shiflett's store.

"Things are finally settling down." Miranda watched the girls, smiling, enter the grocery store.

"Thank God." Harry tossed a catalog into the Tucker post box. "Now if my truck would just get fixed! I'm getting spoiled driving Blair's Dually and I don't want to wear out my welcome."

"Think of all the string and rubber bands they have to remove," Pewter quipped sarcastically. "What are Jody and Karen doing out of school?"

"Hookey," Tucker thought out loud.

Mrs. Murphy said, "*There's a big field hockey game after school today, and a huge football game Friday. Maybe their coach got them out of class.*"

"*Wish we'd get out of work early.*" Pewter rubbed the plastic comb Harry had just installed on the corner of the post boxes. It was advertised as a cat-grooming aid.

" '*Course St. E's won't be worth squat—they lost too much practice time, but Crozet High ought to have a good game.*" The tiger enjoyed sports.

"*St. E's practiced,*" Tucker said. "*Of course, how well they practiced with all the uproar is anyone's guess.*"

Jody and Karen came out of the store, placed a big carton in the back of Karen's old car, and drove off.

Susan zoomed into the post office through the backdoor. "Good news!"

"*What?*" came the animal and human chorus.

"Sean Hallahan has regained consciousness." She beamed. "He's not out of the woods yet, but he knows his name, where he is, he recognizes his parents. He's still in intensive care. Still no visitors."

"That's great news." Harry smiled.

"Once he's really clear, off some of the painkillers, he'll have other pains to deal with . . . still, isn't it wonderful?"

65

The deep golden rays of the late afternoon sun slanted over the manicured field hockey pitch. The high winds and snow of the previous
week had stripped the trees of their leaves, but the mild temperature
balanced the starkness of early winter.

Knowing how rapidly the mercury could fall, Harry tossed four
blankets over her shoulder.

As she made her way to the bleachers, the Reverend Herb Jones
called out, "You opening a trading post?"

"Four beaver pelts for one heavy blanket." She draped a royal-
blue buffalo plaid blanket over her arm as if to display her wares.

Miranda, warm in her MacLeod tartan kilt with a matching tam-
o'-shanter, soon joined them. She carried two hot thermoses, one of
tea, the other of chocolate.

"You come sit by me." Herb patted the hard wooden bleacher
seat next to him.

Sandy Brashiers, beaming, shook the hands of parents, telling each of them how grateful he was that St. Elizabeth's frightful ordeal was behind them. He thanked everyone for their support, and he promised the best for the remainder of the semester.

Coach Hallvard, about to face the formidable St. Catherine's team from Richmond, had not a second to glad-hand anyone.

Mim accompanied her daughter, which put Little Mim's nose out of joint because she wanted to be accompanied by Blair Bainbridge. He, however, had been roped into setting up the hot dog stand since his Dually, the newest in town, could pull the structure. Not only did Blair's Dually have a setup for a gooseneck trailer, he also had a Reese hitch welded to the frame.

"Mother, why don't you sit with the girls?" Little Mim waved broadly at Miranda in MacLeod tartan splendor.

Mim, sotto voce, replied, "Trying to get rid of me?"

"Why, Mother, whatever gave you such a silly idea?"

"Humph. You need me to extract money out of these tightwads, Marilyn. You haven't been a raging success."

"Considering all that's happened here, I've done pretty damn well, Mother. And I don't need you to advertise my shortcomings. I'm conversant with them."

"Well, aren't we testy?"

"Yes, we are." Little Mim gave her a sickeningly sweet smile.

These last two years Little Mim had found some backbone. Her mother enjoyed friction on the odd occasion, although she wasn't accustomed to receiving it from her formerly obsequious daughter. However, it did spice up the day.

"Mimsy," Miranda called out, knowing Mim hated "Mimsy." She felt devilish. "Sit with us."

Mim, throwing her alpaca shawl, deep raspberry, over her wildly overpriced Wathne coat, paraded grandly to the bleachers, leaving Little Mim to scoot to the hot dog stand where she found, to her dismay, Cynthia Cooper helping Blair set up shop.

The home team trotted across the field as the rhythm section of the band beat the drums.

Karen Jensen ran with Brooks. "Toni Freeman has moves like a snake," Karen said about the opponent who would be covering Brooks.

"I'll be a mongoose."

"This is going to be a tough game." Karen grew increasingly fierce before the game.

"Zone. You'll be in the zone."

"Yeah. There's Rog."

Brooks waved back at Roger.

"Tossed salad." Karen laughed, meaning Roger had flipped over Brooks.

Jody loped up from behind. "Let's skin 'em alive, pound 'em senseless! *Yes!*" She moved by them.

As the team approached the bench, the stands erupted in a roar. St. Catherine's also shouted. The entire senior class had trekked out from Richmond. This was a grudge match because St. Catherine's had edged out St. E's in the semifinals at last year's state tournament.

The three animal friends sat with the humans on the bleachers.

Pewter hated the crowd noises. *"I'm going back to the car."*

"Miranda closed up the Falcon; you can't get in," Mrs. Murphy told her.

"Then I'll go to the hot dog stand." Pewter's eyes glistened.

"Stay with us," Murphy told her loudly.

"Will you two stop fussing at each other!" Harry commanded.

"She started it." Pewter oozed innocence.

A phone rang in Herb's pocket.

"What on earth?" Miranda exclaimed when he pulled a fold-up cellular out of his Norfolk jacket.

"The modern age, Miranda, the modern age." He pulled out the antenna, hit a button, and said, "Hello."

Susan answered, "Herb, tell the gang I'm on my way. Oh, and tell Harry I dropped off BoomBoom to pick up her truck. It's ready."

"Okay. Anything else?"

"No. Be there in ten minutes."

"Fine. 'Bye." He pressed the green button again, sliding the aerial down. "Harry, Susan will be here in ten minutes, and Boom-Boom is bringing your truck. Susan dropped her off."

"BoomBoom? Great. Now I have to be terminally grateful."

"No, you don't. After all, she wrecked your truck in the first place."

"Given the way she drives, she'll wreck it again."

"*Mother, you're irrational about BoomBoom.*" Mrs. Murphy scratched her neck.

"No, she won't," Herb answered. "Here we go!"

The game started with St. Catherine's racing downfield, taking a shot on goal, saved.

"Jeez, that was fast." Harry hoped St. Elizabeth's defense would kick in soon.

"May I see that?"

"Sure." Herb handed Miranda the cellular phone.

She slipped the aerial out and held it to her ear. "It's so light."

"I'll pick up my messages; listen to how clear it is." He punched in what must have been seventeen or more numbers and held the phone to Miranda's ear.

"Amazing." Suddenly her face changed. "Herbie, look."

Parading in front of the bleachers was April Shively wearing a St. Elizabeth's jacket. She was carrying three closed cartons that she dumped at Sandy Brashiers's feet.

Blair noticed this from the hot dog stand. Cynthia hurried over, Little Mim at her heels.

"Deputy Cooper." A surprised Sandy put his hand on the boxes. "Marilyn."

"I'll take those." Little Mim bent over and picked up a rather heavy carton.

"No." Sandy smiled falsely.

April, her grin widening, turned on her heel and left. "Ta-ta!"

"Damn her," Sandy said under his breath.

"Cynthia, you can't have these." Little Mim squared her shoulders.

"Why don't we examine them together? It will only help St. Elizabeth's if everything is aboveboard from the start." Cynthia made a strong argument.

"As headmaster, I'll take charge of those documents."

"Down in front!" a fan, oblivious to the drama, yelled at them.

"Without me you won't be headmaster for long." Little Mim clipped her words, then smiled at the deputy as she changed course. "Come on, Cynthia. You're absolutely right. We should do this together."

As they hauled off the cartons, the announcer blared over the loudspeaker, "We are happy to announce that St. Elizabeth's own Sean Hallahan has regained consciousness, and we know all your prayers have helped."

A huge cheer went up from the stands.

66

After the game, won by St. Elizabeth's, Jody, who'd played brilliantly, drove alone to the University of Virginia Hospital.

Sean, removed to a private room, no longer had a guard since Kendrick had confessed. His father was sitting with him when Jody, wearing a visitor's pass, lightly knocked on the door.

"May I come in?"

Sean turned his head toward her, stared blankly for a moment, then focused. "Sure."

"Hello, Mr. Hallahan."

"Hello, Jody. I'm sorry this is such a troubling time for you."

"It can't be as bad as what you're going through." She walked over to Sean. "Hey."

"Hey." He turned his head to address his father. "Dad, could we be alone?"

In that moment Mr. Hallahan knew Jody was the girl in question, for his wife had told him Sean's words during his first, brief moment of lucidity when Cynthia Cooper was on guard.

"I'll be just down the hall if you need me."

When he had left, Jody leaned over, kissing Sean on the cheek. "I'm sorry, I'm really sorry."

"I was stupid. It wasn't your fault."

"Yes, it was. I told you—well, the news—when I was pissed off at you and the world."

"I'll marry you if you like," he gallantly offered.

"No. Sean, I was angry because you were paying attention to Karen. I wanted to hurt you."

"You mean you aren't pregnant?" His eyes brightened.

"No, I am."

"Oh." He dropped his head back on the pillow. "Jody, you can't face this alone. Lying here has given me a lot of time to think."

"Do you love Karen?"

"No. I haven't even gone out with her."

"But you want to."

He drew a long breath. "Yeah. But that was then. This is now."

"Will you walk again?"

"Yes." He spoke with determination. "The doctors say I'll never play football again . . . but they don't know me. I don't care what it takes. I will."

"Everyone's back at school. My dad confessed to the murders."

"Mom told me." He didn't know what to say. "I wish I could be at Homecoming."

"Team won't be worth squat without you."

"Paul Briscoe will do okay. He's just a sophomore, but he'll be good."

"Do you hate me?" Her eyes, misty, implored him.

"No. I hate myself."

"Did you tell anyone—"

"Of course not."

"Don't."

"What are you going to do?"

"Get rid of it."

He breathed hard, remaining quiet for a long time. "I wish you wouldn't do that."

"Sean, the truth is—I'm not ready to be a mother. You're not ready to be a father, either, and besides—it may not be yours."

"But you said—"

"I wanted to hurt you. It may be yours and it may not. So just forget it. Forget everything. My dad's in jail. Just remember—my dad's in jail."

"Why would he kill Mr. Fletcher and Mr. McKinchie?"

"I don't know."

His pain medication was wearing off. Sweat beaded on Sean's forehead. "We were having such a good time." He pushed the button for the nurse. "Jody, I need a shot."

"I'll go. Don't worry. You're sure you didn't tell anyone anything?"

"I didn't."

"I'll see you later." She passed Mr. Hallahan, who walked back into Sean's room the minute she left.

"She's the one."

"No." Grimacing, Sean pleaded, "Dad, get the nurse, will you? I really hurt."

67

That same night Cynthia Cooper and Little Mim sifted through papers at Little Mim's beautiful cottage on her mother's vast estate.

"Why do you think April finally changed her mind?" Little Mim said.

"Had to be that she heard about Roscoe's affair with Irene," Coop answered. "Her hero suddenly had feet of clay."

The minutes from the various committee meetings provided no surprises.

Roscoe's record book containing handwritten notes made after informal meetings or calls on possible donors did pack some punch.

After a meeting with Kendrick Miller, Roscoe had scrawled, "Discussed women's athletics, especially a new training room for the girls. Whirlpool bath. Won't give a penny. Cheap bastard."

On Father Michael's long prayers during assembly: "A simple 'Bless us, dear Lord' would suffice."

After a particularly bruising staff meeting where a small but well-organized contingent opposed athletic expansion and a film department, he wrote concerning Sandy Brashiers, "Judas."

As Little Mim occasionally read pungent passages aloud, Cynthia, using a pocket calculator, went through the accounting books.

"I had no idea it cost so much money to run St. E's." She double-checked the figures.

"What hurts most is maintenance. The older buildings suck up money."

"Guess they were built before insulation."

"Old Main was put up in 1834."

Cynthia picked up the last book, a green clothbound book, longer than it was wide. She opened it to the figures page without checking the front. As she merrily clicked in numbers, she hummed. "Do you remember what cost five thousand dollars the first week of September? It says 'W.T.' " She pointed to the ledger.

"Doesn't ring a bell."

Cynthia punched in more numbers.

"Hey, here's a good one." Little Mim laughed, reading out loud. " 'Big Mim suggested I butter up Darla McKinchie and get her to pry money out of Kendrick. I told her Darla has no interest in St. Elizabeth's, in her husband's career and, as best I can tell, no affection for the state of Virginia. She replied, "How common!" ' "

Little Mim shook her head. "Leave it to Mother. She can't ever let me have something for myself. I'm on the board, she isn't."

"She's trying to help."

Marilyn's hazel eyes clouded. "Help? My mother wants to run every committee, organization, potential campaign. She's indefatigable."

"What cost forty-one thousand dollars?"

Little Mim put down Roscoe's record book to look at the ledger. "Forty-one thousand dollars October twenty-eighth. Roscoe was dead by then." She grabbed the ledger, flipping back to the front. "Slush fund. What the hell is this?"

Coop couldn't believe she'd heard Little Mim swear. "I suppose most organizations have a kitty, although this is quite a large one."

"I'll say." Little Mim glanced over the incoming sums. "We'll get to the bottom of this." She reached for the phone, punching numbers as she exhaled loudly. "April, it's Marilyn Sanburne." She pressed the "speaker" button so that Coop could hear as well.

"Are you enjoying yourself?"

"Actually, I am," came the curt reply. "Roscoe's record book is priceless. What is this green ledger?"

"I have no idea."

"April, don't expect me to believe you. Why else would you remove these papers and accounting books? You must have known about the slush fund."

"First of all, given everyone's temper these days, a public reading of Roscoe's record book is not a good idea. Second, I have no idea what the slush fund was. Roscoe never once mentioned it to me. I found that book in his desk."

"Could Maury have started giving St. Elizabeth's an endowment?"

"Without fanfare? He was going to give, all right, but we were going to have to kiss his ass in Macy's window."

Little Mim bit her lip. "April, I've misjudged you."

"Is that a formal apology?" April asked.

"Yes."

"I accept."

"Sandy Brashiers couldn't have handled this," Little Mim admitted.

"He'd have fumbled the ball. All we need is for the papers to get wind of this before we know what it's all about," April said.

"You have no idea?" Little Mim pressed.

"No. But you'll notice the incoming sums are large and regular. Usually between the tenth and fifteenth of each month."

"Let me see that." Coop snatched the green book out of Little Mim's hands. "Damn!"

"What?" Little Mim said.

Cynthia grabbed the phone. "April, seventy-five thousand dollars came in the week after Roscoe died. It's not reflected in the ledger, but there is a red dot by October tenth. For the other deposits, there's a red dot with a black line through it."

"Primitive but effective bookkeeping," April said.

"Did you know a Jiffy bag with seventy-five thousand dollars arrived in Roscoe's mailbox at Crozet on October"—she figured a moment—"twelfth. I'm pretty sure it was the twelfth."

"I didn't know a thing about it."

"But sometimes you would pick up Roscoe's personal mail for him?"

"Infrequently . . . but yes."

"Do you remember other Jiffy bags?"

"Cooper, most books are sent in bags like that."

"Do you swear to me you don't know what this money represents?"

"I swear, but I know it represents something not right. That's why I cleaned everything out. I didn't mind sitting in jail. I felt safe."

"One last question."

"Shoot."

"Do you believe that Kendrick Miller killed Roscoe and Maury?"

"Roscoe loathed him. But, no, I don't."

"He says he blew up in a rage."

"Show him the ledger."

"I'm going to do just that. One more question. I promise this is the last one. Do you think Naomi knows about the ledger?"

A pause. "If she did, we'd see the money. Even if just a pair of expensive earrings."

"Thanks, April."

"Are you going to prosecute me for obstructing justice?"

"I'm not the legal eagle, but I'll do what I can."

"Okay." April hung up, satisfied.

"Marilyn, I need this ledger. I won't publicize it, but I need to show it to Kendrick and Naomi. This is starting to look like money-laundering. Question is, was Kendrick Miller involved in it?"

The next day Kendrick examined the figures closely but said nothing. Cynthia could have bashed him.

Naomi appeared genuinely shocked by the secret bookkeeping.

All Rick Shaw said when he read through the book was, "Dammit to hell!"

68

"Stick Vicks VapoRub up your nose." Rick handed over the small blue glass jar to Cynthia Cooper as they cut the motor to the squad car.

She fished out a big dab, smoothing it inside each nostril. The tears sprang from her eyes.

"Ready?"

"Yep." She noticed that the photographer was already there. The rescue squad would soon follow. "Boy, George Bowden looks rough."

"Probably puked his guts out. Natural reaction."

"George." Rick walked over, leaves crunching underfoot. "Feel up to some questions?"

"Uh-huh." He nodded.

"What time did you discover the body?"

"Well, now, let me see. I set the alarm for four o'clock 'cause I wanted to be at the edge of the oat fields just on my way down to the hayfields. Good year for grouse, I can tell you. Anyway, uh"—he rubbed his back pockets in an upward motion—"got here about four forty-five, thereabouts. The kids set up a ruckus. Followed them." He indicated his hunting dogs as the kids.

Cynthia carefully walked around the car. The Vicks killed the stench but couldn't do much about the sight. She dusted each door handle. As she was quietly doing her job, another member of the department, Tom Kline, arrived. He gagged.

"Vicks." She pointed to the squad car.

He jammed the stuff up his nose, then returned, carefully investigating the car.

"Guys, I'm going to open the door. It'll be a real hit even with the Vicks. We need to dust the inside door handles, the glove compartment, just hope we're lucky. We aren't going to get anything off the body."

When the door was opened, George, although twenty yards away, stepped backward. "My God."

"Walk on back here with me." Rick led him out of olfactory range. "It's overpowering. The carbon cycle."

"What?"

"Carbon. The breakdown of flesh." Since George wasn't getting it, Rick switched back to business. "Did you notice anything unusual apart from the corpse? Footprints?"

"Sheriff, that thing's been out here so long, any footprints would be washed out."

"A month to six weeks. 'Course, we've had some cold spells. Bill Moscowitz can pinpoint the time for us. Bad as it is, the corpse would be torn apart if it had been out of the car. The fact that it's relatively intact may help us."

"Tire tracks washed out, too. I mean, I would have noticed tire tracks before. Would have come on down."

"You haven't been over here?"

"Been up on the mountain fields, no reason to come down here. Hay's not worth cutting this year anyway. Forgot to fertilize. Mostly I've been working on the mountainside of the farm because of the apples. Good year."

"What about grapes?"

"Got them in 'fore the rains. Be real sweet 'cause of the light drought this summer."

"Do you recognize that corpse?"

"How would I?"

"Odd though it may seem, if that body belonged to someone you knew, you would probably recognize it even in its current condition. Nine times out of ten people do."

"You mean, you show people something like that?"

"Only if we can't make an identification by any other means. Naturally, you try to spare the family as much pain as possible."

"I don't know that"—he gesticulated—"don't know the car. Don't know why she came down this lane. Don't know nothing."

"George, I'm sorry this has happened to you. Why don't you go on home? If I need you, I'll call or come by."

"You gonna take that outta here, aren't you?"

"As soon as we finish dusting the car and taking photos."

"Something in the air, Sheriff."

"I beg pardon?" Rick leaned forward as if to draw closer to George's meaning.

"Evil. Something in the air. The headmaster fella at the rich kids' school and then that Hollywood blowhard stabbed by Kendrick Miller. Sometimes I think a door to the underworld opens and bad spirits fly out."

"That's very interesting," said Rick, who thought George was slightly demented: nice but tilted.

"I was saying to Hilary the other day, evil flowing down the mountain with that cold wind. Life is an endless struggle between good and evil."

"I expect it is." Rick patted him on the back. "You go on home, now."

George nodded good-bye. The dogs tagged at his heels. George, not more than thirty-five, thought and acted like a man in his sixties.

"Boss, we're finished down here. You want a look before we wrap up?"

"Yeah." Rick ambled over. There were no weapons in the car or in the trunk, which ruled out a self-inflicted wound. There was no purse. Usually if someone committed suicide by drug overdose, the vial would be around. Given the body's state of decay, how she died would have to be determined by the coroner. "You satisfied?"

"Yes," Cooper replied, holding out the car registration. "Winifred Thalman."

"Okay." He nodded to the rescue squad.

Diana Robb moved forward with a net. When a body was decomposed, they placed a net around it to keep bones and disintegrating flesh together as much as possible.

"I'm going back to the office," Rick told Cynthia. "I'll call New York Department of Motor Vehicles and start from there. If there's a super at her address, I'll call him, too. I want you to make the rounds."

"You thinking what I'm thinking?"

"Yeah."

"She would have been killed close to the time of Roscoe's death."

He picked up a brittle leaf, pulling away the drying upper epidermis, exposing the veins. "Could have." He released the leaf to fall dizzily back to earth. "It's the why."

They looked at each other a long time. "Boss, how we gonna prove it?"

He shrugged. "Wait for a mistake."

69

The drive back from Richmond, hypnotic in its boredom, found Irene and Jody silent. Irene swung onto the exit at Manakin-Sabot.

"Why are you getting off sixty-four?"

"I'll stay more alert on two-fifty. More to see."

"Oh." Jody slumped back in her seat.

"Do you feel all right?"

"Tired."

"That's natural after what your body has just been through."

"Mom, did you ever have an abortion?"

Irene cleared her throat. "No."

"Would you?"

"I don't know. I was never in your position. Your father thinks it's murder." Her brow furrowed. "How are you going to break this to him?"

"He should talk."

"Don't start, today. He's a flawed man but he's not a killer. Now, I'm going to tell him you had a miscarriage. Leave it to me."

"We're lucky he's in jail." Jody smiled weakly, adding, "If he was home he'd kill us!"

"Jody!"

"I'm sorry, but, Mom, he's confused. People do have secret lives, and Dad is weird."

Irene raised her voice. "You think he did it, don't you? You think he killed Roscoe and McKinchie. I don't know why. You ought to give your father more support."

"Dad's got an evil temper."

"Not that evil."

"You were going to divorce him. All of a sudden he's this great guy. He's not so great. Even in jail he's not much different from when he was out of jail."

A strangled silence followed. Then Irene said, "Everyone can change and learn. I know your pregnancy shocked him into looking at himself. He can't change the past, but he can certainly improve the future."

"Not if he gets convicted, he can't."

"Jody, shut up. I don't want to hear another word about your father getting convicted."

"It's better to be prepared for the worst."

"I'm taking this a day at a time. I can't handle any more than I'm handling now, and you aren't helping. You know your father is innocent."

"I almost don't care." Jody sat up straight. "Just let me have what's left of this year, Mom, please."

Irene considered what her daughter said. Jody could seem so controlled on the outside, like her father, but her moods could also shift violently and quickly. Her outburst at the field hockey game, which now seemed years away, was proof of how unhappy Jody had been. She hadn't seen her daughter's problems because she was too wrapped up in her own. A wave of guilt engulfed her. A tear trickled down Irene's pale cheek.

Jody noticed. "We'll be okay."

"Yes, but we'll never be the same."

"Good."

Irene breathed in deeply. "I guess things were worse than I realized. The lack of affection at home sent you looking for it from other people . . . Sean in particular."

"It was nice being"—she considered the next word—"important."

They swooped right into the Crozet exit. As they decelerated to the stop sign, Irene asked, "Did you tell anyone else you were pregnant?"

"No!"

"I don't believe you. You can't resist talking to your girlfriends."

"And you never talk to anyone."

"Not about family secrets."

"Maybe you should have, Mother. What's the big deal about keeping up appearances? It didn't work, did it?"

"Did you tell anyone?"

"No."

"You told Karen Jensen."

"I did not."

"You two are as thick as thieves."

"She hangs out with Brooks Tucker as much as she hangs out with me." A thin edge of jealousy lined Jody's voice. "Mom, hang it up."

Irene burst into tears. "This will come back to haunt you. You'll feel so guilty."

"It was the right thing to do."

"It violates everything we've been taught. Oh, why did I agree to this? I am so ashamed of myself."

"Mother, get a grip." Icy control and icy fury were in Jody's young face. "Dad's accused of murder. You're going to run the business. I'm going to college so I can come home and run the business. You can't take care of a baby. I can't take care of a baby."

"You should have thought of that in the first place," Irene, a hard edge now in her voice, too, shot back.

"Maybe you should have thought about your actions, too." Jody's glacial tone frosted the interior of the car.

"What do you mean?" Irene paused. "That silly idea you had that I was sleeping with Samson Coles. Where do you get those ideas? And then to accuse the poor man in the post office."

"To cover your ass."

"What!" Irene's eyes bugged out of her head.

"You heard what I said—to cover your ass. You'd been sleeping with Roscoe. You thought I didn't know."

Irene sputtered, her hands gripping the steering wheel until her knuckles were white. "How dare you."

"Save it, Mom. I know because he told me."

"The bastard!"

"Got that right."

Irene calmed down a moment. "Why would he tell you?" She still hadn't admitted to Jody the veracity of the accusation.

"Because I was sleeping with him, too."

"Oh, my God." Irene's foot dropped heavier on the gas pedal.

"So don't tell me right from wrong." Jody half smiled.

"I'm glad he's dead."

Jody smiled fully. "He didn't tell me, really—I figured it out for myself."

"You—" Irene sputtered.

"It doesn't matter." Jody shrugged.

"The hell it doesn't." She slowed down a bit since the red speedometer needle had surged past eighty. "Did you sleep with him?"

"Yes. Each year Roscoe picked his chosen one. My turn, I guess."

"Why?" Irene moaned.

"Because he'd give me anything I wanted and because I'd get into whatever school I wanted. Roscoe would fix it."

"Jody, I'm having a hard time taking all this in." Irene's lower lip trembled.

"Stop," Jody commanded.

"Stop what?"

"The car!"

"Why?"

"We need to pick up the mail."

"I'm too shook up to see people."

"Well, I'm not. So stop the damned car and I'll get the mail."

Irene parked at the post office, while Jody got out. Then she worried about what her daughter would say to Harry and Miranda, so she followed her inside.

Harry called out, "In the nick of time."

Miranda, busy cleaning, called out a hello.

"Irene, you look peaked. Come on back here and sit down. I'll make you a cup of tea."

Irene burst into tears at Miranda's kindness. "Everything is so awful. I want my husband out of jail."

"Mom, come on." Jody tugged at her, smiling weakly at Miranda and Harry.

"*Poor Irene.*" Tucker hated to see humans cry.

"*She's better off without him,*" Pewter stated matter-of-factly.

Two squad cars roared by the post office, sirens wailing, followed by the rescue squad. Cynthia trailed in her squad car. But she pulled away and stopped at the post office. She opened the door and saw Irene and Jody.

"What's going on?" Miranda asked.

"A corpse was found at Bowden's farm." She cleared her throat. "The car is registered to Winifred Thalman of New York City."

"I wonder who—" Miranda never finished her sentence.

"Mom, I'm really tired."

"Okay, honey." Irene wiped her eyes. "You can't accuse Kendrick of this one! He's in jail."

Cooper quietly replied, "I don't know about that, Mrs. Miller, she's been dead quite some time."

Tears of frustration and rage flooded Irene's cheeks. She slapped Cynthia hard.

"Mom!" Jody pulled her mother out of there.

"Striking an officer is a serious offense, isn't it?" Harry asked.

"Under the circumstances, let's just forget it."

"*They finally found the body.*" Tucker sighed.

"*Yes.*" The tiger squinted as the dying sun sparked off Irene's windshield as she pulled away from the post office. "*They're getting closer to the truth.*"

"*What is the truth?*" Pewter said philosophically.

"*Oh, shut up.*" Mrs. Murphy cuffed her friend's ears.

"*I couldn't resist.*" The gray cat giggled.

"*We might as well laugh now,*" Tucker said. "*We aren't going to laugh later.*"

70

Mrs. Murphy worked feverishly catching field mice, moles, shrews, and one sickly baby bunny, which she quickly put out of its misery. Pewter opened the kitchen cabinets while Harry slept. She had a knack for flipping open cabinet doors. She'd grab the knob and then fall back. She rooted around the shelf until she found a bottle of catsup. Fortunately, the bottle was plastic because she knocked it out of the cabinet, shoving it onto the floor for Tucker to pick up.

The corgi's jaws were strong enough to carry the oddly shaped object out to the truck.

"I can put all the kill here in the bed," Mrs. Murphy directed the other two. "If you'll help me, Pewter."

"Harry's going to find all this."

"Not if Tucker can drag out the old barn towel."

"How are we going to get it up in the bed of the truck?"

"Pewter, let me do the thinking. Just help me, will you?"

"What do you want me to do with this bottle of catsup?"

"Put it behind the front wheel of the truck. When Harry opens the door for us, pick it up and jump in the truck. Pewter and I will distract her. You can drop it and kick it under the seat. Remember, gang, she's not looking for this stuff. She won't notice."

Tucker hid the catsup behind the front wheel, then strolled into the barn and yanked the towel off the tack trunk with Harry's maiden initials on it, MM. She tripped over the towel as she walked to the truck, so she dragged it sideways.

Murphy and Pewter placed the small dead prey at the back corner of the truck bed. ·

"Pewter, perch on the bumper step."

"You'd better do it. You're thinner." Pewter hated to admit that she was overweight.

"All right." Murphy jumped down on the back bumper step while Pewter hoisted herself over the side of the tailgate. Tucker sat patiently, the towel in her mouth.

Simon, returning home in the early dawn from foraging, stopped to wonder at this activity. *"What are you-all doing?"*

"Trying to get the towel into the bed of the truck. It's too big to put in my mouth and jump in," Mrs. Murphy informed him. *"Okay, Tucker, stand on your hind legs and see if you can reach Pewter."*

Tucker put her paws on the bumper, her nose edging over the top.

Mrs. Murphy leaned down, grabbing the towel with her left paw. *"Got it."*

Pewter, half hanging over the tailgate, quickly snatched the towel before Murphy dropped it—it was heavy. With Pewter pulling and Mrs. Murphy pushing, the two cats dumped the towel into the truck bed. Mrs. Murphy gaily leapt in, and the two of them placed the towel over the kill, bunching it up to avoid its looking obvious.

"I'll be," Simon said admiringly.

"Teamwork," Mrs. Murphy triumphantly replied.

"What are you going to do with those bodies?" Simon giggled.

"Lay a trail to the killer. Mom's going over to St. Elizabeth's today, so I think we can get the job done."

The possum scoffed. "*The humans won't notice, or, if they do, they'll discount it.*"

The tiger and the gray cat peeped over the side of the truck. "*You might be right, but the killer will notice. That's what we want.*"

"*I don't know.*" Simon shook his head.

"*Anything is better than nothing,*" Murphy said forcefully. "*And if this doesn't work, we'll find something else.*"

"*Why are you so worried?*" Simon's furry nose twitched.

"*Because Mother will eventually figure out who the murderer really is.*"

"Oh." The possum pondered. "*We can't let anything happen to Harry.*" He didn't want to sound soft on any human. "*Who else will feed me marshmallows?*"

71

The animals, exhausted from running back and forth across the playing fields, sacked out immediately after eating.

Pewter and Mrs. Murphy curled up on either side of Tucker on the sofa in front of the fire. Pewter snored, a tiny little nasal gurgle.

Fair brought Chinese food. Harry, good with chopsticks, greedily shoved pork chow mein into her mouth. A light knock on the door was followed by Cynthia Cooper, sticking her head in. She pulled up a chair and joined them.

"Where are the critters?"

"Knocked out. Every time I called them, they were running across the football field today. Having their own Homecoming game, I guess. Can I get you anything else?"

"Catsup." She pointed at her plate. "My noodles."

"You're kidding me." Harry thought of catsup on noodles as

she opened her cabinet. "Damn, I had a brand-new bottle of catsup, and it walked away."

"Catsup ghost." Fair bit into a succulent egg roll, the tiny shrimp bits assaulting his taste buds.

"What were you doing at St. E's?"

"Like a fool, I agreed to help Renee Hallvard referee the field hockey games if she can't find anyone else. She can't for the next game, so I went over to review the rules. I wish I'd never said yes."

"I have a hard time saying no, too. The year I agreed to coach Little League I lost twenty pounds"—Fair laughed—"from worrying about the kids, my work, getting to practice on time."

"Is this a social call, Cynthia? Come on," Harry teased her.

"Yes and no. The corpse, Winifred Thalman, was a freelance cinematographer. I called April Shively before anyone else—after I stopped at the post office. She says Thalman was the person who shot the little movies the seniors made their first week back at school."

"Wouldn't someone have missed her in New York? Family?"

Cooper put down her egg roll. "She was estranged from her only brother. Parents dead. As a cinematographer, her neighbors were accustomed to her being absent for months at a time. No pets. No plants. No relationships. Rick tracked down the super in her building."

"You didn't stop at the post office to tell me the news first, did you?" Harry smiled.

"Saw Irene's car."

"Ah."

"Kendrick's got to be lying. Only reason we can come up with for him to do that is he's protecting his wife or his daughter."

"They killed Roscoe and Maury?" Fair was incredulous.

"We think one of them did. Rick's spent hours going over Kendrick's books and bank accounts, and there's just no evidence of any financial misdoing. Even if you buy the sexual jealousy motive, why would he have killed this Thalman woman?"

"Well, why would Irene or Jody have done it?" Harry asked.

"If we knew that, we'd know everything." Cynthia broke the

egg roll in two. "Irene will be at the field hockey game tomorrow. We'll have her covered by a plainclothesman from Waynesboro's department. You'll be on the field. Keep your eyes open."

"Irene or Jody stabbed Maury? Jeesh," Fair exclaimed. "Takes a lot of nerve to get that close at a public gathering."

"Wasn't that hard to do," Harry said. "Sometimes the easiest crimes are the ones committed in crowds."

"The killer confessed twice to Father Michael. Since Kendrick has confessed, Father Michael hasn't heard a peep. Nothing unusual about that—if you're a murderer and someone has taken the rap for you. Still, the impulse to confess is curious. Guilt?"

"Pride," Harry rejoined.

"Irene or Jody . . . I still can't get over it."

"Do you think they know? I mean, does one of them know the other is a killer?" Harry asked.

"I don't know. But I hope whoever it is gets sloppy or gets rattled."

"Guess this new murder will be on the eleven o'clock news"— Harry checked the old wall clock—"and in the papers."

"Whole town will be talking." Cynthia poured half a carton of noodles on her plate. "Maybe that'll rattle our killer. I don't know, she's been cold as ice."

"Yeah, well, even ice has a melting point." Fair tinkled the ice in his water glass.

"Harry, because you're in the middle of the field, you're secure. If it is Jody, she can't stab you or poison you without revealing herself. Are you willing to bait her? If we're wrong, there will be plenty of time to apologize."

"I'll do it." She nodded her head, "Can you set a trap for Irene?"

"Fair?"

"Oh, hell!" He put down his glass.

72

The colored cars and trucks filling the St. Elizabeth's back parking lot looked like jelly beans. The St. Elizabeth's supporters flew pennants off their antennas. So did the Chatham Hall fans. When the wind picked up, it resembled a used-car parking lot. All that was missing were the prices in thick grease crayon on the windshields.

Harry, despite all, read and reread the rule book in the faculty locker room. She knew the hardest part of refereeing would be blowing the whistle. Once she grew confident, she'd overcome that. And she had to establish her authority early on because if the kids thought they could get away with fouling, some would.

Mrs. Murphy sat on the wooden bench next to her. Pewter and Tucker guarded the door. Deputy Cooper waited in the hall.

The noise of a locker being pulled over, followed by shouting, reverberated down the hall.

"What the hell?" Harry ran out the door toward the commotion.

Cooper jerked her head in the direction of the noise. "It's World War Three in there, and the game hasn't even started."

"Well, it is the qualifier for state." Harry tucked her whistle in the whistle pocket.

Pewter giggled. *"She found it."*

The animals ran down the hall. Tucker, losing her hind footing on the slick waxed surface, spun around once. They reached the locker room and crept along the aisle.

"What a dirty trick! I'll kill whoever did this!" Jody kicked her locker again for good measure. Dead mice, moles, and shrews were scattered over the floor. A bottle of catsup, red stuff oozing out of the bite marks, splattered everywhere. Jody's stick had catsup on it, too.

"Gross." Karen Jensen jumped backward as the tiny dead animals spilled everywhere.

"You did this!" Jody lost her composure, accusing the last person who would do such a thing.

"You're crazy," Karen shot back.

Jody picked up her hockey stick and swung at Karen's head. Fortunately, Karen, the best player on the team and blessed with lightning reflexes, ducked. Brooks grabbed Jody from behind, but Jody, six inches taller, was hard to hold.

Coach Hallvard dashed into the room. "Cut it out!" She surveyed the mess. "All right. Out of here. Everyone out of here."

"Someone filled my locker with dead mice and catsup!" Jody shrieked. "And it's your fault. You won't let us keep locks on our lockers anymore!"

"We'll solve this after the game." Coach put her hands on her hips. "It could have been someone from Chatham Hall. It certainly would benefit them to rattle one of our best players and set this team fighting among ourselves, wouldn't it?"

The girls drank in this motivating theory, none of which Hallvard believed. However, it provided a temporary solution. She'd talk to Deputy Cooper after the game. Coach was intelligent enough to know that anything out of the ordinary at St. Elizabeth's must be treated with the utmost suspicion, and Cynthia had briefed her to be alert. She didn't identify Jody as a possible suspect.

"You're right, Coach." Jensen, the natural leader of the team, finally spoke. "Let's wipe them off the face of the earth!"

The girls cheered. As they grabbed their sticks and filed out of the room, Brooks noticed Mrs. Murphy.

"Murphy, hi, kitty."

"*Keep your cool, Brooks, this will be a hell of a game.*"

When the home team ran across the field to the benches, the home crowd roared.

Fair sat next to Irene, as he promised Cynthia he would. The plainclothes officer from Waynesboro sat behind her, pretending to be a Chatham Hall supporter.

Miranda, also alerted, huddled with Mim in the center of the bleachers.

Cynthia stayed behind the Chatham Hall bench, which gave her a shorter sprint to the gym if need be. She knew Irene was well covered, so she watched Jody.

Herb Jones joined Sandy Brashiers and some of the faculty on the lower bench seats.

Harry met her co-official, Lily Norton, a former All-American, who drove over from Richmond.

"I'm a last minute fill-in, Miss Norton. Bear with me." Harry shook her hand.

"I was a freshman at Lee High the year you-all won state." She warmly returned the handshake. "You'll do fine, and please, call me Lily."

"Okay." Harry smiled.

They both synchronized their watches, then Lily put the whistle to her lips, blew, and the two captains trotted out to the center of the field.

Mrs. Murphy, Pewter, and Tucker, on the gym side of the field, watched closely, too.

"*Tucker, stay on the center line on this side. You know what to do?*"

"*Yes,*" Tucker answered forcefully.

"*Pewter, you hang out by the north goal. There's a maple tree about twenty yards back from the goal. If you get up in there, you can see what's going on. If anything worries you, holler."*

"You-all won't be able to hear me because of the crowd noise."

"Well"—Mrs. Murphy thought a minute—*"about all you can do is run down the tree. We'll keep glancing in your direction."*

"Why can't we stay on the edges of the field?" Tucker said.

"The referees will chase us off. Mom will put us in the truck. We've got to work with what we have."

"That field is a lot of territory to cover," Pewter, not the fastest cat in the world, noted.

"We'll do what we can. I'll stay under the St. Elizabeth's bench. If I get shooed away from there, I'll head down to the south goal. We clear?"

"Yes," they both said.

"Why can't Coop shoot if Jody or Irene goes nuts?"

"She can, but let's hope she doesn't need to do that." Murphy exhaled from her delicate nostrils. *"Good luck."*

The three animals fanned out to their places. Mrs. Murphy ducked feet and the squeals of the players who saw her. She scrunched up under the players' bench, listening intently.

The first quarter provided no fireworks but showed off each team's defensive skills. Jody blocked an onrushing Chatham Hall player but got knocked sideways in the process. She leapt up, ready to sock the girl, but Karen yelled at her, "Stay in your zone, Miller."

"Up yours," Jody shot back, but she obeyed.

The first half passed, back and forth but no real excitement.

Pewter wished she were under the bench because the wind was picking up. Her perch was getting colder and colder.

The second half opened with Brooks stealing a Chatham Hall pass and running like mad toward the goal where, at the last minute, now covered, she fired off a pinpoint pass to Karen Jensen, who blazed her shot past the goalie. A roar went up from the St. Elizabeth's bleachers.

Susan jumped up and down. Irene, too, was screaming. Even Sandy Brashiers, not especially interested in athletics, was caught up in the moment.

The big girl whom Jody had blocked took advantage of the run back to the center to tell Jody just what she thought of her. "Asshole."

"It's not my fault you're fat and slow," Jody needled her.

"Very funny. There's a lot of game left. You'd better watch out."

"Yeah, sure." Jody ignored her.

Chatham Hall grabbed the ball out of the knock-in. The big player, a midfielder, took the pass and barreled straight at Jody, who stepped out of the way, pretended to be hit, rolled, and flicked her stick out to catch the girl on the back of the leg.

Harry blew the whistle and called the foul.

Jody glared at Harry, and as Chatham Hall moved downfield, she brushed by Harry, close enough to make Harry step back and close enough for Harry to say, "Jody, you're the killer."

A hard shot on goal was saved by the St. Elizabeth's goalie. Another roar erupted on the sidelines. But the game became tougher, faster, and rougher. By the end of the third quarter both sides, drenched in sweat, settled in for a last quarter of attrition.

Whether by design or under the leadership of the big Chatham Hall midfielder, their team kept taking the ball down Jody's side. Jody, in excellent condition and built for running, couldn't be worn down, but they picked at her. Each time she'd lose her temper, they'd get the ball by her.

Finally Coach Hallvard took her off the field, substituting a talented but green sophomore, Biff Carstairs.

Jody paced in front of the bench, imploring Renee Hallvard, "Put me back in. Come on. Biff can't handle it."

True enough. As they flew down the right side of the field, Biff stayed with them, but she hadn't been in a game this good, this fast, or this physically punishing.

Chatham Hall scored on that series of plays, which made Jody scream at the top of her lungs. Finally, Hallvard, fearing another quick score, put Jody back in. The St. Elizabeth's side cheered anew.

Fair murmured in a low voice as the crowd cheered, "Irene, give yourself up. We all know it wasn't Kendrick."

She whirled around. "How dare you!"

A pair of hands behind her dropped to her shoulders so she

couldn't move. The plainclothesman ordered, "Stay very still." He removed one hand and slipped it inside his coat to retrieve a badge.

"I didn't kill those people." Irene's anger ebbed.

"Okay, just sit tight," the plainclothesman said quietly.

Perhaps Jody felt an extra surge of adrenaline. Whatever, she could do no wrong. She checked her woman, she stole the ball, she cracked the ball right up to her forwards. She felt invincible. She really could do no wrong. With Jody playing all out at midfield and Karen and Brooks lethal up front, St. Elizabeth's crushed Chatham Hall in the last quarter. The final score was four to two. The crowd ran off the bleachers and spilled onto the field. Mrs. Murphy streaked down the sidelines to escape the feet. Pewter climbed down from the tree, relieved that nothing dangerous had happened. The animals rendezvoused at the far sideline at center with Tucker.

"I thought she'd whack at Mom with her stick. I thought we rattled her enough." Pewter was dejected that Jody had proved so self-possessed.

"Oh, well." Tucker sat down.

Mrs. Murphy scanned the wild celebration. Harry and Lily slowly walked off the field. Jody watched out of the corner of her eye even as she jumped all over her teammates.

"Nice to work with you." Lily shook Harry's hand. "You did a good job."

"Thanks. Aren't you going back to change?"

"No, I'd better get on the road." Lily headed toward the parking lot behind the gym.

As Harry entered the gym, Jody drifted away from the group. There was nothing unusual in a player heading back to the gym.

Cynthia, caught in the crowd, fought to get through the bodies when she saw Jody leave.

The three animals raced across the grass, little tufts of it floating up in the wind as it flew off their claws. They reached the door just as Harry opened it.

"Hi, guys." She was tired.

Within a minute Jody, stick in hand, was also in the gym. As Harry turned right down the hall toward the faculty changing room,

Jody, on tiptoes now, moved down the hall, carefully listening for another footfall. Without speaking to one another, the animals ducked in doorways. Only Murphy stayed with Harry in case Tucker and Pewter failed.

Jody passed Pewter, who ran out and grabbed the back of her leg with her front claws. Jody howled, whirled around, and slapped at the cat, who let go just as Tucker emerged from the janitor's door. She ran hard at Jody, jumped up, and smashed into her knees. Dog and human collapsed in a heap, and the hockey stick clattered on the shiny floor.

"Goddammit!" Jody reached for her stick as Tucker grabbed the end of it.

They tugged from opposite ends. Tucker slid along the floor, but she wouldn't let go. Jody kicked at the dog, then twisted the stick to force her jaws loose. It didn't work. Pewter jumped on Jody's leg again as Harry, hearing the scramble, opened the locker room door and came back into the hall. Mrs. Murphy stuck with Harry.

"Good work," the tiger encouraged her pals.

Jody, seeing Harry, dropped her hockey stick, lunging for Harry's throat.

Harry raised her forearm to protect herself. She stumbled back against the concrete wall of the gym, which gave her support. She lifted up her knee, catching Jody in the crotch. It slowed Jody, but not enough. Pewter, still hanging on to Jody's right leg, was joined by Murphy on the left. They sank their fangs in as deep as they'd go.

Jody screamed, loosening her grip on Harry's neck. The enraged girl lurched for her hockey stick. Tucker was dragging it down the hallway, but the corgi couldn't go fast, she being small and the stick being large.

Jody yanked the stick hard out of the dog's jaws. Tucker jumped for the stick, but Jody held it over her head and ran for Harry, who crouched. The hallway was long and narrow. She would use the walls to her benefit. Harry, a good athlete, steadied for the attack.

Jody swung the stick at her head. Harry ducked lower and

shifted her weight. The tip of the hockey stick grazed the wall. Harry moved closer to the wall. She prayed Jody would crack her stick on the wall.

Jody, oblivious to the damage the cats were doing to her legs, she was so obsessed, swung again. The stick splintered, and that fast Harry pushed off the wall and flung herself at Jody. The two went down hard on the floor as the cats let go of their quarry. Tucker ran alongside the fighting humans, waiting for an opening. Her fangs, longer than the cats', could do more damage.

Sounds down the hall stopped Jody for a split second. She wriggled from Harry's grasp and raced away from the noise. Tucker caught her quickly and grabbed her ankle. Jody stopped to beat off the dog just as Cynthia Cooper rounded the corner and dropped to one knee, gun out.

"Stop or I'll shoot."

Jody, eyes glazed, stared down the barrel of a .357, stared at the bloody fangs of Tucker, then held up her hands.

73

Because of their bravery, the animals were rewarded with filet mignon cooked by Miranda Hogendobber. Harry, Fair, Susan, Brooks, Cynthia, and the Reverend Jones joined them. The animals had place settings at the big dinner table. Miranda went all out.

"This is heaven," Pewter purred.

"I didn't know Pewter had it in her." Susan smiled at the plump kitty.

"There's a lion beneath that lard," Mrs. Murphy joked.

As the humans put together the pieces of the murderous puzzle, Tucker said, "Murphy, how did you figure it out?"

"Mother was on the right track when she said that whoever killed Roscoe Fletcher did it at the car wash. Any one of the suspects could have done it, but not one person recalled anyone giving Roscoe candy, although he offered it to them. Jody walked past the Texaco station on her way to the deli. The station blocks the view from the car wash. She gave him the candy; no one saw her, and no car was behind Roscoe yet. She could have worked fast, then run back to the office. It would give her a good alibi. She was waiting for an opportunity. She was smart enough to know this was a good shot. Who knows how long she carried that candy around?"

"I don't know whether to pity Jody or hate her," Susan Tucker mused.

" 'Behold, these are the ungodly, who prosper in the world; they increase in riches!' Psalm Seventy-three, verse twelve," Miranda recited. "Roscoe and Maury did increase in riches, but they paid for it. As for Jody, she was very pretty and vulnerable. But so are many other young people. She participated in her own corruption."

"The slush fund ledger gave me part of the motive—money—but I couldn't find the slushers. Drugs weren't it." Cynthia folded her arms across her chest. "Never would I have thought of porno movies."

"It is ghastly." The Reverend Jones shuddered.

"What tipped you off?" Pewter asked Murphy.

"It took me a long time to figure it out. I think finding that address label at the bottom of Roscoe's desk was my first inkling. Neptune Film Lab. And wonderful though it might be to have a film department at a private secondary school—it seemed like a great expense even if Maury was supposedly going to make a huge contribution."

"Kendrick was more of a man than we've given him credit for," Susan said.

"He guessed Jody was the killer. He didn't know why." Cynthia recalled the expression on his face when Jody confessed. "She'd told Irene and Kendrick that she was pregnant by Sean. It was actually Roscoe."

"I'd kill him myself." Fair's face flushed. "Sorry, Herb."

"Quite understandable under the circumstances."

"She had slept with Sean and told him he was the father of her child. That's when he stole the BMW. He was running away and asking for help at the same time," Cynthia continued. "But she now says the father might be Roscoe. And she said this is the second film made at St. Elizabeth's. Last year they used Courtney Frere. He'd pick one favorite girl for his films. We tracked her down at Tulane. Poor kid. That's what the sleeping pills were about, not low board scores. The film she was in was shot at Maury's house, but then Roscoe and

Maury got bolder. They came up with the bright idea of setting up shop at St. Elizabeth's. It certainly gave them the opportunity to troll for victims.''

''Monsters.'' Miranda shook her head.

''There have always been bad people.'' Brooks surprised everyone by speaking up. ''Bad as Mr. Fletcher and Mr. McKinchie were, she didn't have to kill them.''

''She snapped.'' Susan thought out loud. ''All of a sudden she must have realized that one mistake—that movie—could ruin the rest of her life.''

''Exactly.'' Cynthia confirmed this. ''She drove out with Winifred Thalman, thinking she could get the footage back, but Winifred had already mailed the rough cut to Neptune Lab. She only had outtakes with her, so Jody killed her. She threw the outtakes in the pond.''

''How,'' Harry asked, ''did she kill her?''

''Blow to the head. Maybe used her hockey stick. She walked across the fields after dark and arrived home in time for supper. After that she was driven by revenge. She wanted power over the people she felt had humiliated her—even though she'd agreed to be in these movies for money.''

''The slush fund?'' Harry asked.

''Right. Forty-one thousand dollars withdrawn by Maury, as it turns out. Forty-one thousand dollars for her BMW . . . it all added up. Imagine how Kendrick must have felt when he saw that figure in Roscoe's secret ledger. The deposits were from other films. Maury and Roscoe shot porno movies in New York, too. There they used professionals. Roscoe's fund-raising trips were successful on both counts,'' Cynthia said.

''How'd she kill Maury?'' Brooks was curious.

''She slipped into the girls' locker room, put on the Musketeer outfit, and rejoined the party. She saw Maury start to leave and stabbed him, with plenty of time to get back to the locker and change into her skeleton costume. She may even have lured Maury out of the dance, but she says she didn't,'' Cynthia answered.

''Does she feel any remorse?'' Miranda hoped she did.

"For killing three people? No, not a bit. But she feels terrible that she lied to Sean about being the father. About goading him into calling in the false obituary and about following Roger on his paper route and stuffing in the Maury obit. That's the extent of her remorse!"

"Do you believe she's crazy?" Fair said.

"No. And I am sick of that defense. She knows right from wrong. Revenge and power. She should be tried as an adult. The truth is: she enjoyed the killing." Cynthia stabbed her broccoli.

"Why would a human pay to watch another human have sex?" Pewter laughed.

"Boredom." Tucker ate table scraps slipped her by Fair.

"I wouldn't pay to watch another cat, would you?" Pewter addressed Murphy.

"Of course not, but we're cats. We're superior to humans." She glanced at Tucker.

"I wouldn't do it, I'm superior, too," Tucker swiftly said, around a mouthful.

"Yes—but not quite as superior as we are." Mrs. Murphy laughed.